THE
GROUND
BENEATH
HER FEET

SALMAN RUSHDIE

THE GROUND BENEATH HER FEET

A Novel

HENRY HOLT AND COMPANY · NEW YORK

Henry Holt and Company, Inc.
Publishers since 1866
115 West 18th Street
New York, New York 10011

Henry Holt® is a registered trademark of
Henry Holt and Company, Inc.

Grateful acknowledgement is made to the following for
permission to reprint previously published material:

"Jailhouse Rock" by Jerry Leiber, Mike Stoller
© 1957 (Renewed) Jerry Leiber Music, Mike Stoller Music;
All rights reserved; Used by permission.

"What a Wonderful World" by George David Weiss,
Bob Thiele © 1967 (Renewed) Quartet Music, Inc.,
Range Road Music, Abilene Music;
All rights reserved; Used by permission.

"Rubber Ball," words and music by Aaron Schroeder and
Anne.Orlowski; Published by Rachel's Own Music and Dandy
Dittys; Used by permission; International Copyright Secured.

"The Great Pretender" by Buck Ram
© 1955 (Renewed) by Panther Music Corporation;
All rights reserved; Used by permission;
International Copyright Secured.

"Orpheus. Eurydice. Hermes," by Rainer Maria Rilke in *Neue
Gedichte: New Poems,* trans. Stephen Cohn (Evanston, Ill.:
Northwestern University Press). © 1992, 1997 Stephen Cohn;
All rights reserved.

LIBRARY OF CONGRESS CATALOGING-IN-PUBLICATION DATA
Rushdie, Salman.
The ground beneath her feet: a novel / Salman Rushdie.
p. cm.
ISBN 0-8050-5308-5 (alk. paper)
I. Title.
PR6068.U757G76 1999   98-42407
823'.914—dc21   CIP

Henry Holt books are available for special promotions and
premiums. For details contact: Director, Special Markets.

First Edition—1999

DESIGNED BY LUCY ALBANESE

Printed in the United States of America
All first editions are printed on acid-free paper. ∞

1   3   5   7   9   10   8   6   4   2

FOR MILAN

Set up no stone to his memory.
Just let the rose bloom each year for his sake.
For it is Orpheus. His metamorphosis
into this and that. We should not trouble

about other names. Once and for all
it's Orpheus when there's singing.

—R. M. Rilke, *Sonnets to Orpheus*
translated by M. D. Herter Norton

CONTENTS

THE GROUND BENEATH HER FEET

1

THE KEEPER OF BEES

On St. Valentine's Day, 1989, the last day of her life, the legendary popular singer Vina Apsara woke sobbing from a dream of human sacrifice in which she had been the intended victim. Bare-torsoed men resembling the actor Christopher Plummer had been gripping her by the wrists and ankles. Her body was splayed out, naked and writhing, over a polished stone bearing the graven image of the snakebird Quetzalcoatl. The open mouth of the plumed serpent surrounded a dark hollow scooped out of the stone, and although her own mouth was stretched wide by her screams the only noise she could hear was the popping of flashbulbs; but before they could slit her throat, before her lifeblood could bubble into that terrible cup, she awoke at noon in the city of Guadalajara, Mexico, in an unfamiliar bed with a half-dead stranger by her side, a naked mestizo male in his early twenties, identified in the interminable press coverage that followed the catastrophe as Raúl Páramo, the playboy heir of a well-known local construction baron, one of whose corporations owned the hotel.

She had been perspiring heavily and the sodden bedsheets stank of the meaningless misery of the nocturnal encounter. Raúl Páramo was unconscious, white-lipped, and his body was galvanized, every few moments, by spasms which Vina recognized as being identical to her own dream writhings. After a few moments he began to make frightful noises deep in his windpipe, as if someone were slitting his throat, as if his blood were flowing out through the scarlet smile of an invisible wound into a phantom goblet. Vina, panicking, leapt from the bed, snatched up her clothes, the leather pants and gold-sequinned bustier in which she had made her final exit, the night before, from the stage of the city's convention centre. Contemptuously, despairingly, she had surrendered herself to this nobody, this boy less than half her age, she had selected him more or less at random from the backstage throng, the lounge lizards, the slick, flower-bearing suitors, the industrial magnates, the aristotrash, the drug underlords, the tequila princes, all with limousines and champagne and cocaine and maybe even diamonds to bestow upon the evening's star.

The man had begun to introduce himself, to preen and fawn, but she didn't want to know his name or the size of his bank balance. She had picked him like a flower and now she wanted him between her teeth, she had ordered him like a take-home meal and now she alarmed him by the ferocity of her appetites, because she began to feast upon him the moment the door of the limo was closed, before the chauffeur had time to raise the partition that gave the passengers their privacy. Afterwards he, the chauffeur, spoke with reverence of her naked body, while the newspapermen plied him with tequila he whispered about her swarming and predatory nudity as if it were a miracle, who'd have thought she was way the wrong side of forty, I guess somebody upstairs wanted to keep her just the way she was. I would have done anything for such a woman, the chauffeur moaned, I would have driven at two hundred kilometres per hour for her if it were speed she wanted, I would have crashed into a concrete wall for her if it had been her desire to die.

Only when she lurched into the eleventh-floor corridor of the hotel, half dressed and confused, stumbling over the unclaimed newspapers, whose headlines about French nuclear tests in the Pacific and political unrest in the southern province of Chiapas smudged the bare soles of her feet with their shrieking ink, only then did she understand that the suite of rooms she had abandoned was her own, she had slammed the door and didn't have the key, and it was lucky for her in that moment of vulnerability that the person she bumped into was me, Mr. Umeed Merchant, photographer, a.k.a. "Rai," her so to speak chum ever since the old days in Bombay and the only shutterbug within one thousand and one miles who would not dream of photographing her in such delicious and scandalous disarray, her whole self momentarily out of focus and worst of all looking her age, the only image-stealer who would never have stolen from her that frayed and hunted look, that bleary and unarguably bag-eyed helplessness, her tangled fountain of wiry dyed red hair quivering above her head in a woodpeckerish topknot, her lovely mouth trembling and uncertain, with the tiny fjords of the pitiless years deepening at the edges of her lips, the very archetype of the wild rock goddess halfway down the road to desolation and ruin. She had decided to become a redhead for this tour because at the age of forty-four she was making a new start, a solo career without Him, for the first time in years she was on the road without Ormus, so it wasn't really surprising that she was disoriented and off balance most of the time. And lonely. It has to be admitted. Public life or private life, makes no difference, that's the truth: when she wasn't with him, it didn't matter who she was with, she was always alone.

Disorientation: loss of the East. And of Ormus Cama, her sun.

And it wasn't just dumb luck, her bumping into me. I was always there for her. Always looking out for her, always waiting for her call. If she'd wanted it, there could have been dozens of us, hundreds, thousands. But I believe there was only me. And the last time she called for help, I couldn't give it, and she died. She ended in the middle of the story of her life, she was an unfinished song abandoned at the bridge, deprived of the right to follow her life's verses to their final, fulfilling rhyme.

Two hours after I rescued her from the unfathomable chasm of her hotel corridor, a helicopter flew us to Tequila, where Don Ángel Cruz, the owner of one of the largest plantations of blue agave cactus and of the celebrated Ángel distillery, a gentleman fabled for the sweet amplitude of his countertenor voice, the great rotunda of his belly and the lavishness of his hospitality, was scheduled to hold a banquet in her honour. Meanwhile, Vina's playboy lover had been taken to hospital, in the grip of drug-induced seizures so extreme that they eventually proved fatal, and for days afterwards, because of what happened to Vina, the world was treated to detailed analyses of the contents of the dead man's bloodstream, his stomach, his intestines, his scrotum, his eye sockets, his appendix, his hair, in fact everything except his brain, which was not thought to contain anything of interest, and had been so thoroughly scrambled by narcotics that nobody could understand his last words, spoken during his final, comatose delirium. Some days later, however, when the information had found its way on to the Internet, a fantasy-fiction wonk hailing from the Castro district of San Francisco and nicknamed <elrond@rivendel.com> explained that Raúl Páramo had been speaking Orcish, the infernal speech devised for the servants of the Dark Lord Sauron by the writer Tolkien: *Ash nazg durbatulûk, ash nazg gimbatul, ash nazg thrakatulûk agh burzum-ishi krimpatul.* After that, rumours of Satanic, or perhaps Sauronic, practices spread unstoppably across the Web. The idea was put about that the mestizo lover had been a devil worshipper, a blood servant of the Underworld, and had given Vina Apsara a priceless but malignant ring, which had caused the subsequent catastrophe and dragged her down to Hell. But by then Vina was already passing into myth, becoming a vessel into which any moron could pour his stupidities, or let us say a mirror of the culture, and we can best understand the nature of this culture if we say that it found its truest mirror in a corpse.

One ring to rule them all, one ring to find them, one ring to bring them all and in the darkness bind them. I sat next to Vina Apsara in the helicopter to Tequila, and I saw no ring on her finger, except for the talismanic moonstone she always wore, her link to Ormus Cama, her reminder of his love.

She had sent her entourage by road, selecting me as her only aerial companion, "of all of you bastards he's the only one I can trust," she'd snarled. They had set off an hour ahead of us, the whole damn zoo, her serpentine tour manager, her hyena of a personal assistant, the security gorillas, the peacock of a hairdresser, the publicity dragon, but now, as the chopper swooped over their motorcade, the darkness that had enveloped her since our departure seemed to lift, and she ordered the pilot to make a series of low passes over the cars below, lower and lower, I saw his eyes widen with fear, the pupils were black pinpricks, but he was under her spell like all of us, and did her bidding. I was the one yelling *higher, get higher* into the microphone attached to our ear-defender headsets, while her laughter clattered in my ears like a door banging in the wind, and when I looked across at her to tell her I was scared I saw that she was weeping. The police had been surprisingly gentle with her when they arrived at the scene of Raúl Páramo's over-dose, contenting themselves with cautioning her that she might become the subject of an investigation herself. Her lawyers had termi-nated the encounter at that point, but afterwards she looked stretched, unstable, too bright, as if she were on the point of flying apart like an exploding lightbulb, like a supernova, like the universe.

Then we were past the vehicles and flying over the hills and valleys turned smoky blue by the agave plantations, and her mood swung again, she began to giggle into her microphone and to insist that we were taking her to a place that did not exist, a fantasy location, a won-derland, because how was it possible that there could be a place called Tequila, "it's like saying that whisky comes from Whisky, or gin is made in Gin," she cried. "Is the Vodka a river in Russia? Do they make rum in Rúm?" And then a sudden darkening, her voice dropping low, becoming almost inaudible beneath the noise of the rotors, "And heroin comes from heroes, and crack from the Crack of Doom." It was possible that I was hearing the birth of a song. Afterwards, when the captain and copilot were interviewed about her helicopter ride, they loyally refused to divulge any details of that in-flight monologue in which she swung moment by moment between elation and despair. "She was in high spirits," they said, "and spoke in English, so we did not understand."

Not only in English. Because it was only me, she could prattle on in Bombay's garbage argot, *Mumbai ki kachrapati baat-cheet,* in which a sentence could begin in one language, swoop through a second and even a third and then swing back round to the first. Our acronymic name for it was *Hug-me.* Hindi Urdu Gujarati Marathi English. Bom-bayites like me were people who spoke five languages badly and no language well.

Separated from Ormus Cama on this tour, Vina had discovered the limitations, musical and verbal, of her own material. She had written new songs to show off that celestial voice of hers, that multiple-octave, Yma Sumac stairway to heaven of an instrument which, she now claimed, had never been sufficiently stretched by Ormus's compositions; but in Buenos Aires, São Paulo, Mexico City and Guadalajara she heard for herself the public's tepid responses to these songs, in spite of the presence of her three demented Brazilian percussionists and her pair of duelling Argentine guitarists who threatened to end each performance with a knife fight. Even the guest appearance of the veteran Mexican superstar Chico Estefan had failed to enthuse her audiences; instead, his surgery-smoothed face with its mouthful of unreal teeth only drew attention to her own fading youth, which was mirrored in the average age of the crowds. The kids had not come, or not enough of them, not nearly enough.

But roars of acclaim followed each of the old hits from the VTO back catalogue, and the inescapable truth was that during these numbers the percussionists' madness came closest to divinity, the duelling guitars spiralled upwards towards the sublime, and even the old roué Estefan seemed to come back from his green pastures over the hill. Vina Apsara sang Ormus Cama's words and music, and at once the minority of youngsters in the audiences perked up and started going crazy, the crowd's thousand thousand hands began moving in unison, forming in sign language the name of the great band, in time to their thundering cheers:

V! T! O!

V! T! O!

Go back to him, they were saying. We need you to be together. Don't throw your love away. Instead of breaking up, we wish that you were making up again.

Vertical Take-Off. Or, Vina To Ormus. Or, "We two" translated into Hug-me as V-to. Or, a reference to the V-2 rocket. Or, V for peace, for which they longed, and T for two, the two of them, and O for love, their love. Or, a homage to one of the great buildings of Ormus's home town: Victoria Terminus Orchestra. Or, a name invented long ago when Vina saw a neon sign for the old-time soft drink Vimto, with only three letters illuminated, Vimto without the *im*.

V . . . T . . . Ohh.

V . . . T . . . Ohh.

Two shrieks and a sigh. The orgasm of the past, whose ring she wore on her finger. To which perhaps she knew she must, in spite of me, return.

The afternoon heat was dry and fierce, which she loved. Before we landed, the pilot had been informed of mild earth tremors in the region, but they had passed, he reassured us, there was no reason to abort the landing. Then he cursed the French. "After each one of those tests you can count five days, one, two, three, four, five, and the ground shakes." He set the helicopter down in a dusty football field in the centre of the little town of Tequila. What must have been the town's entire police force was keeping the local population at bay. As Vina Apsara majestically descended (always a princess, she was growing into queenliness) a cry went up, just her name, *Veeenaaa,* the vowels elongated by pure longing, and I recognized, not for the first time, that in spite of all the hyperbolic revelry and public display of her life, in spite of all her star antics, her *nakhras,* she was never resented, something in her manner disarmed people, and what bubbled out of them instead of bile was a miraculous, unconditional affection, as if she were the whole earth's very own new-born child.

Call it love.

Small boys burst through the cordon, chased by perspiring cops, and then there was Don Ángel Cruz with his two silver Bentleys that exactly matched the colour of his hair, apologizing for not greeting us with an aria, but the dust, the unfortunate dust, it is always a difficulty but now with the tremor the air is full of it, please, señora, señor, and with a small cough against the back of his wrist he shepherded us into the lead Bentley, we will go at once, please, and commence the programme. He seated himself in the second vehicle, mopping himself with giant kerchiefs, the huge smile on his face held there by a great effort of will. You could almost see the heaving distraction beneath that surface of a perfect host. "That's a worried man," I said to Vina as our car drove towards the plantation. She shrugged. She had crossed the Oakland Bay Bridge going west in October 1984, test driving a luxury car for a promotional feature in *Vanity Fair,* and on the far side she drove into a gas station, climbed out of the car and saw it lift off the ground, all four wheels, and hang there in the air like something from the future, or *Back to the Future,* anyway. At that moment the Bay Bridge was collapsing like a children's toy. Therefore, "Don't you earthquake me," she said to me in her tough-broad, disaster-vet voice as we arrived at the plantation, where Don Ángel's employees waited with straw cowboy hats to shield us from the sun and machete maestros prepared to demonstrate how one hacked an agave plant down into a big blue "pineapple" ready for the pulping machine. "Don't try and Richter me, Rai, honey. I been scaled before."

The animals were misbehaving. Brindled mongrels ran in circles, yelping, and there was a whinnying of horses. Oracular birds wheeled noisily overhead. Subcutaneous seismic activity increased, too, beneath the increasingly distended affability of Don Ángel Cruz as he dragged us round the distillery, these are our traditional wooden vats, and here are our shining new technological marvels, our capital investment for the future, our enormous investment, our investment beyond price. Fear had begun to ooze from him in globules of rancid sweat. Absently he dabbed his sodden hankies at the odorous flow, and in the bottling plant his eyes widened further with misery as he gazed upon the fragility of his fortune, liquid cradled in glass, and the fear of an earthquake began to seep damply from the corners of his eyes.

"Sales of French wines and liquors have been down since the testing began, maybe as much as twenty percent," he muttered, shaking his head. "The wineries of Chile and our own people here in Tequila have both been beneficiaries. Export demand has shot up to such a degree you would not credit it." He wiped his eyes with the back of an unsteady hand. "Why should God give us such a gift only to take it away again? Why must He test our faith?" He peered at us, as if we might genuinely be able to offer him an answer. When he understood that no answer was available, he clutched suddenly at Vina Apsara's hands, he became a supplicant at her court, driven to this act of excessive familiarity by the force of his great need. She made no attempt to free herself from his grasp.

"I have not been a bad man," Don Ángel said to Vina, in imploring tones, as if he were praying to her. "I have been fair to my employees and amiable to my children and even faithful to my wife, excepting only, let me be honest, a couple of small incidents, and these were maybe twenty years ago, señora, you are a sophisticated lady, you can understand the weaknesses of middle age. Why then should such a day come to me?" He actually bowed his head before her, relinquishing her hands now to lock his own together and rest them fearfully against his teeth.

She was used to giving absolution. Placing her freed hands on his shoulders, she began to speak to him in That Voice, she began to murmur to him as if they were lovers, dismissing the feared earthquake like a naughty child, sending it to stand in the corner, forbidding it to create any trouble for the excellent Don Ángel, and such was the miracle of her vocal powers, of the sound of her voice more than anything it might have been saying, that the distressed fellow actually stopped sweating and, with a hesitant, tentative rebirth of good cheer, raised his cherubic head and smiled. "Good," said Vina Apsara. "Now let's have lunch."

At the family firm's old hacienda, which was nowadays used only for great feasts such as this, we found a long table set in the cloisters overlooking a fountained courtyard, and as Vina entered, a mariachi band began to play. Then the motorcade arrived, and out tumbled the whole appalling menagerie of the rock world, squealing and flurrying, knocking back their host's vintage tequila as if it were beer from a party can, or wine-in-a-box, and boasting about their ride through the earth tremors, the personal assistant hissing hatred at the unstable earth as if he were planning to sue it, the tour manager laughing with the glee he usually displayed only when he signed up a new act on disgracefully exploitative terms, the peacock flouncing and exclamatory, the gorillas grunting monosyllabically, the Argentine guitarists at each other's throats as usual, and the drummers—ach, drummers!—shutting out the memory of their panic by launching into a tequila-lubricated series of high-volume criticisms of the mariachi band, whose leader, resplendent in a black-and-silver outfit, hurled his sombrero to the floor and was on the point of reaching for the silver six-gun strapped to his thigh, when Don Ángel intervened and, to promote a convivial spirit, offered benevolently, "Please. If you permit it, I will intent, for your diversion, to sing."

A genuine countertenor voice silences all arguments, its sidereal sweetness shaming our pettiness, like the music of the spheres. Don

Ángel Cruz gave us Gluck, *"Trionfi Amore,"* and the mariachi singers did a creditable job as Chorus to his Orfeo.

> *Trionfi Amore!*
> *E il mondo intiero*
> *Serva all'impero*
> *Della beltà.*

The unhappy conclusion of the Orpheus story, Eurydice lost forever because of Orpheus's backwards look, was always a problem for composers and their librettists.—Hey, Calzabigi, what's this ending you're giving me here? Such a downer, I should send folks home with their faces long like a wurst? *Hello?* Happy it up, ja!—Sure, Herr Gluck, don't get so agitato. No problem! Love, it is stronger than Hades. Love, it make the gods merciful. How's about they send her back anyway? "Get outa here, kid, the guy's crazy for you! What's one little peek?" Then the lovers throw a party, and what a party! Dancing, wine, the whole nine yards. So you got your big finish, everybody goes out humming.—Works for me. Nice going, Raniero.—Sure thing, Willibald. Forget about it.

And here it was, that showstopper finale. Love's triumph over death. *The whole world obeys the rule of beauty.* To everyone's astonishment, mine included, Vina Apsara the rock star rose to her feet and sang both soprano parts, Amor as well as Euridice, and though I'm no expert she sounded word and note perfect, her voice in an ecstasy of fulfilment, finally, it seemed to be saying, you've worked out what I'm for.

> *. . . E quel sospetto*
> *Che il cor tormenta*
> *Al fin diventa*
> *Felicità.*

The tormented heart doesn't just find happiness, okay: it *becomes happiness.* That's the story, anyway. That's the way the song goes.

The earth began to shake just as she finished, applauding her performance. The great still life of the banquet, the plates of meats and bowls of fruits and bottles of the best Cruz tequila, and even the banquet table itself, now commenced to jump and dance in Disney fashion, inanimate objects animated by the little sorcerer's apprentice, that over-weening mouse; or as if moved by the sheer power of her song to join in the closing *chaconne*. As I try to remember the exact sequence of events, I find that my memory has become a silent movie. There must have been noise. Pandemonium, city of devils and their torments, could scarcely have been noisier than that Mexican town, as cracks scurried like lizards along the walls of its buildings, prying apart the walls of Don Ángel's hacienda with their long creepy fingers, until it simply fell away like an illusion, a movie façade, and through the surg-ing dust cloud of its collapse we were returned to the pitching, buck-ing streets, running for our lives, not knowing which way to run but running, anyway, while tiles fell from roofs and trees were flung into the air and sewage burst upwards from the streets and houses exploded and suitcases long stored in attics began to rain down from the sky.

But I remember only silence, the silence of great horror. The silence, to be more exact, of photography, because that was my profession, so naturally it was what I turned to the moment the earthquake began. All my thoughts were of the little squares of film passing through my old cameras, Voigtländer Leica Pentax, of the forms and colours being registered therein by the accidents of movement and event, and of course by the skill or lack of it with which I managed to point the lens in the right or wrong direction at the wrong or right time. Here was the eternal silence of faces and bodies and animals and even nature itself, caught—yes—by my camera, but caught also in the grip of the fear of the unforeseeable and the anguish of loss, in the clutches of this hated metamorphosis, the appalling silence of a way of life at the moment of its annihilation, its transformation into a golden past that could never wholly be rebuilt, because once you have been in an earthquake you know, even if you survive without a scratch, that like a stroke in the heart, it remains in the earth's breast, horribly potential, always promising to return, to hit you again, with an even more dev-astating force.

A photograph is a moral decision taken in one eighth of a second, or one sixteenth, or one one-hundred-and-twenty-eighth. Snap your fingers; a snapshot's faster. Halfway between voyeur and witness, high artist and low scum, that's where I've made my life, making my eye-blink choices. That's okay, that's cool. I'm still alive, and I've been spat at and called names only a couple of hundred times. I can live with the name-calling. It's the men with the heavy weaponry who worry me. (And they are men, almost always, all those arnolds carrying termina-tors, all those zealous suicidists with their toilet-brush beards and no hair on their baby-naked upper lips; but when women do such work, they're often worse.)

I've been an event junkie, me. Action has been my stimulant of choice. I always liked to stick my face right up against the hot sweaty broken surface of what was being done, with my eyes open, drinking, and the rest of my senses switched off. I never cared if it stank, or if its slimy touch made you want to throw up, or what it might do to your taste buds if you licked it, or even how loud it screamed. Just the way it looked. That's where for a long time I went for feeling, and truth.

What Actually Happens: nothing to beat it, when you're pressed up against it, as long as you don't get your face torn off. No rush like it on earth.

Long ago I developed a knack for invisibility. It allowed me to go right up to the actors in the world's drama, the sick, the dying, the crazed, the mourning, the rich, the greedy, the ecstatic, the bereft, the angry, the murderous, the secretive, the bad, the children, the good, the newsworthy; to shimmy into their charmed space, into the midst of their rage or grief or transcendent arousal, to penetrate the defining instant of their being-in-the-world and get my fucking picture. On many occasions this gift of dematerialisation has saved my life. When people said to me, do not drive down that sniper-infested road, do not enter that warlord's stronghold, you'd do well to circumnavigate that militia's fiefdom, I was drawn towards it almost irresistibly. Nobody has ever gone in there with a camera and come out alive, somebody would warn, and at once I'd head off past the checkpoint of no return. When I got back people looked at me oddly, as if seeing a ghost, and asked how I managed it. I shook my head. Truthfully, I often didn't know. Perhaps if I knew I wouldn't be able to do it any more and then I'd get killed in some half-baked combat zone. One day that may happen.

The closest I can get to it is that I know how to make myself small. Not physically small, for I am a tallish guy, heavy-set, but psychically.

I just smile my self-deprecating smile and shrink into insignificance. By my manner I persuade the sniper I do not merit his bullet, my way of carrying myself convinces the warlord to keep his great axe clean. I make them understand that I'm not worthy of their violence. Maybe it works because I'm being sincere, because I truly mean to deprecate myself. There are experiences I carry around with me, memories I can draw on when I want to remind myself of my low value. Thus a form of acquired modesty, the product of my early life and misdeeds, has succeeded in keeping me alive.

"Bullshit," was Vina Apsara's view. "It's just another version of your technique for pulling chicks."

Modesty works with women, that's true. But with women I'm faking it. My nice, shy smile, my recessive body language. The more I back off in my suede jacket and combat boots, smiling shyly beneath my bald head (how often I've been told what a beautiful head I have!), the more insistently they advance. In love one advances by retreating. But then what I mean by love and what Ormus Cama, for example, meant by the same word were two different things. For me, it was always a skill, the *ars amatoria:* the first approach, the deflection of anxieties, the arousal of interest, the feint of departure, the slow inexorable return. The leisurely inward spiral of desire. *Kama.* The art of love.

Whereas for Ormus Cama it was just a simple matter of life and death. Love was for life, and endured beyond death. Love was Vina, and beyond Vina there was nothing but the void.

I've never been invisible to the earth's little creatures, however. Those six-legged dwarf terrorists have got my number, no question about it. Show me (or, preferably, don't show me) an ant, lead me (don't lead me) to a wasp, a bee, a mosquito, a flea. It'll have me for breakfast; also for other, more substantial repasts. What's small and bites, bites me. So at a certain moment in the heart of the earthquake, as I photographed a lost child crying for her parents, I was stung, once, hard, as if by conscience, on the cheek, and as I jerked my face away from my camera I was just in time (thank you, I guess, to whatever horrible *aguijón-*wielding thing it was; not conscience, probably, but a snapper's sixth sense) to see the beginning of the tequila flood. The town's many giant storage vats had burst.

The streets were like whips, snaking and cracking. The Ángel distillery was one of the first to succumb to this lashing. Old wood burst open, new metal buckled and split. The urinous river of tequila made its frothing way into the lanes of the town, the leading wave of the torrent overtook the fleeing populace and turned it head over heels, and such was the potency of the brew that those who swallowed mouthfuls of that angelic surf came up not only wet and gasping but drunk. The last time I saw Don Ángel Cruz, he was scurrying in the tequila-drowning squares with a saucepan in his hand and two kettles on strings slung around his neck, trying pathetically to save what he could.

This is how people behave when their dailiness is destroyed, when for a few moments they see, plain and unadorned, one of the great shaping forces of life. Calamity fixes them with her mesmeric eye, and they begin to scoop and paw at the rubble of their days, trying to pluck the memory of the quotidian—a toy, a book, a garment, even a photograph—from the garbage heaps of the irretrievable, of their overwhelming loss. Don Ángel Cruz turned panhandler was the childlike, fabulous image I needed, a figure eerily reminiscent of the surreal Saucepan Man from some of Vina Apsara's favourite books, the Faraway Tree series of Enid Blyton that travelled with her wherever she went. Cloaking myself in invisibility, I began to shoot.

I don't know how long all this took. The shaking table, the collapse of the hacienda, the roller-coaster streets, the people gasping and tumbling in the tequila river, the descent of hysteria, the deathly laughter of the unhoused, the bankrupted, the unemployed, the orphaned, the dead . . . ask me to put an estimate on it and I'd come up empty. Twenty seconds? Half an hour? Search me. The invisibility cloak, and my other trick of switching off all my senses and channelling all my powers of perception through my mechanical eyes—these things have, as they say, a downside. When I'm facing the enormities of the actual, when that great monster is roaring into my lens, I lose control of other things. What time is it? Where is Vina? Who's dead? Who's alive? Is that an abyss opening beneath my combat boots? What did you say? There's a medical team trying to reach this dying woman? What are you talking about? Why are you getting in my way, who the fuck do you think you're trying to push around? *Can't you see I'm working?*

Who was alive? Who was dead? Where was Vina? Where was Vina? Where was Vina?

I snapped out of it. Insects stung my neck. The torrent of tequila ceased, the precious river poured away into the cracking earth. The town looked like a picture postcard torn up by an angry child and then painstakingly reassembled by its mother. It had acquired the quality of brokenness, had become kin to the great family of the broken: broken plates, broken dolls, broken English, broken promises, broken hearts. Vina Apsara lurched towards me through the dust. "Rai, thank God." For all her fooling with Buddhist wisemen (Rinpoche Hollywood and the Ginsberg Lama) and Krishna Consciousness cymbalists and Tantric gurus (those *kundalini* flashers) and Transcendental™ rishis and masters of this or that crazy wisdom, Zen and the Art of the Deal, the Tao of Promiscuous Sex, Self-Love and Enlightenment, for all her spiritual faddishness, I always in my own godless way found it hard to believe that she actually believed in an actually existing god. But she probably did; I was probably wrong about that too; and anyway, what other word is there? When there's that gratitude in you for life's dumb luck, when there's nobody to thank and you need to thank somebody, what do you say? God, Vina said. The word sounded to me like a way of disposing of emotion. It was a place to put something that had no place else to go.

From the sky, a larger insect bore down upon us, burdening us with the insistent downdraft of its raucous wings. The helicopter had taken off just in time to escape destruction. Now the pilot brought it down almost to ground zero, and beckoned, hovering. "Let's get out of here," Vina shouted. I shook my head. "You go," I yelled back at her. Work before play. I had to get my pictures on to the wires. "I'll see you later," I bellowed. "What?" "Later." "What?"

The plan had been for the helicopter to fly us, for a weekend's relaxation, to a remote villa on the Pacific coast, the Villa Huracán, co-owned by the president of the Colchis record company and located to the north of Puerto Vallarta, in privileged isolation, sandwiched like a magic kingdom between the jungle and the sea. Now there was no way of knowing if the villa still stood. The world had changed. Yet, like the townspeople clinging to their framed photographs, like Don Ángel with his saucepans, Vina Apsara clung to the idea of continuity, of the prearranged itinerary. She was staying with the programme. Until my kidnapped images were off to the world's news desks to be ransomed, however, there could be no tropical Shangri-la for me.

"I'm going, then," she screamed.

"I can't go."

"What?"

"Go."

"Fuck you."

"What?"

Then she was in the helicopter, and it was rising, and I had not gone with her, and I never saw her again, none of us did, and the last words she screamed down at me break my heart every time I think of them, and I think of them a few hundred times a day, every day, and then there are the endless, sleepless nights.

"Goodbye, Hope."

I began to use the workname "Rai" when I was taken on by the famous Nebuchadnezzar Agency. Pseudonyms, stage names, worknames: for writers, for actors, for spies, these are useful masks, hiding or altering one's true identity. But when I began to call myself *Rai,* prince, it felt like removing a disguise, because I was letting the world in on my most cherished secret, which was that ever since childhood this had been Vina's private pet name for me, the badge of my puppy love. "Because you carry yourself like a little rajah," she'd told me, fondly, when I was only nine and had braces on my teeth, "so it's only your friends who know you're just some no-account jerk."

That was Rai: a boy princeling. But childhood ends, and in adult life it was Ormus Cama who became Vina's Prince Charming, not I. Still, the nickname clung to me. And Ormus was good enough to use it too, or let's say he caught it off Vina like an infection, or let's say he never dreamed I could give him any competition, that I could be a threat, and that's why he could think of me as a friend. . . . But never mind that just now. *Rai.* It also meant desire: a man's personal inclination, the direction he chose to go in; and will, the force of a man's character. All that I liked. I liked that it was a name that travelled easily; everyone could say it, it sounded good on every tongue. And if on occasion I

turned into "Hey, Ray" in that mighty democracy of mispronuncia-
tion, the United States, then I was not disposed to argue, I just took
the plum assignments and left town. And in another part of the world,
Rai was music. In the home of this music, alas, religious fanatics have
lately started killing the musicians. They think the music is an insult to
god, who gave us voices but does not wish us to sing, who gave us free
will, *rai,* but prefers us not to be free.

Anyway, now everybody says it: Rai. Just the one name, it's easy, it's
a style. Most people don't even know my real name. Umeed Merchant,
did I mention that? Umeed Merchant, raised in a different universe, a
different dimension of time, in a bungalow on Cuffe Parade, Bombay,
which burned down long ago. The name Merchant, I should perhaps
explain, means "merchant." Bombay families often bear names derived
from some deceased ancestor's line of work. Engineers, Contractors,
Doctors. And let's not forget the Readymoneys, the Cashondeliveris,
the Fishwalas. And a Mistry is a mason and a Wadia is a shipbuilder and
a lawyer is a Vakil and a banker is a Shroff. And from the thirsty city's
long love affair with aerated drinks comes not only Batliwala but also
Sodawaterbatliwala, and not only Sodawaterbatliwala but Sodawater-
batli*opener*wala too.

Cross my heart and hope to die.

"Goodbye, Hope," cried Vina, and the helicopter went into a steep
banking climb and was gone.

Umeed, you see. Noun, feminine. Meaning hope.

Why do we care about singers? Wherein lies the power of songs?
Maybe it derives from the sheer strangeness of there being singing in
the world. The note, the scale, the chord; melodies, harmonies, arrangements; symphonies, ragas, Chinese operas, jazz, the blues: that such
things should exist, that we should have discovered the magical intervals and distances that yield the poor cluster of notes, all within the
span of a human hand, from which we can build our cathedrals of
sound, is as alchemical a mystery as mathematics, or wine, or love.
Maybe the birds taught us. Maybe not. Maybe we are just creatures in
search of exaltation. We don't have much of it. Our lives are not what
we deserve; they are, let us agree, in many painful ways deficient. Song

turns them into something else. Song shows us a world that is worthy of our yearning, it shows us our selves as they might be, if we were worthy of the world.

Five mysteries hold the keys to the unseen: the act of love, and the birth of a baby, and the contemplation of great art, and being in the presence of death or disaster, and hearing the human voice lifted in song. These are the occasions when the bolts of the universe fly open and we are given a glimpse of what is hidden; an eff of the ineffable. Glory bursts upon us in such hours: the dark glory of earthquakes, the slippery wonder of new life, the radiance of Vina's singing.

Vina, to whom even strangers would come, following her star, hoping to receive redemption from her voice, her large, damp eyes, her touch. How was it that so explosive, even amoral, a woman came to be seen as an emblem, an ideal, by more than half the population of the world? Because she was no angel, let me tell you that, but try saying so to Don Ángel. Maybe it's just as well she was not born a Christian, or they'd have tried to make her a saint. Our Lady of the Stadiums, our arena madonna, baring her scars to the masses like Alexander the Great rousing his soldiers for war; our plastered Unvirgin, bleeding red tears from her eyes and hot music from her throat. As we retreat from religion, our ancient opiate, there are bound to be withdrawal symptoms, there will be many side effects of this Apsaran variety. The habit of worship is not easily broken. In the museums, the rooms with the icons are crowded. We always did prefer our iconic figures injured, stuck full of arrows or crucified upside down; we need them flayed and naked, we want to watch their beauty crumble slowly and to observe their narcissistic grief. Not in spite of their faults but *for* their faults we adore them, worshipping their weaknesses, their pettinesses, their bad marriages, their substance abuse, their spite. Seeing ourselves in Vina's mirror, and forgiving her, we also forgave ourselves. She redeemed us by her sins.

I was no different. I always needed her to make things all right: some botched job, some bruise on my pride, some departing woman whose last cruel words succeeded in getting under my skin. But it was only near the very end of her life that I found the courage to ask for her love, to make my bid for her, and for a heady moment I truly believed I might tear her from Ormus's clutches. Then she died, leaving me with a pain that only her magic touch could have assuaged. But she wasn't there to kiss my brow and say, It's okay, Rai, you little jerk, let it pass, let me put my witchy ointment on those bad, naughty stings, come here to mama and watch the good times roll.

This is what I feel now when I think of Don Ángel Cruz weeping before her in his fragile distillery: envy. And jealousy too. *I wish I'd done that, opened my heart and begged for her before it was too late, and also I wish she hadn't touched you, you snivelling squeaky-voiced bankrupt capitalist worm.*

We all looked to her for peace, yet she herself was not at peace. And so I've chosen to write here, publicly, what I can no longer whisper into her private ear: that is, everything. I have chosen to tell our story, hers and mine and Ormus Cama's, all of it, every last detail, and then maybe she can find a sort of peace here, on the page, in this under-world of ink and lies, that respite which was denied her by life. So I stand at the gate of the inferno of language, there's a barking dog and a ferryman waiting and a coin under my tongue for the fare.

"I have not been a bad man," Don Ángel Cruz whimpered. Okay, I'll do some whimpering of my own. Listen, Vina: I am not a bad man, either. Though, as I will fully confess, I have been a traitor in love, and being an only child have as yet no child, and in the name of art have stolen the images of the stricken and the dead, and philandered, and shrugged (dislodging from their perch on my shoulders the angels that watched over me), and worse things too, yet I hold myself to be a man among men, a man as men are, no better nor no worse. Though I be condemned to the stinging of insects, yet have I not led a wicked vil-lain's life. Depend upon it: I have not.

Do you know the Fourth *Georgic* of the bard of Mantua, P. Vergilius Maro? Ormus Cama's father, the redoubtable Sir Darius Xerxes Cama, classicist and honey-lover, knew his Virgil, and through him I learned some too. Sir Darius was an Aristaeus admirer, of course; Aristaeus, the first beekeeper in world literature, whose unwelcome advances to the dryad Eurydice led her to step on a snake, whereupon the wood nymph perished and mountains wept. Virgil's treatment of the Orpheus story is extraordinary: he tells it in seventy-six blazing lines, writing with all the stops pulled out, and then, in a perfunctory thirty lines more, he allows Aristaeus to perform his expiatory ritual sacrifice, and that's that, end of poem, no more need to worry about those foolish doomed lovers. The real hero of the poem is the keeper of bees, the "Arcadian master," the maker of a miracle far greater than that wretched Thracian singer's art, which could not even raise his lover from the dead. This is what Aristaeus could do: *he could spontaneously generate new bees from the rotting carcase of a cow.* His was "the heavenly gift of honey from the air."

Well, then. And Don Ángel could produce tequila from blue agave. And I, Umeed Merchant, photographer, can spontaneously generate new meaning from the putrefying carcase of what is the case. Mine is the hellish gift of conjuring response, feeling, perhaps even comprehension, from uncaring eyes, by placing before them the silent faces of the real. I, too, am compromised, no man knows better than I how irredeemably. Nor are there any sacrifices I can perform, or gods I can propitiate. Yet my names mean "hope" and "will," and that counts for something, right? Vina, am I right?

Sure, baby. Sure, Rai, honey. It counts.

Music, love, death. Certainly a triangle of sorts; maybe even an eternal one. But Aristaeus, who brought death, also brought life, a little like Lord Shiva back home. Not just a dancer, but Creator and Destroyer, both. Not only stung by bees but a bringer into being of bee stings. So, music, love and life-death: these three. As once we also were three. Ormus, Vina and I. We did not spare each other. In this telling, therefore, nothing will be spared. Vina, I must betray you, so that I can let you go.

Begin.

2

MELODIES AND SILENCES

Ormus Cama was born in Bombay, India, in the early hours of May 27, 1937, and within moments of his birth began making the strange, rapid finger movements with both hands which any guitarist could have identified as chord progressions. However, no guitar players were included among those invited to coo over the new-born baby at the Sisters of Maria Gratiaplena Nursing Home on Altamount Road, or, later, at the family apartment on Apollo Bunder, and the miracle might have gone unnoticed had it not been for the single reel of 8 mm monochrome film shot on June 17 on a hand-held Paillard Bolex, the property of my own father, Mr. V. V. Merchant, a keen amateur of home movies. The "Vivvy movie," as it came to be known, luckily survived in reasonable condition until, many years later, the new computer technologies of film enhancement allowed the world to see, in digitally magnified close-ups, the pudgy hands of baby Ormus incontestably playing air guitar, moving soundlessly through a complex series of monster riffs and dizzy licks with a speed, and feeling, of which the instrument's greatest practitioners would have been proud.

Back at the beginning, though, music was the last thing on anyone's mind. Ormus's mother, Lady Spenta Cama, had been told in the thirty-fifth week of pregnancy that the child she was carrying had died in her womb. At that late date she had no choice but to go through the full agony of labour, and when she saw the stillborn corpse of Ormus's elder brother Gayo, his non-identical, dizygotic twin, her wretchedness was so great that she believed the continued movement within her was her own death trying to be born, so that she could be united with her lifeless child at once.

Until that unhappy moment she had been a placid individual, an astigmatic endomorph, heavy-spectacled and heavy-bodied, given to a certain bovine rotation of the jaw, which her voluble, irascible, erratic husband, Sir Darius Xerxes Cama, tall, ectomorphic, extravagantly moustachioed, and gimlet-eyed under his red, golden-tasselled fez, often deliberately mistook for stupidity. It was not stupidity. It was the unflappability of a soul fully occupied on the spiritual level, or, more exactly, a soul who found in her everyday routines a means of communing with the divine. Lady Spenta Cama was on speaking terms with two of the Parsi angels, the Amesha Spentas for whom she was named: the Angel Good Thoughts, silent conversations with whom occupied her for an hour each morning (she steadfastly declined to reveal the nature of these chats to her husband or anyone else); and the Angel Orderly Righteousness, under whose tutelage she became minutely attentive to household affairs, the supervision of which took up most of her afternoons. Of the various supernatural Spentas, this was the duo with whom Lady Spenta Cama felt the most affinity. The Angel Excellence and the Angel Immortality were far beyond her, she humbly allowed, and as to the Angel Perfect Sovereignty and the Angel Divine Piety, it would have been immodest to claim too close a connection with them.

The Christian and Muslim concept of angels, she liked to boast, was "derived" from these Zoroastrian originals, just as devils descended from "our own Daevas"; such was her proprietorial feeling, her pride in Parsi primacy, that she spoke of these malignant forces as if they were personal pets, or one of the many china ornaments with which she littered the Camas' thing-stuffed Apollo Bunder apartment, that much-coveted Bombay belvedere with its five high windows facing saltily out to sea. It was nevertheless startling that one so close to virtue should give way so spectacularly to the Daevas Misery, False Appearance and Evil Mind, and wretchedly cry out for woe.

"Arré, come on, then, take me, why not, O death be my dominion," Lady Spenta squalled. The two grandly Valkyrian ladies by her bedside frowned disapprovingly. Ute Schaapsteker, the chief consultant gynaecologist at the Maria Gratiaplena (known throughout the city's upper echelons as "Snooty Utie" or, alternatively, "Sister Adolf"), made a number of sharply admonitory remarks concerning the impropriety of prematurely wishing for death, which would certainly come, unwished for, at the proper time. Her aide, the midwife Sister John, was still young in those days but was well on the way to becoming that dark galleon of a bedside presence whose formidable gloom and upper-lip mole blighted many a Bombay birth over the next fifty years. "Great tidings of gladness and joy!" she boomed sourly. "For He that is Mighty hath harvested unto Himself the soul of this fortunate infant, like as though it were a grain of blessed rice." The pair of them would no doubt have continued in this vein for some considerable time, had Lady Spenta not suddenly added, in entirely altered, indeed comprehensively astonished tones, "Such pressure on my back passage, either I am in danger of passing a stool or else there is some other *chokra* trying to make an appearance."

It had not been her death wriggling inside her, of course. Nor were her bowels in danger of opening. She quickly gave birth to a small but healthy baby, a little four-and-a-half-pound eel of a boy whose living form had been concealed from Dr. Schaapsteker's examinations, during both pregnancy and labour, by his dead twin's larger body. Remarkably, the Camas already had a five-year-old pair of dizygotic male twins, Khusro and Ardaviraf, known to one and all as "Cyrus and Virus." Sir Darius Xerxes Cama, who knew his Greek mythology, was familiar with the Olympian deities' practice of inserting a babe (Idas, Polydeuces) of semi-divine parentage into a womb that was also preparing to bear (Lynceus, Castor) a fully human child. In the case of the precocious, multi-talented Khusro—a child with the genuinely malign ruthlessness of a true hero—and the slow-witted, sweet-natured Ardaviraf, the ancient Greeks would have had little difficulty in identifying the child with a god for a father. On this second occasion, presumably, the dead Gayo was the earthly child and the living Ormus the one with the immortal pedigree as well as yearnings. Thus Sir Darius would be deemed the father of one duffer and one corpse, an inglorious fate. But scholarship is one thing, parenthood quite another, and Sir Darius Xerxes Cama, "the Apollonian of Apollo Bunder," was a staunch Cantabrigian rationalist and an eminent barrister-at-law who had "eaten his dinners" at Middle Temple and had subsequently dedicated his life to what he called, in an intentionally oxymoronic flash of wit, "the miracle of reason." He yielded up rights of paternity to no god, whatever his origin, took up the reins of fatherhood and, in strict fairness, oppressed all his children equally.

The living baby was taken away to the incubator by scowling Sister John, who found it harder to celebrate a birth than a "harvesting." The dead baby was removed (there are sights too powerful for mere men's eyes), and at last Sir Darius Xerxes Cama was allowed to enter the delivery room. Spenta was gripped by remorse. "In the moment of his birth I allowed the servants of the Lie to seize my tongue," she confessed. Sir Darius had long found the various manifestations of his wife's literalist religiosity difficult to handle. He did his best to conceal his unease, but could not shut out the image of Lady Spenta's tongue being worked by little bat-winged creatures despatched by Angra Mainyu, a.k.a. Ahriman himself. He closed his eyes and shuddered.

Lady Spenta rallied. "Whose idea was it to name that poor boy Gayo, anyway?" she demanded, forgetting in the heat and emotional ambiguity of the moment that it had been her own. Her husband, too gallant to remind her, bowed his head and took the blame. The First-Created Man, Gayomart, had indeed been killed by Angra Mainyu long ago. "*Bad* choice of name," Lady Spenta cried, bursting once again into tears. Sir Darius Xerxes Cama's head bowed lower; Lady Spenta found herself addressing the tasselled top of his fez. She knocked on it, firmly. It yielded a hollow sound. "The only way of compensating," she insisted, sobbing, "is at once to name the surviving boy with the name of god."

Hormuz or Ormazd, local derivatives of Ahura Mazda, were her stated options, which Sir Darius Xerxes Cama the classicist at once Latinized as Ormus. His wife was placated. She dried her eyes and together the couple visited the incubator room, where Ute Schaapsteker confirmed that the child was expected to live. "My little

Ormie," Lady Spenta Cama purred at the under-sized little fellow through incubator glass. "My little shrimpy boy. Now you're safe from Hell. Now they can't open up the ground and take you down."

Sir Darius, having received Snooty Utie's reassurances about little Ormus's prospects, made his excuses, went so far as to kiss his wife and rushed off, somewhat too eagerly for Lady Spenta's taste, to play cricket. It was a big match. That year the annual Quadrangular Tournament between the city's British, Hindu, Muslim and Parsi teams had become Pentangular, and on this day Sir Darius had been put down to turn out for the Parsis against the new boys, The Rest, an XI drawn from the ranks of Bombay's Christians, Anglo-Indians and Jews. Sir Darius Xerxes Cama at forty-three still possessed the physical strength and godlike musculature of an all-round sporting hero, body-builder and ex–amateur wrestling champion. His elegant left-handed batsmanship remained much in demand; his trademark stroke was a lazily executed, and therefore alarming, but still highly effective late cut. And in short spells he could still produce bowling of discomforting speed: "the thunderbolts of Darius," as they had long been known. When he pulled on his whites, divesting himself of the long coat and high fez of a Parsi gentleman after his anxious nocturnal hours at the nursing home, he felt a sense of proud relief steal over him. No longer was he obliged to prowl peripherally at the edges of women's business! He was a tiger unchained, and his bursting pride at becoming the father of a third male child would shortly be visited upon the enemy in the form of doughty deeds with bat and ball. This transformation from citizen to sportsman in the privacy of a changing tent at the edge of the great Maidan was, of all life's rituals, the one Sir Darius most keenly enjoyed. (When, after a day's ferocious advocacy, he would strip away the gown and wig of the Law and take up his willow cudgel, he felt as if he were entering into his better nature, into a finer self of Olympian fibre and grace.) His fellow opening batsman, a dashing young blade named Homi Catrack, asked him if he felt able to play after missing a night's sleep. "Pish!" cried Sir Darius, and strode forth to do battle for his race.

On the Maidan, a large, noisy crowd awaited his coming. Sir Darius had always disapproved of the behaviour of Bombay's spectators. It was the one small blemish on these otherwise delightful days. The hooting, the shrieking, the blaring of tin horns, the banging of *dhols,* the rising chant as a pace merchant ran in to bowl, the barracking, the cries of snack vendors, the howling laughter, in short the incessant clamour, created, in Sir Darius's opinion, an unsuitable environment for the practice of the game's noble arts. The country's imperial overlords, observing the bawdiness of the populace, could only feel disappointed at the continuing backwardness of those over whom they had ruled so wisely for so long. Sir Darius Xerxes Cama, walking out to bat, wanted to cry aloud, "Brace up! Do yourselves justice! The British are watching."

It was a "fine day," the day of Ormus Cama's birth. This old Bombay term, long fallen into disuse, used to mean a day on which unexpected cloud cover brought cool relief from the heat. Schoolchildren had been given a "fine day holiday," as was the occasional practice in those far-off times. This particular fine day, however, was ill-starred. True, a child had been born alive, but another had been born dead. Demons, Daevas, had been conjured, and there were disapprovals hanging in the air. At the Sisters of Maria Gratiaplena Nursing Home, Snooty Utie Schaapsteker's disapproval of Lady Spenta's self-pity had mingled with Sir Darius's disapproval of what he might on another occasion have called his wife's "superstitions," to create a less than celebratory mood. Here at the cricket ground, too, there were unexpected noises of reproof. A band of nationalist sympathizers had arrived with a variety of deafening musical instruments, and from the beginning of the game they set out to disrupt the players' concentration by what Sir Darius thought to be a particularly tasteless type of musical heckling.

"Don't be wicket," the hecklers chanted, to the beat of drums and the tooting of trumpets, "Ban communal cricket." Sir Darius Xerxes Cama was aware that Mahatma Gandhi and his followers had denounced the Pentangular Tournament as a communally divisive, anti-national throwback, in which men of colonialized mentality performed like monkeys for the amusement of the British and gave unhelpful assistance to the policy of divide-and-rule. Sir Darius was no Independence merchant. Nationalists! He entertained the gravest doubts about the wisdom of surrendering the governance of India to men of such limited musical sense. For Mr. Gandhi personally he conceded a grudging respect but felt that if he could only persuade the great man to don flannels and learn the basics of the game, the Mahatma was bound to be persuaded of the tournament's value in honing that spirit of competition without which no people can take its place at the forefront of the world community.

As he arrived at the crease, one of the hecklers sang out, "Lady Daria's come to play!" At once a distressingly large section of the crowd—must be Christians, Anglos or Jews, huffed Sir Darius in displeasure—took up the insulting chant. "Lady Cama, give us drama! Give a catch and be a charmer!" Toot, rattle, clank. "Give us drama, Lady Cama."

Now Sir Darius noticed that his own boys, the five-year-old twins Cyrus and Virus, were sitting with their ayah on the grass close by the nationalist hecklers, grinning happily, giving every appearance of enjoying the spoilsports' antics. He moved a few paces towards them, waving his bat. "Khusro! Ardaviraf! Move on!" he called. The boys and the ayah were unable to hear him in the din and assumed he was waving. They all waved back. The hecklers, thinking he was shaking his bat at them, and happy to have so provoked him, redoubled their efforts. The music of their merry hostility clamoured in his ears. Sir Darius Xerxes Cama faced the bowling in an imperfect frame of mind.

Mr. Aaron Abraham, opening the bowling for The Rest, was able to make the new ball swing discomfortingly in those overcast conditions. Sir Darius was lucky to survive his first three deliveries. Seeing him struggle, the nationalist claque grew even noisier. Clank, rattle, toot. The drummers and trumpeters improvised a tune, and over and over his tormentors sang, "Lady Daria, don't be slack. Make a duck and off you quack." And then came a variant, and evidently popular, version: "Lady Donald, make a duck."

Sir Darius strode down the pitch to confer with his partner.

"Quack, is it?" he fumed, swishing his bat. "I'll soon give them quack, but what is this Donald?" As he asked the question, however, he remembered a recent visit to the cinema with the twins to see Chaplin's *Modern Times,* a film Sir Darius admired for, among other things, staying "silent." In the supporting programme they had seen a cartoon short, "Orphans' Benefit," featuring a new, anarchically violent, web-footed and horribly noisy anti-hero. Sir Darius brightened. "Donald, is it?" he roared. "Ha! Ha! Ha! I'll quickly make those bounders Duck."

Homi Catrack tried in vain to calm him. "Never mind the crowd. Play yourself in; then we'll show them what-for." But Sir Darius had lost his head. The fourth ball of Aaron Abraham's over was a loose delivery, eminently hittable, and Sir Darius seized his chance. He swung with all his might, and there can be no question that he was trying to hit the ball right at the group of heckling nationalist musicians. Afterwards, in the grip of an unassuageable remorse, he conceded that his injured vanity had overcome the fatherly prudence that should have been his uppermost concern, but by then it was too late; the cricket ball had travelled towards the boundary at high velocity and could not be re-called.

It was not going to hit the hecklers and there was no way of correcting its course, but many spectators were diving out of its way, for it was travelling at genuinely frightening speed, and there, smack in its path, moving neither to left nor to right, were Sir Darius Xerxes Cama's non-identical twin sons, standing up to applaud their father's great stroke, fearless, because how could their beloved father possibly cause either of them the slightest harm?

No doubt the ayah's slow reactions were partly responsible for the accident, but from the moment that he saw what was about to happen, Sir Darius never blamed anyone except himself. He bellowed out a warning at the top of his voice, but the drums and horns were louder than his screams, music prevented him from sounding the alarm, and an instant later, sweet, slow Ardaviraf Cama was struck by the rocketing cricket ball, right between the eyes, and fell down flat, as if he were made of wood, like a stump.

Perhaps at the very moment when the story of the Cama family was being re-written forever by the addition of that cruel line, the trajectory of a red cricket ball from a father's bat to a son's forehead, my mother and father were meeting for the first time at the Sisters of Maria Gratiaplena Nursing Home.

When it comes to love there's no telling what people will convince themselves of. In spite of all the evidence that life is discontinuous, a valley of rifts, and that random chance plays a great part in our fates, we go on believing in the continuity of things, in causation and meaning. But we live on a broken mirror, and fresh cracks appear in its surface every day. People (like Virus Cama) may slip through those cracks and be lost. Or, like my parents, they may be thrown by chance into each other's arms, and fall in love. In direct contradiction of their predominantly rational philosophies of life, however, my father and mother always believed that they were drawn together by Destiny, which was so determined to unite them that it manifested itself in no less than four different forms: that is to say, social, genealogical, gastronomical and Sister John.

They had both come to visit Lady Spenta Cama and were both inappropriately dressed in mournful attire, because they had not heard of the birth of little Ormus and were simply and kindly intending to console Lady Spenta for having had to endure the experience of a still-birth. My parents were younger than Sir Darius and Lady Spenta by a generation, and both were relatively recent friends of the family. An unlikely friendship had developed between the two men, who had found common ground in the subject of Bombay itself; Bombay, that great metropolitan creation of the British, whose foremost chronicler my father—the England-returned architect and devoted local historian V. V. Merchant (soon to be the diffident *auteur* of a subsequently celebrated home movie)—would in time become. Sir Darius Xerxes Cama, honoured with a baronetcy for services to the Indian Bar, liked to say with a great laugh that he, too, was a great metropolitan creation of the British, and proud of it. "When you write this city's history, Merchant," he roared one night over a clubhouse dinner of mulligatawny and pomfret, "you might just find it's my biography you've penned." As for my mother, she had come to know Lady Spenta Cama at meetings of the Bombay Literary Society. Lady Spenta was the least well read of women, but her serene insouciance in the face of her almost Himalayan ignorance inspired in the younger (and immensely more brilliant) Ameer a kind of amused awe that, had events taken a different course, might have deepened towards friendship.

In the nursing home's waiting room, surrounded by the beaming relatives of new-born male children and the determinedly cheerful relatives of new-born girls, my future parents made an odd pair, he wearing a dark suit and a lugubrious expression, she in a plain white sari, without jewellery, and wearing minimal make-up. (Many years later, she confided to me that "I was always certain of your father's love, because when he fell for me I was looking less attractive than a water buffalo.") As the only mourners in a place of rejoicing, it was natural that they should move towards each other and introduce themselves.

Both of them would have been feeling awkward at the prospect of facing Lady Spenta and Sir Darius in what they believed to be a moment of deep grief. My mild, tender-hearted father would have been shifting his weight and smiling his embarrassed, buck-toothed smile on account of a strangling emotional inarticulacy that made it hard for him to reveal to the outside world the great depths of feeling within his breast, and an unworldly temperament that led him to prefer the mustinesses of records offices to the unfathomable messiness of Bombay life. Ameer, my mother—"rich by name, and the real money in the family," in her own subsequent, sardonic self-description— would also have been ill at ease, because neither condolences nor congratulations came easily to her lips. I do not mean to suggest that she was unfeeling or cold; quite the contrary. My mother was a disappointed altruist, an angry woman who had come down to earth expecting a better place, who had landed in the lap of luxury and never recovered from the disillusioning discovery that dismal suffering, not easeful joy, was the human norm. Neither her philanthropy nor her temper tantrums—though both were impressive—sufficed to assuage her disappointment in the planet and her own species. Her reactions to birth and death, shaped and coloured as they were by her sense of having been let down by the cosmos, could therefore seem, to the untutored ear, just a trifle, well, cynical. Or, to be frank, heartless, brutal and mortally offensive too. *Dead baby? What else to expect? He's well out of it, anyway. Living baby? Poor kid. Think what he's got in store.* That was her natural style.

However, before she could launch on some such speech and alienate my future father forever, she was forestalled by a startling discovery, and history moved, like a railway train diverted by a sudden switching of points, down an entirely different path.

"I am Merchant," my father introduced himself. "Like Vijay, but no relation, though I am also V. In fact, V. V." Ameer frowned, not because she was unaware that Vijay Merchant was a rising star of Indian cricket, but . . .

"How can you be 'Merchant'?" she objected. "You can not be 'Merchant'. I," she pointed at her chest for emphasis, "*I* am Merchant. Ameer."

"You?" (Bewildered.)

"I." (Emphatic.)

"Are Merchant?" (A shake of the head.)

"*A*. Merchant. Miss." (A shrug.)

"Then we are both Merchants," confirmed V. V., wonderingly.

"Don't be silly," Ameer rejoined.

Now V. V. Merchant emitted a long blurt. "Until my grandfather's time we were Shettys or Shetias or Sheths. He Englished it up, standardized it. Also, he converted. Became a sort of bad Muslim. Strictly non-practising, as we have all remained. You may ask, Then why bother? To which I answer only, Why not?"

"Sheths, you say," Ameer mused, sticking to the point.

"And now Merchant."

"So you *are* Merchant," she conceded.

"At your service."

"But not related."

"Misfortunately not."

My mother had come to an important, if still provisional, decision during the above conversation. Beneath V. V. Merchant's shyness and behind his buck teeth she had divined the existence of a great soul, a soul of profound constancy, a rock upon which, as she afterwards liked blasphemously to boast, she could build her church. Therefore, and with great daring, she declared in a voice that permitted no arguments, "Between one merchant and another there is no middle way. Either we must be sworn rivals or we must merge, as partners."

My father blushed, so deeply that his unkempt and already thinning hair began to quiver with delight.

What social circumstances initiated and nomenclatural coincidence encouraged was further confirmed by the small consoling gifts they had brought for Lady Spenta. With surprise, Mr. V. V. Merchant saw the small bag in Miss Ameer Merchant's hand; with equal surprise, Miss Ameer Merchant noted that Mr. V. V. Merchant was carrying an identical bag. Prominently displayed on both bags was the name of a certain highly respected food store near Kemp's Corner; and within the bags, identical glass jars lay concealed.

"Honey," explained V. V. Merchant. "Honey from the Kashmir Valley. To remind her of the sweetness of life."

"How can it be Kashmiri honey?" cried Ameer. "*This* is Kashmiri honey."

She showed him her jar; he showed her his. She began to be angry, and then, instead, started laughing. My father also laughed.

The handiwork of distant bees had eased the path of love.

Finally, and conclusively, their destiny was incarnated as an angry nun, for at this moment they found themselves faced with the stern, voluminous presence of a woman with a penumbra like a partial eclipse of the sun. "Yes?" barked Sister John, so savagely that, alas, it plunged the already tickled Merchants into a fit of the giggles. "We are here," explained V. V. Merchant, splitting his sides, "to comfort Lady Spenta Cama in her tragic hour."

"Such a terrible thing," my mother lamented, wiping away tears of mirth. "The birth of a dead child."

"Beware," said Sister John, in a voice like Judgement Day. "Or you may burn in hell-fire for your sins."

The waiting room fell silent. The two Merchants, stung by the midwife's admonition, instinctively moved closer together: closing ranks. A hand (his, hers) brushed against another hand (hers, his). In the years that followed, they would always enjoyably disagree about who had made the first move, whose fingers had reached for whose, which of them had been the clasper and which the claspee. What cannot be denied—"forward" and "loose" as the behaviour must undoubtedly be termed—is that Sister John united their hands, which were not often thereafter untwined. Until, many years later, they were driven apart by a third party. Yes, a lover of sorts, or, at any rate, a Beloved. An old lady who was not even a human being. I mean the city itself.

"Anyway," added Sister John, shrugging, "there is a birth as well."

From Sister John the two Merchants now received news of the unlooked-for live arrival whom nobody knew quite how to celebrate, because his birth was so mixed up with the tragedy of Gayomart Cama, who was finished before he began. In Sir Darius's absence, the surly nun was in charge and stood barring my parents' way. "Lady Spenta rests now. Come later." After much persuasion, this embattled quinquereme of a midwife agreed to take Vivvy and Ameer to see the under-sized but undoubtedly finger-wiggling Baby Ormus asleep in his light-filled incubator of glass, lying on his back with one knee raised, not at all unlike a god, with, on his left eyelid, a small purplish bruise, like the shadow of an eyeball. When my mother saw him glowing in that case she could not forbear to say, "Little tom thumb looks more like a snow white in this glass coffin," whereupon two sharp intakes of breath informed her that this ill-advised simile had shocked not only Sister John but Lady Spenta Cama herself, Lady Spenta who had risen to greet her visitors and tottered up behind them to be hit with this ice-cold verbal douche right between the eyes. "Oh," Lady Spenta said, blinking with shock, rooted to the spot, rotating her slack jaw. "A coffin, you say. Oh, my, my. A witch has come to put a curse upon my child."

My father tried stumblingly to pacify her, but it was too late. Too late to salvage things on that not-so-fine day.

I repeat: until the day of Ormus's birth Lady Spenta Cama had been, by nature, almost preternaturally calm. The new wildness of her formulations was thus an indication of the moment's star-crossed, transformational nature. From that time onwards her personality changed, becoming nervy, unsettled, easily flustered. Also, after hearing my mother's so-called curse, Spenta became incapable of loving the accursed child as he deserved. Instead, she shied away from him, as if he bore a disease.

It was thanks to the Ratty-and-Mole affection between Sir Darius Cama and V.V. Merchant—the older man a flamboyant, blazered sportsman and bon vivant, the younger one of life's subfusc burrowers—that an opportunity for making amends was given, and speedily accepted, three weeks later. By then Ameer and Vivvy had become inseparable. They went to Apollo Bunder arm in arm. V.V. Merchant took his Paillard Bolex along, filmed the infant Ormus in his crib and presented the film to Lady Spenta as a peace offering, which she, outwardly restored to her habitual evenness of nature, was prepared to accept. My mother and Ormus's mother, however, never became really close.

But I mustn't get too far ahead of my tale.

After Miss Ameer Merchant's unintentional faux pas, my father quickly escorted my grumpily unembarrassed mother away from the scene. Lady Spenta Cama took to her bed in a frenzy of superstition. Her son Ormus's birthday, already an ambiguous event, had been further stained by Ameer's image of glass-coffined death. And when, soon afterwards, Sister John dolorously brought her the news that Sir Darius Xerxes Cama had run all the way from the cricket match on the Oval Maidan to the emergency room of the Parsi Lying-In Hospital with the limp body of his son Virus in his arms, Lady Spenta's hold on her sanity was, for a time, released.

Ardaviraf Cama regained consciousness in the intensive care unit a few hours later, apparently suffering from nothing worse than concussion and double vision. His reluctance to speak was ascribed by doctors to shock. Soon, however, it became plain that his mind had been impaired. He stopped speaking entirely, and responded to questions with slow, sad nods or melancholic shakes of the head. However, gradually even these gestures ceased, and Virus retreated into an impassive silence from which he would never emerge. As if he had become a photograph of himself. As if he were a motion picture, a "talkie" unaccountably denuded of its sound track, restored to the era before sound, without so much as the addition of title cards or piano accompaniment. As if his father's misdirected drive had so damaged his faith in all fathers, his trust in trust itself, as to necessitate this permanent retreat.

Though he would not speak, he did react to simple requests and commands. If told there was food on the table, he would quietly sit down to eat. When instructed that it was time for bed, he went to his room without a word and lay with his face to the wall. It was not long before the best medical opinion in town declared itself incapable of helping him any further. He went back to his studies at the Cathedral School, where, during lessons, he sat at his desk much as before, but never raised his hand to speak or deigned to answer any teacher's questions. After an initial period of adjustment the school accepted the new state of affairs. Virus had always been a slow child, and was slower now, but the teachers were willing to let him stay on and listen in the hope that he might improve over time.

It also became obvious that Virus no longer wished to participate in games of any sort. At school, in break periods, he sat cross-legged in a corner of the quad with, on his face, a yogi's look of perfect meditative calm, apparently oblivious to the rackety mayhem around him. Wordlessly, as he grew, he absented himself from all sporting activities, field hockey as well as cricket, and athletics too. That was the year the Maharaja of Patiala found time to open the great Brabourne Stadium in between his various extramarital liaisons, and the School Sports Day was held in that august location thereafter. On Sports Day, however, Virus would simply stay in bed, wearing his customary look of serene absence, and nobody had the heart to force him out of doors. After school hours, his twin brother Cyrus and his friends often tried, without luck, to entice him into their street games of seven-tiles or gillidanda. Even board and card games were banished from Virus's life: Carrom and rummy, Totopoly and Happy Families, Chinese chequers and Snap. He had moved into the mystery of inner space and had no time for play.

Faced with a child who, at the age of five, had decided to put away childish things, Sir Darius Xerxes Cama punished himself by giving up his beloved game of cricket forever; also his lesser loves, wrestling, fencing, swimming and squash. And because as well as himself he blamed music for having caused the accident, music of all types was banned from the Cama apartment, without hope of return. Sir Darius sold the radiogram and broke every record in his collection, and when, during the wedding season, rowdy processions would pass along Apollo Bunder en route to receptions at the Taj Hotel, he would rush about in a frenzy, slamming windows so as to shut out the wedding guests' songs. Cyrus and Virus had begun to receive lessons on the piano and the Indian flute. These were halted. The teacher was dismissed and the baby grand in the drawing room was locked. At her husband's request, Lady Spenta Cama placed the key in a silver locket, which for many years she wore around her neck.

Virus's silence became familiar, even pleasant. Sir Darius realized he was actually relieved that his afflicted son never disturbed the peace of the breakfast table by chirping up with goodness knows what meaningless childish remarks. His silence had gravitas. It was, Sir Darius decided, eloquent. History was going the wrong way. Virus's silence began to look like a grand refusal. The Independence bandwagon was rolling now—Independence, whose mob of hooligan supporters had provoked Sir Darius into injuring his own child!—and the *Pax Britannica* would shortly be at an end. "Bad times ahead," Sir Darius took to saying. "Too many people spouting too many words, and in the end those words will turn to bullets and stones. Ardaviraf's silence speaks for all of us who fear the power of these metamorphic words."

So it was that Sir Darius Xerxes Cama half persuaded himself that his son Virus's muteness was in fact a kind of sophisticated speech. This made him feel a little better, but curiously, as he exonerated himself from at least some portion of blame, his anti-musical rhetoric grew more extreme. He began to hold music responsible for the world's ills and would even argue, in his cups, that its practitioners should be wiped out, eradicated, like a disease. Music was a virus, an infection, and music-lovers were comparable to those globe-trotting sexual immoralists whose nameless activities had resulted in the global spread of syphilis. They were sick, and it was Virus Cama, with his dignified silence, who was well.

After Virus's retreat into silence, Lady Spenta beat a retreat of her own, into that spiritual world which now, more than ever, seemed like a better habitation than our own. "I know where my son has gone," she announced to her husband in a tone that brooked no argument. "He has crossed the Chinvat Bridge on his soul's journey. It is for us to keep his body safe until his soul's return." With the aid of her ally the Angel Orderly Righteousness, she dedicated herself to this task, washing Virus's body in the bath as if he were a baby, spoon-feeding him at mealtimes as if he did not know how to use his own hands. "All his efforts are engaged in his mighty journey through the otherworld," she explained. "So we must spare him worldly exertion of all types." To all these ministrations Virus Cama passively submitted, showing neither pleasure nor dislike. Nor could Sir Darius, with his heavy burden of guilt, find it in his heart to object.

The washing and feeding of Baby Ormus, however, was left in the hands of the household's employees.

Virus Cama had been named after a Zoroastrian mystic who lived at some point between the third and seventh centuries of the Christian Era and left behind him a detailed account of the journey on which Lady Spenta was convinced that her son had also embarked. If she was right, then on the Chinvat Bridge to the world of the spirit Virus Cama first witnessed a dead soul's encounter with the incarnation of his own good deeds, a beautiful girl whose enormous breasts "swelled downwards, which is charming to heart and soul," and was then guided by the Angel Divine Obedience and the Angel Flaming Fire of Thought on a tour of the limbo of the Permanently Still, where those who were equally good and sinful were transformed into statues; the place of the stars and the moon, where those who were irreligious but good in other ways had ended up; and past higher levels of virtue and radiance to the pure light of Ahura Mazda himself; and then—for this was a journey in the opposite direction to Dante's—he had a good long look at Hell, where snakes crawled into men's arseholes and emerged from their mouths, etc. He would have noted the extraordinary concentration upon the female breast and also on excreta, and the ferocious glee with which the legions of the sinful were gnawed by Noxious Beasts. Adulteresses were hung by their breasts, or forced to gash their breasts with iron combs; women who had not breast-fed their children were obliged to use their breasts to dig into rocky hills. Urinating while standing up was punished especially harshly, and women who approached water or fire during menstruation were forced to eat cup after cup of male piss and shit. It is scarcely to be wondered at that Lady Spenta, imagining her Ardaviraf following her namesake on this jaunt, should become obsessed with keeping him clean and feeding him from less vilely replenished cups.

The longer Virus Cama's silence lasted, the more desperate Lady Spenta grew. She had come to rely so much upon the fantasy of her son's journey, from which he must surely return, that it began to engulf her, as if she were the soul crossing the Chinvat Bridge to see great and terrible sights, to be faced with the droopy-bosomed evidence of her good deeds and the suppurating manifestations of her sins. When she was not busy with Virus and his needs, she wore an absent yet uncalm look, and behaved in a manner at once agitated and remote. (To Ormus she continued to be distant, never fond. Events had neutered her maternal feelings towards him. Raised by servants, he was left to find love where he could.)

What a cricket ball started could not be stopped. One by one, the members of the Cama family were seceding from reality into private worlds of their own.

Sir Darius Xerxes Cama himself became the next member of his family to withdraw from everyday life. The Law, which had given him such moral sustenance all his adult life, had become, as many of his colleagues had begun openly to proclaim, "an ass." In this period the imperial administration had begun to use the full force of the legal system against the nationalists, and even though Sir Darius was a leading advocate of British civilisation and opponent of the Congress, he began to experience a profound sense of unease at what was going on. Many of his respected colleagues had joined the Independence johnnies, whose leader, Mr. Gandhi, was after all a pretty crafty legal eagle himself. Taken by surprise by the storm within himself, Sir Darius Xerxes Cama gave up his practice and retreated into the sumptuous library of classical texts which was the glory of the Apollo Bunder apartment, and he sought in the groves of scholarship that peace of mind which had been so comprehensively destroyed by the private and public history of his time.

Along with his fellow Freemason William Methwold, Sir Darius began an investigation of Indo-European myths. Methwold was a wealthy Englishman from a family of landowners and diplomats, and as a property developer had had a hand in many of the new villas and apartment blocks springing up on Malabar Hill and along Warden Road. Rendered egg-bald by alopecia, a condition which he concealed beneath a wig, he was a brilliant Greek scholar, and plunged into Sir Darius's library with the thirst of a parched wanderer who stumbles upon the purest mountain stream. Sir Darius Xerxes Cama had in his younger days fallen under the influence of the German-born scholar Max Müller, whose work in comparative mythology had led him to the conclusion that all the ancient myths of the Proto-Indo-European or Aryan cultures—Zoroastrians, Indians, Greeks—were in essence stories about the sun. This theory pleased a secularized Parsi

like Sir Darius, who saw in it the rational source of the spiritual flum-
mery that had gained almost complete mastery over his beloved wife.
(Ahura Mazda, Ormazd, Hormuz was after all nothing else but Light;
and Apollo was the sun.) However, after Müller's disciples attempted
to prove that Jesus Christ and his disciples were nothing more than
fairy-tale versions of the sun and the twelve signs of the zodiac,
William Methwold had turned against "solar mythology," and at meetings of the Malabar Hill Lodge, to which they both belonged, he outraged Sir Darius by a brilliant series of spoof monologues in which he
proved, first, that the Emperor Napoleon and his dozen generals were,
like Christ and his followers, no more than zodiacal fictions; and, second, that Oxford University and Professor Müller himself could not
possibly exist, either. Methwold hurled at Müller's philosophy the
attacks formulated by the Scots journalist Andrew Lang, who held that
there was no need for these unprovable Aryan theories; the gods of the
Greeks had simply emerged from the large number of savage beliefs
the world over. "Savage beliefs?" Sir Darius had roared, coming to his
feet, brandy in hand, and silencing the lodge. "Including ours, I suppose?" William Methwold held his ground. "There are barbarians the
world over, my dear fellow," he equably rejoined. "Present company
excepted, of course."

For a time, the two friends saw little of each other. They patched
things up when William Methwold came over a few months before the
day of Ormus's birth and Virus's accident to applaud Sir Darius's victory
in a local badminton tourney. Over tumblers of Scotch, Methwold
admitted that he had been lured back into the Aryan fold by the work
of the Frenchman Georges Dumézil, who had "shown" that the Greek
god Ouranos was none other than India's own Varuna, thus proving the
common heritage of all Aryan culture. "Good show," cried Sir Darius,
happily. "We both turned out to be barbarians, after all."

During the next few years, Sir Darius and Methwold met from time
to time to explore the relationships between the Homeric and Indian
mythological traditions. The abduction of Helen of Troy by Paris and
that of Sita of Ayodhya by the demon king Ravana; the relationship
between Hanuman, the wily monkey god, and the devious Odysseus;
the parallels between the tragedy of the House of Atreus and that of
Rama's clan: these and many other matters, like the gentlemen schol-

ars they were, they expatiated upon and enjoyed. Sir Darius was particularly drawn to the so-called tripartite theory of Dumézil. Could it
be true that all Aryan cultures rested on the triple concept of religious
sovereignty, physical force and fertility—that this was the real Trinity
that defined both Eastern and Western civilisation, their common
bond? In the time after he gave up the Bar, this became the great question of Sir Darius Xerxes Cama's life. With William Methwold by his
side, he plunged deeper and deeper into the technical aspects of the
problem, and the further from the surface of life they journeyed, the
happier they became. Outside the library, the last phases of the colonial history of England and India took their well-known course, and a
great war, greater than the wars over Helen and Sita, was brewing. But
Sir Darius and William Methwold had sealed themselves away from the
contemporary and sought refuge in the eternal. Inside the Cama
library, Odysseus became a monkey god and Paris a demon king, and
the Parsi knight and the English property-wallah grew so close that it
became hard to tell them apart. Sir Darius lost much of his hair;
William Methwold divested himself of his black wig and hung it on
the back of his chair. And in the privacy of the universe of books, at
an oak table groaning with ancient learning, they worked in joyful
solitude, eternally alone except, on occasion, for the silent phantom-
like figure of Virus Cama, sitting solemnly on a step stool in a corner.

One day, however, Sir Darius took off his half-rimmed spectacles,
banged his fist on the table and shouted: "It isn't enough."

William Methwold looked up from his books, startled. What wasn't
enough? Could Sir Darius conceivably be tiring of this idyllic existence, which had given them both such pleasure? "P-perhaps you
could reconsider your self-denying ordinance," he stammered, "and we
could have a game of squash. *Mens sana,* you know, *in* bally *corpore
sano.*" Sir Darius made a dismissive noise. He was trembling on the
edge of new knowledge, and this was no time for squash.

"Three functions aren't enough," he said feverishly. "There must be
a fourth."

"Can't be," said Methwold. "Those three concepts of old Georges's
fill out the insides of the whole social picture."

"Yes," said Sir Darius. "But what about *outsideness*? What about all
that which is beyond the pale, above the fray, beneath notice? What

about outcastes, lepers, pariahs, exiles, enemies, spooks, paradoxes? What about those who are remote? Damn it," and here he turned to face his silent child, sitting in the shadows of the room, *what about Virus?*"

"I'm not sure I understand." William Methwold was out of his depth.

"What about people who just don't belong?"

"Where? Belong where?"

"Anywhere. To anything, to anyone. The psychically unattached. Comets travelling through space, staying free of all gravitational fields."

"If there are people like that," Methwold offered, "aren't they, well, *rarae aves*? Few and far between? Does one really need a fourth concept to explain them? Aren't they, well, like waste paper, and all the stuff one puts in the bin? Aren't they simply surplus to requirements? Not wanted on the voyage? Don't we just cross them off the list? Cut them? Blackball them out of the club?"

But Sir Darius Xerxes Cama wasn't listening. He was standing at the great window of the library, staring out at the Arabian Sea. "The only people who see the whole picture," he murmured, "are the ones who step out of the frame."

Try to imagine the scene: the Parsi grandee in the sanctum of his library, with his English friend and the living ghost of his child, a man driven by life into books, standing by an open window. So he's not completely sealed off, the library isn't a closed tomb, and through the window comes all the tumultuous sensation of the city: the scents of channa and bhel, of tamarind and jasmine; the shouting voices, because nobody ever says anything in these parts without first raising his voice; and the quarrel of traffic, the hooves, the sputtering exhausts, the bicycle bells; the brilliant light of the sun on the harbour, the hooting of warships and the electricity of a society at a point of transformation.

Now imagine a gust of wind, sweeping a crumpled page of newsprint off the filthy street, tossing it upwards in slow spirals like a dirty butterfly; until at last it passes through the window, the outside world penetrates the world within, and lands neatly by Sir Darius's polished oxfords, pleading for attention. This is a picture I keep seeing, although it couldn't be, could it, how it really happened. Maybe someone wrote Sir Darius a letter, or he chanced upon a learned journal which contained the information that broke his heart. Prefer, if you please, some such prosaic version, but I'll stick with mine. Through the window came the newspaper, and Sir Darius, picking it up distastefully, was on the point of disposing of it when four words caught his eye. *Aryan, Nazi, Müller, Dumézil.*

Neither Sir Darius Xerxes Cama nor William Methwold ever believed for a moment that either of the great maligned scholars, dead Max or living Georges, had had a single racial-supremacist cell in his body. But when language is stolen and poisoned, the poison works its way backwards through time and sideways into the reputations of innocent men. The word "Aryan," which, for Max Müller and his generation, had a purely linguistic meaning, was now in the hands of less academic persons, poisoners, who were speaking of races of men, races of masters and races of servants and other races too, races whose fundamental impurity necessitated drastic measures, races who were not wanted on the voyage, who were surplus to requirements, races to be cut, blackballed and deposited in the bin of history. By one of the wild improbabilities that, taken collectively, represent the history of the human race, the arcane field of research in which Sir Darius and William Methwold had chosen to sequester themselves had been twisted and pressed into the service of the great evil of the age. History had captured their field, and their love of it had placed them on the wrong side—the side of the poisoners, of the unutterable, of those whose crime was beyond words.

At the moment when things changed for them, Sir Darius and Methwold had been full of the delight of examining the parallels between the Viewing from the Walls in the *Iliad* (when the Trojans survey the besieging army while, for their benefit, Helen identifies Agamemnon, Odysseus, Idomeneus and the greater Ajax) and the similar scene in the *Ramayana* (in which a pair of spies, standing with the abductor Ravana on the ramparts of his fortress, identify the heroes Rama, Lakshmana, Vibhishana and Hanuman). Sir Darius read the scrap of newspaper that had blown in through the window and passed it to Methwold without saying a word. When the Englishman had finished reading, he shook himself, as if emerging from a long sleep, and said, "Let's call it quits." Sir Darius inclined his head and began to close the beloved books. It was September 1939. Rip van Cama and William Winkle stumbled blinking into the light, the roar, the stink of the real world.

"One of these days," Sir Darius mumbled as Methwold replaced his wig on his head and took his leave, "let's have that game of squash."

After he gave up the study of comparative mythology, Sir Darius Xerxes Cama began to change. He saw little of William Methwold, who, it was rumoured, had developed a predilection for Indian women from the bottom of the social scale. Breaking the vow he had made after injuring his son Ardaviraf, Sir Darius also returned to the pursuit of sporting excellence: not cricket, admittedly, but wrestling, badminton, squash. His regular opponent was the much younger Homi Catrack, and even though Sir Darius was the more gifted athlete of the two, and a tormented soul who needed the release of physical effort, the years had taken their toll, and he lost more contests than he won. The two individuals who suffered most as a result of Sir Darius's decline were his sons Cyrus and Ormus, both of whom he took to berating regularly on the subject of the decay of Parsi youth, whose alleged feebleness Sir Darius had begun to hold in contempt. The worse he played, the more vociferously he accused the next generation of decadence, of defeatism, of weakness, of homosexuality. He made the boys arm-wrestle him and laughed in their faces when he won. In that apartment which had grown accustomed to many different kinds of tragic silence, to those collected silences which had driven away friends, colleagues, even my own parents, this new, bullying sound of bombast was doubly shocking.

Three years went by. Sir Darius Xerxes Cama took to drink. (It was a time of total prohibition, but for men of Sir Darius's breeding and connections, there was always a bottle to be found.) He took to hemp and opium. Homi Catrack led him into the dark side of the city and showed him a world whose existence he had never suspected. The lower he sank, the louder grew his remonstrations. Returning from the cages of Kamathipura, from the rooms of the dancing whores, he would often shake his sons awake to accuse them of moral turpitude, of going to hell, to the dogs, to pot. Ten-year-old Cyrus and five-year-old Ormus heard him out and never said a word. Being Camas, they knew how to armour themselves in dumbness. Whatever they said would have fanned his hypocritical fire; elder and younger child knew enough to remain mute.

The early years of Ormus Cama imprisoned him within an emotional isolation so oppressive that he temporarily lost the ability to sing. From the moment of his birth, he had given many extraordinary indications of the depth of his precocious musical talent—not only the chord progressions of his finger movements but also the syncopated drumming of his tiny feet against his crib and the perfect-pitch gurgles that went up and down the musical scale, *saregama padhanisa, sanidhapa magaresa*. But his mother was lost in mysticism, his brother Virus was cocooned in silence, and his father wasn't listening. Only Cyrus Cama, his older brother, was paying attention, and Cyrus's heart was full of hatred.

Unnerved by his twin brother Ardaviraf's transformation into a zip-lipped zombie, and unwilling to blame either his father or poor Virus himself for the calamity, Cyrus had decided to blame his baby brother. "If Daddy hadn't been up all night waiting for Ormus to get himself born," he wrote in the diary he kept hidden under his mattress, "then it is certain-sure that his hit would have gone straight down one of those stupid hecklers' throats." In those days Cyrus worshipped his father and spared no effort to please him. But when he topped the class he returned home, report card in hand, to hear a tirade on the decline of the intellect of Parsi children; when he starred in junior races at the Brabourne Stadium Sports Day, his father declined to come and watch. Afterwards, when Cyrus came home loaded with little silver trophies, Sir Darius would pour scorn on his competitors. "Such namby-pamby weaklings you must've run and jumped against, no wonder you beat the lot." Cyrus, unable to blame his father for these cruelties, directed all his anger towards his brother Ormus instead.

One night in 1942, Cyrus Cama was woken in the middle of the night by the sound of little Ormus, with whom he still shared a room, singing in his sleep, so sweetly that birds had woken, thinking the dawn had come, and gathered on his windowsill to listen. This sleeper's melody contained such joy in life, such optimism and hope, that it drove Cyrus Cama insane, and clutching his pillow in his hand he went to Ormus's bed, intent on murder. The family ayah, Roxana, was asleep on a mat on the bedroom floor. This was the same slow-reacting ayah who had been standing beside Virus Cama when the cricket ball struck him, but on this occasion she more than redeemed herself, because she too had been woken by Ormus's singing, she had been lying peacefully on her mat in the moonlit bedroom, enjoying the sleeping child's song, so she saw Cyrus place his pillow over his brother's face and hold it there. The song stopped, the birds screamed, little Ormus's arms and legs began to kick, and Roxana threw herself at Cyrus Cama and dragged him weeping away.

"I couldn't stand it," was Cyrus's only explanation to his parents, Lady Spenta loose of hair and wild of eye, Sir Darius in his dressing gown, rubbing his head. "I couldn't stand the noise."

Sound and silence, silence and sound. This is a story of lives pulled together and pushed apart by what happens in (and between) our ears. Cyrus Cama was sent away to boarding school, still with murder in his eyes, banished to an implacable hill-station establishment which based its methods upon the tried and true British principles of cold baths, bad food, regular beatings and high-quality academic instruction, and which helped him to develop into the full-blooded psychopath he afterwards became.

And Ormus? Ormus Cama did not sing again for fourteen years. Not a ditty, not a warble, not a note. Not until Vina Apsara set his music free.

Sir Darius Xerxes Cama's gradual decline slowly stripped away the stiff veneer of decorum beneath which his true nature had lain concealed most of his life, revealing the prodigious vanity under that formal exterior, taking the brakes off the love of showing off which was his Achilles' heel. At the wealthy Malabar Hill Masonic Lodge, where he spent much of his leisure time among the leading officials of the fraying Raj and their local cronies, there was ample opportunity for self-display. In 1942, at one of the grand, men-only, bimonthly dinners held by the lodge, Sir Darius Xerxes Cama in his cups gave a performance that nobody who witnessed it ever forgot. After eating heartily, in a manner resolutely unaffected by the food shortages and rationing laws, the membership retired to a noble smoking room complete with humidor and string quartet, where the blackout drapes over the windows were the only concessions to the realities of the age; however, by way of compensation, an excellent supply of imported brandies and whiskies was available to members, in spite of the prohibition laws. In this congenial setting, the great men relaxed, telling ribald jokes, demonstrating bits of card magic, oiling the wheels of business and Empire, and doing party tricks. Sir Darius—drunk, opium-addled, filled with self-hatred—ordered the tail-coated musicians to "have a bash" at the movie tune "We're Off to See the Wizard (The Wonderful Wizard of Oz)." Sir Darius, the music hater! Sir Darius, the declaimer of interminable jeremiads against anything with a tune, making a musical request! Well, *that* got everyone's attention.

As the band struck up, Sir Darius Xerxes Cama stripped off his dress shirt and treated the cream of British-Indian Bombay—wartime Bombay, in which the nationalist movement was gathering momentum and every one of these high colonial nights felt a little more like a last waltz than the one before—to the idiosyncratic art of Musical Muscle Control. His pectoral and abdominal muscles jerking along to the music like tango dancers with roses between their teeth, or skirt-swirling, sliding and twirling queens of the jitterbug or lindy hop, he cried out, "This is what we could do in our heyday! Behold mind and body working as one! Behold the perfect union of the intellectual and physical spheres!" At the end of the performance, buttoning up his shirt, he bowed and declared, like a fabulist delivering the moral of his tale: *"Mens sana in corpore sano."* His fellow Masons responded with a weary politeness that concealed their mild, end-of-Empire ennui.

I can only imagine that Sir Darius was introduced to this garish skill by some louche crony of his fellow Mason Homi Catrack's, in a den on Falkland Road. That he had not walked away from the demonstration with a haughty laugh, that he had, in fact, returned week after week and actually learned the trick of it, is a sign of how far he had fallen, of the vulgarity that had entered that once noble soul. Or to put it another way: it showed that for all his bluster, he was indeed his son's father. His son Ormus, I mean, the future star of stars.

In more robust imperial times such outré exhibitionism—too extreme even by Masonic standards—would undoubtedly have tarnished Sir Darius's reputation and might have damaged his legal practice, but he had retired and was therefore invulnerable; besides, these were demoralized, rudderless days for the smart set that revolved around the British Presence in India. Suicides and crack-ups were not infrequent events. A cigar-smoking Parsi grandee removing his shirt and twitching his muscles to music seemed relatively mild by comparison. All present understood his pain and could foretell the future: his future, their own. Anglophilia, for so long the basis of these people's ascendancy, would henceforth be like the mark of Cain. It would be the dark star hanging over their interminable but also irreversible decline.

One day in 1942, soon after the Quit India Resolution was launched from the maidan at Gowalia Tank, leading to the eruption across the city of violent demonstrations, lootings and acts of arson in the wake of Mr. Gandhi's immediate arrest, Sir Darius Xerxes Cama spoke heated words on the subject of the "country's surrender to mob rule and firestarters" and added, for the first time, a thought that was to become an obsession. "Anyway, Bombay isn't India. The British built her and the Parsis gave her her character. Let them have their independence elsewhere if they must, but leave us our Bombay under beneficent Parsi-British rule."

Sir Darius was persuaded by Homi Catrack, to whom he had addressed this *cri de coeur,* to venture out of his shrinking Anglocentric milieu and "meet the future." Homi was a cards-and-horses gambler and a movie producer with—in spite of his rolled trouser leg and his activities "on the square"—a surprising commitment to the nationalist movement concealed behind his Brylcreem-and-cravat, playboy-or-gigolo smoothery. Sir Darius had started regarding him as something of a race traitor (for were not the Parsis' interests inseparable from those of the British, whose presence they had so vigorously supported, whose culture they had so successfully integrated with their own?). But the fellow's charm was irresistible, and his prowess at badminton and squash and even golf was the equal—all too often, gallingly, more than the equal!—of Sir Darius's own. "Rackets and clubs," Homi Catrack panted as they sweated happily in the nude democracy of the Wellesley Club locker room. "That's the kind of guy you're dealing with here. A clubman, *par excellence.* And, in his very water, a racketeer." He actually winked at Sir Darius to emphasize the play on words.

Wink or no wink, Homi was telling the simple truth, for in addition to being a member of every worthwhile club in the city, from the (now-defunct) Wellesley to the Governors of the Mahalaxmi Race-course, he had also, during those days of scarcities, made a rogue's fortune by cornering the market in cement, and also from a chain of bootleg stills and illegal speakeasies. It is said that Homi Catrack was the first man to use the term "parallel economy" and that his stashes of black money would, if piled high, have formed an edifice larger than the Gateway of India. It is one of the paradoxes of human nature that this same Homi, who profited so greatly from the turmoil of the 1940s, was one of the greatest admirers of the "honest men who would clean up India," as he called the Congress leadership. His rage at Gandhi's arrest was genuine and intense.

In the locker room after a keen contest which, for once, he had narrowly won, Sir Darius Xerxes Cama was in generous mood, imagining himself in ancient Greece or Persia, sweating among philosophers, discoboli, chariot racers, sprinters, maguses and kings. In the grip of such a reverie, he was inclined to forgive a wink, and an invitation to the future seemed appropriate enough. "Very well," he glowered, tolerantly. "Let us see what type of scum is presently rising to the top."

The future turned out to be a bunch of bohemians, painters, writers and movie people, who gathered to drink whisky and discuss civil disobedience in Homi's substantial apartment (with partially obstructed sea view) in an Art Deco apartment block called Côte d' Azur on Warden Road. Within minutes Sir Darius Xerxes Cama knew it had been a mistake to come. He felt like a visitor from the moon, an alienated alien, unable to breathe this heady, illicit air. He moved uncertainly at the fringes of the night, largely ignored in spite of his striking physical presence—the fez, the moustache, the long frock coat, the natural physical grace of his movements, the fierce shine of power in his eyes: human power, that is, the force that comes from a man's nature and cannot be learned, or bought, or bestowed.

Clusters of intellectuals had formed around certain beautiful women—the starlet Pia Aziz, the artist Aurora Zogoiby—while most of the other women in the room were sitting at the feet of a boozy but celebrated Muslim writer of low-life stories who was shocking them by providing, in the most exquisite and ornate Urdu Sir Darius Xerxes Cama had ever heard, detailed and hair-raising descriptions of the worst things in the world, undisguised by circumlocution, unfettered by good taste. He spoke naturally in that famous glittering prose which was somehow both voluptuous and precise, at once dainty and appalling, telling tales of the degraded interiors of the local insane asylums, of the brutal murders and casual rapes that were the city's hidden news, of the corruption of those in authority and the violence in the hearts of the poor, of incestuous love affairs in high society and the killing of daughters in the slums, of the caged whores of Falkland Road and of the mafias who ran the city's organized crime as well as its prostitution and would order men's penises to be severed as casually as they would call for a bunch of red bananas in the bazaar. The contradiction between the high jewellery work of the writer's language and the pornographic nature of his material left Sir Darius more shocked and revolted than he felt able to show. Also, of course, he was rather more familiar with some of the storyteller's source material than he cared to reveal.

He turned away and half collided with the only Englishman at the gathering. It was William Methwold, whom he hadn't seen in years. "And how do *you* come to be here?" Sir Darius in his unnerved condition found himself speaking more bluntly than was polite, and immediately attempted to apologize. "I'm afraid I'm out of sorts," he began, but Methwold stopped him, and greeted him with evident affection.

"I'm a little disoriented myself," he said. "But then that's our destiny, as most of the assembled company would readily agree. And to answer your question, I have a house Mr. Catrack wants to buy. And there will come a time when I want to sell it."

They left it at that and began to drink seriously. Human history clanked along, and the hot, blind stars wheeled overhead. They mentioned neither Homer nor Max Müller, neither the *Ramayana* nor Dumézil. It was a night for whisky and defeat. Sir Darius Xerxes Cama forgot his wife waiting for him in the Apollo Bunder apartment, forgot his sleeping sons, forgot where he was, forgot himself, drank too heavily, and at a certain point he tore open his shirt and, bellowing out the words of "Let's Do It (Let's Fall in Love)," introduced the gathering to the gentle art of Musical Muscle Control. His fellow guests fell silent; even the obscene writer's oral narratives were stilled; and when Sir Darius Xerxes Cama finished, with a blurted *"Mens sana in corpore sano,"* he understood in spite of his drunken stupor that what was acceptable among the bread-roll-hurling, jolly-jape-urinating, Eton-and-Oxford, men-only Freemasonry of the last years of British India had led, on this occasion, in more radical, and mixed, society, to his making a great ass of himself. Nobody spoke for a long moment, though there were several suppressed giggles and loud, irrepressible snorts of joy. Then Aurora Zogoiby, that damned painter woman with the sharp tongue, spoke up loud and clear, and stabbed him in the heart.

"Quoteofy your Latin tags by all means, Daryoosh darling," she drawled, "but the general opinion round here is that this *corpore* of yours is stark raving *insano.* As, quite possibly, Sir Circus Camasaurus, are you."

Sir Darius Xerxes Cama never met Aurora Zogoiby again. They lived in a great city, a metropolis of many narratives that converged briefly and then separated for ever, discovering their different dooms in that crowd of stories through which all of us, following our own destinies, had to push and shove to find our way through, or out. In Bombay the stories jostled you in the street, you stepped over their sleeping forms on the sidewalks or in the doorways of pharmacies, they hung off the local trains and fell to their deaths from the doors of B.E.S.T. buses or—once upon a time but no more—under an onrushing tram. Aurora the painter forgot the inebriated lawyer soon enough, never gave him another thought, but Sir Darius carried her words to the grave, like a spear.

He came to a decision. Homi Catrack and his vaunted "future" had nothing to offer him. He would dissociate himself from them both. He was, after all, a clown, a dinosaur, a species on the verge of extinction. Something immense was about to strike his world, and the cloud the impact threw up would obliterate the likes of him. Very well. Let it be so. He would make of his remaining days a lament for the mistakes of progress and the failure of the young to learn the lessons of the past. He would be a terror, as the great lizards had been, the terror of the earth, until the long night fell.

He was a natural leader of men caught in a dead end of history and deprived of followers. Where he led was backwards, in a direction nobody wanted to go. He was a father who loved his sons and came to be hated by all of them because of the harangue that never ended, the critique that reached no final summation but surged on through the days of their youth, while they, swimmers caught by the mighty wave of his disappointment, fought for breath and feared at every moment that they might drown.

And Ormus Cama, who ran furthest from his shadow, was the child most shaped by him, the only one in all the family who would always secretly acknowledge his own kinship with his father's exhibitionist streak, and of course his muscles' vulnerability to cheap music, which made them bop and twitch.

My own mother, Mrs. Ameer Merchant, correctly prophesied a further problem for young Ormus. While everyone's attention was focused on the accident to Virus, on Cyrus's murderous streak, on the mystical absentness of Lady Spenta and the decay of Sir Darius, it was Ameer who kept her eye on the ball. "It is not Cyrus or Virus who is that boy's twin," she pointed out. "The disaster that sealed his fate didn't happen on any cricket pitch but inside his mother, before he was even born." For many years after Ormus and I unexpectedly became pals, in spite of the ten-year difference in our ages, my mother would return to her theme. "Born in his dead brother's shadow," she would say, tut-tutting, shaking her head. "He never could get out of it. Doesn't matter how far he ran, that dead boy's shadow was stuck hard to his heels. Doesn't matter that he ran right round the world a hundred and one times. His fate was sealed there and then, before he took one step down his bad-mash road."

Such were the factors that detached Ormus Cama from the ordinary ties of family life. The ties that strangle us, which we call love. Because of the loosening of these ties he became, with all the attendant pain of such becoming, free.

But love is what we want, not freedom. Who then is the unluckier man? The beloved, who is given his heart's desire and must for ever after fear its loss, or the free man, with his unlooked-for liberty, naked and alone between the captive armies of the earth?

My mother's intuition proved to be correct. Born in his dead twin's shadow, Ormus Cama turned out to be what the ancients called a psychopomp, one concerned with the retrieval of lost souls, the souls of the beloved dead. As he grew older, he began to suffer from the family affliction of silence, of inwardness. In the beginning, until the miracle of the music, he feared, but could do nothing to resist, these spells of what he called "Cama obscura." During these "darknesses," Ormus would lie still, with his eyes shut, for hours on end, while the purple stain on his eyelid seemed to be searching the empires of the unseen, probing the depths of the worlds that lay concealed beneath the surface of the apparent, hunting (and eventually finding) Gayomart.

After the death by spearing of mortal Castor, Polydeuces the son of Zeus spent alternate days below the earth with his dead brother, at a place named Therapne; and in return the dead twin was allowed to spend alternate days with his brother on the surface, with the ground beneath his feet instead of over his head. Gayomart Cama did not return, however; unless it was in the form my mother named, as Ormus's shadow, conceived of as something like that roguish, independent silhouette which once escaped from Peter Pan until sewn back to his feet by Wendy Darling. For it was true that Ormus had shadow selves, the many Others who plagued and came to define his life. It might not be so fanciful (my own nature has a weakness for fancy) to say that his dead twin was, in the shifting shape of Ormus's monochrome, protean shade, still alive.

"My little Ormie," Lady Spenta Cama had once greeted her unexpected son. *"My little shrimpy boy. Now you're safe from Hell. Now they can't open up the ground and take you down."* But Lady Spenta was wrong about the ground beneath his feet. I'm not saying that he was carried by demons down to some ancient supernatural inferno. No, no. But chasms did open. They can, and did. They consumed his love, stole his Vina from him and would not give her up. And they did send him, as we shall see, all the way to Hell and back.

The ground, the ground beneath our feet. My father the mole could have told Lady Spenta a thing or two about the unsolidity of solid ground. The tunnels of pipe and cable, the sunken graveyards, the layered uncertainty of the past. The gaps in the earth through which our history seeps and is at once lost, and retained in metamorphosed form. The underworlds at which we dare not guess.

We find ground on which to make our stand. In India, that place obsessed by place, belonging-to-your-place, knowing-your-place, we are mostly given that territory, and that's that, no arguments, get on with it. But Ormus and Vina and I, we couldn't accept that, we came loose. Among the great struggles of man—good/evil, reason/unreason, etc.—there is also this mighty conflict between the fantasy of Home and the fantasy of Away, the dream of roots and the mirage of the journey. And if you are Ormus Cama, if you are Vina Apsara, whose songs could cross all frontiers, even the frontiers of people's hearts, then perhaps you believed all ground could be skipped over, all frontiers would crumble before the sorcery of the tune. Off you'd go, off your turf, beyond family and clan and nation and race, flying untouchably over the minefields of taboo, until you stood at last at the last gateway, the most forbidden of all doors. Where your blood sings in your ears, *Don't even think about it*. And you think about it, you cross that final frontier, and perhaps, perhaps—we'll see how the tale works out—you have finally gone too far, and are destroyed.

"At the frontier of the skin." They made a song about it, as they did about everything. You remember it. You remember the nasal elongation of his phrasing, and above and behind him the high purity of her voice. You remember his words, her words. If you remember the music the words are impossible to forget. At the frontier of the skin no dogs patrol. That was it. At the frontier of the skin. Where I end and you begin. Where I cross from sin to sin. Abandon hope and enter in. And lose my soul. At the frontier of the skin no guards patrol.

Yeah, but there was a second verse. At the frontier of the skin mad dogs patrol. At the frontier of the skin. Where they kill to keep you in. Where you must not slip your skin. Or change your rôle. You can't pass out I can't pass in. You must end as you begin. Or lose your soul. At the frontier of the skin armed guards patrol.

Vina Apsara, the beautiful, the dead. Her very name, too good for this world. Vina, the Indian lyre. Apsara, from *apsaras*, a swanlike water nymph. (In Western terms, a naiad, not a dryad.) Look out, Vina. Nymph, watch your step. Beware the ground beneath your feet.

3

LEGENDS OF THRACE

Nobody in my family could sing a note, let alone hold a line or carry a tune. Nor could any of us produce a credible sequence of musical sounds by any other means. No string instruments were played, no flutes blown, no keyboards thumped. We couldn't even whistle. From deep within the dusty trunk of childhood I can still dig out the memory of my mother Ameer when young, Ameer on our Cuffe Parade verandah, sitting on a low stool facing the sea, with an old-fashioned churn between her knees, making mango ice cream and trying, unwisely, to whistle while she worked. The churning and the whistling made for hard, hot labour, they furrowed and moistened her high-arched brow, but when I tasted the result of her struggles I gagged and retched; her off-key *siti-bajana* had curdled my favourite dessert. I begged her to desist in future, knowing she would not. "Ma, keep mum." "Silent ice is wholly nice." "Ice cream not youce cream." And, parodying the Kwality brand's famous slogan, "A dream without scream." That was how we spoke, my mother and I: in puns and games and rhymes. In, you might say, lyrics. This was our tragedy. We were language's magpies by nature, stealing whatever sounded bright and

shiny. We were tinpan alleycats, but the gift of music had been withheld. We could not sing along, though we always knew the words. Still,
defiantly, we roared our tuneless roars, we fell off the high notes and
were trampled by the low ones. And if bitter ices were the consequence, well, there were worse fates in the world than that.

Villa Thracia, where I was raised, was one of the series of wedding-
cake fantasy bungalows that formerly lined that gracious promenade
like proud courtiers standing in a row before their queen, the sea. On
Cuffe Parade in the cool of Bombay evenings, the city's strollers, complete with kids and pets, would come out to amble and flirt and "eat
the air." From itinerant vendors they would buy channa for the children, Gold Flake cigarettes for the gents, and fragile garlands of cham-
beli flowers to wind into the ladies' hair. My memories of that
childhood home seem now like dreams of Olympus, of a sojourn with
the gods in the days before I was cast out into the world. Clutching at
what remains of the past, I hear its spooky laughter as it eludes me. I
snatch at wisps of faery dresses but yesterday's creatures no longer
return. I must do the best I can with echoes.

That Cuffe Parade has gone now, and the process of its going was
assisted, if one believes certain unsubstantiated suggestions regarding
the laying of a fire, by the young Vina Apsara; and what Vina may or
may not have facilitated was completed by my mother, who loved the
city but for whom the future was a force more powerful than love.
Cities are not immortal; nor are memories; nor are gods. Of the deities
of childhood's Olympus, hardly any now remain.

For many Indians, our parents are as gods. Vina, who had most reason to deny her parentage, took to saying, at the height of her fame
and after reading Erich von Däniken, that her true ancestors had been
godlike entities who arrived in silver chariots from outer space, tall,
lucent, androgynous beings one of whom had extruded her painlessly
from "her" navel. "They watch over me always," she told more than
one bewildered reporter. "I am in permanent contact. Permanent." In
those days she was presenting herself as an androgynous alien on stage
as well as off, and no doubt such guff was good for business. But I
could hear the savagery beneath her airhead quotes. I could hear the
goat songs of her past.

("Goat songs"? Excuse me. A literal translation, from the Greek, of a more familiar word: "tragedies." And Vina's story, with its echoes of the high old yarns of, oh, Helen, Eurydice, Sita, Rati and Persephone—tall Vina's tall tale, which in my circumambulatory way I am hastening to tell, certainly had a tragic dimension. But it also had a good deal to do with goats.)

If our parents are to be thought of as godlike, might the gods actually be our parents? Tales of divine paternity began, let us agree, at the beginning of things, and will end only at the end of time. As I learned in boyhood from my father, the gods themselves quarrelled over the "putative procreative interventions" of other deities. Shiva, suspecting that the new-born Ganesh might not be his son, struck off the baby's head; then remorse set in, and in a panic, he replaced the lost head with the first that came to hand: viz., the trunker's noddle we know and love today. And who was the father of Orpheus, by the by; Apollo the glorious Sun God, or merely Oeagrus, ruler of the outlying, the more than somewhat hickish, province of Thrace? For that matter, who was the father of Jesus Christ?

As we grow, we lose our belief in our progenitors' superhuman nature. They shrivel into more or less unimpressive men and women. Apollo turns out to be Oeagrus, god and Joseph the carpenter end up being one and the same. The gods we worship, we discover, are not different from ourselves.

I'm in this god-bothered mood because it's time to unveil the central mysteries of my own family life. Without further ado, therefore, I present you with an image from childhood of my own at-that-time divine-seeming father, Mr. V. V. Merchant. On Juhu Beach, *circa* 1956, in his middle forties, skinny as an excuse, earnest as a promise, joyful as a birth, grinning his shy, buck-toothed grin; bare-footed, hairlessly bare-chested, with his trouser legs rolled up; straw hat on head, sweat pouring down his cheeks, spade in hand; and digging.

How my father loved to dig! Other parents stood by, bored, while their eager children scrabbled in sand; or, leaving the world of silicon to urchins and ayahs, strolled off to take (and also shoot) the breeze. In my case, it was a question of having to go flat out to keep up with my feverishly burrowing sire. At the age of nine I was, I must admit, hankering for forms of beach life existing beyond the bucket and spade. Juhu Beach was an idyllic spot in those days, not the urbanized

Bombay-Bondi it has become. A journey there felt like a trip beyond the frontier of the city into enchanted space. And slowly, as I grew older and raised my eyes from the sand and beyond the conventional weekend pleasures of snack vendors, and boys shinning up coco-palms, and racing camels, I heard a new voice speaking to me, not in any language I had ever learned, but in the secret language of my heart.

It was the sea. Its come-hither murmur, its seductive roar. That was the music that could wash my soul. The lure of a different element, its promises of elsewhere, gave me my first intimation of something hidden within me that would pull me across the water, leaving my parents stranded. The sea, the wine-dark, the fish-rich. The lap and suck of waves dying on sand. Rumours of mermaids. Touch the sea and at once you're joined to its farthest shore, to Araby (it was the Arabian Sea), Suez (it was the year of the Crisis), and Europa beyond. Perhaps even—I remember the thrill of the whispered word on my young lips—America. America, the open-sesame. America, which got rid of the British long before we did. Let Sir Darius Xerxes Cama dream his colonialist dreams of England. My dream-ocean led to America, my private, my unfound land.

(Allow me to add: while you're in the sea, the bugs don't bite.)

I was, I remain, a strong swimmer. Even my nine-year-old self would strike boldly out beyond my depth, heedless of danger. My mother would wade anxiously after me, her sari ballooning in the water like a jellyfish. When I swam safely back to shore, she cuffed me on the ear. "Don't you know the Old Man of the Sea is waiting to drag you down?" Mother, I know, I know.

That sandy shore, on which my barefoot father dug like an overworked undertaker, that beloved homeland, came to seem like a prison to me. The sea—over the sea, under the sea, it scarcely seemed to matter—the sea and only the sea would take me where I could be free.

V.V. Merchant, however, dreamed of the past. That was his promised land. The past was the truth, and like all truths, it lay hidden. You had to dig it out. Not just any past; just the city's. V.V. was a Bombayite through and through. And yes, many Bombayites now associate those initials with the crooked billionaire financier V.V. "Crocodile" Nandy, but my father is not under any circumstances to be confused with that mighty rogue. Of all Nandy's many embezzlements, swindles and thefts, his purloining of Vivvy Merchant's initial letters is the one that rankles most with me. But that's life, I guess. A big crook counts for more in the world than a small and honest man.

My father's given names were Vasim Vaqar, in case you were wondering, the inaccurate Ws of his names' traditional transliterations from the Urdu having been replaced by phonetically correct Vs. However, in spite of the switch, my strongly secularist father much disliked the "unacceptably religious iambs" of his names and wouldn't have been pleased to see them given an airing here; the more informal, and ideologically neutral, "Vivvy" had long been good enough for him. Still, he was the Digger of Bombay, and even if he did choose to bury his own names, he'd be on shaky ground if he complained that I'd dug them up.

(He's dead. He can't complain.)

The rest of India held no interest for Vivvy, while his home town— that single grain of sand whirling through the immensity of the cosmos—contained, for him, all the mysteries of the universe. And as his only son, I, of course, was his preferred repository of knowledge, his deposit account, his security box. Every father wishes his son to inherit the best of himself, and Bombay was what my father gave to me. Instead of children's books, I got local legends. The *Chronicles of Bimb,* or *Bimbakyan.*

In the end I ran a mile from the place. Hundreds of miles. Thousands.

Bombay? Don't ask. I could pass any exam you care to set. I can see the ghosts of old times walking down new streets. Take me to Churchgate and I'll show you where the Church Gate once stood. Show me Rampart Row and I'll show you the Ropewalk, where the British Navy's ropemakers plied their twisting, twining trade. I can tell you where the bodies are buried (F. W. Stevens, the city's architect supreme, d. 5 March 1900, lies in the Sewri cemetery), where the ashes are spilled, where the vultures fly. Graveyards, burning ghats, doongerwadis. I can even locate the bodies of islands, reclaimed long ago into the downtown peninsula. Old Woman's Island—dig into that name and you get *Al-Oman*—is now a somewhat raised lump of ground on the east side of Colaba Bazaar. My father liked digging into place names, so allow me to inform you, just off the top of my head, that Chinchpokli is "tamarind hollow" and Cumballa Hill is named after the lotus flower and Bhendi Bazaar is situated where once the ladies'-fingers grew.

From this kindergarten vegetable stuff, this urban "eatymology," as Vivvy Merchant called it, we proceeded on to more adult territory. Vivvy is digging on Juhu Beach, but what of Chowpatty? No problem. "Four rivulets," though nobody now knows where they might trickle . . . And Foras Road? If you know it, you'll know it's a street of whores. But V.V. dug down beneath the brothels, dug down in time as well as earth, down through one meaning to another, and showed me the building of the "foras dykes" which had reclaimed this old marshland from the sea. Where a swamp of morals now stands, was once simply a swamp. . . . And Apollo Bunder, where Ormus Cama grew up? Originally Palva Bunder, of course. "Apollo," my father pronounced, "was a nomenclatural interloper." He spoke like that. Nomenclatural interloper, putative procreative interventions, subterranean veracity. "Greek gods, like everybody else, have invaded India from time to time."

Apollo grabbed the Bunder, but it was Dionysus who really made his mark. Came this way when young, conquering and boozing, and taught us Indians how to make wine. (Alas, we forgot his lessons, and had to settle for arrack and toddy, until the British taught us, much later, about beer and rum and yo-ho-ho.) Dionysus won all his battles, did his share of slaughtering and laying waste, and departed with many elephants; the usual. That kind of show-off behaviour just doesn't impress us any more. Sounds like the old colonial boasting to me. No place for it in today's world.

Dionysiac goddesses: that's closer to my personal experience. What I know about is Vina. Vina, who came to us from abroad, who laid waste to all she saw, who conquered and then devastated every heart. Vina as female Dionysus. Vina, the first bacchante. That, I could buy.

Deeper and deeper my father delved beneath the ferocity of the Juhu sun, perhaps hoping to find Portuguese moidores (he dug into the name, naturally. *Moedas de ouros,* if you want to know; coins of gold) or maybe just the petrified skeletons of primeval fish. See him scoop away the present, behold the sands of time climb up around him in surprised dunes crawling with tiny see-through crabs! Listen for his scholarly cries, "Aha! Oho!" as lo! he chances upon a buried bottle, empty, broken, containing no message, he pounces on it as if it were a relic of ancient kingdoms, Rome, Mohenjo-Daro, Gondwana, perhaps even Gondwanaland, the proto-continent upon which no man ever walked, let alone blew glass into bottle shapes, or poured Dionysian liquid into the same; but Gondwanaland is still where India began, if you dig down deep enough in time. India broke off it, sailed across the ocean and smashed into what remained of the northern proto-continent, thus bringing into being the Himalayas. (My father liked to shock me by saying, "The collision is still taking place, India continues to experience impactual consequences, meaning that the mountains are getting bigger.") Now he's invisible from the waist down, glowing, happy; and now only his hat can be seen; and down and down he digs, towards Hell or the Antipodes, while I splash about in the future, further and further out to sea until my mother the jellyfish calls me in.

For twenty years, through one of the greatest upheavals in the history of nations, the end of the British Empire, my father, architect, excavator and local historian, burrowed away into the underground memory of the city the British built, becoming the undisputed master of a subject in which nobody else had the slightest interest; for Bombay forgets its history with each sunset and rewrites itself anew with the coming of the dawn. Can it be that his preoccupations blinded him to the momentous nature of those years, to the Navy Strike and Partition and all that followed? In those days of upheaval the ground itself seemed uncertain, the land, the physical land, seemed to cry out for reconstruction, and before you took a step you had to test the earth to see if it would bear your weight. A great transformation was afoot; and if my father found the uncertainty too much to bear, if he dug himself into the past, seeking fixity in knowledge, seeking solid ground beneath the shifting sands of the age, well, there's no shame in that.

We all have to deal with the uncertainty of the modern. The ground shivers, and we shake. To this day, when I'm strolling down a sidewalk, I always avoid the joins. Step on one of those cracks and they could widen, all of a sudden they could swallow you with a lazy yawn. And of course I know that superstition is a retreat, a way of not facing the real. But the real was Vina, and it's still hard to look her ending in the face.

I will. When I come to it, I will.

Finally, my father gave up his digging. We had ignored him for an eternity, the indolent beach-world had turned its gaze away from his absurd hyperactivity. Exhausted, he needed help to climb out of the hole he'd dug. Grinning coconut salesmen lent him their hands, keeping their baskets balanced on their heads. Even though I had not yet learned the word, I recognized, with some embarrassment, the kitschiness of the image. My father was wearily unconcerned. Happily smacking the sand off his body with his hat, he bought us coconuts from his helpers, waited while they hacked the tops off with their great knives, and then gulped down the coco-milk making loud gluggy noises, like a bath. A moment later, he was asleep in the shade of a coco-palm; whereupon, placing a finger against her lips for silence, smiling secretly, my mother embarked upon some sand madness of her own.

Like Michelangelo, who believed that the figures of his Titans lay imprisoned within lumps of Carrara marble from which it was his duty as an artist to release them, who sculpted the *David* by simply removing everything in the stone that was not David, Ameer Merchant detected a form concealed within the great mound of sand flung up by V.V.'s beach archaeology. But my mother was no artist. She was an entrepreneur, a "developer," to use the new word of those days. She saw no godly figures in the hill of moisture-darkened sand. "I will build," she declared, "my mansions fit for gods, but men will live in them." While V.V. snored, Ameer shaped the maquette of such a mansion out of sand. While he dreamed of unknown depths, she brought into being a dream of heights. Painstakingly, she worked from the top down, in the manner of the master builders of the great Kailash temple at Ellora, that overwhelming monolith hewn by successive generations out of the living rock. And yes, it was a building that appeared, but one entirely free of devotional content. It is true that a tall spire was seen first, but this was a radio mast. And though the building

seemed to soar from the sand like a steeple, yet the profusion of delicate indentations suggestive of windows showed that this was a design
on an altogether grander scale than any sacred site. Small twigs, carefully inserted by Ameer into her fragile vision, served as gargoyles, and
the building's surfaces were distinguished by its architect's addition of
much geometric decoration along its various planes. Surplus sand fell
away from her creation like a redundant garment, until at length it
stood before me in magnificent nudity.

"Skyscraper," she named it. "How'd you like to own a penthouse at
the top?" Skywhatter? Where was a penthouse pent? These were words
I did not know. I found myself disliking them: the words, and the
building to which they belonged. Besides, I was bored and wanted to
swim.

"Looks like a big matchbox to me." I shrugged. "Live in it? As if."

Ameer bristled at this assault upon her handiwork. I deemed it a
good time to head for the water. "You don't know anything," she
cried, rounding on me like an eight-year-old. "Just wait on and see.
One day they'll be all over the place." Then she heard herself sulking
and began to giggle. "They'll be here," she waved an arm gaily. "All
along here." That set me off too. "Beachscrapers," I said. "Sandscrapers,"
she agreed. "Camelscrapers, cocoscrapers, fishscrapers." We were both
laughing now. "And I suppose chowscrapers at Chowpatty Beach," I
wondered. "And hillscrapers on Malabar Hill. And on *Cuffe Parade?*"

"Cuffescrapers," laughed my mother. "Go and swim now and stop
being so *bad-tameez*."

"Where are you going to put them, anyway?" Emboldened by her
good humour, I delivered an unanswerable last word on the subject.
"Here, nobody'll want them, and in town, there are houses everywhere
already."

"No room, then," she mused, pensively.

"Exactly," I confirmed, turning towards the water. "No room at all."

On that momentous day at the beach, I had my unforgettable first
glimpse of Vina. It was the day of my instant infatuation, the com-
mencement of a lifelong enslavement. . . . But at once I halt myself. It
is possible I am pouring the wine of several beach weekends into the
bottle of a single day. Damn it, there are things I can't remember. Was

it on this day, or another day? In November, or the following January? While my father was snoozing, or after I went for a swim? So much is lost. Hard to believe that all this sand has accumulated, obscuring the years. Hard to believe that it's so long ago, that flesh is mortal, that everything slides towards its end. Once, I belonged to the future. The beloved future of my beloved mother, that was what counted; the present was a means, and the past no more than a dull shard of pottery, a bottle dug up by my father on the beach. Now, however, I belong to yesterday.

Is that a line from a song? I forget. Is it?

At any rate: on this golden afternoon or another, bronzer p.m., at this instant or that one, the celebrated Mr. Piloo Doodhwala and his famous "magnificentourage" marched forth on to Juhu's sands. I should say that at the time, I knew nothing about him whatsoever. I was wholly ignorant of his growing citywide renown as a "character" and "coming man" and statewide purveyor of milk; I had no idea that his real name was Shetty—just as our family's had been until it got Englished years ago—but nobody called him that any more, because, as he himself liked to say, "milkman by fame, I am Milkman by name"; I had never heard of the term he had coined to describe the intimate clique of family members and servitors with which he liked to surround himself—a term gleefully taken up by the local rags and much satirised ("magnificentestine," "arrogantourage," etc.); but Piloo Shetty alias Doodhwala was impervious to satire. I simply beheld a small, plump, white-kurta-pajamaed man in his middle twenties, a young man with so great a sense of his own value that he already looked middle-aged, a fellow with a strutting walk like a peacock's and plentiful dark hair so sleekly plastered down with oil that it resembled a sleeping mongoose. He carried himself like a king, Caligula or Akbar, monarchs who entertained fantasies of being divine. Behind him strode a tall Pathan bearer in full sash-and-turban regalia, holding a large, many-coloured parasol, winking with sequins and mirrorwork, over the little emperor's head.

Piloo was preceded by musicians—a drummer, a raucous flautist, a horn player as blaringly aggressive as a motorist, and a pair of writhing, mumming singer-dancers who were probably hired *hijras,* transsexuals—whose appalling racket launched an irresistible assault upon the late-afternoon gentility of the beach. Scurrying along at his right and left elbows were male secretaries, leaning in to hear the great man's words and taking rapid shorthand notes. Following this extraordinary group was a tiny, almost spherical lady, Piloo's unusually but accurately named wife Golmatol, sheltering her mottled skin beneath a black umbrella; two little girls, aged about seven and eight, whose names, Halva and Rasgulla, bore witness to their parents' sweet teeth; and another, much taller, darker girl of around twelve or thirteen, whose face was entirely obscured beneath an enormous, low-brimmed straw hat, so that all I could see was her Stars-and-Stripes swimsuit and the white lungi she was wearing over it, tied at the hip. There was an ayah and there were two domestic servants bearing picnic hampers. A trinity of security guards sweltered in militaristic uniforms. The primary responsibility of these guards—which they discharged with enthusiasm, vigour and the liberal use of long lathi sticks—was to bat away the cluster of anxious individuals who swarmed and buzzed in the wake of the magnificentourage, for a great man will always attract supplicants and hangers-on, and must be protected from same when he is trying to have a nice day out.

Who was this pocket giant, this mighty mouse? What might be the source of such display? Whence came his power, his wealth? Ameer Merchant, her good humour befouled by the Doodhwala party's noisy advent, was in no mood for questions. "Goats," was her snappish reply. I didn't know what to make of that. He'd got *her* goat, that was plain. "Mummy? Excuse me?" She actually bleated at me in annoyance. "You don't know goats? *Mè-è-è?* Billies, nannies. Don't be stupid now. *Bakra-bakri* is all." And that was all the explanation I could get.

V. V. Merchant came awake in a confused state, jolted out of deep sleep by the noise; whereupon, to his further bewilderment, his beloved wife rounded on him. "Blasted *tamasha,*" she snorted, explosively. "Seems like one side of this family never learned how to behave."

Well, *that* was a bombshell. "We're related? How? Where?"

The Piloo gang had come to a halt no more than forty feet away, and its less exalted members were busy laying out sheets and sweets, acting on Golmatol's stentorian instructions, and raising a gay *shamiana* mar-

quee on poles over the festive spread. A card school got going, and Piloo
soon showed himself to be a fierce bidder and big winner, although
perhaps his servitors, understanding where their interests lay, allowed
him his successes. From a thermos flask a bearer poured Piloo a large
aluminum tumblerful of thin, blue-white goat's milk. He drank open-
mouthed, careless of dribbles. Halva and Rasgulla began to wail for
their own drinks, but the girl in the straw hat and swimsuit had walked
off and was standing at some distance with her back to the Doodhwalas,
hugging herself, and slowly shaking a disenchanted (though still largely
invisible) head. And what with the musicians' noise, the supplicants'
pleas, the thwacking of lathi sticks, the shrieks of the wounded, the
young girls' wails and the orders bellowed by Golmatol Doodhwala, it
was necessary to raise one's voice; my enquiries about these high-
decibel family members were made at top volume.

Ameer clutched at her brow. "Oh God, Umeed, get out of my head
just now. They're nothing to do with me, I can tell you. Ask your father
about his relatives."

"Distant relatives," yelled V. V. Merchant, on the defensive.

"Poor relations," rudely shouted Ameer Merchant.

"They don't look so poor to me," I objected, at the top of my voice.

"Rich in goats," Ameer bellowed into a sudden pause in the music,
and her words hung irretrievably in the air, as inescapable as if they'd
been lit up in neon like the Jeep sign on Marine Drive, "but poor in
quality. Shoddy human goods."

An awful stillness descended. It was a hot year, 1956, one of the
hottest on record; the afternoon was well advanced, but the heat had
not diminished. Now the temperature actually seemed to rise, the air
began to buzz, the way it's supposed to do before lightning strikes, and
Shri Piloo Doodhwala began to swell in the heat, to redden, to exude
liquid from every pore, as if he were filling up so fast with words that
there wasn't room for anything else inside him. His younger daughter,
Halva, emitted a nervy giggle, got two tight slaps from her mother,
began to cry, saw Golmatol Doodhwala's hand rising again, and shut
up fast. War was very close. The sand between the Doodhwala encamp-
ment and our own had become a no-man's-land. Heavy artillery was
moving into position. And at this moment the tall girl, the twelve- or
thirteen-year-old in the Stars-and-Stripes swimsuit, strolled idly into

that embattled zone, looked interestedly from Doodhwalas to Merchants and back again, and tilted back her big straw hat. I regret to report that I failed to control myself when I saw her face. That Egyptian profile which, many years later, I saw again in a portrait of the female pharaoh, Queen Hatshepsut, the first woman in recorded history, whom dismissive Vina, unimpressed by divine monarchs even though she became a sort of god-queen herself, referred to as Hat Cheap Suit; those sardonic eyes, that mouth so dryly twisted, caused me to let out a gasp. No, it was more than a gasp. It was a loud, strangled noise, choking, formless, and it ended in something like a sob. In short, I made, for the only time in my life, the noise of a badly smitten human male falling instantly, heavily, painfully in love. And I was only nine years old.

Let me try and remember the great moment with maximum accuracy. I had, I think, only recently emerged from the sea, my tooth braces were smarting, and I was feeling a little peckish—or else I had been planning a swim when I was distracted by the arrival of the magnificentourage. At any rate, when Ameer Merchant spoke the sentence that Piloo Doodhwala heard as a declaration of war, I had just reached down into a bag of fruit and come up with a juicy apple in my fist. Apple in hand, I gazed upon the beautiful dark girl in the Old Glory swimsuit, apple in hand I emitted my awful, naked noise of adoration; and when my feet began to move of their own accord and propelled me forward until I stood before her, gazing up into the light of her beauty, I was still holding that apple out in front of me, like an offering, like a prize.

She smiled, amused. "Is that for me?" But before I could articulate a reply, the two other girls—damn it, the two ugly sisters!—had run up with gleaming faces, ignoring their ayah's injunctions to return. "Appo," said Halva Doodhwala, making baby eyes and affecting baby talk in a doomed attempt at appearing winsome; and Rasgulla Doodhwala, older but no wiser, poutingly confirmed, "Ppl." The tall girl laughed, rather cruelly, and struck an attitude, head cocked sideways, hand on hip. "You see, you must choose, young master. To which of us will you offer your good gift?"

That's easy, I wanted to say, for it is the gift of my heart. But Piloo and (especially) Golmatol were glaring at me in savage anticipation of my decision, and when, hesitating for a moment, I cast a glance at my own parents, I saw that they were unable to help me make a choice that would affect their lives as much as mine. I did not know then (though it would have been easy to guess) that the tall girl was not the younger girls' sibling, that her place in the entourage was more Cinderella than Helen; or a curious amalgam of the two, a sort of Cinderella of Troy. But it wouldn't have made any difference if I had known; for though my tongue said nothing, my heart was speaking loud and clear. Without a word, I held out the apple to my beloved; who, with a curt nod, somewhat ungraciously received the gift and gave it a goodly bite.

So it was that my deliberate spurning of the charms of Halva and Rasgulla, those little mistresses of the insincerely batted eyelash, was added by the Doodhwalas to my mother's more accidental insult, and that was that. The Hindustani word *kutti* is inadequate for my purposes, suggesting as it does a rather petulant, almost childish level of quarrel. This was not *kutti*. This was vendetta. And in Piloo Doodhwala—who was now, to my horror, beckoning me to approach—I'd made a powerful enemy, and for life.

"Boy!"

Now that the point of no return had passed, Piloo had miraculously relaxed. He had lost the swollen look of a man over-full of furious vocabulary, and even the sweating had stopped. I, however, found myself being bitten by insects. It was that moment of the late afternoon when the mordant armies of the air manifest themselves, appearing like little clouds from some aerial dormitory. As I approached Piloo, who was reclining in splendour on *gao-takia* bolsters beneath his mirrorwork marquee, I was obliged to slap and rub at my face and neck, for all the world as if I were punishing myself for my judgement in the matter of the apple. Piloo smiled his deadly, glittering smile and continued to beckon.

"And your goodname, please?" I told him my name. "Umeed," he repeated. "Hop. That is good. All persons should be having hop, even when their situation is hopliss." He fell into a period of contemplation, munching on a morsel of dried bummelo; then spoke again, waving a piece of the fish in his hand. "Bombay duck," he smiled. "You know what is it? You know that this *bombil* phish declined to help Lord Rama to build the bridge to Lanka, phor purpose of rescuing Lady Sita? And therephore he squeezed it tight-tight and crushed all its bones, so now it is boneless wonder? No, how can you know, for you are conwerts." This word led to much shaking of the head, and many more mouth-fuls of the fish, before he renewed his harangue. "Conwert," he said. "You know what is it? I will tell. Religious conwersion, it is like get-ting on a train. Afterwards, only the train itself is where you are belong-ing. Not departure platform, not arriwal platform. In both these places you are totally despised. Such is conwert. It is your goodfather's phore-father."

I opened my mouth; he indicated that I should close it. "Seen and not heard," he stated. "Keep your trap shut is best policy." He munched on mango. "When man conwerts," he mused, "it is like a powver cut. Load shedding. He is shedding, you see?, the Load of Human Destiny in a basically cowvardly way. Phundamentally an unserious phashion. In doing so he detaches himself from the history of his race, isn't it? Like pulling out a plug, okay? And then the toaster will not work. What is life, boy? I will tell. Life is not just a single hair plucked out phrom the head of God, okay? Life is a cycle. In this poor life of ours we must pay phor the sins of our past existence, and also if appropri-ate reap reward of prewious good behawiour. The conwert is like a guest in a hotel who will not pay his bill. Therephore conwersely he cannot expect benephits if there is billing error in his phavour."

Piloo's thesis wasn't easy to grasp, what with all the trains, toasters, cycles and hotels tumbling around in there, but I understood the essen-tial point: he was insulting my father, and my father's (Muslim) branch of the family, and therefore, by extension, me. Now, however, as my adult self observes the scene through my nine-year-old eyes and ears, I see and hear other things too: the class differences, for example, the note of snobbishness in my mother's disdain for Piloo's coarser behav-iour and vulgar accent; and of course communal differences. The old Hindu-Muslim rift. My parents gave me the gift of irreligion, of grow-ing up without bothering to ask people what gods they held dear, assuming that in fact, like my parents, they weren't interested in gods, and that this uninterest was "normal." You may argue that the gift was a poisoned chalice, but even if so, that's a cup from which I'd happily drink again.

In spite of my parents' godlessness, however, the old family rift persisted. It was so deep that the family's two branches, converts and unconverted, had erased each other from their social maps. At the age of nine I had not even known of the Doodhwalas' existence, and I'm sure Halva and Rasgulla had been equally unaware of their distant cousin Umeed Merchant. As for the tall girl, the swimsuit queen with my apple in her mouth, I still had no clue as to how and where she fitted in.

"Umeed," called my mother, and her voice was angry, "come back here, now."

"Go, little Hop." Piloo dismissed me. He had begun idly to roll a set of poker dice on his carpet. "But I wonder, when you are a big Hop, what-all you will be."

I already knew the answer to that. "Ji, a photographer, ji."

"So," he said. "Then you must learn how a picture can be false. Take my photo just now, isn't it? What do you see? Only some big sahib acting big. But this is a dastardly lie. I am a man of the people, Hop. Simple phellow, humble origins, and because I am accustomed to hard work, so I also know how to enjoy. Just now I am enjoying. But you, Hop, you and your daddy-mummy, you are the guys acting big. Too big, maybe, for boots." He paused. There were milky crescents rimming the pupils of his eyes. "I think perhaps we have phought bephore, in other lives. Today we will not phight. But one day we will surely phight again."

"Umeed!"

"Say also to your goodmother," murmured Piloo Doodhwala, the smile fading from his lips, "that this sand building like a *Shiv-lingam* is a philthy blasphemy. To all decent eyes it is offensiwe and obscene."

In my mind's eye I see again my nine-year-old self, an envoy leaving the enemy camp and returning to his own. But I can also see what's really going on, the process by which power, like heat, is slowly draining from the world of my angry mother to that of Piloo the newly cool. Which is not fancy but hindsight. He hated us; and in time he would inherit, if not *the* earth, then *ours*.

"I hate India," my swimsuit queen mentioned savagely as I passed her. "And there's plenty of it to hate. I hate the heat, and it's always hot, even when it rains, and I really hate that rain. I hate the food, and you can't drink the water. I hate the poor people, and they're all over the place. I hate the rich people, they're so goddamn pleased with themselves. I hate the crowds, and you're never out of them. I hate the way people speak too loud and dress in purple and ask too many questions and order you around. I hate the dirt and I hate the smell and I specially hate squatting down to shit. I hate the money because it can't buy anything, and I hate the stores because there's nothing to buy. I hate the movies, I hate the dancing, I hate the music. I hate the languages because they're not plain English and I hate the English because it's not plain English either. I hate the cars except the American cars and I hate those too because they're all ten years out of date. I hate the schools because they're really jails and I hate the holidays because you're not free even then. I hate the old people and I hate the kids. I hate the radio and there's no tv. Most of all I hate all the goddamn gods." It was an astonishing utterance, spoken in a casual, world-weary monotone, with her eyes fixed on the horizon. I had no idea how to reply, but a reply did not appear to be required. At that time I did not understand her anger, and it shocked me deeply. Was this the girl with whom I had fallen so hopelessly in love? "I hate the apples too," she added, driving a sword into my heart. (But she'd eaten mine, I noticed.) Lovelorn, slapping at bugs, I turned to go on my difficult way. "Want to know what I like, what's the only thing I like?" she called after me. I paused and turned back to face her.

"Yes, please," I humbly said. I may even have bowed my head in misery.

"I love the sea," she said, and ran off to swim. My heart almost burst with joy.

I heard Piloo's dice begin to click and roll; and then, at Golmatol Doodhwala's command, the musicians started up again, and I heard nothing else.

For a long while I have believed—this is perhaps my version of Sir Darius Xerxes Cama's belief in a fourth function of *outsideness*—that in every generation there are a few souls, call them lucky or cursed, who are simply *born not belonging*, who come into the world semi-detached, if you like, without strong affiliation to family or location or nation or race; that there may even be millions, billions of such souls, as many non-belongers as belongers, perhaps; that, in sum, the phenomenon may be as "natural" a manifestation of human nature as its opposite, but one that has been mostly frustrated, throughout human history, by lack of opportunity. And not only by that: for those who value stability, who fear transience, uncertainty, change, have erected a powerful system of stigmas and taboos against rootlessness, that disruptive, anti-social force, so that we mostly conform, we pretend to be motivated by loyalties and solidarities we do not really feel, we hide our secret identities beneath the false skins of those identities which bear the belongers' seal of approval. But the truth leaks out in our dreams; alone in our beds (because we are all alone at night, even if we do not sleep by ourselves), we soar, we fly, we flee. And in the waking dreams our societies permit, in our myths, our arts, our songs, we celebrate the non-belongers, the different ones, the outlaws, the freaks. What we forbid ourselves we pay good money to watch, in a playhouse or movie theatre, or to read about between the secret covers of a book. Our libraries, our palaces of entertainment tell the truth. The tramp, the assassin, the rebel, the thief, the mutant, the outcast, the delinquent, the devil, the sinner, the traveller, the gangster, the runner, the mask: if we did not recognize in them our least-fulfilled needs, we would not invent them over and over again, in every place, in every language, in every time.

No sooner did we have ships than we rushed to sea, sailing across oceans in paper boats. No sooner did we have cars than we hit the road. No sooner did we have airplanes than we zoomed to the furthest corners of the globe. Now we yearn for the moon's dark side, the rocky plains of Mars, the rings of Saturn, the interstellar deeps. We send mechanical photographers into orbit, or on one-way journeys to the stars, and we weep at the wonders they transmit; we are humbled by the mighty images of far-off galaxies standing like cloud pillars in the sky, and we give names to alien rocks, as if they were our pets. We hunger for warp space, for the outlying rim of time. And this is the species that kids itself it likes to stay at home, to bind itself with—what are they called again?—*ties.*

That's my view. You don't have to buy it. Maybe there aren't so many of us, after all. Maybe we are disruptive and anti-social and we shouldn't be allowed. You're entitled to your opinion. All I will say is: sleep soundly, baby. Sleep tight and sweet dreams.

According to the Doodhwala version of the universe, it all started because my paternal great-grandfather "embraced Islam," as they say: Islam, that least huggable of faiths. As a result of that prickly embrace, Vivvy Merchant (and Ameer too, and indeed every Muslim in the sub-continent, for we are all the children of converts, whether we admit it or not, every single one of us) lost his connection with history. Thus we can interpret my father's desperate diggings into the city's past as a quest for his mislaid personal identity; and Ameer Merchant, dreaming of Cuffescrapers and such, was likewise seeking lost certainties in visions of high-rise apartment blocks and Art Deco cinemas, in bricks and mortar, in reinforced cement-concrete.

No shortage of explanations for life's mysteries. Explanations are two a penny these days. The truth, however, is altogether harder to find.

Always, from my earliest remembered days, I longed above all to be— to use once more a phrase to which I remain (perhaps excessively) attached—worthy of the world. To this end I was fully prepared to be tested, to perform labours. I began to learn about the heroes of Greece and Rome through Nathaniel Hawthorne's *Tanglewood Tales,* and of Camelot I became aware thanks to MGM's *Knights of the Round Table,* starring Robert Taylor as Lancelot and Mel Ferrer as Arthur, and as Guinevere, if memory serves, the incomparable Ava, that palindromic goddess who looked just as good when seen from the back as from the front. I devoured children's versions of the Norse Sagas (I particularly recall epic journeys made in a boat called Skidbladnir, the "ship that flew") and of the adventures of Hatim Tai and Haroun al-Rashid and Sindbad the Sailor and Marco Polo and Ibn Battuta and Rama and Lakshmana and the Kurus and Pandavas and anything else that came to hand. However, this high moral formulation, "being worthy of the world," was too abstract to be easily applicable to daily life. I told the truth and was a reasonably upstanding, if also rather solitary and inward, child; but heroism escaped me. There was even a brief inter-lude, at around the time I am describing, when I began to believe the world to be unworthy of me. Its false notes, its constant fallings-short. This was, perhaps, my mother's disappointed idealism, her growing cynicism, leaking into me. Now, looking back, I can say that we have been more or less on a par, the world and I. We have both risen to occasions and let the side down. To speak only for myself, however (I do not presume to speak for the world): at my worst, I have been a cacophony, a mass of human noises that did not add up to the symphony of an integrated self. At my best, however, the world sang out to me, and through me, like ringing crystal.

When I met Vina at the beach, I knew for the first time how to measure my worth. I would look for my answers in her eyes. I would ask only to wear my lady's favour on my helm.

I must say that I had the best possible start in life. I was the fortunate and only son of loving parents who, in order to do justice to their beloved child without giving up their own private and professional passions, chose to have no more children after me. Looking over the foregoing account of fun at the beach, I see that I have omitted to touch on the many small affectionate gestures with which V.V. and Ameer Merchant habitually demonstrated their love: her wry but adoring smiles at her digging husband, his shy, toothy grins in return, the brushings of her hand against his cheek, of his hand against the nape of her neck, the tiny solicitudes of a happy marriage—sit here, it's more shady; drink this, it's cool and sweet—that, though they be murmured ever so privately, do not escape the camera-eyed, antenna-eared, all-recording child. I, too, was well loved, and had never for a day been left in an ayah's care, a fact that aroused amazement, and attracted considerable criticism, in our social circle. Lady Spenta Cama, who never wholly forgave Ameer for her faux pas on the day of Ormus's birth, was in the habit of telling people that any woman who would not even look for a good ayah "must have a little too much of the servant in her own family background." The remark reached Ameer's ears at high speed, malice being the most eager of postmen, and relations between the two women were further strained. My parents' resolve was only strengthened by such gibes. During my babyhood and early infancy, they drew up a weekly rota of duties and pleasures on a rigorously fifty-fifty basis, arranging their work schedules and even their sleep patterns to fit the principle of parental equality. I was not breast-fed; my father would not allow it, for then he would be unable to do his share of feeding. And in his gentle way he insisted on fulfilling his appointed quota of bottom-wiping and nappy-boiling and colic-comforting and play. My mother sang her tuneless songs, and my father also sang his. So it was that I grew up thinking of this, too, as "normal." The world had many shocks in store for me.

They gave up most of their social lives without even noticing that they had done so. The arrival of a child (me) had completed them in some profound way, and they no longer appeared to need other people. Their friends remonstrated with them at first. Some were hurt. Many believed, with Lady Spenta Cama, that there was something "unhealthy" in the Merchants' "obsessive" behaviour. In the end, however, everyone simply accepted the new pattern of life as a fact, as merely one eccentricity among life's many perplexities. V.V. and Ameer were able to concentrate on their boy (me) without concerning themselves about injured feelings or wagging tongues.

Was it on account of their smothering love, or something less explicable in myself, that I began to look out to sea, and dream of America? Was it because, between them, they had possessed the city so completely—was it because I felt that the land was theirs—that I decided to award myself the sea? Did I quit Bombay, in other words, because the whole damn city felt like my mother's womb and I had to go abroad to get myself born? Such are the psychological explanations on offer, readily available from stock.

I would like to reject them all. My parents, I repeat, loved me and gave me the best they could afford. No childhood home could be more evocative, or linger more sweetly in the memory, than Villa Thracia on Cuffe Parade; and in addition to the best of homes, I had good friends, went to a good school, and had excellent prospects. How churlish, then, to blame one's parents for providing precisely what every parent hopes to offer! How disgustingly improper to hold against them just that loving attentiveness which is every father and mother's ideal! You will not hear such words from me, be sure that you won't. Detachment, a weakened sense of affiliation, was simply in my nature. Already, at the age of nine, I not only had secrets but was proud of them. My high longings, my dreams of ancient knights and heroes, I hugged to myself; to reveal them would have been to shame myself, to plunge into the humiliating gulf between the greatness of my intentions and the paltry nature of my few achievements. I cultivated silence, while dreaming that, one day, I might sing.

This overly defended self of mine had certain uses. Sometimes, of an evening, I played poker with Vivvy and Ameer. Almost always, I ended up with the largest pile of matchsticks in front of me. "Maybe you should go in for pro gambling when you grow up," my mother shockingly suggested. "Because, darling boy, that poker face of yours is already working fine." I nodded. Success loosened my tongue a little. "Nobody ever knows what I'm thinking," I told her. "That's the way I like it."

I saw the shock on both their faces, and the bewilderment too. They simply had no idea what to say to me. "It's better to speak your heart, Umeed," my father finally got out. "Better to show your hand than hide it, eh?" My father, the very model of the upstanding gent, the most honourable of men, the most honest, the least corruptible, the gentlest of manner but also the most iron-principled, the most tolerant, was in short the best of men, a godless saint (how he'd have hated the term!) who could be sold a cheap watch in the street and think it an Omega, who always lost at cards and later, tragically, lost at life. And I, his crafty, feigning son, I grinned wide-eyed at this genuinely unworldly innocent man, I made as if to echo his innocence, and then made my checkmate move. "In that case," I murmured, "why aren't all the matchsticks piled up in front of you?"

In retrospect it seems plain that the sea was just a metaphor for me. Certainly I liked to swim, but I was just as happy to do so at, for example, the Willingdon Club swimming pool, just as content with fresh water as with salty. Nor did I ever learn to sail, or regret not learning. Water was simply the magic element that would bear me away on its tides; when I grew up, and air was offered instead, I switched allegiances at once. But I remain grateful to water, because Vina loved it, and we could swim in it together.

Air and water, earth and fire: all four shaped our stories (I mean, of course, Ormus's story, Vina's tale, and mine). In the first two was our beginning. But then came middles, and ends.

. . .

When you grow up, as I did, in a great city, during what just happens to be its golden age, you think of it as eternal. Always was there, always will be. The grandeur of the metropolis creates the illusion of permanence. The peninsular Bombay into which I was born certainly seemed perennial to me. Colaba Causeway was my Via Appia, Malabar and Cumballa hills were our Capitol and Palatine, the Brabourne Stadium was our Colosseum, and as for the glittering Art Deco sweep of Marine Drive, well, that was something not even Rome could boast. I actually grew up believing Art Deco to be the "Bombay style," a local invention, its name derived, in all probability, from the imperative of the verb "to see." *Art dekho.* Lo and behold art. (When I began to be familiar with images of New York, I at first felt a sort of anger. The Americans had so much; did they have to possess our "style" as well? But in another, more secret part of my heart, the Art Deco of Manhattan, built on a scale so much grander than our own, only increased America's allure, made it both familiar and awe-inspiring, our little Bombay writ large.)

In reality that Bombay was almost brand-new when I knew it; what's more, my parents' construction firm of Merchant & Merchant had been prominent in its making. In the ten years between the birth of Ormus Cama and my own coming into the world, the city had been a gigantic building site; as if it were in a hurry to become, as if it knew it had to provide itself in finished condition by the time I was able to start paying attention to it. . . . No, no, I don't really think along such solipsistic lines. I'm not over-attached to history, or Bombay. Me, I'm the under-attached type.

I return to my muttons. It is true, though it's got nothing to do with me, that the building boom that created the Bombay of my childhood went into overdrive in the years before my birth and then slowed down for about twenty years; and that time of relative stability tricked me into believing in the city's timeless qualities. After that, of course, it turned into a monster, and I fled. Ran for my wretched life.

Me? I was a Bombay *chokra* through and through. But let me confess that, even as a child, I was insanely jealous of the city in which I was raised, because it was my parents' other love, the daughter they never had. They loved each other (good), they loved me (very good), and they loved her (not so good). Bombay was my rival. It was on account of their romance with the city that they drew up that weekly rota of shared parental responsibilities. When my mother wasn't with me—when I was riding on my father's shoulders, or staring, with him, at the fish in the Taraporewala Aquarium—she was out there with *her*, with Bombay; out there bringing her into being. (For of course construction work never stops completely, and supervising such work was Ameer's particular genius. My mother the master builder. Like her dead father before her.) And when my father handed me over to her—when we sang our hideous ditties and ate our curdled ice-cream—he went off, wearing his local-history hat and a khaki jacket full of pockets, to dig in the foundations of building sites for the secrets of the city's past, or else sat hatless and coatless at a designing board and dreamed his lo-and-behold dreams.

V. V. Merchant's first love would always be the city's pre-history; it was as if he were more interested in the infant's conception than in her actuality. Give him his head and he would prattle happily for hours of the Chalukya settlements on Elephanta and Salsette islands two and a half thousand years ago, or Raja Bhimdev's legendary capital at Mahim in the eleventh or twelfth century. He could recite the clauses of the Treaty of Bassein under which the Mughal emperor Bahadur Shah ceded the Seven Isles to the Portuguese, and was fond of pointing out that Queen Catherine of Braganza, wife of Charles II, was the secret link between the cities of Bombay and New York. Bombay came to England in her dowry; but she was also the Queen in the N.Y. borough of Queens.

Maps of the early town afforded him great joy, and his collection of old photographs of the edifices and *objets* of the vanished city was second to none. In these faded images were resurrected the demolished Fort, the slummy "breakfast bazaar" market outside the Teen Darvaza or Bazaargate, and the humble mutton shops and umbrella hospitals of the poor, as well as the fallen palaces of the great. The early city's relics filled his imagination as well as his photo albums. Hats were of particular interest. "Time was, you could tell a man's community at once by the thing he wore on his head," he lamented. Sir Darius Xerxes Cama with his chimney-pot fez was a last relic of those days when Parsis were called Topazes on account of their headgear. And banias had round hats and the chow-chow Bohras crying their unlistably various wares in the streets seemed to be carrying balls upon their heads. . . . It was from my father that I learned of Bombay's first great photographers, Raja Deen Dayal and A. R. Haseler, whose portraits of the city became my first artistic influences, if only by showing me what I did not want to do. Dayal climbed the Rajabai tower to create his sweeping panoramas of the birth of the city; Haseler went one better and took to the air. Their images were awe-inspiring, unforgettable, but they also inspired in me a desperate need to get back down to ground level. From the heights you see only pinnacles. I yearned for the city streets, the knife grinders, the water carriers, the Chowpatty pickpockets, the pavement moneylenders, the peremptory soldiers, the whoring dancers, the horse-drawn carriages with their fodder-thieving drivers, the railway hordes, the chess players in the Irani restaurants, the snake-buckled schoolchildren, the beggars, the fishermen, the servants, the wild throng of Crawford Market shoppers, the oiled wrestlers, the moviemakers, the dockers, the book sewers, the urchins, the cripples, the loom operators, the bully boys, the priests, the throat slitters, the frauds. I yearned for life.

When I said this to my father he showed me still lives of hats and storefronts and piers and told me I was too young to understand. "Comprehension of historical appurtenances," he assured me, "reveals the human factor." This required translation. "See where people lived and worked and shopped," he clarified, with a rare flash of irritation, "and it becomes plain what they were like." For all his digging, Vivvy Merchant was content with the surfaces of his world. I, his photographer son, set out to prove him wrong, to show that a camera can see beyond the surface, beyond the trappings of the actual, and penetrate to its bloody flesh and heart.

The family construction business had been developed by his late father-in-law, Ishak Merchant, a man so interminably choleric that at the age of forty-three his inner organs literally burst with anger and he died, bleeding copiously inside his skin. This was soon after his daughter's marriage. The daughter of an angry man, my mother had chosen a partner wholly lacking in anger, but couldn't handle even his gentle—and rare—reproofs; the mildest of cavils would unleash in her an astonishing storm of emotion that was more tearful than explosive, but otherwise, in respect of its extreme and damaging force, not at all unlike her dead father's rage. V. V. treated her gingerly, like the fragile thoroughbred she was. Which was necessary; but also spoke of trouble ahead, or would have, had either of the happy couple been listening. But they turned a deaf ear to all words of warning. They were deeply in love; which beats earplugs.

The happy newlyweds, Vivvy and Ameer, were plunged in at the deep end. Fortunately for them, the city needed every builder it could get. Two decades later, they could point out several of the *art dekho* mansion blocks along the west side of the Oval Maidan, and on Marine Drive too, and say with justifiable pride, "We built that" or "This one's ours." Now they were busy further afield, in Worli and Pali Hill and so on. As we drove home from Juhu, we made a number of detours to take a look at this or that site, and not only those with Merchant & Merchant boards on the wire perimeter fences. Building sites are, to a family of builders, what tourist sights are to the rest of the populace. I had grown accustomed to such behaviour and, in addition, was so excited about my encounter with my swimsuit goddess that I didn't even bother to complain. I did, however, ask questions.

"What's her name?"

"Arré, whose name? What do I know? Ask your father."

"What's her name?"

"I'm not sure. Nissa or some such."

"Nissa what? Nissa Doodhwala? Nissa Shetty? What?"

"I can't remember. She grew up far from here, in America."

"America? Where in America? New York?"

But my father had run out of information; or else there were things he did not wish to reveal. Ameer, however, knew it all.

"New York State," she said. "Some stupid *gaon* in the backyard of beyond."

"What *gaon*? Oh, Ammi, come on."

"You think I know every village in the U.S.? Some Chickaboom-type name."

"That's not a name. Is it?"

She shrugged. "Who knows what-all kind of crazy names they have there. Not just Hiawatha-Minnehaha but also Susquehanna, Shenandoah, Sheboygan, Okefenokee, Onondaga, Oshkosh, Chittenango, Chikasha, Canandaigua, Chuinouga, Tomatosauga, Chickaboom." They were her last words on the subject. Chickaboom, N.Y., it was.

"Anyway," added my mother, "you don't want anything to do with her. For one thing, that Piloo is her guardian now, and plus, she is well known to be nothing but trouble. One thousand and one percent bad egg. She has had a life of tragedy, that is so, my heart goes out to her, but just keep away from her. You heard how she talks. No discipline. She's too old, anyway; find friends your own age. And plus," as if this clinched it, "she's a vegetarian."

"I liked her," I said. My parents both ignored me.

"You know," my mother changed the subject, "those Red Indian names sound darn South Indian to me. Chattanooga, Ootacamund, Thekkady, Schenectady, Gitchee-Gummee, Ticklegummy, Chittoor, Chitaldroog, Chickaboom. Maybe some of our Dravidian co-nationals sailed off to America yonks ago in a beautiful pea-green boat. Indians get everywhere, isn't it? Like sand."

"Maybe they took some honey and plenty of money," my father joined in. I saw that we had embarked on one of our traditional family kidabouts and there was no point trying to get things back on track.

"What's the point of wrapping honey in a five-pound note, anyway," I said, giving in. "And, p.s.," I added, my thoughts turning back to my swimsuit girl, "what self-respecting pussycat would marry a stupid owl?"

"Minnehaha, Laughing Water," Ameer followed her own train of thought. "So *haha* must be laughing, which means *Minne* is water. Then what's Mickey?"

"Mickey," said my father sternly, "is a mouse."

The philosopher Aristotle was dismissive of mythology. Myths were just fanciful yarns, or so he opined, containing no valuable truths about our natures or our surroundings. Only by reason, he argued, will men understand themselves and master the world in which they live. For this view Aristotle had, in my childhood, some minority local support. "The true miracle of reason," Sir Darius Xerxes Cama once (or, actually, rather too often) said, "is reason's victory over the miraculous." Most other leading minds, I'm bound to report, disagreed; Lady Spenta

Cama, for example, for whom the miraculous had long ago supplanted the quotidian as the norm, and who would have been utterly lost, without her angels and devils, in the tragic jungle of the everyday.

Also ranged against Aristotle and Sir Darius was Giovanni Battista Vico (1668–1744). In Vico, as for so many present-day theorists of childhood, the early years are the crucial ones. The themes and dramas of those first moments set the pattern for all that follows. For Vico, mythology is the family album or storehouse of a culture's childhood, containing that society's future, codified as tales that are both poems and oracles. The private drama of the vanished Villa Thracia colours and prophesies our subsequent way of living in the world.

"Keep away from her," said Ameer Merchant, but once the inexorable dynamic of the mythic has been set in motion, you might as well try and keep bees from honey, crooks from money, politicians from babies, philosophers from maybes. Vina had her hooks in me, and the consequence was the story of my life. "Bad egg," Ameer called her, and "rotten apple" too. And then, dripping and bruised, she arrived at our door in the middle of the night, begging to be taken in.

Just seven days after our Juhu experiences, at six o'clock in the evening, it began to rain out of a clear sky, in hot, fat drops. Heavy rain, whose warmth did nothing to cool down the maximum-humidity heat wave. And as the rain increased in force, so too, in a freak of nature, the temperature also rose, so that the water, falling, evaporated before it hit the ground and turned to mist. Wet and white, rarest of all Bombay's meteorological phenomena, the mist rolled in across the Back Bay. The citizenry, strolling on the Parade for the customary "eating of the air," fled in search of shelter. Mist obliterated the city; the world was a white sheet, waiting to be written upon. V.V., Ameer and I stayed indoors, clutching our poker hands, and in that bizarre whiteness our bidding became extreme, reckless, as if we intuited that the moment required extravagant gestures of us all. My father lost even more matchsticks than usual, and at higher speed. A white night fell.

We went to our beds, but none of us could sleep. When Ameer came to kiss me good night, I said, "I keep waiting for something to happen." Ameer nodded. "I know."

Later, after midnight, it was Ameer who first heard the noises outside, the bumping and thumping, as if an animal were loose on the front verandah, and then an exhausted, tearful panting. She sat straight up in bed and said, "Sounds like whatever Umeed was hoping for has turned up at last."

By the time we reached the verandah the girl had passed out on the boards. She had a black eye and there were cuts on her forearms, some of them deep. Glistening serpents of hair lay across the wooden verandah floor. Medusa. It crossed my mind that we should look at her face only in a burnished shield, lest we be turned to stone. Her white T-shirt and jeans were sodden. I could not help looking at the outlines of her thick nipples. Her breathing was too fast, too heavy, and she was groaning as she breathed. "It's her," I said, stupidly.

"And we have no choice," my mother said. "And what will be will be."

Dry, warm, bandaged, and eating hot porridge from a bowl, with a towel wound over her hair like a pharaoh's crown, the girl held court in my parents' bed, and we three Merchants stood before her like courtiers; like bears. "He tried to kill me," she said. "Piloo, the yellow-belly. He attacked me. So I ran away." Her voice failed. "Well, he threw me out," she said. "But I won't go back, anyway; whatever happens." And Ameer, who had warned me off her, said fiercely, "Go back? Out of the question. Nissa Doodhwala, you will kindly just stay put." Which utterance was rewarded by a tentative, though still suspicious, smile.

"Don't call me by that bastard's name, okay?" the girl said. "I left there with nothing. From now on I'll be whatever name I choose."

And a few moments later: "Vina Apsara. That's my name."

My mother soothed her, reassured her—"Yes, Vina, okay, baby, whatever you want"—and then probed: what had provoked so violent an attack? Vina's face slammed shut, like a book. But the next morning the answer arrived on our doorstep, anxiously ringing the bell: Ormus Cama, beautiful and dangerous as the revenant sun, nineteen years old, with a "reputation." And in search of forbidden fruit.

It was the beginning of the end of my days of joy, spent with those Thracian deities, my parents, amidst legends of the city's past and visions of its future. After a childhood of being loved, of believing in the safety of our little world, things would begin to crumble for me, my parents would quarrel horribly and die before their time. Fleeing this frightful disintegration, I turned towards my own life, and there, too, I found love; but that existence also came to an untimely end. Then for a long time there was just me, and my painful remembering.

Now there is at last a new flowering of happiness in my life. (This, too, will be told at the proper time.) Perhaps this is why I can face the horror of the past. It's tough to speak of the beauty of the world when one has lost one's sight, an anguish to sing music's praises when your ear trumpet has failed. So also it is hard to write about love, even harder to write lovingly, when one has a broken heart. Which is no excuse; happens to everyone. One must simply overcome, always overcome. Pain and loss are "normal" too. Heartbreak is what there is.

4

THE INVENTION
OF MUSIC

Even though Ormus Cama, our absurdly handsome and impossibly gifted hero, has just returned to the centre of my stage—a little too late to provide prompt comfort to the young lady for whose distress he is largely to blame!—I must briefly halt my runaway bus of a narrative, so that I may help the reader to a better understanding of how matters had arrived at so sorry a pass. And so I take you back to Ormus's father, Sir Darius Xerxes Cama, now in his middle sixties, stretched out on a British-style button-back leather chesterfield sofa in his Apollo Bunder library; with his eyes closed and a cut-glass tumbler and a decanter of whisky by his side; and dreaming.

Whenever he dreamed, he dreamed of England: England as a pure, white Palladian mansion set upon a hill above a silver winding river, with a spreading parterre of brilliant green lawns edged by ancient oaks and elms, and the classic geometry of flower beds orchestrated by unseen master gardeners into a four-seasons symphony of colour. White curtains were blowing at the open French windows of the great house's orangery wing. In the dream Sir Darius was once again a young boy in short trousers, and the mansion was a magnet drawing him forward across its perfect lawns, past the topiary hedges and the ornamental fountain pullulating with figures from ancient Greece and Rome, the hirsute, lecherous gods, the naked heroes with their upraised swords, the serpents, the ravished women, the severed heads, the centaurs. The curtains wound themselves around him, but he fought free, for somewhere in this house, waiting for him, combing her long hair and singing a sweet song, was his mother, whom he had lost so long ago, whom he mourned every day, and to whose bosom his dreaming self hastened to return.

He couldn't find her. He searched the house in vain, scurrying through the interconnecting grandeur of anachronistic state rooms; boudoirs of murderous Restoration miladies who had hidden their daggers and poisons in secret cavities behind fleur-de-lys panelling; Baroque offices of power where bewigged grandees with perfumed kerchiefs had once dispensed patronage and largesse to their malodorous, genuflecting protégés, and where, too, conspiracies of state had been hissed by great men into the ears of murderers and thieves; grand carpeted *Jugendstil* stairways down which betrayed princesses had hurled themselves in fits of lonely despair; and medieval star chambers where summary justice had once been handed down beneath artists' impressions of whirling galaxies and dying suns . . . until he stumbled out into an inner courtyard of the white house, where at the far end of a pool of cold black water stood the naked figure of a beautiful and blindfolded woman, her arms spread wide, as if she was preparing to dive. But she did not dive. The palms of her hands turned invitingly towards him, and he couldn't resist, he was no longer a boy in short trousers but a man full of desire; he ran towards her, even though he knew the scandal would unmake him. Dreaming, he intuited that the dream spoke of something buried in his past, buried so deep that he himself had entirely forgotten what it was.

"Yes, come to me," whispered Scandal, enfolding him in her arms, "my darling, my favourite servant of the Lie."

When he was awake, and the memory of the blindfolded nude by the swimming pool had faded into the limbo of things half remembered and uncertain, and the whisky had loosened his tongue, Sir Darius Xerxes Cama would soliloquize yearningly about the country houses of old England—Boot Magna, Castle Howard, Blandings, Chequers, Brideshead, Cliveden, Styles. As he grew older and thickened by drink, certain boundaries blurred in his memory, and nowadays he drew only the vaguest of distinctions between Toad Hall and Blenheim Palace, Longleat and Gormenghast. His nostalgia applied equally to the dream houses of fiction and the real country seats of "bluebloods" and prime ministers and rich arrivistes like the Astor clan. Real or fictional, these mighty piles represented for Sir Darius the closest approximation to earthly Paradise that human imagination and ingenuity had managed to create. He spoke more and more often of moving the family to England on a permanent basis. On Ormus Cama's nineteenth birthday his father gave him the first volume of Sir Winston Churchill's new *History of the English-Speaking Peoples.* "Not content with winning the war," Sir Darius said, shaking his head admiringly, "the old bulldog went off and won the Nobel Prize in Literature also. No wonder they call him Winnie. British youth looks up to him, seeks to follow where he trod. Great things are consequently expected of the younger generation in England. Our youth, by sad contrast," he said, looking disapprovingly at Ormus, "is in a state of advanced decay. Old virtues— service of community, discipline of personality, memorizing of poetry, mastery of firearms, pleasure in falconry, formal dancing, building of character through sport—these things have lost meaning. Only in the mother country can they be rediscovered."

"On the cover of this book the King of England has an arrow stuck in his eye," Ormus pointed out. "I guess archery must not be a specialty of the bulldog breed."

Sir Darius was predictably provoked, and would have relieved himself of a further tirade had Lady Spenta not added, immovably, "If you are dreaming again of relocating in London, be assured that I personally will never consent to upping sticks." Which turned out, like all prophecies, to be untrue.

Ormus Cama withdrew. Abandoning his parents to their ancient rituals of disagreement, he wandered through the sprawling Apollo Bunder apartment. While he remained in Sir Darius's field of vision his movements were exaggeratedly adolescent, that is, indolent and listless, the very picture of decadent Parsi youth. Once he was out of his father's sight, however, a remarkable transformation occurred. It should be remembered that Ormus, a born singer, had not opened his lips in song since the night he was almost smothered in his bed by his elder brother Cyrus; and a stranger, watching him now, might easily have concluded that all the unsung music of his silenced years had accumulated in him, causing acute discomfort, even agony; and that the pent-up melodies were actually trying to burst out of his body as he walked.

Oh, how he swayed and twitched!

If I say that Ormus Cama was the greatest popular singer of all, the one whose genius exceeded all others, who was never caught by the pursuing pack, then I am confident that even my toughest-minded reader will readily concede the point. He was a musical sorcerer whose melodies could make city streets begin to dance and high buildings sway to their rhythm, a golden troubadour the jouncy poetry of whose lyrics could unlock the very gates of Hell; he incarnated the singer and songwriter as shaman and spokesman, and became the age's unholy unfool. But by his own account he was more than that; for he claimed to be nothing less than the secret originator, the prime innovator, of the music that courses in our blood, that possesses and moves us, wherever we may be, the music that speaks the secret language of all humanity, our common heritage, whatever mother tongue we speak, whatever dances we first learned to dance.

From the beginning he claimed that he was literally years ahead of his time.

At the moment of which I now speak, the butterfly was still in its chrysalis, the oracle had not found its voice. And if I mention, as I must, the grinding rotation of his hips as he moved through the apartment on Apollo Bunder, and the increasing explicitness of his pelvic thrusts and the dervish thrashings of his arms; if I linger upon the baby-cruel curl of his upper lip, or the thick black hair hanging in sensual coils around his brow, or the sideburns that were straight out of a Victorian melodrama—if, above all, I attempt to reproduce the few strange sounds he was managing to produce, those *unnhhs, uhh-hhhs,* those *ohhs*—then you, stranger, might excusably write him off as a mere echo, just another of that legion of impersonators who first rejoiced in, and afterwards rendered grotesque, the fame of a young truck driver from Tupelo, Miss., born in a shotgun shack with a dead twin by his side.

I don't deny that, one day in early 1956, a girl named Persis Kalamanja—with whom Lady Spenta Cama was hoping to arrange Ormus's marriage; indeed, Lady Spenta was in those days actively and urgently negotiating the same with Kalamanja *père et mère*—took Ormus Cama down to the Rhythm Center store in Fort, Bombay, that rhinestone treasure chest full of the antiquated ditties of an older generation's moonsters, junesters and toupéed croonsters, which just occasionally came into possession of true jewels, perhaps from sailors on shore leave from an American naval vessel in the harbour. There, in a listening booth, hoping to impress her putative husband-to-be by her cultural savvy (for Persis was much taken with the idea of the match; Ormus, as I may have mentioned before, and will no doubt have occasion enviously to repeat, was an almost irresistibly sweet-featured fellow), eager Persis played Ormus a new, but already crackly, 78 rpm record, and to her deep, though short-lived, satisfaction, the young man's eyes widened in what might have been terror, or love, just like any other teenager hearing in the voice of Jesse Garon Parker, as he sang "Heartbreak Hotel," the sound of his own unarticulated miseries, his own hunger, isolation and dreams.

But Ormus was no ordinary teenager. What Persis had mistaken for enchanted bliss was actually surging anger, an uncontainable rage spreading in him like the plague. Halfway through the song it burst out of him. "Who is he?" shouted Ormus Cama. "What's the name of this blasted thief?"

He came out of the booth at high speed, as if he believed he might be able to grab the singer by the collar of his shirt if he moved fast enough. Facing him was a tall, amused girl, perhaps twelve or thirteen years old, but sophisticated enough for both of them, in a baggy sweatshirt that declared its allegiance to certain unnamed Giants in New York. "Thief?" she enquired. "I've heard him called lots of names, but that's a new one on me."

Many different versions of the first encounter between Vina Apsara and Ormus Cama are presently in circulation, thanks to the clouds of mythologisation, regurgitation, falsification and denigration that have surrounded their story for years: depending which journal you read, you might have heard that he transformed himself into a white bull and carried her away on his back while she, warbling gaily, clutched with erotic delight at his two long, curved and gleaming horns; or that she was indeed an alien from a galaxy far, far away who, having identified Ormus as the most perfectly desirable male specimen on the planet, beamed down smack in front of him at the Gateway of India, holding a space flower in her hand. The Rhythm Center encounter is dismissed as "apocryphal" by many commentators; too contrived, they shrug, too banal, and what *is* all that about having written the song? Plus, these cynics add, if you want yet more proof that the story is phoney baloney, try this for size. The whole thing simply makes no sense at all unless you accept that Ormus Cama, quiffed, sideburned and pelvis-swivelling Ormus, had never previously heard of the reigning king of rock 'n' roll. "This was apparently *1956,*" the critics jeer. "In 1956 even the Pope had heard of Jesse Parker. Even the Man in the Moon."

In Bombay in those days, however, communications technology was in its infancy. There was no tv, and radios were bulky items under strict parental control. Also, the state broadcasting corporation, All-India Radio, was forbidden to play Western popular music, and the only Western records pressed in India, at the Dum Dum factory in Calcutta, tended to be selections from Placido Lanza, or the sound-track music from the MGM movie *Tom Thumb*. Print media were likewise parochial. I cannot remember seeing a single photograph of American singing stars in any local showbiz magazine, let alone the daily papers. But of course there were imported American magazines, and Ormus could have seen pictures of Jesse Parker (perhaps alongside the sinister figure of "Colonel" Tom Presley, his manager) in *Photoplay* or *Movie Screen*. And that was also the year of *Treat Me Tender,* Jesse's first movie, which played at the New Empire cinema, certified for adults only. However, Ormus Cama always insisted he had neither heard of Parker nor seen his photograph until that day in the Rhythm Center store; he always claimed that his dead twin Gayomart was his only style guru— Gayomart, who apparently came to him in dreams.

So I will cling to my record shop anecdote, if only because I heard Ormus and Vina repeat it a hundred times during the years of their great love, fondly lingering here or there, in the booth or outside it, now on one part of the tale, now on another. Each loving couple cherishes the tale of its coming together, and Ormus and Vina were no exception. However, as they were—it must be said—consummate mythologisers of themselves, the tale they told was inaccurate in one important particular: Miss Persis Kalamanja was omitted completely from their reminiscing. This is an injustice which I am now able to put right. I call the heartbroken Miss K., my witness, to the stand.

Poor Persis, who had already lost her loving heart to Ormus Cama, lost a great deal more that day in the Rhythm Center store. She lost Ormus himself, and with him her whole future. Once he had come face-to-face with Vina, it was all over for Persis; she could see that at a glance. Vina and Ormus hadn't even touched, they didn't know each other's names, but already their eyes were making love. After Ormus dumped Persis she learned how a human being may believe two contradictory things at once. For a long time she believed he would surely return to her once he realized how true a love he had spurned, truer than anything that America-returned child could give him; and at the same time she also knew he would never come back. These two propositions, of equal and opposite power, paralysed her, and she never married, nor did she stop loving him until the very end, when, after the cycle of catastrophes had run its course, I received a letter from her. Poor Persis, still in Ormus's power even though he no longer lived, poured out her heart to me in an elegant, mature hand that spoke of her strong character. Yet even this impressive woman had been defenceless against the sheer force of Ormus Cama, his desirability, his voltage, his charm, his casual cruelty, his life. He broke her and forgot her. They did that to people, both of them, Vina too, as if the vastness of their own love excused them from the ordinary decencies, from responsibility, from care. Vina did it to me. Which didn't set me free, either.

"The worst thing," Persis wrote, "was that he rubbed me out of the picture, as if I hadn't been there, as if I'd never existed, as if it wasn't me who took him there that day and started everything up." I attempted, in my reply, to offer what comfort I could. She was by no means the only part of their story that Vina and Ormus tried to erase. For much of their public lives, they chose to conceal their origins, to shed the skin of the past, and Persis was shucked off along with every-thing else; it was, one might say, nothing personal. That's what I told Persis, anyway, while privately believing that in her case it might indeed have been very personal indeed. Sometimes I thought of Ormus and Vina as worshippers at the altar of their own love, which they spoke of in the most elevated language. Never were there such lovers, never had feelings of such depth, such magnificence, been felt by other mortals. . . . The presence of another woman at the meeting of such godlike *amants* was a detail the deities preferred to gloss over.

But Persis existed; she still exists. Ormus and Vina have gone, and Persis, like me, is a part of what remains.

In the record store, while Ormus and Vina's eyes made love, Persis tried to defend her territory. "Listen, jailbait," she hissed, "shouldn't you be in KG?"

"Kindergarten's out, grandma," said Vina, and turned her back on the Kalamanja heiress, bathing Ormus Cama in the cascade of her liq-uid regard. Distantly, like a sleepwalker, he answered her question. "I called him a thief because that's what he is. That's my song. I wrote it years ago. Two years, eight months and twenty-eight days ago, if you want to know."

"Oh, come on, Ormie," Persis Kalamanja battled on. "The record only came out a month ago, and that was in America. Here, it's hot off the boat." But Vina had begun to hum another tune; and Ormus's eyes blazed once again. "How do you know that song?" he demanded. "How could anyone have sung to you what only ever existed in my own head?"

"I suppose you wrote this one too," Vina challenged him, and sang a snatch of a third melody. "And this, and this."

"Yes, all of them," he said, seriously. "The music, I mean; and the vowel sounds. Those cockeyed words may be somebody else's—a song about *blue shoes*? What *bakvaas*, I swear!—but the vowel sounds are mine."

"When you're married to me, Mr. Ormus Cama," said Persis Kala-manja in a loud voice, gripping his arm tightly, "you're going to have to start acting a lot more sensible than you are right now." At which reproof the object of her affections simply laughed: merrily, in her face. Weeping, routed, Persis fled the scene of her humiliation. The process of removing her from the record had begun.

From the beginning, Vina accepted Ormus's prophetic status without question. He claimed to be the true author of some of the most celebrated songs of the day, and did so with such uncontrolled intensity that she found she had no option but to believe him. "Either that," she told me many years later, "or else he was dangerously insane, and the way I was feeling about living in Bombay, the way things were for me in old Uncle Piloo's clutches, a madman for a boyfriend was just fine." After Persis fled, a brief awkwardness hung in the air; and then Vina, to hold the interest of the man to whose life she had already privately joined her own, asked if he knew the story of the invention of music.

Once upon a time the winged serpent Quetzalcoatl ruled the air and the waters, while the god of war ruled the land. Theirs were rich days, full of battles and the exercise of power, but there was no music, and they both longed for a decent tune. The god of war was powerless to change the situation, but the winged serpent was not. He flew away towards the house of the sun, which was the home of music. He passed a number of planets, and from each of them he heard musical sounds, but there were no musicians to be found. At last he came to the house of the sun, where the musicians lived. The anger of the sun at the serpent's invasion was a terrible thing to witness, but Quetzalcoatl was not afraid, and unleashed the mighty storms that were his personal specialty. The storms were so fearsome that even the house of the sun began to shake, and the musicians were scared and fled in all directions. And some of them fell to earth, and so, thanks to the winged serpent, we have music.

"Where is that story from?" Ormus asked. He was hooked.

"Mexico," said Vina. She came towards him and brazenly took his hand in her own. "And I am the winged serpent, and this is the house of the sun, and you, and you, are music."

Ormus Cama stared at his hand lying in hers; and felt something lift from him, the shadow, perhaps, of a pillow with which, long ago, his brother had smothered his voice.

"Would you like," he asked, amazing himself by the question, "maybe one day soon, to hear me sing?"

What's a "culture"? Look it up. "A group of micro-organisms grown in a nutrient substance under controlled conditions." A squirm of germs on a glass slide is all, a laboratory experiment calling itself a society. Most of us wrigglers make do with life on that slide; we even agree to feel proud of that "culture." Like slaves voting for slavery or brains for lobotomy, we kneel down before the god of all moronic micro-organisms and pray to be homogenized or killed or engineered; we promise to obey. But if Vina and Ormus were bacteria too, they were a pair of bugs who wouldn't take life lying down. One way of understanding their story is to think of it as an account of the creation of two bespoke identities, tailored for the wearers by themselves. The rest of us get our personae off the peg, our religion, language, prejudices, demeanour, the works; but Vina and Ormus insisted on what one might call auto-couture.

And music, popular music, was the key that unlocked the door for them, the door to magic lands.

In India it is often said that the music I'm talking about is precisely one of those viruses with which the almighty West has infected the East, one of the great weapons of cultural imperialism, against which all right-minded persons must fight and fight again. Why then offer up paeans to culture traitors like Ormus Cama, who betrayed his roots and spent his pathetic lifetime pouring the trash of America into our children's ears? Why raise low culture so high, and glorify what is base? Why defend impurity, that vice, as if it were a virtue?

Such are the noisome slithers of the enslaved micro-organisms, twisting and hissing as they protect the inviolability of their sacred homeland, the glass laboratory slide.

This is what Ormus and Vina always claimed, never wavering for a moment: that the genius of Ormus Cama did not emerge in response to, or in imitation of, America; that his early music, the music he heard in his head during the unsinging childhood years, was not of the West, except in the sense that the West was in Bombay from the beginning, impure old Bombay where West, East, North and South had always been scrambled, like codes, like eggs, and so Westernness was a legitimate part of Ormus, a Bombay part, inseparable from the rest of him.

It was an amazing proposition: that the music came to Ormus before it ever visited the Sun Records studio or the Brill Building or the Cavern Club. That he was the one who heard it first. Rock music, the music of the city, of the present, which crossed all frontiers, which belonged equally to everyone—but to my generation most of all, because it was born when we were children, it spent its adolescence in our teenage years, it became adult when we did, growing paunchy and bald right along with us: this was the music that was allegedly first revealed to a Parsi Indian boy named Ormus Cama, who heard all the songs in advance, two years, eight months and twenty-eight days before anyone else. So according to Ormus and Vina's variant version of history, their alternative reality, we Bombayites can claim that it was in truth our music, born in Bombay like Ormus and me, not "goods from foreign" but made in India, and maybe it was the foreigners who stole it from us.

Two years, eight months and twenty-eight days, by the way, adds up (except in a leap year) to one thousand and one nights. Nineteen fifty-six, however, was a leap year. Go figure. This kind of spooky parallel doesn't always exactly work out.

How could such a thing happen?

We must wait a little longer for the answer, until Ormus Cama has returned home from the record store, stunned by joy (because of his meeting with that under-age nymphet, Vina Apsara) and horror (because of his discovery of the "theft" of his secret music by Jesse Parker, Jack Haley's Meteors and sundry other quiffed and finger-snapping Yanks). The answer cannot be given until Ormus has first encountered his inquisitive matchmaker of a mother, who is anxious to know how things went with "dear Persis, such an able girl, with so many good qualities, so dutiful, so well educated, such good marks in her Matric and Senior Cambridge, and quite pretty in a way, don't you think so, Ormus dear," to which somewhat perfunctory encomium he makes no other reply than a shrug. Then he must lounge lazily through the dining room, past the decrepit old domestic servant pretending to polish the silver candelabrum on the sideboard, Gieve, the kleptomaniac head bearer, whom his father took on from the departed William Methwold and who now bears the title of "butler," thanks to Sir Darius's fondness for Lord Emsworth's immortal Beach, and who has been very, very slowly stealing the family silver for years. (The disappearances have been so petty and so rare that Lady Spenta, guided by the Angel Good Thoughts, to say nothing of the Angel Blind Stupidity, has ascribed them to her own carelessness. Hardly anything except this candelabrum still remains, and even though the identity of the thief is well known to Ormus, he has never mentioned it to his parents, on account of his lofty disdain for material possessions.) And—at last!—Ormus must, he does, enter his own room, he stretches out on his bed, he looks up at the slow ceiling fan and drifts—now!—into reverie. A shadow falls. This is the fabled "Cama obscura," his stricken family's curse of inwardness, which he and he alone has learned how to harness, to transform into a gift.

There is a trick he can play on his mind. As he stares at the fan he can "make" the room turn upside down, so that he seems to be lying on the ceiling looking down at the fan which is growing like a metal flower from the floor. Then he can change the scale of things, so that the fan seems gigantic, and he can imagine himself sitting beneath it. Where is this? (His eyes close. The purple birthmark on his left eyelid seems to pulse and throb.) It's an oasis in the sands, and he's stretched out in the shade of a tall date palm, whose head tosses slowly in the warm breeze. Now, by dint of deeper dreaming, he populates that desert-ceiling; large airplanes land on the runway of the curtain rail, and all the raucous medley of a magical metropolis pours out of them, roads, tall buildings, taxicabs, policemen with guns, gangsters, saps, pianists dripping cigarettes from their lips and composing songs to other men's wives, poker games, big rooms featuring star entertainers, wheels of fortune, lumberjacks with money to burn, whores saving up for that little dress shop back home.

He is no longer in an oasis but in a city of dazzling lights, standing in front of a building that might be a theatre or a casino or some other secular temple of delights. He plunges in and at once he knows who he's looking for. He can hear his brother, whose voice is faint but not so very far away. His dead twin is singing to him, but he can't make out the song. "Gayomart, where are you going," Ormus calls. "Gayo, I'm coming, wait for me."

The place is swarming with people, all of them in too much of a hurry, spending too much money, kissing each other too lubriciously, eating too quickly so that meat juices and ketchup dribble down their chins, getting into fights over nothing, laughing too loud, crying too hard. At one end of the room is a giant silver screen, bathing the great room in glittering light. From time to time, the people in the room look up to it longingly, as if towards a god, but then shake their heads regretfully and continue with their carousing, which is oddly melancholy. All the people give off an air of incompleteness, as if they have not fully come into being. There are soldiers boasting to their fiancées about their deeds. There is a blonde with a fabulous décolletage wading through a fountain in full evening dress. In a corner, Death plays chess with a knight on his way home from the Crusades, and in another corner a Japanese samurai scratches desperately at an itch he cannot reach. Outside, in the street, a beautiful woman with cropped blond hair is hawking copies of the *Herald Tribune*.

Like a dark shade detached from its owner, Gayomart Cama slips through this gathering of brighter shadows, singing his elusive song. Ormus, pursuing him, is jostled and obstructed by a bald policeman sucking a lollipop, two absurd Indian clowns who speak in rhymes, and an underworld gang boss with cotton-wool padding in his cheeks. Their eyes fix briefly upon him, interrogating him fiercely. *Are you the one?* they seem to ask. *Is it you who will save us from this appalling place, this anteroom, this limbo, and give us the key to the silver screen?* But at once they know he is useless to them, he's not the one, and they return to their zombie dances.

Gayomart slips through a door at the far end of this first chamber, and Ormus struggles after him. The chase continues down staircases of decreasing grandeur, through rooms of growing gloom. Less glamorous than the hall of uncreated film and television characters is the room of unmade stage rôles, and tawdrier still is the parliament chamber of future betrayals, and the saloon bar of uninvented books, and the back alley of uncommitted crimes, until finally there is just a series of narrow iron steps descending into pitch blackness, and Ormus knows his twin brother is down there, waiting, but he's too afraid to descend.

Sitting on the top step of his dreamworld, staring into the dark, the purple stain on his eyelid glowing with the effort of searching out his lost sibling, his shadow self, who is down there somewhere in the blackness, Ormus Cama can hear Gayo singing his songs. Gayo has a fine, even a great, singing voice: perfect pitch, immense vocal range, effortless control, expert modulation. But he's too far away; Ormus can't make out the words. Just the vowel sounds.

The noise without the meaning. Absurdity.

Eck-eck eye ay-ee eck ee, ack-eye-ack er ay oo eck, eye oock er aw ow oh-ee ee, oo . . . ah-ay oh-eck . . .

Two years, eight months and twenty-eight days later he burst out of a listening booth in Bombay, having heard the same sounds issuing from the throat of the new American phenomenon, the first blazing star of the new music, and in the midst of his bewilderment he saw in his mind's eye the expressions on the faces of the shadows he had seen in his dream underworld, the melancholy and desperation of proto-entities longing to become and fearing their great day would never dawn; and he knew that his own face wore the selfsame expression, for the same terror was snatching at his own heart, *someone was stealing his place in history,* and it was to that look of naked fear that Vina had responded when she caught at his trembling nineteen-year-old hand and squeezed it tightly between her own, precocious palms.

I'm the least supernaturally inclined of men, but this tall story I have no option but to believe.

Three people, two living, one dead—I mean his ghostly brother, Gayomart, his lover, Vina, and his father, Sir Darius Xerxes Cama—were severally responsible for making sure that Ormus's day did, in the end, show up. On Gayo's lip-curled features he modelled his own sensualist's scowl; and Gayomart's elusive songs, those devil-tunes wafting up from satanic darkness, became Ormus's own. In Gayo, Ormus found the Other into which he dreamed of metamorphosing, the dark self that first fuelled his art.

Of Vina's part in his story, much more will soon be said. As for Sir Darius, who dreamed whisky dreams of England while asleep on his leather chesterfield and yearned for fictional mansions when he was awake, his son certainly inherited his capacity for leading a vivid dream-life. And more; Sir Darius's disenchantment with his home town became Ormus's too. The son inherited his father's discontent. But the land of Ormus's dreams was never England. No white mansion for him, but that other house, the place of light and horror, of speculation and danger and power and wonder, the place where the future was waiting to be born. America! America! It pulled him; it would have him; as it pulls so many of us, and like Pinocchio on Pleasure Island, like all the little donkeys, we laugh (as it devours us) for joy.

Hee-haw!

America, the Great Attractor, whispered in my ears too. But on the topic of Bombay, the city we would both leave behind, Ormus and I never agreed. Bombay was always something of a hick town, a hayseed provincial ville, in his eyes. The greater stage, the true Metropolis, was to be found elsewhere, in Shanghai, in Tokyo, in Buenos Aires, in Rio, and above all in the fabled cities of America, with their pinnacled architecture, the outsize moon rockets and giant hypodermic syringes towering over their cavernous streets. It is no longer permissible to speak of places like Bombay, as people spoke of them in those days, as being situated on the *periphery;* or to describe Ormus's yearnings, which were also Vina's and mine, as some sort of *centripetal force.* Yet finding the centre was what drove Ormus and Vina on.

My reasons were different. Not contempt, but surfeit and claustrophobia, made me leave. Bombay belonged too completely to my parents, V.V. and Ameer. It was an extension of their bodies, and, after their deaths, of their souls. My father, Vivvy, who adored both my mother and the city of Bombay so deeply that he sometimes referred to himself, only half jokingly, as a polygamist, had taken to referring to Ameer as if she were a metropolis herself: her fortifications, her esplanades, her traffic flow, her new developments, her crime rate. Sir Darius Xerxes Cama had once equated himself, the arch-Anglophile product of the city the British built, with Bombay; but Vivvy's heart-city would never be Darius's. It was his own wife, Ameer.

Many youngsters leave home to find themselves; I had to cross oceans just to exit *Wombay,* the parental body. I flew away to get myself born. But like a longtime cigarette smoker who manages to quit, I have never forgotten the taste and kick of the old abandoned drug. Imagine, if you will, the elaborately ritualised (yes, and marriage-obsessed) formal society of Jane Austen, grafted on to the stenchy, pullulating London beloved of Dickens, as full of chaos and surprises as a rotting fish is full of writhing worms; swash & rollick the whole into a Shandy-and-arrack cocktail; colour it magenta, vermilion, scarlet, lime; sprinkle with crooks & bawds, and you have something like my fabulous home town. I gave it up, true enough; but don't ask me to say it wasn't one hell of a place.

(And there were other reasons too, let's be frank. For example, the threats against my person. If I'd stayed, it could have cost me my life.)

Now my story begins to strain in opposite directions, backwards, forwards. The forward pull, which every storyteller ignores at his peril, and to which for the moment I must yield, is nothing less than the tug of forbidden love. For even as the twenty-year-old German poet Novalis, "he who clears new territory," took a single look at twelve-year-old Sophie von Kühn and was doomed, in that instant, to an absurd love, followed by tuberculosis and Romanticism, just so the nineteen-year-old Ormus Cama, the most handsome young fellow in Bombay (though not, on account of the shadow that had lain over his family ever since the accident to Ardaviraf, the most eligible), fell for twelve-year-old Vina, fell flat, as if someone had pushed him in the back.

But their love was not absurd. Never that. We all filled it up with meanings, a surfeit of meanings; as we did their deaths.

"He was a proper gentleman," Vina as an adult would say with genuine pride in her voice—Vina, whose taste ran to the roughest low-lifes, the most louche, least gentlemanly types on earth! "The second time we met," she would continue, "he declared his love?, and also swore a solemn oath that he would not so much as touch me until the day after my sixteenth birthday. My Ormus and his goddamn oaths." I suspected her of whitewashing the past, and said as much more than once. It never failed to rile her. "Extremes of experience is one thing," she'd snarl. "You know my views on that: I'm for 'em. Bring 'em on! I want to have them for myself?, not just read about them in the paper. But Bombay's Lolita I was not." She'd shake her head, angry at herself for being angry. "I'm telling you something beautiful, you bastard. I'm telling you it was over three years before I even got to hold his hand again! All we did was sing. And ride those goddamn trams." Then she laughed; she could never resist the memory, and gave up her wrath. "Ding-ding!" she pealed. "Ding!"

Anyone who has listened to the lyrics of Ormus Cama will certainly know of the central place reserved in his personal iconography for tramcars. They recur many times, along with street entertainers, card-players, pickpockets, wizards, devils, union men, evil priests, fisher-women, wrestlers, harlequins, vagabonds, chameleons, whores, eclipses, motorbikes and cheap dark rum; and without fail, they lead to love. *Your love is bearing down on me, there can be no escape*, he sings. *Oh cut my captured heart in two, oh crush me like a grape. No, I don't care. It's who I am. Oh you can tram me, baby, but I will derail your tram.*

It was on the tramcars of Bombay, now departed, much mourned by those who remember them, that Ormus and Vina conducted their long courtship: she playing truant from school, he absenting himself from the Apollo Bunder apartment without explanation. Back then young people were kept on a tighter leash, so it was inevitable that a day of reckoning would come, but in the meanwhile they clattered round the city, hour after enchanted hour, and learned each other's stories. And so I, too, am—at last!—able to go backwards into the past; Vina's past. Satisfying my narrative's other need, I offer up for general consumption what Vina whispered into her future lover's ear.

The making of a bad girl: Born Nissa Shetty, she grew up in a shack in the middle of a cornfield outside Chester, Virginia, above Hopewell, between Screamersville and Blanco Mount, down a nothing track snaking east from 295. Corn on both sides of her and goats in the back. Her mother, Helen, Greek-American, full-figured, nervy, a reader of books, a dreamer, a woman of humble origins who carried herself well and hoped for much, fell during the World War II man shortage for a sweet-talking Indian gent, a lawyer—how'd he get all the way out there? *Indians get everywhere, isn't it? Like sand*—who married her, fathered three daughters in three years (Nissa, born during the Nor-mandy landings, was the middle one), went to jail for malpractice, got struck off the register, came out of jail after Nagasaki, told his wife he had revised his sexual preferences, went off to Newport News to set

up as a butcher with his beefy male lover, "as the female in the relationship," in Vina's words, and never wrote or called or sent money or
presents for his daughters on their birthdays or Christmas. Helen
Shetty in that loveless peace tumbled into a downward spiral of drink,
pills and debt, couldn't hold a job, and the kids went to hell at high
speed, until she was rescued by a jack-of-all-trades builder, John Poe, a
widower with four kids of his own, who met her drunk and blurting
in a bar, heard her out, reckoned she had good reason to despair, called
her a good-looking woman who deserved a break, swore to look after
her, got her off the sauce, took her and her three kids into his simple
home and never differentiated between her children and his own,
never commented on their dark skins, gave the girls his own name (so
that at the age of three Nissa Shetty became Nissy Poe), worked hard
earning money to put food in his family's mouths and clothes on their
backs, asked nothing from Helen in return but conventional woman's
work and an agreement that they have no more children, and though
she had hoped for high things in her life, she knew how close she'd
come to the gutter, so she was lucky to have found this instead, stability, a kind of gruff monosyllabic average love, a generous-hearted man,
solid ground under her feet, and if he wanted things old-fashioned,
that was an adjustment she was prepared uncomplainingly to make, so
the shack was kept spotless, the clothes were cleaned, the children fed
and bathed, John Poe's dinner was hot on the table every night when
he came home, and he was right about the children thing too, so she
went into the city and had the operation, and that was okay, that was
really okay, she had her hands full and this made things easy, he was
old-fashioned in bed as well as out of it, didn't hold with rubbers and
such, and now everything was just fine, it was finer than fine, it was
fine. Once a week they all went out to the drive-in in John's pickup,
and Helen Poe looked at the stars above instead of those on the screen
and thanked them, with certain reservations, for her luck.

If John Poe had a dream, it was of goats. In the corral behind his
home there was a white Saanen doe who provided the family with
milk, and a small, transient population of Spanish and myotonic goats
being bred for the slaughter. Nissy Poe grew up without knowing the
taste of cow milk. John Poe told her that goat milk was easier to digest,
and even encouraged her to wash her face in it as a beauty treatment,

as Queen Cleopatra used to do. She had learned from her mother never to contradict this big, kindly but dominating man, and she meekly drank down that thin bluish rancid-smelling liquid which she had come to hate. And after the doomed Spanish goats were taken off to the abattoir in their season, there would be nothing but chevon, goat meat, to eat for weeks at a stretch. Helen Poe was not a woman of great culinary skills, and little Nissy came to fear mealtimes above all things, because of the smile she had to paint on her face. John Poe was a man who needed regular thanking for the blessings he bestowed.

After a big goat dinner he would push back his chair and tell the future. These few creatures out back, in the paddock surrounded by a five-foot-high fence with the wire spaces just five inches or so apart, these were just the start, Nissy's stepfather declared. He wasn't going to labour for other folks all his days, you bet. A goat farm was what he had in mind. Not a meat farm, though; he held meat goats in some-thing like contempt, especially the myotonics, whose genetic disorders caused them to fall over stiff-legged if they were startled. Some nights, John Poe looked forward to the day when he would go into the dairy-goat business, in Oregon, maybe, or Florida. He rhapsodised about the virtues of the "Swiss" Alpines and Toggenburgs and the "desert" Nubians. He spoke of the delights of goat cheese and goats' milk soap. On other nights, his vision was of angora and cashmere, and a future in fibre farming in Texas or Colorado. "You'll like that, with your Ori-ental blood, huh," he told Helen's daughters. "Cashmere is from Kash-mir, India, originally, and angora came from Ankara, Turkey, and the name mohair, which is what we call the cloth made from the hair of the angora goat, is Arabic or such, meaning 'what we prefer.' " The Uzbek black goat, whose wool fibre was longer than the guard hairs and was of high, cashmere-type quality, often cropped up in these reveries. Nissy Poe, Eastern blood and all, came to detest the very words mohair, cashmere and Uzbek. But she smiled and said thank you as required. And John Poe, beer in hand, wafted off into his private Oriental fantasy.

Ormus Cama and I, growing up in India, felt our hearts striving towards the West; how strange it is to think of Vina's early years under the aegis of that good plain man with his lust for the East, or at least its hairy beasts.

Sometimes John Poe told goat jokes. (Two goats break into the projection room at the drive-in and start munching. "God, this film is good," sez the first, and the second goes, "Yeah, but I thought the book was better.") However, he did not tolerate such levity in others. A new neighbour dropped by once and said, "Goats, hey. Sure, we dig goats, we were thinking of getting a pet goat, but this guy said to us, 'Thing about goats is, they'll eat your car.' "After he left, John Poe placed him, his family and their land off limits. The man received a life sentence without ever knowing what he'd done, and John Poe being the man he was, it was a sentence from which there was no possibility of appeal.

It was a home without privacy, the children stacked in their bunks three and four to a room. Some of them grew up quiet, inward, defended. Nissy ran wild. In kindergarten she became notorious as a biter of other kids and teachers too, and she had to be withdrawn from class. John Poe whaled her soundly and she went back and bit harder. The war escalated and then suddenly stopped, because both combatants realized that if it went any further there might be a fatality. John Poe told Nissy he loved her and put away his belt, and Nissy Poe told her terrorised classmates, "It's okay, I ain't gonna kill ya."

In the matter of race John Poe was close to being a liberal. He went with Helen to see the school authorities to explain that the girls' darkness was not Negro darkness, they were Indians from India and didn't need to be discriminated against, they could ride on the bus along with the regular kids. This argument the school accepted, though it brought problems of its own.

As Nissy grew older she learned that the other kids, the white kids, called her Blackfoot Indian, and also goatgirl. And then there were these three neighborhood boys, they looked Negro and spoke Spanish—boy, were *they* confused—and they used to jeer at Nissy Poe because she could ride on the bus to the white folks' school. And then one day the three boys were waiting for her bus, they kept saying there was a law now and they were going to her school too, except the driver wouldn't let them aboard, not on his bus. As she climbed on, she heard them shouting insults at her, something about her family's *cabritos* when she was the *kid* of a *cabronito*. She looked it up. *Cabrito* meant kid goat and *cabronito* meant small homosexual. The next day they were waiting for the bus again, with their daddy this time, but so what, she just took them all on. The father pulled her off his boys, she was kicking and punching air as he hauled her away, but she was satisfied, because in that short time she had inflicted a startlingly disproportionate amount of damage on the slanderers. John Poe got his belt out again, but his heart wasn't in it, because he knew that her will was greater than his. He began to ignore her, and didn't accompany Helen when she went to the school to plead with the staff to let her daughter stay on, and get an education, and escape from the trap of poverty, as she herself had once hoped to do. "It is a hard thing," Helen Poe told her daughter's class teacher, "for a child to live without hope."

Goatgirl. Not far from the shack, up towards Redwater Creek, there was a wooded hollow called Jefferson Lick. According to local legend, a kind of centaur lived there, a refugee from a Canadian travelling circus, mad and dangerous on account of all those years spent in a cage for the pleasure of the public, whipped and half starved. The Goat Monster of Jefferson Lick was the local bogeyman, used to frighten small children into obedience, and at the annual fancy-dress dance during the summer fair there would always be a Lick Man or two, the great god Pan come to Virginia, dressed in rags. When children were sure they were far enough away from Nissy Poe to be safe, they would call her the Goat Man's daughter and then run for their lives.

Helen attempted to steer her daughter on to a better road. When the girl was almost ten years old the mother stood with her (this was Memorial Day weekend, 1954) and looked up at the galaxy blazing out of the night sky. "Just follow your star, honey, don't get sidetracked by anyone or anything," Helen said, with a tremor in her voice that made Nissy glance at her sharply. The mother broke out a quick, thin, hard little smile that didn't fool Nissy for a minute. "Not like me, hey," Helen grinned, like a skull. "Just pick one of those beauties and follow where it leads." A meteor flashed. "I'll take that one," said Nissy Poe. "Looks like it's going places." Don't pick that one, her mother thought, a shooting star's bad luck. But she didn't say it, and the girl nodded firmly. "Yes, ma'am. That's the one that I want."

That weekend, after finishing her chores, Nissy Poe went down to Jefferson Lick on her own, unafraid. She didn't expect to meet any monsters but she did want to be in there, as far in as she could go. The woods were lovely, dark and deep, and as she pushed her way through springy foliage into the depths of the hollow she felt something quite unknown fall upon her, like a blessing. It was solitude. To see the birds, you have to become part of the silence. Who said that? Some num-skull. In here it was like *Snow White*. Birds everywhere, like butterfly clouds, and if you sang, they sang right along with you. Hooded war-blers, yellow-breasted warblers, provided back-up vocals; woodpeckers laid down the beat. Nissy Poe let everything go, and sang. Shake, rattle and roll! This was her great secret, this voice like a rocket blast of power. Sometimes when John Poe was at work, and when John Poe's children were all out of the house, so they couldn't tell tales—John Poe might treat everyone alike, but the kids were another thing entirely—Helen would turn on the radio and find a station that played the new stuff, the Driftwoods, Jack Haley, Ronnie "Man" Ray. Sometimes they'd even find one of the Negro rhythm and blues stations, and Helen would swing her hips and join in with that music, the segre-gated music, the music John Poe called the devil's boogie. "Come on, honey," Helen urged, "sing up here along with me," but Nissy Poe would always refuse and press her mouth into a white, bloodless line, and Helen would shake her head. "I don't know what it'd take to get you to have a good time," she'd say, and then the music would seize her again, she'd roll her eyes, and dance, and whoop it up, under the loyal, impassive eyes of her own daughters. (Two out of three; the youngest was usually placed on sentry duty in the front yard, in case John Poe returned unexpectedly.) Helen seemed in those moments to be a child herself, to be reaching out for a version of herself that had been crushed beneath the adult she had been forced by necessity to become.

Nissy Poe never sang for her mother but would go to Jefferson Lick to be alone, and only then, far from the world, protected by an apoc-ryphal ogre, would she unleash the voice that revealed her heart's deepest desire. Music! It was all she wanted in life; to be a part not of silence, but of sound.

If there had been a Lick Monster present, he would have applauded. From the beginning, Vina had the voice, and the relentless attack. She sang her young heart out, then lay back on a bank of earth though she knew she would have to suffer for her dirty clothes later on, fell asleep, woke with a start, to find it was dark, scrambled out of the Lick and began to run, and when she got home she found she could have taken her time, because everybody was dead.

The children had been murdered in their beds, stabbed in their hearts with a large kitchen knife. They died without waking up. But John Poe had had his throat cut, and from the wreckage in the room it was plain he had staggered around for long moments before crashing down on top of the old tv cabinet. Blood was smeared down the tv screen, and he lay at its feet in a great sticky puddle, the swamp of his lost life. The tv was on, and somebody was saying something about a war starting up involving the Vietwhat? At Dienbienwhere? In Indochina, right. That was between India and China? And really had a whole lot to do with a girl in a shack near Hopewell, Va., standing knee-deep in her dead family's blood.

Helen wasn't in the shack, but Nissy found her soon enough, because all the goats were dead too, and Helen was hanging by her neck from one of the cross-beams of the three-sided loafing shed John Poe had built with his own hands to give the livestock someplace to stand when the weather turned mean. In the dirt below her dangling feet was a large kitchen knife coated thickly with dark, congealing blood.

Because she didn't go for help until morning; because she set up a stepladder and cut her mother down with the murder weapon; because she stayed out there in the loafing shed all night, alone with the knife and her mother and the dead goats and the universe on fire in the sky, the shooting stars shooting every which way, the Milky Way pouring down (it was probably made of fucking goat milk and smelled like fucking piss); because of her bad-girl track record, the biting, the fighting, she was a suspect for about five minutes, five minutes in which she, goatgirl, the goat monster's daughter of Jefferson Lick, saw the thing in the officers' eyes that's there only when they look at big-time killers. Call it respect. But after five minutes even Sheriff Henry had worked out it would've been pretty tough for the kid to have done it, hanged her mother, for Chrissake, she was only ten. It wasn't a hard case to crack, crazy woman ran amuck, big handsome woman like her, still plenty there for a man to hold on to and be comforted by, too bad, things got to her, she snapped. Shit happens.

. . .

After that, her father, Butcher Shetty, showed up with his lover, but she didn't like the sound of Newport News, she'd had enough of butchery for one lifetime, she'd be a vegetarian for the rest of her days. She finally agreed to go live with Helen's distant relatives the Egiptuses of Chickaboom, up near the Finger Lakes in western New York State: and all the way there, alone on the bus, she was wondering why her mother had chosen that precise moment to crack, that Memorial Day when her middle daughter had fallen asleep in Jefferson Lick. Maybe it wasn't a spur-of-the-moment thing. Maybe Helen had waited until she, Nissa, was out of danger. She had been picked to survive, selected by her mother as the only one in the family who deserved life. Her mother had seen or heard something in her, something other than the wildness and violence, and so had spared her life. Nissa, her shooting star.

"She heard me!" The power of her sudden realization made her shout the words aloud. The passengers nearest her looked at her, shifted in their seats, but she was oblivious to their unease. *Helen heard me. She must've followed me to the Lick one day, and I never knew, and that's why she waited, she knew I'd be gone for a long while. I'm alive because she wanted me to sing.*

Welcome to Chickaboom, said a sign.

Of the year or so she spent in that northern clime, in that Egiptian exile, Vina Apsara never told anyone very much. Ask her a question too many and she'd turn on you like a snake. She spoke to me about it only a couple of times in her life. The moment she arrived, she buried poor Nissy Poe, I know that. Mr. Egiptus offered her the use of his family name and said he had always wanted a daughter named Diana. She became Diana Egiptus without regret. The new name was not, however, lucky. "There was a woman who was not good to me," she said. "I was not treated well in that family." I could hardly get her to speak their given names. "The woman who I stayed with then," she called her chief tormentor, Mrs. Marion Egiptus; the other family members were "the people I was not happy with." These people ran, I was able to establish, the Egypt, a small cigar store, outside which stood the half-size figure of a pharaonic charioteer holding, in one hand, the reins of his single horse and, in the other, a fistful of stogies. "It was a one-horse town," Vina said, "and the one horse was made of wood." This small town was her first Troy. Bombay would be her second, and the rest of her life her third; and wherever she went, there was war. Men fought over her. In her own way, she was a Helen too.

What happened in Chickaboom? I can't tell you much; Vina told me very little, and those who have investigated the story since have given conflicting, often purely fictitious accounts. Marion Egiptus was foulmouthed and harsh and repulsed by the future Vina's dark skin. Other members of the Egiptus household saw the same dark skin as an invitation to sexual relations. The young Nissy-Diana-Vina had to fight her cousins off.

The Egypt faltered, or was bought out. There was a fire, or there was not. It was an insurance scam, or arson, or it didn't happen. Marion Egiptus, the "woman she stayed with then," the "woman who was not good to her," refused, perhaps on account of the blow to the family's fortunes, or (if there was not, in fact, such a blow) on account of her profound aversion to the girl, to keep Diana Egiptus with her any more. There are suggestions that Vina's delinquency continued, the truancy, the violence, the excessive use of pills.

Rejected by Mrs. Egiptus, she was sent to India because no American options remained. Butcher Shetty of Newport News wrote a begging letter to his rich relations the Doodhwalas of Bandra, Bombay, failing to mention he was no longer a lawyer, no longer a fat cat getting fatter off a daily diet of high-calorie American mice, but that omission was a matter of honour, a way of preserving his self-respect. He also omitted to mention his daughter's many run-ins with authority, and somewhat overstated young Nissa Shetty's girlish charms (in this letter she reverted to her original name). At any rate, the rich Doodhwalas, seduced by the glamorous prospect of acquiring an America-returned niece, agreed to take her in. Nissa Shetty's father met her off the Greyhound at the Port Authority Terminal and spent a night with her in Manhattan. He took her to dinner at the Rainbow Room and danced with her on the revolving stage and held her close; and she understood what he was telling her; not only that business was good but also that he was saying goodbye for ever, she couldn't count on him any more. Don't call, don't write, have a good life, goodbye. The next morning she went to Idlewild by herself, took a deep breath and headed east. East to Bombay, where Ormus and I were waiting.

If we are to understand Vina's rage, which drove her art and damaged her life, we must try to imagine what she would not tell us, the myriad petty cruelties of the unjust relations, the absence of fairy godmothers and glass slippers, the impossibility of princes. When I met her on Juhu Beach and she delivered herself of that astonishing tirade against the whole of India, past, present and future, she was in reality only indulging in a kind of masquerade, concealing herself from me behind her bitter ironies. In cosmopolitan Bombay it was she who was provincial; if she praised American sophistication at our expense, it was because sophistication was a quality she utterly lacked. After a lifetime of poverty, it was India, in the overblown form of Piloo Doodhwala, that had offered her a first taste of affluence; therefore, by inversion, she filled her dialogue with ersatz rich-American contempt for the impoverishment of the Orient. In Chickaboom the winters had been savage (that was a detail I did manage to extract from her); loathing the cold, she complained, in warm Bombay, about the heat.

Finally, and above all else, if we are to understand Vina's rage, we must put ourselves in her shoes and try to imagine her sentiments when, after a gruelling journey across the planet to Bombay's Santa Cruz airport, she disembarked from the Pan American Douglas DC-6, to find that her father—oh, the unforgivable thoughtlessness of the man!—had delivered her once more, and with scant hope of escape, into the hated company of goats.

Ding-ding! Ding!

For a big city, Bombay can operate remarkably like a small village; it isn't long before everyone knows everything, especially about a cocky twelve-year-old beauty taking tramcar rides with a grown nineteen-year-old man with movie star good looks and a whispered success rate with the girls that is fast acquiring legendary proportions. Memories being what they are, none of the three of us could agree on how long it took, days, weeks, months. What is beyond doubt is that when the news reached the ears of Piloo Doodhwala he tried to beat her up;

whereupon she attacked him with an abandoned savagery that obliged Golmatol, Halva, Rasgulla and several other members of the "magnif-icentourage" to help subdue her, a process during which she both inflicted and received a number of wounds. The rain came; she was put out of doors; she arrived on our doorstep; and Ormus, who loved her, who swore he had not touched her, let alone defiled her honour, was not far behind.

And this in the far-off 1950s! In "underdeveloped" India, where boy-girl relations were so strictly controlled! True, true: but permit me to say, "underdeveloped nation" or not, one of our prime cultural arti-facts was a highly developed apparatus of hypocritical disapproval, not only of any incipient change in social mores, but also of our own his-torically proven and presently hyperactive erotic natures. What's the *Kama Sutra*? A Disney comic? Who built the Khajuraho temples? The Japanese? And of course in the 1950s there were no girl tarts in Kamathipura working eighteen hours a day, and child marriages never took place, and the pursuit of the very young by lecherous old hum-berts—yes, we'd already heard of the new Nabokov shocker—was utterly unknown. (Not.) To hear some people talk, you'd conclude that sex hadn't been discovered in India by the mid-twentieth century, and the population explosion must have been made possible by some alter-native method of fertilisation.

So: Ormus Cama, in spite of being an Indian, had a way with girls; and Vina, in spite of being just twelve, had a history of extreme vio-lence towards males who stepped out of line. Yet their meeting trans-formed them both. From that moment on, Ormus lost interest in all other females of the species, and never regained it, even after Vina's death. And Vina had found, for the first and only time, a man whose approval she constantly needed, to whom she turned, after everything she said or did, for confirmation, for validation, for meaning. He became the meaning of her life, and she of his. Also, she owned a bat-tered old acoustic guitar, and on those long afternoons riding the tramcars or sitting on the rocks at Scandal Point or walking in the Hanging Gardens or fooling around the Old Woman's Shoe in Kamala Nehru Park, she taught him how to play. What's more, when she'd lis-tened to his incoherent, eavesdropped songs, the prophetic ditties of the late Gayomart Cama, she gave him the advice that led to his second, true birth into music and made possible the whole astonishing Cama songbook, the long stream of hits by which he will always be remembered. "It's good you love your brother, and want to follow where he's leading. But maybe it's the wrong way. Try another room in that dream-palace of yours. Or another one, or another one, or another one. Maybe you'll find your own noises someplace in there. Maybe then you'll be able to hear the words."

At the end of one cycle of time, they say, we experience *kenosis,* an emptying. Things lose meaning, they erode. This is what had been happening, I believe, not only to Ormus Cama and Vina Apsara, but also to all those whose lives touched theirs. The decay of time, at the end of a cycle, leads to all manner of poisonous, degrading, defiling effects. A cleansing is required. The love that was born between Ormus and Vina, the love that was prepared to wait years for fulfilment, provided that new cleanness, and a new cycle of time began. *Plerosis,* the filling of time with new beginnings, is characterised by a time of superabundant power, of wild, fruitful excess. Alas, however, such shapely theories are never quite up to the task of accounting for the messiness of real life. The cleansing and renewal of time did indeed have some beneficial results, but only on the lives of the lovers themselves. They were, it's true, greatly energized by their new love; but all around them, the catastrophes continued.

He loved her like an addict: the more of her he had, the more he needed. She loved him like a student, needing his good opinion, playing up to him in the hope of drawing forth the magic of his smile. But she also, from the very beginning, needed to leave him and go elsewhere to play. He was her seriousness, he was the depths of her being, but he could not also be her frivolity. That light relief, that serpent in the garden, I must confess, was me.

5

GOAT SONGS

Begin, today, with an animal sacrifice. (Or, at least, an account of same.)

O twice-born Dionysus, O madness-strengthened bull, inexhaustible fount of life energy, divine drunkard, conqueror of India, god of women, master of the snake-changing maenads, the chewers of laurels! In lieu of burnt offerings, accept from us, ere we proceed with our humble entertainments, a bloody tale of slaughtered milk-givers; and, being pleased, bestow upon our poor efforts the benison of your crazy, lethal grin!

Whereas the large-scale farming of goats had been, for Vina Apsara's late stepfather, John Poe, no more than a distant, utopian fantasy, Shri Piloo Doodhwala, her most recent "loco parentis," as my mother called him, "more loco than parentish," was the dairy-goat king of what became the state of Maharashtra, a person of immense, even feudal significance in the rural areas where the care and handling of his herds accounted for almost all local employment. From his earliest days to his present pre-eminence, Piloo the milkman thought of his "little business," his "milk round," as a mere stepping-stone to far higher things:

that is to say, public office, and the immense wealth that such office can bring to a man who knows how the world works. The opening of the Exwyzee Milk Colony, and its promise to provide the Bombay citizenry with top-grade, full-cream, pasteurized cows' milk, was therefore an event which Piloo took as a personal insult.

"Cowvs?" he shrieked at his wife, Golmatol. "Let them worship cowvs, but leawe their udders alone! A person should not squveeze the titties of a goddess! Isn't it, wife? What do you say?" To which Golmatol hesitantly replied, "But and all, the milk is OK." Piloo exploded. "OK? To my phace you are saying it? Arré, how to surwiwe when I am beset by traitors? When I must phight not only these sacred mooing gods but also my own wife as vell."

Golmatol, colouring, eyes downcast, retreated. "No, dear, I only said." But Piloo's anger had been re-targeted at the primary enemy. "Exwyzee," he snorted. "If they are so wyzee, then they will surely know that pretty soon they will be ex."

Piloo went to war. Attended by the scurrying magnificentourage, he stalked the corridors of power in the Bombay Sachivalaya, dispensing bribes and threats in equal measure, demanding the investigation, condemnation and cancellation, as a matter of priority, of the "blasphemous cow-abuse phacility just opened north of Town." He sought out zoning inspectors, tax inspectors, livestock inspectors, hygiene inspectors and of course police inspectors. He paid for giant advertising billboards on which, in a large speech-bubble issuing from his own leering face, and under the legend *Your Milkman Says,* the following argument was made: *EX—means Expensive! WY—means Why Buy It?? ZEE—means Zero Enjoyment Exists!!!* And at the bottom, next to his trademark cartoon goat, the slogan: *Vote Goat—Buy PILOO—the Dude with Doodh.*

It didn't work. In all his life he never suffered a more complete, a more humiliating rebuff. The city authorities declined even to investigate, let alone condemn or cancel the Milk Colony's licenses. Neither blasphemy nor abuse was being committed, all analysts agreed. Zoning inspectors declined to cancel permits, tax inspectors refused to harass, livestock and hygiene inspectors heaped Exwyzee with praise, police inspectors said they had nothing to inspect. Worse still, the Exwyzee grounds became a popular weekend picnic resort; and worst of all,

month by month Piloo's sales figures declined, while those of the hated
cows went from strength to strength. The goat villages, blaming Piloo
for the crisis, simmered with the possibility of violence. Faced with the
erosion of his power base, Piloo Doodhwala admitted to his lady wife
that he had no idea what to do.

"And my poor Halva and Rasgulla?" demanded Golmatol Doodhwala, sheltering one weeping daughter under each arm. "What will you
say to them? You think they have an idea in their dear heads? They are
not lovely! Their skin is not wheatish! In education they are deficient!
Sweets by name, they are sour by nature! All their hope was pinned on
you! And now if you remove from them even their fortune, then what?
Will husbands drop from the skies? Poor girls have no chance—no
hope in hell!"

Into this time of crisis came that half-breed girl, all the way from New
York. She turned out to be poor, badly connected, with more scandals
in her history than a Pompadour: damaged goods, in short. The
Doodhwalas closed ranks against her, barely acknowledging her existence. They offered her the bare minimum: food (though their dining
table groaned with dishes, she was usually served rice and lentils in the
kitchen, in ungenerous quantities, and often went hungry to bed); simple clothing (the swimsuit had come with her from America, a gift
from her absentee father); and an education (this was what Piloo
begrudged most, because the fees cost good money, and the brat didn't
seem to want to learn anything, anyway). Other than providing her
with these necessities, they abandoned her to her fate. She quickly perceived that rich Bombay offered her the worst of both her previous,
much poorer worlds: the detested goats of John Poe and the heartless
cruelties of the Egiptus family of cigar store fame.

Now that day at Juhu Beach begins to look very different. It becomes
clear that, strangely enough, Piloo and Vina had both come to the same
conclusion: all they had left in life was attitude, but it was a steed which
would get you a long way if you knew how to stay on its back. So
Piloo and his magnificentourage had come to perform, in public, a
masque of power, to enact the lie of continued success in the hope that
the sheer force of the performance would somehow make it true,

would reverse the slow defeat that Exwyzee cows were inflicting upon the Doodh-Dude's goats. And Vina, too, was struggling to survive: in reality she wasn't Piloo's spoiled rich American bitch kid, but a poor brat brazening it out while staring the bleakest of futures in the eye.

The future of the milk business became Piloo Doodhwala's only topic of discussion, his fixation. At home in his Bandra villa, pacing up and down in the garden, he would shriek and gibber like a caged langur. He was a man of his generation, the last for whom breast-beating and hair-tearing were still legitimate pursuits. His family and the magnificentourage, both, in different ways, fearful of the future, would hear him out in silence. His weepings, his shakings of fists, his speeches addressed to the empty, cloudless heavens. His complaints about the injustice of human life. Vina, who had seen too many things in her short life, was less tight-lipped, and the day came when she could stand it no longer.

"Oh, to hell with your stupid goats," Vina burst out. "Why don't you just cut their horrible throats and turn them into meat and coats?" Parrots flew from the trees, alarmed by the timbre of her voice; their droppings polluted Piloo's garments and, indeed, his agitated hair. She herself, tickled by the accident of the triple rhyme, began, in spite of her profound annoyance, to giggle.

The watching Doodhwala girls braced themselves delightedly for the lashing fury with which their father would now surely chastise the upstart pauper. But—in spite of her blatant insubordination, and what Ameer Merchant would have called her "fit of the gigglics"; in spite of the rain of parrot shit—no such fury manifested itself. Like unlooked-for sunshine when there has been talk of storms, Piloo Doodhwala's smile arrived, first a little hesitantly, and then breaking out in all its full-beam glory. "Thanking you, Miss America," he said. "Meat phor the interior, owercoat phor exterior. Idea is good, but"—and here he tapped a finger against his temple—"it has prompted one further idea, which is ewen betterer. It may be, madamoozel, that you hawe rescued, albeit inadwertently, our poor phamily phortunes." At which unexpected (and, in their view, entirely inappropriate) lavishing of praise upon the household's Cinderella, Halva and Rasgulla knew not whether to take umbrage or rejoice.

After this unusual exchange, Piloo Doodhwala ordered the slaughter of all his herds and the distribution of the meat, gratis, to the deserving and non-vegetarian poor. It was a royal massacre; the gutters near the abattoirs bubbled over with blood, flooding the streets, which grew sticky and stank. Flies crowded so thickly that in places it became inadvisable, for reasons of low visibility, to drive. But the meat was good, and plentiful, and Piloo's political prospects began to improve. Vote goat indeed. If Piloo had run for governor that week, no man could have stood against him.

His distressed goatherds, seeing the approach of destitution as clearly as if it were the mail train from the north, sought urgent assurances. Piloo toured the countryside, whispering conundrums in their ears. "Newer phear," he said. "The goats we will hawe in phuture could not be depheated by Exwyzee or any other alphabetists. They will be top-quality goats, and you will all grow phat and lazy, becaase you will still get all your pay, though the goats will not require any maintenance, and also, they will not cost one single rupee to pheed. Phrom now on," he concluded cryptically, "we will raise not simply goats but ghoasts."

The riddle of the "ghoasts"—or ghoats, or goasts, or what you will—must remain unsolved awhile. We have arrived once again, by recirculation, at the moment of Vina's expulsion from Piloo's portals. News of her scandalous liaison with Ormus Cama has reached her latest guardian's ears; a quarrel, which has already been alluded to, has already taken place. I offer no further details of those vituperative exchanges, or of the violent struggles that immediately preceded Vina's flight south in the pouring rain, which took her all the way from the Doodhwalas' Bandra mansion to our doorstep at Villa Thracia, Cuffe Parade. Instead, I take up the story from its last resting place: namely, the arrival of Ormus at our family home on Cuffe Parade, urgent with concern for Vina's well-being; and the further arrival, hard on Ormus's heels, of Shri Piloo Doodhwala, accompanied by wife, daughters and the full "magnificentourage."

My mother, Ameer, had telephoned him earlier to inform him that Vina was safe and well, and had gone on to speak a few home truths about his treatment of her. "She will not return to your house," Ameer finished. "Return?" barked Piloo. "Madam, I hawe put her out of doors, like a common bitch. Return is not the question." In the light of this telephonic washing of hands, the arrival of Piloo & Co. was something of a surprise. Vina sprang up and retreated at high speed to the room my mother had given her. Ormus rushed forward to stand face-to-face with his beloved's tormentor. It was left to my mild father to ask Piloo his business. The milkman shrugged. "Regarding that ungratephul girl," he said. "Monies hawe been paid. Phees, cash, spending on account. There has been major outlay of phunds, and in consequence one is considerably out of pocket. Reimbursement is not unreasonably required."

"You're asking us to purchase her?" My fine, high-minded father took a moment to grasp the horrible truth. Piloo made a face. "Not as such purchase," he insisted. "I do not insist on a profit. But you are an honourable man, isn't it? I am certain you would not ask me to swallow the loss."

"We are not speaking here of goods and chattels—" began V.V. Merchant, in outrage, but at this point Ormus Cama interrupted him. We were all standing like statues in our living room—the shock of the encounter had driven all thoughts of relaxation from our minds—and Ormus Cama's eye had fallen upon a pack of cards and a heap of matchsticks on a low table in a corner, the remnants of a light-hearted game of poker a couple of nights back, before the world began to change. He riffled the pack under Piloo's nose. "Hey, big-mouth," he said. "I'll play you for her. What do you say, hot shot? All or nothing. Do you dare to do it, or are you a gutless cutlass?"

Ameer began to protest, but my father—whose own fatal weakness would turn out to be gambling—silenced her. Piloo's eyes were gleaming, and the members of his magnificentourage, who were eavesdropping on the confrontation from the porch outside, began to hoot and cheer. Piloo nodded slowly. His voice grew very soft. "All or nothing, is it. Either I must giwe up 'all' my legitimate claim to recompense or . . . but what is 'or'? What is 'nothing'? If you lose, what do I win?"

"You win me," said Ormus. "I will work for you, any work you name, until I have worked off Vina's debt."

"Stop it, Ormus," said Ameer Merchant. "This is childish, absurd."

"I accept," sighed Piloo Doodhwala, and bowed.

Ormus bowed back. "One cut each," he said. "High card wins all.

Suit immaterial. Aces high, jokers beat aces. Further cuts to decide if we draw equal cards."

"Agreed," breathed Piloo. "But we will play vith my pack." He snapped his fingers. His Pathan bearer marched into our living room carrying, on the white-gloved palm of his outstretched right hand, a silver salver upon which lay a pack of red playing cards whose seal had not been broken. "Don't," I begged Ormus. "There's some trick." But Ormus picked up the pack, broke the seal and nodded. "Let's begin."

"No shuffle," Piloo whispered. "Just cut."

"Good," said Ormus, and did so. And drew the two of hearts.

Piloo laughed. And cut. And drew the two of spades. The smile died on his lips, and the Pathan bearer recoiled from the ferocity of his master's glare.

Ormus cut again. The ten of diamonds. Piloo became very stiff. His hand jerked forward to the salver. He drew the ten of clubs. The Pathan bearer's arm began to tremble. "Hold the tray with both hands," Piloo snarled, "or else phind somebody whose shit hasn't turned to water."

On the third cut they both drew eights. On the fourth it was one-eyed jacks and on the fifth, the jacks with both eyes. By the sixth round, when they both drew fives, the silence in the room had become so noisy that even Vina emerged from her retreat to find out what all the fuss was about. Piloo Doodhwala was sweating heavily; his white kurta was sticking to the curve of his belly as well as the small of his back. Ormus Cama, however, was perfectly calm. In the seventh round both men drew kings; in the eighth, nines. In the ninth it was kings again, and in the tenth it was fours.

"That's enough," Piloo broke the silence. "From now on I'm drawing first."

On the eleventh cut, Piloo Doodhwala drew the ace of spades, and gave a great, deep sigh. Before he had finished exhaling, Ormus had cut for his card. It was the joker. Ormus remained impassive, looking down at the grinning clown on the silver dish. Piloo Doodhwala sagged visibly. Then he rallied, clicked his fingers under Ormus's nose, snapped, "Keep the bitch," and walked out.

Ormus Cama went over to Vina, who was looking, for once, like a scared twelve-year-old. "You heard the man," he grinned. "I won you fair and square. Now you belong to me."

He was wrong. Vina belonged to no man, not even to him, though she loved him till the day she died. She reached out towards him, offering a caress of thanks. He stepped back, seriously. "No touching," he reminded her. "Not until you are sixteen years and one day old."

"And not then, not until you're decently married," said my mother, "if I have anything to do with it."

It is time to accentuate the positive. For are there no noble qualities, no high achievements, no exaltations of the spirit to praise in the life of the great sub-continent? Must it always be violence or gambling or crooks? These are touchy times. National sensitivities are on permanent alert, and it is getting harder by the moment to say boo to a goose, lest the goose in question belong to the paranoid majority (goosism under threat), the thin-skinned minority (victims of goosophobia), the militant fringe (Goose Sena), the separatists (Goosistan Liberation Front), the increasingly well organized cohorts of society's historical outcasts (the ungoosables, or Scheduled Geese), or the devout followers of that ultimate guruduck, the sainted Mother Goose. Why, after all, would any sensible person wish to say boo in the first place? By constantly throwing dirt, such booers disqualify themselves from serious consideration (they cook their own goose).

It is in the most constructive spirit imaginable, therefore, that I record the heartwarming news that Vina Apsara, who once, while standing on a beach wrapped up in Old Glory, hurled abuse at all things Indian, began at Villa Thracia to fall in love with her biological father's great country of origin. She had to wait for Ormus Cama until after her sixteenth birthday, but this other love entailed no waiting period. She consummated it right away.

To her last day, I could always see in her the skittish, disintegrated creature she'd been when she first came to us, looking as if she might run away again at any moment. What a piece of jetsam she was then, what a casualty! Literally selfless, her personality smashed, like a mirror, by the fist of her life. Her name, her mother and family, her sense of place and home and safety and belonging and being loved, her belief in the future, all these things had been pulled out from under her, like a rug. She was floating in a void, denatured, dehistoried, clawing at the shapelessness, trying to make some sort of mark. An oddity. She put me

in mind of one of Columbus's sailors, close to mutiny, fearing that at
any moment she might plunge off the edge of the earth, staring longingly at the lookout in the crow's-nest, whose spyglass probed the liquid emptiness, searching vainly for land. Later, when she was famous,
she herself often mentioned Columbus. "He went looking for Indians
and found America. I hadn't planned on going anywhere, but I found
more Indians than I could handle." Vina's smart mouth, her lippiness.
That, at the age of twelve, she already had.

She was a rag-bag of selves, torn fragments of people she might have
become. Some days she sat crumpled in a corner like a string-cut puppet, and when she jerked into life you never knew who would be
there, in her skin. Sweet or savage, serene or stormy, funny or sad: she
had as many moods as the Old Man of the Sea, who would transform
himself over and over again if you tried to grab him, for he knew that
if you did capture him he would have to grant your deepest wish. Fortunately for her, she found Ormus, who just hung on to her, held her
spirit tight in his love without laying a finger on her body, until at last
she stopped changing, was no longer ocean then fire then avalanche
then wind, and was just herself, one day after her sixteenth birthday, in
his arms. And then she kept her side of the bargain and, for one night,
gave him his heart's desire.

That she was in bad trouble, she already knew. That sassiness, delinquency, nihilism and unpredictability didn't add up to a person, she had
worked out for herself. In her own way, and in spite of all her surface
insouciance and defiance, she possessed a constructive spirit, and it's my
belief that she was spurred on in her heroic act of self-construction by
the experience of living *chez nous,* where talk of building was constant
(these were the days when V. V. and Ameer started work on the great
Orpheum movie theatre, the project that would eventually ruin them).
What she set about constructing was put together with the materials
that came immediately to hand: that is to say, Indian goods. What she
built was "Vina Apsara," the goddess, the Galatea with whom the
whole world would fall, as Ormus fell, as I fell, in love.

She began with music. "Vina." She'd heard a musician in Piloo's
entourage playing, coarsely and without feeling, an instrument that in
spite of such brutalisation "made a sound like god; and when I found
out what it was called, I knew that was the name for me." The music

of India, from northern sitar ragas to southern Carnatic melodies, always created in her a mood of inexpressible longing. She could listen to recordings of ghazals for hours at a stretch, and was entranced, too, by the complex devotional music of the leading *qawwals*. Longing for what? Not, surely, for an "authentic" Indianness that she could never attain? Rather, I must conclude—and this is hard for a lifelong sceptic like me to write—that what Vina wanted was a glimpse of the unknowable. The music offered the tantalising possibility of being borne on the waves of sound through the curtain of *maya* that supposedly limits our knowing, through the gates of perception to the divine melody beyond.

A religious experience, to be brief, was what she wanted. In a sense, this meant she understood the music far better than I, for its spiritual element is of central importance to so many people, not least the musicians themselves. I, however, am my parents' child, in that I have always been deaf to religious communications of all types. Unable to take them at face value—what, you *really* think there was an angel there? Reincarnation, *honestly?*—I have made the mistake (encouraged by a childhood in which I hardly ever heard the name of any deity mentioned with approval in our home) of assuming that everyone else was of the same mind, and thought of such speech as metaphorical, and nothing more. This has not always proved a happy assumption to make. It gets one into arguments. And yet—though I know that dead myths were once live religions, that Quetzalcoatl and Dionysus may be fairy tales now but people, to say nothing of goats, once died for them in large numbers—I can still give no credence whatsoever to systems of belief. They seem flimsy, unpersuasive examples of the literary genre known as "unreliable narration." I think of faith as irony, which is perhaps why the only leaps of faith I'm capable of are those required by the creative imagination, by fictions that don't pretend to be fact, and so end up telling the truth. I am fond of saying that all religions have one thing in common, namely that their answers to the great question of our origins are all quite simply wrong. So when Vina made, as she would repeatedly make, announcements of her latest conversion, I would reply, "Oh, sure," and convince myself that she was, in a profound sense, just kidding. But she wasn't. She meant it, every time. If Vina had decided to worship the Great Pumpkin, then assuredly, come

Hallowe'en, hers—and not poor Linus's—would have been the sincer-est pumpkin patch of all.

"Apsara" was a clue too, if I hadn't been too stupid to pick it up. It indicated a quantity of serious reading, and even though Vina liked to claim that she'd taken the name from a magazine advertisement in *Femina* or *Filmfare* for beauty soap or luxury silks or some such frip-pery, hindsight shows up that subterfuge for the ruse it was. She had plunged into the great matter of this strange, huge land in which she had been exiled, far from everything she'd ever thought or been or known. A refusal of the customary marginalised rôle of the exile, it was—I see it now—heroic.

"Vina Apsara" sounded to her twelve-year-old self like someone who might plausibly exist. She would bring her into being, using, as her tools, her love for Ormus Cama, her incredible will, her fabulous hunger for life, and her voice. A woman who can sing is never entirely beyond salvation. She can open her mouth and set her spirit free. And Vina's singing needs no paeans of praise from me. Put on one of her records, lie back and float downstream. She was a great river, which could bear us all away. Sometimes I try to imagine how she would have sounded singing ghazals. For even though she dedicated her life to another music entirely, the pull of India, its songs, its languages, its life, worked upon her always, like the moon.

I do not flatter myself (or not always) that she came back for me.

To my parents, Vina was the daughter they never had, the child they had chosen to forgo so that they could concentrate on me and on their work; she was the life they thought they did not have room for in their lives. But now that she had arrived, they were filled with joy, and there turned out to be time for everything, after all. She picked up languages as easily as, throughout her life, she picked up lovers. It was in those years that she perfected her use of "Hug-me," our polyglot trash-talk. "Chinese khana ka big mood hai," she learned to say, when she wanted a plate of noodles, or—for she was a great hobbit fancier—"Apun J.R.R. Tolkien's *Angootiyan-ka-Seth* ko too-much admire karta chhé." Ameer Merchant, the family's great word-gamester, paid Vina the com-pliment of incorporating many of the girl's locutions into her own personal lexicon. Ameer and Vina were, linguistically at least, two of a kind. (And my mother saw, in her new ward, some deeper echoes of her own unconventional spirit.) Ameer was always convinced of the deep meanings hidden in euphony and rhyme: that is to say, she was a popster *manqué.* So, in her increasingly intimate moments of Vina-teasing and general raillery, Ameer would conflate Ormus Cama and Vasco da Gama—"Ormie da Cama, your great explorer, discovering you like a new world full of spices"—and it was a short step from Gama to *Gana,* song, and between Cama and *Kama,* the god of love, the distance was even less. Ormus Kama, Ormus Gana. The embodiment of love, and also of song itself. My mother was right. Her word games said more than she knew.

Vina was already much the same size and build as my mother, and Ameer let her dress up, not only in saris of lavish silk, but also in the slinky sequinned sheath dresses—plunging necklines and all—with which Ameer loved to display her figure to the city's sophisticated set. Vina grew her hair long, and once a week Ameer personally applied fresh coconut oil to the growing tresses and massaged the young girl's scalp. She showed Vina the traditional way of drying long hair, spreading it over a wickerwork surface, under which she set a pot of live coals sprinkled with incense. For her skin, Vina learned how to mix rose water and *multani mitti,* a clay named after Multan in Pakistan, and apply it as a face mask. Ameer rubbed ghee into Vina's feet to keep them soft and to draw out "surplus temperature" from the body during the hot season. Best of all, she taught Vina the connection between jewellery and good fortune; godless Ameer was not without her superstitious foibles. Vina took to wearing a gold chain round her waist. (However, nothing could induce her to wear toe rings, once she had been told that they heightened a woman's fertility.) And for the rest of her life, the great singer would never wear a precious stone until she had "road-tested" it by putting it under her pillow every night for a week, to see what effect it had on her dreams. This tried the tolerance of various illustrious international jewellery stores, but for a good customer, and a star, people were willing to stretch a point.

(If she had known that her last sexual companion, the playboy Raúl Páramo, had covertly slipped the gift of a ruby necklace under her pillow during their night of befuddled love—rubies had been absolutely forbidden her, years before, by Ameer's personal astrologer—she would have understood at once why she had dreamed of blood sacrifice, and been warned, perhaps, of the nearness of her doom. But she never found the necklace. It was discovered by the police during their search of her hotel room, and before she could be informed, it was all over.

And besides, all this jewel reading is pure malarkey. Nothing to it at all.)

As well as Hindi-Urdu and the secrets of beauty and gems, Vina also drank down the city of Bombay in great thirsty gulps—in particular, to the delight of my father, the language of its buildings. V.V. became her eager instructor, and she his star pupil. My parents had just sunk a great deal of money in a prime property near the Bombay Central railway terminus, the site of the proposed Orpheum theatre, which, my father was determined, would be built in the Deco style that Bombay had made her own, even though the city's other Deco movie houses were already twenty years old and more "modern" theatres were presently the rage. Vina wanted to know everything. After a while, whenever we went to English-language movies, she paid more attention to the cinemas than to anything on the screen. At the great Deco masterpiece, the red-sandstone-and-cream Eros Cinema (Paramount Pictures, in VistaVision: Danny Kaye in *The Court Jester,* warning that on account of the pellet with the poison, the chalice from the palace was the one you must shun, while the vessel with the pestle had the brew that was true), Vina couldn't remember the plot but was able to mention casually that while the building had been designed by local boy Sohrabji Bhedwar, the fabulous interiors, black, white, gold and chromium, were the work of Fritz von Drieberg, who also renovated the New Empire (20th Century–Fox, Todd-AO, Rodgers, Hammerstein, a bright golden haze on the meadow, surreys with fringes, Rod Steiger singing his great self-pitying ditty, none of it enough to get her to remember a word of the fabulous score of *Ooooooo-klahoma!*). At the Metro with its MGM spectaculars—Stewart Granger in *Scaramouche,* winning the longest sword fight in movie history—her attention wandered to the chairs and carpets (American, imported) and the murals (by students at the J.J. School of Arts, where once Rudyard Kipling's dad had been in charge). And at the Regal—Maria Montez unforgettable in Universal's *Cobra Woman*—architecture-obsessed Vina failed to notice that La Montez was playing twins, but whispered credit was duly given to the Czech Karl Schara for the dazzling sun-ray design of the auditorium. At the Hindi movies, she behaved better and seemed more interested, though we did learn of the merits of Angelo Molle (interior, Broadway Cinema, Dadar). Vina professed unoriginally to be in love with Raj Kapoor, and Ormus was touchingly annoyed. I, however, was half sick of cinemas. Fortunately, the hot-season holidays came, and we went to Kashmir.

Vina blossoming towards womanhood in that once blessed valley is one of my most treasured memories. I remember her in the Shalimar Gardens beside running water, slowing suddenly from a child's gallop to a woman's walk and beginning to turn heads. I remember her on a palomino pony in the mountain meadow of Baisaran, her hair streaming behind her as she rode. I remember her on the Bund in Srinagar, falling in love with the names of the magic emporia full of papier mâché and carved walnut furniture and numdah rugs: Suffering Moses and Cheap John and Subhana the Worst. I remember her on a pony trek through the high hamlet of Aru, being horrified that the villagers pretended they had no food to sell us, because they heard me call her "Vina" and assumed we were Hindus, and I also remember the equally intense disgust on her face when, having heard we were Muslims, these same villagers brought us a feast of shirmal and meatballs and refused to let us pay.

I remember her reading voraciously, devouring books—all in English, for she never could read Indian languages as well as she spoke them. In a field of flowers at Gulmarg, she read *On the Road* (she and Ormus could recite passages by heart, and when she did the book's elegiac conclusion, *I think of Dean . . . I think of Dean Moriarty,* there were tears in her eyes). Or, in a wood of tall trees near Pahalgam, she wondered if any of these conifers might be Enid Blyton's Faraway Tree, which—in an inspired inversion of the normal rules of travel—was regularly visited, at its cloud-concealed top, by fantastic lands. Most heart-piercingly of all, I remember her at the Kolahoi Glacier, talking excitedly about Jules Verne's *Journey to the Centre of the Earth,* and her dream of travelling to another high snowscape, that of the Snaefellsjokull in Iceland, so that on the summer solstice she could position herself in the right place at the right time and watch a rock's shadow point its swivelling finger, exactly at noon, to the entrance to the Underworld—an Arctic Taenarus Gate. In the light of what happened to her, this memory, I must confess, now gives me a bad attack of the creeps.

(All those cinemas show Hindi movies now. And Kashmir is a battle zone. But the past is not less valuable because it is no longer the present. In fact, it's more important, because forever unseen. Call it my brand of mysticism, one of the rare spiritual propositions I am prepared to make.)

Ormus Cama did not accompany us on holiday, or to the movies. On the subject of Vina's extraordinary liaison, Ameer Merchant had laid down the law. With great tolerance—and in spite of vociferous opposition from Lady Spenta Cama, whom, you will recall, she didn't much care for—she accepted the possibility that this was the beginning of a genuine love match, "but all proprieties must be observed." Ormus was allowed to call five times a week at tea-time and stay for one hour exactly. My mother agreed not to inform Lady Spenta of Ormus's visits, on the understanding that she herself would be present throughout them, or, if business appointments made it impossible for her to be there, that the entire encounter take place out of doors, on the porch. Vina agreed without argument. This was not the mutinous inwardness of Nissy Poe, or the frightened yielding of a girl with no options in life. Family life had begun to mend Vina, to make her whole, and she submitted happily to Ameer's maternal discipline because it sounded like love. Indeed, it was love; hard to say which of them needed the other more.

(Besides, as it turned out, Vina and Ormus had another, unexpected ally, who made possible a series of more private trysts.)

For me, Ormus's visits were the worst hours of the week. I tried to be absent as often as I could. When I was home, I sulked in my room. After he'd gone, however, things would look up. She'd come to see me. "Come on, Rai," she'd say. "You know how it is. I'm just killing time with Ormie, waiting for you to grow up and be my man." She'd stroke my cheek and even kiss me lightly on the mouth. And the years passed, and I turned thirteen, and her sixteenth birthday was round the corner, and still Ormus Cama refused to touch her, whether chaperones were present or not, and still I sulked in my room, and in she came,

"Come on, Rai," and caressed me. In the light touch of her fingers and lips I could feel all the weight of her forbidden love for Ormus, all that inexpressible desire. I was forbidden fruit too, oppositely vetoed on account of my youth rather than hers. But although there wasn't anybody chaperoning us, because my parents were just too innocent to think of the possibility of my becoming Ormus's surrogate, his body double, I would have been prepared to settle for that lesser rôle, to be his shadow, his echo; in fact I was longing for it. But she refused to gratify me, she left me feeling worse than before, she kept me waiting.

It was a long wait. But Vina was worth waiting for.

Vina's weakness for mentors, for leaders and teachers, the addiction to mumbo jumbo which was her way of papering over the radical uncertainties of life, meant that Ormus could always, and effortlessly, claim her for his own. But I repeat: she was never wholly his possession. Card-game victories and worldwide celebrity notwithstanding, she kept coming back to me.

From Death Valley, the lowest point in the continental United States, you can see Mount Whitney, the highest. So, from the depths of my frustrated misery when Ormus Cama came to tea, I offer the following remembered glimpse of the high days when she and I were lovers:

Many years later in New York, in my third-floor walk-up on a block near St. Mark's noted for its population of gay Cuban refugees, Vina rolled off my sweating body immediately after we had finished making love, and lit a cigarette. (I have always perspired freely, a slight disadvantage in daily life but a definite plus during sex, when slipperinesses of all sorts, including moral, are efficacious.) "Did I tell you? I saw a light on him," she said. "A radiance, an aura, that first day in the record store. Not excessive?, but definitely emanating. About equivalent to a hundred-watt bulb, that is to say, enough to illuminate an average-size room. Which was plenty."

Vina was never one for the niceties of sexual betrayal. She thought nothing of discussing her *fidanzato* with her back-door man twenty seconds after reaching orgasm, which she reached easily and which, in that period of her life, was noisy and prolonged. (Later, after their marriage, she still came easily but her pleasure would last only an instant before she switched it off, zap, as if she were responding to some invisible conductor's baton. As if she were playing that beautiful instrument, her own body, and suddenly heard a shockingly false note.) I had learned to accommodate myself to her conversational indelicacies. However, then as now, I lacked the patience for such low-grade material as this "aura," this "light."

"Bushwah," I retorted. "Ormus is no god-man with portable lighting effects. Trouble with you is, you came to India and caught a dose of Wisdom-of-the-East-itis, a.k.a. gurushitia, our incurable killer brain disease. I told you not to drink the water if it wasn't boiled."

"Trouble with *you*," her smoke blew in my face, "is that you *never* drink the water unless it's been boiled for a fucking *year.*"

She caught India, and it almost killed her. She contracted malaria, typhoid, cholera and hepatitis, and they didn't reduce her appetite for the place at all. She wolfed it down like a cheap snack from a roadside stall. Then it rejected her, as cruelly as she had been rejected in Virginia or New York State. By that time, however, she had grown strong enough to absorb the blow. She had Ormus, and the future was no longer in anyone else's gift. She could hit back and survive. But her years of good behaviour ended at that moment. After it, she embraced instability, her own and the world's, and made up her own rules as she went along. Nothing was certain in her vicinity any more, the ground was always trembling, and of course the fault lines spread through her from top to toe, and faults in human beings always open up in the end, like cracks in the groaning earth.

"The Swimmer," one of the last songs Ormus Cama wrote for himself and Vina, was recorded on the island of Montserrat beneath a grumbling volcano. The hard rhythm-and-blues guitar riff that drives the song had been in his head for days. He had woken with it pounding in his ears, and grabbed a guitar and a tape deck to record it before it went away. They weren't getting along in those days, and the studio sessions were scratchy, wasteful, clenched. Finally, he plugged into the poisoned atmosphere, he turned towards what was blocking things and harnessed it, made the quarrel his subject, and that bitter, prophetic song of doomed love was the result. For himself, he wrote some of his darkest lines. "I swam across the Golden Horn, until my heart just burst. The best in her nature was drowning in the worst." This in a nasal, dragging delivery that alarmed his admirers, was described by one notoriously waspish music critic (who was unconsciously echoing the singer's father, Sir Darius Xerxes Cama) as resembling the dying agonies of an aged goat, and proved that he had begun to sink even before the tragedy. But because he still loved her, even in their worst moments he couldn't deny it, he gave her high, hopeful lines to sing against his own low despair, lines as seductive as the sirens' song; as if he were both John and Paul, both sour and sweet.

There's a candle in my window, Vina sang, but I don't have to tell you, you're feeling it already, the memory of it, pulling at your emotions. *Swim to me.* I can't listen to it myself. Not any more.

The best in our natures is drowning in the worst. It was Ormus's mother who used to say that. Lady Spenta Cama in the late 1950s fell into a deep sadness, under whose influence she became blasphemously convinced that the Monster of the Lie, Ahriman or Angra Mainyu, was gaining the victory over Ahura Mazda and the Light, in spite of what was prophesied in the great books, the Avesta, the Yasna and the Bundahish. Priests in their white garments were invited with increasing frequency into the apartment on Apollo Bunder, and they brought their little fires with them and chanted nobly. "Hear ye then with your ears, and see the bright flames with the eyes of the Better Mind." Ardaviraf Cama, Lady Spenta's silent son, would sit with her and haltingly participate in the fire rituals, wearing that sweet expression which was his hallmark; Ormus, however, absented himself. As for her ageing, drink-blurred husband, his impatience with her orisons only increased with the passing years. "Blasted priests make the place look like a blasted hospital," he would grumble, passing through the chamber of her devotions. "Blasted fire'll probably end up burning the blasted house down."

The house of Cama was indeed in danger, but not from holy fire. On the tenth anniversary of the independence of India, Spenta received a letter from William Methwold, who was now a peer of the realm, a Foreign Office grandee, and wrote to wish his old friends well "on so auspicious a date." However, the letter also had a less auspicious purpose. "If I address this to you, my dear Spenta, rather than to

Brother D.X.C., it is because I have, I fear, difficult tidings to impart." Then followed a series of contorted, digressive animadversions on the general subject of banquets he had recently attended, in particular one "rather jolly affair" involving a re-staging of *Twelfth Night* at Middle Temple on Twelfth Night, Middle Temple being the place where *Twelfth Night* had first been staged on an earlier Twelfth Night; at any rate—and at last Lord Methwold accelerated towards his dreadful point—he had been seated by the purest chance next to the eminent judge Henry "Hang'em" Higham, who turned out to be a former classmate of "Brother D.X.C.'s" and revealed, over the brandy, that while Sir Darius Xerxes Cama had been an enthusiastic eater of dinners, in his legal studies he "hadn't come up to scratch." He had flunked his examinations, and had never been admitted to the Bar "in any shape or form."

Lord Methwold had "found the accusation well-nigh impossible to credit." In London he had required enquiries to be made, and found, to his dismay, that Henry Higham had been right. "I can only conclude," he wrote in his letter, "that your husband's papers were forgeries, forgeries of the highest quality, may I say; that he simply decided to brazen it out, on the assumption that nobody in India would bother to check; and if they did, it is not impossible, as you must know, nor indeed overly expensive, to buy a fellow's silence in that great country of yours, for which I have never ceased to feel the keenest nostalgia."

Lady Spenta Cama loved her husband in spite of everything, and he loved her. Ormus Cama always believed that the foundation of his parents' mutual affection was a sexual compatibility which old age had done nothing to erode. "The old folks went at it most nights," he'd say. "We all had to pretend we hadn't heard anything, which wasn't easy, because they made plenty of noise, particularly when my boozy father insisted upon what he called the English position, which I don't think my mother enjoyed. Those shrieks weren't really of pleasure, but she was prepared to suffer a lot for the sake of love." After she discovered that Sir Darius had built his entire professional life on a falsehood— that he was, covertly, a Servant of the Lie—Lady Spenta moved into a separate bedroom, and at night the apartment was full of the sad silence of that ending. She never gave Sir Darius a reason for her departure from the conjugal bed, and wrote to Lord Methwold imploring him, in the name of their long friendship, to keep her husband's secret. "He has not practised law for many years, and when he did, all agreed that he gave sterling service, so no harm done, eh?" Methwold wrote back to agree, "on the single condition, my very dear Spenta, that you continue to write and give me all the news, as I no longer feel comfortable about writing to D.X.C. himself, knowing what I now know."

"I fear I may be succumbing to error," Spenta confided unhappily in a later letter to Lord Methwold. "As Parsis we are proud to believe in a forward-moving view of the cosmos. Our words and deeds are part, in their small way, of the battle in which Ahura Mazda will vanquish Ahriman. But how may I believe in the perfectibility of the universe, when in my small backwater there are so many slippery slopes? Maybe our Hindu friends are right, and there is no progress but only an eternal cycle, and right now it is the long age of darkness, *kalyug*."

To combat her doubts and justify the prophet Zarathustra's innovative world picture, Lady Spenta Cama plunged into good works. Under the tutelage of the Angel Health, late-night hospital visits became her specialty. Small, heavy, bustling Spenta in her horn-rim specs, leaning forward slightly as she scuttled along, with her handbag held tightly in both hands, became a familiar figure in the neon-lit nocturnal corridors of the Lying-In Hospital and the Gratiaplena Nursing Home, particularly in those grim wards and intensive care units reserved for the gravely ill, the incurables, the horribly crippled and the dying. The nursing staff at these institutions—even the Gratiaplena's redoubtable Sister John—quickly formed a high opinion of the little lady. She seemed instinctively to know when to prattle on to the patients—gossiping about little Bombay nothings, the latest shop, the latest scandal—and when to maintain a pure silence that somehow exuded comfort. In the matter of silences she appeared to have learned something from her son Ardaviraf. Virus Cama began accompanying his mother on her rounds, and his tranquil muteness, too, brought the succour of serenity to the sick. Deeply affected by what she saw at the hospital—the many cases of malnutrition, and polio, and tuberculosis, and other poverty-related illnesses, including the self-inflicted injuries of unsuccessful suicides—Lady Spenta became, with Mrs. Dolly Kalamanja of Malabar Hill, the joint convenor and driving force of a group of Parsi ladies like herself, whose purpose was to alleviate the suffering of their community, which was widely believed to be exclusively composed of prosperous and powerful citizens, but which was, in reality, plunging into extreme hardship and even, in some cases, destitution. Sir Darius Xerxes Cama, an increasingly remote figure, disapproved of the morning teas at which the ladies would plan their fund-raising work. "Stupid beggars've only got themselves to blame," he would mutter, passing through the drawing room like a ghost. "No backbone. Weaklings. Sissies. I'm sorry, but it's the truth." The ladies ignored him and got on with their work.

There were malicious whisperers who opined that Lady Spenta Cama's sickbed visits were themselves unhealthy, that they smacked of obsession, that she had become addicted to holding the hands of the dying and playing the sainted, bountiful grande dame. I do not agree. If I am to criticise Lady Spenta's high-energy charity offensive, I would say only this: that charity begins at home.

In 1947, at the age of fifteen, Cyrus Cama had made his own declaration of independence. By then he had spent five years at the famous—and famously disciplinarian—Templars School in the southern hill station of Kodaikanal, as a punishment for his attempted smothering of his brother Ormus. During his early days at the Templars School he had given every sign of being a disturbed child, capable of violence towards his fellow students and also towards members of staff. However, at other times, he came across as a completely different child, possessed of a sweetness of nature fully as disarming and winsome as his brother Ardaviraf's. This "second self" earned him more chances than another such child would have been allowed.

Sir Darius and Lady Spenta had chosen the Templars' "year round" option, which permitted Cyrus to live at school during the holidays as well as term time, an option normally taken up only for boys whose parents were abroad or deceased. In the early days the school had twice written to the Camas asking them to reconsider this decision, because the boy appeared troubled and would no doubt benefit from a family environment; but Lady Spenta, in particular, had been adamant. "The boy needs an iron hand," she wrote back, "and you have boasted of having such a hand. Do you say that your school's reputation is undeserved?" Sir Darius, too, was of the opinion that, as the British used to say, "board is best." One may ascribe the Camas' harsh decision to the widespread Indian abhorrence of psychiatric problems and mental illness, but to explain is not to condone.

At any rate, after Lady Spenta's challenge, Cyrus was treated with maximum severity. Corporal punishment was frequent, prolonged and intense. He responded quickly. The violence ceased, his academic performance improved dramatically, Cyrus the delinquent vanished, and Cyrus the charmer took over completely. In addition, he developed a passionate interest in fitness and gymnastics, becoming the star of the school gymnasium, equally adept on horizontal and parallel bars, pommel horse and rings. His reports began to glow with his teachers' pride and satisfaction, and no doubt Lady Spenta felt herself justified by these reports.

In August 1947 the Templars School was in recess. Cyrus Cama was still in residence, along with half a dozen other boys, mostly the sons of diplomats whose fathers were newly taking up ambassadorial posts around the world. The mass murder of these children—all smothered in their beds while they slept—was an atrocity that would at any other time have captured the nation's full attention. However, the agony of the Partition massacres and the counterpointing ecstasy of the Independence festivities, coupled with the fact that these murders had taken place not in Delhi, Calcutta or Bombay but in remote Kodaikanal, meant that the deaths were ignored by the national newspapers, in spite of the eminence of the dead boys' families. The disappearance of Cyrus Cama did not initially cause him to be suspected of wrongdoing. The attempted smothering of little Ormus was a family matter, which the Camas had kept to themselves; nor, when they learned of the atrocity, did they volunteer any information to the police.

Cyrus was thought either to have escaped the assassin, in which case he was hiding out somewhere, perhaps wounded and certainly terrified, and would probably emerge after a time (he did not); or to have been taken hostage by the criminal, in which case a ransom demand might follow, or else his body would be found later, in another place (it was not). The assassin's purposes were obscure, but those were murderous days, and the Kodaikanal C.I.D., with its limited resources, did not succeed in establishing motive.

The "Pillowman," as the psychopathic serial killer Cyrus Cama later came to be known, was as intellectually brilliant and physically strong as his father longed for all young Parsi men to be, and was, in addition, responsible in the next few weeks for murders in Mysore, Bangalore and Madras. Owing to the dispersed locations of his crimes, the lack of a communal factor and the overwrought temper of the times, no connection was at first made between these separate killings—though the use of an identical method, smothering by pillows, provided an obvious link—nor was Cyrus implicated. (By now the Kodaikanal police were favouring the hostage-and-subsequent-murder theory and waiting for his dead body to turn up.) Finally, Cyrus could no longer stand the anonymity, and sent a fifteen-year-old's boastful letter to all the relevant police chiefs, incriminating himself while insisting that he would never be caught by duffers such as they.

When Lady Spenta was informed of these facts, she wept shocked tears. "Our world has lost its moorings," she told her husband. "Nothing is certain. Common humanity, what is it? How to counter so much violence, so many betrayals, such fear?" *The best in our natures is drowning in the worst.* Then for a time she retreated, as was the family practice, into a suffocated silence, emerging from it to declare in an airless voice that she no longer had a son called Khusro alias Cyrus Cama and that his name was never to be spoken in her presence again; with which Sir Darius Xerxes Cama grimly concurred. The disowning of Cyrus Cama was formalized. Sir Darius changed his will, disinheriting his murderous child. Which Virus, his twin brother, accepted without saying a word.

Cyrus Cama's technique was to charm people to their deaths. He looked and acted several years older than his age, and in respectable public places—cinemas, coffeehouses, restaurants—he befriended his victims, usually foolish young people with money to burn, to whom he came across as an unusually attractive and original young man with an exceptional force of intellect. They asked him what a young Parsi blade might be doing travelling in south India by himself (in those days few Indians travelled for pleasure in their own country, even to Kashmir); he replied in well-modulated, articulate, boarding-school accents, singing the praises of his liberal parents, C.B. and Hebe Jeebeebhoy of Cusrow Baag, Bombay, who understood that a young man must do his growing up on his own, and had acceded to his wish to see the glories of newly independent India, travelling solo on a kind of pilgrim's *yatra*, before he went up to read Law at Oxford University, England, in one year's time. He regaled his victims with traveller's tales of the great sub-continent, describing glittering cities and mountain ranges like the devil's teeth, and river deltas prowled by tigers, and lost temples in distant cornfields, in such idiosyncratic detail that it was impossible to doubt the authenticity of his entirely fictional accounts. By the end of the first evening the intrepid traveller had so completely seduced his marks that they invited him into their homes as their house guest.

Then he would transfix them by speaking passionately, night after eloquent night, of the "moral short circuit" of the age, the nationwide "loss of soul-greatness" of which he had been made so painfully aware on his journeyings, and of his dream of forming a "people's movement for the salvation by spiritual energy-force of this poor, bloodied land." Such was his charisma, and his skill at identifying his dupes, that the victims quickly began to think of him as some sort of great new leader, a guru or even a prophet, and willingly handed over substantial sums of money for the foundation of his movement and the propagation of his ideas; whereupon he visited them softly in their idiotic bedrooms and allowed the pillows, which seemed to move of their own volition into his hands, to do their work, which was necessary work, for the foolish did not deserve to live. To be killable was also to be worthy of being killed. (Adulatory descriptions of Cyrus Cama had also been found in the private diaries of the boys he killed at the Templars School, with whose freely donated pocket money he had financed his initial flight.)

Cyrus was prone to exaggerated mood swings, however, plunging at times into a lightless, cavernous underworld of self-loathing; and it was during one of these periods, early in 1948, that he returned to Kodaikanal, walked into the town police station and surrendered to the terrified duty officer, saying, "I could do with a rest, yaar." Only just sixteen, he admitted sole responsibility for a total of nineteen smotherings, was adjudged by the courts to be "profoundly disordered, utterly immoral and highly dangerous," and was transported north to be locked up for the rest of his days, "for the protection of the public," in a cell without a pillow at the maximum security facility of Tihar

Jail, Delhi. Within weeks he had made a favourable impression on his jailers, who spoke effusively of his wisdom, learning, excellent manners and immense personal charm.

This was the living skeleton in Ormus's family cupboard, and another thing he had in common with Vina. There was a multiple murderer in his family too.

When I think about the three brothers Cama, I see them as men who were all incarcerated for a time, enclosed within their own bodies by the circumstances of their lives. A cricket ball jailed Virus within his silence; a pillow silenced Ormus's music for fourteen years; banishment and punishment caused Cyrus, too, to conceal himself beneath a falsehood, a self he had borrowed from his sweet-natured twin, which was not truly his. Each found something different in that internal exile. Cyrus found the wellspring of mayhem, Virus discovered the nature of peace, and Ormus, first by chasing Gayomart's shade through his dreams, and then—following Vina's advice—by learning how to listen to his own inner voices, found his art.

They were also, all three of them, men who attracted followers. Cyrus had his victims, and Ormus had his fans. Virus, however, attracted children.

Not long after Ormus Cama's epochal encounter with Vina Apsara at the Rhythm Center record store, his brother Ardaviraf was wandering, as was his habit, along the seafront to the Gateway of India in the cool hour between the heat and the darkness. He had started in those days to acquire a following of street urchins, who neither asked him for money nor offered to shine his shoes, but simply grinned at him in the hope (usually fulfilled) that he would smile back. The beautiful smile of Virus Cama had become infectious; it was spreading through the street urchin community at high speed and dramatically increasing their earning power. Few foreign visitors could resist its winsome innocence. Even seasoned Bombayites, hardened by years of refusing the children's entreaties, were melted by its warmth and gave out handfuls of silver *chavanni* bits to the incredulous brats.

It is true that there were times when Ardaviraf Cama did not smile. At these times he was assailed by feelings of claustrophobia, and of a malevolence so powerful that he had to sit down on the sea wall and gasp for breath. Terrible thoughts arrived in his head from nowhere.

"Eight years. Can you imagine how much bitterness can accumulate during eight years in jail, how great a flood of vengeance must be unleashed to wash away such pain?" He couldn't answer the question. He didn't want to know the answer. But he knew that his twin brother was still alive and crazy and dreaming only of the day of his inevitable escape. Virus closed his eyes and breathed deeply, and the transmission from the Pillowboy—now a Pillowman of twenty-four—came to an end. Children clustered around him, offering up their smiles, which were also his. He smiled back. The children cheered.

"Who dat man?" Who can forget the immortal Harpo and his infant followers in *A Day at the Races*? Although Virus Cama's habitual mode of attire was nattily printed bush shirt and cream slacks, his ragamuffin-wreathed strolls always put me in mind of that beloved (and voluntarily mute) genius in his clown's battered hat and tattered coat. Virus's shock of curly hair increased his resemblance to Mr. Adolph Marx . . . and maybe one of his little ruffian pals had sneaked a look at the old movie, because one day this little fellow came up to Virus, grinning widely and bold as brass, and wordlessly held out a wooden flute; which Virus wonderingly examined; and put to his lips; and blew.

Rooty-toot-toot! Music came naturally to all the Cama boys, including the late Gayomart, and the hunger and ease with which Ardaviraf now played his flute—instinctively, with a few inevitable hesitations, but on the whole with a fluency that bordered on the magical—said much about the pain of melody's long absence from his life. The haunting, ghostly notes of the evening raga stopped the promenaders in their tracks. Children squatted down at his feet; the birds forbore to sing. The flute's sound was like the weeping of the soul, the soul at the Chinvat Bridge, perhaps, waiting for judgement. After a time, as the dusk closed in and the street lights glowed, Ardaviraf stopped, and looked gawkily, goofily pleased. "Come on, Mister Virus," pleaded the boy who had handed him the flute, "something with a smile." Virus set the flute against his lips once more; and played, with considerable gusto, "The Saints." And now he was not only Harpo but the Pied Piper too, leading his children nowhere; and after that he was Mickey Mouse as the Sorcerer's Apprentice, surrounded by Walt Disney's uncontrollable brooms, because the urchins' gleeful dancing had spiralled out of control, they were twirling in the headlights of

motor cars and scooters, running wild, until the whistling of policemen scattered them, leaving Virus, flute in hand, to look dumbly
shamefaced and hang his head as a white-gloved officer lectured him
about the dangers of obstructing traffic.

The next morning, a Sunday, Ardaviraf Cama broke his father's
nineteen-year-old embargo on music and brought melody back to the
flat at Apollo Bunder. When Sir Darius was closeted in his library and
Lady Spenta was taking "charitea" at Dolly Kalamanja's, Virus searched
his mother's boudoir; found what he was looking for in a small chest
of jewellery that sat on his mother's dressing table; knocked on
Ormus's door; and held out, for his amazed brother to inspect, a silver
locket containing a small key. Ormus Cama, hardly able to believe his
eyes, meekly followed the newly determined Virus into the drawing
room, where his silent sibling removed the dust cover from the long-
forbidden baby grand, unlocked the magic keys with his own magic
key, sat down, and launched into what had already become one of the
most celebrated riffs in popular music. Ormus shook his head, amazed.
"When did *you* learn about Bo Diddley?" he demanded; received no
answer; and began to sing.

Enter Sir Darius Xerxes Cama, his hands over his ears, listing slightly
to port, followed by the butler Gieve bearing a whiskey tumbler on a
tray. "You sound like a goat with its throat cut," he raged at Ormus, in
unconscious imitation of all the fathers raging at that very moment, all
around the world, against these devil's tunes. But then Sir Darius
caught Ardaviraf's eye and stopped, discomfited. Virus began to smile.

"It was because of you," Sir Darius said weakly. "Because of the
injury to you. But of course, if you want—I can't stop you—how can
I deny?"

Virus's smile grew broader. In that awesome instant, which signalled
the end of his patriarchal power over his own home, and in spite of the
turbulence of his emotions, Sir Darius felt his own facial muscles
twitch, as if a smile were trying to climb on to his face, like a spider,
against his will. He turned and fled. "Tell Spenta," he called over his
shoulder, "I've gone to the club."

Virus launched into a new tune. *Oh, yes, I'm the Great Pretender,* sang
Ormus Cama, *pretending that I'm over you.*

• • •

His tongue untied by his tongue-tied brother, Ormus Cama at last began to utilize his prodigious gifts; for he was a prodigy from the start, he had only to touch an instrument to become a virtuoso player, only to attempt a style of singing to master it. Music flooded from him. Liberated, he sat beside smiling Ardaviraf at the piano every day and taught him a dozen new tunes. And when he visited Vina at Villa Thracia he plucked and strummed and whanged away at her battered old three-quarter-size guitar (Piloo Doodhwala had sent her few possessions round the day after Ormus's joker trumped his ace), and our house too grew full of the new music. At first Ormus played only the songs he had half learned from Gayomart in his dreams, singing those strange vowel sequences of his that made no sense to anyone, or fitting nonsensical words to them that utterly undermined the mysterious authority of the dream-music:

"The ganja, my friend, is growing in the tin; the ganja is growing in the tin."

(And then, diminuendo:)

"The dancer is glowing with her sin. The gardener is mowing with a grin. The ganja is growing in the tin."

"For Pete's sake, Ormus," Vina protested, giggling.

"But that's what it sounds like," he'd complain, sheepishly. "It's hard to hear."

After a few such failures he agreed to stick to the current hit parade. Sure enough, however, one thousand and one nights later, "Blowin' in the Wind" hit the airwaves in its authentic version and Ormus shouted at me, "Do you see now? Don't you see?"

Such things kept happening, there's no denying it; and whenever one of Gayomart Cama's melodies burst through from the world of dreams into the real world, those of us who had heard them for the first time in garbled form in a Bombay villa on the old Cuffe Parade were forced to concede the reality of Ormus's magic gift.

If he found opportunities to play Vina his other creations, the ones she had sent him in search of—I mean his own songs, the music that belonged to him alone—I never knew it. But it was during these years of waiting, when he was writing copiously, flowing like an undammed stream, that he wrote those first, naked love songs. *I didn't know how to be in love,* he wrote, *until she came home from Rome. And I believed in god above until she came home from Rome.* (Well, no, he didn't, as a matter of fact, but truth yielded to the harsh necessities of rhyme.) *But now you fit me like a glove. You be my hawk, I'll be your dove. And we don't need no god above, now that you're home from Rome.* And even more devotional than that was the joyful genuflection, the teenage prayer, of the anthemic "Beneath Her Feet": *What she touches, I will worship it. The clothes she wears, her classroom seat. Her evening meal, her driving wheel. The ground beneath her feet.*

This is the tale of Ormus Cama, who found the music first.

Lady Spenta Cama's feelings for Ormus remained, let us say, muted. Ardaviraf was her darling, however, and so, although she shared her husband's low opinion of the grunts and hiccups of Ormus's so-called singing, she was unable to ask the brothers to desist. The return of music to Apollo Bunder only increased her determination to marry off her youngest son as soon as possible. Ever since he had finished school with an academic record that brought shame and dishonour to his family, Ormus had been on the loaf: idle, without direction, except with regard to girls. Parents of students at the Cathedral Girls' School had lately started complaining to Lady Spenta that her son was in the habit of lounging against a wall across the road from the school entrance, idly picking his teeth while allowing his hips, very slowly, to gyrate, and that these gyrations were putting the girls off their homework. Ormus, when confronted by Lady Spenta, did not attempt to deny the charge. From the start the extreme sensuality of his body was an effect he produced unconsciously; he never felt responsible for it and so, naturally, accepted no responsibility for its effects. He had music on the brain, he shrugged, and it made his body move without his knowing why or how. What the girls thought about it was neither his business nor his fault. "Boy seems feckless," Lady Spenta complained to Sir Darius. "Lacking in ambition, giving backchat, nothing but music between his ears. Good for nothing, he will turn bad for everything if we do not intervene."

Persis Kalamanja was the perfect answer. The girl was beautiful, had the disposition of a saint, and unaccountably gave every sign of adoring Ormus. Also, her parents were loaded. Sir Darius's long retirement had severely eroded the Cama bank balances, and—at least in Lady Spenta's opinion—Ormus owed it to his mother and father to restore the family's financial health. Patangbaz "Pat" Kalamanja and his wife Dolly hailed from Kenya but had made their fortune in post-war London, manufacturing cheap radios and alarm clocks under the Dollytone name, and diversifying, as Kalatours, into the travel agency business, specializing in flights between the countries of the then-exploding Indian diaspora. Business was booming in fifties Britain, and Pat Kalamanja was obliged to base himself in Wembley most of the year, but Dolly had "fully relocated to the mother country," bought one of the finest old bungalows on Malabar Hill from old Mr. Evans of the Bombay Company, spent a fortune on ruining it, developed a hunger for respectability, and wanted a piece of Sir Darius's baronetcy as passionately as Lady Spenta wanted Pat Kalamanja's cash.

"Wants to sing, eh?" Lady Spenta snorted at her husband. "Dollytone radios will sing for him. Wants to dance up a storm? Travel business will lead him to calmer waters. Also, there is the British connection," she added, slyly, knowing the effect it would have on Sir Darius the arch-Anglophile.

Sir Darius's eyes glittered. He agreed at once to his wife's plan. "Older families are put off by the mistakes of you-know-who," she reasoned (it was the closest she would come to mentioning Cyrus Cama's nineteen murders), "so these Kalamanjas have fallen from the heavens, like a beautiful cut kite."

The problem was Vina. After their meeting, Ormus gravely informed his mother that as he had inadvertently fallen in love, the engagement to the beauteous Persis was unfortunately out of the question. When he identified the object of his improbable affections, his mother—who had assumed that the new light in Ormus's eye, the new lightness in his step, the new eagerness with which he greeted each new day, was because of Persis, and was therefore the result of her parental good judgement—flew into a pop-eyed rage. "You devil! That twelve-year-old penniless brat from nobody and nowhere?" she shrieked. "Get this into your head: that's a non-starter, sonny jim." Lady Spenta and Dolly Kalamanja both agreed to proceed with their plans as if nothing had happened. "It will blow over," Dolly assured her friend determinedly. "Boys will be boys, before and after marriage, but they can still be good husbands and all." This remark rather shocked Lady Spenta, but she held her tongue.

A few days later, Persis Kalamanja and Ormus Cama were taken by their respective parents on a joint family outing to the Exwyzee Milk Colony. They were encouraged to wander off by themselves among the greenery and cows, and when they were out of earshot, gorgeous Persis, whom most young men would happily have died for, asked about her under-age rival. "Look, you can tell me, it's okay, I won't be upset," she said. "Never mind what our mothers want. Love is too important to lie about." Ormus, looking awkward for once in his graceful life, confessed that he had no idea how it had happened, but that day at the record store he had met the only girl he would ever love. Persis took it on the chin, set aside all her own hopes, nodded seriously and promised to help. From that moment until Vina's six-teenth birthday, Persis joined Ormus and Vina in a conspiracy of small and large deceits. For a start, she announced to her mother that she was not at all sure about this supposed god's gift, Ormus Cama; she was one pretty high-calibre female herself and did not intend to buy the first goods her mother picked off the peg, and if it was to be Ormus then she would need a good long period in which to satisfy herself that he was an option which she was prepared, after weighing all the pros and cons, to select. "Girls today, too modern, I swear," sighed Dolly Kala-manja, and might have tried to force the marriage through, except that Persis appealed to her father Pat in England, and Patangbaz Kalamanja told Dolly that his beloved daughter wasn't going to be parcelled off to anybody if she didn't want to be posted, so that was that: Dolly sulked, but settled for a long "pre-engagement." Every month or so, Dolly would complain that her daughter was taking too long to decide, and Persis would invariably reply, "But a wife is for life, and that's too long to be wrong." Persis the Great Pretender, the beard. At night she would cry herself to sleep. And Ormus and Vina were so wrapped up in each other that they never really paid attention to the beautiful girl who gave up her own hope for their sake. Yet it is Persis who, in many ways, was the true heroine of the story of their love.

She would tell her mother she had arranged to meet Ormus for coffee, or "chips and swimming at the Willingdon"; or that he was taking her to one of the Sunday morning jazz "jam sessions" that were becoming popular, back then, in certain Colaba restaurants; or that there was a "good flick" on. "Love picture?" Dolly would greedily enquire, and Persis would nod, giving every appearance of excitement. *"Love Is a Many-Splendored Thing,"* she would reply, or, later, *"An Affair to Remember,"* and Dolly would nod, "Excellent! Get him in the mood!" And off Persis would go, driving herself down Malabar Hill in her Hindustan Ambassador to her empty assignation. For indeed she did meet Ormus at the club or restaurant or café or cinema in question, so that technically she had not lied to her mother; but a few moments later, Vina would arrive, and Persis would leave without a word. Those lonely hours, when she roamed the city alone until she could go home without blowing the lovers' alibi, were like a hole in her life, a wound through which all her hope and much of her joy seeped out. "I think of those times covering up for Ormie as the love affair we never had," she wrote to me. "He was with me, I told myself, he was right there by my side, but of course he wasn't, it was all foolishness. Not many-splendoured. Not worth remembering. But me, I couldn't forget."

Between the self and the other, between the visionary and the psychopath, between the lover and his love, between the overworld and the underworld, falls the Shadow.

Time passes. Now, in his dreams, Ormus still chases Gayomart through that Las Vegas of the subterranean world, but as often, or perhaps more often, he stands face-to-face with himself on the streets of an unknown but familiar city, and listens to what his own dream-image has to say. He is still young.

The world is not cyclical, not eternal or immutable, but endlessly transforms itself, and never goes back, and we can assist in that transformation.

Live on, survive, for the earth gives forth wonders. It may swallow your heart, but the wonders keep on coming. You stand before them bareheaded, shriven. What is expected of you is attention.

Your songs are your planets. Live on them but make no home there.

What you write about, you lose. What you sing, leaves you on the wings of song.

Sing against death. Command the wildness of the city.

Freedom to reject is the only freedom. Freedom to uphold is dangerous.

Life is elsewhere. Cross frontiers. Fly away.

Vina Apsara is looking for someone to follow, and Ormus is discovering how to lead. They read books together, looking for answers. In the beginning was water and slime, Vina reads aloud. Out of this, Time was born, three-headed, a snake. Time made the shining air and a yawning gulf, and in the air he hung a silver egg. The egg split, and so on. The part that interests Ormus is the twofold nature of man. Who is both Titanic and Dionysiac, both earthly and divine. By purification, asceticism and ritual, we may purge the Titanic element, we may cleanse ourselves of what is earthly, physical. The flesh is weak, evil, contaminated and corrupt. We must strip ourselves of it. We must prepare for becoming divine.

No, Ormus shouts. They are in the Hanging Gardens, surrounded by topiary elephants and evening hedonists, and his cry attracts attention. He moderates his voice. It is the opposite that's true. We must purge ourselves of the divine and prepare to enter fully into the flesh. We must purge ourselves of the natural and prepare to enter fully into what we ourselves have built, the man-made, the artificial, the artifice, the construct, the trick, the joke, the song.

Yes, she murmurs. The flesh, the living flesh.

What is apparent is what there is. The hidden world is a lie.

There are contradictions here. Even as she believes him, believes with the force of her needing to believe, the force of her need of him, she is half aware of another side, not only to her nature, but to his. For she is—will be—Dionysiac, divine, and so is—so will—he. They will drive people mad with desire, with music, will leave behind them long trails of destruction and delight. Is pleasure an aspect of reason or of dreams?

She asks: Why do you look for your brother in that dream-house?

My brother is dead, he shouts, turning more heads. Leave him out of this. My brother Gayomart who was never even alive.

Touch me, she pleads. Hold me, hold my hand.

He will not. He has sworn an oath.

He cannot touch her. She is not a child, not remotely a child, and yet she is a child. In his dreams, and in waking visions, he sees her body growing, sees her breasts begin to bud and flower, the coming of bodily hair and the red blood staining her thighs. He feels her move beneath his hand, feels himself tense and grow at her rough and tender touch. In the privacy of his thoughts he is a voluptuary, feral, criminal, but in the real world, which feels daily more unreal, he plays, for the first time in his life, the perfect gentleman.

She, Vina, will always boast about this on his behalf. "He waited for me." It makes her proud: of him, but also of herself. To be worth so serious a love. (I waited for her too, but she did not boast about me.)

The bruise on his eyelid is sore. His mother and father fight in him, Lady Spenta's angels and mysteries, Sir Darius's vaunted Apollonian rationalism. Though it could also be said that Lady Spenta with her good works is battling with the real world, its diseases, its cruelties, while Sir Darius, sunk in the unreality of his library, is living more than one kind of lie.

Living brothers fight in him too, violent and serene. His dead twin recedes.

Reason and the imagination, the light and the light, do not coexist peacefully.

They are both powerful lights. Separately or together, they can blind you.

Some people see well in the dark.

Vina, watching him grow, hearing the struggle of his thoughts, feeling the anguish of his controlled desires, sees a light around him. It is the future, perhaps. He will be bathed in light. He will be her perfect lover. He will command multitudes.

He is fragile too. Without her love, terminally alienated, he might go horribly wrong. The idea of family, of community, is almost dead in him. There is only silent Virus and their piano sessions. Otherwise he has come loose, like an astronaut floating away from a space capsule. He is a layabout who hears only the vowel sounds of cheap music, who makes meaningless noises. He could easily amount to nothing. He might fail to add up to a person.

• • •

(It is said that when Kama, the love god, committed the crime of trying to shoot mighty Shiva with a dart of love, the great god burned
him to ashes with a thunderbolt. Kama's wife, the goddess Rati,
pleaded for his life, and softened Shiva's heart. In an inversion of the
Orpheus myth, it was the woman who interceded with the deity and
brought Love—Love itself!—back from the dead. . . . So also Ormus
Cama, exiled from love by the parents whom he had failed to transfix
with love's arrow, shrivelled by their lack of affection, is restored to the
world of love by Vina.)

He clings to her, without touching her. They meet and whisper and
shout and make each other up. Each is Pygmalion, both are Galatea.
They are a single entity in two bodies: male and female constructed
they themselves. You are my only family, he tells her. You are my only
earth. These are heavy burdens, but she bears them willingly, asks for
more, burdens him identically in return. They have both been damaged, are both repairers of damage. Later, entering that world of ruined
selves, music's world, they will already have learned that such damage
is the normal condition of life, as is the closeness of the crumbling
edge, as is the fissured ground. In that inferno, they will feel at home.

6

DISORIENTATIONS

In the autumn of 1960, when Vina Apsara was about to reach the magic age of sixteen, Sir Darius Xerxes Cama at last made the journey to England of which he had dreamed for so many years. In these latter days of his life Sir Darius had yielded to his wife's entreaties and resumed his studies in the field of Indo-European myth. (Lady Spenta hoped for the eradication of her husband's ruinous whisky addiction by an earlier, more valuable intoxication.) A new generation of European scholars, including many brilliant young Englishmen, was ridding the field of its unjust Nazi taint and introducing new levels of sophistication to what now looked like the first stumblings of Müller, Dumézil and the rest. Sir Darius in his library tried to excite Lady Spenta, as he himself was excited, by this new thinking, which had done so much to refine and amplify understanding of "sovereignty," "physical force" and "fertility," the three primary concepts of the Indo-European worldview. However, no sooner had he begun to explain the thrilling new proposition that each member of the conceptual triad also functioned as a sub-concept within each category than Lady Spenta's heavy body appeared to deliquesce into a languid jelly. Sir Darius, pressing on, insisted that "sovereignty" was now to be sub-divided into "sovereignty within sovereignty," "force within sovereignty," and "fertility within sovereignty"; while "physical force" and "fertility" were likewise, "by the same token," to be rendered tripartite. "I have a headache," said the jelly at this point, and wobbled off at high speed.

Sir Darius did indeed turn away from whisky. However, his distress at what he saw as the culture's general decline did not diminish. Left to his own devices, Sir Darius reflected on how his own family circumstances reflected this decline. As head of the household, he possessed sovereignty within sovereignty by right, both in its magical, terrifying and remote aspect and in the more legalistic and familiar meaning of the term; but while he had certainly grown remote from his children, it was a long time since anyone had thought him the smallest whit magical or terrifying. As for force within sovereignty, which he interpreted as the protection of the family's solidarity and continuity, especially by its younger members, its "warriors," well, that was just a joke. "We have slipped," he reflected aloud, "to the point at which we are mired in the lowest sub-section of the third concept, fertility within fertility, which, in our case, means no more than indolence, dreams and music."

Sir Darius's own scholarly efforts received their reward: a paper under his name—" 'Sent to Coventry': or, Is There a Fourth Function?"—was accepted for publication in the esteemed *Proceedings of the Society of Euro-Asiatic Studies,* and he was invited to deliver it, in the form of a lecture, at the Society's annual general meeting in Burlington House. His subject was the hypothetical "fourth concept" of "outsiderness," the condition of the leper, pariah, outcast or exile, whose necessity he had intuited long ago, and his evidence in support of his arguments ranged from the casteless Untouchables of India (Gandhi's Harijans, Ambedkar's Dalits) to the Judgement of Paris; for did not Paris himself embody the outsider in this vitally significant myth? Alternatively, the outsider was Strife, the goddess who produced the golden apple. Either way, the example stood.

Now that he was sober, Sir Darius's terrible secret had begun to prey upon him ever more hungrily, in his waking hours as well as during his recurring dreams of the naked figure of Scandal in the pure white country house, and the growing conviction that he himself was a pariah such as those of whom he wrote, or ought to be, and might yet become one if his great Lie became known, lent his work a passion that made his sentences blaze from the page. He was an isolated old gentleman by this time. Even the consolations of Freemasonry were no longer available; the order's Indian membership had drifted away after the end of Empire, and Sir Darius had long since ceased to participate in such threadbare encounters as continued to take place in a new lodge as shabbily paltry as the old lodge had been grand. (Lately he had been remembering his estranged friend, brother Mason and erstwhile squash partner Homi Catrack, and had even suggested to his wife that they should ask the fellow over and renew the old association; where-upon Lady Spenta had to remind him gently that Catrack was dead, sensationally gunned down with his paramour in their love nest by a cuckolded naval officer some three years previously. The case had filled the newspapers for months, but Sir Darius had somehow failed to notice.)

The invitation to England offered an end to this shadow life of his, in which he flitted through the background of events in which he took no part. "And there is Methwold too," he said to Lady Spenta, brightening. "What times we'll have! The grouse moors! The Athenaeum! English honey! What larks!"

Lady Spenta bit her lip. Sir Darius's Anglophilia had intensified with the passage of the years. He frequently praised "U.K." for the grace of its withdrawal from Empire, and also for the "pluck" with which that war-battered nation had rebuilt itself. (No mention was made of Marshall Aid.) India, by contrast, he constantly chided for its "stasis," its "backwardness." He wrote innumerable letters to the newspapers deriding the Five-Year Plans. "What use are steel mills if we sink into ignorance of our natures?" he would thunder. "The greatness of Britain stands squarely upon the Three Concepts . . ." These letters were not published, but he continued to write them. In the end Lady Spenta did not bother to have them posted, but destroyed them privately, without hurting his feelings.

Why did William Methwold no longer write? Sir Darius frequently asked this question, without guessing that Lady Spenta could answer the question if she chose to do so. "Perhaps it is because of my research," Sir Darius wondered. "Possibly he is still squeamish about the old stigma attached to the field. He is a public servant, of course, and must be careful. No matter! When we dine together I will put him straight."

"Go if you must. I will not go with you," Lady Spenta told her husband. Not knowing how to warn him of the humiliation that awaited him in his beloved England, she chose not to witness his destruction. He left on a BOAC Super Constellation, wearing a courtroom shirt of Egyptian cotton with stiffly starched collar and cuffs, and a three-piece suit of finest worsted, with a fob chain glinting upon his belly. Lady Spenta saw on his face the look of tragic innocence worn by goats on their way to the slaughterhouse. She had written to Lord Methwold begging him "if possible, to be kind."

Methwold was not kind. In spite of Sir Darius's urgent letters, and Lady Spenta's own private pleas, he neither met his old friend at Heathrow Airport, nor sent anyone to meet him, nor invited him to stay, nor offered to put him up at his club. Lady Spenta had taken the precaution of asking Dolly Kalamanja to send her husband Patangbaz to the airport, and it was Pat's jolly round face that greeted Sir Darius in the crude arrivals shed (the airport was still under construction at that time, and facilities for passengers were substantially worse than those at Bombay's Santa Cruz). Sir Darius looked haggard and dishevelled at the end of his gruelling journey and equally gruelling interrogation by immigration officials who were bewilderingly unimpressed by his explanations, his credentials or even his knighthood, news of which they treated with extreme scepticism. His repeated references to the eminent Lord Methwold elicited only hollow laughter. After several hours of questioning, Sir Darius was finally released into England, a confused and somewhat punctured man.

Pat Kalamanja's Wembley home was a spacious suburban mansion in red brick equipped with fake white pilasters and columns to give it a more classically impressive air. Kalamanja himself was affable, good-natured, anxious to do the right thing by the father of his future son-in-law, and extremely busy, so that while Sir Darius was given the run of the house he saw his host for no more than a few snatched meals. During these brief encounters Sir Darius was terse and preoccupied. At breakfast, Pat Kalamanja, a business tycoon down to his well-pared fingernails and a man uneasy with small talk, did his best to put his guest at ease. "Nawab of Pataudi! What a cricketer! Blanchflower's Hotspurs! Hell of a football team!" At dinner, he offered political commentary. In the forthcoming American elections, Mr. Kalamanja strongly favoured Richard M. Nixon, because of that gentleman's "plain speaking" to the Russki leader Khrushchev during a visit to a model kitchen in a Moscow trade fair. "Kennedy? Too pretty; means too tricky, what do you say?" But Sir Darius's thoughts were elsewhere.

He spent the empty days telephoning his friend Methwold without reaching him, sending reply-paid telegrams to which no reply was given, and even, on one occasion, making the long journey by bus and Tube train to the door of the Methwold mansion in Campden Hill Square, to leave a long and injured letter of reproach. Finally Lord Methwold did get in touch. A terse note arrived at Wembley, inviting Sir Darius to walk with him, the next morning, in the grounds of Middle Temple, "of which you no doubt have many memories you may possibly wish to re-live."

It was enough. Sir Darius Xerxes Cama understood everything. All spirit left him, and he deflated completely. Mr. Kalamanja, returning home in the evening, found a darkened living room and his guest slumped in a chair beside a cold fire with an empty bottle of Johnnie Walker rolling at his feet. He feared the worst until Sir Darius moaned loudly in his sleep, the moan of a soul caught in the burning pincers of a demon. In his dream Sir Darius was surrendering to Scandal's embrace. He felt his body catch fire as he was consumed by his disgrace and shame, and screamed out at the top of his voice. Patangbaz Kalamanja rushed forward and hugged him. He awoke red-eyed and shivering, pushed good-hearted Pat aside and rushed from the room. The next morning, a crumpled and haunted figure, he asked Kalamanja if his travel agency could get him on an earlier flight home. He offered no explanation and his host did not know him well enough to ask for one. Sir Darius flew back to Bombay without meeting William

Methwold, without delivering his paper on the Fourth Function, and without any remaining ambition in life except one—to die in peace— which he would also fail to fulfil. On his return he unearthed his proudest possessions from the Godrej steel filing cabinet where they had lain under lock and key for half a lifetime, the precious letters patent pertaining to his knighthood, and returned them to the British Consulate in Bombay. His story was over. He shut himself up in his library with a bottle, and waited for the end.

We leave home not only to make room for ourselves but to avoid the sight of our elders running out of steam. We don't want to see the consequences of their natures and histories catching up with them and beating them, the closing of the trap of life. Feet of clay will cripple us, too, in our turn. Life's bruises demythologise us all. The earth gapes. It can wait. There's plenty of time.

Two visions broke my family: my mother Ameer's vision of the "scrapers," the giant concrete-and-steel exclamations that destroyed forever the quieter syntax of the old city of Bombay; and my father's fantasy of a cinema. It was Vina Apsara's great misfortune to put down roots in us, and to idealize my parents as the joint architects of a storybook happy home, just as our little clan started to come apart. "Rai," she once said to me, "you're a lucky bastard, but also a sweetheart, because you don't mind sharing your luck."

Luck runs out. My parents had fallen off their pedestals well before their early demises. Easy to list their faults. My father's great weakness was gambling, in the indulgence of which he took heavy losses. By 1960 these had moved beyond the mere forfeit of small mountains of matchsticks and grown into debts as sizeable but less easily redeemed. He lost at cards, he lost on the horses, he lost at dice, and he had fallen, too, into the clutches of a "private bookmaker" who called himself Raja Jua, "for Chance is the King of all, from our Betters to the Best," and who permitted serious Bombay gamblers to bet on whatever they chose: the outcome of a murder trial, the likelihood of an Indian invasion of Goa, the number of clouds that might cross the western sky in a day, the crucial first week's gross of a new movie, the size of a dancer's breasts. Even the ancient rain game, the *barsaat-ka-satta,* a bet on when the rains would come and how much would fall, was a gamble against which Raja Jua, the prince of bookmakers, would give odds. Bombay has always been a high rollers' town. However, my innocent father, V. V. Merchant, was not so much the roller as the rolled.

As for my mother: her cynicism, once just a pose, an idealist's armour, her defence against the corruption that was all around her, had itself corroded her youthful principles. I accuse her of being willing to destroy what was beautiful for the sake of what was profitable, and to rename these categories "yesterday" and "tomorrow." She was at the forefront of the builders' lobby that was working flat out to scupper the "second city" project for a New Bombay across the harbour in favour of more immediately lucrative land reclamation schemes at Nariman Point and—yes!—at Cuffe Parade as well. It was the proposed Cuffe Parade redevelopment that horrified Vivvy Merchant. All his life my father had faced the internal struggle between his love for the history and glories of the old Bombay and his professional involvement in the creation of the city's future. The prospect of the destruction of the most beautiful stretch of seafront in the city drove him into permanent, but unfortunately silent, opposition to his wife. Silent, because Ameer was still a woman who could brook no criticism. The merest hint that she might be acting improperly would have been enough to induce a storm of weeping and a quarrel that would not end until he abased himself and agreed that he had utterly and cruelly wronged her, and that her injured innocence fully justified her high dudgeon and copious tears. V. V. Merchant, unable to talk to her about his grave concerns, was obliged, instead, to follow the dictates of his nature, and dig.

He could dig in people as easily as in sand. Digging into me, as I grew, he found out one of my secrets. "This photography of yours," he said, speaking for once in short, clear words, "no doubt it is very much liked by pretty young girls?" And I was too inhibited to reply, Yes, Father, but that isn't the point. Your Paillard Bolex, your Rolleiflex and Leica, your collection of the works of Dayal and Haseler: those are my inspirations and spurs. And photography, too, is a kind of digging. I said none of that, though it would have made him proud to hear it. Instead

I quipped, "Yeah, that's it, Daddy-o." He winced faintly, smiled a vague smile and turned away.

But when he dug in my mother, he didn't turn away. He went on until he dug up what would ruin her; and thus destroyed himself.

And that whitest of white elephants, the Orpheum cinema, into which he sank the business's capital with a wanton zeal that even Ameer Merchant was unable to restrain—wasn't that, in its suicidal way, an answer to his wife and her cartel of futurist vandals? In his vision of the theatre, he saw it as a Deco temple for the 1960s, at once a tribute to the city's golden period and a money-spinning Mecca for our movie-crazy city's host of "fillum" fans. But this, too, was a gamble that went badly wrong. Building costs spiralled upwards, the borrowing requirement got out of control, and the dishonesty of sub-contractors resulted in the use of materials and fittings well below specification. Rival cinema bosses bribed municipal inspectors to quibble over approvals and tie up the project in red tape. Ameer, her attention elsewhere, left the Orpheum to Vivvy; unwisely, as it turned out. In the end, Vivvy's gambling debts obliged him to offer the deeds to the new cinema as collateral to Raja Jua. He did not know, at that time, the name of the man for whom this Jua worked.

On my thirteenth birthday my father gave me a pretty serious German camera, a Voigtländer Vito CL, with a built-in light meter and a hot-shoe port for a flash gun, and the first photographs I took were of Vina Apsara, singing. She was better than Radio Ceylon. Most evenings, we'd gather round and she'd let fly with that perfect voice, which grew bigger and richer by the week, by turns dirty-knowledgeable and angel-pure. That voice which had started on its road to immortality. To listen to Carly Simon sing "Bridge Over Troubled Water" is to understand how much Guinevere Garfunkel brought to the table in that partnership. So it was in the great days of VTO. There are bands that are hit machines, bands that earn the respect of the music crowd, bands that fill stadiums, bands that drip sex; transcendent bands and ephemeral, boy bands and girl bands, gimmick bands and inept bands, beach and driving bands, summer and winter bands, bands to make love by and bands that make you memorize the words to every song they play. Most bands are awful, and if there are aliens from other galaxies monitoring our radio and tv waves, they're probably being driven crazy by the din. And in the whole half-century-long history of rock music there is a small number of bands, a number so small you could count to it without running out of fingers, who steal into your heart and become a part of how you see the world, how you tell and understand the truth, even when you're old and deaf and foolish. On your deathbed you'll hear them sing to you as you drift down the tunnel towards the light: Shh . . . Sha-sha . . . Sha-la-la-la-la . . . Shang-a-lang,   shang-a-lang . . . Sh-boom . . . Shoop . . . Shoop . . . Shh. It's all over now.

VTO was one of those bands. And Ormus had the vision, but Vina had the voice, and it was the voice that did it, it's always the voice; the beat catches your attention and the melody makes you remember but it's the voice against which you're defenceless, the unholy cantor, the profane muezzin, the siren call that knows its way directly to the rhythm center, the soul. Never mind what kind of music. Never mind what kind of voice. When you hear it, the real thing, you're done for, trust me on this. Finito, unless you're tied like Odysseus to the mast of your ship, with clay stopping up your ears. That goose of yours? It's fried.

I think, now, that it was Vina's singing that was holding us together in those days. She was our rock, not the other way around. While V.V. Merchant plunged into debt, and also, silently, investigated his wife, assembling a thick dossier on her illegal manipulation of the city's decision makers—while, in short, a time bomb was ticking beneath our lives—Vina sang to us, reminding us of love.

O fierce intensity of childhood seeing! As children we're all photographers, needing no cameras, burning images into memories. I remember our neighbours on Cuffe Parade, their pretensions, their happy and unhappy marriages, their quarrels, their motor cars, their sunglasses, their handbags, their discoloured smiles, their kindnesses, their dogs. I remember the weekends with their odd, imported pastimes. My parents playing golf at the Willingdon, my father doing his best to lose to my mother in order to preserve her good mood. I remember a couple of Navjotes spent guzzling food served on the leaves of plantain trees, several Holis drenched in colour, and at least one visit to the giant prayer maidan on Big Eid, which sticks in the mind because it was so rare. I think my father just wanted me to appreciate what I was missing and why. I remember my friend sweet Neelam Nath, who grew up to die with her children in the Air-India crash off the Irish coast. I remember Jimmy King with his pasty complexion and spiky black fringe; he died young, suddenly, at school. All the classroom doors and windows were closed so that we couldn't see his father driving into the quadrangle to take his son's body home. I remember a long, skinny boy clambering across the rocks at Scandal Point with his friends. He looked through me as if I weren't there. Gold Flake posters, the Royal Barber Shop, the pungent mingled smells of putrefaction and hope. Forget Mumbai. I remember Bombay.

Then they gave me a camera, a mechanical eye to replace the mind's eye, and after that, much of what I remember is what the camera managed to snatch out of time. No longer a memoirist but a voyeur, I remember photographs.

Here's one. It's Vina's sixteenth birthday, and we're at the Gaylord restaurant on Vir Nariman Road, eating chicken Kiev. My mother and father both wear unfamiliar expressions. He looks angry, she seems distracted, vague. Vina, by contrast, glows. All the light in the photograph seems to have been sucked towards her. We are shadowy bodies revolving around her sun. Ormus Cama sits beside her, like a dog begging to be fed. Half of me is in the picture too. I asked a waiter to take the photo but he didn't frame it right. It doesn't matter. I remember what I looked like. I looked the way you look when you're about to lose the thing that matters most.

On the ring finger of Vina's right hand was a glowing moonstone, her birthday gift from Ormus. She had already slept with the ring under her pillow for a week, to test it out before agreeing to accept it, and her dreams had been so erotic that she had awoken each night in the small hours, trembling with happiness and drenched in yellow sweat.

Ormus is asking permission to take Vina to a "concert." V.V. and Ameer are avoiding each other's eyes, skirting the edges of a fight. "The Five Pennies," Ormus says. "Take Umeed also," says Ameer, waving a hand. Vina looks daggers. They pierce my thirteen-year-old breast.

After the success of the Danny Kaye biopic *The Five Pennies,* its subject, the real-life bandleader Red Nichols, had come to Bombay on tour with a new, reformed bunch of Five. Jazz, stimulated by the weekend-morning jam-session brunches, was still hot in town, and a big crowd gathered. I've got the photographs to prove it, but I can't remember where the concert was. Azad Maidan, Cross Maidan, the Cooperage, or somewhere else. Out of doors, anyhow. I remember a raised stage in the open air. Because my mother had sent me along, Ormus brought Virus as well. The four of us got there early and stood near the front. I was disappointed when the Pennies appeared, because Red Nichols was only a little fellow, and his hair was short and white, not a bit like Danny Kaye's flowing carroty locks. Then he picked up his horn and blew. Trad jazz. I liked it, once in a while, I'll confess. But then Vina always said I had bad taste.

That Five Pennies concert is famous for what happened at the very end of an average sort of set that had failed to get anyone's pulse going. After less than wild applause had died down, the crimson-tuxedoed quintet made ready to go into their encore. "The Saints," what else, but no sooner had Red Nichols named the tune than a member of the audience vaulted on to the stage, waving an Indian wooden flute and grinning his goofy, but also infectious, grin.

"Oh, my God," shouted Ormus Cama, and leapt up on stage after his brother.

"Wait for me," yelled Vina, radiance bursting from her as she followed the Cama boys towards her own inescapable destiny; and that made three invaders. Me, I'm a coward. I stayed in the crowd and took photographs.

Click. Red Nichols's horrified face. He has been warned about India, its huge crowds that can turn, in an instant, into murderous mobs. Had he been resuscitated by Danny Kaye, only to die by being trampled under-foot in Bombay? *Click.* Virus Cama's smile works its magic, and the old bandleader's horror is replaced by a look of amused indulgence. *Click.* What the hey. Let the dumb guy play. And you, both of you? What do you do? *Click.* Vina Apsara steps up to the microphone. "We sing."

> *Oh when the sun (oh when the sun)*
> *begin to shine (begin to shine).*

Ardaviraf Cama's playing was undoubtedly skilful, but the music came out of his flute sounding inappropriate; it was a sound in a different currency, an anna trying to be a penny, but it didn't matter, partly because he was happy enough tootling away, and partly because the crafty Nichols had turned off his mike, so if you weren't in the first couple of rows you couldn't hear him at all; but mostly because the minute Ormus and Vina opened their mouths and began to sing, everybody just stopped thinking about anything else. When they had finished, the audience was cheering wildly, and Nichols paid them the compliment of saying they were so good that he didn't mind being upstaged.

The concert was over, the crowd was drifting away, but I stood rooted to the spot, taking photographs. The world was cracking. Ormus and Vina were deep in conversation with the musicians, who were packing up their instruments and shouting at the local stage-hands to watch what they were doing. My heart was breaking. While Ormus and Vina chatted to the jazzmen, their hands and bodies were talking to each other. *Click, click.* I can see you, you two. *Click.* Peek-aboo! Do you know I'm doing this? Are you letting me watch, is that it, even though I'm getting the goods on you, in here, in my little German box of wonders? You don't care any more, is that it? You want it all out in the open. *Click.* And what about me, Vina? I'll grow up too. He waited for you. Why wouldn't you wait for me? I want to be in that number!

From the start my place was in a corner of their lives, in the shadow of their achievements. Yet I will always believe I deserved better. And there was a time when I almost had it. Not just Vina's body, but her attention. Almost.

The musicians were piling their equipment into a small bus. An invitation had been extended and accepted, and it didn't include me. Ormus came over to chase me off: Ormus rampant, full of sex and music.

"Okay, Rai," quoth he, officiously. "Go with Ardaviraf now, okay? Virus'll get you home." Who do you think you are? I wanted to shout. Do you think I am a baby, to be seen home by the village idiot? But he was already walking away, he was embracing Vina, swinging her off her feet, kissing her, kissing her.

The sky was falling. Virus Cama bared his teeth at me, smiling his idiot smile.

They made love that night in Nichols's suite in the Taj Hotel, a stone's throw from the Cama residence. The great cornet player found himself another room and sent up a lovers' feast, and also the messages that had started to arrive for them, which were sent to the band because nobody knew how else to contact the two singers. There were offers to perform all over town, starting at the hotel itself. But as Vina was proud of recounting, the food and drink was not touched, nor were the letters opened until morning. They had better things to do.

The details of the deflowering of Vina Apsara by Ormus Cama are a matter of public record, placed there long ago by Vina herself, so there's no need to dwell on the exact degree of discomfort (considerable), or on Ormus's compensating expertise as a seducer of virgins (a few years after the event, Vina proudly named and numbered Ormus's previous conquests, thus unleashing a pandemic of scandals throughout Bombay society), or on their early difficulties (he was too gentle for her, too reverent, which annoyed her and made her too aggressive, and too physically rough, for his taste), or on their equally early successes (his caressing of the tiny hollow at the base of her spine, his exploration with the tip of his tongue of the edges of her nostrils, his slow sucking of her closed eyes, the head of his penis pressing into her navel, his finger moving along her perineum, her legs around his neck, her buttocks moving against his sex, her generous mouth, and above all her discovery of the extreme sensitivity, unusual in a man, of his nipples: as you observe, I have not forgotten one single jot or tittle of the lubricious catalogue). Suffice to say that the deed—the deeds—were done; that the lovers did not return to their own beds that night; so that on this occasion joy came at night, and it was the morning that was dark and full of sorrow.

The willingness of Vina Apsara to talk publicly about private matters—her catastrophic childhood, her love affairs, her sexual preferences, her abortions—was as important as her talent, perhaps even more important, in the creation of the gigantic, even oppressively symbolic figure she became. For two generations of women she was something like a megaphone, broadcasting their common secrets to the world. Some felt liberated, others exposed; all commenced to hang upon her every word. (Men, too, were both divided and enthralled, many desiring her greatly, some affecting to find her whorish and repulsive; many loving her for her music, others hating her for the same reason—for whatever elicits great love will invariably call forth hatred also; many fearing her for her mouth, some celebrating her and claiming that she had liberated them as well.) But because she frequently changed her mind, abandoning fervently held positions in favour of their opposites, to which she then also adhered with a flaming certainty that brooked no argument, many women had begun, by the time of the earthquake in Mexico, to see her as a traitor to the very attitudes with which she had helped to set them free.

If she had not died, she might have sunk into a cranky, ignored old age, out of step in a way that was merely wrong- or pig- or muddle-headed, whereas once she had defiantly, triumphantly, been the only one in the parade marching in step, until the other marchers took their lead from her. However, eccentric irrelevance was a fate she was spared. Instead, her death unleashed the full power of the symbol she had constructed. Power, like love, most fully reveals its dimensions only when it is irrevocably lost.

Whenever I think of these events, the Saints start marching through my brain. I picture Ormus and Vina waking in bloodied sheets, held fast in each other's arms. I see them opening the unopened messages and allowing themselves to begin to dream about their professional future as well as the future of their love. I see them dressing, saying their farewells to the American musicians and catching a yellow-and-black taxicab to Cuffe Parade, ready to face the music. And throughout this sequence, there's Red Nichols's cornet playing, or maybe it's Louis Armstrong's trumpet I'm hearing. Oh, when the band begin to play. Oh, when the band begin to play.

The first cloud is about to appear on the horizon. Ormus is speaking important words. "Marry me." He takes the moonstone ring off her right hand and tries to slip it on to her engagement finger. "Marry me right away."

Vina grows tense, resists the moving of the ring. No, she will not marry him. She refuses, turns him down flat, doesn't even need time to think about it. But she does not resist the ring, she accepts it, can't stop looking at it. (The taxi driver, inquisitive, Sikh, is all ears.) "Why not?" Ormus's howl is piteous, even a little pathetic. Vina gives the driver more to enjoy than he could have hoped for. "You are the only man I will ever love," she promises Ormus. "But do you seriously suppose you're also the only guy I will ever fuck?"

(A trumpet—it's definitely Satchmo—comes blaring in. Armstrong's instrument is the golden horn of experience, the trump of worldly wisdom. It laughs—*wuah, wuah*—at the worst that life throws up. It's heard it all before.)

There must be somewhere better than this. It's what we all thought in our different ways. For Sir Darius Xerxes Cama, "somewhere better" was England, but England turned against him, and left him shipwrecked, marooned. For Lady Spenta, the good place was the place of pure illumination, where dwell Ahura Mazda and his angels and the blessed; but that place was far off, and Bombay increasingly felt to her like a labyrinth without an exit. For Ormus Cama, "better" meant abroad, but the choice of that destiny meant the severing of all family ties. For Vina Apsara, the right place was always the one she wasn't in. Always in the wrong place, in a condition of perpetual loss, she could (she did) unaccountably take flight and disappear; and then discover that the new place she'd reached was just as wrong as the place she'd left.

For Ameer Merchant, my cosmopolitan mother, the better place was the city she was going to build. V.V. Merchant, true provincial that he was, was tormented by the idea that the good place had existed, we had possessed and occupied it, and now it was being destroyed, and in its obliteration his beloved wife was profoundly implicated.

It was the year of divisions, 1960. The year the state of Bombay was cut in half, and while new Gujarat was left to its own devices, we Bombayites were informed that our city was now the capital of

Maharashtra. Many of us found this hard to take. Collectively, we began to live in a private Bombay that floated a little way out to sea and held itself apart from the rest of the country; while, individually, each of us became our own Bombay. You can't just keep dividing and slicing—India-Pakistan, Maharashtra-Gujarat—without the effects being felt at the level of the family unit, the loving couple, the hidden soul. Everything starts shifting, changing, getting partitioned, separated by frontiers, splitting, re-splitting, coming apart. Centrifugal forces begin to pull harder than their centripetal opposites. Gravity dies. People fly off into space.

I returned to Cuffe Parade on foot after the Five Pennies concert, having with some difficulty shaken off Virus, to find our home transformed into a war zone: or, more exactly, into a pit of dreadful loss. My parents circled the living-room rug like wrestlers, or as if the Isfahani rug were no longer covering a solid floor of mahogany boards but had become a flimsy cloth flung over a bubbling abyss. Glaring red-eyed at each other, they were facing something worse than the loss of the future, worse than the loss of the past. It was the loss of their love.

Piloo Doodhwala had come to call during my absence: not the over-blown Piloo reclining on a cloud of satraps, whom you have already encountered, but a quieter Piloo, accompanied by a single male associate whom he introduced as Sisodia, a business-suited man in his late thirties, astonishingly small, very heavily bespectacled and balding. He had a terrible stammer and a bulging leather attaché case, out of which he now produced a folder concerning the Cuffe Parade development plan, among whose sponsors, listed on the cover of the dossier, was Mrs. Ameer Merchant of Merchant & Merchant (Pvt.) Ltd. As V. V. Merchant had begun to learn by digging, Ameer had joined forces with Piloo's people to push the scheme through. On a coffee table, Piloo's aide spread out a copy of the official survey map of Cuffe Parade. Many of the villa plots were coloured green for "go." Several were covered in green and white stripes, meaning "under negotiation." Only a very few were coloured red. One of these was Villa Thracia, our home. "Your goodwife has already ist ist stated her con consent to the sus sus sale," explained Mr. Sisodia. "All relevant dada documents are hee hee here. As property is technically under your goo goodname, it will be neck neck necessary for you to sign. Just here," he added, pointing, and holding out a Sheaffer fountain pen.

Vivvy Merchant looked at his wife. Her eyes were stone.

"The scheme is fantastic," she said. "The opportunity is incredible."

Piloo leaned forward in his seat. "Lots of cash," he explained in confidential tones. "Plenty phor all."

My mild father spoke mildly, but his thoughts were not mild. "I knew something was up," he said. "But it has gone much further than I guessed. I take it the city is in your pocket. Land use regulations waived, building height regulations to be flouted with impunity."

"Phixed," nodded Piloo, amiably. "No trouble at all."

Mr. Sisodia rolled out a second chart, the plan of the proposed development. A substantial land reclamation scheme was proposed. "More Cuffe," quipped Piloo, "phor our Parade." But Vivvy was looking elsewhere. "The promenade," he said. "Must be sacriphiced, alas," said Piloo, twisting his mouth downwards in a gesture of regret. "And the mangrove forest," Vivvy wondered. Piloo began to sound a little tetchy. "Sir, we are not building tree houses here, isn't it?"

Vivvy opened his mouth. "Bephore you rephuse," said Piloo, holding up a hand for silence, "consider, please, the phollowing."

Mr. Sisodia rose, went to the front door and let in a second aide, who had evidently been asked to wait outside for his cue. When he entered the living room, V.V. Merchant gasped and seemed visibly to diminish.

The second aide was Raja Jua, the king of bookies. He, too, carried a leather attaché case. From it he now produced a folder containing a full record of my father's debts and all the papers relating to the Orpheum cinema, which he passed to the first aide. "Out of his ha ha high pup pup personal esteem for your lay lady why wife," said Mr. Sisodia, "and to avoid all agra agra aggravations, Pilooji is disposed to dismiss these bag bag bagatelles. Development pot potential runs into sue sue super crores. These outstanding ma ma matters are petty. Only sigh sigh sign the agreement of iss iss sale for Villa Thracia, and all dead dead debts will be wiped clean."

"The deeds to the Orpheum," Ameer said. "How could you do it?"

"And our home," V.V. replied. "How could *you?*"

Piloo's face darkened. "If I was a king phrom the time of the great heroes," he said, "I would challenge you to one more gamble. Win it, and the slate is wiped clean. Lose, and I take your lady wife." He smiled. His teeth glittered in the lamplight. "But I am only a humble man," he said. "So I will settle phor your honour, and your home. Also, Mrs. Merchant agrees to appoint Mr. Sisodia as your cinema in-charge. Good phiscal practice must be restored in our partnership. Mowies are Sisodia's second passion, but money is his phirst."

V.V. Merchant rose to his feet. "I agree to nothing," he said in his mild way. "Now get out." Ameer also rose, but her manner was very different. "What do you mean, get out?" she shouted. "We must just lose everything, everything I have built, we must be cleaned out, because of your weaknesses? Lose the cinema, lose control of the company, lose the biggest capital opportunity of the last twenty years and live in poverty until we have to sell the house anyway, just to eat? Is that what you want?"

"I am sorry," said V.V. Merchant. "I will not sign."

There must be somewhere better. Oh, most lethal of ideas! For Piloo Doodhwala was the only one of us who accepted the condition of life as it was, as a given. He did not fritter away his energies on deranged utopian fantasies. How then could he fail to emerge as the big winner? Our lives lay at his mercy, at his feet. How could it ever have been otherwise?

Piloo slaughtered more than goats. He made big killings in many fields. My life has taken a different route, but I have never forgotten the lesson he taught my father—the lesson my parents' catastrophe taught *me*—while, elsewhere in Bombay, Vina and Ormus were making endless love.

Things are what they are.

All evening, all night, my parents fought. I lay awake in my room unblinking as a lizard and listened to their duelling broken hearts. At dawn my father went to bed but Ameer continued to circle the living room like a spoon in a bowl, stirring up the most poisonous of all rages, the wrath churned in the body by the thrashings of dying love. And then Vina and Ormus walked in, and Ameer, possessed by her rage, rounded upon her young ward.

I am unable in all decency to write down the abuses heaped by my mother upon both the lovers, but particularly on Vina. She screamed at her for three hours and twenty-one minutes without appearing to draw breath, pouring out over the young girl what was meant for Vivvy. When she was done she staggered out of the house, exhausted, and collapsed into her beloved old Packard. It bore her away like a runaway horse. A moment later my hollow-faced father lurched out to the Buick. He, too, drove off so erratically—in the opposite direction to Ameer—that I feared for his life. But neither of them suffered the irrelevance of a traffic accident. They had already been in a near-fatal wreck before leaving home.

Insults are mysteries. What seems to the bystander to be the cruellest, most destructive sledgehammer of an assault, *whore! slut! tart!,* can leave its target undamaged, while an apparently lesser gibe, *thank god you're not my child,* can fatally penetrate the finest suits of armour, *you're nothing to me, you're less than the dirt on the soles of my shoes,* and strike directly at the heart. If I offer no exhaustive catalogue of my mother's harsh remarks, it is also because I am unable to judge their several effects. Was it this phrase or that phrase, this blow or that lash? Was it the mere fact of the tirade, or the cumulative effect of that vitriolic tour de force which left both Ameer and Vina physically drained, like fighters who have wrestled each other to a standstill?

Vina Apsara, a young person who had seen too much, whose trust in the world had been horribly eroded, had slowly allowed herself to believe, during her years at Villa Thracia, that she might be able to stand confidently upon the solid ground of our love. Our love as well as Ormus's. Therefore she in her turn had fallen in love not only with us but with our preoccupations, our city, and our country too, to which she had begun to half believe she might be able, in her own way, to belong. And what my mother did that day pulled away the Isfahani rug of Vina's trust in love itself, and revealed the abyss below.

Vina stood still, no more than semi-conscious, with the palms of her hands facing forward, questioning, expecting no answers, like the survivor of a massacre staring into the face of death. Ormus took her face between the palms of his hands. Very slowly she swayed back and away from his touch. At that moment his great love must have seemed to her like a great trap. To fall into it would be to make possible her utter annihilation at some point in the future, when he would turn on her with a sneer on his face and hatred in his voice. No more risks, her face said. This stops, right now.

Villa Thracia, my beautiful childhood home, burned to the ground three days later. Whoever was responsible took care not to commit murder. No doubt the house was watched until the arsonist was certain it was empty, and then it was thoroughly torched. One by one we returned and assembled on the promenade, to stand with bowed heads while black snow fell all around.

Vina Apsara, however, did not return.

You will forgive me a small lump in the throat as I say farewell to Villa Thracia. It was one of the smaller bungalow-villas on the old Edwardian Cuffe Parade, but ours was only a small family, and it had suited us very well. There was half-timbering around the front-facing casement windows, but the rest of the place was brick, trimmed here and there with stone. Red tiled gables stood over them, and over the front door too, making a quaint little porch. Up above was the house's somewhat pompous—or let us say *confident*—defining feature, a square, centrally positioned neo-classical turret, complete with pilasters and pediments on all four sides. This supported a little dome of scalloped green ceramic tiles, with a rather self-aggrandising mini-spire on top. In this ornate upper chamber my parents had lain during their long happy married years. "It's like sleeping in a bell tower," my mother used to say, and my father would reply, squeezing her hand, "And, my dearest, you indubitably are the tower's belle."

Up in smoke it went. Stripped of possessions, memories and happiness, we thought of the touch of falling ashes on our cheeks as our home's farewell caress. Eyewitnesses to the blaze reported that the fire itself had loved the dying house, hugging it tightly, so that for a few instants Villa Thracia seemed to have been re-created in flame. Then smoke, black, unfeeling smoke, took over, the illusion was destroyed, and darkness covered all.

The destruction of your childhood home—a villa, a city—is like the death of a parent: an orphaning. A tombstone "scraper" stands upon the site of this forgotten cremation. A tombstone city stands upon the graveyard of the lost.

· · ·

Where once stood "Dil Kush," Dolly Kalamanja's lavish three-story mansion on Ridge Road, Malabar Hill, that old-world masterpiece, all galleries and verandahs and light, with its marbled halls, its hurriedly acquired collection of paintings by Souza, Zogoiby and Hussain, and above all its mature tropical gardens boasting some of the oldest tamarind, jackfruit and plane trees in the city, and some of the finest bougainvillaea creeper too, you would now find neither trees nor creepers, neither grace nor space. Sitting like a squat missile on its launch pad, the skyscraper Everest Vilas fills that territory with its grey, discolouring concrete and is unlikely to yield possession any time soon. Everest Vilas is twenty-nine storeys high, but mercifully those are stories I do not need to tell. The phantom past is still standing on Ridge Road whenever I take a look. "Dil Kush" lives, as does the day when Villa Thracia burned and Dolly kindly insisted on giving us shelter under her ample, low-pitched roof.

Ormus arrived, at once exhausted and frenzied. It was late at night, but nobody was going to sleep. Vina was still missing. Ormus had searched high and low for her, rushing around all their favourite haunts, until he began to vomit from the stress. Finally, spent, disoriented, he staggered into "Dil Kush," and such was his shaky, giddy, rudderless wretchedness that Ameer Merchant—who was, it must be said, beginning to be eaten alive by remorse—buttoned her lip. Convinced that Vina had died in the fire, that she'd been turned to smoke and blown away, bereft Ormus spoke of following her beyond the grave. Life had lost all value; death at least had this merit, that it was the only experience he and his beloved could now share. He spoke ominously of self-immolation. It was my father, alarmed by the young man's state of mind, who comforted him. "Keep an open mind," said V.V. Merchant, though the words sounded hollow to us all. "No pertinent evidence of her perishing has as yet been obtained."

Persis Kalamanja, I must say, was looking a little shifty, which at the time I put down to the evident ambiguity of her position; for we could all work out that her hopes of marrying Ormus had received an undeniable, if horrible, fillip. Saintly as she was, Persis could not have failed to wonder about the future: might not her own joyful beginning rise from the ashes of Vina's tragic end? And then, being the tender-hearted young woman she was, she would have worked furiously to suppress such vile imaginings (which were rendered yet more vile by the sensation of delicious anticipation they released in her breast). She lowered her eyes and scrupulously supported my father's position. Vina might be not dead but merely delinquent. She laid her hand on Ormus's; he jerked his away, glaring savagely. With trembling lip she backed off and left him to his fears.

Who lit the fire?

The morning brought news, and two C.I.D. officers, the insufferably preening Detective Inspector Sohrab and the contrastingly self-effacing Detective Constable Rustam. These gentlemen informed us that as a result of interviews with neighbours and public-spirited passers-by who had contacted the police, the time of the fire's beginning had been definitively fixed at one p.m. Unfortunately, said D.I. Sohrab, "no miscreants were witnessed absconding from the site." A thorough search of the charred ruins of Villa Thracia had now been completed, and luckily no corpses had been found. (When Ormus heard that Vina had not been burned to death, he looked so happy that my mother had to remind him sternly that a great tragedy had nevertheless occurred.)

The three live-in household servants, cook, bearer and hamal, had all been located. They had been hiding out in the nearby colony of Koli fisherfolk, terrified both of the fire and of being held responsible for it. The police did not, however, believe that the fire was the domestics' fault. Their stories checked out, even though it was a little unusual for all three of them to have been running household errands at the time in question, leaving the villa unattended. Still, there was "clear evidence of an arson attack," Inspector Sohrab said keenly, "though details must be withheld for the nonce." Slowly we realized that we were under suspicion of having burned down our own home. Oleaginously, Sohrab now suggested that the firm of Merchant & Merchant was in alleged financial difficulties; that Shri Merchant himself had reportedly accrued gambling debts. Insurance claims could be beneficial, wasn't it so? My father was outraged at these "foul imputations." "Enquire of those who stand to benefit," he instructed the C.I.D. wallahs, with an unwonted edge to his voice. "Visit Shri Doodhwala and his cronies, and you will be in far greater propinquity to the luciferous rogues."

The cops left, but the doubts remained. The awful truth is that my tempestuous mother half suspected my father of the crime, and even my gentle father had begun to harbour suspicions of his own regarding Ameer. For three days, since their quarrel, my parents had lived apart: she at Villa Thracia, he with friends in Colaba. The fire had brought them together again, if only for my sake. Awkwardly, to keep up appearances, they were sharing one of Dolly's spacious guest bedrooms. But the atmosphere between them was icy.

I was in the room next door, and at night, once again, I could hear them hiss and fight. Ameer was angry enough with her husband to insinuate that he had tried to murder her, and all of us, in our beds. He pointed out mildly that the fire had started in broad daylight, at a time when she was unlikely to have been sleeping. She snorted contemptuously at so nitpicking a reply. V.V., for his part, wondered if she had turned arsonist in order to force his hand. "Is it possible that you would go to such reprehensible extremes in pursuit of those barbarous 'Cuffescrapers'?" At which Ameer shrieked, so that the whole night-time house could hear, "Oh God, look what filthy *galis* he's giving me now!"

Alas, the Piloo faction had indeed won the day in the battle against my father's intransigence. Now that Villa Thracia was gone, V.V. dejectedly gave in and sold Piloo, for a far lower price than the one he had initially refused, the plot of land on which our burned husk of a villa stood like a memorial to the death of idealism. The huge Doodhwala development project moved a step closer to success. The monster edifices of his imagination would bestride the city like the Martian spaceships in *The War of the Worlds*. In cases involving the pursuit of such very large pots of gold, a little firebuggery is not so very unusual.

But Piloo Doodhwala was an influential man. Influence, according to the astrologers, is an ethereal fluid emanating from the stars, which affects the actions of mere mortals such as we. Let us say, then, that Piloo uncorked his ethereal fluids—for he possessed influence of more than one variety—and let them freely flow down, from the highest echelons of the Bombay C.I.D. to the humble detectives assigned to the case. Within a matter of days, these officers announced that they had "conclusively eliminated" him from their investigations. When my father expressed astonishment, Inspector Sohrab told him with some asperity, "You should be grateful. You personally and your goodwife also have generously been included in the said elimination."

The investigation had been "redirected along more profitable avenues of inquiry." These concerned the vanished U.S. citizen, Miss Nissa Shetty alias Vina Apsara. Inquiries at Santa Cruz airport had established that Miss Apsara exited Bombay within hours of the fire, on a TWA aircraft travelling to London and New York. Her unexplained flight was deemed to be of the highest significance. Further detective work, in collaboration with Scotland Yard via the Interpol network, revealed that Miss Apsara's plane ticket had been purchased in pounds sterling in the U.K., and that the issuing agency was Mr. P. Kalamanja's London-based Kalatours outfit. Mr. Kalamanja himself had paid Miss Apsara's fare.

Mrs. Dolly Kalamanja was a small woman wearing big jewellery, a new-rich grande dame who believed in "putting on a show." Her hair was the blue of steel and its style was modelled on the Queen of England's, with those distinctive Ionic squirls adorning the temples. Her bust too—a single, solid bolster without hint of undulations, stretching across her chest like a sleeping policeman, a speed bump prominent enough to slow down anyone unwise enough to make too fast an approach—was reminiscent of Elizabeth II's. She was strong-willed, more conservative than most of Bombay's broad-minded Parsi community, and her high voice was in the habit of being obeyed. Much of what she felt about her own life was formulaic, which did not prevent the emotions from being felt strongly. Thus her husband Patangbaz Kalamanja was her "rock," and her daughter Persis, her "pride and joy." The news of Pat's involvement in the escape to "foreign parts" of a suspected arsonist hit her hard. She reeled. The universe seemed to lose shape and meaning. The earth trembled. The "rock" wobbled, cracked. Persis helped her mother to a chair, and she fell into it with her head "in a whirl," fanning herself with a hankie.

The grand formal drawing room at "Dil Kush" was as well

appointed, with its teak sideboards and mirrors in extravagant geometric shapes and overstuffed Biedermeier sofas and priceless Deco
lamps and genuine tigerskin rugs and bad oil paintings (and, to be fair,
some good ones), as the saloon of a great ocean liner: the *Titanic,* perhaps. Certainly it felt to baffled Dolly like the deck of a badly holed
ship. In her "condition," the room seemed to tilt and start sliding
slowly towards some dreadful netherworld.

"How did that girl get to my Pat?" she wailed, faintly. "Just now I'll
book a call to U.K. and box his blooming ears!"

It was like a scene from a Poirot story. We were all standing or sitting around the room, watching Dolly's melodramatic conniption. Persis was pouring her a glass of water, and the C.I.D.'s finest were
positioned on a tigerskin, well satisfied with the impact of their news.
But neither cocky Sohrab nor dumb Rustam could have been expecting what followed, which was not the threatened telephone call to
Patangbaz in Wembley. For as it happened, there was no need to trouble the international operator. Persis Kalamanja sat at her mother's feet,
massaging them with her hands, looked directly and without wavering
into the eyes of Ormus Cama, and confessed.

Not only confessed, but gave Vina Apsara an unbreakable alibi.

When the impossible becomes a necessity, it can sometimes be achieved.
Hours after Ameer Merchant's tirade had destroyed her faith in the reality of love, Vina called Persis and asked to meet her at (where else?) the
Rhythm Center record store. Her uncharacteristically faltering manner
persuaded Persis to set aside her reservations, and she agreed.

And at the store they went into a listening booth, pretending to
check out the sound-track album of the year's big musical hit, Gordon
MacRae and Shirley Jones in Rodgers and Hammerstein's *South
Pacific.* And while Miss Jones sang about washing some man out of her
hair, Vina—Vina in a frightening, cracked-mirror, off-centre mood that
Persis had never seen in her before—threw herself upon her rival's
mercy for much the same reason. I have to go, she said, and don't ask
me to talk about it because I won't, and don't think I'll change my
mind because I won't. And you have to help me, because there's
nobody else, and because you can, and because you're so fucking sweet

that you won't tell me to fuck off, and anyway, because you want to. You want to in the worst way.

Then she talked about it, anyway. They're fucking with me, she said, they think they can put their feelings inside me and then just rip them out, it's like they're Martians or something, I've got to get away. Persis asked, who. Shut the fuck up, Vina snapped, I said I didn't want to talk.

And more of the same, much more, through "Bali H'ai" and "Happy Talk" and so on. Can you pay, Persis asked her, and she answered I'll get the money, but you have to go ahead and fix up the ticket right now, I mean *now,* and I'm good for it, I'll get it to you somehow—*she was begging openly, winging it, dangling at the end of her rope,* Persis said boldly in the drawing room at "Dil Kush," *god knows how she got that way but somebody had to catch her, so I reached out my hand, I helped her, that's all. And besides, she was right,* she added, staring on and on into Ormus Cama's bewildered face, begging for help, in her own way, as shamelessly, as desperately, as Vina had begged her. Asking for the smallest of words, the faintest reassuring movement of the eyebrow, or perhaps, just possibly, the miraculous comfort of his smile. Asking to be told, yes, now you have a chance.

She was quite right. I did want to. So I did.

Persis had called her father, and Pat Kalamanja had never been able to say no to his little girl; it's for a friend, she said, it's too complicated, she said. Okay, forget it, it's fixed, he gave in, I'll send through the PTA today, so you can pick the ticket at the airline bureau tomorrow, or day after, latest. So you see, Persis said to Inspector Sohrab, you mustn't blame him, he knew nothing, it was me.

PTA is passenger ticket advice, Persis explained. You pay at one end, the ticket gets issued at the other. And I never expected her to have the cash, I knew Daddy would eat the bill anyway when he knew why I wanted the ticket, but she showed up here before noon on the day of the fire with two fat suitcases and a pillowcase full of jewels, and I knew where she got the jewellery from, Ameer auntie, don't think I had the slightest intention of holding on to it, but then all this started, this C.I.D. *tamasha,* and I got scared, I didn't know what to say, so I kept my trap shut, but I've opened it now, please excuse delay. She was with me all the time after that. I took her to the airport and put her on the plane myself and she's gone, and I hope she never comes back.

She may be a thief, said honest Persis, but she didn't start any fire.

The interrogation of Persis Kalamanja by Messrs. Sohrab and Rustam took place behind closed doors in a private room of her family home, lasted several hours, often grew heated, and failed to shake her testimony to the slightest degree. She did, however, fill in the story's blanks. It transpired that Pat Kalamanja had forked out only for a ticket as far as London, not the United States. At Persis's request, he had good-heartedly met Vina off the plane and taken her home to Wembley, because she had nowhere else to go. The next morning she had borrowed a small quantity of English currency from him, left her bags and gone into central London alone. She did not return that night, and agitated Pat was on the verge of calling the police when she walked in the following morning, offered no account of her absence, returned his money in full—the money for her ticket as well as the borrowed cash—and told him she was "all set," called a taxi, refused to allow Pat to help her with her bags, muttered a cursory thank-you and disappeared. Her present whereabouts remained unknown.

Soon after Persis was questioned, Vina Apsara was formally declared to be "no longer under suspicion of arson." Nor was Ameer Merchant prepared to accuse her of theft, because as Persis's story unfolded my mother's remorseful agonies had intensified sharply. She knew that Vina's flight was her doing, that she was the assassin of the runaway girl's joy, and although Ameer was a mistress of the flinty exterior, I could see through her dikes and embankments to the great flood tide of grief behind. Mourning the loss of a girl whom she had, in her own way, truly loved, Ameer cared little for her lost baubles. Vina's removal of jewels from Villa Thracia had resulted, after all, in the preservation and return of at least some of the family treasures. And if she had left the country with her suitcases bulging with Ameer's finest slinky sequinned dresses and dripping with the rest of my mother's diamond rings and emerald earrings and pearl necklaces, which no doubt she had sold in London to raise cash, Ameer waved it all away, what of it, she shrugged, the poor child is more than welcome, for if she had not pinched them, they would have been consumed by fire. Then my mother retired to her room, to weep long and hard for Vina, and for herself and her own departed happiness as well.

Thus Persis Kalamanja not only helped Vina to leave Bombay, as she wished, but also saved her from being wrongfully accused of a crime she did not commit. The police did not break Persis down, and I will not suggest here that the alibi she gave Vina was anything but the whole, the nothing-but-the truth.

When she was worried, she could twist her beautiful mouth until it looked as if it was being wrung by a dhobi. The effect was almost unbearably erotic. In those days there was a whole generation of young men hoping she would twist her mouth in their direction. But the man at whom she was twisting it now, twisting it with all her heart, as she emerged from the police interrogation to face the questions in his eyes, was utterly unmoved. This was her reward for helping Vina: that Ormus Cama completed, at that moment, the process of wiping her off his personal map and out of the history of his life. He looked at her with open hatred; then with contempt; then with indifference; then as if he no longer remembered who she was. He left "Dil Kush" as if withdrawing from a stranger's house into which he had stumbled by mistake. And Persis became "poor Persis" then, and "poor Persis" she remained for the rest of her old maid's life.

Nobody was ever charged with the crime of burning down Villa Thracia. The C.I.D.'s heroes, Sohrab and Rustam, concluded that "criminal intervention" was "off the agenda" and withdrew from the case. Many Bombay properties had old and dangerous wiring systems, and it was easy enough, finally, to believe in an electrical fault as the blaze's probable cause.

Easy enough, especially when the influence kept on flowing down from the top, until all possible suspects were, in the satisfied words of Piloo's aide Sisodia, "Foo fool fully Exxon Exxon exonerated."

Disorientation is loss of the East. Ask any navigator: the east is what you sail by. Lose the east and you lose your bearings, your certainties, your knowledge of what is and what may be, perhaps even your life. Where was that star you followed to that manger? That's right. The east orients. That's the official version. The language says so, and you should never argue with the language.

But let's just suppose. What if the whole deal—orientation, knowing where you are, and so on—what if it's all a scam? What if all of it—

home, kinship, the whole enchilada—is just the biggest, most truly global, and centuries-oldest piece of brainwashing? Suppose that it's only when you dare to let go that your real life begins? When you're whirling free of the mother ship, when you cut your ropes, slip your chain, step off the map, go absent without leave, scram, vamoose, whatever: suppose that it's then, and only then, that you're actually free to act! To lead the life nobody tells you how to live, or when, or why. In which nobody orders you to go forth and die for them, or for god, or comes to get you because you broke one of the rules, or because you're one of those people who are, for reasons which unfortunately you can't be given, simply not allowed. Suppose you've got to go through the feeling of being lost, into the chaos and beyond; you've got to accept the loneliness, the wild panic of losing your moorings, the vertiginous terror of the horizon spinning round and round like the edge of a coin tossed in the air.

You won't do it. Most of you won't do it. The world's head laundry is pretty good at washing brains: Don't jump off that cliff don't walk through that door don't step into that waterfall don't take that chance don't step across that line don't ruffle my sensitivities I'm warning you now don't make me mad you're doing it you're making me mad. You won't have a chance you haven't got a prayer you're finished you're history you're less than nothing, you're dead to me, dead to your whole family your nation your race, everything you ought to love more than life and listen to like your master's voice and follow blindly and bow down before and worship and obey; you're dead, you hear me, forget about it, you stupid bastard, I don't even know your name.

But just imagine you did it. You stepped off the edge of the earth, or through the fatal waterfall, and there it was: the magic valley at the end of the universe, the blessed kingdom of the air. Great music everywhere. You breathe the music, in and out, it's your element now. It feels better than "belonging" in your lungs.

Vina was the first one of us to do it. Ormus jumped second, and I, as usual, brought up the rear. And we can argue all night about why, did we jump or were we pushed, but you can't deny we all did it. We three kings of Disorient were.

And I'm the only one who lived to tell the tale.

• • •

We Merchants moved into rented accommodation in the Camas' apartment block on Apollo Bunder, separate flats for my mother and father, and me like a yo-yo between the pair of them, learning independence, still playing my cards close to the chest, growing up. In those days Ormus Cama and I were closer than we ever managed before or since, on account of our common loss. I guess we could each tolerate the other's need for Vina because she wasn't around either of us. There wasn't a day when we didn't both spend most of our time thinking about her, and the same questions were in both our hearts. Why had she abandoned us? Wasn't she ours, hadn't we loved her? Ormus had the better claim, as always. He had won her in a bet, he had earned her by waiting through the long self-denying years. And now she was gone, into that immense underworld made up of all the things and places and people we did not know. "I'm going to find her," Ormus repeatedly swore. "No limit to where I'll go. To the ends of the earth, Rai. And even beyond." Yes, yes, I thought, but what if she doesn't want you? What if you were just her Indian fling, her bit of curry powder? What if you're her past, and at the end of your long quest you locate her in a penthouse or trailer park and she slams the door in your face?

Was Ormus ready to plunge even into this inferno, the underworld of doubt? I didn't ask him; and because I was young, it took me a long time to understand that the hell-fires of uncertainty were already burning him up.

Back then it wasn't easy to travel if all you had was an Indian passport. Inside this passport some bureaucrat would laboriously inscribe the few countries you were actually allowed to travel to, most of them countries that had never crossed your mind as possible destinations. All the rest—certainly all the interesting places—were off limits unless you got special permission, and then they would be added to the passport's handwritten list by another bureaucrat, with the same handwriting as the first. And after that there was the problem of foreign exchange. There wasn't any: that was the problem. There was a national shortage of dollars and pounds sterling and other negotiable currencies, so you certainly couldn't have any, and you couldn't travel unless you had some, and if you did buy some at extortionate rates on the black market, you might be called upon to explain how the stuff got into your hands, which would make it even more costly, because of the additional expense of the shut-up money, the bribe.

I offer this brief lesson in nostalgia economics to explain why Ormus wasn't on the first plane in pursuit of his great love. Darius Xerxes Cama—plain Mr. these days—was mostly in his cups, and after his own shaming experience of rejection, by England in general and William Methwold in particular, was unapproachable on the subject of transcontinental travel. Mrs. Spenta Cama (the loss of her title still smarted) flatly refused to buy her least favoured son even the cheapest ticket on a cut-price Arab airline, or the smallest acceptable number (one hundred) of under-the-counter "black pounds." "Chit of a girl is not worth ten pice," she declared flatly. "Just see that beautiful Persis at last, why can't you. Poor girl loves you to pieces. Let the blinkers fall from your eyes once and for all."

But Ormus was blinkered for life. In the next few years I had ample opportunity to observe his character at close quarters, and beneath his brilliant, shifting surface, the mazy, chameleon personality that made every girl he met want to pin him down; beneath his alternately concealing and revealing nature, now open as an invitation, now closed as tight as a trap, now needing, now pushing away, beneath all the improvised melodies of himself, there was this unaltered, unvarying beat. Vina, Vina. He was a slave to that rhythm, for good.

Let me make one thing clear: he wasn't faithful to her absent self, to her memory. He did not withdraw from society and light a nightly candle at her deserter's shrine. No, sir. Instead, he sought her in other women, sought her furiously and inexhaustibly, searching for an inflection of her voice in this beauty, a toss of her hair in another's flowing locks. Most women offered only disappointments. At the end of these encounters he often found even the ritual courtesies of the situation beyond him and would confess the true nature of his quest, and sometimes the real woman who had disappointed him would have the generosity to listen to him speak of the departed shadow woman, for hour after hour, until the dawn, when he would fall silent and slip away.

A few women came close to satisfying him, because in certain lights, if they said very little and lay just so; or if, once he had placed a lace handkerchief or a mask over their faces, their now-anonymous bodies held some echo of hers, a breast, a curve of the thigh, a movement of the neck; then, ah, then he could delude himself for fifteen or twenty seconds that she had returned. But inevitably they would turn, they would speak lovingly to him or arch their bare, strong backs, the light would change, the mask would drop away, the illusion would be destroyed, and he would abandon them where they lay. In spite of maudlin confessions and casual cruelties, however, the young women who showed up at his performances (for he had begun to sing professionally) continued to seek these more private, and almost invariably wounding, audiences.

Nor was his search confined to young hipsters. The catalogue of his substitute loves during these years reads like a cross section of the female population of the city: women of all ages, all walks of life, thin women and fat women, tall women and short, noisy and quiet, gentle and rough, united only in this: that some shard of Vina Apsara dwelt in them, or was believed to do so by the distraught lover she had left behind. Housewives, secretaries, building-site workers, pavement dwellers, sweatshop labourers, domestic servants, whores . . . he hardly seemed to need sleep. By day and by night he would rove the streets, looking for her, the woman who was nowhere, trying to draw her out of the women who were everywhere, finding some fragment to hold on to, some wisp of her to clutch at, in the hope that this *nuage* might at least cause her to visit him in his dreams.

Such was his first pursuit of her. To me it felt almost necrophiliac, vampiric. He was sucking the lifeblood out of living women to keep alive the phantom of the Departed. Often, after a conquest, he would confide in me. Then felt I like Dunyazade, Scheherazade's sister, sitting at the foot of the queen's sleepless bed while she told tall stories to save her life: he would tell me every detail—somehow failing to give the impression that he was boasting—and I, dazed and aroused in equal measure by his passions and descriptions, might on occasion murmur, "Maybe you ought to get over her. Maybe she isn't coming back." Then he would shake his head with its lengthening mane of hair, and shout, "Get thee behind me, Satan. Seek not to come between the lover and his love." Which made me laugh; as it was not meant to do.

What a figure he cut in public! He glittered, he shone. Every room he entered took its shape from his position in it. His smile was a magnet, his frown a crushing defeat. His days "on the loaf" were over. No more hanging around girls'-school gates. He was singing most nights now, playing every instrument in sight, and the girls were flocking to him. The city's hotels and clubs, even the Hindi movie playback producers, were vying for his services. He played the field, signing no contract, committing himself to nobody exclusively, and was hot enough to get away with it. The main attraction of the city's Sunday morning brunches, where, largely thanks to him, jazz was giving way to rock 'n' roll, his gyrations caused the city's demoiselles to swoon. Their mothers, while disapproving strongly, could not take their eyes off him, either. Anybody from the Bombay of those days would remember the young Ormus Cama. His name, his face, became part of the definition of the city in that departed heyday. Mr. Ormus Cama, our women's guiding star.

In conversation, particularly when he leaned close in to some young lovely in big bangs and a spreading pink skirt, his intensity was almost frightening in its sexual power. Celebrate the physical, he would hiss, for we are flesh and blood. What pleases the flesh is good, what warms the blood is fine. The body, not the spirit. Concentrate on that. How does that feel? Yes, it felt good to me too. And that? Oh, yes, baby, my blood too. It's hot.

Our selves, not our souls . . . He spread his erotic gospel with a kind of innocence, a kind of messianic purity, that used to drive me wild. It was the greatest act in town. I did my best to copy it as I moved through my teens, and even my poor mimic version brought fair results with the girls of my generation, but often they'd laugh in my face. Most times, as a matter of fact. I'd count myself lucky to get anywhere with one girl in ten. Which I have in common, as I have since learned, with the male species in general. Rejection is the norm. Knowing this, we long for acceptance all the more. We aren't holding the cards in this game. If we have the knack of it, we learn finesse. . . . Ormus, though, he was an artist, he held the ace of trumps: viz., sincerity. He would take me along to his jam sessions and even to some of his nocturnal songfests (I had two parents vying for my love and favours, so it was easy to twist them round my little finger and get permissions which might otherwise have been refused), and after he finished singing I would watch the maestro at work, sitting in a booth or at a table, with some young female hanging on his every word. I watched him with an almost fanatical attention, determined not to miss the small unwary moment, the tiniest of off-guard instants, when his mask slipped, when he revealed to his disciple-spy that it was just a performance, a calculated series of effects, a fraud.

The moment never came. It was because he meant it, meant it from the depths of his being, that he won followers, fans, hearts, lovers; that he won the game. That Dionysiac credo of his, reject the spirit and trust the flesh, with which he had once wooed Vina, was now knocking half the city for six.

There was only one woman he would not attempt to seduce, and that was Persis Kalamanja. Maybe this was her punishment for having helped Vina get away from him, that she would never taste even a night of his fabled delights; or perhaps it was something else, a mark of his high opinion of her, an indication that had it not been for Vina Apsara, she would indeed have stood a chance.

But Vina existed, and so "poor Persis" was erased.

The private Ormus, the one I was privileged to observe at Apollo Bunder, was very different from this public love god. The bruise on his eyelid itched. Often his old darkness would descend upon him, and he would lie motionless for hours at a time, turning upon that inward eye that saw such strange apocalyptic sights. He no longer spoke much of Gayomart, but I knew his dead twin was in there, fleeing endlessly down some descending labyrinth of the mind, at the end of which not only music waited, but also danger, monsters, death. I knew it because Ormus still came back out of the "Cama obscura" with batches of new songs. And maybe he was going in deeper, taking more risks, or perhaps Gayo was coming back towards him and singing right into his ear, because now Ormus was bringing back more than vowel sequences or misheard, nonsensical lines (though sometimes, for example when he first played me a number called "Da Doo Ron Ron," it was hard to tell the difference). He was being given whole songs now. Songs from the future. Songs with names that meant nothing in 1962 and 1963. "Eve of Destruction." "I Got You, Babe." "Like a Rolling Stone."

Ormus liked to compose his own songs up on the flat roof of the apartment block, and spent eternities up there, lost within himself, searching for the points at which his inner life intersected the life of the greater world outside, and calling those points of intersection "songs." Just once he let me photograph him while he worked, picking away at a guitar laid on his lap across his crossed legs, eyes shut, gone. My Voigtländer camera had escaped the Villa Thracia fire because I had become inseparable from it and had taken it with me to school. I had read in a book called *Photography for Beginners* that a true photographer was never parted from the tool of his trade, and had taken the advice to heart. Ormus liked my attitude, found it "serious," he said, and in spite of my store of jealousy regarding Vina I was always anxious for his good words, so I puffed up horribly when he praised me. His personal nickname for me, in those days, was "Juicy." "My friend Juicy Rai," he'd introduce me—just sixteen in 1963—to his louche club-world set. "You never heard anyone like him. Always seeing photographs—three strangers in a bus queue all lifting their legs at the same time like in a dance routine, or people waving from the deck of a departing steamer, and one of the waving arms is a gorilla's—and then he hollers out, Juicy this? Juicy that? And of course nobody did see it but him, but what do you know, it turns up on his film. Young Juicy," he'd slap me on the back, and his female partners would bestow upon me their most groin-melting, glamorous looks. "Fastest shot in the East." At which I, humiliatingly, youthfully, would blush.

So in November 1963 he let me photograph him while he worked. A lot of the songs he was writing then were of the protest type, idealistic, strong. In the matter of worthiness, which so often exercised my private thoughts, Ormus was of the party that believed there was more wrong with the world in general than its ordinary citizens. In this he was like my mother; except that she, disillusioned, had decided she couldn't beat the world's corruption and had joined forces with it instead. Ormus Cama had not given up on the perfectibility of man and of his social groupings as well. That day on the roof, however, eyes closed, talking to himself, he sounded puzzled. "This isn't how things should be," he'd murmur every few minutes. "Everything's off the rails. Sometimes a little off, sometimes a lot. But things should be different. Just . . . different."

It became a song, in the end: "It Shouldn't Be This Way." But watching him, making myself invisible so that I didn't inhibit him, moving around the roof on cat's paws, I had the strange sense that he wasn't speaking figuratively. Just as Ormus could surprise by the depth of his sincerity, so also his literalness could catch one off guard. I felt the hairs on the back of my neck begin to rise. The muscles in my stomach knotted. "Things aren't like this," he kept repeating. "It shouldn't be this way." As if he had access to some other plane of existence, some parallel, "right" universe, and had sensed that our time had somehow been put out of joint. Such was his vehemence that I found myself believing him, believing, for example, in the possibility of that other life in which Vina had never left and we were making our lives together, all three of us, ascending together to the stars. Then he shook his head, and the spell broke. He opened his eyes, grinning ruefully. As if he knew his thoughts had infected mine. As if he knew his power. "Better get on with it," he said. "Make do with what there is."

Later, as I drifted off to sleep in my room, Ormus's rooftop torment came back to haunt me: his sudden possession by the idea that, like a runaway freight train, the world had veered sideways off its proper track and was now banging about, out of control, upon a great iron web of switched points. In my pre-sleep drowsiness, it was a notion that unnerved me; for if the world itself were metamorphosing unpredictably, then nothing could be relied upon any more. What could one trust? How to find moorings, foundations, fixed points, in a broken, altered time? I came awake fast and hard, with my heart pounding. It's okay. It's okay. Only a waking dream.

The world is what it is.

I thought then that Ormus's doubts about reality might be a kind of revenge of the spirit, an irruption, into a life dedicated to the actual and the sensual, of the irrational, the incorporeal. He, who had rejected the unknowable, was being plagued by the unknown.

• • •

The day after the President of the United States had that narrow escape in Dallas, Texas, and we were all becoming familiar with the names of the would-be assassins, Oswald, whose rifle jammed, and Steel, who was overpowered on some kind of grassy knoll by a genuine hero, a middle-aged amateur cameraman called Zapruder, who saw the killer's gun and hit him over the head with an 8 mm ciné camera . . . on that extraordinary day, Ormus Cama had a different name to conjure with, because he arrived at the Regal Café, Colaba, to be informed that among the audience for his late-night set would be a party from the United States of America, including Mr. Yul Singh himself. Even then most music-loving metropolitan Indians had heard of Yul Singh, the blind Indian record producer who founded Colchis Records in New York City in 1948 with a ten-thousand-dollar loan from his optician. After Colchis struck gold by playing "race music," rhythm and blues, to white radio audiences, that optician, Tommy J. Eckleburg, briefly became a Manhattan celebrity himself. He even showed up with Yul Singh on the talk-show promo circuit.

"So why does a blind man need an optician, Yul?"

"Optimism, Johnny. Optimism."

"And why does an optician need a blind man, T.J.?"

"Don't go insulting my good friend now, Mr. C. He's differently sighted is all."

When Ormus arrived at the Regal and was told about the Yul Singh party, he frowned hard and began to complain of a terrible headache. He took pills and lay down in his dressing room with an ice pack on his head, and I sat beside him, massaging his temples. "Yul *Singh*," he kept repeating. "*Yul* Singh."

"The top banana," I said, proud of my newly acquired knowledge. "Aretha, Ray, the Beatles. Everybody." Ormus winced, as if the pain in his head had intensified.

"What's the matter?" I asked. "Pills not working?"

"There's no such man," he whispered. "He doesn't fucking exist."

That was ridiculous. "You're hallucinating," I told him. "You'll be telling me next there's no Jesse Garon Parker." He took the point, and covered his face with his hands. I heard a snatch of song.

> *It's not supposed to be this way*
> *it's not supposed to be this day*
> *it's not supposed to be this night*
> *but you're not here to put it right*
> *and you're not here to hold me tight*
> *it shouldn't be this way.*

Then his head seemed to clear; the pills had kicked in. He sat up on his couch.

"What's wrong with me?" he said. "This is no time to be cracking up."

"Break a leg," I told him, and he went out to play.

At the end of the set, which, in honour of the visiting Americans, Ormus had dedicated to President Kennedy's survival, I was with him in his tiny dressing room, along with three young women (no room for more). Ormus was stripped to the waist, towelling himself down, to the delight of the ladies. Then Yul Singh knocked at the door. Ormus shooed the women out but told me I could stay.

"Kid brother?" Yul Singh asked, and Ormus grinned. "Something like that."

Singh was a piece of work. He was wearing the most beautiful blue silk suit I had ever seen, his shirts bore his personal monogram, his two-tone shoes made my feet ache with envy. He was fortyish, small, dark, goateed, and his sunglasses—the work, no doubt, of that ocular couturier *par excellence,* Dr. T.J. Eckleburg—were made to fit the curve of his head, so that you never could catch a glimpse of those sightless eyes, no matter how much you craned your curious neck. In his hand was a white cane, made of pure ivory, with a silver head.

"Okay, listen to me," he said: straight to the point. "I don't come to Bombay to find acts, okay? I come to see my mother. Who god bless her she's over seventy now but still rides a horse. You don't need to know that. So, I heard your music, and what, you think I don't know anything, who the fuck are you trying to kid?"

All this spoken through teeth glittering in the most courteous of smiles. I had never seen Ormus so discomfited. "I don't understand,

Mr. Singh," he said, suddenly sounding very young. "You didn't like my performance?"

"Who cares what I like? I told you, I'm off duty. My mother's out there. She heard you, I heard you, the whole town heard you. What is it, a kind of tribute act, right? I'll give you this, you've got those songs down, and the phrasing, you could be those guys. So, okay. I'm not interested. You're doing it to get women, pocket money, what? You get women? Is that what you're looking for?"

"Just one woman," Ormus said faintly, shocked into honesty.

That made Singh stop and cock his head. "She ran out on you, huh. You were singing these cockamamie tribute numbers, and she'd had enough."

Ormus pulled the shreds of his dignity around him. "I get the point, Mr. Singh, thank you for your honesty. I wasn't singing my own songs today. Another night, maybe I'll give them a try." Singh smacked his cane on the bare floor. "Did I say I was finished? I'll tell you when I'm finished, and I won't be finished until you tell me, boy, where you got hold of that last number you sang, what bootlegging motherfucker stole it for you, that's what I said when you started singing, you see what you made me do, you made me swear in front of my white-haired mother, I hate to do that. She was knitting, it made her drop a stitch. You don't need to know that."

The last song had been a tender ballad, slow, full of longing: a song for Vina, I thought, one of Ormus's rooftop compositions, written while dreaming of lost love. But I was wrong. The name of the song was "Yesterday."

"I heard it," Ormus said, lamely, and Yul Singh rammed the tip of his cane into the floor once more. "Impossible, okay?" he said. "That song, we aren't putting it out until next year. We haven't even recorded it yet. There isn't even a fucking demo. The guy just wrote it, he just played it to me on his fucking piano in London, okay, and then I fly to Bombay to see my sweet old mother who god bless her I've now left out there for many minutes wondering why is her son swearing in front of her, you understand what I'm saying, this is not right. It shouldn't be this way."

Ormus was silent, stopped in his tracks. How could he say, I have a dead twin, I follow him in my dreams, he sings, I listen, and these days I'm getting better at hearing the words? Getting better all the time?

Yul Singh stood. "Let me tell you two things. One, if you ever sing that song again, I'll have lawyers on you tighter than a straitjacket and your balls will be on my table beside my cornflakes in a little china bowl. Two, I never swear. Never. I'm famous for my clean tongue. Therefore comprehend, please, my distress."

He was going through the door. I caught a glimpse of two burly aides in tuxes. He turned for a parting shot.

"I didn't say you didn't have talent. Did I say that? I don't believe so. You have talent. Maybe great talent. What you don't have is material, except what you stole, beats me how and you aren't going to say. What you also don't have is a band, because those guys in pink jackets with their big-band haircuts are definitely going nowhere except back home on the bus. Further, motivation. This it seems to me you are also short on. When you've got material you think it's up to snuff, when you've got an act you think it'll travel, don't come and see me. When you've got motivation, that's different, if someday you get it, but maybe you won't, which don't worry I won't be waiting. Maybe if you find that girl, yeah. Find her and she'll be the making of you. I owe everything personally to my own lovely wife who unfortunately she's not accompanying me on this trip. You don't need to know that. Good night."

"So he doesn't exist," I said to Ormus. "That's lucky, then."

Ormus looked like he'd been hit by lightning. "It's all wrong," he mumbled stupidly. "But maybe this is how it has to be."

7

MORE THAN LOVE

I must confess that I never completely accepted the passport/foreign exchange explanation of Ormus's non-pursuit of Vina. Where there's a will, etc., I couldn't help thinking; so when Yul Singh shrewdly queried the singer's motivation, I realized he'd put his finger on the problem and was only saying aloud what I already knew. Such was Ormus's outward confidence, however—his sexual swagger, his ease with his body and voice, his charm—that I had allowed myself to believe (more exactly, I had kidded myself that I believed) that those private inwardnesses of his, and even those panicky outbursts about errors in reality, could be ascribed to his intense artistic sensibility, which drew him inexorably towards what Browning calls the dangerous edge of things.

"The honest thief, the tender murderer." Interesting as such paradoxes undoubtedly are, Ormus Cama sought an edge more dangerous by far, an edge in the mind, beyond which he pursued his dead brother, returning with prophetic music but risking, each time, that he might not return at all. It was unsurprising, I thought with teenage omniscience, that such journeys into the unknown should take their toll, and leave the voyager moody and erratic. In short, I believed Ormus Cama to be a little touched in the head, knocked off balance by loss, as separated twins (and jilted lovers) sometimes are. The surviving male Camas were, all of them in their various ways, a couple of annas short of the full rupee; Ormus, neither homicidal nor mute nor sunk in a whisky stupor of defeat and shame, was both gifted and charismatic, and his strangeness only increased the attraction. So there were many ways for me to set aside my early doubts, to stop articulating, even to myself, the obvious insight that Vina's sudden desertion, immediately after their long-postponed and profoundly satisfying first (and only) night of love, had badly damaged Ormus's sense of himself, had left him holed below the waterline, listing in the water, bailing furiously and trying not to drown. Now that Yul Singh's clear-sightedness had opened my own eyes, I could see the thick, paralysing fog of fear enveloping Ormus Cama, the sense of deep inadequacy revealed by his Bombay Casanova act, his unstoppable Don Juanism. If Aphrodite had resigned from Olympus, if Venus had announced that her job wasn't worth doing any longer, it could not have hit Ormus harder than Vina Apsara's disillusionment with love. He too had lost confidence, and faith in the very idea of Vina, the idea of there being an eternal and perfect partner whom he might perfectly and eternally love and by whom he might in his turn be rendered perfect and eternal. "I'll follow her to the ends of the earth," he boasted, but he wouldn't even go as far as the airport.

He had begun to fear what he desired most. On the greatest day of his professional life he developed a migraine, and then failed to perform a single song of his own to the celebrated producer sitting beside his knitting mother in the audience. Instead, he sang his Gayo ditties, those cover versions of the well-known hits of the day which he had so uselessly heard long before, in dreams; and so he was mistaken by the producer for a novelty act, a provincial echo of the big-city action, a hick. It was the same with Vina; he'd lost his nerve. The fear that she might no longer love him—that she might, indeed, slam that trailer door in his face—had grown stronger than his love, kept him at home.

In the thirteen months after Yul Singh's exposure of his secret timorousness, Ormus Cama's loss of nerve gradually became apparent to everyone. Until that day the house musicians at the various clubs and coffeehouses, such as the Pink Flamingoes backing combo at the Regal Café, had treated Ormus like a demi-god, one of those mythological heroes whose fate it is to end up twinkling in the heavens. After the boss of Colchis Records gave him the thumbs-down, however, the musicians of Bombay wasted no time in letting Ormus Cama know that it was no good his putting on airs any more, he might think he was the Mod God (a title—more alliterative than accurate—which he'd been given by a critic), but as far as they were concerned he was no better than they were, just the singer with the band, and singers were two a penny, so he'd better watch his step. And to complete his discomfiture, he also lost what we used to call "the knack."

The first women to reject his advances, the starlets Fadia Wadia and Tipple Billimoria, briefly became famous in the city's café society as the bubble bursters of Ormus's lady-killer reputation. Within weeks of those first refusals, however, the whole of "Ormie's Army" had deserted him. Only Persis Kalamanja remained, magnificently waiting in ardent solitude in her mother's Malabar Hill mansion. But that was a phone call Ormus Cama never made. To call Persis would be to admit he was finished. It would be like calling a tower of silence to rent space on the vulture-crowded roof. Persis Kalamanja, infinitely patient Persis, who bore no malice towards any human being, Persis the beautiful, every mother's ideal daughter and most men's dream of a bride, had been transformed by Ormus's tormented fancy into an avatar of the Angel of Death.

He became an increasingly forlorn, frayed figure during the course of that year, and still he made no effort to go in search of Vina. Even Mrs. Spenta Cama, who had never succeeded in loving her youngest child and had opposed with all her force Ormus's obsession with the under-age Vina, found herself saying, with a kind of irritation, "What do you think she's going to do after all this time? Plop down the chimney on Christmas Day, all tied up with ribbon and a card?"

The Cama apartment boasted no chimney; the family was not in the habit of celebrating Christmas; Vina Apsara did not come to call, with or without gift wrapping. But someone did return. And after that, Christmas Day was still nothing for Camas to celebrate, but it was also impossible to forget.

• • •

Cyrus Cama broke out of jail that Christmas Eve, disguised as a Syriac priest, having convinced a guard that he was a great seer whose murdering days were behind him and who would be of far greater value to the nation as a free man, spreading his unique message around the land. He emerged into a nation in dire need of guidance. Jawaharlal Nehru was dead. His successor, Indira Gandhi, was little more than a pawn in the hands of the Congress kingmakers, Shastri, Morarji Desai and Kamaraj. A fanatical gang of political bully boys, Mumbai's Axis, was on the verge of seizing control of Bombay, and Hindu nationalism was sweeping the country. There was a general feeling that things were going too fast, that the national railway train was roaring ahead without a driver, and that the decision to drop international tariff barriers and deregulate the economy had been too hastily taken. "Maybe in twenty years' time, when we are stronger," said an *Indian Express* editorial, "but why now? Where's the fire?"

On the night of Cyrus's escape, his twin brother Ardaviraf woke up suddenly, shuddering, as if something evil had moved lightly along his spine. He remained in that position, sitting up in bed, shivering, until he was discovered by his mother, who wrapped him in blankets and fed him chicken soup until the colour returned to his cheeks. "It's like he saw a ghost," Spenta said on the phone to Dolly Kalamanja, whose briskly matter-of-fact pooh-poohing of all paranormal gibberish always made the mystically inclined Spenta secretly feel a good deal better. "Poor fellow," clucked Dolly sympathetically. "Devil knows what foolish notions course through that boy's head."

The next morning brought news of Cyrus's escape, and Spenta gave Virus a long look, but he only grinned his innocent grin and turned away. Spenta Cama was gripped by an undefined fear. She knew it was no good discussing the alarming development with her increasingly withdrawn husband. Instead, she called her closest ally. "What won't my Khusro do this time," she wailed at Dolly. "What shame won't he now bring down on my head?" But Dolly Kalamanja, who knew her friend well, heard some deeper terror beneath Spenta's lamentations, a fear which had driven Spenta to talk openly about a subject whose very existence she had never before liked to admit. Dolly was no longer an innocent arriviste, and had found out about jailed Cyrus some while back. Such was her fondness for Spenta, and her own good nature (which she had passed on to Persis), that she had never once raised the topic. "If mum is the word Spenta wants," she had told Persis, "then mum's what she'll get from me."

The two women had a busy programme that day. There was a Kalamanja "charitea" at Dolly's place, followed by a special fund-raising fashion show, or Xtraordinary Xmas Xtravaganza, at the Orpheum cinema, and after that a round of hospital visits. "Come over early," Dolly advised Spenta. "Get your mind off it. Masses to plan." Mrs. Spenta Cama, plagued by anxiety, scurried gratefully across to Malabar Hill at once, and plunged into good works with energy and relief.

Ormus, too, would say afterwards that he had left home feeling nervous and on edge, but then in those hard days he often was. He shrugged off the feeling and went to work. He had been booked, that evening, to croon supper-club material at the Cosmic Dancer Hotel on Marine Drive, whose restaurant had been given a Christmas theme by the addition of much cotton wool and a few plastic trees. Ormus was forced to dress up in a red outfit with a white beard and sing a selection ranging from "White Christmas" to Eartha Kitt's "Santa Baby," even though this last song was so clearly written to be sung only by a woman. It was a B-list booking that said much about his declining reputation.

Sometimes it is necessary to touch bottom in order to know which way is up; to go a long distance down the wrong road before you know the right way. Ormus Cama had been allowing himself slowly to sink, crippled by a terrible, lassitudinous inertia that bore a marked resemblance to his father's. On the night of Darius's murder, however, Ormus Cama at last saw himself plain. At the end of his set at the Cosmic Dancer Hotel, those two purgatorial hours spent singing old songs through a Santa Claus beard, he listened to the sparse, uninterested applause and began to laugh. He removed his beard and Father Christmas hat and laughed until the tears streamed down his face. Afterwards many Bombayites would claim to have been present at Ormus Cama's last show in the city, enough people to fill the Wankhede Stadium several times over, and the accounts they gave of his farewell remarks were many and various. He was said to have spoken angrily, or humbly, or arrogantly, or in French. He was accused of having harangued the audience about the future of popular music, or berated them for their inattention, or begged them to give him one more chance, at which he had been booed from the stage. Some said he had made a political speech, attacking the assembled B-list fat cats for their corruption and greed; or that he had blasphemed, not only against Christmas and the Christians, but against all gods and rites—"charades"—of worship. According to these hordes of self-styled witnesses, he had been magnificent or pathetic, a hero or a clown.

The truth was that he couldn't stop laughing, and the only thing he said wasn't addressed to anyone present. "Shit, Vina," he said, holding his sides. "I'm sorry it took me so long to understand."

Meanwhile, back at the Apollo Bunder apartment, Gieve the butler had served dinner to Darius and Ardaviraf Cama and then retired to the servants' quarters, where he found, to his amazement, that all the resident domestics had run off, except for the cook, who was in the process of leaving. "And where do you think you're going?" Gieve asked this fellow, who just shook his head and exited at top speed via the servants' outside staircase, a clanking cast-iron spiral fixed to the rear of the building. It is plain that Gieve himself felt no warning pangs of terror, because he lay down on his cot as usual and was soon asleep.

Mr. Darius Cama spent the last hours of his life alone in his beloved library, fuddled by old age, mythology and booze. He had become obsessed by the notion that the Greek figures of the Titans Prometheus, "forethought," and his brother Epimetheus, "afterthought," the sons of the "First Father," Uranus, might have been derived from the Puranic heroes Pramanthu and Manthu, and that the swastika, that ancient Indian fire symbol, could also be connected to Prometheus's symbolic rôle as the thief of Olympic fire for the benefit of his creation, mankind. The Nazis had stolen the swastika and defiled it—as the Nazi connection had sullied the entire field—and the old gentleman scholar hoped in his muddled fashion that these, his last researches, might in some small way redeem both the swastika and the study of Aryan myth from the terrible deformation to which history had subjected them. However, he was unable to think clearly enough to follow his arguments through. His notes wandered from the point, digressing from Prometheus and Epimetheus to their youngest uncle, Cronus, who took a cruel sickle and cut off his father's balls. The last words Darius Xerxes Cama wrote slid away from scholarship entirely to reveal all his confusion and pain. *No need to cut off my balls,* he wrote. *Did it all by myself,* and then his head fell forward and rested upon his papers, and he slept.

Spenta came home late and went quietly to her room; Ormus, wreathed in radiance, returned an hour before dawn, singing without restraint, and switched on a great blaze of chandeliers and standard lamps. Exhausted Spenta in her room saw no lights, heard no songs and did not awake. Blinking rapidly, as if he were emerging into the light after years spent hiding from the world in a darkened attic, Ormus retired, having spent the night prowling the city streets, laughing, calling out Vina's name, drunk on nothing but excitement, burning with need. He entered his room noisily, fell down on to his bed and passed out fully clothed. The apartment slept, innocent of the tragedy within its walls.

Morning came, rapid and intolerant, the way morning is in the tropics. As usual it was the city that woke Spenta with its shrugging, careless noise of shouts and engines and bicycle bells. Crows sat on the windowsills, bold as brass, and cawed her out of bed. But in spite of all this noise, it was a silence that dragged Spenta upright, a silence where there should have been sound. A part of the morning orchestra was missing: there were no household noises. Spenta, pulling a floaty chiffon peignoir over her nightdress, went forth into the apartment, where she found neither the sweeper woman and her daughter, squatting with their brooms, nor the hamal, busy with the dusting and polishing. The kitchen was empty. Gieve was nowhere to be found. She called aloud: *"Arré, koi hai?"* No answer. Such laziness was unforgivable. Spenta stormed through the kitchen towards the servants' quarters, grim of face, determined to give her indolent household the rough edge of her tongue; and came back an instant later, running, with one hand over her mouth as if she were stifling a scream. She flung open the door to Ardaviraf Cama's bedroom. He was asleep, snoring beatifically. Then she went into Ormus's quarters. He tossed blearily and grunted. Darius's bedchamber was empty. Spenta went towards the library, then came to a standstill outside the closed double doors, as though she could not bear to open them because she was unprepared for the sight she would then be required to see. With a hand on each doorknob, she leaned forward, until her forehead was pressing painfully against the shining mahogany; and she wept.

It is said that after an anointed king passed away, his soul took refuge in the body of a crow. It may also be that the name of Cronus, who killed his father, derived from the Greek word for crow and not, as is more often thought, from the word for time. And it is a fact that when Spenta opened the library door, a single crow was sitting on her husband's desk, right beside his uncaring head. When it saw Spenta, it cawed loudly, took flight in a panicky circle, colliding twice with the leather spines of old books, and then made its escape through the room's high windows, which had—unusually—been left wide open, even though the air conditioner was on. Spenta Cama gently laid the back of her right hand against her husband's cheek. Which was cold.

Darius Xerxes Cama and his manservant Gieve had both died of suffocation, which was the murderous "trademark" of Cyrus the Pillowman. The time of death was fixed at around ten-thirty in the evening. The butler had resisted his murderer energetically. There were traces of blood—possibly the killer's—under his long fingernails. Darius did not seem to have resisted at all. His face was calm, nor were there any signs of a struggle. It was as if he had given up his life's breath gladly, as if he were happy to yield it up to his own son.

Good mythology makes bad detective work. The Greeks would have us believe that the First Father was murdered by his youngest son at the instigation of the First Mother, Gaia, Mother Earth herself. But at the time of the Cama killings, Ormus had been singing to a room full of unimpressed diners, and Spenta had been caressing the hands of mortally ill patients at the Lying-In Hospital.

Inspector Sohrab of the Bombay C.I.D., arching a disapproving eyebrow, noted his surprise at having occasion to interview Camas,

Kalamanjas and (as near neighbours who might have seen something significant) Merchants too, so relatively soon after the mysterious fire at Cuffe Parade. However, there could be no doubt that the prime suspect in the present case was the psychopathic escaped killer Khusro alias Cyrus Cama, whose blood was of the same type as the stuff under the dead butler's nails. The motive for the murders was of minor significance in the case of "crazies," who could, as Inspector Sohrab pointed out, "do anything you can think of at the drop of a hat." It was his best guess that Gieve had been killed first, just to get him out of the way. Darius Xerxes Cama had been the real target, perhaps—"just a wild surmise, see"—because Cyrus resented having been first banished from his home, chastised by his teachers more or less at his parents' request, and then legally disowned. Sohrab and Rustam looked at Spenta Cama with open hostility. "Lucky you were out," said Inspector Sohrab viciously, "or you too may have received your deserts."

Some side issues had resolved themselves. The domestic staff had all returned, shuffling and surly, claiming that as Christians they had simply been attending Midnight Mass at the Cathedral and had then gone to visit their family members in the city's outlying suburbs. It was Christmas, after all, and they had been determined to observe it even if their heartless employers had refused to give them the night off. Gieve had not been a Christian. There was nothing else to explain.

There were only two matters, according to Sohrab and Rustam, that still required clarification. Firstly, on the same night as the double killing at Apollo Bunder a person answering closely to the description of the said psychopathic killer Khusro Cama had been seen leaving the scene of a murder by asphyxiation in the city of Lucknow, halfway across the sub-continent. And secondly, the profile of the blood under the dead Gieve's fingernails also corresponded precisely to that of Khusro's twin, the speechless Ardaviraf Cama, on whose forearms there were undeniable scratches, deep enough to have drawn blood.

Virus sat in a corner of the library, his eyes fixed upon the desk at which his father had been found. His feet were up on the chair, and his arms were locked around his knees, and he was rocking slowly back and forth. Sohrab questioned him, badgered him, cajoled him, threatened him, all to no avail. Virus said nothing. "Leave the boy alone,"

Spenta Cama shouted at the C.I.D. inspector at last. "Can't you see he is grieving? Can't you smell how we are all stinking with misery? Go away and do your job, and when you catch," and here she broke into tears, "when you find my other boy, you keep him safe and sound."

On New Year's Day, 1965, Cyrus Cama walked up to the main gate of Tihar Jail and surrendered. Under interrogation, he denied all knowledge of the murder in Lucknow (for which another man was eventually arrested and hanged, protesting his innocence to his last breath). However, he freely confessed to the parricide, and confirmed that the death of the manservant had been—and here he quoted Auden—a "necessary murder." He pointed to the gouges on his arms, wounds far more severe than Virus's scratches, categorically denied that they were self-inflicted, and gave a description of the double crime, so detailed and so closely in line with the known facts and forensic evidence as to terminate all discussion. He was returned to solitary confinement in the jail's maximum-security psychiatric wing, and it was decreed that the teams of prison officers who guarded him should be changed "with high frequency," so that no other poor sucker could ever fall under Cyrus's passionate, erudite, fanatical, lethal spell.

After the fire at Villa Thracia, Persis Kalamanja's alibi had freed Vina from suspicion. Now it was Cyrus Cama's turn to exonerate his brother. All these alibis, all these alternative story lines, that we must abandon! The story, for example, in which our seafront home was destroyed by Vina's revenge; in which the fire inside that much-abused child burst out and consumed my childhood too. And the even stranger story of how Virus Cama, his mysterious mind somehow linked to his twin brother's, carried out the Apollo Bunder murders for him; of how Cyrus could be in two places at once and know, thanks to the unfathomable communication between identical twins, every detail of the murders he forced his silent brother to commit. These stories float, now, in the limbo of lost possibilities. We simply have no grounds for believing them to be true.

And yet, and yet. After her husband's murder Spenta Cama never went to sleep without locking her bedroom door. Nor did Ormus join his dumb brother, whose smile was as sweet as ever, for any more sessions at the family piano.

Impossible stories, stories with No Entry signs on them, change our lives, and our minds, as often as the authorized versions, the stories we are expected to trust, upon which we are asked, or told, to build our judgements, and our lives.

Nine feet from wing tip to wing tip, the vultures hover over the *dokhma,* the Tower of Silence, in the gardens of the *Doongerwadi* on Malabar Hill. Their circling reminds Ormus of the fly-past of aircraft at the funerals of the great. *Between the Parsi and the vulture there exists the great binding intimacy of last things. For us there is no rush. We have our whole lives to wait, I for you, you for me. Each knows the other will keep his appointment.*

We pass through rooms lined with portraits of our famous dead and come to the long funeral hall. Here is the priest and here is the sandalwood man and here is the fire which is the representation of god but is not god. Here are the pallbearers, the nassasalars. *Here is my brother, Ardaviraf the silent. Holding a white scarf between us, we lead the procession into the gardens where the tow-ers stand. There are plenty of birds today, thirty birds, like the thirty in Attar's great poem who made the journey to the Simurg and became the god they sought. The thirty vultures joining together and becoming Vulture. That is the kind of thought my father might have thought, the kind of connection he might have made. You must know who comes to see you today, O vulture, I must explain him to you, in silence, accompanied by my brother of silence, before the silent towers.*

He was a distant father, but we had no other. He was disappointed in us. We were not what he had hoped for. We were less than his dreams. But he praised you, vulture, for your rational, scientific mind. He praised our last meeting, in which the cycle of life is renewed. And on his desk, among the notes he had been working on when he died, he spoke thus of you:

Prometheus chained to a pillar in the high Caucasus, with Zeus's vulture gnawing at his liver all day long. By night the liver regenerates. Unending punishment of pain. The vulture of Prometheus seen as proof of the vindictiveness of Z. With each bite it shows us why we should turn aside from gods & take the rational path. The gods lie, accuse us falsely. (Re: Prometheus, some trumped-up business about a secret love affair with P. Athene.) The gods are whimsical, irrational, divine. For the crime of being ourselves they turn us into rocks, spiders, plants. The agony inflicted by the mordant v. is nothing less than the agony of reason. Joyful agony. It shows Prometheus who he is, how he should live, why the gods are wrong, why he is right. Vulture, we are in your debt. And forever joined to you by ties of our lives' blood. Which may be more powerful than love.

Prometheus the creator of mankind, who saved us from Zeus's wrath by warning Deucalion to build an ark against the Flood. Prometheus father of science & knowledge, who gave us fire and received the vulture in return. What is Titanic in us, let us seek. What is Olympian, let us expunge. I am my father's son. I had thought myself free of him, self-made, but that was vanity. Death shows us the power of blood.

I am my father's son. The punishment of Prometheus I take upon myself. O Promethean vulture of reason, help my father find his way to his deserved rest.

Spenta Cama sent news of Darius's passing to his old friend Lord Methwold, who had continued to write to her with surprising frequency. By return of post she received a long letter of condolence, which spoke of Darius in the warmest terms, much regretted the gulf that had grown up between them, and invited Spenta and her sons to England. "Though it is winter here, yet these different skies, these unfamiliar surroundings, may by virtue of that very difference help to soothe, if not assuage, your pain." On receiving this letter Spenta Cama had a number of thoughts more or less at once: that she was not in as much pain as she had expected; that after the years of Darius's decline, his death felt almost like blessed relief, not least—as the absence of struggle had hinted—to himself; that having refused for half a lifetime to share her husband's English dream, she now found that the prospect of an English winter was filling her with excitement, anticipation, even joy; and that it would be very nice to see William Methwold again after all these years, very nice indeed.

And then there was the problem of money. Darius had died a poor man, and Ormus Cama's income—on which the household had relied to a far greater extent than his disapproving mother had been prepared to admit—had declined sharply. In recent months Spenta had sold off a few "trinkets and baubles" to help maintain standards. Her money worries had etched themselves deeply on her formerly unlined brow and thus come to the attention of Dolly Kalamanja, who had not been so graceless as to speak of them openly. Instead, like a true friend, she had found disingenuous excuses for sending Spenta "little gifties"— silk sari lengths, baskets of laddoos, hot-tiffin carriers laden with the latest international cuisine from the celebrated "Dil Kush" kitchens— in short, the bare necessities of life. For her part, Spenta received the presents lightly, as if they were no more than the trivial evidences of a good friendship, and made sure that she, in her turn, sent Dolly the occasional gift of love: a small ivory carving from the secret treasure chest she kept under her bed, or a novel filched from Darius's library.

Thus Spenta was able to accept her friend's largesse without losing face. But she was practised enough in the codes of polite society to know that her financial situation would soon be the talk of the town, for what Dolly could perceive and keep to herself, less loving eyes would also see soon enough, and less respectful tongues would feel no compulsion to be discreet. Widowhood had only served to underline the crisis by revealing to Spenta the extent of Darius's debts. It seemed inevitable that the Apollo Bunder apartment would have to be sold and the family would be forced to move into humbler accommoda-tion, joining the swelling ranks of distressed Parsi gentlefolk whose extreme indigence was a phenomenon of the age and another mark of the passing of the Empire upon which they had gambled and lost.

Into this growing crisis Lord Methwold's letter of invitation dropped like a blessing from her guardian angels. Spenta hugged it to her bosom and giggled, most improperly for one so recently bereaved. An interested male party with a fortune is a boon to the spirits. *Lady Methwold,* Spenta murmured, and then had the decency to blush, and think of her sons.

Naturally, there was no way of leaving helpless Ardaviraf behind, but once they were in England, Lord Methwold would know what to do for the best; and as for Ormus, that loafer, that immoral nightclub singer who had turned out so poorly, she did not feel able—for she was an honest woman—to decamp without telling him that he had also been invited. When she did tell him, she made it very plain that she was not expecting him to accept Lord Methwold's invitation and would quite understand if he decided his life must take a different, more "bohemian" course. (With what delicate disdain she articulated that word "bohemian"!) In short, she went as close as her nature allowed to telling him he was not wanted on the voyage. To her hor-

ror, however, Ormus Cama accepted, with what looked very like elation. "It's high time I got out of this two-bit town," he said. "So, if it's
okay, I'll tag along for the ride."

Spenta Cama left Bombay at the end of January 1965, accompanied by
her sons. None of the three ever returned to India. By the end of the
year Spenta had become Lady Methwold. At Methwold's insistence,
Virus Cama had been placed in a sanatorium where he would receive
the finest care, and also twice-weekly flute lessons from a professional
flautist of Indian extraction. As for Ormus, he had vanished into the
rest of his life, about which there will be a great deal to say hereafter.
The newlyweds Spenta and Methwold were left to their own devices,
as was only right. Spenta's new husband was full of remorse for his
cold-shouldering of Darius in the matter of the faked legal qualifica-
tions. "In his way he was a giant," Methwold said. "But a giant out of
time. The age of giants has gone, and we mortals grow careless of the
few that remain. But the two of us can hold hands through this long
winter, and remember." These words were spoken on the broad, frosty
parterre of an ample residence in the Home Counties, of which Spenta
was the new châtelaine: a white Palladian mansion set upon a hill
above the winding Thames. White curtains blew at the French windows of the orangery. There was a fountain crawling with gods.
    It was the mansion of Darius Cama's dreams.

Death is more than love or is it. Art is more than love or is it. Love is
more than death and art, or not. This is the subject. This is the subject.
This is it.
    What deflects us from the subject is loss. Of those we love, of the
Orient, of hope, of our place in the book. Loss is more than love or is
it. More than death or is it. More than art, or not. Darius Cama's
"fourth function" added, to the tripartite system of Indo-European
culture (religious sovereignty, physical force, fertility), the necessary
additional concept of the existential outsider, the separated man, the
banished divorcé, the expelled schoolboy, the cashiered officer, the
legal alien, the uprooted wanderer, the out-of-step marcher, the rebel,
the transgressor, the outlaw, the anathematized thinker, the crucified
revolutionary, the lost soul.

The only people who see the whole picture are the ones who step out of the frame. If he was right then this is the subject also. If he was wrong, then the lost are merely lost. Stepping out of the frame, they simply cease to exist.

I am writing here about the end of something, not just the end of a phase of my life but the end of my connection with a country, my country of origin as we say now, my home country I was brought up to say, India. I am trying to say goodbye, goodbye again, goodbye a quarter century after I physically left. This ending is oddly positioned, coming as it does in the middle of my story, but without it the second half of my life could not have happened as it did. Also, it takes time to come to terms with the truth: that what's over is over. Because as it happens I didn't go of my own free will. As it happens I was driven out, like a dog. I had to run for my life.

Small earthquakes were recorded in several parts of India during the late 1960s and early 1970s; nothing serious, no loss of life and minimal damage to property, but enough to make us sleep a little less easily in our beds. One shook the Golden Temple in the Sikh holy city of Amritsar in the Punjab, another rattled teeth in the small southern town of Sriperumbudur. A third scared the children of Nellie in Assam. Finally, the picturesque waters of a Kashmiri lake, high Shishnag, that cold mirror in the sky, began to roil and spume.

Geology as metaphor. There were plenty of rishis and mahagurus, and even political columnists and editorial writers, who were prepared—eager!—to link these tremors with the great public events of those years, such as Mrs. Gandhi's emergence as a formidable leader, "Mrs. Mover-and-Shaker," and her victory over Pakistan in the great War of 1965, which lasted exactly twenty-two days and was fought on two fronts simultaneously, in Kashmir (the "Kashquake") and in Bangladesh (the "Banglashake"). "Old Order Cracks Up," cried the pundits, and, once the allegations about Mrs. G.'s electoral malpractices began, "Dark Rumbles Shake Gandhi Administration."

I, however, did not need geology to explain the upheavals in my immediate circle. I, Umeed Merchant, a.k.a. Rai, turned eighteen in the year of the War. Ormus had gone, and Vina was a fading memory, and I was shuttling between my estranged parents' apartments along with the household servants, because they shared the domestic help as well as me, and when I was angry with them, and at that age one is often angry, I would say that I felt as if I were just another one of their underpaid employees. Then my mother's inoperable brain tumour was diagnosed and within weeks she just died, click, as if somebody had turned out her light, and left me burdened with whole volumes of gentler sentences that I had left unsaid. She was fifty-one years old.

The evening after we buried my mother, my father and I drove out to take a look at Cuffe Parade. The long process of levelling and reclamation was almost complete. The villas, promenade and mangrove forest were long gone, and the sea had retreated before the power of the great machines. An immense brown expanse of land stretched before us, an almost blank slate upon which history was only just beginning to write. The huge dusty space was broken up, articulated, by metal fencing, and large signs forbidding various activities, and the concrete and steel foundations of the first tall buildings; also pile drivers, steam-rollers, trucks, wheelbarrows, cranes. And though the day's work was over, we could still see clumps of workers in the near and middle distance, men were leaning against concrete stumps out of which steel rods twisted like the branches of trees created by some botanical Frankenstein, women with hitched-up saris were holding their earth-carrying metal bowls against their hips and smoking beedis under the No Smoking signs, laughing harshly out of grim gap-toothed faces which knew that life was nothing to laugh about.

This was not the emptiness of the desert but a desert of the spirit, I thought.

"No," said my father, reading my mind. "It is an empty canvas, primed and waiting for the intervention of the artist's hand. Your mother was a visionary. Here, from this propagatory enclave—seedbed wrested from seabed—her Ozymandian colossi will rise, and the mighty will look upon Bombay and despair." He was speaking of his rival, the only one who could have parted two people who loved each other so deeply, and in that moment I did not know whether to hate the city that had torn them apart or to take my lead from V.V.'s desperate generosity in his time of inconsolable grief, his compassionate irony, and forgive Bombay as he forgave it, and also pity it as he did, in the name of that dear, lost love. I thought of sand castles and ice cream and tunelessness and puns, and I thought anew of Vina, in whom there was more of Ameer Merchant than could now be found anywhere else on earth.

It had grown dark, and the evening bugs were biting me to bits. "Let's go," I said, but he didn't hear me. It was my turn to read his mind. She became cynical, he was thinking, she made a pact with the devil, and the devil sent a monster into her head and bore her away. "That isn't it," I said. "It wasn't anything to do with that. You don't believe in the devil, anyway. It was just a stupid disease." He snapped out of his reverie with such a wretchedness upon him that I embraced him. I was six or seven inches taller than him by this time and his scrawny head with its wild wisps of grey hair lay against my chest and he sobbed. The lights of the city—Malabar Hill far away, the Queen's Necklace of Marine Drive curving towards us—hung around us like a noose.

Back then I was partial to science fiction novels. There was a European novel, Polish, I think, about a planet that could bring people's thoughts to life. Think of your dead wife, and there she is in your bed. Think of a monster, and it will crawl into your brain, through your ear. That sort of thing.

Lights like a noose. These were words that came to mind as my father wept on my breast. I should have been more careful with my thoughts. I should have stayed with him that night, but I wanted to be alone, I wanted to sit and stand and walk in Ameer Merchant's rooms and breathe in the past, before it changed for ever. I should have wondered why he told me to turn off the fan as I left him sitting on his bed in his stripey nightsuit. No moon, and stenchy air. I should have stayed with him. The darkness of the city fell around him like a noose.

Some people can sleep under a moving fan and some just can't. Ormus Cama could turn the room upside down and rest under his fan like a man at a mechanical oasis. Vina, however, once told me she could never get rid of the idea that the damned thing would come loose and fly at her while she slept. She had nightmares of decapitation by those whirling blades. Personally, I always liked my fan. I would set the control at minimum and lie back with that slow familiar disturbance of air rolling softly over my skin. The disturbance that calmed. It made me dream of lying stretched out at the edge of an equatorial ocean, lapped

by tides warmer than blood. My father was the opposite. "Doesn't matter how hot it is," Vivvy Merchant said. "The dratted downdraft
induces a cold and tremulous sensation. Shivers my timbers, in sum."

Because I knew this about him, I turned off the fan without argument and left him by himself, left him to choose between the living
and the dead, which was an easy choice, I guess, when Ameer was
among the ranks of the expired, while the cohorts of the extant
included only me. Love is more than death, or is it. There are those
who say that the songsmith Orpheus was a coward because he refused
to die for love, because instead of joining Eurydice in the afterlife he
tried to drag her back to the life before; which was against nature, and
so failed. Judged by this standard, my father was a braver man than the
Thracian lyre player, for in his pursuit of Ameer he sought no special
privileges from the guardians of the hereafter, he requested no return
tickets from the monsters at the gates. But Eurydice and Orpheus were
childless, and my parents were not.

I am the one who has to live with the choice my father made.

O Nissy Poe with your pendant mother in the goats' shed in Virginia long ago. Vina, we are linked by the thing we have seen, by the
burden we have to bear. They didn't want to see us growing up. They
didn't love us enough to wait. Suppose we hadn't turned out okay?
Suppose we needed them? Suppose a thousand things and a thing.

Murder is a crime of violence against the murdered person. Suicide
is a crime of violence against those who remain alive.

The servants woke me early and took me to his bedroom. They clustered in the doorway, wide-eyed, driven half mad by what they saw,
like Goya figures at a witches' sabbath, goggling in fascinated terror at
the Goat. V.V. Merchant was hanging from the ceiling fan. Lights like
a noose. He had used the flex from a standard lamp to fashion the
instrument of his ending. He was rotating slowly, turning in the breeze.
This is what got to me, broke through my reserve, prevented me from
suppressing my feelings and casting a cold eye on the event: that somebody had come in here and switched on the fan. "Who did it?" I
shrieked. "Who turned the damn thing on?"

"Sahib, it was hot, sahib," said the Goya figures. "Sahib, and there is
the question of the smell."

• • •

He had never really believed in their separation, always hoped to win her back. One day she would wake up, he imagined, and wonder why he wasn't in the bed beside her, she would see the error of her ways. That mattered, her seeing the error of her ways, because the Ameer he wanted back was the woman he'd married, not the cynical Mammon worshipper who had joined forces with Piloo Doodhwala. His own grievous fault caused him much daily torment. In his determination to break his gambling addiction, he had gone so far as to ask for my help. What he wanted was for me to become his bookmaker, and so I opened a book. When the cardplaying bug bit him, we played cards. Evening after evening of matchstick poker. I would make entries in the book each time we played, and kept an exact tally of his matchstick losses, which were, as ever, heavy. As for the racetrack, he managed to keep away from it, except on gymkhana days when families were welcome. Then I would accompany him, having made sure he was carrying no money, and instead of making bets we would take photographs of the horses he fancied. If he backed a winner we kept the photograph and pasted it into the book alongside a note of the odds; if not, we ripped it up and hurled it into a trash can as if it were a useless betting slip from the Tote. However, details of these "losses" were also entered in the book of his withdrawal from addiction. When he wanted to bet on the weather, I took the bet. He would see two flies on a windowpane and want to bet on which of them would take off first. As he went about town he would often get into disputes about cricket scores, movie credits, the authorship of songs, and instead of betting real money, he would ring me, and I would enter the bet in the book, afterwards adding a note saying whether he was right or wrong. In this way, very slowly, he had cured himself. The fantasy bets in my little copybook—which was yellow and bore, on the cover, the legend *Globe Copy* and a picture of a saturnine ringed planet—gradually weaned him off the real thing. Each month there were fewer entries for me to make, until at last there came a month in which I was not required to make any entries at all. He took the book and showed it to Ameer. "It's over," he said. "Why not give Piloo the bum's rush and we can resume?"

"You're right about one thing," she told him. "It's over, that's for sure." Two weeks later the tumour made its appearance. Six weeks after that she was dead.

Sometimes it's just over and you can't make it all right. Justification by works: an overrated idea. There are the dumpers and there are the dumped, and if you fall into the latter category no amount of fantasy gambling can save you. In my life I have done my share of dumping (mostly women) and have not often been the spurned party. Except, of course, that my father—for whom Ameer's last rejection was perhaps even more painful than her death—strung himself up and left me dangling. Thus making himself both dumper and dumpee. Except, also, that Vina always turned away from me whenever her love of Ormus, her addiction to him, her Ormus habit, required her attention.

But even Ormus Cama had to learn what it felt like to be cast out, fourth functional, dispensable; to be exiled beyond an unbreachable pale.

8

THE DECISIVE MOMENT

Let us now praise unjustly neglected men. The first permanent photograph was taken in 1826, in Paris, by Joseph Nicéphore Niépce, but his place in our collective memory has been usurped by his later collaborator, Louis Daguerre, who sold their invention, their magic box, the "caméra," to the French government after Niépce's death. It must therefore be stated without equivocation that the celebrated daguerreotype plates could not have been created without Niépce's scientific knowledge, which far exceeded that of his partner. Nor was the art of photography Niépce's only child; for he was also the creator of the mighty pyréolophore, or combustion engine. Truly, a father of the New.

What was it like, that First Photograph, forerunner of the Age of the Image? Technically: a direct positive image on a treated pewter plate, requiring many long hours of exposure time. Its subject: nothing more elevated than the view from the Nicéphorean workroom window. Walls, sloping roofs, a tower wearing a conical hat, and open country-side beyond. All is dull, still, dim. No hint here that this is the first quiet note of what will become a thundering symphony, or it may be more honest to say a deafening cacophony. But (I switch metaphors in my excitement) a floodgate has been opened, an unstoppable torrent of pictures is to follow, haunting and forgettable, hideous and beautiful, pornographic and revelatory, pictures that will create the very idea of the Modern, that will overpower language itself, and cover and distort and define the earth, like water, like gossip, like democracy.

Niépce, I bow my head to you. Great Nicéphore, I doff my beret. If Daguerre—like the Titan Epimetheus—was the one who opened this Pandoran box, unleashing the ceaseless click and snap, the interminable flash and sprocket of photography, still it was you, great Anarch!, who stole the gods' gift of permanent vision, of the transformation of sight into memory, of the actual into the eternal—that is, the gift of immortality—and bestowed it upon mankind. Where are you now, O Titanic seer, Prometheus of film? If the gods have punished you, if you're chained to a pillar high up on an Alp while a vulture munches your guts, take comfort in the news. This just in: the gods are dead, but photography is alive & kicking. Olympus? Pah! It's just a camera now.

Photography is my way of understanding the world.

When my mother died I photographed her, cold in bed. Her profile was shockingly gaunt, but still beautiful. Brightly lit against a darkness, with shadows gathering great scoops from her cheeks, she resembled an Egyptian queen. I thought of the female pharaoh Hatshepsut, whom Vina also mirrored, and then it hit me. *My mother looked like Vina;* or, as Vina might have looked, had she grown old and died in her bed. When I made eight-by-ten prints of the photograph I liked best, I wrote "Hat Cheap Suit" on the back with a thick black marking pen.

When my father died I took his picture before they cut him down. I asked to be left alone with him and used a roll of film. Most of the shots avoided his face. I was more interested in the way the shadows fell across his dangling body, and the shadow he himself cast in the early light, a long shadow for a smallish man.

I thought of these acts as respectful.

After they were gone I walked the streets of the city they had both loved in their different, irreconcilable ways. Though that love had often oppressed and stifled me, I now wanted it for myself, wanted to have my parents back by loving what they loved and so becoming what they had been. And photography was my means of gaining an education in their love. So I photographed the workers at the Cuffe Parade development site as they walked with perfect, nonchalant balance along the beam of a crane a hundred feet above ground. I seized for myself the maelstrom of straw baskets at Crawford Market, and took possession, too, of the inert figures who were everywhere, sleeping on the hard pillows of the sidewalks, their faces turned towards urinous walls, beneath the lurid movie posters of buxom goddesses with sofa-cushion lips. I photographed political slogans on *art dekho* buildings, and children grinning out through the toe of the giant Old Woman's Shoe. It was easy to be a lazy photographer in Bombay. It was easy to take an interesting picture and almost impossible to take a good one. The city seethed, gathered to stare, turned its back and didn't care. By showing me everything it told me nothing. Wherever I pointed my camera—*Juicy that? Juicy* that?—I seemed to glimpse something worth having, but usually it was just something excessive: too colourful, too grotesque, too apt. The city was expressionistic, it screamed at you, but it wore a domino mask. There were whores, tightrope walkers, transsexuals, movie stars, cripples, billionaires, all of them exhibitionists, all of them obscure. There was the thrilling, appalling infinity of the crowd at Churchgate Station in the morning, but that same infinity made the crowd unknowable; there were the fish being sorted on the pier at the Sassoon dock, but all the activity showed me nothing: it was just activity. Lunch runners carried the city's tiffin boxes to their destinations, but the boxes guarded their mystery. There was too much money, too much poverty, too much nakedness, too much disguise, too much anger, too much vermilion, too much purple. There were too many dashed hopes and narrowed minds. There was far, far too much light.

I began to look at the darkness instead. This led me towards the use of illusion. I composed pictures with sharply delineated areas of light and dark, composed them with such manic care that the light area of one image corresponded precisely to the blackness in another. In the darkroom I had set up for myself in my father's old apartment I blended these images. The composite pictures that resulted were sometimes dazzling in their mixed perspectives, often confused, sometimes unreadable. I preferred the composite darknesses. For a time I began to shoot deliberately into the dark, picking human life out of lightless-ness, delineating it with as little light as I could get away with.

I decided not to go to college but to concentrate on my pho-tographs. I also wanted to move. I could not bear to go on living in those two separate sets of rooms under the same roof, within the schizoid structure of my parents' fatal unhappiness. Then the much larger Cama apartment was put up for sale by the firm of Cox's & King's, acting as local agents for the new Lady Methwold, who had no plans to return. I got hold of the keys and went to take a look. I shut the door behind me and for a while I did not turn on any lights, but allowed the darkness to take what shape it chose. As my eyes adjusted, I saw soft Himalayas of dust-sheeted furniture ribbed faintly with the sly light that had sidled in between the closed imperfect shutters. In the library I stood beside the shrouded bodies of Darius's desk and chair and peered at the shelves of naked, staring books. It was the books that at first glance seemed dead, like withered leaves. The furniture, beneath the winter of the white dust sheets, looked as if it were simply waiting for the return of spring. I was intrigued to note that the apartment did not trouble me; not even this room in which a world had ended retained any power to move. I had seen other such rooms. I pointed my camera, and working very quickly, feeling an eagerness take hold of me, I took several shots.

After I moved into the apartment, however, it was the books that came to life and spoke to me. Darius's lifetime of learning was of no long-term interest to his sons, for all Ormus Cama's noble funeral thoughts and Cyrus's high, if warped, intelligence; so it—the library, the old man's unquiet shade—adopted me instead. On an impulse I bought it along with the apartment, and began to read.

For a while I became a photographer of exits. It isn't easy to take pho-tographs of strangers' funerals. People get annoyed. Yet it interested me that Indian funeral practices dealt so openly, so directly, with the phys-icality of the corpse. The body on the pyre or on the *dokhma,* or in its close-sewn Muslim shroud. Christians were the only community to conceal their dead in boxes. I didn't know what it meant, but I knew how it looked. Coffins forbade intimacy. In my stolen photographs—for the photographer must be a thief, he must steal instants of other people's time to make his own tiny eternities—it was this intimacy I sought, the closeness of the living and the dead. The secretary staring through eyes made garish with grief at the body of his great master dressed in fire. The son standing in an open grave, holding his father's shrouded head in his cupped hand, laying it tenderly upon deep earth.

Sandalwood plays its perfumed part in all these rites. Sandalwood chips in the Muslim bier, in the Parsi fire, on the Hindu pyre. The odour of death is an intimacy too far. But a camera cannot smell. Dispensing with nosegays, it can stick its nose as far in as it is permitted to go, it can intrude. Often I had to turn on my heels and run, pursued by insults and stones. Murderer! Assassin! the mourners shouted after me, as if I were responsible for the death they mourned. And there was a truth in the insults. A photographer shoots. Like a gunman standing by a little gate in a prime minister's garden, like an assassin in a hotel lobby, he must line up a clear shot, he must try not to miss. He has a target, and there are crosshairs in his eyepiece. He wants light from his subjects, he takes their light and their darkness too, which is to say, their lives. Yet I also thought of these pictures, these forbidden images, as gestures of respect. The camera's respect has nothing to do with seriousness, sanctimony, privacy, or even taste. It has to do with attention. It has to do with clarity, of the actual, of the imagined. And there is also the issue of honesty, a virtue which everyone routinely extols and recommends, until it is directed, in all its uncushioned force, at themselves.

Honesty is not the best policy in life. Only, perhaps, in art.

Deaths are not the only exits, of course, and in my new rôle as exit photographer I sought also to document more quotidian departures. At the airport, spying upon the sorrows of parting, I sought out the single dry-eyed member of a weeping throng. Outside the city's cinemas I examined the faces of audiences emerging from dreams into the pungency of the real, with the illusion still hanging in their eyes. I tried to find narratives, mysteries, in the come and go at the doors of great hotels. After a time I no longer knew why I was doing these things, and it was at this point, I believe, that the pictures started to improve, because they were no longer about myself. I had learned the secret of becoming invisible, of disappearing into the work.

Invisibility was simply extraordinary. Now, when I went in search of exits, I could walk right up to the edge of a grave and photograph an argument between those who wanted flowers scattered over the body and those who argued that the religion permitted no such effete indulgences—or I might eavesdrop on a quayside family quarrel at the docks in order to capture the moment when the newlywed young daughter of old parents, a girl who had refused an arranged marriage and insisted on a "love match," stormed away from her disapproving mother and boarded the waiting steamer, clinging to her awkwardly grinning, weak-moustachioed disaster of a husband, and set out into her new life carrying the burden of a remorse she would never be able to shed—or I might sidle into any of the secret moments we hide from the world, a last kiss before parting, a last piss before starting, and snap happily away. I was too excited by my power to be scrupulous about its use. The inhibited photographer should set down his camera, I thought, and never work again.

As my parents' sole heir, I had become a young gentleman of means. The family business, Merchant & Merchant, with its thick folder of architectural contracts and its important interest in the Cuffe Parade and Nariman Point developments, I sold for a handsome sum to the consortium of developers headed by Piloo Doodhwala. The Orpheum cinema, now flourishing under new management, I likewise disposed of to the glinting Mr. Sisodia, who had already leased a lot in Film City and founded the Orpheum movie studios that would make his reputation and fortune. "Or or always welcome at the awfu awfu Orpheum," Mr. Sisodia assured me as I signed the papers. But I had washed my hands of my parents' work. In these old stories, I sought no further part. I snapped Sisodia's picture—thick black glasses, cadaverous teeth, Methwold-hairless head, ruthless, charming, insincere, every inch the embryonic movie mogul—and quickly took my leave.

By the start of the 1970s the city's air had become badly polluted, and public commentators, ready as ever to allegorize, called it a sign of the filth in the national atmosphere. The city's doctors noted an alarming rise in migraine sufferers, and the oculists revealed that many patients had started complaining of double vision, though they couldn't remember bumping their heads, and there was no other evidence of concussion. Wherever you went you saw men and women standing in the street scratching their heads, frowning. There was a growing general sense of disorder, of things being out of kilter, off the rails. *It shouldn't be this way.*

Bombay had become Mumbai, by order of its rulers, the MA party, of which, it unsurprisingly emerged, Shri Piloo Doodhwala was a principal benefactor and power broker. I dropped in on Persis Kalamanja to complain about the new name. "And what are we supposed to call Trombay, then? 'Trumbai'? And how about the Back Bay? 'Backbai'? And what's to be done with Bollywood? I suppose it's 'Mollywood' now." But Persis had a bad headache and didn't laugh. "Something's going to happen," she said seriously. "I can feel the ground beginning to shift."

Persis had turned thirty. Her beauty, which had reached its full womanly bloom, had also become oddly asexual, neutered, in my opinion, by her development of an enigmatic little smile which I found almost insufferably pious. My sarcastic carpings aside, however, her saintly personality and the zeal with which she had joined her mother in a heavy programme of good works had earned her much respect all over town, while her continued celibacy, at first the subject of giggles and whispers, then a cause for pity, nowadays engendered in most of us a kind of unholy awe. There was something otherworldly about Persis these days, and I was not surprised when her mystical side, which lies beneath all our surfaces like a fault, began to manifest itself, and she took to making gloomy predictions of the future. She sat dressed in simple homespun amid the splendours of "Dil Kush" and foretold doom, and if she was our Cassandra, then maybe—just maybe—Bombay was about to fall, like Troy.

Ours was an unlikely intimacy, a friendship of opposites, born of loss. After Vina and Ormus had gone, Persis and I gravitated towards each other, like disciples after the departure of their masters, like echoes of a silenced sound. But as the years passed we became each other's bad habit. I disapproved of her self-denying saint act. No more old maid, go get laid, I would tell her in my best social-butterfly manner; enough with the soup kitchens, get into some hot water of your own. For her part, she scolded me for my many undoubted failings, and in this unexpected way we grew fond, even inordinately fond, of each other. She never gave the slightest sign of wanting anything from me other than platonic, brother and sister friendship, and fortunately that madonna rictus of hers, her smile like a holy sword, had chopped off my own desire at the root.

It was the day of the kite festival. The rooftops were already filling up with children and adults, launching their technicolor diamonds into the air. I had arrived at "Dil Kush" with my own selection of kites and *manja* reels, including the kite fighters' special battle thread, black gut dipped in a suspension full of tiny shards of broken glass. *Kala manja.* How did a family that must have originally got its name by selling such a ferocious weapon, the H-bomb of the kite world, produce a namby-pamby like you, I asked Persis, who was in an uncharacteristically foul humour today, too sour even to smile her infuriating smile. "I guess I just looked past the dirty kites to the pure heavens above," she snapped, meaning it. She was worried about something, more worried than she was willing to admit.

Dolly Kalamanja came into the room with her house guest, a tall, sloping Frenchman in his sixties, wearing an absurd trilby pulled down so low it all but touched his nose. He was armed with a small Leica pocket camera, and eager for the roof. "Persis, come, no," cried Dolly. "Don't just sit on and miss the fun." But Persis shook her head muti-nously. We left her by herself and made our ascent.

Kite dogfights raged overhead. I hurled my warriors into the fray and slew my foes, one, two, three. In the crowded sky it was impossi-ble to be sure whose kite attacked, whose fell. They became unidenti-fied flying objects. One stopped thinking of them as having owners. They were their own masters, kites-errant, duelling to the death.

Dolly had half introduced me to the Frenchman on the stairs to the roof, calling him simply "our Mr. H.," showing off her bit of French. *"Notre très cher Monsieur Ach'."* I noticed with some annoyance that he hardly ever looked up at the sky, and paid no attention whatsoever to my victories. The rooftops—flat or sloping, ridged or domed, and all crowded with people—held his attention entirely. He took small steps, this way, that way, until he settled. Then, frozen in a half stoop, he waited, Leica at the ready. His patience, his stillness, was inhuman, predatory. I understood that I was watching a master of invisibility at work, an artist, an occultist. He would dissolve while I watched him, he became simply not-there, an absence, until the little scene he was stalking satisfied him, and then, click, he would fire off a single shot and re-materialize. He must indeed be a master marksman, I thought, to need no more than one. Then he would make his little dance of steps again, settle again, vanish again, click, and so on. Watching him, I lost my favourite kite. Someone else's *kala manja* cut me down. I didn't care. I had seen enough to know the Frenchman's name.

At that moment the earthquake began. My first thought, when I felt the tremor, was that this was an impossibility, a piece of make-believe, a mistake, because we did not have earthquakes in Bombay. In those years when many parts of the country had begun to shake, Bombayites had prided themselves on being quake-free. Good communal relations and good solid ground, we boasted. No fault lines under our town. But now Piloo Doodhwala's MA boys were stoking the fires of discord, and the city had begun to shake.

It was what Persis had foretold. There could be no denying that she had developed some sort of sixth sense, some preternatural sensitivity to the treacheries of life. In China they were predicting earthquakes by watching the behaviour of cattle, sheep and goats. In Bombay, apparently, one now needed only to keep Persis Kalamanja under observation.

The truth is that it was not a bad earthquake, low on the scale and of short duration. But there was widespread damage, because the city was unprepared. Many shanties, hutments, *jopadpatti* lean-to shacks and slum dwellings fell, as well as three tenement *chawls* and a couple of derelict villas on Cumballa Hill. Cracks appeared in large structures, including the façade of the Orpheum cinema, and in roads and underground drains, and there was much smashed furniture and glass. There were fires. The sea wall at Hornby Vellard broke and for the first time in more than a century the tides swept in through the Great Breach, and the Mahalaxmi racetrack and the Willingdon Club's golf course were both swamped under a foot of briny water until the damage was repaired. When the sea retreated it left behind its mysteries: unknown fishes, lost children, pirate flags.

An unspecified number of construction workers and kite fighters fell to their deaths. A dozen or so citizens were crushed beneath falling masonry. The tram lines twisted madly up from the roads, and after that they were ripped up for good. For three days the city seemed hardly to move. Offices remained closed, the monstrous traffic jams vanished, pedestrians were few and far between. In the open spaces, however, crowds gathered, huddling far from the buildings, but casting anxious glances, too, at the earth of the maidans, as if it had become an adversary, sly, malign.

In the months that followed, as Mrs. Gandhi's dictatorial Emergency tightened its grip, the national mood grew sombre and fearful. But the worst excesses of the Emergency occurred elsewhere; in Bombay it was the earthquake that people remembered, the earthquake that gave us the shock that shook our confidence in who we were and how we had chosen to live. An op-ed columnist of the local edition of *The Times of India* went so far as to wonder if the country might literally be breaking apart. "Long aeons ago," he reminded us, "India made a tryst with destiny, breaking away from the mighty southern proto-continent of Gondwanaland and linking her destiny to the northern landmass of Laurasia. The Himalaya mountains are the evidence of that coming together; they are the kiss that joined us to our fate. Is it a kiss that failed? Are these new movements of the earth the prelude to a titanic divorce? Will the Himalayas begin, very slowly, to shrink?" Eight hundred words of questions without answers, of traumatized predictions that India would become the "new Atlantis" as the waters of the Bay of Bengal and the Arabian Sea closed over the Deccan plateau. The paper's publication of so panicky a text indicated the depth of local concern.

On the roof, during the few, but impossibly elongated, seconds of the quake, the great French photographer M. Henri Hulot turned his camera perversely towards the sky. All over town terrified kite flyers had let go of their controlling reels. The heavens were full of dying kites, kites nosediving towards the earth, kites being smashed in mid-air by collisions with other kites, kites being torn to shreds by the boiling winds and by the Dionysiac madness of their sudden freedom, that fatal liberty acquired in the midst of catastrophe and then stolen away again, almost at once, by the inexorable gravitational pull of the cracking earth below. Click, went the Leica. The result is the famous image "Earthquake 1971," in which the tearing mid-air explosion of a single kite tells us everything about the unseen mayhem below. The air becomes a metaphor for the earth.

"Dil Kush" was a solidly constructed mansion, its foundations driven deep into the living rock, and so it trembled but did not break. One of the water tanks on the roof did split, however, and I pulled Hulot away from the path of the gushing water, which he gave no sign of having seen. Dolly Kalamanja was already running downstairs, shouting out her daughter's name. The Frenchman thanked me courteously, touching his hat, then tapping his camera with a self-deprecating shrug.

Downstairs, Persis sat sobbing amid broken glass, inconsolable, like a homespun princess surrounded by opulent jewels, like a lonely woman amid the ruins of her memories. The earthquake had shaken up feelings which she had tried to bury long before, and now they were pouring out of her, like water from a burst tank. Dolly flapped helplessly around her with a large handkerchief, mopping at her face. Persis brushed her mother away as if she were a moth.

"Everybody leaves," she wailed. "They all go away and we're left here to wither and die by ourselves. No wonder the whole place cracks to bits and falls down, it's all shrivelled up and old and on its own."

M. Hulot, clearing his throat, extending an arm, not knowing whether to touch her or not, allowed his fingers to flutter helplessly by her shoulder. A second moth, which she was too polite to swat. He essayed gallantry. "Mademoiselle, I assure you, the only rotten fruit here is imported from France."

She laughed, a little crazily. "You are wrong, monsieur. You may be over sixty, but me, I am five thousand years old, five thousand years of stagnation and decay, and now I am going to pieces and everyone is going away." She whirled towards me then, and glared savagely. "You, why don't you also go? He has been trying to leave for years," she snarled at the alarmed Hulot, with sudden, shocking vehemence. "Always photoing exits. What are all these ways out but rehearsals for his own? All he wants is to run away to his beloved Europe, his Amrika, but as yet he hasn't found the guts."

"You take photographs?" Hulot asked me. I nodded, dumbly. I could never have imagined that I could have a chance to discuss my obsession with such a figure. Now that the chance had come it was impossible to take it, because Persis Kalamanja was on fire.

"Living in that place of dead men, dumb men, killers and evacuees," Persis jeered in a loud, unsteady voice. "What for? To be their lost shadow, their last camp follower, like one of those club bearers or ancient fogeys who are sitting waiting for the British to return?"

"This is a lot to deduce from a change of address," I said, trying to make light of her hostility, of the thing that had burst out of her depths and attacked me for the crime of not being another man; of living in his home and not being he.

"You were born with everything," she raged, having moved beyond all restraint, "and you're throwing it away. Family business, everything. Next you will throw us away also. Of course! You are leaving, but you are so confused you don't know it. Walking the city streets with your stupid camera, thinking you're saying hullo when really it's one long goodbye. Arré, you're mixed up about everything, Umeed, I'm sorry. You want so much to be loved but you don't know how to let people love you. What do you want, hein? Plenty-women-lots-of-money? White birdies, black chickies, pounds sterling, U.S. greenbacks? Will that satisfy you? Is it what you're looking for?"

Even as she said the unsayable, the unforgivable, I was unsaying her words, forgiving her, because I knew I was taking another man's beating. I was struck by the fact that the questions she was hurling at me were such close variants of what Yul Singh had asked Ormus Cama years before. And as she asked it I knew that my answer was the same as his. It was an answer I couldn't bring myself to give her, but she saw it on my face anyway, and snorted with contempt.

"Always second in line," she said. "And if you never get her? Then what?"

I had no answer. Fortunately, as things turned out, I didn't need one.

M. Hulot asked to see my work, and we made our escape. I drove him through the chaos of the city—the fallen trees, the collapsed balconies like soldiers' chevron stripes, the demented birds, the screaming—to what was now my apartment. He spoke uninhibitedly about his own technique; about the "pre-composition" of an image in the imagination, and then the intense stillness, the waiting for the decisive moment. He mentioned Bergson's idea of the self as "pure duration," *no longer situated under the sign of the permanence of the* cogito, *but in the intuition of the duration.* "Like a Japanese artist," he said. "An hour of being there before the empty canvas, learning the void, and then three seconds of strokes, *paf! paf!,* like swordsmanship, very exact. You want to go to the West," he said. "But I have learned most from the East."

I was surprised that a man as unassuming, as determinedly everyday as he, should speak so much about magic, about the "soul of the real," an oxymoron that reminded me of Darius Cama's "miracle of reason." "It was Balzac," Hulot said, "who told Nadar that photographs stripped away the subject's personality. The idea of the camera has always been closely related to the older, but parallel, idea of ghosts. The still camera, yes, and the film camera even more so."

There was a film he greatly admired, he said: *Ugetsu,* by the Japanese master Mizoguchi. A poor man is taken up by a great lady, kept in style and offered unimaginable delights, but she is a phantom. "It is easy for a film to convince us of this proposition so improbable, because on the screen, all are equally wraithlike, equally irreal." A more recent film, *Les Carabiniers* by Jean-Luc Godard, proved Balzac's point by extension. "Two young country boys go off to war, promising their girls that when they return they will bring back all the wonders of the world. They return, penniless, with nothing more than a battered suitcase to show for their adventures. But the girls do not excuse them, they want their promised wonders. The soldiers open the suitcase, and *voilà!* The Statue of Liberty, the Taj Mahal, the Sphinx, I don't know what other things beyond any price. The girls are completely satisfy; their beaux have kept their word. Afterwards the soldiers are killed: a machine gun in a cellar. What remains of them is the treasure they brought home. The wonders of the world.

"Picture postcards," he laughed. "The souls of things."

In the former library of Sir Darius Xerxes Cama, upon the same table at which Darius and William Methwold had pursued their studies, I spread out my portfolio for Hulot. The chandelier lay in pieces on the floor, and books had tumbled from the shelves. To keep myself busy while Hulot examined my pictures, I began to pick up the fallen volumes. I had been reading my way through the old texts and commentaries. The books in Greek and Sanskrit were beyond me, I readily admit, but the ones I could read had captured me, drawing me into their cosmos of savage divinity, of destiny that could be neither diluted nor avoided, but only heroically endured, because one's fate and one's nature were not separate things, only different words for the same phenomenon.

"Have you looked at the past?"

At first, lost in the contemplation of the fallen books, I didn't understand the Frenchman's question. Then in a rush I began to jabber about my father's photograph collection, about Haseler and Dayal. I was aware of how provincial I must sound, so, like an over-enthusiastic schoolboy, I dropped the more cosmopolitan names of Niépce and Talbot, of the daguerreotype and the calotype. I referred to Nadar's portraits, Muybridge's horses, Atget's Paris, Man Ray's surrealism; to *Life* magazine and *Picture Post*.

"Are you really so serious a young man?" he teased me, gravely. "Did you never see any dirty postcards or look for porno magazines?"

That made me blush, but then he became serious and changed my life, or rather allowed me to believe what I had not until then really dared to believe: that I could have the life I most desired. "You have understood something about attention and surprise," he said. "Something of the double self of the photographer, the ruthless *tant-pis* killer and the giver of immortality also. But there is a danger of mannerism, what do you think."

Of course, thank you, maestro. Mannerism, yes, a great danger, a terrible thing, I will be on my guard against it in future, maestro, be assured of it. Thank you. Attention, surprise. Exactly. These will be my watchwords. Have no fear.

He turned away from my babbling to look out of the high windows towards the Gateway, and changed the subject. "Your friend Persis is like many remarkable people I have met in Asia," he said. "Her prediction of the tremor. Extraordinary, yes? It is perhaps her asceticism that has enabled her, that has opened her to such things. She is a seer without a camera, an *illuminée* of the decisive moment. It is quite normal after such a feat prodigious that there should be some uncontrollable emotional release." He swung round to see how his statement had gone down, and caught me in the act of pulling a face. He roared with laughter. "Oho, you don't like that," he observed.

An answer was expected, and so, even though I had no explanation for Persis's astonishing prescience, I took a sternly rationalist line. "Excuse me, monsieur, but hereabouts we are plagued by godness masquerading as goodness. The supernatural level is our lifetime detention centre. And every so often our deep spiritualism leads us to massacre one another like wild beasts. Excuse me, but some of us aren't falling for it, some of us are trying to break free into the real."

"Good," he said, mildly. "Good. Find your enemy. When you know what you're against you have taken the first step to discovering what you're for."

He made as if to go. I offered him my services as a driver, but he declined them. He wanted to stalk the shaken city for the images he was pre-composing in his mind. As he left, he gave me his card. "Call me when you come," he said. "Maybe I am able to be of a little help."

M. Hulot had told me ghost stories: the spectre of a Japanese woman, the postcards of the dead *carabiniers.* Images on film were the ghosts in the machine. Three days after the earthquake, I saw a ghost of my own; not a photograph, but a genuine apparition, a revenant from the past. I was at home at Apollo Bunder, participating in the great clear-up of broken glass and tumbled books. The phones weren't working and there were power outages—"load shedding"—during the hottest hours of the day. I was sweating and short-tempered and not at all prepared for a loud banging on the apartment's front door. I opened up with a scowl on my face and found myself facing the phantom of Vina Apsara, which looked as shocked as I.

"This isn't right," she said, clutching her brow, as if she had a headache. "This isn't supposed to be you."

It seemed that ghosts could grow up. She was ten years older than when I'd last seen her: a ravishing twenty-six. Her hair exploded from her head in a huge halo of frizz (it was the first Afro I'd ever seen), and she wore the wised-up, not remotely innocent, expression that was mandatory for the "alternative" women of the period, especially singers who were politically involved. But Vina was always good at putting out mixed signals. As well as the single black glove of the black

American radicals, she had painted the *Om* symbol in scarlet on her right cheek and wore an English dress from a boutique called The Witch Flies High, one of the dark wisps of Indianized occult-chic couture characteristic of the period, which very approximately covered a part of her long and outrageous body. Her dark skin had a burnished quality to it: a heightening. I did not know it then, but it was the gleam created by the brilliant gaze of the public eye, the first rough licks of the tigerish tongue of fame.

"You're years too late for him," I said, a little too cruelly. "Nobody waits for ever, not even for you."

She pushed past me into the apartment, as if it belonged to her. Knowing she came from nowhere, had nothing but what she made of herself, she had learned to treat the whole world as her possession, and I, like the rest of the planet, meekly acquiesced, and acknowledged her dominion over me and mine.

"What a train wreck," she said, surveying the smashed apartment. "Did anybody get out of this alive?"

Her delivery was unimpressed-tough-broad, but her voice trembled briefly. That was when I understood that the earthquake had jolted Vina into the realization that she was still tied to Ormus, that he was still the only man for her, and the fear that he might be dead or injured had overridden all the uncertainties that had driven her away and led her to create her hard-boiled persona. The earthquake hurled her on to a plane and brought her back to Bombay, to Ormus's door; only it wasn't his door any longer. Other upheavals had placed me in his space. I made her coffee, and slowly, as if rediscovering an old habit, she stopped striking attitudes and metamorphosed back into the girl I had known and, yes, damn it, loved.

She had completed her apprenticeship in the coffee bars and clubs of London, from beatnik folk dives like Jumpy's to the bubbling psychedelia of Middle Earth and UFO, and then moved to New York. There, she went down a blind alley to Folkville, where she shared star billing with Joan Baez but felt alien and ill at ease. She then disgusted and lost her folkie fans by moving into the "mainstream" and doing a season in a sequinned fishtail dress (as it happens, one of the outfits she had stolen from my mother), opening for the Supremes at the Copacabana, because she wanted to be the first brown woman supporting the first black women to play that exalted and conservative gig. Also because she wanted to upstage Diana Ross; which she did. After that she changed direction again, becoming an early pioneer of the trail that led from the Wrong End Café to Sam's Pleasure Island and Amos Voight's Slaughterhouse, where the worlds of art, film and music met and fucked, while Voight mildly, ruthlessly, watched.

She was becoming notorious as an unashamed exhibitionist—a reputation that her largely absent Witch dress did nothing to disprove. To wear such a garment in Bombay could be dangerous, but Vina didn't care. She was an ornery loudmouth too. She appeared regularly on the covers of underground magazines, those new cracks in the media façade caused by the Western youthquake. By pouring out her rage and passion in those journals of narcotic typography, and posing pneumatically for their porno-liberal pix, she became one of the first sacred monsters of the counter-culture, an aggressive iconoclast, half genius, half egomaniac, who lost no opportunity to roar and suck and boo and preen and demolish and cheerlead and revolutionise and innovate and flash and boast and scold. The truth is that this noisy-noisome, pestilential-pest act of hers had set her singing career back. Nowadays such fuck-you, in-your-face aggression would be merely conventional, almost necessary for the wannabe rockette; but in those days such battles had not yet been won. People could still be, and often were, insulted and shocked. You could shoot yourself in the foot.

So while her marvellous voice ensured her a full slate of bookings, her bad mouth lost her many of them. The Copacabana engagement, for example, was terminated after one week, when she casually referred to her stuffed-shirt audience as "dead Kennedys." The United States, still at war both with itself and in Indochina, had been plunged into deep mourning by the freak double killing of President Bobby Kennedy and his elder brother and predecessor, ex-President Jack, both slain by a single bullet fired by a delusional Palestinian gunman. This was the so-called magic bullet which bounced around the lobby of the Ambassador Hotel, L.A., whining like a demented hornet, and ended up scoring an appalling double hit. In that grief-charged atmosphere, when hundreds of thousands of Americans reported sledgehammer migraine headaches and violent dizzy spells, and people stood dazed on street corners murmuring "It shouldn't be this way," Vina was probably lucky that her gibe only lost her a job. She could have been run out of town on a rail. She could have been lynched.

Once, casually, she had married and divorced, and the list of her lovers was long. Interestingly, though she liked to hint at bisexuality, the list was exclusively male. Professionally unconventional Vina was a traditionalist in this area, at least, though her promiscuity was extreme even by the standards of the times.

When Vina arrived on my doorstep, her celebrity as a singer had not spread outside a medium-size circle of cognoscenti; she had belatedly been signed to a recording contract by Yul Singh's Colchis label, but thus far word of her talents had not travelled back east. Nor was her mouthy notoriety locally known. Distraught, anonymous, she stretched out on one of my sofas and smoked a joint. I am ashamed to say that I had never previously been offered what I still quaintly called a "reefer," and its effect on me was rapid and potent. I lay down beside her, and she drew close. We stayed like that for a long time, allowing the distant past to make its connection with the present, letting the silence erase the intervening years. It grew dark. The power was back, but I switched on no lights.

"I'm not too young any more, am I," I said at last.

"No," she said, kissing my chest. "Am I too old?"

After we made love—in the bed in which Ormus Cama had been conceived—she wept, then slept, then awoke to weep again. Like many women of the time, she had used abortion as a supplementary birth control technique, and the fourth time—she had recently learned—had left her barren. Unable to have children, and following her normal practice of drawing universal conclusions from her own idiosyncratic experience, she had responded by developing a great polemic against Western birth control methods, a jeremiad against the scientific manip- ulation of women's bodies for men's pleasure, which hit a number of bull's-eyes and then turned into a cockeyed eulogy of the wisdom of the more "natural" habits of the women of the East. At some point during that night, when I confess my mind was on other matters, she muttered that her main reason for returning had been her desire to go out into the villages and learn the secrets of natural birth control from the women of India. This remark, made in profound seriousness, had the effect of making me laugh. No doubt it was the residual effect of the hashish, but I laughed until the tears ran down my face. "And when you've finished praising them for being so sophisticated about rhythm and withdrawal and all," I cackled, "they'll ask you if you can spare a diaphragm, and a few rubbers too." By the time I had finished making this observation, Vina was fully dressed, operatically choleric and on her way out.

"That isn't why you came, anyway," I giggled loudly. "I'm sorry you had a wasted trip." She threw something fragile at me from the doorway, but I was used to broken pottery and glassware. "You're a low-life runt, Rai," she snarled. I didn't know then about her penchant for this type of behaviour, the easy conquests followed by the vicious scorn. It seemed to me that, once again, I was taking someone else's knocks, being punished for occupying another man's space.

I sobered up once she'd gone. When a woman who obsesses you hands down harsh judgements, they go deep. And when the chance to make those judgements come true offers itself, maybe you take them, maybe you live down to her low opinion of you and spend the rest of your life with the no-longer-deniable accusation stabbing you in the heart.

After one night with Ormus Cama, Vina flew away for a decade. After one night with me, she took off again. One measly night, and then poof! Do you see why she felt like a phantom to me, why her visit felt like that of the ghostly sisters in *The Manuscript Found at Saragossa*, who can make love to the hero only in his dreams? And yet this night, at the end of which she went away almost before she had arrived, changed everything. It was the night Persis's prophecy came true, and I, too, came unstuck from India and began to drift away.

Withdrawal, the method of prophylaxis favoured in the Indian villages, which has done so much to control the exploding Indian population, was subsequently recommended by Vina Apsara to her American and European sisters in a series of controversial interventions. I am at least able to confirm that she herself remained a devotee, if not entirely a mistress, of the art.

The official version of Vina's one-night-only return engagement in Bombay, when she neither sang nor shot her mouth off but merely rekindled an old flame, then poured cold water all over him and flew off again, leaving him drenched and quaking, was somewhat different. All her life, the story she told everyone, perhaps even Ormus Cama, was that when she heard the news of the Bombay earthquake she had indeed rushed to the airport, possessed by the sudden realization of her undimmed love for a man she had not seen for ten long years. "Just my luck," she would say. "Most romantic thing I ever did, and he wasn't even there."

But the thirty-six-hour trip had not been wasted. By a stroke of good fortune, she had been able to meet in her hotel suite with that great honorary Indian Mother Teresa, a true saint, who had endorsed Vina's views wholeheartedly. A meeting with leading Indian feminists had also been arranged. These impressive women told her about the rumoured plans of Mr. Sanjay Gandhi to force sterilisation upon an unwilling population. Vina launched a pre-emptive strike against this atrocity in the making. "Once again Western technology and medicine go hand in hand with tyranny and oppression," she said in a celebrated press conference. "We must not let this man conquer Indian women's wombs." In those days the West's love affair with Indian mysticism was at its height, so her statements gained wide-spread support.

To return to the personal, to the love story the whole world was happy to hear a thousand times and a time, the tale of the birth of the immortal VTO: At the end of her brief stay (Vina would say), she had been granted a kind of miracle. Just before leaving for the new Sahar International Airport, having a few minutes to waste, she had turned on the radio and twiddled the knob, looking for the Voice of America wavelength. All of a sudden she heard a familiar voice. "My heart stopped, except that it also went crazy, like a horse," she'd explain, in a charming self-contradiction, which she would usually follow with another. "I couldn't bear for the song to finish, but I also needed it to stop at once, so I could hear what the DJ said." The song was called "Beneath Her Feet," one half of a double-A-side release (the flip, which was driving the disc towards #1, was called "It Shouldn't Be This Way"). The band was named Rhythm Center, on Colchis.

"Ridiculous, huh?" she told a thousand and one journalists over the years. "After all that time it turned out we were signed to the same label. I guess we both owe Mr. Yul Singh a great big thank-you."

Persis complained of having been erased from the record by Ormus; I could say the same of Vina's treatment of me. But in truth it was different between us. True, I couldn't cure myself of her, and that was the same as what Persis felt for Ormus. But Ormus had forgotten Persis Kalamanja; whereas Vina, whatever she said or didn't say, kept coming back to wherever I was to be found. I was her favourite thorn; she couldn't get me out from under her skin.

Maybe she really did hear Ormus on the radio. I'll buy into that, what the hell, I like fairy tales too. She heard him sing his great love song to her, heard him clean across the world, and felt a loop in time closing, felt herself slip back a decade, moving towards a crossroads she had reached once before; or, like a railway train, approaching an old familiar set of points. Last time she had gone one way. Now she could switch tracks and skip across into the alternative future she had foolishly denied herself. Picture her in the Taj Hotel, looking across Bombay harbour, hearing her lover's song. She looks sixteen again. She is under the spell of the music. And this time she chooses love.

And now I must sing the last song of India that will ever pass my lips; I must quit my old stamping grounds once and for all. Here's an irony worth a shake of the head or a rueful grin: that the severance of my connection with the country of my birth should come to pass at the point of my deepest intimacy with it, my broadest knowledge, my most genuine feelings of belonging. For whatever Persis thought, my years as a photographer had opened my eyes to the old place, and my heart as well. I had started by searching for what my parents had seen in it, but soon I began to see it for myself, to make my own portrait, my own selection from the overwhelming abundance that was everywhere on offer. After a period of feeling an odd, alienated disconnection, feeling it as something not chosen but simply *so,* I was seeing my way, through the camera lens, of being a "proper" Indian. Yet it was the thing I most rejoiced in, my photographer's craft, that ensured my banishment. For a while this created problems for me of value, of defining right thought, right action. I didn't know which way was up any more: what was ground, what sky. The two seemed equally insubstantial to me.

Do you remember Piloo's goats? It is a long time since I left them to their own devices. Now, however, I must return to those spectral animals. It is a goat song that I must sing.

At the time of the earthquake, all manner of bizarre rumours were in the air. Those about Mrs. Gandhi—her electoral fraud, which could very well lead to the Allahabad High Court barring her from holding public office—were so sensational that they fully occupied most people's attention. Would the Prime Minister resign, or try to cling to power? The unthinkable was becoming thinkable. At every dinner table, every water well, every *dhaba* and street corner in the country, people argued over the issue's rights and wrongs. New rumours spread every day. In Bombay, the earthquake raised the general hysteria level to an even higher pitch. In such a climate, it has to be said, nobody was very interested in goats.

The day after Vina's disorienting flying visit, however, I was telephoned by Anita Dharkar, a bright young editor at the *Illustrated Weekly,* which had published individual pictures and photo-essays of mine from time to time. "So, wanna hear the red-hot scuttlebutt on Piloo?" she enquired. She knew of my loathing for the man who had wrecked my parents' marriage. Find your enemy, Henri Hulot had advised. I knew who my enemy was. I just didn't know what I could do to harm him; not until shrewd Anita made her call.

(I must reveal that between Anita and myself there was, well, something. A light occasional thing between colleagues, but with enough substance to it to make me disguise the confusion within me that Vina's visit had left behind. My old gift for playing the cards close to my chest came in useful. I don't think Anita suspected anything was up.)

"Piloo? Did the earthquake gobble him up?" I asked, optimistically. "Or is he climbing into Mrs. G.'s back pocket like every other cheap crook around?"

"How much do you know about his goat farms?" asked Anita, ignoring me.

Officially, Piloo was out of the milk industry now, having given in gracefully to his competitors at the Exwyzee Milk Colony. Instead, he had gone into the mutton-and-wool business in a big way. "Why don't you just turn them into meat and coats?" a petulant young Vina had once asked him. Well, so he had. His ranches were spread across rural Maharashtra and Madhya Pradesh from the baking lowlands of the Godavari River valley to the slopes of the many hill ranges of central India, from the Harishandra range, the Ajanta plateau and the Ellora hills to the Sirpur hills and Satmala plateau in the east, and the Miraj hills near Sangli in the south. Fearlessly, he had established large herds near the bandit-infested gulches of Madhya Pradesh, and Andhra Pradesh as well. He was now one of the national goat industry's largest employers, and his famously high standards of hygiene and quality control had won nationwide awards, and entitled him, as well as the standard fodder subsidies, calculated per head of livestock, to the substantial tax rebates and improvement grants available to such enlightened rural entrepreneurs.

"Enough," I answered Anita. "But why do you care? You're vegetarian, and allergic to mohair too." I liked Anita. I liked her looks, which were lavish, and her singing voice, which was the best I'd heard since Vina's. I liked the gleam of her dark, naked body, its black light, its definition, its boldness. I liked, too, that she appreciated my pictures and championed them inside the *Weekly*, where there were certain opponents.

"Suppose I told you," Anita was saying, "that those goats don't exist?"

The creative imagination possessed by a great scam artist is of a high order; one can't help but admire. What surrealist boldness he displays in the conception of his deceits; what high-wire daring, what mastery of illusion in their execution! The flim-flam maestro is a superman for our times, disdaining norms, scorning convention, soaring far beyond the gravitational pull of plausibility, shucking off the puritan naturalism that would hold most ordinary mortals back. And if in the end he comes unstuck, if his ruses fail like the melting wings of Icarus, then we love him all the more for revealing his human frailty, for falling fatally to earth. In his moment of failure he deepens our love and renders it eternal.

We have been privileged, in India, to observe at close quarters some of the very best—the best of the best—members of the trickster hall of fame. As a result, we are not easily impressed, we demand the highest levels of performance from our public crooks. We have seen too much, yet we still want to be made to laugh and shake our heads in disbelief; we rely upon the scamster to rekindle a sense of wonder dulled by the excess of our daily lives.

Since Piloo's pioneering work, we have marvelled at the People's Car scam of the later 1970s (huge sums of public money disappeared from a project headed by Sanjay G.), the Swedish Cannons scam of the 1980s (huge sums of public money went astray from an international arms deal that besmirched the reputation of Rajiv G.), and the Stock Exchange scam of the 1990s (strenuous efforts were made to fix the movements of certain key stocks, using, naturally, huge sums of public money). Yet when students of the topic gather together—that is to say, whenever and wherever two or more Indians meet for coffee and a chat—they will generally agree that the Great Goat Scam gets their vote for the all-comers gold-medal position. Just as *Citizen Kane* is always chosen in movie polls as the best film of all time, and VTO's *Quakershaker (How the Earth Learned to Rock & Roll)* invariably beats *Sgt. Pepper* into second place in the voting for best ever album; just as *Hamlet* is Best Play and Pelé is Best Football Player and Michael Jordan is the Hoop Dreamboat and Joe DiMaggio is forever Best American, even if he needed the famous line in the famous song explained to him, he thought he was being sent up, didn't understand the reverence in which he was held, so also Piloo Doodhwala is unshakeably ensconced as India's Scambaba Deluxe.

And the fellow who put him up there was me.

Fodder fraud does not, at first glance, look as romantic a diddle as gun-running commissions or manipulating the investment market. Goats, after all, famously eat anything, so the subventions to farmers are necessarily small: on the order of one hundred rupees per goat per annum, or around three dollars a head. Goat feed = chicken feed, you may scornfully conclude. Not much scope there for one of the great confidence tricks of all time. Doubter, be reassured. Mistake not flamboyance for genius, or glistering garbage for gold. It was the very smallness of the sums involved that enabled Piloo to set up his glorious scheme, the sheer banality of the project that protected it from public scrutiny for so many years. For while one hundred chips is a mere bagatelle, it is, nevertheless, one hundred chips in your pocket, as long as your goat is of the Non-Existent type. And because the Non-Existent Goat breeds faster, and requires less attention, or indeed space, than any other variety, what is to stop the energetic goat farmer from increasing the quantity of his livestock at high speed, almost ad infinitum? For the Non-Existent Goat never falls ill, never lets you down, never dies unless it is required to do so, and—uniquely—multiplies at the precise rate stipulated by its owner. Truly, the most obliging and likeable of goats, it makes no noise, nor is there any shit to shovel.

The scale of the Great Goat Scam was almost beyond comprehension. Piloo Doodhwala was the proud owner of one hundred million wholly fictitious goats, goats of the highest quality, the softness of whose wool had passed into legend, whose flesh was a byword for tenderness. The flexibility of the Non-Existent Goat allowed him to defy the received wisdom of centuries of goat husbandry. Deep in the heart of central India he achieved the incredible feat of rearing top-quality cashmere goats—who were conventionally thought to need high mountain pastures—in the heat of the plains. Nor had communal issues restricted him. His meat goats could be raised by vegetarians, whose work with these magical creatures involved no loss of caste. It was an operation of immense beauty, requiring no work at all, except for the effort of maintaining the fiction of the goats' Existence. The financial outlay required to ensure the silence of thousands upon thousands of villagers and government inspectors and other officials, and to pay off the border bandits, was very considerable, but entirely within tolerable limits if considered as a percentage of the enterprise's turnover, and it was, after all (see above), cushioned by tax breaks and capital subsidies to boot.

One hundred times one hundred million is ten billion rupees, one hundred thousand crores. Two hundred million pounds sterling. Three hundred million dollars per annum, free of taxes. Hush money and protection money payments, annual salaries to the villagers employed to tend the Non-Existents, and miscellaneous expenses added up to less than five percent of this exquisite sum and represented nothing worse than a tiny mole, a sort of financial beauty spot, upon the immortally lovely face of this magnificent scam, which Piloo operated without hindrance—indeed, with the enthusiastic support of many of Maharashtra's greatest figures—for almost fifteen years.

Three hundred million times fifteen is four and a half billion dollars. One and a half million crores of rupees. Less expenses, certainly. Let's not exaggerate. Call it four billion dollars, net.

I went in to the office to discuss the brief. Anita Dharkar had a satirical spread in mind. On the left, Piloo's deserted "ranches"; on the right, a more typical goat farming operation. "Presenting Piloo's Invisible Goats," she extemporised, enjoying herself. "Here you see them, not being seen. Unlike these Ordinary Goats, which, as you can see, you can see."

I, who had boasted about my talent for invisibility, was commissioned to photograph these phantoms, Doodhwala's "ghoasts." Anita wanted Piloo's magic herds on film. "Piloo is not only protected by corruption," she said, becoming serious. "Also, there is the infinite indifference of India. *Chalta-hai,* isn't it? So it goes. We expect our Piloos to get up to tricks, and we shrug and turn away. Only if you get the pictures proving the case beyond all doubt will we be able to make anything happen."

She had acquired a full list of all Piloo's registered goat-rearing facilities. "How'd you do that?" I asked, impressed. But she was too savvy to betray a source, even to me. "Truth will out," she said. "In the end, there's always an honest Injun somewhere, if you can find him. Even in Inja."

"Or maybe," I said, less idealistically, "there's someone Piloo forgot to buy."

"Or maybe," Anita took up the thread, "it's just in the nature of secrets to come out, because the only way to keep a secret is not to tell anybody, which is why I'm not answering your disgraceful question about my informant. And Piloo's secret was shared by too many people. The wonder is it didn't leak years ago. Piloo must've been paying damn, damn well."

"Or maybe," I responded, "your source is a kind of patriot. People are always complaining, right?, that India is too busy aping the West. But here is our very own special talent; we should celebrate it. About scams we don't need to learn a thing. We can teach. Listen, I'm sort of proud of Piloo. I hate the bastard, but he has done a beautiful thing."

"Sure," said Anita. "So let's try to give him what he deserves. The Padmashri, even the Bharat Ratna. No; these honours are not big enough. How about a pair of official portraits, front view, side view, wearing stripey outfit, and holding a card with name and serial number also, if poss?"

It sounded good to me. "Just get the photos, Rai, okay?" she said, and walked out of the room.

She didn't tell me about the other photographer, the one she'd sent before me, the one who hadn't returned: not because she was anxious to avoid alarming me, but because she knew I would be offended at being her second choice. She wanted to come with me, too; she had it all planned out. We would fly to Aurangabad, acting like newlyweds on honeymoon, not a camera in sight. For verisimilitude and other reasons, we would check in at the Rambagh Palace Hotel and make love all night. To keep up the honeymoon cover story—for we were going into Piloo country, where any doorman, any *chaprassi*, could be a stool pigeon—we would go to Ajanta and stand in the darkness of the caves while a guide switched a light on and off and the Buddhist master-pieces appeared and vanished. The bodhisattvas, the pink elephants, the half-clad women with their hourglass figures and perfect globes of breasts. Anita's body was the equal of any fresco and the offer was an attractive one, but I left Bombay without telling her and plunged into the hard heart of India, intent upon doing what I had laughed at Vina for wanting to do, what city dwellers almost never do in India. I would enter rural India. Not to learn about rhythm or withdrawal, but to get old Piloo's goat.

After that strange, jangling single night with Vina, it did me good to get away. *Of course I never set any fire. You think I burned your house down? Did your mother think so? Gee, thanks. I may have been a thief, but I wasn't crazy.* She had wanted to meet my mother, to offer restitution. New jewellery for old. But it was too late for things like that. The rifts in our world could not be mended. What was burned could not be unburned, what was broken could not be fixed. A dead mother, a father rotating slowly and reeking of bitter perfume as his bedroom fan turned. Strange fruit. I tried to imagine how Ameer Merchant might have reacted to Vina's return. I think she would simply have opened her arms and taken Vina right back into her heart.

To think about those days again—Ameer, V.V., the fire, the lost love, the wasted chances—was upsetting. The size of the countryside, its stark unsentimental lines, its obduracy: these things did me good. To be moving within its great dusty sweep, its lack of interest, helped restore a sense of proportion; it put one in one's place. I drove my Jeep—laden with supplies of dry and tinned food, jerry cans of petrol and of water, spare tyres, my favourite hiking boots (the ones with the secrets in their heels) and even a small tent—into the far east of Maharashtra. I was in Piloo's empire, looking for the back door.

Always the back-door man.

A journey to the centre of the earth. The air grew hotter with every mile, the wind seemed to blaze more fiercely on my cheeks. The local bugs seemed larger and hungrier than their city cousins, and I was, as usual, lunch. The road never emptied: bikes, horse-drawn carts, burst pipes, the blare of buses and trucks. People, people. Roadside saints in plaster. Men in a circle at dawn pissing on an ancient monument, some dead king's tomb. Running dogs, lounging cattle, exploded rubber tyres prominent among the piles of detritus that were everywhere, like the future. Groups of youths with orange headbands and flags. Politics painted on passing walls. Tea stalls. Monkeys, camels, performing bears on a leash. A man who pressed your trousers while you waited. Ochre smoke from factory chimneys. Accidents. *Bed On Roof Rs 2/=*. Prostitutes. The omnipresence of gods. Boys in cheap rayon bush shirts. Everywhere around me, life was striving, pullulating. The roaches, the beasts of burden, the enervated parrots, fought for food, shelter, the right to see another day of life. The young men with their oiled hair strutted and preened like skinny gladiators, while the old watched their children suspiciously, waiting to be abandoned, to be shouldered aside, tossed into some ditch. This was life in its pure form, life seeking no more than to remain alive. In the universe of the road, the survival instinct was the only law, the hustle the only game in town, the game you played until you dropped. To be here was to understand why Piloo Doodhwala was popular. The Great Goat Scam was the life of the road writ large. It was a mega-hustle which freed his people from the daily hustles that drove them into early graves. He was a miracle man, a prophet. It would not be easy to bring him down.

My plan—more a notion than a strategy, really—was to get as far off the beaten track as possible. I had seen from Anita's list that many of Piloo's ghost farms were located in the most remote parts of the state, in highly inhospitable territory, with a communications infrastructure that was poor to non-existent. Any farmer of Actually Existing Goats would have had the greatest difficulty, and would also have incurred inordinate and crippling expenses, in simply bringing his herds to the slaughterhouse or shearing shed. Non-Existent Goats caused no such problems, naturally, and the inaccessibility of the "ranches" made the true nature of Piloo's operation easier to conceal. I was gambling on the over-confidence of his minions in these far-flung places. A photographer from the *Illustrated Weekly* would be the last person on earth they'd expect to see.

At that time, a much ballyhooed Trans-India Auto Rally was taking place, and it was my intention to pose as a lost driver in need of food, water, rest and guidance. This would, I hoped, buy me a few hours of time in the company of Piloo's phantoms. Then it would be up to my powers of photographic invisibility to seize the opportunity. Dusty, exhausted, I turned my Jeep off the main highway on to ever smaller and more broken roads, and headed for the hills.

After travelling for two days I came to a river, a trickle down the centre of a dry, rocky bed. There was a peasant passing, as there always is, with a stick over one shoulder and a water pot hanging from each end of the stick. I asked him the river's name, and when he answered "Wainganga," I had the odd feeling of having taken a wrong turning out of the real world, of having slipped somehow into fiction. As if I had accidentally crossed the border of Maharashtra not into Madhya Pradesh but into a parallel, magic land. In contemporary India those hills ahead of me, a low range with jungled ravines, would have been the Seoni range, but in the magic sphere I had entered they were still called, in the old fashion, Seeonee. In their jungles I might chance upon legendary beasts, talking animals who never were, created by a writer who put them in this faraway wilderness without ever seeing it with his own eyes: a panther and a bear and a tiger and a jackal and an elephant and monkeys and a snake. And on the hills' high ridges I might at any moment glimpse the mythic figure of a human boy, a Non-Existent Boy, a figment, a man-cub dancing with wolves.

> *Now Chil the Kite brings home the night*
> *That Mang the Bat sets free.*

I had reached my destination. A deeply rutted dirt path led off the country road towards Piloo Doodhwala's mysteries. Still in the grip of my curious mood of unreality, I drove towards my fate.

The sheer unchartedness of rural India in its most profound depths never failed to amaze. You turned off the road on to the rural tracks and at once felt as the earth's early navigators must have done; like a Cabot or Magellan of the land.

Here the polyphonic reality of the road disappeared and was replaced by silences, mutenesses as vast as the land. Here was a wordless truth, one that came before language, a being, not a becoming. No cartographer had fully mapped these endless spaces. There were villages buried in the backlands that never knew about the British Empire, villagers to whom the names of the nation's leaders and founding fathers would mean nothing, even though Wardha, where the Mahatma founded his ashram, was only a hundred-odd miles away. To journey down some of these tracks was to travel back in time for over a thousand years.

City dwellers were constantly told that village India was the "real" India, a space of timelessness and gods, of moral certainties and natural laws, of the eternal fixities of caste and faith, gender and class, landowner and sharecropper and bonded labourer and serf. Such statements were made as if the real were solid, immutable, tangible. Whereas the most obvious lesson of travelling between the city and the village, between the crowded street and the open field, was that reality shifted. Where the plates of different realities met, there were shudders and rifts. Chasms opened. A man could lose his life.

I am writing about a journey into the heart of the country but it's just another way of saying goodbye. I'm taking the long way round to the exit because I can't agree with myself to let go, to be done with it, to turn away towards my new life, just to settle for that fortunate existence. Lucky me: America.

But it's also because my life hinges on what happened out there, on the banks of the Wainganga River, within sight of the Seeonee hills. That was the decisive moment that created the secret image which I have never revealed to anyone, the hidden self-portrait, the ghost in my machine.

Nowadays I can behave, most of the time, as if it never happened. I'm a happy man, I can throw sticks for my dog on an American beach and let the turn-ups on my stone-grey chinos get wet in the Atlantic tides, but sometimes in the night I wake and the past is hanging there in front of me, rotating slowly, and all around me the jungle beasts are growling, the fire grows dim, and they are closing in.

Vina: I promised you I would open my heart, I swore that nothing would be spared. So I must find the courage to reveal this also, this terrible thing I know about myself. I must confess it and stand defenceless before the court of anyone who can be bothered to judge. If anyone remains. You know the old song. Even the President of the United States sometimes must stand naked.

Or I washed my hands in muddy waters, I washed my hands but they wouldn't come clean.

At a certain point I left the Jeep behind, off the track, and proceeded on foot. As I crept towards my goal I felt an excitement—no, it was more than a mere kick, it was fulfilment—which left me in no doubt that I had discovered what I wanted most. More than money, more than fame, maybe even more than love.

To look with one's own eyes into the eyes of the truth, and stare it down. To see what was *thus,* and show it *so.* To strip away the veils and turn the thunderous racket of revelation into the pure silence of the image and so possess it, to put the world's secret wonders in your suitcase and go home from the war to your once-in-a-lifetime woman, or even to the picture editor you slept with twice a week.

But this world was not rackety. Its stillness was unnatural, it was much more than country hush. I had entered the territory of the four-billion-dollar phantom goat, and the goat is, of course, an ancient avatar of the devil. Allow me to concede that in that occult silence I felt a little scared and far from help.

> The herds are shut in byre and hut
> For loosed till dawn are we.

There was a cluster of buildings ahead. Huts and byres, but where were the villagers' herds? Yet more silence burst from Piloo's scam sheds, eloquent as a lion's roar. I reached into the patch pocket on my right trouser leg and felt the reassuring presence of the slim little Leica which I'd bought myself in honour of my encounter with the great Henri Hulot. Then men carrying field implements rose up all around me, seeming to burst from the very earth, and that, as far as photography was concerned, was that.

They had seen me coming a mile off, which didn't in itself matter too much. In my long and various professional life, I have bribed and sweet-talked my way past the roadblocks of regional warlords in Angola and former Yugoslavia, I have found routes in and out of twenty-seven different revolutions and major wars. The security cordons at the Milan and Paris fashion collections, the concentric circles of armed and unarmed aides guarding the route to the man or woman of real power, the maître d's at the leading Manhattan restaurants, pah! I snap my fingers under their collective nose. Even on that early adventure, rookie that I was, I felt confident of my ability to hoodwink these back-of-beyond yokels and then get the goods on their little livestock swindle.

Unless, of course, they weren't yokels. Unless they were members of one of the feared gangs of killer bandits who roamed these invisible parts. Unless Piloo was actually using the bandits to police his operation. Unless they murdered me there and then and left my body for the vultures and carrion crows.

My captors and I turned out to have no language in common. They spoke a local dialect that made no sense at all to me. However, conversation quickly became redundant. After they had removed my cameras and rolls of film and the keys to my Jeep and robbed me of all my money, they took me to the place of imaginary goats. Here I met the other journalist, the one of whose existence I had previously been unaware. He was waiting for me in one of the byres, hanging from a low beam, rotating slowly in the hot draughts of wind, and dressed very like myself. The same patch pockets on his trousers, the same hiking boots. The same empty camera bag at his feet. He had been dead for much too long, and even as I started vomiting I understood that my yarn about the Trans-India Rally was probably not going to be believed.

Why didn't they string me up right away? I don't know. Boredom, probably. There's not much to do out there in the boondocks when you don't even have real goats to fuck. You've got to spread out your pleasures. The anticipation is more than half the fun. Crocodiles do the same thing. They keep their quarry half alive for days sometimes, saving them for later. So I'm told.

Boredom and laziness saved my life. These husbanders of fictive billies and nannies were people who had made their illicit living for one and a half decades by doing nothing at all. If they were bandits (which I increasingly doubted), they were bandits who had lost their edge. Many of them were stout, soft-bodied, which was rarely true of peasants and dacoits. Corruption had both fattened their bodies and eroded their spirits. They bound me and abandoned me, left me retching emptily on account of the stench of my dead colleague, and at the mercy also of the one zillion crawling things to whom a dead body is the occasion for a grand inter-species reunion.

At night the phantom goatherds got drunk in another hut, and the loud noises of their carousing stopped only when they were all unconscious. I managed to free myself of the badly tied ropes around my arms and legs, and after a few moments more I made my escape. The Jeep was where I'd left it, looted but with enough gas in the tank to get me to a town. I managed to hot-wire it and drove away as fast as the surface would permit. I did not turn on the headlights. Fortunately there was a bright-yellow gibbous moon to light my way.

"Thank god," Anita Dharkar said, when I reached a telephone and reversed the charges and woke her up. "Thank god." I was so angry she'd said such a thing that I shouted abuse at her down the phone. Fear, danger, panic, flight, stress: these things have odd, displaced consequences.

Thank god? No, no, *no.* Let's not invent anything as cruel, vicious, vengeful, intolerant, unloving, immoral and arrogant as god just to explain a stroke of dumb, undeserved luck. I don't need some multi-limbed Cosmic Dancer or white-bearded Ineffable, some virgin-raping metamorphic Thunderbolt Hurler or world-destroying flood and fire Maniac, to take the credit for saving my skin. Nobody saved the other fellow, did they? Nobody saved the Indochinese or the Angkorans or the Kennedys or the Jews.

"I know the list," she said. I was calming down. "Yeah, well," I said, awkwardly. "I just needed to make the point."

The photographs I brought back to Bombay created a great sensation, though considered purely from the aesthetic viewpoint they were as dull and uninspired as the First Photo itself, that ancient monochrome view of walls and roofs as seen from the studio window of Joseph Nicéphore Niépce. They were pictures of emptiness, of corrals and pastures, byres and sheds, in which no animals could be seen; of fences, doors, fields, stalls. Photographs of absences. But tell-tale Doodhwala Industries stencils were visible everywhere, on wooden walls and fence posts and on the occasional vehicle: a cart, a truck. Just as the banality of goat fodder had enabled Piloo to construct his mighty fraud, so the banality of these images, what one might call their *decisive voiding,* served to deconstruct the swindle. Within weeks of their publication, a major fraud squad investigation was in progress, and within three months warrants were issued for the arrest of Piloo Doodhwala, most of the "magnificentourage," and several dozen lesser associates across two states.

The bizarre character of the scandal attracted international attention. The photographs were widely re-published, and as a result I received a brief handwritten note from M. Hulot, offering his congratulations on my "scoop de foudre" and inviting me to join the world-famous Nebuchadnezzar photographers' agency, which he had founded in the year of my birth, along with the American Bobby Flow, "Chip" Boleyn from England and a second French photographer, Paul

Willy. It was as if Zeus had tapped me on the shoulder and asked me to join him and the other naked, omnipotent pranksters on top of their storied hill.

It was the beginning of the life I have led ever since, the first day, one might say, of my life as a man. And yet, as the attentive reader will already have divined, something was badly amiss.

It is time, after all these years, to answer certain questions.

Rai—here's the first question—*how does a man shoot a roll of film while bound hand and foot? How does a man film a "goat farm" which he has never visited (for the pictures clearly showed images of at least two separate establishments in different parts of the country)? Most puzzlingly of all, how does a man take photographs after his camera equipment has been removed?*

I could say there was another loaded camera hidden in the Jeep, taped under the offside rear wheel arch, and the murderous bastards missed it. I could say I was goaded into passionate, dangerous action by the experience of spending a day retching and gagging in the company of a hanged man, who wore the same clothes and boots as myself, whose swollen, blackened face might have—or so it seemed to me, in my torment—borne more than a passing resemblance to my own. I did it for him, I could tell you, for my murdered, stinking companion, *mon semblable, mon frère*. I did it for the dead twin I did not know I had.

I became careful, circumspect. I found a hiding place during the night from which I could work by day. I became invisible, motionless, invincible. I got the pictures. Here they are. The bastards went to jail, okay? Can I do anything else for you? Anything else you want to know? What's that? What did you say?

Why didn't you buy more film?

Oh, for crying out loud. They robbed me. I was broke.

And then Anita came, and brought you home.

Right. Right.

So, when did you go to the second location, far away in the Miraj hills?

Later. I went later. What's your problem?

In that case, why didn't you take more film?

What, you think it was easy to get those photos? Just to get five or six images would have been a sort of miracle. This was one full roll.

Tell us about the boots, Rai. Talk about the hiking boots.
Stop it. Shut up. I can't.
Oh, but you must.

Okay: the thing you could do with these special, imported hiking boots: if you slightly loosened a screw at the base of the heel, you could twist the whole heel section round to reveal a small cavity. A cavity just about large enough to hold a roll of film. I'd used the trick a few times, for example when photographing Mumbai's Axis rallies. As a matter of fact, I'd used it this time. When I left my Jeep to go "ghoast"-busting, I had a spare film in each heel.

The hanged man and I were alone for a long time. His feet swung not far from my revolted nose and yes I wondered about the heels of his boots yes when I got the ropes off I made myself approach him yes in spite of his pong like the end of the world and the biting insects yes and the rawness of my throat and my eyes sore from bulging as I puked I took hold of his heels one after the other yes I twisted the left heel it came up empty but the right heel did the right thing the film just plopped down in my hand yes and I put an unused film in its place from my own boot yes and I could feel his body all perfume and my heart was going like mad and I made my escape with Piloo's fate and my own golden future in my hand yes and to hell with everything I said yes because it might as well be me as another so yes I will yes I did yes.

I've seen that film now, *Ugetsu Monogatari,* the Japanese picture Hulot praised so highly. I must have seen it a dozen times. It's not only a ghost story; there's a sub-plot. A poor man wants to be a great samurai warrior. One day he sees a famous fighter being killed. Afterwards he boasts that he is the one who bested the hero. It makes his reputation. For a while.

I never actually said the photographs were mine. I just processed them and handed the results to Anita at the *Weekly* offices and allowed everyone else to give me the credit; which I took. Which isn't quite the same thing as boasting.

Who am I kidding?

There. Now I've removed my mask, and you can see what I really am. In this quaking, unreliable time, I have built my house—morally speaking—upon shifting Indian sands. *Terra infirma.*

Piloo Doodhwala had his scam; and as you see, I had mine. He made four billion dollars. I just made my name.

I brought the film out, but it hadn't been shot by me. It would never have seen the light of day if I hadn't found it, but it wasn't my work. Piloo might never have been arraigned, might never have been sent to jail, might have gone on earning his goaty billions for the rest of his life, if not for me. But the photographs weren't mine. It was over a quarter of a century ago, and since then I've earned my spurs, I deserve my goddamn reputation, I've worked for everything I've got. But the pictures that made my name, that brought me to the world's attention? They weren't mine, they weren't mine, they weren't mine.

Too human for the Wolf Pack, too vulpine for Man, Mowgli in the Seeonee hills resolved to hunt alone. Not a bad resolve for a photographer. After my experiences by the banks of the Wainganga, I made the Man Cub's vow my own.

Another bitter pill: the Piloo exposé jailed him, but instead of ruining him, it actually made him bigger. The size of the pro-Piloo demonstrations in the rural areas of Maharashtra and Madhya Pradesh alarmed and impressed the Bombay and Delhi power élite. Prosecuting Piloo began to be described as an act of vengeance by the "English medium" liberal élite against a true man of the masses, a son of the soil. The moment he was jailed he announced his intention to run for public office, and his campaign quickly became unstoppable. The Bombay jailkhana became Piloo's royal court. His cell was furnished like a throne room, and banquets were brought in daily by Golmatol and his daughters. Mighty figures came to visit and offer obeisance. Mumbai's Axis grandees supported Piloo's bid for mayor, and within six months of being jailed he had been elected to the post. A pardon was sought for him and swiftly granted by the President of India, acting on the urgent advice of the increasingly powerful Sanjay Gandhi, a shoo-in for the next Indian Premier. A general election was called, and the Indira Congress, in association with its new Hindu nationalist allies across the country, including Mumbai's Axis in Bombay and Maharashtra, swept back to power. Emergency rule was ended. No longer necessary: the electorate had endorsed tyranny and corruption. *Chalta hai.*

So it goes.

• • •

Much of this, the apotheosis of Piloo, the total victory of Pilooist values over everything in India that I had slowly come to love, happened after I had gone. Listen: once I received the invitation from Nebuchadnezzar I'd have left anyway, but I'd have kept my links to the old country, like Hulot himself I'd have made it one of my subjects, because there it was inside me, colonizing every cell, an addiction so deep it could not be destroyed without killing the addict too; or so I naïvely believed. What happened instead was that Anita Dharkar was beaten and raped in her own home in the middle of the night the weekend after Piloo went to jail, and her assailants, who hadn't even bothered to hide their faces, told her to be sure and tell me that I was their next port of call, only in my case they didn't intend to be so gentle and considerate.

"Is there somewhere you can go?" she asked. I wanted to go to her, but she told me not to come round on any account, her family was looking after her, she would be fine. I knew she would not be fine. "You should leave the country," she said. "Things will get much worse before they get better." I asked her if she would come with me. Her voice was thick-lipped, juddering, broken, and her body, I didn't know how to think about what had been done to her body. But she would not leave. "They have finished with me now," she said. "So, no problem." She meant that India was still the only place on earth to which she could imagine herself belonging, corrupt and crooked and heartless and violent as it was. She belonged, and optimism and hope were still not dead in her in spite of her appalling violation. She could not define herself, could not give herself any meaning, except here, where her roots had gone too deep and spread too wide.

Something required me to leave. Something else required her to stay. In my story, which is also that of Ormus Cama and Vina Apsara, Anita Dharkar, poignant, lovely, sweetly singing Anita who was defiled for the crime of possessing integrity, Anita the photo editor, heroine and patriot, is a boat against the current, moving determinedly in the opposite direction to the tale.

Her dream was of an India which would deserve her, which would show that it had been right for her to remain. There are noble women who remain married to coarse wife-beaters for similar reasons. They see the good in their bad men.

And of course there was somewhere I could go. I locked up my home, dismissed the servants and went to see Persis. *Get me a ticket, Persis. Fix it with your airline contacts that I can travel under a false name. Don't ask me why, Persis. You don't want to know. Persis, I'm going, as you always said I would. Thank you. I'm sorry. Goodbye.*

Persis, gentle gatekeeper of our lives. Who stood by the river that separates the worlds and helped us to cross, but could not do so herself.

Even after the assault on Anita, it did not occur to me, when I left my Apollo Bunder apartment, that I was going for good, that I would never again set foot in those rooms; nor on that street, to brush off Virus Cama's troop of urchins; nor in that city, to witness its surge towards the skies; nor in any part of India, though it remained a part of me, as essential as a limb. India, where my parents lay buried, and the smells were the smells of home. I was heading full of anticipation towards a new life, the life I wanted, but I had no sense of having burned my boats. Sure, I'd go back. Things would cool down. Piloo, now rising, would take a tumble soon enough. Nobody remembered anything, anyway, and to return as a big-deal Nebu Agency photographer would ensure me open-arms treatment and the widest possible access. Of course it would. Real life was not like an earthquake. Rifts might appear, but most of them mended, after a fashion. It's not as if some science fiction chasm had appeared, so wide that there was no way across. It was just end-of-part-one, start-of-part-two, is all.

But Pilooism won the day, Pilooism and Sanjayism, its Delhi twin. Delhi and Bombay used to hate each other. Bombay-wallahs sneered at the way Delhi people licked the arse of power, then turned it round and sucked its indifferent cock. Delhi-ites derided Bombay's money-grubbing glitzy materialism. This new alliance united the dark side of both. The corruption of money and the corruption of power, united in a super-corruption that no opponent could withstand. I never foresaw that; but Lady Spenta Cama had intuited it long ago.

The best in our natures is drowning in the worst.

Nothing could touch those two. The law couldn't damage Piloo, and Sanjay, too, led a charmed life. Even when his light aircraft stalled in mid-air while he was looping the loop like a fool over his mother's official residence, he managed to survive the emergency landing. Oh, the utter Caligulan barbarity of India during the consulship of those terrible twins! The beatings, the bullyings, the jailings, the flailings, the burnings, the bannings, the buyings, the sellings, the shamelessness, the shamelessness, the shame.

I know it's different now. The quadruple assassination. I know. People will say I've been away too long, I don't understand the situation, it's not as I say it is, it never was, it was better in some ways, and in others, worse.

But I'll tell you how it feels, after all these years. It feels like an ending in the middle pathway of my life. A necessary ending, without which the second half would have been impossible. Freedom, then? Not exactly. Not quite a liberation, no. It feels like a divorce. In this particular divorce I was the party who didn't want the marriage to break up. I was the one who sat around waiting, telling myself, it'll be okay, she'll think better of it, she'll come back to me and all manner of thing shall be well. But she never came back. And now we're all older, it's too late, the links didn't break, they just wore away years ago. At the end of a marriage the moment comes when you have to turn away from your wife, from the unbearably beautiful memory of the way you were, and turn towards the rest of your life. That's me at this point in this story. Once again, I'm the dumpee.

And so farewell, my country. Don't worry; I won't come knocking at your door. I won't phone you in the middle of the night and hang up when you reply. I won't follow you down the street when you step out with some other guy. My home is burned, my parents dead, and those I loved have mostly gone away. Those whom I still love I must leave behind for good.

I go—I hunt—alone.

India, I have swum in your warm waters and run laughing in your high mountain meadows. Oh, why must everything I say end up sounding like a *filmi gana,* a goddamn cheap Bollywood song? Very well then: I have walked your filthy streets, India, I have ached in my bones from the illnesses engendered by your germs. I have eaten your independent salt and drunk your nauseatingly sugary roadside tea. For many years your malaria mosquitoes would bite me wherever I went, and in deserts and summers around the world I was stung by cool Kashmiri bees. India, my *terra infirma,* my maelstrom, my cornucopia, my crowd. India, my too-muchness, my everything at once, my Hug-me, my fable, my mother, my father and my first great truth. It may be that I am not worthy of you, for I have been imperfect, I confess. I may not comprehend what you are becoming, what perhaps you already are, but I am old enough to say that this new self of yours is an entity I no longer want, or need, to understand.

India, fount of my imagination, source of my savagery, breaker of my heart.

Goodbye.

9

MEMBRANE

One universe shrinks, another expands. Ormus Cama in the middle 1960s quits Bombay for England, restored to himself, feeling his true nature flowing back into his veins. As the plane lifts from his native soil, so his heart lifts also, he sheds his old skin without a second thought, crosses that frontier as if it didn't exist, like a shapeshifter, like a snake. His fellow steerage passengers cocoon themselves in uninterest, they sit jammed up against the lives of strangers but pretend they notice nothing in order to maintain the fiction that they are not themselves observed. Ormus's unleashed personality is unable to contain itself within such demure fictions. His self has taken wing. It overflows its bounds. He stares openly and long at the other travellers, memorising them, *these are the people who are going with me to the New World,* and he even speaks to them, smiling his disarming smile.

Welcome aboard the *Mayflower,* he greets them, seizing their hands as they pass his seat, the terrified uncomprehending peasants from remote inland villages on their way to desert kingdoms, the perspiration-sprinkled executives in cheap suits, the frowning chaperones of a veiled young bride fainting in a pink *gharara* with too much gold braid, the

unwary young student on his way to a miserable four years in an English boarding school, and the children. There are children everywhere,
children running in the aisles imitating aircraft to the dismay of the
cabin staff; or standing up on their seats grave-eyed and motionless,
showing a more than adult understanding of the importance of this
momentous day; or screaming like strapped-down lunatics at their
fastened seat belts; children dressed in spectacularly lumpy woollen
jumpers in functional grey and navy blue, their very garments proclaiming their alienation from the new homes they have never seen,
trumpeting the difficulty they will have in adjusting to life in those
lightless northern climes.

We are the Pilgrim Children, Ormus thinks. Where the first foot
falls, let us call it Bombay Rock. Boom chickaboom, chickaboom
boom.

He himself has dressed carefully for the journey, arraying his body
in the casual wear of America: the Yankees baseball cap, the white Beat
Generation T-shirt with the ragged cutaway sleeves, the Mickey Mouse
watch. There is a touch of Europe too, in the black hipster jeans which
he literally charmed off the legs of an Italian tourist at the Gateway, a
susceptible youth, one of the first longhaired Westerners to arrive in
India in search of beaches and enlightenment, and no match for
Ormus Cama's astonishing powers of persuasion, which left him bare-
legged and dumbfounded with his right fist full of money and Ormus's
gift of a neatly folded lungi hanging over his bemused left arm.

England may be my immediate destination but it is not my goal,
Ormus's clothes announce, old England cannot hold me, it may pretend to be swinging but I know it's just plain hanged. Not funky but
defunct. History moves on. Nowadays England is ersatz America,
America's delayed echo, America driving on the left. Sure, Jesse Garon
Parker was white American trash who wanted to sing like a black boy,
but the Beatles, for goodness' sake, the Beatles are white English trash
trying to sing like American *girls*. Crystals Ronettes Shirelles Chantels
Chiffons Vandellas Marvelettes, why not wear some spangly dresses,
boys, why not get some beehive hairdos instead of those loveable
moptops and have the sex change operations too, go the whole way,
do it right.

These reflections before even setting foot in England or America or any place except the land where he was born, which he is leaving for good, without regrets, without a backward glance: I want to be in America, America where everyone's like me, because everyone comes from somewhere else. All those histories, persecutions, massacres, piracies, slaveries; all those secret ceremonies, hanged witches, weeping wooden virgins and horned unyielding gods; all that yearning, hope, greed, excess, the whole lot adding up to a fabulous noisy historyless self-inventing citizenry of jumbles and confusions; all those variform manglings of English adding up to the livingest English in the world; and above everything else, all that smuggled-in music. The drums of Africa that once beat out messages across a giant landscape in which even the trees made music, for example when they absorbed water after a drought, listen and you'll hear them, yikitaka yikitaka yikitak. The Polish dances, the Italian weddings, the zorba-zithering Greeks. The drunken rhythm of the salsa saints. The cool heart music that heals our aching souls, and the hot democratic music that leaves a hole in the beat and makes our pants want to get up and dance. But it's this boy from Bombay who will complete the American story, who will take the music and throw it up in the air and the way it falls will inspire a generation, two generations, three. Yay, America. Play it as it lays.

While he is required to remain seated he occupies his narrow chair as if it were a throne, managing somehow in that confined space to lounge, to give the impression of consummate, even royal, ease. In the countries below him other kings are going about their business. The King of Afghanistan is acting as tourist guide to well-heeled travellers while blocks of hashish bearing government seals of quality and grade are sold in the high-street stores of his capital city; the Shah of Iran makes love to his wife, whose moans of pleasure mingle with the screams of the vanished thousands in the torture chambers of SAVAK; the Queen of England dines with the Lion of Judah; the King of Egypt lies dying. (And so, in America, a magic land that is swinging slowly but surely towards the top of Ormus's personal Faraway Tree, does Nat "King" Cole.)

And the earth continues, unpredictably, wrongly, to move.

Not everybody is happy to be going West. Virus Cama is sitting bolt upright between his mother and brother, can sense the distance between himself and jailed Cyrus growing, and as the bond of their twinship stretches so his dumb face seems to distend with grief. The pink bride is crying softly behind her veil, ignored by her sweat-stained bodyguards. And Spenta Cama on a wing and a prayer is flying in a state of extreme tension, keeping her fingers crossed, heading for her blind date with William Methwold, the one great gamble on which her future depends.

Ormus closes his eyes and drifts languidly away from consciousness towards turbid airplane sleep. Down the Las Vegas corridors of his mind he chases the dragon, the wisp of smoky nothing that is also Gayomart his dead twin. The past is dropping away from him. Vina has escaped from his yesterdays and is now waiting up ahead, she is his only future. Quake me, Ormus Cama, murmuring down towards sleep, asks of Fate. Rock me like a baby in the bosom of music. Shake me till I rattle, shake me but don't break me, and roll me, roll me, roll me, like thunder, like a stone.

This when they're flying over what's that down there, the Bosphorus is it, or the Golden Horn, or are they the same place, Istanbul, Byzantium, whatever: drugged by flight, detached from the indifferent earth, he feels a certain resistance in the air. Something fighting back against the aircraft's forward movement. As if there's a stretchy translucent membrane across the sky, an ectoplasmic barrier, a Wall. And are there ghostly border guards armed with thunderbolts watching from high pillars of cloud, and might they open fire. But there's nothing for it now, this is the onliest high road into the West, so onward, drive those dogies onward. But it's so springy, this invisible restriction, it keeps pushing the airplane back, boeing!, boeing!, until at last the *Mayflower* breaks through, it's through! Sunlight bounces off the wing into his bleary eye. And as he passes that unseen frontier he sees the tear in the sky, and for a terror-stricken instant glimpses miracles through the gash, visions for which he can find no words, the mysteries at the heart of things, Eleusinian, unspeakable, bright. He intuits that every bone in his body is being irradiated by something pouring through the sky-rip, a mutation is occurring at the level of the cell, of the gene, of the particle. The person who arrives won't be the one who left, or not quite. He has crossed a time zone, moved from the eternal past of early life into the constant now of adulthood, the tense of presence, which will become a different kind of preterite, the past of absence, when he dies.

The visionary moment takes him by surprise, unnerves him. After a few seconds the opening vanishes and there's nothing out there except the cloud columns, the jet streams, the anachronistic, remnant moon, and infinity, spreading. He feels his fingers tremble, there's a biochemical quiver moving through his body, it's the way you feel when somebody slaps your face or impugns your honour or just leans drunkenly into you and calls you an asshole, it's the way you feel when you feel insulted. He does not want this charismatic experience, wants the world to be real, to be what it is and no more, but he knows that he has always been prone to slipping off the edge of things. And now that he has taken flight, the miraculous has assailed him, has surged through the fractured sky and anointed him with magic. A mantle of sunlight settles on his shoulders. Get away from me, he protests. Just let me sing my songs. His right hand, its fingers still unsteady, touches his mother's left; and clasps.

Spenta, shocked by Ormus's unexpected words, unable to avoid the conclusion that they are meant for her, is perplexed by his apparently contradictory capture of her jewelled hand. Physical displays of affection between Spenta and Ormus are uncharacteristic, infrequent. The mother finds herself feeling light-headed, and begins to blush like a young girl. She turns to look at her son, and at once her stomach whirls, as if the plane had dropped a few thousand feet through a hole in the air. Sunlight is falling on Ormus, and she feels there is another light emanating from within him now, a radiance of his own, rhyming with the sun's. Spenta who has walked with angels most of her life looks on her child as if for the first time. This is the son whom she tried to dissuade from accompanying her to England, the last-born flesh of her flesh, whose blood bonds she would have been prepared to cut loose. Remorse consumes her. My goodness, she thinks, my son is already more than a man, he's more than halfway to being a young god, and it's no thanks to me. With unpractised awkwardness she covers his hand with her other hand and asks, Something on your mind, Ormie? Is there maybe something I can do for you? He shakes his head absently, but she insists, driven on by her sudden guilt: Anything, there must be some little service.

As if awakening from sleep, he says, Mother, you must let me go.

Get away from me. So he was saying goodbye after all, she thinks, and foolish tears blub out: What are you saying, Ormie, have I not been, she can't finish the sentence, because she knows the answer, which is No. A good mother? No, no.

Ashamed, she turns her face away. She is sitting between her sons. Ardaviraf Cama sits straight-backed in the window seat, oblivious, silent, smiling his serene smile. That faint empty rictus of idiot joy. We are crossing a bridge in the air, Spenta understands. We, too, are travellers between the worlds, we who have died to our old world to be reborn in the new, and this parabola of air is our Chinvat Bridge. Having embarked, we have no option but to go forward on that soul's journey in which we will be shown what is best, and worst, in human nature. In our own.

Determinedly, she turns back to implore Ormus: Take some money, at least.

He agrees to accept five hundred pounds. Five hundred pounds is a lot of money, you can live on it for six months or more if you're careful. He takes it because he knows that he is the one giving the gift. It is her liberty, not his, that is the subject of this transaction. He is already free. Now she is buying her freedom from him, and he is permitting her to do so. The price is more than fair.

He has passed through the membrane. His new life begins.

Europe unrolls below him like a magic rug, and delivers up an unexpected Cleopatra. A young Indian woman materialises, a stranger, squatting by his aisle seat. Her long hair is worn loose over a long shirt and black tights, the uniform of the arty metropolitan beatnik. Her self-presentation is intimate, sultry. Here I am, darling, she says, surprised to see me? He confesses that yes, he is indeed a tad taken aback. Don't tease me, she cries, making a moue. You weren't so reticent in the hotel room, when you were playing fast and loose with my oiled and perfumed body while the waves at high tide, the aroused and moonlit sea, drowned our noisy cries. You crashed against me like the ocean et cetera. You told me I was the most beautiful girl in the world, at the height of your passion you swore I was the only one for you et cetera et cetera, so how can you be surprised that I'm on this flight as per arrangement, and now we can live happily ever after in jolly old London Town et cetera et cetera et cetera.

He has a good memory, but he does not remember her. She tells him the name of the hotel and the number of the room and then he is sure it isn't true. He has not forgotten—how could he forget?—wearing a Father Christmas outfit at the Cosmic Dancer on Marine Drive, but he never took a room there, with or without sea view. The woman has perched herself on the arm of his seat. I would watch you sleep and even your breath was music, she reminisces. I would bend over your body, my nakedness a beat away from yours and so on, and I felt your melody waft against my skin and so forth. I would inhale your lazy odours and drink the rhythms of your dreams. And so on and so forth. And so often. Once while you slept I held a knife against your throat. Spenta, who has heard every word—every passenger within six rows has heard every word—looks out of sorts, pulling her grumpy bulldog face. Ormus remains calm, begins to let the stranger down gently. Clearly a mistake has been made.

A second woman, older, bespectacled, sari-clad, flustered, comes bustling up, speaks sharply to the first: Maria, how can you bother the gentleman so? You're too intelligent, you should have better sense. Go back to your seat at once! Yes, miss, says the beatnik, demurely. Then swiftly she kisses Ormus on the mouth, thrusting a quick, long tongue between his astonished lips. I will be every woman you have ever wanted, of every shape, of every race, of every wild proclivity et cetera, she whispers. I will be your secret heart's unspeakable desires. Just going, miss, she adds in a different, placatory voice, and retreats. As she passes down the aisle she sings out, over her unembarrassed shoulder, Look for me in your dreams and so on. And send for me when it's time.

Passengers mutter and grouch. She waves lightly, and is gone.

The older woman lingers. Mr. Cama, she says, awkward but resolute, would you allow me to ask you a couple of personal questions, pardon the intrusion?

She introduces herself as the young woman's former teacher at Sophia College: My most brilliant student, it is all so stupid. Such expressiveness in that child, words fail me. But there is a mental problem, what a tragedy, it drives me mad. . . . She says she is taking her protégée on a tour of London galleries and shows. Such strong creativity in the girl, she sighs, but alas, she makes things up.

Taking a breath, she makes her enquiry. Mr. Cama, she has heard you singing, and now she is singing only of you. But her love story. It is important to establish. Do you know her from back home? From where we are from?

She speaks as if her Bombay, her India, were somehow different from mine, Ormus thinks, but lets it pass. Maybe she came to a show, he tells her, but no, I don't know her from a hole in the ground.

These things happen, he tells the lady in the sari. He is as yet only a small-time entertainer, a tiny bulb in the blinding light show of fame, but even for him this isn't the first such encounter. There was a Russian girl, the daughter of a Bombay-based consular official, who sent him seventeen numbered letters in English, each accompanied by a poem in Russian. One letter a day, until on the eighteenth day there was no poem and a melancholy awakening. *Now I know you do not love me, so I will be sending my virginal yearnings to great poet Mr. A. Voznesensky instead.* In the plane to London the sari-clad teacher nods: You can see that I had to ask. I never knew what to think. What a fixation! So much detail, I thought how could it be a fantasy, but of course it could not be true. Don't be angry. You must be furious. Only have pity. When a gifted child is damaged it is all our loss, isn't it? No, never mind, it's nothing to do with you. We are not a part of your world. Thanking you all the same.

Ormus delays her with questions of his own.

The teacher looks shifty. Yes, unfortunately it has been going on for some time, she confirms. Apparently the two of you have a love nest in Worli, but of course you don't have it. And she says you want to marry her but she wants to be free of ties, even though she is bound to you in far deeper ways than any ordinary married persons can comprehend, it is a marriage of mythological proportions and when you die you will take up residence in the stars et cetera. But of course you do not want this, she has been drawn into your penumbra and it has become more real than her own. It is not real. I mean it is real for you but not for her.

Once again, the odd locutions. There is mystery here.

She has written poetry, the teacher bursts out, painted paintings, learned the words to the songs that you have sung. Her room a shrine to your not existing love. You should understand that the paintings are good paintings, the poems are not without talent, her singing voice is strong and it can additionally be sweet. Maybe once you said a friendly word to her after a show. Maybe one day you smiled and touched her hand. And when we got on to the plane you said Welcome to the *Mayflower*. That was unwise, it would have been better not to say it. And the *Mayflower* is not the name of this plane. The name of the plane is *Wainganga*. Oh, it doesn't matter what the name is.

And her name is Maria, Ormus asks. He twists round in his seat, trying to see where she's sitting. The teacher shakes her head. No need for names-shames, she says, leaving. A sick stranger and her friend, you must be happy with that. Why names? You'll never talk to us again.

But as he watches the teacher scurry down the aisle, Ormus hears Gayomart whispering in his ear: The obsessed young woman's name is not an irrelevance. She's not from the past. She's the future.

Mr. John Mullens Standish XII, the radio pirate, known as Mull, Ormus Cama tells me (years later, in the period we have both come to think of as A.V., that is to say, After Vina), I would call the first man of genuine consequence to take me under his wing, an entrepreneur of real acumen, exceptional leadership qualities, a certain ruthless charm, a deep thinker, the first honourable gent I encountered on my journey West, and what was he? A common buccaneer, a desperado, a man facing possible arrest at Heathrow Airport an hour or two after our meeting. This, however, troubled me not in the slightest. Quite the contrary. Ever since boyhood, I'd had a head full of criminals of the sea. Captain Blood, Captain Morgan, Blackbeard, the Barbary Corsairs, Captain Kidd. The great Brynner, with hair and a moustache, as Jean Lafitte in Quinn and DeMille's movie about the Battle of New Orleans. The novels of Rafael Sabatini, the feats of the Elizabethan privateers. Nor was I limited to storybook stuff. You, Rai, with your darker perspective, there's too much of the world's horror in your eye, so you don't see. How to relish the seafaring criminals of our own childhood coastline. Yet there they were, all the time, plying their trade right under our noses. Looking out to sea from Cuffe Parade or Apollo Bunder, we— you and I!—we saw the Arab dhows, the dirty little engine-driven fish-

ing launches. Silhouettes on the horizon, red sails in the sunset. Carrying who knows what booty to who knew where—

Save this guff for the magazines, I interrupt. Narcotics smuggling is
not so romantic, that's the truth. Criminal mafias, ditto.

He ignores me, lost in rhetoric: And if the pirate Drake hadn't
beaten the Armada, and the Spanish had conquered India instead of
the British? You'd have liked that, I guess? (Such moments, when Sir
Darius Xerxes Cama's Anglophile xenophobia emerges from his son's
mouth, are genuinely spooky.)

British, Spanish, what's the difference? I cry, to provoke him.

Well, he rises to the bait, if you'd . . . then he sees my game, restrains
himself and grins ruefully. Anyway, he shrugs, when Standish
approached me, it seemed as if Jason himself was inviting me aboard
the *Argo* to join the quest for the Golden Fleece. And all I had to do
was play music.

They are already in German airspace when the stewardess—Ormus,
perhaps excusably in view of the date and his own Bombay English,
still thinks of her as an air hostess—summons Mr. Cama into first class.
Mull Standish rises to welcome him: tall, Bostonian, not yet fifty but
already silvery and patrician, reeking of old money, dressed in Savile
Row silk and Lobb leather. Don't be fooled by appearances, he greets
Ormus, handing him a Scotch and soda without troubling to ask,
adding: It's mostly phoney. You'll find I'm pretty much a rogue.

I caught your Santa act, he mentions further, twinkling. On an earlier visit. That was some exit you made.

Ormus shrugs, is unamused by the happenstance of it: the Cosmic
Dancer Hotel again. As if Nataraja, the old Lord of the Dance, were
out there somewhere, choreographing the steps of his petty human
destiny. I was going through a bad time, he snaps. I'm better now. He
doesn't add that the excitement of England, as it approaches, is flooding through him, as if he were a drain-blocked Bombay street in the
monsoon. Standish, a big man, sees it, anyway: Ormus's aroused condition, his readiness for whatever may come. His so to speak protagony.
You're the vigorous type, he notes. Good. We have that in common,
for a start.

Standish's own vigour is so great that it seems he might burst out of his suit and shoes at any moment, like Tarzan in the City, like the Hulk. This is a person who has business with the world, who expects events to fall in with his plans. An actor and a maker. His highly manicured nails, his equally well attended hair, speak of a certain *amour propre.* Near the end of this long plane flight he looks daisy-fresh. That takes some doing. That takes an exercise of will.

Is there something I can do for you?

Ormus's question actually makes Standish applaud. You're in even more of a hurry than I'd hoped, the older man congratulates the younger. And here I am thinking it's the East that's timeless, and us transatlantic rats who can't stop racing to Hell and back again.

No, Ormus answers. Actually it's the West that's exotic, fabulous, unreal. We underworlders . . . He realizes that Standish isn't listening. Don't go chippy on me, Mr. Cama, the American says: distantly, even idly. We may be working together for some time, and we're going to have to be able to speak our minds, any way we choose. Even a pirate can cleave to his First Amendment rights, as I hope you will allow. (The twinkle is back in his eyes.)

He's a Cambridge man—Cambridge, England; two years of graduate school. In his day he was a brilliant Chinese scholar, with dreams of setting up an academic institution of his own once he was through studying. Things have not worked out as he hoped. An early marriage to a woman in the rag trade failed, though not before it produced two sons, who stayed in England with his angry, resentful ex-wife when he went back across the Atlantic. For a time he taught Chinese at Amherst College. Then, frustrated at failing to gain the rapid advancement he expected, he made a curious, flamboyant decision. He would drive long-haul trucks across America for a few years, work his ass off, save money, start his dreamed-of Chinese school. From teacher to Teamster: a metamorphosis that represented the first stage of his true coming to be, his American way. He lit out, without illusions or regrets.

He quotes Sal Paradise by heart: *So began the part of my life you could call my life on the road. Before that I'd often dreamed of going West to see the country, always vaguely planning and never taking off.* For two years, maybe three, time was kind of stretchy then, you never knew how long things were taking, I crisscrossed America, carrying its produce to those who needed it, who were addicted to it as badly as any junkie, or had been told they needed it so often that they became addicted to the telling. A heavily fatigued speedhead, blissed out on distance and music and harsh, hungry freedom. Of course I never saved any money at all, spent it right away on women and substances, and most of all I spent it at Vegas, where the big wheels kept taking me, the spinning roulette wheels of my monster trucks.

Standish is away with his thoughts. Ormus, sipping Scotch, understands that a full opening of the self is being offered here, an absolute honesty, offered at once and without restraints as the proof of the soliloquist's bona fides. Listening, Ormus closes his eyes for an instant, and there is his own Vegas, that blaze of light through which his dead brother ducks and dives. So they have Las Vegas in common too.

Like Byron, like Talleyrand . . . I do not hesitate, Ormus Cama tells me A.V., to compare Mull Standish to such men; for he often made the comparison himself, and these days, a person's self-description is quickly adopted by all and sundry—Clown Prince, Comeback Kid, Sister of Mercy, Honest John—so why deny Standish his chosen similes? . . . like Joyce's Nausicaä, Gertie MacDowell, the American has a club foot. The Lobb shoes have to be specially built to accommodate and support it. In the matter of sexual attraction, it is well known that neither Talleyrand nor Byron was adversely affected by his damaged limb. However, in the younger days about which he has chosen to tell Ormus, Mull Standish was still more of a Gertie: his foot crippled his self-belief. Then, while he was losing his stash in an early round of the World Championship of Poker, he was approached by a young man, who spoke appreciatively of his physical beauty and offered him a substantial sum of money to accompany him to a suite at the Tropicana. Standish, feeling broke, absurd and flattered, agreed, and the encounter changed his life.

This was the beginning of my voyage across a frontier I'd thought forever closed to me. (His voice is languorous now, his body stretches out and grows dreamy with remembered joy.) Through that slash in the iron curtain between heterosex and homosex, I saw a vision of sublimity. After that, I gave up the trucks, and for a passage of years I stayed in Vegas, as a working male.

Prostitution taught him he was beautiful and desired, it allowed him to dream, to construct the Mull Standish who would dare to enter the zeitgeist and shake it all about. From Las Vegas to New York's Forty-second Street was a predictable next step, and it was here that he became the beneficiary of a classic only-in-America moment. A limousine pulled up; its window motored open; out leaned that selfsame young man, the trick from the Tropicana, his transforming angel. *Jesus. I've been looking for you for months. Jesus Christ.* It turned out that Mr. Tropicana had come *(a)* into his inheritance, and *(b)* to the conclusion that Mull Standish was his one true love. As a token of this love he gave Mull a brownstone apartment building in St. Mark's. In a trice the midnight cowboy was transformed into a member of the propertied classes, a respectable member of the Greater Gotham Business Guild of gay businessmen, and a pillar of the community. Thereafter Standish rapidly parlayed his early, lucky break into the beginnings of a jaw-dropping real estate portfolio, thanks to his continuing, long-term relationship with the Tropicana Kid—let's call him Sam—and, therefore, honorary membership of the inner circle of one of New York's true First Families, the great construction dynasties, the master builders, the high grammarians of the city's present tense.

Mayors, bankers, movie stars, basketball stars, representatives, Mull Standish says, and it is the first time Ormus hears a note of boastfulness in his voice, These people have been, let us say, frequently at my disposal.

America is not so unlike India, after all.

Why aren't you there now? Ormus has perspicacity of his own. There is a hidden dimension here, a side to the tale that has not been disclosed. Mull Standish raises a glass, acknowledging the question's shrewdness. I have certain issues with the IRS, he confesses. Corners were cut. There was a degree of clumsiness. It suits me to be in England for a time. England, where it's still illegal to be queer. As for India, I go there for my spiritual needs. I see this is a remark of which you do not approve. What shall I say? You have lived in the wood all your life and so you cannot see the trees. To provide the planet with good air to breathe, we have been given the Amazon rain forest. To provide for the planet's soul, there is India. One goes there as one goes to the bank, to refill the pocketbook of the psyche. Excuse the vulgar money-oriented metaphor. I have a refined act but I am not at bottom the refined type. Leopardskin briefs under the sober suit. Lycanthropic tendencies at the time of the full moon. A certain loucherie. In spite of which I have my spiritual hunger, the needs of my soul.

The stewardess tells me you've been calling this plane the *Mayflower,* it has pleased you to make that joke. Did you know that Standish is a famous *Mayflower* name? I guess nobody reads Longfellow any more, especially in Bombay. Still, it's a poem of more than a thousand lines, a long and vile thing. Miles Standish, a professional soldier, suffering from soldierly inarticulacy, wishes to marry a certain Puritan maiden, Priscilla Mullens or Molines, and makes what you might call the Cyrano error, sending his friend John Alden to plead his cause because the cat had gotten his tongue and wouldn't let go. Young Alden, a cooper, a signatory of the Mayflower Compact, the founder of Plymouth Colony, a man of fortunate looks and pleasing manner, is unfortunately much in love with the same damsel, and yet in friendship's name agrees to do as he is bid. Well! Mistress Molines or Mullens, she hears him out, then looks him squarely, forwardly in the eye and asks, Why don't you speak for yourself, John? Tedious hundreds of lines later they are married, and the gruff old soldier, my vanquished—and distant—ancestor, is left to make the best of it. I tell you this because, though I'm no Puritan, Mistress Priscilla's words are now my motto. I ask nothing on others' behalf, but am shameless and inexorable in my own interest. As now, this minute, in making my approach to you.

Ormus reddens, and Standish, seeing his embarrassment, laughs. No, not sex, he reassures him. Piracy on the high seas.

England rushes towards them, then stops. Air traffic congestion, even in 1965. Unable to make their approach, they circle in the sky. Down below them, the pirate navy has assembled, an invasion is in progress. Here is a decommissioned old passenger ferry, flying the Jolly Roger, moored in the North Sea. The *Frederica*. Here's another, the *Georgia,* anchored off the Essex coast, near Frinton. Look down at the Thames Estuary: those three tiny dots, see them?, are also part of this cutthroat fleet. Ormus, tired, exhilarated, is in an airplane state of mind; hollow, unreal, a condition in which it's hard to keep a grip on things. Mull Standish seems utterly unfazed, and is talking, now, about childhood:

There was a heavy glass ball that used to sit on the windowsill of my bedroom. My father would turn it to catch and refract light. There were bubbles in it, like galaxies, like dreams. The small things of our earliest days move us, and we don't know we don't know why. Now that I've started this pirate fleet thing, I keep seeing that ball. Maybe it's innocence, freedom, I couldn't say. Maybe it's about a transparent world: you can see through it to the light. Maybe it's just a ball of glass, but somehow it's moving me, it's making me do this.

It occurs to Ormus as Standish talks on that he's giving too many reasons for doing what he is doing: over-explaining what is, after all, a nakedly commercial enterprise, news of which has already reached India. At a brilliant moment in British music, British radio is deadly dull. Restrictions on "needle time" mean that when you want the latest hit records—John Lennon singing "Satisfaction," the Kinks' "Pretty Woman," or "My Generation," by the new super-group High Numbers, who changed their name from The Who and immediately made the big time—all you get is Joe Loss or Victor Sylvester, music for dead people. But because commercial radio isn't illegal if it's not land based, the pirate ships have come to give the kids what they want. Needle time and adverts. Hello pop pickers this is Radio Freddie broadcasting on 199 . . . this is Radio Gaga . . . this is the Big M. The pirates aim their sounds at Britain and the country surrenders. And Mull Standish is the Lord High Desperadio: the music brigands' king.

Reasons go on pouring out of him. Maybe he's in England because, to be absolutely frank, things with his lover, Sam Tropicana, are no longer what they were, the bloom is off. Or maybe he just plain got bored with the construction industry, all those hard hats and girders, all those empty rooms for other lives to fill. Or maybe it's the fault of the CIA, because, yes, they approached him on several occasions, a Chinese-language expert is assumed to be top-grade spy material, so they try and sign you up before the Yellow Peril gets to you and turns you to the dark side, and the second time he refused them—a man called Michael Baxter or Baxter Michaels had made the approach right in the foyer of the Sherry Netherland—he was accused of having an attitude and threatened with the confiscation of his passport. *I crossed some line when that happened, it changed America for me, and it became possible to leave.* And then, of course, it's surprising he's taken so long to get round to mentioning it, there's the war, America is at war. Ballot boxes have been stuffed full of votes for President Kennedy, war is always good for sitting presidents, his numbers are up from the tight squeeze against Nixon in 1960, he's got four more years of power and priapism at Pennsylvania Avenue, and now it's the voters, the young generation of soldier electors out there in jungled, swamped, incomprehensible Indochina, who are being stuffed into boxes in shocking quantities and being sent home to various addresses less exalted than JFK's. Their numbers, too, are up.

Mull Standish is against the war, but that's not exactly what he wants to say. He wants to say—his eyes are gleaming now, and the energy pours from him with redoubled, frightening force—that the war has turned him on to its consequent music, because in this dark time it's the rock music that represents the country's most profound artistic engagement with the death of its children, not just the music of peace and psychotropic drugs but the music of rage and horror and despair. Also of youth, youth surviving in spite of everything, in spite of the children's crusade that's blowing it apart. (A mine, a sniper, a knife in the night: childhood's bitter end.)

That's when I really fell in love with rock, Standish is off and rolling, because I admired so much what it was doing, the humane democratic spirit-food fullness of its response. It was not just saying fuck you, Uncle Sam, or give peace a chance, or I feel like I'm fixin' to die, or even making patriotic noises, zap zap zappin' the Cong. Rather, it was making love in a combat zone, insisting on the remembrance of beauty and innocence in a time of death and guilt; it privileged life over death and asked life to take its chance, let's dance, honey honey, in the street, on the phone, and we'll have fun fun fun on the eve of destruction.

His manner has changed completely, from patrician Bostonian to eager-beaver muso peacenik, and Ormus, watching the transformation, begins to see who he really is. Never mind all his explanations, the truth is he's just another one of us chameleons, just another looking-glass transformer. Not only an incarnation of Jason the Argonaut but also perhaps of Proteus, the metamorphic Old Man of the Sea. And once we've learned how to change our skins, we Proteans, sometimes we can't stop, we career between selves, lane-hopping wildly, trying not to run off the road and crash. Mull Standish, too, is a slip-slider, Ormus understands: a shape-shifter, a man who knows what it's like to wake up as a giant bug. That's why he picked me out, he can see we're of the same tribe, the same sub-species of the human race. Like aliens on a strange planet we can recognize each other in any crowd. At present we have adopted human form, here on the third rock from the sun.

Standish, this new, exhilarated, high-as-a-kite Standish, says: I came to England to get away from a country at war. One month after I arrived, the new Labour government decided to join forces with the Americans and ship its own kids out to die. Things here stopped being theoretical. British boys and girls, too, started being mailed home in small packages. I couldn't believe it, as an American I felt *responsible,* as if I'd flouted quarantine regulations and imported a deadly epidemic, I felt like a flea carrier. A plague dog. This development was not as per programme. In a spin, I flew out to India, which is what I do when I need to regain equilibrium. That's when I looked in at your big moment at the Cosmic Dancer, by the way.

After Bombay, Standish had gone to sit at the feet of a teenage ma-haguru in Bangalore, and then up to Dharmsala to spend time at the Buddhist Shugden temple. *Again*—I find myself thinking when Ormus tells me the story—*again the curious possessive fascination of the hedonistic West with the ascetic East. The arch-disciples of linearity, of the myth of progress want, from the Orient, only its fabled unchangingness, its myth of eternity.* It was the god-boy who came through. He's an old soul in a young body, Mull says reverentially, a Tantric Master in his final incarnation. I confessed everything to that wise child, my alienation, my guilt, my despair, and he smiled his pure smile and said, The music is the glass is the glass ball. Let it shine.

I understood then that the limit on needle time was the enemy, the censor. The limit was General Waste-More-Land's broadcasting ally, General Haig's whore. Enough with big bands and men in white tuxes with bow ties pretending nothing was going on. I mean come *on.* A nation at war deserves to hear the music that's going *mano a mano* with the war machine, that's sticking flowers down its gun barrels and baring its breasts to the missiles. The soldiers are singing these songs as they die. But this is not the way soldiers used to sing, marching into battle bellowing hymns, kidding themselves they had god on their side; these aren't patriotic-bullshit, get-yourself-up-for-it songs. These kids are using singing, instead, as an affirmation of what's natural and true, singing against the unnatural lie of the war. Using song as a banner of their doomed youth. Not *morituri te salutant,* but *morituri* say up yours, Jack, those about to die give you the fucking finger. That's why I got the ships.

He slumps back in his seat, almost talked out. He has sold up a chunk of his American real estate holdings to purchase, equip and staff up these barely seaworthy little boats. A complete encirclement of England and Scotland is envisaged, seagoing conditions permitting. Now we're blasting the material at them round the clock, he says, Hendrix and Joplin and Zappa, making war on war. Certainly, the loveable moptops too. Also the Lovin' Spoonful, Love, Mr. James Brown feelin like a sex machine, Carly Simon and Guinevere Garfunkel feelin groovy et cetera. My one regret is that we can't moor a boat on the Thames, right outside the Houses of Parliament, mount giant speakers on the deck and blow those complacent bastards right out of their murderous seats. But never say die; this project, too, is in development. So what do you say? Are you with us or withered? There or square?

He had me badly off balance, just the way he wanted me, Ormus tells me, A.V.: I was ripe for adventure, and he'd taken me by storm.

The pilot announces the flight's clearance to land. The air hostess approaches, asks Ormus to resume his own seat. Ormus, rising to go, asks Mull Standish, Why me?

Call it a hunch, he replies, No, let's say inspiration. I flatter myself that I am a judge of men. Something about the way you tore off the Santa beard that night. Something about you struck me, strikes me, as, ah, ah.

Piratical? Ormus suggests.

Emblematic, Mull Standish finds the word, with what looks suspiciously like the makings of a blush mounting above the semi-stiff collar of his Turnbull & Asser shirt. I asked around a little, you know. Seems you're capable of generating a following. People look to you. Maybe you'll get 'em listening to us.

But I'm trying to be a singer, not a DJ on a cold, wet boat, Ormus makes his last, wavering stand. His imagination has been captured, and Standish knows it.

You will be, Standish promises. As a matter of fact you already are, and a good one, might I add. Yes, sir. At this very moment—hark at you—I could swear you're singing right now. Yes. I can hear your song.

As the plane touches down, Ormus Cama's head starts pounding. There is something about this England in which he has just arrived. There are things he cannot trust. There's a rip, once again, in the surface of the real. Uncertainty pours down on him, its dark radiance opens his eyes. As his foot alights upon Heathrow, he succumbs to the illusion that nothing is solid, nothing exists except the precise piece of concrete his foot now rests upon. The homecoming passengers notice none of this, they stride confidently forward through the familiar, the quotidian, but the new arrivals look fearfully at the deliquescent land. They seem to be splashing through what should be solid ground. As his own feet move gingerly forward, he feels small pieces of England solidify beneath them. His footprints are the only fixed points in his universe. He checks out Virus: who is untroubled, serene. As for Spenta Cama, her eyes are fixed on the crowd of waving greeters high above. Trying to pick out a familiar face, she has no time to look down. Never look down, Ormus thinks. That way you won't see the danger, you won't plunge through the deceptive softness of the apparent into the burning abyss below.

Everything must be made real, step by step, he tells himself. This is a mirage, a ghost world, which becomes real only beneath our magic touch, our loving footfall, our kiss. We have to imagine it into being, from the ground up.

But he will spend his early days on the sea, within sight of land, which will remain just out of reach but which will listen, as though hypnotized, to his seductive, imagining voice.

Beyond the barrier, William Methwold and Mull Standish are waiting, two large pinkish thumbs sticking out of a rackety Indian crowd, the land children running at top speed to greet their cousins from the air, outpacing the astonishingly stentorian shouts of the older women in their heavy-framed spectacles and wine-dark overcoats worn over brilliant saris, and the bellowed rebukes of the older men with jutting lower lips and jangling car keys. The younger women, not in fact demure, group together to perform demureness; they lower their eyelids, whisper, simper. The younger men, not in reality half as backslapping and juvenile as they seem, likewise gather in clutches, their arms around one another's shoulders, to yell and joke, giggle and nudge. Ormus, emerging into England, finds himself momentarily, dizzyingly, back in India, hearing an echo of home. Nostalgia tugs at him for an instant. He jerks himself free of it. There's new music in the air.

Out of the migrant throng, this new way of being British, the two white men rise like Alps. Methwold is a walking antique, with mottled skin blotched over his hairless unwigged dome, making his baldness look like a map of the moon, with its dry seas of shadow and tranquillity, its veiny lines, its pocks. Limp fleshfolds flap above the collar that has grown too large for his neck. He walks with a stick, and he looks, Spenta is happy to note, as pleased to see her as she is to see (indeed, to recognize) him. As for Mull Standish, he has evidently evaded arrest. Perhaps the IRS isn't as hot on his trail as he fears; and as for his pirate ships, technically they are breaking no law, though the state's lawyers are working overtime to come up with pretexts on which they can be closed down.

The Camas pause. They are at their crossroads. Their futures tug them apart.

Okay, then, Ormus says to his mother.

Okay, then, in a muffled voice she replies.

Okay, then, Ormus punches Virus on the shoulder.

Virus makes a tiny sideways motion of the head.

Okay, see you, then, Ormus repeats. Nobody is touching him, but he feels himself held. He pulls against the force field, turns a shoulder and tugs hard.

Okay, see you, then. Spenta seems incapable of offering more than echoes, is herself becoming no more than a member of that crowd of echoes bouncing around them, fading, fading.

Ormus goes towards Standish, parts from his mother without looking back. Though his last image of her is a trembling lip and a lace kerchief at the corner of an eye, still in the rear-view mirror of his mind he can see her looking grateful. He can see her future shining like a diamond on her brow, the great mansion, the silver thread of river, the green and pleasant land. Though he abhors the countryside, he is happy for her. She has given him what she has been able to give, though she

could never love him. It has been less than enough by ordinary standards, but he is prepared to call it sufficient. In a way it is this lack of
emotional enthusiasm, this absence of unconditional love, that has prepared him for his great future, has gotten him on to the runway, so to
speak, like a jet aircraft, ready to fly. And she herself is husband hunting now. She's a fishing fleet of one. Best for her to arrive as unen-
cumbered as possible. Virus grins mutely at her side at the approaching
English milord, but Ormus makes himself scarce. Spenta, preparing her
smile for Methwold, has no time for a sentimental farewell. Mother
and son go their ways: she into the arms of an old England, he into the
new country that's in the process of being born. Destiny summons
them both, breaking their family ties.

Music in the air, from a crackly transistor. Soft brushes coax a whispered beat from a drum, a big bass line is laid down, a high riff
screams from an invisible clarinet. All that's needed is for a singer to
grab some of that stuff and go for broke. Here she comes, her bluesy
coloratura spiralling over and around the jazzy rhythm of the tune.
Vina! It sounds like her voice, drowned in crackles and arrivals-
lounge ruckus as it is, but high, strong, who else could it be. As she
will one day hear him on a Bombay radio, so today, at the beginning
of his journey back into her heart, he thinks he hears her, and even
when, after their reunion, she promises him it couldn't have been, she
didn't have a recording contract back in '65, he refuses to accept his
mistake. The long-haul terminal was a chamber of echoes that day,
and that's how he heard her voice, an echo returning from the future
to summon up his love.

He is clear about his purpose: by his labours to make himself worthy of her again. And when he's ready he'll find her, he'll make her real
by touching her kissing her caressing her, and she'll do the same for
him. Vina I'll be the ground beneath your feet and you, in this happy
ending, will be all the earth I need.

He walks towards her, away from his mother, into the music.

The rapid disenchantment of Ormus Cama with his fantasy of the
West, which will be the making of him as an artist and almost the
unmaking of him as a man, begins the instant he lays eyes on Radio
Freddie, that seven-hundred-ton rust bucket, pitching uncertainly, like

a super-annuated rodeo rider, upon the saddle of the sea. His heart sinks. His imagined journey from periphery to centre has never included the low, dank northern flats of Lincolnshire, nor this biting, sou'westered journey out from shore. He feels "out of land," the land-lubber's version of fish-out-of-water. Briefly he wants out, but there's nowhere to go, no other course but the one on which he's set. Indentured Indian labourers arriving in Mauritius and erasing from their Bhojpuri vocabularies such words as "return" or "hope" would have felt, in Ormus's shoes, no less enslaved.

By contrast, Standish, erect at the prow of the motor launch that is transporting him to his kingdom, aquiline of profile, silver hair streaming, looks exalted, haloed. A man with a mission is a dangerous man, Ormus thinks, feeling for the first time in their admittedly brief acquaintance a jolt of something resembling fear. Then Standish turns his head, gleaming with anticipation, points. There they are, he shouts. Look at them, Hook and Smee. The two Tweedles. They hate me, naturally; as you will soon discover. (This in an odd voice pitched halfway between tragedy and pride.) Mr. Nathaniel Hawthorne Crossley and Mr. Waldo Emerson Crossley, he finishes, raising an arm in salute, Your new colleagues. My sons.

The men standing at the *Frederica*'s rail do not return his greeting.

Hawthorne Crossley—greatcoated, long-silk-scarved, corduroy-jeaned, the sole of one shoe coming loose—has inherited his father's looks and volubility. He uses his mother's surname, but he's Standish translated into English, filled up with alcohol and spite, and aged twenty-four or -five. Hail Standish, he mocks, as Ormus follows Mull aboard Radio Freddie, Hail the pioneer hero, maker of charts, conqueror of nations. So must the empire builders have looked in their prime, eh, Waldorf? My baby brother, he explains to Ormus. Not named as Mr. Standish would have you believe in honour of a great philosopher but after a fucking salad, as eaten by his presently divorced parents on the night he was conceived.

Rheumy-eyed Waldo, smaller, fuzzy-headed, leather-jacketed, Lennon-bespectacled, his mother's boy, beams, nods, sneezes. In his personal universe Hawthorne is a blazing star.

Hail Standish, Waldo eagerly agrees.

Think of stout Cortez in the Keats poem, only it was really Balboa, gazing at the Pacific, Hawthorne exhorts. Consider Clive of India on the battlefield at Plassey, Captain Cook sailing into Sydney harbour. The Islamic conquerors bursting out of Arabia to face the might of Persia, only to find the once mighty superpower rotten and decayed. They blew it away like sand. It's what Standish hopes to do to the BBC Light Programme.

Why isn't one of you in the studio? Mull Standish fondly interjects.

Because we decided to play the whole fucking Floyd album, Hawthorne answers, every last bubble and shriek. So we've got hours. We reckoned we could trust Eno to flip the disc while we greeted the aged parent. He takes an uncorked bottle of bourbon from his great-coat pocket. Mull Standish takes it from him, wipes off the neck, prepares to drink.

Robert Johnson was poisoned by a theatre owner who suspected Johnson of fucking his chick, muses Hawthorne, thoughtfully, Sonny Boy Williamson tried to save him, knocked away the bottle he was going to drink from. Don't ever drink from an open bottle, he said. You never know what's in it. Johnson didn't like the advice. Don't ever knock a whisky bottle away from me, he said, and drank from another open bottle, and bango! End of story.

Mull Standish drinks, hands back the bottle, introduces Ormus.

Aha, the Indian nightingale!, says Hawthorne. (It is raining now, a fine icy drizzle that inserts itself between the men and their clothes, between Ormus and his happiness, between the father and his sons.) The bulbul of Bombay! He found you, then. About fucking time. And now you're his Koh-i-noor diamond, the fucking jewel in his arse. A little on the old side for the work, I'd have thought. All I can say is I hope you wash your mouth before applying it to my fucking microphone.

Hawthorne, *Jesus Christ*. Standish's voice is low and dangerous, and the younger man's tongue stumbles, dries. But it's too late, the cat's out of the bag. Why me? Ormus had asked, and Standish had replied, Call it inspiration. But of course it had nothing to do with inspiration. It's love.

Bareheaded in the rain, Mull Standish, exposed, shamed, confesses and apologizes to Ormus Cama: I have been less than frank. I asked around about you, I told you that. I should have admitted that my personal feelings were in fact engaged. The eagerness. The eagerness of my enquiries. I suppressed that information, which was culpably wrong. However, you have my one thousand per cent guarantee that it won't become a problem between us. . . . Hawthorne snorts with mirthless laughter. Runny-nosed Waldo, not to be outdone, snorts too. Mucus explodes from his nose, like a glutinous flag. He wipes it off his face with the back of his chilblained hand.

Ormus is hearing echoes again. In Hawthorne Crossley he sees Vina reborn, Vina in her childhood incarnation of Nissy Poe, in whose family history there are poignant parallels to the tale of this smart-mouthed, bitter child of a broken home. He sees, too, that Mull Standish's long autobiographical reminiscence about his lover, "Sam Tropicana," who pursued him for months, then found him and changed his life, was a parable, a tale told in code, its real meaning being: *This is what I can do for you. It's true: I hunted you, you have been the quarry of my own obsessive love. But now I can change your life, it is my turn to give as once I was given, to be the bringer of good things as once they were brought to me. I want nothing from you except that you permit me to be your Santa Claus.*

I want nothing from you, Mull Standish is saying, miserably. For you, however, I want very much indeed.

Let me out of here, Ormus Cama demands, and Mull Standish, who has abruptly run out of all his words, can do nothing but drip in the rain and extend, in a profound, involuntary gesture, both of his trembling, supplicant arms. Their palms are upturned, and empty.

Hawthorne Crossley relents. Oh, stay. Will you stay, for fucksake. Stay for the same reason we do: viz., that here there's booze and music, no dope, alas, because the law keeps boarding us to see if there's the tiniest chance of fucking us up, but really the only thing to be afraid of is that one of these fine days the sea god might decide to open up his great gob and swallow us down. Whereas out there—he gestures vaguely with the emptying bottle of Beam towards the land—out there it's just too fucking terrifying for words.

Out there there's kinky bishops, Waldo elucidates. And dodgy Scotch eggs and takeaway chop suey and bent coppers and voodoo dolls and napalm. There's anabolic steroids and cows and anti-personnel strikes

north of the DMZ. And Bideford Parva and Piddletrenthide and
Ashby-de-la-Zouch and country people in wellies and the Mekong
delta where wellies aren't much use and Tet which isn't a place but a
date, like Christmas, that's out there too. There's Arsenal F.C. and
Ringo marries his hairdresser and Harold Wilson and Russians walking in space. And axe murderers and mother-rapers and father-rapers.

The draft as well, Hawthorne concedes, belching, We're all blowing
in *that* wind. What we're hoping is, if we do this long enough, and
throw in a spot of littering and creating a nuisance on the side, we may
be thought not moral enough to be in the army. If we're lucky we
might be not moral enough to blow up women and children and such.
We might even be not moral enough to die.

Like Arlo Guthrie, explains Waldo, swaying. (They've finished the
bottle of Beam.) Meanwhile, out there, the wrong people are escaping
bullets. King Jigme Wangchuk of Bhutan escapes assassination attempt.
A machine-gun attempt on the Shah of Iran's life fails. President
Sukarno survives a communist coup.

Race riots in Watts, Hawthorne picks up the thread, Edward Heath
elected Tory leader. Two charged with Moors murders. Churchill dead.
Albert Schweitzer dead. T. S. Eliot dead. Stan Laurel dead. The British
believe in God but prefer tv, polls prove. China has the A-bomb. India
and Pakistan on brink of war. And England swings like a fucking
pendulum do. It scares me to fucking death and back again.

Stay, repeats Waldo, showing his teeth and offering a bottle of sherry,
Harveys Bristol Cream. Best we can do at the moment. Welcome to
wonderful 199.

Ormus takes the bottle. And who's Eno? he asks. The third Stooge?

You don't have to worry about Eno, Hawthorne shrugs. Eno's a
prince. A man among men. A needle in a haystack. Eno's the business.
He's OK.

It's raining harder. Mull Standish makes as if to go. His sons ignore
him.

His real name's Enoch, Hawthorne says, turning his soaked back on
his father. He dropped the *ch* because he understandably didn't want a
racist handle, what with him being a person of tint. It's as if you were
a person of Jewishness who got named Hitler by accident and decided

to be a Hit instead. Or if your name was unfortunately Stalin and you shortened it to Star.

Mao's a tough one, says Waldo. But you could always answer to Dong.

Hawthorne confides, Actually, he's called Eno because e knows how all this fucking equipment works and we don't have a clue.

Or, Waldo offers, because e no say very much.

Or, Hawthorne continues, because he takes a lot of fruit salts, poor love. It's his third-world digestion. Anyway, when you get to know him you call him Ali. Eno Barber, Ali Barber. I expect that's a joke you'll find funny. I expect that's a joke with a cultural reference that isn't too fucking tough for you to pick up.

He doesn't get it, Waldo pouts. He hasn't had halfway enough to drink, he says.

Hawthorne leans in on Ormus, blasting him with a fog of whisky breath. Listen, Mowgli, he says, not without aggression, you're our fucking guest here, see. How'd you expect to understand the fucking host culture if you insist on remaining teetotal, if you obstinately refuse to fucking integrate in this obstinate fucking Paki obstinate bastard way?

Maybe he's too good for us, Waldo ponders. Too good for Harveys Bristol Cream. Too good for the finest British sherry our father's money can buy.

Mull Standish, with the help of the motor-launch captain, leaves the *Frederica*. Now that you boys have started getting on so well, he says, I'm sure the station will just go from strength to strength.

God save the Queen, Hawthorne Crossley salutes his father extravagantly, And he probably ought to keep an eye on that Elizabeth Windsor as well.

In Ormus Cama's classic rock 'n' roll belter "Ooh Tar Baby"—an encrypted remembrance of his English years, sung in the sour-sour, down-and-dirty cool-cat growl that became his abiding gift to the male singers of the New York underground—the Tar Baby is England itself. England kidnaps people, he says in interviews, when, on his comeback tour, late in his career, he breaks the habit of a lifetime and consents to a few journalistic encounters. England seizes hold, he says, and won't let go. It's uncanny. You arrive for whatever reason, just passing through en route to the rest of your life, but watch out, or you'll get stuck for years. That old Tar Baby, you can greet her courteously but she won't give you the time of day, you can speak to her as nice as pie but she won't act polite, 'til finally you're so ticked off that you bust her in the mouth, and then, too late!, you're held fast. Once you attack her you're in her thrall. It's a strange kind of love, what I call stuck love, but you can't get away. You're only some dumb rabbit anyhow, how smart can you be to be punching out that sticky old sister, if you know what I mean. So you're hanging there, and you can't help yourself, you're beginning to think in a way she's cute, but then you start worrying that maybe in the bushes there's that hungry fox, lying low and saying nothing and waiting for his supper.

Ooh Tar Baby yeah you got me stuck on you. Ooh Tar Baby and I can't get loose it's true. Come on Tar Baby won't you hold me tight, we can stick together all through the night. Ooh Tar Baby and maybe I'm in love with you.

10

SEASON OF THE WITCH

At first the music is the only thing he can get a grip on. Mull
Standish XII, who chooses the playlists for all his boats, has a
good ear and sure instincts. As he becomes familiar with these lists,
Ormus privately concedes that his premature dismissal of cisatlantic
rock music was way off beam. This is the golden age of British rock 'n'
roll. After Sinatra and Parker, this is the third revolution.

Mull visits each boat once in every two-week period. (The terms
of employment for DJs aboard Radio Freddie are also based on a
fourteen-day rotation, two weeks on, two weeks off.) He arrives with a
clattering canvas bag of the latest platters and announces the musical
marching orders for the next fortnight: push this, spotlight that, play this
one once in a while but only because we can't not play it, listen to this
one, you guys, this kid's going to be vast. There is a sense of an audience
building, and the terrestrial bosses are definitely getting nervous. You
can tell this is so because the frequency of the drug-squad raids is
increasing. In Ormus's first shift they are boarded twice, the boat is
turned upside down, its human cargo is strip-searched, there is a good
deal of sneering and shoving, and finally they are left alone again.

My fucking rectum's getting so habituated to being probed by these rozzers' rubber-gloved fingers, announces Hawthorne, it's beginning to fucking like it.

Waldo gravely assents. Probably something in the genes.

Ormus, however, finds it hard to see the funny side. Naked and innocent before the officers of the law, suffering their jolly rogerings, he shakes with rage and shame. This is an England his father never knew, at whose existence he could not have guessed.

Except during the police searches, Cap'n Pugwash (not his real name) and the crew of the *Frederica* have little time for the broadcasting staff. Their quarters are separate, and few words are exchanged. The raids, however, are forging a curious bond between the two camps. The bluebottles' stings act as a unifying force. The invasions, the gibes, transcend the gulfs of world-view and class between the mariners and the radio upstarts. After one raid Pugwash himself—a stubbly, beer-bellied grouch with an appropriately piratical moustache—unbends so far as to say to Hawthorne Crossley, *You keep at it, mate, yeah? You give 'em what bleeding for.* Then, gradually, the surly standoff resumes.

Such are the shock troops of Mull Standish's conquering navy, the navy of peace and music, to whom all England must—according to the chief pirate's strategy—inevitably succumb. In spite of his new-found admiration for the music, Ormus is finding it hard to get a handle on England. Water slurps beneath his feet. Everything shifts. He is told that the kids are crazy for Freddie, but the England he sees on the horizon is a low dark shape below a low grey sky, distantly mooing with uninterest.

Drunkenly, clumsily, the station gets through the days and nights. The weather is continuously dreadful: rain, wind, more wind, more rain. The *Frederica* pitches and rolls. Waldo Crossley is frequently sick, and not always over the side. Somehow, a minimum level of hygiene is maintained, so that the health inspectors, when they make their raids, are unable to close the show down, and leave angry and frustrated. Ormus, learning the art of gonzo broadcasting, comes to see that Eno, the person of tint, is the key. Eno dresses in immaculate whites and sports a cream Borsalino hat, and he is a world unto himself, wanting nothing to do with DJs or crew. He appears not to eat or drink or sleep or (in spite of the Crossleys' fruit-salts slur) even shit or piss. In the ship's studio he keeps things moving from his position behind a desk that looks like an electric hedgehog, bristling with switches. That's where he stays, on the far side of his glass window, Ali Barber in Aladdin's cave, and there's a large sign on the wall behind him saying *Know Your Place.* Eno believes in apartheid, Hawthorne explains, and that means you too. You know that in South Africa the blacks hate the Indians more than they hate the whites.

He's from South Africa, then? Ormus surmises.

Waldo shakes his head gravely. No. Stockwell.

The music is extraordinary. Keening slow-hand guitar playing, the old wise voices of ridiculously young blues rockers, the hard-edged raunch 'n' roll women and the soft ethereal crystal-voiced maidens, the screaming feedback swirls of psychedelia, the ballads of war and love, the hallucinated visions of the great troubadours. By clinging to the music Ormus can keep a hold on what's real. The music tells him truths he finds he already knows. The music is a great wild bird calling out to the bird of the same species that lies hidden in his own throat, in the egg of his Adam's apple, hatching, nearing its time.

Ormus, Hawthorne and Waldo set up a sleep rota. They crowd into the confined studio space two at a time, Ormus and Hawthorne, Hawthorne and Waldo, Waldo and Ormus. Time stretches endlessly before them, the land drifts off like a fantasy, and cocooned as they are in rain and alcohol it's easy for them to imagine they're talking to themselves. What goes out over the air in between songs: their interior monologues, the fatigue-and-whisky-polluted streams of their wrecked consciousness.

Ormus, during one night shift, in the small hours when the monsters crawl, notices that his co-jockey Waldo has fallen asleep. Whispering, as if speaking privately to his beloved, he calls out across the skies for Vina. Eno, impassive in his booth, offers no comment. He is lost in electricity, devoted to the maintenance of the signal, dedicated to purity of sound. Perhaps he isn't even listening to Ormus's cry, just hearing the level and timbre of it, throwing his switches, watching his gauges, the flickering of illuminated needles reflected in his eyes.

Are you there, my love, Ormus murmurs. Oh my long-lost love. You did not trust me and I was wounded, proud, I let you go away. Now I must prove myself worthy, I must perform labours, pursue quests, shoulder the burdensome world.

Mull Standish sends an urgent message via the ship's radio. The first mate, who is also the radio operator, transcribes the text, and Cap'n Pugwash—who has been tuning in to Ormus's soliloquy—is sufficiently moved (he's a big lump-in-throat softy, really) to bring Standish's message personally to Eno, who flattens the paper against the glass window. This is an inspiration, Ormus reads. Who is she? Is she real? Did you make her up? Certainly you mustn't find her too soon. Keep it going. Instalments every night. This will build the audience like nothing else. The lovesick floating romeo sings to his unheeding love. You want a singing career? You just found the door. This will give you profile, saliency, share of mind. This will make your make your name.

Vina Apsara has not heard Ormus's appeal. She's in America and doesn't know he's floating off the coast of England, damp and yearning, and calling out her name.

Nobody tells her. It isn't time.

The migraines come. They're getting worse. Sometimes he is unable to sleep at all during his allotted hours. He picks up one of the paperbacks abandoned in his cabin—it must be Mull Standish who brought them aboard in the hope of pushing a little culture into his sons, who have promptly tossed them into the spare cabin, the one they never enter, the one that's now Ormus's little hole of privacy. Books by famous American writers, Sal Paradise's odes to wanderlust, Nathan Zuckerman's *Carnovsky,* science fiction by Kilgore Trout, a playscript—*Von Trenck*—by Charlie Citrine, who would go on to write the hit movie *Caldofreddo.* The poetry of John Shade. Also Europeans: Dedalus, Matzerath. The one and only *Don Quixote* by the immortal Pierre Ménard. F. Alexander's *A Clockwork Orange.*

Here's the year's hit fantasy-thriller, *The Watergate Affair,* in which the future President Nixon (President Nixon! that's how wild a fantasy it is) has to leave office after trying to bug the Democrats' offices, an accusation that's finally proved true, in a wildly implausible twist, when it turns out that Nixon also bugged himself, ha ha ha, the things these guys think of to make us laugh.

But every time he picks up one of these books his brain swirls and thumps, and he is forced to put them down unread. His head bursts with confusions and when he closes his eyes he finds that behind his eyelids his dead twin Gayo has changed his behaviour. Gayomart no longer runs away but comes towards, stands up close, staring at Ormus like a man gazing into a mirror. You're a changed man, Gayomart Cama grins. Maybe that's Gayomart out there and you're in here now, trapped in unreality. Maybe now I'm dreaming you. Ormus is appalled by the hostility in Gayomart's glittering grin. Why do you hate me, he asks. Why do you think, his brother replies. I'm the one who died.

To keep Gayo away he must keep his eyes open. He is so tired that he has to use his fingers to push the heavy lids apart. He switches on the monitor in his tiny cabin and tries to concentrate on the brothers Crossley doing their shift.

If you're listening, Antoinette Corinth, you witchy insomniac, and I know you're listening because you always are, then this one's for you. This one comes to you from Hawthorne with love. And Waldo would add his personal salutations but alas at present he's being somewhat indisposed in the bin. This one is to honour your genius, O queen of the black arts, princess of the pentangle, Baroness Samedi, priestess of Wicca, adept of the secrets of the Great Pyramid, dispenser of all good things, dressmaker extraordinaire, O Mother who gave us suck. We took your name and you at once let it go, espousing, instead, the noble Corinthian tradition. Mother forgive us for we are royally arseholed. Forgive us Mother for we have taken the shilling of him what done you wrong. As you have surmounted your bitterness towards him, as you have found it in your mighty soul to transcend your most righteous anger, so also let us not come into your bad books, if that's at all possible, because we really needed the spondulicks the cash the moolah the bread the bread. Forgive us Mother for we are soldiers of the Queen our Father and this is wonderful 199, Radio Freddie, and for all you night owls and our own dear Mum here's Manfred Mann to promise us that god is on our side.

Listening to Hawthorne's tirade, Ormus Cama is reminded of Sanjay Gandhi's legendary resentment of his mother Indira for abandoning his father Feroze. Mull Standish is Indira metamorphosed, he thinks, Indira who was powerless against her savage son, who endowed Sanjay with a lifetime's supply of rage.

Is there a god? wonders Waldo Crossley between Manfred Mann and the Searchers. Biggish question. Take your time.

If there's no god, why do men have nipples, Hawthorne ripostes between the Searchers and the Temptations.

On the other hand, if there's no god, it does explain why we have to have Peter, Paul and Mary, reasons Waldo persuasively, between the Temptations and the Righteous Brothers.

If there's no god, who left the tap running up there? Hawthorne roars at the end of "Unchained Melody," thumping the studio table. Check*mate,* I *think.*

The Miracles begin to sing. It goes on raining.

At the end of the first fortnight, the Crossley brothers bring Ormus Cama home to mother, where he is to take up residence in the spare room. Home is a maisonette above their mother's clothes shop in a red-brick row-house backwater at the wrong end of Chelsea, past too many kinks in the King's Road, tucked away between the gasworks and Wandsworth Bridge Road; yet time seems to eddy and swirl around this spot, it knows the difference between size and mass. Only the truly massive can push it around. Here, in limbo, time has located a mighty gravitational force, an omnivorous black hole.

Vina once came here. She bought a flimsy frock.

The boutique—a new word that will not last—is called The Witch Flies High and it is already legendary: that is, the arbiters of these matters have agreed that it is one of the enclaves by which the zeitgeist—another fashionable word that will fall from favour—will come in time to be defined. The kiss of posterity is deemed to have blessed The Witch already. She pulls the city into her gravitational field, shapes the moment to her will. Within its event horizon, the laws of the universe cease to apply. Darkness reigns. Antoinette Corinth is the only law.

Mick Jagger is rumoured to wear the dresses, those brief concoctions of velvet and lace. John Lennon's white limo stops outside once a week and a chauffeur takes away whole racks of clothes for the great man and his wife to try on. German photographers with stone-faced models arrive to use The Witch's windows as backdrops for their fashion spreads. The boutique has famous painted windows, featuring the Wicked Witch of the West from the land of Oz. She flies over Emerald City, cackling. Her smoking broom does sign writing in the sky. *Surrender Dorothy.* (The ignorant and unfashionable mistake this for the name of the shop. Such persons are invariably refused admission. Antoinette Corinth loathes Dorothy Gale, her dog and all inhabitants of Kansas, Kansas-as-metaphor, flat, empty, uncool. Antoinette Corinth is Miss Gulch.)

Antoinette lounges in the boutique's doorway, illuminated by a yellow tungsten street lamp, an ample woman wearing a groin-length black lace mini-dress with matching shawl and talking to a waistcoated dandy who turns out to be a celebrated society couturier, and her first backer, Tommy Gin. She permits her sons to peck her on the cheek, ignores Ormus's polite greeting. Gin, too, cuts him dead. Ormus follows Hawthorne and Waldo into The Witch.

Inside, it's pitch dark. You go through a heavy bead curtain and are instantly blinded. The air is heavy with incense and patchouli oil and with, too, the aroma of substances forbidden aboard Radio Freddie. Psychedelic music terrorizes your eardrums. After a time you become aware of a low purple glow, in which you can make out a few motionless shapes. These are probably clothes, probably for sale. You don't like to ask. The Witch is a scary place.

In the depths of the boutique is a dimly discernible presence. This is She. She runs the shop, and makes Twiggy look like a teenager with a puppy-fat problem. She is very pale, probably because she spends her life sitting in the dark. Her lips are shiny black. She also wears a black mini-dress, but hers is velvet, not lace. This is her urban vampire look. (Her other style, black smocks worn with smudged black eyes, is described by Antoinette Corinth as "dead baby.") She stands knock-kneed and pigeon-toed after the fashion of the period, her feet forming a tiny ferocious T. She wears immense silver knuckle-duster rings and a black flower in her hair. Half love child, half zombie, She is a sign of the times.

Ormus attempts charm, introduces himself, mentions his recent arrival in England, says some words about his first stint aboard Radio

Freddie, and at this point, faced with the glint of her basilisk eyes in the purple haze, runs out of words and sputters to a halt.

Talk radio's over, she says, Dialogue's dead.

This is stunning information. In five words the neo-Kantian, Bakhtinian definition of human nature—that we change each other constantly through dialogue, through intersubjectivity, the creative interplay of our several incompletenesses—is laid to rest. The essentially Apollonian universe of communication shrivels beneath the contemptuous force of She's Dionysiac post-verbalism. Before Ormus can absorb so revolutionary a change, however, Tommy Gin comes into the store at speed, pursued by a hooting Antoinette Corinth. Listen, man, I'm sorry, man, Gin expostulates, clasping both of Ormus Cama's hands, It's the Witch, man, she likes her joke. I mean, you're Indian, I love India. The Maharishi, man. And the Buddha, and Lord Krishna. Beautiful.

And Ravi Shankar, offers Ormus, trying to be friendly. But Tommy Gin has run out of Indians and can only nod furiously. Right, right, he nods, beaming.

Right, Ormus Cama concurs.

But what I'm saying—Gin returns to his embarrassed apology—is, back there, man, I laid a heavy trip on you, but it's only because she's always shitting with people's heads, I mean, if you can believe it, she told me you were *Jewish*. You can dig that, man, you can see how that would, yeah. But you're not, man, you're just not. Oh, wow.

Hey, Indian guy, shouts Antoinette Corinth, waving a joint in a long cigarette holder. Perhaps you should teach me a few of your whatchoumacallit rope tricks. You seem to have tied the Queen up in knots, unless I'm *very* much mistaken.

Ormus Cama faced with Gin and Antoinette has the sense of having come into the presence of malignity. Gin doesn't count: he's a nasty pinprick, a squib. But from Antoinette Corinth there pours a barely disguised and vengeful malevolence. This is not that wise woman free of all bitterness eulogized by her sons over the pirate airwaves. This is a woman of such palpable vindictiveness that, even though he has no reason to believe he is the target of her venom, Ormus feels physically endangered. He begins, involuntarily, to back away, and bumps into something hard in the dark. A rack of dresses falls to the floor, hangers clattering.

Hah! Hah! (Antoinette Corinth's laugh is a heavy smoker's retch.) The little dear. He's simply terrified. Ormus, baby. Welcome to Unfold Road.

Mull Standish telephones that evening: Everything fine? She acting OK? And before Ormus can answer: Your musical future. I'm working on it. My plans are close to firmed up. Did you know the Georgie Fame record couldn't get played on the BBC, and now, thanks to us, it's a top three hit? That's a big step. It proves the pirates' power. And the next proof is you. Because if we can do it with an unknown, then we're really calling the shots. We need to talk material. We need to talk musicians. We need to talk, period. Don't ask me when. I'm on it. I'm way ahead of you. I'm already there. Be prepared.

There can be no doubting, in retrospect, that Mull Standish was in love with Ormus Cama: in pie-eyed, adolescent, moon-calf love. But he was also a man of quality, a person of character, and he kept his word. Never in all the years of their partnership did he sexually importune the artist whom he helped to build into a world superstar. Without Mull Standish—who put the band together, provided the instruments, booked the recording studios at his own cost and acted as his own promo man—there would certainly have been no Rhythm Center. And without Rhythm Center, there would have been no VTO.

That night on the phone, his first night at the maisonette over The Witch, Ormus remains sceptical: What do you want from me? he wants to know.

Mull Standish's voice wavers fractionally, loses much of its rich timbre. My sons, he says, faltering. Put in a good word for me with my sons.

Which isn't easy. Released from the captivity of Radio Freddie, Hawthorne and Waldo Crossley are busily opening the doors of perception. In their mother's lair—zodiac on the ceiling, astrolabes, Ching sticks, fliers advertising Tibetan overtone chanting, cat, broomstick, the works—they lie semi-conscious, blissing out, with Mummy's help.

They do like their lump sugar, Antoinette Corinth beams. After two weeks, their poor tongues were just hanging out. And you, my Oriental prince? One lump or two?

In spite of a life spent in the allegedly exotic East, Ormus is not accustomed to meeting witches. Awkwardly cross-legged on an Afghan rug, he shifts his weight from haunch to haunch and declines the offered drug. Squinting through Antoinette's chosen darkness, he registers the caged parrot, the Mexican chac-mool, the Brazilian samba drums. Books about the old religions of human sacrifice and blood. A sorceress with Latin accents. Ormus begins to finds it hard to take her seriously. This is an act, isn't it, a posture, a game. In this "culture," people have time for games. Maybe they never get past games. A "culture" of grown-up children.

Germs on a slide.

Antoinette notes Ormus's interest in her paraphernalia, senses his scepticism, launches into a long self-justifying oration. "People are looking for something better. An alternative. And here's this simply immense body of forbidden knowledge, absolutely coherent, fantastically erudite, the hidden learning of the entire human race, and all placed beyond the respectable pale. Why? Well, obviously. Because they don't want us to have access to the power. The *nuclear* power of the secret arts."

That's some of it. Now Ormus begins to see and hear her more clearly. She sounds like a demagogue: self-righteous, a True Believer. She sounds like somebody covering up, using the half-digested rhetoric of the age's lunatic fringe to lend colour to a life story of whose painful banality she is perhaps afraid. What is she, anyway? A tailor who got lucky in trade, but was unlucky in love. Two grown sons and an empty bed. It seems to Ormus that she infantilises her children, that feeding them hallucinogens is her way of keeping them babyish, helpless, dependent; of keeping them hers. In the grip of a sudden wave of nauseous revulsion against the spirit of the age, Ormus finds Antoinette Corinth hard to like: clutchy, a self-dramatist, shrill.

He asks if it's permitted to use the drums. She is disappearing down the smoke rings of her mind, and waves, vaguely. Softly, eagerly, the silky twisting rhythms flow from his fingertips. It is as if the drums have been yearning to speak to him, and he to them. Finally, he thinks: at long last, here are friends.

Fucking Paradise, grunts Antoinette Corinth, and passes out. Ormus doesn't care; he is lost in the samba, the carnival under his flying, beating hands.

Long after he has gone to bed on the floor below her he hears her wake and crash around upstairs. He hears odd chanting, the chinking of finger cymbals, a woman's voice howling at the moon.

This England, addled by mysticism, mesmerised by the miraculous, the psychotropic, in love with alien gods, has begun to horrify him. This England is a disaster area, the old are destroying the young by sending them to die in distant fields, and in response the young are destroying themselves. He is having an essentially conservative response not only to the war but also to the countervailing laissez-faire of the age, a response that will intensify as he learns more about the place. A revolt against the damage, the waste, the self-inflicted wounds, the bedspread jackets, the swallowing of various forms of gibberish that has replaced the exercise of intelligence, the susceptibility to gurus and other phoney leaders, the flight from reason, the descent into an inferno of privilege.

In time he will write songs about this disaster area, songs that excoriate a generation lost in space, songs bursting with a savage indignation that will make them, by one of the ironic inversions of the culture, into anthems for the very people he is attacking. The dying, drifting, broken generation, which has told itself a great lie—that it represents hope and beauty—will hear the truth in Ormus Cama's earthquake songs; will look in those cruel mirrors and see themselves. Ormus Cama will find his Western voice, in the words of M. Henri Hulot, by understanding what he is against. And, in the form of Vina, his one and only love, who he's for.

When Sir Darius Xerxes Cama returned from his spirit-destroying trip to England he was interrogated about that country by his butler, Gieve, who had heard certain lies which he knew were too absurd to be true; but he needed Darius to confirm their falsehood:

They say, sir, that in U.K., if a man does not have a job, the government gives him money. If he does not have a house, the government gives him a pukka residence, not a *jopadpatti* shack on the pavement but a solid construction. If he or his family are sick, the government pays for the hospital. If he can't send his children to school, the government sends them free. And when he is old and useless, the government gives the good-for-nothing cash money every week for the rest of his life.

The idea that a government might behave in such a way seemed to offend Gieve's sense of the natural order. When Darius confirmed the approximate accuracy of the assertions, the butler couldn't stand it. He smacked his brow, shook his head, couldn't speak for a moment. Then he said, "In this case, sir, *why is anyone in U.K. ever unhappy?*"

Why is anyone unhappy in this privileged corner of the globe? Yes, OK, the war, Ormus concedes. But does that excuse everything? Does it mean people can pour themselves down a drain and call it peace? Does it mean people can untie the strings of the world—*and hark, what discord follows*—and call it freedom?

His horror, his sense of foreboding, of wrongness and impending doom—cracks in the world, abysses, the four horsemen, all the anachronistic apparatus of millenarian eschatology—is increased by the knowledge of his own involuntary gift of visions, the holes in the real that manifest themselves to show him another reality, which he resists, though it beckons him to enter; for entry would feel—he knows this—very like insanity. Can it be this visionary madness, the thing he most fears within himself, that's most in tune with his new world?

She comes to him near the end of the night, matter-of-factly joins him on his mattress, without emotion, under some sort of narcotic influence. Their sex, performed in the red-rimmed, bad-breath hours after the cold dawn, is unconvincing, bony, brief; dry frottage, like a duty. Like sex's end: an old married couple's last parched congress. Exhaustion claims them, and they sleep. In two weeks he'll go back to the ship, and if somebody else sleeps here, She may also come to him, sleepwalking.

In the sky above them, Major Ed White is walking in space. He has stepped out of the frame. For fourteen minutes he is the ultimate outsider, the only sentient creature hanging above the Earth, outside the Gemini 4 spacecraft. Ecstatic, he has to be coaxed back into Gemini by his co-astronaut, his space twin.

There is a horse on tv called Mister Ed and Ormus Cama drifting towards sleep allows himself to confuse the two. First centaur in space. Or Pegasus, the last of the winged horses, returning to our corrupt, post-classical times.

She takes him to a club called UFO to satisfy people's need to believe in space creatures other than Major or even Mister Ed. Coloured oils squeezed between glass slides pulse to the music. Hairy heads nod in time, like windscreen poodles. There is much pungent smoke. What is he doing here in this wasted dark when Vina is somewhere else, waiting. Or not waiting. While beside him, concealed in inarticulacy, She doodles on a napkin, decorating the word "unfold." Her calligraphy finds the name of the club in the name of the street. *UnFOld Road.*

Even here, underground, he feels like the Gemini astronaut, floating, above, outside, watching. Bursting with ecstasy. Waiting to become.

By day he walks the city streets, looking for other Englands, older Englands, making them real. He eschews narcotic assistance. He is high on the place itself, its brilliant, familiar strangeness. To be utterly lost amidst buildings you recognize, to know nothing about a cityscape of which you have carried around, for years, what you thought to be an ample and sufficient storehouse of images, is a delirious enough experience. No funny cigarettes required. On the loaf, elated by the great dirty river, the grimy sunsets, Ormus Cama loses his heart, without warning, to the smell of fresh, leavened, white bread.

There was leavened bread in Bombay, but it was sorry fare: dry, crumbling, tasteless, unleavened bread's paler, unluckier relation. It wasn't "real." "Real" bread was the chapati, or phulka, served piping hot; the tandoori nan and its sweeter Frontier variant, the Peshawari nan; and for luxury, the reshmi roti, the shirmal, the paratha. Compared to these aristocrats, the leavened white loaves of Ormus's childhood seemed to merit the description which Shaw's immortal dustman, Alfred Doolittle, dreamed up for people like himself: they were, in truth, the undeserving poor. They were nothing like the lavish loaves sitting plump and enticing, and for sale, in the windows of the capital's many bakeries—the ABC chain, the Chelsea Bakery itself. Ormus Cama plunges into this new world, betraying, without a backward glance, the fabled breads of home.

Whenever he passes a bakery, he feels compelled to enter. The daily purchase and consumption of quantities of bread is, in a way, his first wholeheartedly erotic encounter with London life. Ah, the soft pillowy mattressiness of it. The well-sprung bounciness of it between his teeth. Hard crust and soft centre: the sensuality of that perfect textural contrast. O White Crusty loaves of 1965, both sliced and unsliced! O small and large Tins, Danish Bloomers, flour-dusted Baps! O bread of heaven, bread of leaven, feed me till I want no more! In the whorehouses of the bakeries Ormus pays without a murmur for his encounters with the amorality of the loaf. It's anybody's, but once coin of the realm has been exchanged, these swallowed morsels, these love bites, are his and his alone. East is East, thinks Ormus Cama; ah, but yeast is West.

Standish has bought him a guitar. His pockets stuffed with fresh bread rolls, Ormus sits in parks and makes technical experiments, looking for the new voice that will match his new being, in this new world. What develops at first differs from the driving hard-rock delivery which he originally favoured, and to which he will always, when the spirit moves him, return. This new voice, however, is sweeter, higher, and the songs it sings have longer lines and more complex melodies that cross over and under one another, lifting and circling, like dancers. Mull Standish will choose to record one of these songs: "She (The Death of Conversation)."

(Tabla drums, rakataka takatak. A bouncing guitar. Horns. Waa whup-whup waa, waa whup-whup waa. A full, lush sound, nothing like the screech and thunder characteristic of the period. It sounds new. So does this voice, speaking in unexplained personal references, but somehow including the listener in its private world. A girl lies down in darkness, she asks why am I right on the floor, why am I right on the floor here, when the rest of my life is so wrong. I need a carnival costume, I want my day in the sunlight, don't want to be a black cat in a back catalogue.)

Ormus has fully regained his touch with the ladies. Arrested by his beauty, by the grace of his long-striding walk, they sweep him off the city streets. The doors of the lonely city open wide. Sometimes he owns up to being the new boy on Radio Freddie, and feels the first astonishing cat-lappings, the addictive caresses, of Western fame.

Soon it begins to feel like a long time ago that he was Indian, with family ties, with roots. In the white heat of the present tense these things have shrivelled and died. Race itself seems less of a fixed point than before. He finds that to these new eyes he looks indeterminate. He has already passed for Jewish, and now as he is noticed by the girls on their scooters and motorbikes, the girls in their bubble cars and Minis, the girls in their false eyelashes and high boots, as they screech to a halt and offer him a ride, he is taken for an Italian, a Spaniard, a Romany, a Frenchman, a Latin American, a "Red" Indian, a Greek. He is none of these, but he denies nothing; during these brief, casual encounters he adopts the protective colouring of how others see him. If asked a direct question he always tells the truth, but it embarrasses him more and more that people, young women particularly, find his true identity so sexually attractive for such phoney, Ginnish reasons. *Oh, that's so spiritual,* they say, slipping out of their clothes. *So spiritual,* galloping him like a horse. *Spiritual,* wagging at him doggy fashion. Mortified, he finds these invitations impossible to refuse. The spiritual Indian, uprising, carnally conquers the West.

Here, he is at the frontier of the skin. Mull Standish meets him for coffee at the Café Braque in Chelsea. We aren't going to conceal anything, Standish announces. We just aren't going to make a big deal out of it, or you'll be stuck in the ethnic ghetto for keeps. We're also going to lie about your age. Pushing thirty is no time to start a career in this business. This here is electric babyland.

Eating his way through plateful after cottony plateful of Wonderloaf and butter—brought to the table with growing irritability and scorn by the Braque's immortally surly waiters—Ormus ponders the link between deracination and success, and persuades himself that the taking of a stage name is not a dishonourable act. Who ever heard of Issur Danielovitch, not to mention Marian Montgomery, Archibald Leach, Bernie Schwartz, Stanley Jefferson, Allen Konigsberg, Betty Joan Perske, Camille Javal, Greta Gustafsson, Diana Fluck, Frances Gumm, or poor dear Julia Jean Mildred Frances Turner, before they changed their names. Erté, Hergé, Ellery Queen, Weegee . . . The whole history of the pseudonym justifies him. Yet in the end he finds he can't do it. He will remain Ormus Cama. This is his compromise: that the band will not bear his name, though the musicians Standish has assembled are a job lot of sessions artistes. He names this, his first outfit, after the site of his first meeting with Vina. Rhythm Center. "She," by Rhythm Center. I like it like it, Mull Standish says, sipping coffee, tapping his cane. Yes that yes that grooves.

Thank Christ, Standish adds. I thought you were going to call it White Bread.

Only when it's too late will Ormus discover that Standish has issued a false biography of his new star, inventing a melting-pot, patchwork-quilt, rainbow-coalition tale of mixed genes, elaborating on the years of struggle in odd dives in European cities, everywhere but Hamburg (to avoid the Beatles comparison). The poverty, the despair, the over-coming, the making of the finished article. When he does find out, he confronts an unrepentant Standish, who lays down the law: The truth won't play. This, however, is a résumé with legs. Long legs. *Fabulous* legs. Sing the songs, sonny, and let Uncle Mull take care of business.

Later in his career, Ormus Cama will be attacked, often and viciously, for denying his origins. By then, however, Mull Standish will be dead.

Standish asks after the boys, and his demeanour alters. The bullish man of the world gives way to a more vulnerable and hesitant persona. What do they say? he probes, wincing slightly, his arms coming up a little way off the table, crossed, as if bracing for a blow. What do they say about me? She's been poisoning them for two decades, turning their thoughts against me. Are they safe with her? God knows. She's crazy, you know, you'll have spotted that. Which cuts no ice with them. She's the parent in place, while I, I have no defence. I left, I deserted them, I changed my what's the new word orientation. My pointing towards the East. I can't help that. But I'm here now, I want to be a, a good one, a real one, but maybe it's too late, maybe I can't.

Father, Ormus says. The word you're avoiding.

So they hate me, right. You can tell me, I can take it. No; lie.

Ormus recounts a conversation with Antoinette Corinth. This may surprise you but I want them to like him, she said. It's up to him to build the bridge, God knows he's starting late, but yes, I can see he's finally decided to try. OK. I want them to be close to their father. I want them even to love him, I want him to have the pleasure of his sons' love, I want him to love their love so profoundly that he can't do without it, I want that, even for him, why would I not want it?

He shakes his head, can't believe it. She said that?

She said, It's what I'm waiting for, Ormus recalls.

What does that mean?

In the sense of hoping for, I suppose. (Ormus is trying to be even-handed, trying not to take sides.) Maybe you're seeing phantoms where none exist. Maybe she just has a more generous side than you're willing to allow.

Yeah. And maybe the moon is made of cheese, Standish surrenders to sarcasm. Hey, look. Up in the sky, above the Pheasantry. Wasn't that a flying pig?

Land, water, water, land. Time drips, floats, stretches, shrinks, passes. The story of the first record by Rhythm Center, its pirate provenance, Standish going from store to store around the country, begging, cajoling, threatening, begging some more: all this is well known. The song does well but not astoundingly well. Ormus's nocturnal apostrophising of his lost love is catching on faster than his music. But Vina isn't there. She lies over the ocean, she's singing with Diana Ross at the Rainbow Room, she's hanging out with Amos Voight and so on, and she hears nothing from her lovesick swain.

There is the war and the protest against the war. A generation is learning how to march, how to riot, it is inventing the chants that turn groups of kids into armies that have the power to frighten the state. What do we want when do we want it. One two three four, two four six eight. Ho ho ho.

The non-war news also feels high, spaced out, out of joint. In Spain a group of aristocrats has been unable to leave the grand salon of the urban mansion in which they recently enjoyed a sumptuous banquet. Nothing impedes them, yet they do not leave. At the gates of the compound in which the mansion stands, a similar invisible impediment prevents anyone from entering. Gawpers, the mansion's domestic staff, the emergency services, press at the open gate but do not pass through. There is talk of a divine curse. Some claim to have heard the beating wings of the angel Azrael overhead. His dark shadow passes like a cloud.

A Polish patriot, Zbigniew Cybulski, has been murdered in a back yard, amid sheets blowing from washing lines. Blood spread across a white sheet held against his midriff. A battered tin mug that fell from his hand has become a symbol of resistance. No: it is a holy relic, worthy of worship. Bow down.

An American girl in Paris is becoming an object of reverence. There are those who call her the reincarnation of the armoured virgin, St. Joan. A cult is in the process of being born.

These are not secular times. In the sphere of the secular all is bombs and death. Against which, it seems, sex and music may not be bulwarks enough.

A great movie star has tragically died. She was in love with two friends, who told her that her face, her smile, put them in mind of an ancient carving. They quarrelled over her. At length, after lunch in a small café, she took one of the friends for a ride in her car and deliberately drove straight off the end of a washed-out bridge, into the water. Both of them were killed. The other man, still seated at the café table, watched his beloved and his friend vanish for ever.

Not long before dying, the actress made a hit record, accompanying herself on acoustic guitar. Now the record is played constantly, the first French song to zoom up the British charts, paving the way for Françoise Hardy and others. Ormus, whose French is poor, strains to understand the lyrics.

Everyone to his taste, turning, turning, in the whirlpool of life?

Is that it?

On board the *Frederica,* Ormus Cama notices that the sign on the wall in Eno's cubicle has changed. *Keep your distance.* After that he makes a point of checking, and the changes continue. One week the sign says, *Don't get too close.* Another, *Mend no fences.* Another, *Love not that ye be not loved.* Another, *Fight that sweet tooth. Save more than your teeth.* One message is long and in blank verse:

> *May the gods save me from becoming*
> *a stateless refugee!*
> *Dragging out an intolerable life*
> *in desperate helplessness!*
> *That is the most pitiful of all griefs;*
> *death is better.*

Ali's cracking up, Hawthorne Crossley says, Must be the sleep deprivation.

Must be the hat, Waldo opines, Or is he, by any chance, illegal?

If he was illegal they'd have closed us down by now, Hawthorne reasons.

Ormus says nothing when he sees the long text. He understands that Eno is sending a message directly to him. He feels the hot sting of its criticism and tries to catch the engineer's eye. But Eno seems far away.

Many years will pass before Ormus Cama learns that the author of the long text is not Eno Barber but Euripides. The shorter texts, however, are Eno's own.

Mind your backs. Mind your heads. And these messages? Who are they for?

At The Witch, too, Ormus is receiving messages. She still sometimes comes to his bed when the whim takes her. Dialogue being over, they do not speak. They greet, fuck, part in silence: the copulation of ghosts. But sometimes she, too, leaves him notes. Some are melancholy, opaque. *If music could cure sorrow it would be precious. But no one thought of using songs and stringed instruments to banish the bitterness and pain of life.* Most of the notes, however, are about Antoinette, whose dominant personality seems entirely to have subjugated She's. Antoinette's hard life and times. Disowned by her wealthy family for marrying the club-footed Standish, and then abandoned by the bastard with two small children and no income, she dragged herself out of the gutter by her own talents and round-the-clock work. *She is a frightening woman; no one who makes an enemy of her will carry off an easy victory.*

The notes are confused. Sometimes they are fearful of Antoinette's rage, at other times they praise her generous love. Towards Tommy Gin, with his vain tousle of carefully teased red hair, his floral waistcoats, his preening, his bigotry, She's scribblings are unreservedly hostile. *He thinks he invented her, he thinks he invented everything, the clothes, the music, the attitude, the protest marches, the peace sign, the women's movement, Black is Beautiful, the drugs, the books, the magazines, the whole generation. I guess none of us would have anything in our heads if not for him, but in fact he's not important, just an evil little shit who knows how to get himself noticed, but she's a real artist, she doesn't go in for all that crap, she creates beauty from the depths of her wounded soul, and you wait and see, she'll break off with him any day now, she'll cut him out completely, the Witch doesn't need a Wizard, and once she's dumped him he'll just shrivel and die like a vampire in the sun.* It seems that silent She has a lot of words locked up inside her, after all. Apollo is in there. Behind the black Dionysiac clouds enveloping this young woman, the sun god is struggling to release his light. It doesn't take Ormus long to understand that She is deeply in love with her boss. Men may come and men may go but the two dark ladies, the large flamboyant one upstairs and the small wasted one sitting in the purple dark below, are in it for the duration.

Distracted by this realization, Ormus perhaps fails to grasp what he is being told, on land by She, at sea by Eno Barber. That there is danger here, coming steadily closer. That the earth is beginning to tremble. Like most protagonists he is deaf to the warnings of the chorus. Even when he dreams a terrible dream—the boys tumbling down the maisonette stairs with the tops of their heads exploded, standing open like burst cans of beans—he attaches no weight to the portent. He is trying to keep a lid on his visionary tendency, in this milieu of cabbalistic nonsense he is making an effort to shun omens and keep a grip on the actual, to concentrate on the music and stand firm upon the dailiness of English life.

To hold on to the elation, the joy he brought with him, the idea of renewal.

His thoughts turn more and more towards Vina. The Vina that exists only in his imagination, whom he knows more intimately than any living being, is being confronted on the stage of that same imagination by another Vina, her adult self, her unknown twin. Life has happened to her and turned her into a stranger. New life, and the eternal haunting of the past. The dead family, the slaughtered goats, the murdering mother hanged in the loafing shed. Piloo, Chickaboom, those too, but above all the dead, pendant mother, and Nissy sitting with her, calling nobody, fearing that this present foretells her future. The dangling ankles, the long bare calves are the image of her own.

Ormus's old fears creep back; he imagines Vina looking him blankly in the eye, saying, *No, that's the past,* and walking off into some alien sunset, leaving his life emptied of meaning. But such dark fancies fail to overpower him. He is filled with light, radiant with possibility. He hit bottom at the Cosmic Dancer and it showed him the way up. Now he is soaring towards the skies, none of his argosies shall fail, and at the appropriate moment he will find her, take her hand, and they will fly together over the bright glow of Metropolis at night. Like fairies, like long-tailed comets. Like stars. That's his story, the one he's written for himself, to which reality has no option but to conform.

But at present he's caught up in another story. They say another galaxy is presently invading the Milky Way, swirling its otherness into our familiar neighbourhood, bringing its story into ours. It's small, we're (relatively) big; we'll pull it to pieces, destroy its suns, rip its atoms up. So long, small galaxy, goodbye baby and amen.

Ormus's story and the story of The Witch Flies High are swirled together now. Which will pull the other apart?

Even worse: will they turn out to be the same story after all?

I've been thinking about what you might call the Medea issue. A witchy lady, Ms. Corinth, undeniably; with sons, and a deserter father too. Can't deny the similarities, especially as Antoinette has chosen to play them up, abandoning "Crossley" for "Corinth." What is she trying to do, scare people? Or just Mull Standish? Is she genuinely capable of tragedy, of going so far beyond the frontiers of motherhood and sanity that her deeds acquire the stature of destiny? Is she *fated*? Ormus, who at first found her malevolent, has come to think of her as half posturing phoney, half lunatic-fringista, more insubstantial than shady, a designer witch, using numerology to help her pick her lovers, using occult signs not to conjure devils but only to decorate the busts of her nightmare-black baby-doll dresses. Unlike the note-writers—She, Eno—he isn't buying. And the two silent scribblers, after all, are individuals whose own dysfunctionality erodes their credibility as analysts. Ormus Cama, finally, cannot believe that he has walked on to the stage of some fearsome contemporary goat song. Antoinette Corinth cannot, will not, be responsible for his fate.

We underestimate our fellow humans because we underestimate ourselves. They—we—are capable of being much more than we seem. Many of us are able to answer life's darkest questions. We just don't know if we can come up with the answers to the riddles until we're asked.

There will be a tragedy. Antoinette Corinth will not be held responsible.

Mull Standish perseveres with his wooing of his children, and Hawthorne and Waldo slowly respond. As the cycles of their pirate world accumulate into a year, then two, his sons' bantering treatment of him acquires a quality of genuine affection. There are loving gestures: an arm around a shoulder, a playful, filial punch to the cheek that opens out, at the last instant, into a brief stroking gesture of the fingertips. The needs of blood draw them close. The day comes when one of them—Waldo, inevitably, the less defended personality of the pair—accidentally calls Standish "Dad," and even though Hawthorne subjects him to prolonged abuse for this gaffe, Standish is moved to tears. And Hawthorne isn't really cross. "Dad" feels like the right word, even to him. After all these years.

Adversity helps, of course. Laws are being passed that will close the pirates down. The weather, which once scattered and wrecked the Spanish Armada, has not dealt kindly with Standish's pirate fleet. These are old tubs, and they leak. Batter them with storms and they threaten to break. There are growing problems of insurance, and the boats are, beyond a doubt, dangerous.

There is a new terrestrial station, Radio 1. It steals many of Standish's most talented broadcasters. His ships begin to shut up shop, one by one. Soon there is only Radio Freddie, the first to start broadcasting and the last to remain.

The *Frederica*, rusting, knows her time of rest cannot be far removed.

Rhythm Center, Ormus's first band, has had a series of small successes, making the Fifty, seeming never to reach the modest plenty of the Forty. In part the failure to make a real breakthrough is because the band plays no live gigs, it being Standish's view that the club audience wouldn't "buy" them. His strategy is to keep it mysterious, build a cult, an underground groundswell. There are also the difficulties associated with recording on a small independent label, Standish's own Mayflower franchise: the distribution problems, the limited promotional budgets. The death is reported of the American DJ Alan Freed, who has finally drunk himself into an early grave after giving currency to the word "payola," that's pay plus Victrola. Freed is dead but the practice of accepting bribes to play records is not, and Mull Standish may be rich but he can't go up against the big boys in this bidding war. His pirates will play Rhythm Center's 45s but the other pirates won't. And the BBC, well, nobody ever proved a corruption charge against the BBC, but Ormus hasn't made their playlist, either. In spite of his reasonable success. The BBC makes its own decisions, it isn't led by the common herd. What, they should let the kids decide what they put on the air? *Please.*

Outside England, forget it, no dice. No pay, no play. Vina is in America but Ormus's voice is trapped on the other side of the Atlantic. She can't hear his plea.

The songs themselves are the real problem. Something unreconciled in the writing. There are too many people inside Ormus, a whole band is gathered within his frontiers, playing different instruments, creating different music, and he hasn't yet discovered how to bring them under control: the lover yearning for his vanished love, swooning for Vina into the North Sea night; and the dreaming eavesdropper following his dead twin brother who sings him the songs of the future; and the simple rock 'n' roller in love with a banging-heartbeat beat; and the impish comic penning ironic faux-country odes to bread; and the angry moralist railing against the addle-brained age, its fakeola, its fuddled death wish; and finally, the reluctant visionary who is given glimpses of another possible universe, glimpses he would prefer not to see.

He hasn't fully grasped how to make of multiplicity an accumulating strength rather than a frittery weakness. How the many selves can be, in song, a single multitude. Not a cacophony but an orchestra, a choir, a dazzling plural voice. He worries, as Standish does, about being too old; hasn't understood that this can be set aside, rendered irrelevant. In short, he is still trying to settle on the one true line to follow. Still looking for ground to stand on, for the hard centre of his art.

The crucial change comes, as all true Ormus fans will readily know, in mid-1967, in a recording studio in a Bayswater backwater, behind the Whiteleys department store. The story of the recording of Ormus

Cama's song "It Shouldn't Be This Way," and of the subsequent three-year delay in its commercial release, has been told so often that it barely needs repeating. The popularly known version of the event is broadly true, and even if it weren't, the advice of the Wild West newspaper editor is well worth taking.

If the facts don't fit the legend, print the legend.

Mull Standish is waiting by the mixing desk when Ormus arrives, looking grim. Okay, I'm ready, he says. Get rid of the musicians.

Standish stiffens, grows very still. All of them? he asks.

Every last one, assents Ormus, flopping down on a squashy corner seating unit and closing his eyes. And wake me when they've gone, he adds.

Now Rhythm Center is Ormus and only Ormus. He's alone in the studio with guitars, keyboards, drums, horns, woodwinds, a big bass, an early Moog synthesizer. He sits down behind the drums and starts to play.

What, you're going to play them all, the sound mixer wants to know. What am I supposed to do, I'm on four-track here.

(Who is this guy, he means. This is the real world here, feller; sixteen-track, thirty-two-track, forty-eight-track recording tape, that's fantasyland, it's the future, and this in front of me it's just a mixing desk, ain't got no time machine.)

We'll just have to bounce the tracks down as we go, Ormus snarls. Something's got into him today. It's not a good idea to argue.

Bounce them down, the engineer says. Sure, why not.

Bouncing down is what you do when you need to keep tracks free. You mix together two tracks and transfer the mixed sound to a third track. Then you can re-use the first two tracks to record two more parts of the music and you bounce these down to the free fourth track. Now you've got two tracks containing mixes of two tracks each. If you've still got a lot of parts to record, you can bounce these two tracks down into one, giving you a single track with four parts on it and three free tracks.

And so on.

The problem is that once you've done this you can never separate the tracks again. The mix you make is what you're stuck with. You can't pull the music apart and play with it any more. You're making final, irrevocable decisions as you go. It's a recipe for disaster, unless the person doing it is a genius.

Ormus Cama is a genius.

Each time he lays down a track—he can play every instrument in the studio better than the sessions guys he's just fired—he comes into the booth, lies down on the seating unit, closes his eyes. The sound mixer moves his slides, turns his dials, and Ormus directs him until the music coming out of the speakers is the secret music in his head. Pull these up, push those back, he says. Bring this in here, fade that away there. Okay, it's okay. That's it. Don't change a thing. Go.

You're sure, now, the mixer says. Because this is it. No turning back.

Bouncey bouncey, Ormus grins, and the mixer laughs and sings back at him.

And like a rubber ball I come bouncing back to you.

The sound grows, becomes fat, exciting. The mixer's a big unfazeable guy, he's getting paid, what's to worry. He's good at what he does, he's worked with everyone, he doesn't get impressed. But look at this, his shoulders are going, boom, to the music, dip, to the beat. This Indian bloke running in and out of the studio, blowing a horn, mixing it in, bouncing it down, then strings, then a bubbling electro beat, he's got the ear, he's got the chops.

Bouncey bouncey!

It's time to sing. *But you're not here to put it right, And you're not here to hold me tight. It shouldn't be this way.*

When it's done, the mixer stands up and holds out a huge paw. I wish you all the best with your song, he says. I've had a good day today.

Ormus stands toe-to-toe with Mull Standish. The rage is still on him.

So, he asks, quietly, furiously. Am I ready or what?

Standish nods. You're ready.

But this famous scene is the aftermath of a scene people don't talk about:

On the last night of Radio Freddie, at the emotional closing-down ceremony aboard the erstwhile ferryboat, Cap'n Pugwash and his fellow pirates are moved to tears on behalf of their beloved rusting tub.

Listen, Pugwash keens, as if speaking by the bedside of a dying lover, you lot are only going off the air, but she's going off the water, the poor old girl. Yes, it's the knacker's yard for the *Frederica,* and nothing to be done about it but drink.

Much is imbibed. Eno Barber sits behind his glass window with a bottle of rum. The sign on the wall behind him reads, *Go away.* Hawthorne and Waldo sing schoolboy rugby songs. This amazing loss of cool passes unnoticed in the general stupor, and actually endears them to the Pugwash bunch, which joins in lustily. Dinah Dinah show us your leg, a yard above your knee. If I were the marrying kind which thank the Lord I'm not sir. Ugly, boastful, male, ultimately innocent songs.

Ormus confronts Mull on deck. They're both drunk. Mull steadies himself against the movement of the boat by putting a hand on Ormus's shoulder. The singer pushes it away, and Mull staggers briefly, then gathers himself. You bastard, Ormus tells his friend, you've been holding me back. Two fucking years. What am I supposed to do? How long am I supposed to wait? Optimism is the fuel of art, and ecstasy, and elation, and the supply of these commodities is not endless. Maybe you don't want me to make it. You want me to stay small-time, not even a has-been but a never-was, beholden to you, a hanger-on, a fly in your goddamn web.

Mull Standish keeps his temper. It's true, he says, mildly. I haven't pushed you as I might. My small indie label, et cetera. You call that holding you back, then okay, I held you back. I'm holding you back because if I let you go now you'll fail, you'll fall to earth. You haven't found the courage to fly. Maybe you won't. The problem is not technical. You're worried about wings? Look on your shoulders. There they are. The problem, pal, is not wings but balls. Maybe you're just a no-balls eunuch and you'll sleep on a mattress at The Witch for the rest of your eunuch life.

The boat sways and so do they. Ormus Cama is being given a great gift. Words are being said which will oblige him to face the issue of himself.

Whatever you want to say about yourself is fine with me, Standish says. You say you've got a dead twin in your head who's listening to the chart-toppers of tomorrow, I could care less. You talk about visions, baby, I say follow that star all the way to Bethlehem and check out the kid in the manger. The trouble is you're running away from it all, there's too much of you missing from your music. You're phoning it in. People notice. I tell you what, just fuck off, why don't you. What I see is potential that is not being realized. This as an investor I do not care for. What I know is that music comes out of the self, the self as given, the self in itself. *Le soi en soi*. The silk in silk, as we used to say in my punning Francophone youth.

Standish is breathing heavily now. His entire being is crackling at the edges of his body. St. Elmo's fire; like that. Because he loves this man, he's straining at his physical frontiers to show him the way. Is it Vina you need, he roars. Then find her. Don't whine into a radio mike on a broken-down boat. Find her and sing her your songs. What's the most dangerous thing you can do? Do it. Where's the nearest edge? Jump off it. Enough already! I've said my piece. When you're ready, if you're ever ready, give me a call.

Loud singing explodes from the cabin. I'll come again, you'll come again, we'll both come again together. We'll be all right in the middle of the night, coming again together.

A week passes and then Ormus calls.

Set it up. I'm ready. Set it up.

And later, at the end of the recording session, when they have the precious tape, they're standing toe-to-toe, uncertain whether to fight or kiss.

What I want the music to say is that I don't have to choose, Ormus finally speaks up. I need it to show that I don't have to be this guy or that guy, the fellow from over there or the fellow from here, the person within me that I call my twin, or whoever's out there in whatever it is I get flashes of beyond the sky; or just the man standing in front of you right now. I'll be all of them, I can do that. Here comes everybody, right? That's where it came from, the idea of playing all the instruments. It was to prove that point. You were wrong when you said the problem wasn't technical. The solutions to the problems of art are always technical. Meaning is technical. So is heart.

Technically, then, says Mull Standish, I shouldn't lay a hand on you, because I promised, but now you've made me a happy man, would you allow me a hug?

The release of this song will bring Vina Apsara back to him at last. It will mark the beginning of their almost frighteningly totemic celebrity. And it will not happen for over three years.

The happiness of Mull Standish (with Ormus, with his sons) is what Antoinette has been waiting for. What she means by this, and whether she is to blame for what is soon to follow, the reader must presently judge.

A few weeks go by. Then, in the maisonette above The Witch:

It must be a Saturday, and it's only around noon, so naturally nobody is up, and the shop's shut. The doorbell—the maisonette's bell, not the shop's—rings for such a long time that, leaving She semi-conscious on the mattress, her face dusted lightly with ash, Ormus struggles into a pair of red crushed-velvet flares and staggers downstairs to the door.

On the doorstep is an alien: a man in business suit and matching moustache, with a briefcase in one hand and, in the other, a copy of a glossy magazine open at the page on which a model is wearing one of The Witch's latest offerings.

Good afternoon, says the alien, in excellent English. I have a chain of shops in Yorkshire and Lancashire . . .

She, naked beneath a hopelessly inadequate dressing gown, cigarette dripping from her lips, weaves down the stairs with a hand in her hair. The alien turns puce and his eyes start sliding around. Ormus retreats.

Yeah? enquires She.

Good afternoon, the alien tries again, although his English is giving him difficulty all of a sudden. I have a chain of shops in Yorkshire and Lancashire selling ladies' fashions, and I am most interested in this particular garment as featured here. With whom would I speak with a view to placing a first order for six dozen items, with an option to repeat?

It is the biggest order The Witch has ever had. Halfway up the stairs now, the imposing, black-and-gold-caftanned figure of Antoinette Corinth materialises. Impossible to know her thoughts. Ormus fancies he feels a tingle in the air, the sense of having arrived at a turning point. The alien waits patiently while She considers matters. Then, with great deliberation, the manageress nods a few times, slowly. Fashionably.

We're closed, man, she says, and shuts the door.

Antoinette Corinth comes down and kisses She on the mouth. After which, still in Antoinette's arms, She turns to Ormus and, most unusually, speaks further words.

A fucking artist, she says. This beautiful woman.

At this point the doorbell rings again. She turns and goes back upstairs, this time with Antoinette. She is plainly not planning to return to Ormus's humble mattress. The cushions and silks, the exotic markings and draperies of Antoinette's lair await her. Ormus stands and looks at the closed door.

Again, the bell. He opens the door.

On the doorstep, holding a wickerwork hamper that contains a selection of the finest leavened breads money can buy, is the overlord of the Colchis label, the blind recording angel himself, Yul Singh; and behind him, a limousine half as long as the street.

You see, Mr. Cama. You see before you. Now that you're ready, which I have to say I congratulate you, I didn't expect it, but I heard your tape from your man Mr. Standish who allow me to say you found yourself a good one there, and having ears to hear I have heard what I have heard, so as it turns out it was not required for you to seek me out, which as I remember I advised you on no account to do. As things transpire which I don't mind saying it's a funny old world, and so Mr. Cama with your permission it is I who have come to you.

"Lorelei," from the first VTO album, the self-titled *VTO* (Colchis, 1971):

Certain shapes pursue me, I cannot shake them from my heel. Certain people haunt me, in their faces I will find the things I feel. Uncertain fate it daunts me, but I'm gonna have to live with that raw deal. No authority's vested in me, on what's good or bad or make-believe or even real. But I'm just saying what I see, because the truth can set you free, and even if it hasn't done too much for me, well, I still hope it will.

And I can feel your love, Lorelei. Yes, I can feel your love pour on me. Oh I can feel your love, Lorelei.

• • •

In the summer of 1967, Ormus takes a drive in the country one weekend afternoon with his good friends Hawthorne and Waldo Crossley, in Hawthorne's Mini Cooper S (with Radford conversion), to celebrate his recording contract with Colchis Records. Antoinette Corinth, in an unusual display of maternal affection, insists on packing them a picnic lunch. A thermos of tea, and sandwiches.

I'm so delighted for you, she says to Ormus, magnanimously. And what with your success and the boys taking to him at last, I'm glad for Mull as well. I can't imagine he's ever been happier. Not a cloud on his horizon. Blue skies ahead as far as the eye can see. Bye, darlings, darlings. Have a lovely day.

At first things go swimmingly. They pass a troupe of white-faced mimes in a park playing slow-motion tennis without a ball, and they stop for a while, sipping tea from the hot thermos, to watch the intensely contested game. Their topics of conversation are diverse. They touch on the suicide of the Beatles' manager, Brian Epstein; and the American race riots; and Cassius Clay's refusal to fight in Indochina, the stripping of his title and his transformation into Muhammad Ali; and even the *musique concrète* of Stockhausen. But mostly they talk about driving down to the anti-war music festival taking place at Woburn Abbey, in spite of the widespread fear of violence. Troops as well as armed and mounted police have massed on the outskirts of the Woburn estate, and government spokesmen are warning the musicians and the crowd to avoid inflammatory or seditious behaviour. In response, many musicians have vowed to be as seditious as possible. There are rumours of possible gas attacks, even of the use of automatic weapons.

(The national mood is so ugly that when a daily newspaper, reacting to the growing hippie phenomenon but failing to connect its message of peace to the overwhelming fact of the war, describes the season as a "summer of love," it comes across as a risible piece of government propaganda.)

However, the catastrophe, when it comes, has nothing to do with the protest movement or the forces ranged against it. Ormus Cama is a known opponent of the Wilson government's decision to involve

British troops in Indochina—*why do Labour leaders always have to prove they have the balls for war?*—but he is not stopped at any army barricade, nor is he the subject of a charge of mounties.

What happens is apolitical: a traffic accident.

Hawthorne Crossley is behind the wheel, perhaps driving too fast, certainly losing concentration and seemingly overtired and erratic; and in a sleepy English village off the M1 the Mini Cooper collides with a large heavy-goods vehicle carrying a weighty and odorous cargo of agricultural fertiliser. Hawthorne Crossley is killed outright, Waldo suffers head injuries which cause irreparable damage to his brain, while Ormus, in the back of the car, is also gravely injured. Ordure covers everything. The emergency services have to dig down to them through a little hill of excrement. A rendezvous with a truckload of shit: it would be funny, if it were not so unfunny.

Ormus is in the back seat of the car. He closes his eyes for an instant because alternative universes have begun to spiral out from his eyeballs in rainbow-coloured corkscrews of otherness that fill him with terror, and because he does not know about the impurities in the thermos of tea he thinks he's producing the hallucination all by himself. So he clenches his lids against the twin exfoliating beanstalks of the vision and when he opens them again all the world is truck. The improbably loud drag of metal against metal. The ticking of the seconds slowed down until they sound like the doomy muffled beats of a funeral drum. When you hit a big truck in a small vehicle, he remembers from somewhere, the greatest danger is that you will be sucked underneath it and decapitated or at least crushed. Heavy metal with its wall of sound goes on sliding past. They bounce off the truck's rear wheel arch, spin, hit something else, a house or a tree, and stop. Nobody's wearing a seat belt. Ormus, tumbling dreadfully in the confined space of the car, glimpses rag-doll Waldo lolling in the front passenger seat with his mouth open; and then the driver, Hawthorne Crossley, floats into view, heading wide-eyed for the windscreen. Hawthorne exhales violently, like a madman's laugh, *hahaaa,* and Ormus sees a little white cloud fly out of his mouth and hang there for a moment, like a speech bubble; and disperse. Then like an underwater swimmer reaching the surface Hawthorne's head breaks the windscreen and passes through it and that's that. When Ormus is able to remember things he will remember this as the moment he saw Hawthorne's life leave his body, and what does that mean, does it mean there is a spirit after all, a soul that's in the flesh but not of it, a ghost in the soft machine. That will be a thing for him to wrestle with at another time, but right now all wrestling has to stop, because something hard has punched him, like a fist, in the left eye.

Time accelerates as they decelerate. Fertiliser pours down. He nothing knows.

This is what is reported. The casualties are taken to a nearby cottage hospital. Ormus's American manager, a "hobbling, Svengali-like figure," Mr. Mull Standish, arrives soon afterwards, together with the record company boss Yul Singh, expensively accoutred in a navy-blue suit, Ray Charles shades and black leather gloves, and accompanied, Piloo Doodhwala fashion, by an entourage of aides and bodyguards. Standish, utterly demolished by the fate of his sons, sobs helplessly by their hospital beds; it's reportedly Yul Singh's team of Sikhs who spirit the singer away through a back exit, in spite of his serious wounds and fractures, and remove him to a secret location where he will be given private care. Ormus is reported to be holed up in a village in the Welsh borders, or in the Scottish highlands, or suburban Essex. There are sightings in Paris and Switzerland; in Venice (the masked carnival) and Rio de Janeiro (where he dances, again in the carnival, amid the small-breasted and ample-buttocked women beloved of Brazilian men); in Flagstaff, Arizona, and don't forget Winona—he's getting his kicks on Route 66. He is said to be horribly disfigured; it is rumoured that his vocal cords have been severed; a "definitive" investigation in a Sunday newspaper reveals that he has given up his life as a musician for ever, converted to Islam and joined an obscure sect of devotees—the "Cats of Allah"—based, improbably, in the heart of the Jewish community of Hampstead Garden Suburb. The most persistent rumour is that he is lying, deeply comatose, in a top-secret intensive care unit, isolated in a glass case like Snow White asleep in her coffin.

For three and a quarter years, Ormus will remain in sequestration, far from the public eye. Neither his record label, Colchis, nor his personal representatives at Mull Standish's Mayflower Management offices, will issue any statements.

Stories circulate, and there's no point in arguing with them. Parts of them are accurate enough, except for the bizarre worldwide sightings of the suddenly invisible man, whose disappearance—there is no escape from these bitter ironies—propels him from third-rate popster status to a condition of considerable renown. The longer he stays invisible, the greater grows his fame. A cult develops, whose adherents believe that Ormus Cama will awake to lead them out of these troubled times, beyond our vale of tears to redemption. Reissues of his Mayflower records, as well as bootleg recordings of his early Bombay performances, begin to circulate and sell; a legend grows. People, being people, begin to speak cynically of a publicity stunt. Yul Singh is well known as a wily bird, and Standish, though less known, is no less wily.

The coma story, however, is true. Ormus is not dead but sleeping.

The speculation grows so intense that the human dimension of the tragedy is almost completely obliterated. The people involved cease to be thought of as living, feeling beings; they become abstract, pieces in a riddle, a heartless game. They become empty vessels into which public speculation can be poured.

Certain facts do not come to light. Yul Singh and his inner circle at Colchis work to suppress them, and ironically the cloud of conjectures actually helps.

In the bloodstream of the Crossley brothers, and that of Ormus Cama too, doctors have found dangerously high levels of the hallucinogen lysergic acid diethylamide 25. These medical reports do not become public knowledge, however. Nor does any police action follow from them.

In the wreckage of the Mini Cooper, a thermos flask has been found. Somehow, this flask is not retained in police possession, or subjected to any kind of examination by the authorities. For some reason it is given into the hands of a "family friend." The friend never resurfaces. Nor does the flask.

There is therefore no proof that there was any sugar in the tea.

• • •

A man's worth reveals itself in the hour of his greatest adversity. What is our value when the chips are down? Do we merely flatter to deceive, or are we the real thing, the stuff of alchemists' dreams? These, too, are questions to which most of us, mercifully, are never required to supply answers.

The rising of Mull Standish to the occasion of tragedy, though unsurprising to those who know him, is nonetheless an example to all. Emerging dry-eyed from his cottage-hospital grief, he dedicates himself to the welfare of the living. In the weeks that follow, the fevered energy with which he locates and hires the finest available treatment for Waldo is a marvel to behold. Waldo will recover from his physical injuries. For several years after that he will benefit from the attention of a team of specialists thanks to whose efforts he will be able to resume a limited, but surprisingly contented, existence in the world.

Yul Singh's men follow Standish's orders. Ormus Cama is taken to a white house on a hill overlooking the Thames, a house at whose open French windows white curtains blow in the breeze, to be cared for by his mother. Thus one rift in the world at least is on the way to being healed. Spenta receives her broken child with loud cries of self-reproach, spends a rapid fortune to set up a state-of-the-art sanatorium in the sunny and spacious old orangery, and resolves to nurse Ormus back to health with her own hands, positioning herself constantly by his bedside, although exhaustion obliges her, from time to time, to snatch a few hours' sleep. Lord Methwold is recently dead, peacefully, in his sleep, deceased without issue, and his wife is the sole—and uncontested—beneficiary of his impressive will. This country mansion is now hers; also the town house at Campden Hill Square, the healthy bank accounts, the substantial holdings in gilts and blue-chip equities. A real stash, in sum. The former Lady Spenta Cama has received the news of her good fortune as an admonition from god. To be suddenly rich in worldly goods is to understand the nature of her deeper impoverishment. Of her three sons, one is in jail for murder, a second has been despatched (oh, callous mother!) to a nursing home, so as not to trouble her aged spouse. The youngest has long been estranged from her, thinking himself unloved; now he's badly hurt. She, who believes herself devout, has failed in her soul's duty.

Secretly, away from the failing Methwold, she has been tuning in to Radio Freddie, keeping in touch with her son through his work. The station's closure has been hard to bear: it is a second parting, a second rupture. Her letter to Ormus, maudlin and full of apologies, addressed to him in care of the pirate station, arrives in Standish's hand on the day of the singer's ill-fated car journey. So it is Standish whose intervention returns Ormus to the bosom of his family. (Virus Cama is home too, liberated from his captivity by his stepfather's demise.)

This service nobly performed, Mull Standish returns to London, to Wandsworth Crematorium, for it is time to burn his son.

At the crematorium, he leans on his cane, closes his eyes, at once sees the great fire-jets billow around the young man's body, cleansing him of himself. Though he is an American and has lived an intensely American life, Mull does not weep. Opens his eyes. Antoinette Corinth and She, their arms around each other, are dabbing at kohl-blurred faces under their black lace veils. More than dialogue is dead now. Standish closes his eyes again and sees Waldo Crossley's future. Waldo, made foolish by the accident, smiles sweetly at autumn leaves as he spears them upon a blustery parterre. Above which, looking down at him from the windows of a large white house, is Ormus's mother. Who wishes nothing more than to make eternal reparation for a lifetime of poor mothering. Who will care for Waldo as if he too were her beloved child.

It's over. No more weeping. Standish moves across the aisle to speak quietly to his ex-wife. It's my belief that this is your work, he says, mildly. I didn't think you could do it, but now I'm sure you did. I can't imagine how great the burden of your hatred must be. I can't conceive of carrying so much poison in your heart for so very long. The killing of your children to spite their father. It's like something out of a book.

You loved them and they came to love you. Her voice is ice. Her teeth glitter maliciously. That is what gives me the greatest comfort, and pleasure.

Murderess, he says. Infanticide. May the gods blast your life, he says. She turns on him. They were disturbed boys ever since you abandoned them. For years now they've been doing whatever it takes to escape the truth. Namely, that their faggot father fucked off fast. When they were kids they'd eat a can of boot polish if they thought it would bring them an hour's escape. They'd drink cough medicine by the quart. Glue, pills, bloody plastic-bag erections, that's what was happening, so Mull, don't you fucking start with me. Then you showed up like god almighty, gave them a job, finally decided to love the little bastards. That *really* drove them to drink and everything else. Needle time. Or hadn't you noticed. But then you close down the station, you take it away from them, and you even let the poor runts see that you love some other shitbag more than them. You just don't get it. You never did get it. They were terrified of you, terrified that you were about to fuck off again. Out of their heads with fear. That just after they started loving you, you'd hightail it with your Indian prince.

He will not let her see him tremble; controls himself; accuses her again.

You prepared the picnic, he says. You planned to kill them all.

Or, she counters, they put the stuff in there themselves. To die and take your lover boy with them. Poor darlings. They couldn't even get that right.

Mull Standish waits alone for the ashes. Hawthorne's ashes are his own life. Decisions must be made: to be or not to be. You face up to life, you give it your best shot, you approach it with all the openness and humanity you have, and you get this. One boy in a fake Greek urn, the other a shell without a self. This isn't what was supposed to happen.

He enfolds the urn in his arms and kisses and kisses it. This is my beloved son in whom I am well pleased.

The small galaxy that is passing through the larger galaxy of my story is being torn apart, destroyed. Antoinette Corinth and She close down The Witch and leave for the Pacific coast of Mexico, dressed in fiery tropical colours, exchanging dark silence for brilliant light and noise. No charges are contemplated against them. It is for each of us to decide which truth we choose to follow: the truth of tragedy, of story, Standish's Medean truth, or Antoinette's accusatory version, or the more sober truth of the Law. Innocent till proved guilty, and so on.

Either way, it's not much good to Hawthorne and Waldo.

Soon after the women's departure there is a fire in Unfold Road and the store burns down. Arson is suspected but not proven, and after a delay the insurance companies pay up. Mr. Tommy Gin, as the principal backer, receives the lion's share of the payout, but a cheque of appreciable size is sent to the beautiful seaside resort of Zopilote in the Mexican province of Oaxaca, on the Golfo de Tehuantepec. The cheque is cashed, but no further news of Antoinette Corinth and her companion, She, is received. They have, for the moment, vanished into an impenetrable elsewhere, into which this story cannot go.

Certain patterns recur, seem inescapable. Fire, death, uncertainty. The carpet whipped out from under us to reveal a chasm where the floor should have been.

Disorientation. Loss of the East.

During the later stages of the so-called lost years, after his emergence from the long coma, Ormus Cama will for a time keep an occasional journal, a haphazard thing littered with automatic writing, crazytalk, "poetry," visions, conversations with the dead, and many ideas for songs.

In one of the earliest entries, he will describe a hallucination experienced in the back seat of the fateful Mini Cooper, in all probability just before the encounter with the fertiliser truck:

The top of my head was open, just blown apart as if by an explosion, and he climbed out and ran away. Now he doesn't come to see me any more, because why would he, he's free, he's not running through the corridors and staircases of the casino looking for a way out, he's escaped, he's out there somewhere. If you meet him, remember he's not me. He just looks that way. He's not me.

And this is another early entry:

Vina I know you better now. My darling I have met your lethal mother. I have faced her other, and survived.

11

HIGHER LOVE

In the early days, before the orangery sanatorium is ready, Ormus is placed in Spenta's own bed, attached to drips and monitors. This part of the house is old and flaky, like the England out of which it was born. A fine rain of plaster dust settles slowly on Ormus's cheeks. Spenta at his bedside brushes the pale flecks away with a paisley-patterned silk cloth. Virus Cama, back home again, sits with his hands resting softly on his knees in a corner of the master bedroom, on a carved folding chair in black teak, a chair that was once used by a travelling Collector in what is now Maharashtra and Madhya Pradesh, on his journeys along the Wainganga and into the Seeonee hills. Spenta regards her broken sons, Sleep and Silence, bows her head, and resolves for the one hundred and first time to make it up to these lost boys, to heal them with belated love. It is not, must not be, too late for redemption: theirs and her own. She prays to her angels but they no longer answer. Her sons are her only angels now.

But Cyrus, she mourns dumbly. For Cyrus, it is too late.

Memorabilia of British India are all around. A mirrorwork *chhatri* hangs over a long-armed recliner chair. Company school pictures, hand-coloured Daniell engravings. A silver tea service, a stone god-head, photographs of great days spent shooting birds and beasts, a tiger rug, stone boxes with silver *bidri* inlay work, an *itr*-seller's perfume chest, a harmonium, carpets, cloths. A framed letter from Morgan Forster describing oddly echoing caves in the side of a scrubby hill.

The Indian nurse arrives.

It is only some while later, after Spenta has remembered who she is and where she has seen her before, that they realize nobody can recall letting her in. She seems to materialize from nowhere, hovering solic-itously behind Spenta and Standish, wearing a pristine starchy uniform in pale blue and white, with a small watch pinned at her breast. The agency sent me, she says vaguely, busying herself with sheets and tow-els and reading the chart hooked over the foot of the comatose singer's bed. Spenta and Standish are at a low ebb. Exhaustion and shock have taken their toll, so that even when Virus Cama gets up from his Col-lector's chair to tug worriedly at his mother's sleeve Spenta just shrugs him off and slumps down with her head in her hands. Standish, too, is on the point of collapse, having barely slept since the catastrophe. The Indian nurse turns down the lights in the master bedroom and takes charge with a competence that brooks no argument. She is a good-looking girl, well spoken, knowledgeable about the leading families of Bombay society. She tells Spenta about her time with the Sisters of Maria Gratiaplena, though, she hastens to add, she herself is no nun. It is perhaps because of this reference that Spenta, whose thoughts are much abstracted, begins to call the newcomer Maria, a name to which she readily answers. Rest, Maria says, and Standish and Spenta troop meekly out, followed by Virus Cama, who keeps looking over his shoulder at the nurse and shaking his greying head.

When she is alone with sleeping Ormus, the nurse begins to talk to him in a voice full of smoke and longing. At last, my love. Though it is not our beautiful little nook in Worli, still it will do, for wherever you lie, that place is my palace and so on, whatever bed contains your body is my only desired resting place et cetera, and even when you die my love I will follow you into your grave, into it and beyond, et cetera et cetera et cetera.

Then she goes on to remind the unconscious man of their past love-making, the many wonderful things they have done together, those

supreme proofs of their passion, athleticism and flexibility, to say nothing of the sensual powers of certain natural oils. Her long oration is an
erotic masterwork that would be lost to posterity were it not for the
Grundig tape deck which Mull Standish has installed beneath Ormus's
bed just in case he should return briefly to consciousness and say
something, anything, during his manager's and his mother's simultane-
ous absence from the room. Ormus stays silent, but the thin brown
tape phlegmatically absorbs everything Maria has to say, eavesdropping
on her intimacies just as those other, fictitious tapes listened in on the
imaginary "President Nixon" in the novel *The Watergate Affair*. And at
a certain point she moves on from reminiscence to action, she
describes to the unknowing Ormus in explicit detail how she plans to
rouse him from his slumbers by arousing his carnal desires, there is a
clink of glass containers, then the slippery sounds of oil-slathered hands
moving across one another and applying themselves to the sleeping
figure.

The sound quality on the tape is good. Anyone listening to it can
easily picture Maria as she climbs on to the bed (mattress noises), and
because the human imagination all too easily runs away with its sup-
positions, I must move on quickly to the clearly recorded sound of a
door flying open, and the horrified voices of Spenta and Standish as
they burst in, Spenta having finally summoned up the memory of the
nympho on the plane to London.

They order the Indian nurse to get off, get dressed and get out,
because how dare she, is she so wholly lacking in the faintest scrap of
decency, they will see her disbarred from nursing duties, she should
cover her breasts at once, yes, and her pudenda too, and above all she
should stop laughing, stop it this minute, this is no laughing matter, in
five seconds' time they are going to send for the police.

Her laughter fills the tape as she leaves the room.

Ormus remains asleep; dormant and, in spite of all Maria's ministrations—so the story goes—still soft.

She keeps showing up. Ormus is moved to the new facility in the
orangery and the next night she's there. Spenta goes to the toilet for a
minute and returns to find Maria, naked except for a black veil, bending over Ormus's exposed sex, the movements of her ample mouth

half concealed by gauze. She really is very beautiful, very wanton and very mad, Spenta thinks, but that doesn't explain how the girl got inside. Spenta gives orders for a constant vigil to be maintained, a guard is posted, dogs are unleashed in the nocturnal grounds. Still Maria finds a way in. One night Standish is on duty, reading the latest Yossarian to help him through the night, and in spite of the writer's comic genius he nods off for, he thinks, no more than a couple of minutes. When he awakes he is startled to find her there, fully materialized, oiled, veiled and naked, in spite of the hounds and the locked grilles and the beam-operated alarm system: and this time she is actually straddling Ormus, bouncing vigorously up and down, riding his soft cock horse. You'll never keep me away from him, she crows. I am his destiny, his private need and so on. That woman (she means Vina) can never give him what he wants, but I know what he desires better than he, I give it to him before he knows he's going to ask for it et cetera. I come from his secret world.

Who are you, Standish demands, blinking. He is heavy with sleep, and he's also wearing his reading glasses, so that everything more than nine inches away looks blurry and unreal.

As he tries to focus on her, she disappears. A crack seems to open in the air itself, and she steps through it and is gone.

The human capacity for rationalization is a thing of wonder. It enables us to disbelieve the evidence of our own eyes. Since what Standish has fuzzily seen is impossible, he concludes that he has not seen it. She must have slipped out the door while he was still dozy, he concludes. He gets up and looks, but she's gone. Standish notes the further failure of the security system and suspects an inside job. The crazy girl is probably buying the favours of some staff member, a gardener, a handyman. Someone is smuggling her in and being rewarded, no doubt, with some of that sexual action with which she makes so free. It must be looked into. Meanwhile, no real harm done. Standish returns to his book.

Peacefully, Ormus sleeps on.

Mull Standish, a contemporary man, looks for answers in the everyday. Spenta just as naturally turns towards the paranormal, fears a haunting and summons Parsi priests from London and the local Anglican vicar.

Fire ceremonies and exorcisms are sonorously performed. After these rites there are periods, often very extended, when the Indian woman fails to manifest herself. For these absences, as for her presences, no explanation is given; Spenta, however, gives the credit to the servants of Ahura Mazda and the Christian God.

Then Maria appears again, and the whole cleansing ritual is renewed.

There are days when Spenta feels mortally afraid. Deserted by angels, she fears she and her family may now have fallen prey to demons. At such moments she looks to Mull Standish for comfort. Always immaculately groomed, expensively tricked out in silk-collared camel coat or raffishly cigar-chewing in mink, Standish in these agonizing times still stands foursquare on the unsteady earth, a well-planted man, a tree that has no plans to fall any time soon. His calm tones, his gravitas, his sleek hair: these things reassure Spenta, and a gleam comes into her eye, though she is seven years his senior and can have no realistic expectations. Still, she pays greater attention to her appearance, she lowers her eyelashes, she flirts. Standish, noting the advent of an unrequitable love, has grown fond enough of Spenta to let her dream.

For all his apparent solidity these are years of misfortune for Mull Standish. The sudden collapse of a Newark office block for which one of his U.S. subsidiaries supplied cooling systems has been followed by a more general erosion of confidence in his construction business. Due to the end of his liaison with "Sam Tropicana," his erstwhile lover's family is determinedly putting the poor mouth on him, and New York's City Hall has started frowning on his projects and tenders. The IRS irregularities have been squared, but only after the payment of arrears plus a punitive fine. In Britain the end of the pirate phase has done more than financial harm; it has removed some essential excitement from his life. He has wound up his record label and makes his bread and butter, nowadays, from investments in rental property shrewdly acquired during the pirates' boom years.

Naturally, like any dynamic entrepreneur, and there can be no doubt of the rightness of that description, he continues to have his schemes and dreams. Hippies in Sloane Square sell yo-yos that light up as they rise and fall. He has a piece of this action, also in much else that is gimcrack and union-jacked and over-priced and sold in Carnaby Street.

His gift for what marketing men call gap analysis has led him to launch a listings service, *Where It's At,* which begins as a poor folded sheet guiding the young to pleasures both mainstream and "alternative" and quickly grows into a money-spinning weekly magazine. For ordinary mortals, this slate of activities would be proof of robust health, and robustness is the quality Standish—still, in his early fifties, an indefatigable powerhouse of a fellow—works hardest to project. However, he is a man with a broken heart. If he is to be compared to a great tree, then there is something decaying at its core. One day, without warning, it may suddenly fall. Only then will passers-by be able to see the sickness, and understand.

When he walks with Waldo Crossley in the grounds of Methwold's riverside estate, congratulating his son on the skill with which he has learned to spear leaves and other detritus, flattering him on the way he looks in the Methwold livery, and being rewarded by Waldo's tear-jerkingly wide, happy, brainless smile—or when he keeps vigil by Ormus Cama's bedside, seeing in the comatose singer the shadow of his own dead Hawthorne—then Standish's back is straighter than ever, his jaw firmer, his eye less moist. But he has been poleaxed and no mistake. The danger is that if Ormus fails to awake, Standish may also fall into some final sleep. Their fates are joined. As the months and years go by, and Standish loses hope of an awakening, little threads of his cloak of discipline begin to fray. There's a tic, sometimes, in the corner of an eye. There are days when a few stray hairs elude his formerly omnipotent brush. When he stands, Spenta notices the first signs of a stoop.

If I was a little younger, she says, taking his arm while they walk on the parterre one late afternoon, I might give you a run for your money.

He hears the loneliness, the echo of a woman standing in the empty room of her future, and decides he has no alternative but to be truthful.

I am one of those, he says, almost tongue-tied for once, for whom the love of women was never really the point.

Wonderful, she claps her hands. I also can see no point in such activity at our age. But companionship, isn't it? That we can offer each other as twilight falls.

At which Mull Standish finds himself at a loss for words.

. . .

Abruptly, Maria stops coming, perhaps despairing of Ormus's prospects. Neither Spenta nor Standish says so, but both think her absence a bad omen.

They begin to speak of the unspeakable: of the life support. For more than three years, Ormus Cama has needed monitors, drips, plasma. There have been moments when respiratory equipment has been necessary. His muscles have atrophied, he is weaker than a baby, and without the machines, the nursing staff, the orderlies, he could not possibly survive. Spenta asks Standish the unaskable.

What do you think, honestly, will he wake up.

And Standish is no longer able to offer a convincing Yes in reply.

It would be possible to arrange a mishap, he says. A power cut, plus a failure of the back-up generator. Or a tube might accidentally fall out of the sleeping man's nose, or a life-giving needle drop from a vein. It might be, what's the word, stumbles Standish. Merciful.

I still believe, Spenta obstinately wails. In I don't know what, a miracle. In blessings from above. In, what to call it, higher love.

When Colchis Records releases the double-A-side 45 "Beneath Her Feet" b/w "It Shouldn't Be This Way" by the defunct band Rhythm Center, it is intended as a farewell gesture, a surrender to the inevitable. Ever since the accident Standish has been adamant: Ormus will recover, at that point he will resume his career, and until then it would be both macabre and bad business to put out any discs.

Yul Singh has gone along with this in his equivocal way.

If this is your wish Mr. Standish which I'm offering no opinion then so be it, it's your call. You change your mind you come and see me. The industry moves on at high speed, you don't need to be told, so we'll see about it as and when. God willing I'm still in this seat, maybe I can help you out.

The time comes when Standish and Spenta agree that they want Ormus to sing again, to sing one last time before the machinery ceases to support his life and he departs. Standish asks Yul Singh to set the music free; which request, for all his tough talk and caveats, the ferocious Colchis overlord—understanding that the request is a kind of death sentence—is unable to deny. Whereupon, to everyone's amazement, the record is a hit. And Vina Apsara in a Bombay hotel room hears Ormus singing, and flies back into his life: and saves it.

Here she is at his bedside, whispering into his ear. Here is Spenta, not knowing whether to fear her as another revenant demon, or to grieve with her for their mutual loss, or to hope. Here is Mull Standish holding his breath. Here, hovering like vultures, are a doctor, a nurse, an orderly.

In the doorway, hat in hand, is blind Yul Singh.

Ormus, she whispers. Ormus, it's me.

At which he opens his eyes; it's as simple as that. His mouth trembles. She bends down to hear him.

The doctor swoops, shoulders her aside. Excuse, please. We must establish the degree of damage. Turning to Ormus with a glitter of bedside teeth, he asks: Who am I?

A drug dealer.

The voice surprises everyone by its strength, its sardonic note. The doctor points to Yul Singh in the doorway. And he, who is he?

A commissar.

Then the orderly, carrying clean sheets and towels.

He isn't important.

And how about you, the doctor asks. Do you know who you are. Do you know what you want.

Vina, he calls. She comes close, takes his hand. *Yes,* he answers. *Now I know.*

How shall we sing of the coming together of long-parted lovers, separated by foolish mistrust for a sad decade, reunited at last by music? Shall we say (for in song we are set free from surly pedantry, and may hymn the soaring spirit, rather than the crumpled letter, of the truth): they ran singing through fields of asphodel and drank the nectar of the gods, and their kissing was as beauteous as the evening horizon, where the earth first touches and then becomes the sky? Shall we liken his sweeping caresses to the movement of the winds across the surface of the sea, now raging, now tender, and her arched responses, so eager, so potent, to the surging ocean waves? Shall we go so far as to speak of love divine, all loves excelling, and conclude that there must be a Great Lover looking down upon us from on high, to whose unconditional passion and openness of heart this earthly pair holds up its shining mirror?

No, this is a story of a deep but unstable love, one of breakages and reunions; a love of endless overcoming, defined by the obstacles it must surmount, beyond which greater travails lie. A hurdler's love. The forking, fissured paths of uncertainty, the twisting mazes of suspicion and betrayal, the plunging low road of death itself: along these ways it goes. This is a human love.

Let Vina speak. He in fact died that day, did you know that, she reveals, lying unclothed and overwhelming across my big brass bed one steaming summer's day in the middle 1980s in New York. That's right, she says with a twist of the mouth, he always did have fantastic timing. I come all the way across the world to find him and that's when the bastard decides to cash in his chips. For one hundred and fifty seconds he genuinely checked out, kicked the bucket, bought the farm. Ormus the flatliner. He went down that tunnel towards the light. Then he turned right round and came on back. Afterwards he told me it was on account of me?, he heard my voice calling behind him?, he looked back, and it absolutely saved his life. Blip blippety blip not-fade-away on the monitor screen, the flatline starts jumping, oh doctor, doctor, he's alive, it's a blessing a miracle, he's come back to us, heavens to Betsy, praise the Lawd. Dead for two minutes but in the third minute he rose again from the dead.

He didn't come back to us, Vina boasts, he came back to me. Didn't wake up until I made my appearance, what was the point, right, because I wasn't there. They'd always said there was nothing wrong with him, levels of electrical activity in the brain were normal, the strong probability being that there wasn't any lasting damage, he was just perfect and dandy?, except that he wasn't awake. No, Lady Methwold, there's no explanation, in these cases they either wake up or they don't and that's the whole of it. He could sleep for years, the rest of his life, or he could open his eyes tomorrow. Or in twenty years' time, not knowing he's missed a day, those awakenings are the most difficult, they look at their hands and scream what's this disease that's shrivelling up my skin, you have to judge the moment when you show them a mirror?, and it's a delicate judgement, believe me, there is the danger of suicide.

Vina repeats, proudly: He waited for me, sleeping, all those long years. Nothing in life was interesting any more unless I was by his side. Then I showed up and jeepers if those peepers didn't pop open right on cue. If that's not love then I don't know what. Which doesn't mean I didn't give him a hard time later on. But that's because he's a man.

A hole has appeared in downtown Mexico City, a chasm thirty metres across. It has swallowed buses, kiosks, children. For years water has been sucked out of the swampy sub-soil to sate the thirsty city, and this is the underworld's revenge. The fabric of the surface is being unwoven from below. Right here in Manhattan the buildings themselves are beginning to stagger. Just a few blocks north of my brass bed, there's a brownstone that's started shedding bricks. A net has been erected to protect pedestrians. People have always jumped off buildings in New York, but this is something new. This building is jumping off itself.

The papers are full of such new catastrophes but Vina wants to talk about old ones. In these years of their semi-retirement she has started coming to me more and more often, and as she removes her clothes she can't help showing some resentment of the great Ormus Cama, of the prominence given to his talent in the burgeoning histories of the VTO phenomenon. This is the price I have to pay for enjoying her favours: this ceaseless Ormusic, her personal obsessive Camamania. She comes to me to let off summer steam. If I were to object, she'd stop coming. Sex is never the point with Vina. Sex is trivial, like blowing your nose. She comes to me because I know her story. She's here to write new paragraphs: to complain. That, for Vina, is intimacy. That amuses and arouses her. Vina on the bed, stretching, turning, torments me, knowing I am happy—or at least willing—to be thus tormented. She is forty years old, and fabulous.

So let's never forget I was the one who fetched him out of the underworld, she boasts, like that Hindu goddess?, what's her name, Mousie.

Rati, I correct her.

Yeah, right. Rati who saved Kama the god of love. When the god of love opened his eyes, by the way, the left eyeball was almost colourless. The doctors blamed a blow received in the car accident and regretted that as the pupil was "stuck" in its fully dilated state and could no longer contract?, the eye would see very little, and blurrily. But I told the doctors it wasn't the accident. He looked down the tunnel and the light poured into his eye. One-eyed death at the tunnel's end glaring at Ormus Cama. He's lucky the other eye survived.

(And the left eye saw plenty, anyway. It saw too deeply, too far, too much.)

I don't interrupt. When Vina starts with her fanciful mysteries, all you can do is lie back and wait for her to lose interest, which never takes too long. Here she is, back again at the story of Kama and Rati. Anyhow, without me he'd be stir-fry, baby, she says, referring to the negative effects of Lord Shiva's thunderbolt on the errant love god of Hinduism. Without me he'd be nothing, he'd be ash.

Thus Vina on the great love of her life. When he awoke, I was his mirror, she says. He saw himself in my eyes and liked what he saw. And lived.

When I want to provoke her, when the monologue about Ormus finally gets my goat, I raise the subject of Maria the phantom nympho-maniac. I do it by conjuring up the old show tune from *West Side Story*. Maria, I start humming, and at once Vina stiffens; her skin actually heats up—I feel her temperature rising—and her eyes begin to boil. Then she disguises her jealousy by transforming it into outrageous behaviour. Do you want me to show you, she asks, savagely. Shall I per-form upon you those unnatural acts. Hers, the so-called spectre's. You be Ormus, lie back and close your eyes just like you always wanted, and I'll be her, the slavering succubus. Would you like that, Rai, hey. You'd love it, am I right. Her terrible rising voice, caught halfway between a tear and a shriek, makes my ear whistle.

Keep it down, I say, a little frightened by this undressed ignoble sav-agery. Vina, come on. I don't need this and neither do you.

But perhaps she does need it, she feels injured by the very existence of this Other, it offends her. Other-hatred is for Vina the mirror image of self-love.

· · ·

The young Indian woman, no longer posing as a nurse but still answering to the name of Maria, starts coming to Ormus again, the first manifestation being a few days after Vina awakens him from his big sleep. She is discreet, however; Vina's presence guarantees Maria's absence, as if this were a condition of her appearances, a law of her fantastic realm. Ormus begins both to dread and to desire solitude because of these secret visits.

Fearing quick rejection, Maria has evolved a new strategy of volubility. Instead of tearing off her clothes and jumping on him, she seduces him with talk, fast, interesting talk, and he listens, because ever since he re-opened his pale left eye he has started seeing things he can't understand, things he needs to understand. It's as if his two eyes are looking into slightly different worlds, or rather two variations of the same world, almost the same and yet utterly separate. Double vision: he gets a lot of headaches.

Your eyes have been opened now, Maria murmurs, massaging his temples. He lets her do it. Now I can come to you like this, it's so much easier, whenever I want. Your eye knows, it remembers. Worli, the Cosmic Dancer, our life in the otherworld. These places feel like dreams et cetera, but they are places you have been and so on. I know it's hard for you. You have to live here for now. I understand. You have to blot certain things out to retain your ability to function and so forth. As for her, she's not good enough for you, but even this I can bear. I will never leave you. This is what you were sent to do. You slipped into your mother's womb behind your dead brother and they believed you belonged to them. Your songs will change this world. This is your fate. You will open their eyes and they will follow you towards the light et cetera et cetera. Your time has come to shine. All your dreams are on their way. See how they shine.

Is it possible that such an otherworld exists, he marvels.

And if it exists, he wonders privately, might it not also be possible that in that otherworld this strange girl might still be considered insane?

Her visits to his bedroom are necessarily brief. He is weak, convalescent, rarely left alone. She talks fast, continues to restrain her passions, seeking to present herself as an intelligent and educated person, a person worthy of his love.

Realities are in conflict, she tells him. Your right eye, your left eye, stare into different versions and so on. At such a moment the frontier between right and wrong action also dissolves. I myself have suspended moral judgement and live according to the more profound imperatives of my appetites et cetera.

He closes his left eye, experimentally. Maria disappears, as if someone had thrown a switch.

On her next visit she complains about her abrupt dismissal, insists on being treated with respect. I am here for you in any way you want, she says, but I don't care to be treated meanly and so forth. Just be a little polite.

What she wants to talk about most is earthquakes. There are going to be more of these, she prophesies. There are always earthquakes, Ormus answers. Yes, she says, but these are different. Two worlds in collision. Only one can survive and so on. In the end this world will crumble and fall et cetera and we will be together at home for ever and I will make you mad with joy et cetera et cetera et cetera as you must already know.

When she is not with him, she says, she visits past and present earthquake zones, in China, northern California, Japan, Tajikistan and elsewhere; all those places where the fabric of the earth has put itself in question. To Ormus, there is something ghoulish about this hobby, and about the lyricism with which she describes these high tragedies. She speaks of the earth beginning to sing, and rocking people's houses as if they were swinging cradles. The earth's pounding lullaby, not soothing but turbulent, coaxing human beings and their creations towards not sleep but death. She has spent a lot of time in Turkey, travelling to remote regions—Tochangri, Van—and India, too, gives her plenty to talk about: the devastation of Dharmsala and Palampur in the century's early years, and the narrow escape in Simla of Lady Curzon, the Viceroy's wife, who was just missed by a chimney that fell into her bedroom; also the Monghyr earthquake of 1934, when sulfurous mud and water bubbled up from great apertures in the earth like proofs of the existence of Hell, and Captain Barnard's Flying Circus was hired by the local authorities to overfly the area and assess the damage.

The great cracks in the streets of Orléansville, Algeria, the tidal wave that engulfed Agadir, the tidal wave that drowned Messina, the collapse of Managua and the escape of Howard Hughes, the Tokyo-Yokohama catastrophe of 1933, the endemic instability of Iran, and the strange behaviour of Sir J. A. Sweetenham, British governor of Jamaica, who refused the aid of the American navy after much of Kingston was flattened in the year 1907: about all these she painstakingly informs her bewildered beloved, in rather too much gruesomely relished detail.

Underlying all earthquakes is the idea of Fault, she says. The earth has many faults, of course. Literally millions have been mapped et cetera. But human Faults cause earthquakes too. What is coming is a judgement.

Now I know she's mad, Ormus thinks, but holds his tongue.

Earthquakes, Maria eagerly explains, are the means by which the earth punishes itself and its population for its wrongnesses. In spite of her disavowals of universal morality, she becomes, when she gets carried away, quite a tub-thumping fire-and-brimstone damnation preacher, bringing Ormus her hot gospel. She looks back to a utopian golden age in which there were no quakes, for the world was at peace, there were no conflicting versions, the earth lacked its present tragic quality of irreconcilability. The lithosphere itself, she argues, was originally intact but has been gradually deformed by movements in the planet's slowly convecting interior and so on. This hot, cauldron-like interior may be called the earth's original sin, its First Fault, and earthquakes are its consequences. Too late now to contemplate any return to that original state of balance, of grace. Too late to reconcile the earth with itself. We must brace ourselves for the tectonic movements, the slippages, the tsunamis, the landslides, the rocking, rolling cities et cetera et cetera, the smashing of the real. We must prepare for shocks, for the fragmentation of the planet as it goes to war with itself, for the endgames of the self-contradictory earth.

Human Faults cause earthquakes too. Maria on subsequent visits returns to her wildest notion. It is her view that there are certain individuals in whom the irreconcilability of being is made apparent, in whom the contradictoriness of the real rages like thermonuclear war; and such is the gravitational force of these individuals that space and time are dragged towards them and deformed. There are rifts, tears, slippages, incompatibilities. It is not that they are responsible for deforming the universe, but that they are the instruments through whose agency that growing deformity is clearly and terrifyingly unveiled.

It is her view that Ormus Cama is such an individual.

She says nothing about Vina in this regard.

She has talked enough. Now she has other plans, and advances upon him. He is in bed, too weak to resist her, and she knows she has aroused his interest. This time he will not refuse.

Ormus closes his eye.

It's almost fourteen years since our first night of love back in old Bombay and still Vina lies unclothed on our hot bed without so much as a sheet to cover her. Another sleeping beauty waiting for her prince (not me, not me) to come.

In the middle 1970s I photographed a great Russian ballet dancer who had defected from the Kirov in France, running towards a group of soldiers and shouting, *Help to me, help for me,* in broken English, pursued by KGB goons. *Help by me, help with me.* Soon after his escape he ended up, as we all end up, in Manhattan, and found his way to my studio wrapped in furs, like a high-stepping big-mouthed bear. I stood him on a white sheet in front of an old eight-by-ten plate camera. He was certainly the loveliest creature he had ever seen, the most gorgeous by a long long way, and so with the help of (not very much) white wine I persuaded him to remove first his furs and then more and more of his clothes, until at length he was triumphantly nude, and delighted to be so. I told him to let his head hang down and allow his arms to hang loosely. Then he should slowly raise his head, and as he did so he should also bring his arms up and out from his body, and that was the shape I wanted, he should hold that, the exposure was a full second long and the plate camera's depth of field was also a problem. He did as I asked and as his strong animal's head rose I saw that the eyes were closed, he was lost in a rhapsody of self-love, which was so profound that synchronously with the rising of his arms he also raised, for my camera's unhoped-for benefit, a long and glisteningly happy erection.

Love by me. Love with me, to me, for me. Love of me.

Vina's self-love is not less than this.

Here are some things she actually sings to me, in vengeful retribution for my humming that teasing Bernstein tune and raising the forbidden subject of Maria, her alternative-reality rival. Rai—this part's the spoken intro—you think you're such a fuckin' star. Let me tell you who you really are. (Now comes the song.) You are ass and I like class. I like diamonds, you are glass. You brown mouse, I like black rats. You boy pussy but I like tom cats. Just because you got this dance, don't think you stand a fuckin' chance.

(End of song.)

Rai, you are burger and I have steak at home. You are not what I want, never were, never will be. But I'm a hungry woman. *I want more than what I want.*

Do you know what you want, they asked Ormus, twice: once when he awoke from the big sleep, once later. They never asked me but if they had I'd have had the answer down pat. I learned it from a good teacher, the toughest in the world.

There is a wind in the willows, and perhaps that is a water rat scurrying to his hole. It is a balmy day, soft-breezed, and oarsmen are on the water in lazy sculls and heaving eights. Flags flutter from passing pleasure craft. Beneath taut sails young men *en matelot* lean and strain. Aboard the motor launches all is relaxation. Brass-buttoned blazers, white duck trousers, the long bare legs of pretty girls. An ack-ack popping of corks. Quails' eggs, and smoked salmon on brown bread. The river people wave to one another as they go, and if that is really Jesus Christ wearing a straw boater in that punt, then he too is welcome, he too deserves this moment of blessed beauty, this storybook English peace.

The war seems very far away.

Spenta walks down a path to the river, past a slope of bluebells and Waldo Crossley picking up leaves and an oak where once that old bastard Castlereagh liked to take his ease. He killed himself while staying here, slit his throat from ear to ear, they say, and emerged from his toilette bleeding to death from this second, lethal smile. In spite of the dead man's ghost, this walk is Spenta's favourite journey, along her mile and a half of shore, and it has become her custom to talk to her first husband while she takes the air.

How you would've loved it, Darius, to have guardianship of these historic moments, this riverbank, and oh, Darius, to feel this bliss. Life has vanquished death and even the furniture celebrates. The gloomy old leather chesterfields are shining and the whiskered ancestors posing in their frock coats and whatnot have stopped looking grim and have cracked out in smiles.

Our son has come back to us and all the world's in bloom.

To this place, Darius, the country's grandees would come to let their hair down, believing themselves beyond inspection and above criticism. Lord Methwold was an unbuttoned host and here, in his prime, he offered recherché pleasures to the great. But the old roué Lord Methwold grew lonely and tired and took a widowed Parsi bride. After that the grandees found the house unsuitable for their preferred sports and the carnival moved on. None of those funny goings-on under my roof, Darius, I can promise you that.

But tell me: is a third marriage proof of lax morals? Especially if for example with a younger man? Even if the gentleman concerned has no interest in um?

By taking Darius around with her, by pleasing his shade and seeking his approval, she assuages a certain guilt. She now possesses what he yearned for above all things: a place in England, perhaps even in Englishness. I resisted it all your life, Darius, so you never had it, and now I've got it instead. If I walk these fields with you, if I tell you the stories of the house and make them yours as well as mine, will you forgive me, my true husband, my love. You see what a poor woman I have been. Everyone must forgive me. You and my sons.

Praise God. Our son Ormus has come back.

Darius, he's awake, but we'll lose him soon. He didn't come back for us. My little Ormie. My little shrimpy boy.

Will you look at this shit, Vina scoffs from the parterre, looking down on Spenta and the shining Thames. Ormus is walking again, slowly, resting an arm on her shoulder. He who moved so beautifully now staggers like a drunk puppet. It's a museum, Vina says. Ye old world. For a boy like you, a place like this is living death. No wonder you got stuck in that coma?, but you're out of it now?, and at your age it's time you finally high-tailed it out of the British Empire.

There are butterflies, songbirds, wildflowers. There are onion-domed gazebos in the woods. Vina, voluble, impatient, makes this well-kept, carefully manicured or tidily unkempt country estate sound like the jungle, like some grass-hut Africa. I mean let's go, Ormus. I'm like out of here. Sail away with me.

That's a song about being tricked into slavery, he objects. It's about deceptions and lies. It's ironic.

England's the trick, she says. You're an American, she says. You always were.

He begins to sing about the ways in which America is unlike Africa. America, which is mercifully free of lions, tigers, murderous black mambas. It's the first time since the coma that he's raised his voice in song.

Sonny Terry and Brownie McGhee covered it, she says, turning away from him so he can't see the tears standing in her eyes. You've got to hear them. Newman may have written it but those guys made it hurt.

She gets rid of the throat lump and returns feverishly to the attack: Ormus you got stuck here, but it was an accident, and man, you're not stuck any more. You can either stay and I don't know immigrunt the rest of your life away, and let's not forget immigratitude, that's expected too, along with immigrovelling?, or you can cross the mighty ocean and leap into that old hot pot. You get to be an American just by wanting, and by becoming an American you add to the kinds of American it's possible to be, that's in general I'm talking about?, okay?, and New York City in particular. However you get through your day in New York City, well then that's a New York kind of day, and if you're a Bombay singer singing the Bombay bop or a voodoo cab driver with zombies on the brain or a bomber from Montana or an Islamist beardo from Queens, then whatever's going through your head?, well that's a New York state of mind.

Of course there are Americans you'll never be, she goes on, Boston Brahmins, slave owners' sons from Yoknapatawpha, or those sad sacks on the daytime confession shows, fat men in check shirts sitting with fat women showing too much thigh, wearing their naked subtitles and baring their clumsy souls. Just because they do not remember their history?, it doesn't mean Americans don't have it or they're not doomed to repeat it. You'll never have that stuff, that's for sure. But you don't need it. You'll say things all wrong but they'll at once become American ways of saying things. You won't know shit but it'll right away become an American type of ignorance. Not belonging, that's an old American tradition, see?, that's the American way. You'll never be a child in a haunted Virginia hollow, Ormus, or see your mama swinging in a barn, but that's cool, you've got horror stories of your own. And you don't have to do it?, but if you want to you can pretend, you can start arguing in bars about the Yankees' pitching rotation or stressing over the Mets, you can play remember-when, that's as in remember-when the Brooklyn Dodgers or Runyon's Broadway or the Village in the fifties or the birth of the blues. It's like you have a leg sawn off and you still feel it twitch?, only it's the opposite?, you can start feeling the twitching of legs you never had, and guess what, if you pretend long enough, then baby it becomes a good old American pretend, you can walk on those pretend legs without even crutches and they'll carry you wherever you're going, because what do you know, half the country's faking it just like you, and the other half isn't, but there's no way to tell who's which. So you get your strength back, Ormus, hear what I'm saying, and then you take up thy bed and you don't just walk, you fuckin' fly out of here. With me. America starts today.

Whoo-ee, she thinks, exhausted and astonished by the vehemence of her propaganda. *Whoo.* Well bang that drum, wrap me in the flag and call me Martha. But if I don't get him out of here pronto, I'm the one, because who can breathe this air, that'll suffocate to death.

Vina has been at war with Spenta since the moment she arrived. Mother and lover circle Ormus in his bed, as if they were prizefighters and he the referee.

All this technology, Vina smacks at the array of medical equipment. It may be good for fixing your teeth but it understands nothing, it explains nothing, and that's why it achieved nothing.

The finest money could buy. It kept him alive, Spenta plaintively replies, not knowing why she's sounding so apologetic, unable to get off the defensive.

Imbalances in the doshas, Vina diagnoses. They disrupted the flow of his prana life-energy force?, and impeded the body's fire. Impeded agni leads to the production of ama. Toxins. We must concentrate on panchakarma: on purging him. Focus on his feces, urine, sweat. The three malas are the key.

What are you saying, Spenta says. These words.

It's your culture, Vina gibes. The world's greatest and oldest holistic system. You don't know this? The five basic elements, earth, water, air, fire, ether?

Oh, ayurveda, Spenta sounds relieved. Yes, daughter, I know many of you youngsters are interested in these old ideas again, but this was never our Zoroastrian way. I personally like Ormus's deceased father put my trust in the finest Western care. Developed, like you, darling, over here only, in the West.

I'll plan it all out, Vina says, ignoring her. He'll need masseurs, herbal remedies. I'll teach him yoga as he gets stronger. Breathing exercises too. And a strict vegetarian diet, okay.

Meat is good for muscle, protests Spenta. And fish for brain. Surely it would be best to leave such matters under professional doctors' care. It must be so, that experts' régime affords best hope of recovery.

Did the doctors wake him up, okay? Vina spits at her. Did the experts have that expertise? Okay. Time somebody started paying attention to what works.

Maybe, daughter—I don't know—maybe you're right—

Rasayana, Vina firmly prescribes. It'll make a younger man of him. Means what, child?

Sunbathing, Vina says. And herbs yoga meditation. And chanting.

Chanting, Spenta repeats, helplessly. Why not. He always loved to sing.

This is not a battle over medical treatment, but an inter-generational war of possession, and Spenta, who believes that she has already lost, has no weapons with which to fight. Unexpectedly, however, heavy artillery is offered. Big, shambling, baggy Patangbaz Kalamanja in a loose dark suit comes to call with bad news. Dolly is dead: of a thrombosis that worked its way to her generous and unsuspecting heart.

That earthquake shook something loose in her, opines Pat, his usual good-natured smile stretched by grief into a kind of snarl. Her own blood turned against her and became her killer, isn't it.

He gave the impression he was describing a murder in the family, and that was plainly how he felt. He blamed himself, of course. All these years I have foregrounded business interests and neglected the little lady, he mourned, looking like a lovelorn panda. She had Persis, but her damnfool husband sat on in Wembley, preferring to be a boss. Now she has gone! What good is Dollytone to me without my Dolly's own dear tones?

The Wembley place has been put on the market. Typically, Pat has nothing but good words for the country he is leaving. Britain is best, he says firmly. But Persis, now, she is my only home.

They are on the stone terrace overlooking the formal parterre, and Vina comes out to join them. Pat Kalamanja is rattled by the arrival of the woman whose charms defeated those of his own beloved daughter. He stiffens when introduced. Vina offers routine condolences, then, unable to check her impulses, asks whether the late Dolly lived and ate according to the principles of vegetarianism and traditional medicine; and adds, foot in mouth, that had she done so with due rigour and attention she might not have succumbed to the blood clot that stopped her heart.

The sight of a choleric Patangbaz Kalamanja, beet red of face, arms flailing, is rare indeed; yet this is the surprising Pat who rounds on Vina and lets fly. Who are you to speak of old learning? he cries. Some cheap singer, isn't it? Yet this same ayurveda you praise is expressly opposed— diametrically and inalienably opposed—to your brand of debauched activities. Music, drugs, television, sexual aggression, exciting movies, pornography, personal stereos, booze, cigarettes, the physical arousal of bodily rubbing in nightclubs and discothèques. This degraded material fills your personal environment, isn't it? Yet what are such stimuli but just the things which our learning names unnecessary and harmful? You have the cheek to speak of vegetables when your whole life is an abomination?

Just as rare as angry Pat is the spectacle of a flushed, nearly speech-less Vina. I am an entertainer, yes, she says, shaking her head as if she's been punched. But surely?, as a manufacturer of radios et cetera?, you wouldn't . . .

Your self craves excitement to fill an emptiness born of insecurity, Pat Kalamanja rages. It is an addictive personality that goes for such low-life materials. Probably you have unfulfilled desires from a past life.

Pat, be calm now. (Spenta feels obliged to intervene on her rival's side.)

It is the bad times, roars the Dollytone tycoon. Kalyug, the age of destruction! Now we see the downward mutation of the species and also of knowledge itself. The universe proceeds by mirror images, and each set of imitations and replicas is less than that which it copies. Even in my beloved Persis I see only my Dolly's echo. Charles Darwin! Evo-lution! Just a sham, isn't it? A sham and a shame.

What a thing to say about your daughter, Vina objects, rallying.

You shut off! Pat Kalamanja roars. Leave India's sacred knowledge within India's national boundaries! What is knowledge? It is the Mind of Vishwaroop, the Cosmic Entity. It is the software of universal con-sciousness. Keep out of it, you, you, *virus.*

Come away, coaxes Spenta, taking her friend's elbow. Vina is not the right target for your wrath. Fate has dealt you a cruel blow and you must strive to understand it. It is not a time to indulge.

Patangbaz subsides, panting. He is no longer the god of anger but once more a stooped widower, coming apart at the seams. You should return home also, he advises Spenta as they move away from the stunned Vina. What is here for you now?

Darius is here, she answers. I am living in his Garden of Eden and he is happily by my side. We walk and talk. It's like this.

Everywhere there are women sitting alone because of men who will not return, says Pat Kalamanja, thinking of Persis. And men also, he adds, longing for women who have gone. Life is a broken radio and there are no good songs.

Go to Persis, says Spenta, kissing him on the cheek. Cling to love while you can. At least he has his daughter, she thinks. As for herself, a vegetarian immoralist, whose determination to succeed will now be twice as great, is planning to make off with her son.

It's been ten years, more than ten. Red Nichols is dead and the Five Pennies aren't worth a nickel. When Ormus and Vina speak of love, they may be chasing phantoms. But though the body metamorphoses, it also remembers. They remember each other's moves, each other's need and smell and touch, each other's extremeness.

There's forgetting, too. Her return, his awakening: they feel like they've journeyed to a city they've both visited in dreams. Everything's familiar, there is much that tugs at the heart, but they don't know their way around. And there are whole neighbourhoods they've never seen.

They set out to learn each other again.

I've been alone, she says. Even when there was a man in my bed; maybe particularly then. You don't know, she says. You truly have no notion. A woman alone in this assassin's business, this thief's murderer's rapist's business. Sometimes you don't get paid. And after they steal your money they bootleg your work, they dirty your reputation, they call you whore.

You don't want to know what I have done. I have danced in a G-string in dirty Midwest dives. Bums in Atlantic City bars have put their hands on me, but I always knew I was a queen in exile, I had that in me?, the waiting?, the knowing my kingdom would come. One day, I knew, the poor would beg me for money and I would say, no dice, jack, I did my hustling, go do yours. People. Always hitting you up, always hitching a ride.

He says, weakly, you sound like you've lived a hundred years.

Two hundred, she says. My heart broke open and history fell in. That, and the future too. I go back a century to ugly Ma Rainey preaching Trust No Man, and forward a century to some space kitty floating weightless round the moon and singing to a stadium in the sky. I sat at the feet of Memphis Minnie, who's only just alive?, a fat balloon in a wheelchair now, she stopped crying just long enough to boast how she out-guitared Broonzy and to teach me the Minnie-Jitis. And what Holiday said about herself you know to be true of me. I was a woman when I was sixteen. Now I'm old as money, old as gold. Now I'm old as love.

He staggers in the gardens, struggling for his lost strength, his storied grace.

I want my man, she croons. I want my man. I don't want a skinny man, and I don't want a fat, and I don't want a man who cares about such things as that. And I don't want him angry, and I don't want him mean, and I don't want him sugar sweet or cute or peachy keen. And I found my man. I found my man.

The blues is just another name for not having any place, she sings. The blues is looking down at planet earth when you're stuck in outer space. Now that I've found you baby I can leave the blues behind. I can put my arms around you and ease my troubled mind. Rock and roll, she lets fly with the full force of her voice. My baby taught me how to rock and roll. I was half, he made me whole, if he's the bridge I'll pay his toll. Rock and roll. My baby taught me how to rock and roll.

To restore his energy she gives him aloe vera juice to drink and teaches him yogic breathing. What worries her most are his vibrations. She makes him spread his hand out flat on a board and hangs a crystal pendant over it. At once the crystal begins to swing insanely around, describing intricate patterns in the air, as if in the grip of a force field of unimaginable strength. She gasps and catches at it, even though she's not supposed to. I had to, she explains, it was about to shatter to bits.

It couldn't take the violence of what you're putting out. I don't know what you've got inside you?, but it's stronger than a nuclear bomb.

Three of us went west from Bombay. Of the three, it was Vina, for whom it was a return journey, who first got caught up in the gnaw and churning of the western world's spiritual hunger, its chasms of uncertainty, and turned turtle: a tough shell over insides full of mush. Vina the radical, the word-hooligan, the outlaw, the woman on the edge: open her up and you found crystals and ether, you found someone who longed to be a disciple and be shewn the straight path. Which was a part of Ormus's power over her, and India's too. As for me, she found me anomalous, oxymoronic, an accusation she might profitably have levelled at herself (but never did). Rai, the un-Indian Indian, the easterner without a spiritual side: she needed to conquer me, to show me the truth about myself, which in her forcefully expressed view I was busily denying. So she kept coming back to me, bouncing between Ormus's bed and mine.

Also, of course, she liked illicit sex. *I want more than what I want.*

When he was strong enough to make love it was our turn, his and mine, to circle round the bed, Vina remembers. (I'm in bed myself by this time, and I've had a bellyful of Vina's Ormusings but I can't shut her up, nobody ever could.) Like stringed magnets, she says. Like dancers at a masked ball, only undressed.

Vina, for petesake. It's late.

Okay, but we did. At that moment which should have been a happy time, you know?, after everything?, we both you could say all of a sudden got to the point, a.k.a. our little deficiency in the department of trust.

Now why would that be an issue between you, I wonder, applying my lips to her moderately interested nipple. Why would the two of you mmff have anything to discuss ffwp in that region whatsoever. Is that mmhm mmhm nice.

Which murmured sarcasms, as I should have known, provoke a Vina tirade. Their unspoken sub-text—you were the broken promise, lady, the one who walked out on him, and as your presence within my bedroom walls goes some distance to proving, infidelity's your middle name—brings her bolt upright in bed, pushing angry hands into the depths of her hair as if in search of a weapon. Vina can do five min-utes—*twenty* minutes—on almost any topic under the sun, and I am now given, with many added expletives, which I shall delete, her impromptu but impressively polished riff on trust, argued as is her cus-tom from the general—trust as an aspect of modernity, its possibility and necessity created by our release from the tribe into the self—to the particular, namely, that which existed or did not exist between herself and Ormus; and, peripherally, me.

The allegedly permanent breakdown of trust between men and women: it's a long time since this began to sound unoriginal, even though it has to be admitted she has a right to the subject, as one of the first women to make it her own, and to keep shouting until it became everybody else's. Scarcely more interesting is her argument that women no longer see men purely as individuals, but think of them as repositories and products of the ignoble history of their sex. But then comes a neat twist. If men are not entirely individuals (and nor are women), then they can't be held fully responsible for their actions, since responsibility is a concept that can exist only in the context of the modern idea of the auto-determinant self. As products of history, as mere culturally generated automata, we're excluded from trusting and being trusted, because trust can exist only where responsibility can be—is—taken.

Professor Vina. I seem to remember she did end up holding some sort of honorary chair in one of the newer disciplines at a small, chic liberal-arts college in Annandale-on-Hudson. I certainly remember her amazing years as a lecture tourist. (This was after VTO stopped performing in public and before she attempted that final, fatal solo comeback.) She went on the college circuit with her "chautauquas," a word she stole from Robert Pirsig's Zen best-seller and re-cycled to describe her otherwise impossible to categorize stand-up evenings mixing ideological harangues, comic cabaret turns, autobiographical self-exposure and overpowering songs. The original, authentic chau-tauqua was a Native American talk-gathering, but Vina was never big on discussion or, indeed, on authenticity, which she held to be a per-nicious notion that needed "deconstruction." Her chautauquas were really improvised monologues, whose closest cousins were the oral

narrative sessions of the great Indian storytellers, actually existing Indians from actually existing India, as she liked to say, pulling rank over
the Red kind and meaning it, although it was a part of her magic, the
thing that made her the colossal figure she became, that—publicly, at
any rate—no Native Americans ever took offence.

I remember, I photographed, the rapt upturned faces of the wor-
shipful college young listening to this grand survivor of the heroic age
who prowled the stage attired in wildly eclectic ethnic symbols, mojos,
caftans, quetzal feathers, classical breastplates, tika marks, and held forth
in shockingly explicit detail about her own life, its highs and lows, its
sexual adventures and political encounters (sometimes these strands
became deliciously entwined, as for example in her account of a long
weekend in the private lodge of a Caribbean dictator with too much
beard and not enough chin). Without warning, she'd electrify her
young audiences by surging out of anecdote into heart-stopping *a
capella* renderings of gospel songs, blues standards, jazz-scat Ella music,
soft bossa nova shuffles and rock anthems, all in that voice, Our Mistress's Voice, her true gift to us all, an instrument that was, literally, too
good for this world. Literally, to die for.

On stage or in my bed, Professor Vina was one of Vina's most awesome alter egos, it was some performance, but even as I listened quietly to the battlefield thunder of her arguments, I found myself
noticing the cracks and rifts she was trying to cover up, the divisions
in her soul, and thinking that Maria the disappearing nympho had a
point when she spoke of our inner irreconcilability, the tectonic contradictoriness that has gotten into us all and has commenced to rip us
to pieces like the unstable earth itself.

Professor Vina and Crystal Vina, Holy Vina and Profane Vina, Junkie
Vina and Veggie Vina, Women's Vina and Vina the Sex Machine,
Barren-Childless-Tragic Vina and Traumatized-Childhood-Tragedy
Vina, Leader Vina who blazed a trail for a generation of women and
Disciple Vina who came to think of Ormus as the One she had always
sought. She was all of these and more, and everything she was, she
pitched uncompromisingly high. There was no Self-Effacing Vina to
set against Vina of the Screamingly Stretched Extremes.

That's why people loved her, remember: for making herself the
exaggerated avatar of their own jumbled selves, but pushed to the edge

or, better, driven to the heights: of talent and articulacy and outrageousness and promiscuity and self-destructiveness and intellect and
passion and life. Higher Vina, engendering in the multitude a recipro-
cally higher, though entirely earthly, love.

As for the particular, the matter of trust between Ormus Cama and
herself, an issue in which I myself have been a significant if ultimately
peripheral factor, Vina uses her cockeyed theories of the externally
determined self to bring in a not-guilty verdict on her many infideli-
ties and desertions. The girl can't help it, that's what her position comes
down to, when you strip away all the long words. What's in her nature
is just there, generated by history or genes or sexual politics, it doesn't
finally matter which. It's as if Olive Oyl were to usurp the catchphrase
of Popeye the Sailor Man. *I yam what I yam an' that's what I yam.* It's
like all the justifications of infidelity which men have used since time
began.

Take it or leave it, she said; and Ormus took it—irresistible Ormus,
for love of whom so many women pined, for whom the saintly beauty
Persis Kalamanja had sacrificed all her hopes of joy.

Can there be a great love without trust?

Sho' thing, Rai, honey, she says, doing her panther stretch and ghetto
drawl, sho' nuff they can. An' Ormus and me, we is the ever-livin'
proof.

(*Ever-living,* I find myself thinking. *Vina, don't tempt fate.*)

Aloud I say, You know, Vina, I don't really get it. I never have. The
way you two are together. How does that work exactly?

She laughs. Higher love, she answers. Love on a higher level. Just
think of it like that. Like, exaltation.

She's relaxing now, having talked herself back into a good mood.
When she isn't spaced out or blazing mad she can take a joke. Where
was I, she says, settling back, her head on my stomach. Oh, right. We
were circling the bed. He was out of the orangery by then?, I should
mention that. Adios to that goddamn glass box. Instead this dusty bedroom full of disapproving clubmen frowning off the walls and above
them if you believe plaster copies of classical friezes. And on

Corinthian pedestals, marble busts. Persons in togas with laurel wreaths sitting on their ears. It's the seventies and the world's falling apart?, but we're given the fucking Parthenon to sleep in. The curtains by the way you would otherwise find only in old movie theatres, that dark sea of cloth, I expected them at some point to lift?, and for there to be I don't know trailers, commercials, our feature presentation. But okay, guess what?, the main attraction was us.

When Vina settles in for one of these all-night marathons, once she's started running on her personal movie screen a selection from her library of personal lifetime classics—and it might turn out to be a double or even triple bill—you just pass the popcorn and diet cola and go with the sleep option, having no other. Sleep for me has not for many years been a thing to look forward to. There are pictures in my head too, and at most of them I'd rather not take a second look.

I have much to say about myself, I have my own stories to tell. Mostly they'll wait. (While the gods are occupying centre stage, we mortals must hang about in the wings. But after the stars have finished all their tragic dying, the extras come on stage—it's the end of the big banquet scene—and we get to eat up all the fucking food.) But the pictures are here now. I can't put them back in their box.

A photographer has a second portfolio that he can't show because he never got the images on to film. If he's a photo-journalist many of these pictures visit him in dreams and ruin his fitful nights. Bobby Flow, the control-freak genius of the Nebuchadnezzar Agency, had three words that he said taught you all you needed to be good at the job. *Get up close.* Which he brilliantly did until somebody blew his head off in a swamp in Indochina, that being an occupational hazard. And the other one is when they don't blow your head off, because then it fills up with the actually existing world, the big picture of the world as it is when somebody peels the skin off. Flayed. Red in tooth and claw. Earthrise re-shot as a bleeding broken skull hanging in exploding space.

I got up close enough times, too many, and I have my battle tales, my tall stories, like everyone else. Photographs taken while sheltering from bullets behind the dead bodies of other photographers. Wall-eyed toothless lunatics with Uzis shoving their guns' noses into my stomach, and even, once, into my mouth. The day I was pushed up against an ochre wall and made the subject of a mock execution, a Slav warlord's little joke. Listen: it's nothing. I seek neither to brag nor to complain. I went because it was my thing, my need. Some go because it's their need to die, some to see death, some to boast when they get back alive. (Everyone's a philosopher.) I could say guilt's got nothing to do with it, that film removed from a dead man's shoe is ancient history, but I'd be lying. That is, up to a point I'd be lying, because while I admit, okay, sure, every time I stand up in front of a screaming child with a bazooka I'm trying to prove I deserve to be there, I have the right to be carrying that camera, that accreditation— if you want ten-cent Lucy van Pelt psychoanalysis, there it is. What really interests and scares me is that the drive goes deeper than that, deeper even than the picture of a man hanging from a slowly rotating fan.

Something in me wants the dreadful, wants to stare down the human race's worst-case scenarios.

I need to know that evil exists and how to recognize it if I pass it in the street. I need it not to be abstract; to understand it by feeling its effect on me, the corrosion, the burn. Once in a chemistry exam I dropped concentrated acid on my hand, and the speed with which the brown stain spread across my skin was even more frightening than the acid itself. Science-fictional speed. But the point is I recovered, I'm fine, my hand works. Does this sound like self-justification? That every time I come away from my chicken game against evil, it's like proving at least to myself that the bad guys still lose a few, they can even have a really long loser streak?

It does?

Okay, so I'm just a violence junkie and one day I'll OD. Like Bobby Flow. Hulot's the clever one. He gave up taking pictures and paints watercolours instead. His paintings are truly dreadful, the worst type of *petit-maître* banality. He has discovered sentimentality and good taste in his old age and these two elderly nursemaids will keep him alive.

I don't need to tell you where I've been. You know already. This Southeast Asian swamp burning with eerie napalm fire, that casual pile of heads by the side of a dusty African road, this terrorist attack on a Mideast market square, that Latin American village mourning its busload of land-mined kids. Sure you do. You've seen my work. We all do this work. It's what's wanted.

And when I can't stand hell any more I change my clothes, I put on some of the best casualwear Seventh Avenue has to offer, head for the studio and drop in on pussy heaven: fashion photography, when you can make beautiful women in expensive clothes behave as if they were in a war zone. They stare, leap, spin, gasp, duck, arch, jerk. I've seen machine-gun fire take a body that way.

That's not all I do with them. It depends on the girl. Some of them are calm and I go with that, I create seas of calm around them, oceans of light and shadow. I drown them in peace until it scares them, and then they come alive. Others know something of my more brutal work and want to show me how real they are, how much they know of harshness, of the street. The contrast between harshness and couture usually works, until it becomes a cliché. Then for a while I go with beauty, piling beauty on beauty, making it overwhelming, almost indecent, like a ravishment.

So that, too, ends up being an assault.

And there's portraiture, though I'm not always as lucky as I was with the erection guy. And there's advertising. And there is more private, essayistic work, but maybe I'll save that for another day. I'm tired. The pictures are coming. The pictures you haven't seen, the ones that come at night.

In the beginning was the tribe, clustering around the fire, a single multi-bodied collective entity standing back-to-back against the enemy, which was the rest of everything-that-was. Then for a little while we broke away, we got names and individuality and privacy and big ideas, and that started a wider fracturing, because if we could do it—us, the planet kings, the gobblers with the lock on the food chain, the guys in the catbird seat—if we could cut ourselves loose, then so could everything else, so could event and space and time and description and fact, so could reality itself. Well, we weren't expecting to be followed, we didn't realize we were starting anything, and it looks like it's scared us so profoundly, this fracturing, this tumbling of walls, this forgodsake freedom, that at top speed we're rushing back into our skins and war paint, postmodern into premodern, back to the future. That's what I see when I'm a camera: the battle lines, the corrals, the stockades, the pales, the secret handshakes, the insignia, the uniforms, the lingo, the closing in, the shallow graves, the high priests, the non-negotiable currencies, the junk, the booze, the fifty-year-old ten-year-olds, the blood-dimm'd tide, the slouching towards Bethlehem, the suspicion, the loathing, the closed shutters, the pre-judgements, the scorn, the hunger, the thirst, the cheap lives, the cheap shots, the anathemas, the minefields, the demons, the demonized, the führers, the warriors, the veils, the mutilations, the no-man's-land, the paranoias, the dead, the dead.

Professor Vina's rhetoric: here's where it leads.

Can you hear in my voice that I'm angry? Good. I've been reading a book about anger. It says that anger is evidence of our idealism. Something has gone wrong, but we "know," in our rage, that things could be different. *It shouldn't be this way.* Anger as an inarticulate theory of justice, which, when you act it out, is called revenge. (Alternatively of course I'm just another choleric snappeur, warped by life, by endlessly playing second fiddle to the main event. This is the clickista's indispensable but somehow low-grade work: second-fiddling while Rome burns. . . . And here, in bed, with Vina? No difference. Ormus Cama is in the seat reserved for the first violin.)

When Vina is angry with me, she remembers the rage of my mother, Ameer Merchant, which drove her away from us, away from love. This is why I forgive her the vindictive remarks. I know I'm standing in for Ameer when Vina lets fly, and I can't help thinking she's sort of entitled.

When I'm angry with her, I remember my mother too. I remember Ameer taking Vina under her wing, teaching her, oiling and brushing her, kohling and hennaing her, pouring herself into that brilliant damaged girl. I remember my own unresolved quarrel with my mother, my broken-home anger, my accusations, the pain I heaped on her own bitter unhappiness. I look at Vina and see Ameer in her. Once, I showed her the pictures I'd taken of my mother on the day of her death. I wanted to see if Vina saw it: the likeness.

She saw it right away. Hat Cheap Suit, she said. But she wasn't thinking of the female pharaoh, and nor was I. She was thinking, *this is me. This is a picture of the future, an image of my own death.*

And as things turned out she was almost right; because when she died, there were no deathbed photos. There wasn't a deathbed, or a body to take a picture of.

My mother's photograph was almost all we had.

Vina's still talking, and all at once she's uncertain, now that she's arriving at the point of the story she wants my full attention, but my consciousness is slipping away, I'm all in, done for, crashing.

Rai?

Mmhm?

It's as if we were both watching—for something, you know—in each other, that is—it's like what you do?, when you're taking a photograph?, and sometimes you wait and wait and it doesn't come, but when it comes, you've got it?, bang?, one shot and it's yours? What's that called? Rai? What's that called?

Unhnh.

So that's what happened. All the pretence just slipped away?, all the injury?, all the past?, and we just, just. Clicked. The decisive moment. That's it. *Click*.

Hynhnyhnm.

By the way, his bruise vanished, she's saying, but her voice is fading out. The birthmark on his eyelid. Did you know that? He hasn't got it any more.

I don't care. I'm asleep.

12

TRANSFORMER

In a pool of light on the red-eye to New York there's a sleepless Hispanic kid, baleful of eye, wrestling grimly with a new kind of science fiction plaything. It's some sort of motor car, but he's not interested in playing vroom-vroom, he's pulling the car apart. Its fins swivel, its tires swing out until they're at right angles to the folding table, its body hinges and opens like an anatomy model. Dazzlingly, startling the brain, it unfolds, exfoliates, deconstructs itself and then clicks together in new, unforeseeable configurations. The boy is finding it difficult to grasp the last secrets of this metamorphic riddle. More than once he slams it down on the table, where it lies unfinished, trapped in an unreadable transitional phase. The noise wakes up the masked sleepers around him, and transfers the boy's own annoyance to these adult others. Finally the dozing man in the aisle seat, his father probably, pushes back his sleep mask and with swift irritable hairy hands shows the boy the gimmick of the toy, and then all at once the car has vanished, and what's standing there instead, rearing up on metallic hind legs, is a big little monster, a grotesque techno-being, some sort of fierce robot thing brandishing lurid, finny ray guns in outsize gauntleted fists. The twentieth century—the car—has been supplanted by this visitor from a dystopic future.

The child begins to play. Boom! Boom! The robot annihilates the seat in front, the armrests, many passengers. In a while the boy falls asleep, cradling the monster in his arms, not at all alarmed by the idea that the commonplace machinery of the present contains the secrets of such apocalyptic tomorrows, that we could transform our quotidian roadsters, our unassuming station wagons, our bourgeois sedans, into fearsome war machines if we could but learn the trick.

Boom! Boom! The boy dreams of destroying the world.

Ormus Cama, watching from across the aisle, is caught up in a fantastic fiction of his own; except that it's no fiction. There is a world other than ours and it's bursting through our own continuum's flimsy defenses. If things get much worse the entire fabric of reality could collapse. These are the extraordinary thoughts he's having, trembling intimations of the end of things, and there's one accompanying puzzle: How come he's the only one who can see the vision? An event on this cosmic scale? Is everybody sleepwalking? Don't they even care?

The northern lights hang around the aircraft, blowing in the solar wind like giant golden curtains—like answers—but Ormus isn't interested, he's lost in his questions. What, Vina asks, struck by the hunted look on him. What. She's bewildered by what he's doing with his eyes, he's closing first one, then the other, winking into the night sky over Greenland like an old lecher making a pass.

Ormus, come on, you're scaring me.

You wouldn't believe me anyway.

I believed you before, didn't I? Gayomart, remember? The songs in your head.

That's right. That's right, back then you were the one who did.

Well then. *What.*

So he confesses the truth which he himself finds beyond belief: that ever since she awoke him from his long beauty sleep he's been living in—or rather with—two worlds at once. He tries to describe to her what he first saw on the flight to London, the gash in the real. Is it like a hole?, like a black or some other color hole?, in the sky?, she struggles to picture it. No, he says, and clutches at the billowing aurora for help. Imagine if this, he says, waving an arm, this, us, where we are, all of it, if it was all a movie on a screen and we were in it, a huge screen like at a drive-in or just hanging in space like a curtain, and then suppose there were slashes in the screen, a mad knifeman ran into the cinema and hacked at that curtain, so now there are these great rips going right across everything, across you, across the window, across the wing out there, across the stars, and you can see that behind the screen there's a whole other set of things going on, maybe another whole I don't know level, or maybe another movie screen with another movie playing, and there are people in that movie looking the other way through the rips and maybe seeing us. And beyond that movie another movie and another and another until who can guess.

There are things he doesn't tell her at this time. He doesn't say, some people seem to have found a slip-sliding method of moving between the worlds. He doesn't say, there's this woman, I don't have any way of stopping her, she shows up whenever she feels like it. He doesn't speak the name Maria.

There's an in-flight movie playing in the next sector of the plane, where the insomniacs are seated. Vina can see the small screen hanging in the darkness a way off. A Scottish doctor keeps turning into a twisted monster and back again. It's that remake, she recognizes it, of the old horror picture, Dr. whatever and Mr. right. Looks like a dud. Even the insomniacs haven't lasted the course. The film's images float silently over the airborne cargo of sleepers, dreaming towards America. Vina is on the edge of her seat. She feels elated, panicky, confused all at once, and flounders for the right thing to say. Where's your bruise, she eventually asks, touching his left eyelid gently. What happened to that, your magic bruise. You had an accident and lost a contusion?, that's what?, illogical.

He's gone, Ormus says. His expression is terrible to behold. Gayomart. He burst out of my head and vanished. I'm alone in here now. He's free.

No bruise but his eyes are different colors.

There's more, he says. The bruise has faded, but now the blind eye's the one that's seeing things. If I close it, the manifestation goes away. At least it goes away most of the time. Sometimes it's so powerful I can even see it with both eyes shut. But shutting the eye is maybe ninety-five percent effective. Then if I close my right eye and it's just the left one that's open it's like dying. Everything disappears and only the otherness is left. As if I'm standing in a snowstorm and looking through windows into another place and in that place, I don't know how to explain this, I'm not even sure if I exist.

He does not add, but then there is Maria.

He sounds wired, screechy. He is saying things that cannot be. I've been thinking, he offers shakily. I was wondering, maybe an eye patch.

Voices, she asks, do you hear voices. What are they saying to you, is there any message. Maybe you should be listening for that, a communication, something important for you to pass on.

This would be a good moment to mention the nocturnal visitor, but Ormus sidesteps it. You aren't freaking out, he notes with admiration. There are those who would run screaming. I'm crazy, raving, don't you think so, most people would. I was in a coma for more than a thousand and one nights, maybe I came out doolally which in case you aren't aware is madness from India. Homegrown, the local brand. Deolali. The heat there drove the British soldiers off their heads. But what, you don't think I'm boiling mad, you think it's possible.

I always knew there was something beyond, she says, letting him rest his head on her bosom in the pressurized dark. I always knew it even when you or Rai made fun. What, this dump was all we got?, no higher-rent accommodations to aspire to?, impossible. But I don't know. You took some pretty hard hits in that crash, so it could be—and I'm not a doctor, okay—double vision, some neural hallucination, the brain can do that?, or maybe it's true, you're looking into another whole thing. I always was the open-minded one. I'm expecting aliens to vacuum me up any day now. Or again, yeah, maybe you're nuts. Which also makes no difference. Have you noticed how many people are nuts? I'm beginning to think it's everyone?, only most of them haven't noticed. In which case sanity isn't the crucial issue. The crucial issue is what do I think of you, and I already answered that by taking an earlier plane, the one from Bombay. You called, I answered. And then I called to you and you opened your eyes. Two-way radio. What do you want, a neon sign? I feel the earth move under my feet. This can't be love I get no dizzy spell. Read my lips. I already made my choice.

There's no message, he says.

It's not paradise, he says. It's not so very unlike here. What I catch glimpses of through the shredding—and I'm starting to see more clearly—I'd call them variations, moving like shadows behind the stories we know. This doesn't have to be supernature, it doesn't have to be god. It could be just—don't ask me—physics, okay? It could be some physics beyond our present capacity to comprehend. It could just be I found a way of stepping outside the picture. There's a Pop Art dance pattern piece by Amos Voight, he says. An Arthur Murray School affair with outlines and arrows, left foot right foot, you get up on to it and follow the steps. Except in this case at a certain moment all your weight's on the foot you're supposed to move. So the pattern doesn't work, it's a joke, a trap. Unless you take a foot off it, change your weight and continue. You have to break the rules, deny the frame story, smash the frame. There's this Russian word, he says. *Vnenakhodimost.* Outsideness. It could be I found the outsideness of what we're inside. The way out from the carnival grounds, the secret turnstile. The route through the looking glass. The technique for jumping the points, from one track to the other. Universes like parallel bars, or tv channels. Maybe there are people who can swing from bar to bar, people who can if you understand me channel-hop. Zappers. Maybe I'm a zapper myself, he says. Exercising a kind of remote control.

Remote controls for tv sets were new then. They were just beginning to be used as similes and metaphors.

What's it like, she wants to know. The other world.

I told you, he answers, feeling the onset of the weary blues. The same only different. John Kennedy got shot eight years ago. Don't laugh, Nixon's President. East Pakistan recently seceded from the union. Refugees, guerrillas, genocide, all of that. And the British aren't in Indochina, imagine that; but the war's there all right, even if the places have different names. I don't know how many universes there are but probably that damn war's in every one. And Dow Chemicals and napalm bombs. *Two, four, six, eight, no more naphthene palmitate*—they've got another name for that too, but it burns little girls' skins the same way. Naptate.

He says, there's a ton of singers in sequins and eyeliner, but no trace of Zoo Harrison or Jerry Apple or Icon or The Clouds, and Lou Reed's a *man.* There's Hollywood but they never heard of Elrond Hubbard or Norma Desmond, and Charles Manson's a mass murderer, and Allen Konigsberg never directed a picture and Guido Anselmi doesn't exist. Nor do Dedalus or Caulfield or Jim Dixon, by the way, they never wrote any books, and the classics are different too.

Vina's eyes have been growing wider, she's been emitting suppressed little giggles of disbelief, she can't help it.

The Garden of Forking Paths, he says, naming her favorite nineteenth-century novel, the interminable masterwork of the Chinese genius, the former governor of Yunnan province, Ts'ui Pên.

What about it? Don't tell me they don't . . .

(She's actually angry: this is the last straw, her face says.)

No such book, he says, and she slams fist into palm.

Damn it, Ormus, and then she controls herself, doesn't let her thoughts slip past her lips: *This is a joke, right. Or else you're really mad.*

He reads her mind anyway. All my life, he says—and there's despair dragging at his voice, distorting the way it sounds—it's been the empire of the senses for me. What you can touch and taste and smell and hear and see. All my speeches in praise of the actual, of what is and persists, and no time for the airy-fairy. And now here in spite of it all are fairies from the fucking ether. All that is solid melts into fucking air. What am I supposed to do?

Make it sing, she says. Write it with all your heart and gift and hold on to the hooks, the catchy lyrics, the tunes. Fly me to that moon.

He sings other men's soft, muffled odes into her consoling breast. You are my sunshine. I'm a king bee. Hold me tight.

Music will save us, she comforts him. That, and, and.

Love, he says. The word you want is love.

Yeah that was it, she grins, caressing his cheek. I knew that.

Will you marry me?

No.

Why the fuck not?

Because you're an insane person, asshole. Go to sleep.

The world is irreconcilable, it doesn't add up, but if we cannot agree with ourselves that it does, we can't make judgements or choices. We can't live.

When Ormus Cama saw his vision, he revealed himself to be a true prophet, and I say this as a dyed-in-the-wool unbeliever. I mean: he was genuinely ahead of his time. We've all caught up now. He isn't here to see them, but the contradictions in the real have become so glaring, so inescapable, that we're all learning to take them in our stride. We go to bed thinking—just a random example—that Mr. N—— M—— or Mr. G—— A—— is a notorious terrorist, and wake up hailing him as the savior of his people. One day the islanders inhabiting a particular cold wet lump of godforsaken rock are vile devil worshippers swigging blood and sacrificing babies, the next day it's as if nothing of the sort ever occurred. The leaders of whole countries vanish as if they never were, they're miraculously erased from the record, and then they pop up again as talk show hosts or pizza pluggers, and lo!, they're back in the history books again.

Certain illnesses sweep across large communities, and then we learn that no such illnesses ever existed. Men and women recover memories of having been sexually abused as children. Whoosh, no they don't, their parents are reinstated as the most loving and laudable people you could imagine. Genocide occurs; no it doesn't. Nuclear waste contaminates large swathes of entire continents, and we all learn words like "half-life." But in a flash all the contamination has gone, the sheep aren't ticking, you can happily eat your lamb chops.

The maps are wrong. Frontiers snake across disputed territory, bending and cracking. A road no longer goes where it went yesterday. A lake vanishes. Mountains rise and fall. Well-known books acquire different endings. Color bursts out of black-and-white movies. Art is a hoax. Style is substance. The dead are embarrassing. There are no dead.

You're a sports fan but the rules are different every time you watch. You've got a job! No you don't! That woman powdered the President's johnson! In her dreams—she's a celebrated fantasist! You're a sex god! You're a sex pest! She's to die for! She's a slut! You don't have cancer! April Fool, yes you do! That good man in Nigeria is a murderer! That murderer in Algeria is a good man! That psycho killer is an American patriot! That American psycho is a patriot killer! And is that Pol Pot dying in the Angkoran jungle, or merely No! Not?

These things are bad for you: sex, high-rise buildings, chocolate, lack of exercise, dictatorship, racism! No, *au contraire!* Celibacy damages the brain, high-rise buildings bring us closer to God, tests show that a bar of chocolate a day significantly improves children's academic performance, exercise kills, tyranny is just a part of our culture so I'll thank you to keep your cultural-imperialist ideas off my fucking fiefdom, and as for racism, let's not get all preachy about this, it's better out in the open than under some grubby carpet. That extremist is a moderate! That universal right is culturally specific! This circumcised woman is culturally happy! That Aboriginal whistlecockery is culturally barbaric! Pictures don't lie! This image has been faked! Free the press! Ban nosy journalists! The novel is dead! Honor is dead! God is dead! Aargh, they're all alive, and they're coming after us! That star is rising! No, she's falling! We dined at nine! We dined at eight! You were on time! No, you were late! East is West! Up is down! Yes is No! In is Out! Lies are Truth! Hate is Love! Two and two makes five! And everything is for the best, in this best of all possible worlds.

Music will save us, and love. When reality bites, and it bites me almost every day, I need Ormus's music, his take. Here it is in my hand, shining like a National guitar: "Song of Everything"'s the track I'm choosing, the first song he wrote in America, at Tempe Harbor, within days of his arrival. I'm sitting here at the end of time with my good friend Mira Celano—and there's a lot to tell you about *her* later in the program—so, Mira, this one's for you.

Everything you thought you knew: it's not true. And everything you knew you said, was all in your head. And everything you did and everywhere you went, well you never ever did that and you were not sent. I think you'll find we're trapped in someone else's mind. Yes I think you'll find we're trapped in someone else's mind. And it's only make-believe but we can't leave it behind.

Everything you think you see: it can't be. There's just me.

Darling there's just me, just me.

In a time of constant transformation, beatitude is the joy that comes with belief, with certainty. The beatific bathe in almighty love, wear smug grins and play their harps and acoustic guitars. Safe in their cocoon from the storms of metamorphosis, the blessed give thanks for their unchangingness and ignore the leg irons biting into their ankles. It's eternal bliss, but nix nix, you can keep that jailhouse cell. The Beats and their Generation were wrong. Beatitude is the prisoner's surrender to his chains.

Happiness, now, that's something else again. Happiness is human, not divine, and the pursuit of happiness is what we might call love. This love, earthly love, is a truce between metamorphs, a temporary agreement not to shape-shift while kissing or holding hands. Love is a beach towel spread over shifting sands. Love is intimate democracy, a compact that insists on renewals, and you can be voted out overnight, however big your majority. It's fragile, precarious, and it's all we can get without selling our souls to one party or the other. It's what we can have while remaining free. This is what Vina Apsara meant when she spoke of a love without trust. All treaties can be broken, all promises end up as lies. Sign nothing, make no promises. Make a provisional reconciliation, a fragile peace. If you're lucky it might last five days; or fifty years.

I offer all this—the airplane terror and doubt, my own post facto musings, his lyrics (which some British professor calls poetry, but then there's always a professor; to me, set down on the page without their music, they seem kind of spavined, even hamstrung)—so that you can have a sense of the amazing realizations to which Ormus Cama was quickly coming. He'd been given a second chance at life, a second act in a country whose citizens' lives famously don't have second acts, and he had concluded that he'd been allowed back for a purpose. Chosen. He was struggling for other language, language that didn't imply an allower, a chooser, but the inertia in language is hard to resist, the inexorable advancing weight of its accumulated history. And all this had filled him up with new music. He was bursting with the stuff, and now that we know the stuff he was bursting with, the image of his arrival in America—that pale man in his mid-thirties with haunted eyes, still gaunt-faced and dressed in crummy bluejeans—feels like a hinge moment, around which turned so much that would become our shared experience, part of the way we saw and constructed ourselves.

Ormus Cama sees the mighty pincushion of Manhattan puncturing the haze of the high dawn air and begins to smile the smile of a man who has just discovered that his favorite fiction turns out to be no lie. As the plane banks and drops he recalls my father Vivvy Merchant's love of Queen Catherine of Braganza, through whom Bombay and New York are forever yoked together. But this recollection fades almost at once: because from the start it was the cloudscrapers of the isle of the Manhattoes that pricked Ormus's heart, he shared my mother's dream of conquering the sky, and never itched for the thronged streets of Queens, its bazaars bustling with the polyglot traffic of the world. Vina, on the other hand, Vina whom Ameer Merchant loved, never ceased to be a street urchin in her heart, even when immense celebrity forced her into its glittering cage. But New York, for Ormus, was from the beginning a doorman, an express elevator and a view. You could say it was Malabar Hill.

The city is temporarily withheld, however: in the words of Langston Hughes, a dream deferred. Yul Singh has arranged everything—documents, permissions, limousine—and has placed one of his country residences, for the purpose of "decompression," of effecting a "soft landing," at the disposal of the "lovebirds." This it's a hell of a place which I say so myself, the winery there makes a powerful Pinot Noir, you two should take time out, drink some wine, think about the future, which okay you're not so young Ormus but the old guys are doing okay, you catch my drift, there's potential, and with Vina beside you she's a doll I don't have to tell you and that voice of hers like a fuckin' steamer horn pardon my French, it could work, no promises, it's down to the material which I don't have to tell you you should get to work on right away, but what the hey, take thirty-six hours, take two days, you wouldn't believe the line of talent at my door, longer every day, you know what I'm saying, forget about it.

Ormus receives this welcoming monologue (in which Yul Singh's tongue is shown not to be as clean as he once claimed) on the car phone in the back of a black-windowed stretch driven by one of the legendary tribe of Colchis factotums, those Americanized heavies of Punjabi descent who are Yul's bodyguards and chauffeurs, bouncers and valets, accountants and lawyers, strategists and enforcers, publicists and A&R men; who dress in identical black Valentino suits and molded shades; and who are universally known, though never in their imposing short-fused presences, as Yul's Sikh jokes. Will Singh, Kant Singh, Gota Singh, Beta Singh, Day Singh, Wee Singh, Singh Singh, and so on. If these are not their real names then everyone has long forgotten what those prosaic handles might have been. Ormus and Vina's present companion is the aforementioned Will. I'll be taking you as far as the helipad, he says, barely turning his head. Mr. Yul's personal Sikorsky will take care of your onward journey today.

No point resisting. Give in gracefully. Ormus and Vina settle back into the deep leather upholstery. Where is this honeymoon lodge, Ormus idly asks.

Sir the Finger Lakes area sir. Does that make any sense to you?

Vina sits up. It does to me. Where's it near to?

Yes ma'am, it's located at the southern tip of Lake Chickasauga. Heart of the state wine-growing region. Ma'am, this would be in the neighborhood of a little town, maybe you're familiar with it, by the name of Chickaboom.

Captivity in Egypt, Vina moans, closing her eyes. Even the Israelites didn't have to return once they'd got away.

Excuse me? Ma'am? You lost me there?

No, nothing. Thank you.

Yes ma'am.

The house at Tempe Harbor, in wood painted pale gray with white trimmings and the sort of ornate carved "lacework" more typically glimpsed through the tropical palm fronds and bougainvillea creepers of Key West, is in fact the creation of a perverse Floridan millionaire of Swiss-German origin, Manny Raabe, who escaped in old age from effete Southern warmth (and occasional hurricanes) into these bracingly nostalgic northern latitudes, and promptly died of the cold. Yul Singh has since put in an underfloor heating system and installed numerous extra chimneys and fireplaces. It's a mighty place, with two slated mansard roofs conceived on the grand scale, like Swiss Alps. Singh keeps it hot, and stuffed with parakeets and tropical plants: as if rebuking the late Raabe for his folly. There's a sauna. The chef— Kitchen Singh—is under instructions to concentrate on a strongly spiced sub-continental cuisine. Tempe Harbor has been transformed by its new owner into a shrine to heat. Which if you don't care for it I apologize, Yul Singh is on the phone the moment the chopper sets down, but if you buy a haunted house you should it's my opinion make it unattractive to the ghost.

There's no trace of a ghost but they're not the only guests. Another pair of "lovebirds" is in residence, the art-house-movie director Otto Wing and his newlywed bride, a long, gummy Nordic beauty called Ifredis, who insists on skipping naked across the midnight lawn to go skinny-dipping in Lake Chickasauga's cold black water, pursued by the scholarly, bespectacled body of her similarly nude husband, who can be heard shrieking out the *An die Freude* as the water hits his genitalia. Joy, shrieks Wing in German. Joy, thou lovely spark of God, daughter of Elysium.

There's a lot of shrieking, as it happens. Wing and Ifredis can't get enough of each other and fuck uninhibitedly whenever and wherever the spirit moves them, and it moves them all the time and all over the place. Ormus and Vina witness the lovers' passion again and again, in the mansion's many living rooms, in the lakeside gazebo, on the pool table, the tennis court, the deck.

These people, says Vina, slightly put out. They make us look like virgins.

When they're not fucking and shrieking, Wing and Ifredis are sleeping, or eating quantities of cheese and drinking orange juice by the quart. (They appear to have their own food supplies, and usually forgo Kitchen Singh's lavish banquets. They generate all the heat they can handle without his culinary aid.)

Their conversation, such as it is, touches mostly on Jesus Christ. Ifredis is a hundred-and-ten-percenter, a girl who holds nothing back. She goes in for religion with the same naked, cold-water zeal as she evidences in her shrieking sex bouts. Swiftly identifying the weak point, the wavering heathen, she pursues Ormus into the hot tub in the spa wing and interrogates him with pitying wonder dripping from her wide blue eyes. So is it really true you no god at all have? I guess not, says Ormus, unwilling to discuss his new visionary condition. There follows a long sorrowing silence, until Ormus understands that reciprocity is required of him. Oh, right, he mutters. Er, how about you?

Ifredis whoops, a long orgasmic sound. Uhh, she purrs. I just love Christ Jesus. Wing arrives, leans on the side of the tub and kisses her deeply, as if drinking at a spring, then emerges from her mouth to offer this thought. I adore in this woman her directness, he says. Her lack of irony. At the point we have reached in the century it is important to eschew all ironic communication. Now is it time to speak directly to avoid a chance of misunderstanding. In all circumstances to prioritize such avoidances.

His bride is tugging at his sleeve. Otto, she pleads, making a rubbery moue. Otto, I want to sit on your arm. She rises like a steaming Venus from the tub and they scamper off. Her English is not good, Otto sings out at Ormus over his departing shoulder. To avoid misunderstanding I should explain that at her present vocabularial level she makes occasionally a confusion of the limbs.

If one were of a paranoid disposition (and these are paranoid days) one might suppose that Yul Singh has engineered this long weekend with great deliberation: that even from distant Park Avenue Yul Singh the blind puppeteer is pulling his guests' strings, the way George Bernard Shaw up there on his godlike cloud manipulates his Higgins and Eliza marionettes on the cover of the original *My Fair Lady* cast recording.

Every detail of life at Tempe Harbor, after all, bears witness to the long reach of the mogul's influence. Even in his absence, Cool Yul is a hands-on host. There are the unpredictable but frequent phone calls to both guests and staff, there is the meticulous attention to detail: the vegetarian menu for Vina, the doctor in residence in case Ormus's health should suddenly deteriorate. The décor is a curious mixture of European high good taste and Indo-American flaunt-it brashness: antique Louis Quinze chairs imported from France and reupholstered in monogrammed powder-blue silk. YSL. The monogram (for Yul Singh Lahori, his rarely used full name) is ubiquitous: on most of the furnishings, on the specially rolled in-house cigars and cigarettes, on the silver cufflinks presented as keepsakes by the housekeeper Clea Singh to all male guests, and even on each thick square of the personalized toilet paper rolls and the house range of TH condoms, sanitary napkins and tampons discreetly positioned, according to gender, in the his-and-hers bathrooms that are a feature of each guest suite. Framed gold and platinum records line the walls; also portraits of the great man—who bears more than a passing resemblance to the actor Vincent Price, that smooth nocturnal prince of the fanged classes—and of his aristocratically etiolated and long-suffering French wife Marie-Pierre d'Illiers. Who I must personally admit is my symbolic ideal, my immortal tea cake, who when I taste her lips I remember everything important in life, Yul Singh confides to Ormus on the phone. Okay, so you want to ask now about my, don't bother to pretend you don't know this, on the surface contradictory and also extremely public liaisons with as they say a string of young beauties, he goes on. The famous disarming grin, the helpless spreading of the arms, come across to Ormus even down the telephone. Alas, Singh confesses, quite unabashed—his Indian reticence supplanted by this adopted American confessional style—memory is a great quality, also possessing considerable erotic force, by the way, which strictly speaking you don't need to know that, it's a private matter between myself and the lady, nevertheless as I was saying remembrance is tops, but sometimes by way of contrast it is even better to forget.

Yul is a ruthless visionary, an amoral schemer. Might it not be a part of his grand design to throw cold water over Ormus and Vina's grand renewed passion, by offering them, in the form of Wing and Ifredis, an admonitory pair of Vargas caricatures of themselves? Happiness writes white, Montherlant said, and Yul Singh, an educated man for all his down-market posturing, is able to take a smart tip. Lovebirds bill and coo and don't get much work done. A little trouble in paradise might well be worth stirring up.

And the Jesus-freak material? Just adds an extra piquancy to the sauce.

Is this scripted dialogue and action? Are these *actors*?

Probe a little more deeply into the Tempe Harbor episode, and further reverberations can be felt. YSL is a lifelong philanderer who nevertheless loves, honors and can never get away from his utterly admirable and evidently *complaisante* wife. In Vina, perhaps, he has already discerned a sexual adventuress as daring as he, a woman in search of an anchor, of solid ground from which to make her nocturnal leaps into the unknown. Ormus—Yul Singh has intuited—must be once again that anchor, the still center of her turning wheel. If he's the rock she can be the roll. This will fuel his music and her singing, both; for art must be made secretly, in quiet places, while the singing voice needs to soar into open space and seek the adulation of the crowd. Yul Singh has his own visionary blind eyes, which can see into possible futureworlds, enabling him to bet heavily on them, even, sometimes, to bring them into being. This is what he has seen: that Ormus and

Vina's genius, their future, their ability to become what they have it in themselves to be, depends on the engendering and perpetuation of special forms of pain. The noisy pain of the compulsive wanderer and the dumb pain of the one who's left.

Wing and Ifredis need neither sleep nor food except for their secret cheese. They are found fucking on the kitchen table, and under the living room rug. The whoops and shrieks grow louder, longer, somehow less human, by the hour. Vina and Ormus feel swamped, stalled, by this pornographic operetta. They are rendered temporarily incapable not of desire but of its physical (and vocal) expression. Like a couple of maiden aunts, they sip drinks on Tempe Harbor's farthest-flung terraces, and disapprove.

Up early on the third morning, Vina finds a dead stag lying in the reeds at the lake's edge: not shot, just deceased. Its head is half under water; antlers break the surface like hard weeds. Insects buzz their requiem. The legs are stiff, like a giant toy's. More specifically, it occurs to her, like the legs of a wooden horse. For some reason she cannot at once identify this unbidden thought makes her cry. Huge sobs burst from her; after a few of these, the memory follows. Of, outside the long-vanished Egypt cigar store, a wooden charioteer and his horse. *A one-horse town and the one horse was made of wood.* Vina summons a house limo—driven by Limo Singh, as the turbaned and uniformed chauffeur informs her without a tic of the irony forbidden by the avant-gardist Otto Wing—and, abandoning Ormus to the screaming lovers of Tempe Harbor, is driven at speed into Chickaboom.

Later, searching the grounds for her, Ormus wears his new eye patch in burgundy-colored velvet (run up for him by Clea the obliging housekeeper) and, with his single available eye, spots the stag, roped to a small tractor, being removed from the water by the chief gardener, Lawn Singh. For an instant he thinks it's Vina. Then his good eye mocks his pounding heart. Four legs not two, hooves not feet. Don't tell Vina you made *that* mistake.

He goes indoors, still oppressed by the residue of fear, the jangly biochemicals coursing through his veins. He makes for the music room—it's soundproofed, you can't hear Otto and Ifredis in there—and sits down at the Yamaha baby grand. You see a dead animal, you think it's the woman you love. You can't trust your eyes. You can't trust *her*. There's music pouring out of his fingertips.

Everything you think you see, he sings. *It can't be.*

And if Yul Singh—Machiavelli, Rasputin, he's never minded what people call him as long as the artistes keep signing on and the customers keep buying—is indeed watching his anguished guest through blind eyes from his Shavian cloud up there in the cloudless sky, he will certainly, at this point, be breaking into the widest of self-satisfied smiles.

The cigar store's gone but it's a small town and Egiptus is an uncommon name. It doesn't take much more than an hour of asking around to learn that the old man choked on a bone years ago but the woman is still just about alive, though emphysema should ensure it won't be for much longer. Mrs. Pharaoh, one old-timer called her in a bar. Now Limo Singh is driving down a long straight country road between vines and corn. There's a red silo and one of those newfangled windmills. It's hot when the wind lets up but the wind isn't letting up today, it bites and plans to go on biting.

The road begins to bend and narrow, loses its confidence, becomes uncertain, sputters into sidetracks, with the wind blowing up a dust cloud to blur things even further, and then in a back-road graveyard of machinery, a place that's lost definition and grown jowly like a plain man's ageing jawline, they find the rusting Winnebago, standing at the edge of a cluster of wrecked and cannibalized automobiles and tractors, surrounded by tall grass so it looks like it's hiding.

She's in a trailer, Vina thinks, but there's no movie to follow. The limo stops and she keeps sitting for a few moments, feeling the loop of time close, and feeling, too, the advent of an unexpected sentiment beyond anger and revenge.

Compassion.

She gets out of the limo and walks through the scrap yard. The trailer door opens. A small gray spike of a head sticks out and starts hollering furiously, with intervals for lung-sick gasps.

What you looking at lady I ain't no fucking sight to be seen. I ain't no local curio you can check out just because you read about me in a fucking guidebook. I should charge admission. What is this. Somebody send you up here? You got business with me or did you just come up here in your fancy vehicle to gloat at folks who didn't have your luck?

A fit of wheezing. Vina just stands there.

Do I know you?

Vina takes off her shades. The old woman looks like she's been hit.

Oh, no, Mrs. Pharaoh says. No thank *you*. That's the past.

She slams the trailer door in Vina's face.

Vina stands there.

The door opens an inch.

You hear me I got no comment at this time. You got no entitlement coming here and invading my constitutional right of privacy. To come accusing me. I ain't in your law court missy I'm in my personal fucking place of residence on my personal patch of mangy fucking grass and I ain't in your court of law. You and your flunkey here you're trespassing and maybe I'll call the cops on you. You think because I can't fucking breathe.

The door swings open. The widow Egiptus is holding on to the handle and, with her spare hand, catching at her chest. She sounds like: a mule. Like: death.

Vina waits.

I didn't do right by you, the woman gasps. That's what you think. To you I'm dirt. I took a young life already damaged and treated it like shit. Well looky here how things worked out. You end up in the big time and I end up in the fucking long grass. You don't reckon maybe you owe me for that. You don't reckon maybe I gave you the kick in the butt that put you on your road, and the survival equipment that took care of you on that journey. Look at you, you look like some tough bitch. Meaning, thanks to me. So don't you come here and fucking stand there like judgement day and hand down your verdict. You took my strength and left me to fucking die. Can't you see I'm dying in front of your face. What do you care. You'll go and I'll go on dying behind your fucking back. Maybe they won't find my body for weeks, not until it's blowed up like a airship and stinking up the county like a bad conscience. It ain't your verdict I got to worry about it's another whole fucking court entirely. Another whole sentence. Jesus.

Mrs. Egiptus shuts the Winnebago door once again and Vina listens to the noises of emphysema in its advanced stage. She turns to Limo Singh. I've had all I can handle for now, she says. Give her the address. Invite her to dinner at eight and tell her it'll be informal, she doesn't need to put on her glass slippers and satin gown. I'll wait in the god-damn car.

Thus Cinderella invites her wicked stepmother to the ball.

Pre-dinner drinks and drugs—champagne, cocaine—on the lawn at Tempe Harbor. Which by the way all I ask is you indulge in the conventional manner, through the nose, Yul Singh stipulates in a series of firm telephone calls to his guests. We got a vogue now for rear-end insertion, excuse my frankness, there's a fellow calls himself Rock Bottom, one of Voight's celebrated superstars, maybe you're acquainted with him but in my frank opinion he's the one to blame. Which it's a free country he can do as he pleases but I'm a little old-fashioned, I don't care for my guests feeding their assholes in front of the hired help.

Mrs. Pharaoh—Marion, the widow Egiptus—comes in like gang-busters, concealing her considerable unease behind a barrage of obscenity; getting her retaliation in first. Her spotless floral-printed dress hangs loose on her emaciated birdy frame. Otto Wing, campily entranced, raises his nose from a small mirror and peers at this ancient apparition.

Wow, Vina invited a bag lady, he announces loudly.

So you're rich now, Marion Egiptus says to Vina right there in the entrance vestibule. You're up here with your rich buddies having yourself a high old time. Sure, I know what that means. A shift in the fucking balance of power. I'm done for and you made good. This is America, money gives you rights. You get the right to haul me out here and shame me, and your friend Mr. Asswipe gets to insult me right into my fucking face. That's okay. I know the score. How's this for a deal. Gimme twenty bucks and I'll apologize right now for how I treated you way back when and for twenty more I'll forget what a twisted little whore you always were. For fifty bucks I'll kneel down and kiss your rich foot and I'll suck your black pussy why not for an even hundred. Your four-eyed friend here, I'll cut him in too. Bag lady, huh. I could show him some fancy action. Put a bag over my head, professor, cut a hole for my mouth, and for two hundred bucks I'll give you what not even Mary Magdalene let alone no naked fucking under-age foreign whore could dream up. But sit down to dinner with you stinking scum? You don't got the money could make me do a thing like that.

I like this woman, enthuses bespectacled Otto Wing. So lacking in circumlocution, and her offer also is intriguing. To have intimate relations with a person who stands at the very gates of eternity. This has possibilities.

But the blasphemy, Otto, Ifredis objects, We must loudly to such language exception take. Her evening dress leaves little to the imagination, and she pushes it even further off the shoulders to attract and hold his attention; which works. Holy flagrant youth triumphs over bad-mouthed blasphemous age.

And the pit of eternal fire will surely open beneath her foots before so long, Ifredis victoriously predicts. Also by the way lady I am not under-age and if you care to know it one hell of a performer in the bag.

Sack, Otto corrects her lovingly, running a hand down her exposed back. One hell of a performer in the sack.

Whatever, darling. I am confuse in my words because just now there is overmuch speech of bags.

Vina takes wheezing Marion Egiptus by the arm and more or less drags the unwilling old woman down to the lakeside, to the same spot where the dead stag fell. Okay, Marion, she says, you're right and you're wrong. You're right I drove out to your trailer to put you down, I wanted some kind of closure?, after all these years of refusing even to speak your name I wanted you to know I made it anyway, I wanted your goddamn envy. But about my inviting your ass up here to jerk you around you're wrong. You're so goddamn fucked up, when I saw that it made me want to help you, so I'll do what I can, doctors, medical bills, whatever.

You're offering money?

Yeah. Yeah, I'm offering cash. And you don't even get to vacuum my cunt.

Okay, I'll take it, the old woman says quickly. How much?

Not as much as you think, Vina shrugs, coming clean. All this isn't mine. I'm just the singer and this, it's the label's.

Marion Egiptus cackles, bringing on a coughing fit. Water streams from her eyes. When she recovers, leaning against Vina, she says, Shit, honey, I knew *that*. When you're real rich, not pretend rich which is about your level, you don't care to make war or peace with the past. Baby, you leave it behind. You're *gone*.

For an instant, the widow Egiptus goes on leaning against Vina's side.

I'm glad I didn't leave you behind, Vina says. Their hands touch.

Marion pulls away. Yeah, she snarls. But once you've handed over the money you won't have to carry me on your fucking back no more. Don't think you're doing nothing for me. You're buying your personal freedom is all.

Well, okay, Vina concedes, maybe so. Nobody wants to be a slave.

Maria's at Tempe Harbor too. No locked door can keep her out. She sets off no alarms. She arrives whenever Vina briefly leaves Ormus to his own devices, and she's all done talking, she is physically insistent once again, even urgent, a phantom soul sister of the erotomaniac Ifredis Wing. Her body feels real enough, and she is strong. She grips his wrists and forces him back on to his bed. Still, Ormus resists. He thinks of Vina, and Maria's power ebbs. Her grip fails. A force drains out of her.

You can't help it, she says disconsolately, stepping away. You're stuck in this stupid place, this dirty fork in the true path. This uncertain earth, its troubled water, its belching fires, its poisoned air et cetera. Its wrongness. No wonder it creates these pernicious side effects. You're polluted, poor darling, you're sick of some psychotropical disease and so forth, and you think what you feel is love.

Strangely, Maria's coming and going is no longer entirely unrestricted. It's as though, by coming into his presence through his pale, blinded, other-sighted eye, she has been deprived of her old means of arrival and departure. It seems that now that she has become a part of his vision, of his seeing, he can control her appearances. She can no longer materialize and then vanish simply by turning sideways, as if there were a slot in the middle of nothing. She can't mail herself in and out of this world like a letter; not any more.

So Clea's eye patch makes possible what no security system can manage. Ormus resolves to keep his left eye patched and in darkness.

Vina is all he sees and all he wants to see.

Even with the eye patch in place Ormus Cama has been finding that America defies credibility. In the hall outside his and Vina's suite there is a drinks machine that eats paper money. This astonishes him. Paper is incapable of the simple mechanical feats which are the limits of his scientific imagination. Electronics—scanners, printed circuits, yes/no pathways—these mysteries are beyond his ken, as secret as the mysteries of the ancient Greeks. The paper-triggered automaton is the gate-keeper of a new world of miracles and confusions, a world where the door knobs turn the wrong way and the power switches are upside down.

It is evident from the daily newspapers that the world beyond the frontiers of the United States (except for Indochina) has practically ceased to exist. The rest of the planet is perceived here as essentially fictional, and what is most distressing about the war in Indochina is that this basically imaginary country is depriving American youngsters of their very real lives, to which they have constitutionally guaranteed rights. This is a disturbance in the natural order, and protests are intensifying. On tv, helmeted, shielded figures bearing arms are seen marching across college campuses, reclaiming the God-given right of Americans to kill or maim their own youngsters before the Indochinese get a chance to do so.

Tv is new to Ormus Cama and it has further wonders to reveal.

There are many advertisements for anti-personnel devices ingeniously and variously disguised as edible foodstuffs and designed to turn the stomachs and digestive tracts of the American people into savage, heaving battlegrounds. These alternate with promo films for a wide range of chemical remedies, each claiming to be the only reliable way of restoring intestinal peace. In between the commercials he gets word of the death of Louis Armstrong whom once he loved in the film of *The Five Pennies* and in other films too. He glimpses many families—including a family of talentless musicians—being laughed at in their own homes by invisible strangers who seem easily amused. There is word of foo fighters—flying saucers—landing in the wide open spaces of the Midwest. An old man, an actor whose chief gift is his inability to remember anything he is told for more than fifteen minutes, is running for governor in California and is routinely referred to as an exemplary American.

The music, however, makes him feel at home. In the soundproofed music room he listens with excitement and pleasure to the *200 Motels* album by Uncle Meat, a live tape of the already legendary tour performances by Zoo Harrison's Caledonia Soul Orchestra, Eddie Kendricks singing "Just My Imagination," the Plastic Ono Band's "Imagine." However, when he hears some kid moaning about the end of rock 'n' roll, Ormus gets angry. Died? The music is just getting born. Vina is its mother and he's the father, and anyone who thinks otherwise should get out of their high-speed road.

In his heart of hearts he knows why he's really angry. He's fifteen years late for the party. These should have been his years, and instead they belong to others. Time's running out. Every day there's one day less to seize.

He's up at the house now, watching Vina down below, by the lake, talking to Mrs. Pharaoh and stuffing dollar bills into the dying woman's shabby purse. He shakes off the miasmic state induced by Maria's visits, and is overcome by a rush of great love for the woman who has renewed his life. How extraordinary she is, how much she has had to combat, to overcome. He must marry her at once. She must stop making her joking refusals and agree to marry him without delay, perhaps even here, at Tempe Harbor. Yes, that would be perfect! By confronting the woman who was not good to her in her younger days, she has laid a ghost to rest. Yul Singh exorcised the ghost of old Manny Raabe by the use of heat. Vina has chased her phantoms away by looking them in the face, and giving up her revenge. Her business with the past is done. To be married at this moment would turn a page.

His desire for Vina swells and overflows. Hers is the only love that can—that *will*—unite his broken vision, make him whole. As his are the only arms that can hold her together after all her struggles, all her pain.

There is a field of cosmos wildflowers by the lake. It's the perfect spot.

He glows with love. Soon it will be his wedding day.

· · ·

If she hadn't made that final settlement of accounts with Mrs. Marion Egiptus of Chickaboom, N.Y.—if her childhood suffering had not been assuaged by an adult cash transaction—then Vina Apsara might just have been raw and vulnerable enough to entertain Ormus's renewed proposals. If Otto and Ifredis Wing had not raced up to her on the lawn, passing the departing Mrs. Egiptus, and proposed a little ménage à trois, or, if she insisted on including her solemn and preoccupied gentleman friend, à quatre, then Vina might not have been so thoroughly consumed by disgust, might not have transferred her contempt for the Wings' post-marital antics to the institution of matrimony itself.

But these things have been done and cannot be undone. And so it is that Ormus, approaching her at the water's edge in the last light of day, with a bunch of wildflowers in his hand and a heart full of love, finds her in viperish mood.

We've got to get out of this place, I mean right now, Vina seethes at her fatuously smiling beau, who's come a-romancing only to find his beloved transformed into a hissing harpy. Her former foster mother's soured anger has ignited her own formidable rage. Ormus, Jesus *Christ*. What are we doing?, we must be crazy?, we should be setting fire to this nightmare palazzo instead of acting like Cool Yul's private harem. His eunuchs and what's the word concubines. We should be burning it to the fucking ground. For this we left England? If this is the twentieth century, baby, we should be making urgent plans to exit permanently into some other epoch. Run, comrade, the old world is behind you, the students said in Paris, '68. Down with a world where the guarantee that we won't die of starvation has been purchased with the guarantee that we will die of boredom! Victory will be for those who know how to create disorder without loving it! Come *on,* Ormus. What's the project, right? Are we going to tear down the asylum or just move in here to some fucking padded cell and I don't know begin to *babble*?

I came out just now, he says—knowing it's the wrong time, not able to help himself, sensing that things are about to slip away from him again, that his wildflower wedding has vanished down a fork in reality along which he won't be able to follow it—I came to ask you to marry me.

I already done tol' you, honey, she answers, the cornpone accent only just taking the edge off the rebuff. I ain't the marryin' kind. I'm jus' the girl who cain't say yes.

She won't do it. Can't bring herself to. She loves him, she loves him to hell and back, but she won't put it in writing and sign her name to it. Freed from the nagging pain of her childhood memories, she refuses this new captivity. She offers him the conventional anti-nuptial radicalism of the time. Monogamy is a manacle, fidelity is a chain. A revolutionary not a wifey will she be. A changer of the world not of diapers she'll become.

He isn't listening. High purpose has descended upon him. If you won't marry me now, then I want to know when you will, he demands, with a stubbornness so deep that it has metamorphosed into something else, into, perhaps, destiny. And the force of his wanting it is so palpable that Vina—who loves him with her life, who knows his love is the equal of hers, who can't trust either his love or her own for five minutes at a time—takes the demand seriously. Name the day, he blazes. As far in the future as you want. Your one hundred and first birthday if you want. But name it and hold to it and I'll never ask you again until that day comes. Give me your unsinkable word and it will keep me afloat all my life. Just name the fucking day.

She's twenty-seven years old, and if there's one thing she's learned it's that nothing stays the same for five minutes, not even your goddamn name. So this demand for an immutable day, it's a storybook device, it's some retro Knights-of-the-Round-Table Camelot-and-chivalry deal. A courtly love revival. He's asking her to mortgage the future, but in the future she'll be someone else again, she'll have changed a dozen times, and nobody can expect your unknown future self to be bound by the mistakes and promises of youth. It's like selling the moon. You can sell it if you're able to find a buyer but only a fool would expect you to deliver. Make the fucking promise, she thinks, and after that it's *caveat emptor.* Let the buyer beware.

Okay, she says. Okay, already, keep your rug on. Ah, ten years from now, she says, how's that. (Thinking, ten years is an impossible eternity.

In ten years, the music business being what it is, and taking her own volatile temperament and tempestuous life history into account, she could be mad or dead. Or thirty-seven, which feels worse. In ten years the light dying around them this evening will be fifty-eight thousand six hundred and fifty-seven billion miles from here and she might be pretty far away herself. Ten years is never-never land, you turn right at a star and go straight on till morning. No rules apply. Besides, behind her back, rabbits rabbits, she's crossing her treacherous fingers.)

Ten years from today? From right now?

(He's being serious. Jesus. Never mind, he'll get over it, it'll be fine.)

Sure, Ormie. Ten years, the clock's running, three, two, one, go.

Then he tells her his side of the bargain.

Waiting for her, briefly possessing her, then losing her: this has been his lot. He waited for her to come of age, there was a single night of love, and then at once she vanished. He fell, he rose again, he strove to become worthy of her, to perform great labors, to solve the riddle of her departure, he set himself after many vicissitudes back upon his true course, and then a chance accident felled him once more; suspended his animation. She returned and worked a miracle, which was undeniably a miracle of love, and then for a few moments they were together, while he healed. But in spite of her continued avowals of their love, of hers, she refuses to offer him the fixity that is only natural and which, in his bizarre two-eyed condition, he needs. He finds that the waiting—another ten years, as she has specified—is preferable to her daily vagaries, her whims. The waiting is at least solid, it has a beginning, a middle and an end, he can lean his weight against it knowing it will not step away at the last instant and let him fall. But in waiting there is no inbetweenness, no acceptably nuanced position, no half measures or relativity theory. As there is none in love. One either loves, or waits for love, or banishes love for good. That is the full range of possible choices. As she has chosen waiting, so he chooses now to amplify what waiting means.

For ten years, until she is thirty-seven years old and he has turned forty-four, he will not touch or be touched by her. Not so much as a clasping of hands or a caress upon the cheek will he offer or permit. What he suffered for love when she was under-age he will suffer again now that they are both in their prime. She has made a promise and he has no doubt that she will honor it. She should also be clear that he will honor his. These promises will be their substitutes for marriage vows. This non-performance, this empty vessel—this suspended absence, swinging hammock fashion between the twin poles of their stark choices—will be the bed of their *grand amour*.

To put it another way: for ten years, it will be strictly business between them. Stricter than business; for this is not a parting, not a divorce agreement, but a lovers' pact, that ends in a long-delayed but much-desired tryst. It ends in for ever. Therefore he submits himself to the rules of love. Though he will not *lay a finger* on her for her stipulated decade, he enters freely and without coercion into a condition of celibacy. He will not share with any other woman what he cannot share with his beloved.

All this he swears.

Ten years from now, the time of denial will end and they will enter into joy.

The love of God, as Otto and Ifredis, the beatifically beating Wings of desire, have abundantly proved, need not hinder your sex drive. Alas, mortal love all too easily gets in its own way.

A Russian man goes into a car showroom and is approached by a sales representative. There's no car actually on display in the showroom, they unfortunately don't have any showroom models at present, but, the salesman explains, we have photographs, and certainly, sir, I'll be happy to take your order. The customer quickly signs the purchase papers and asks, How soon can I have it? In two years from now, the salesman replies—Okay. But will it come in the morning or the afternoon?— I'm sorry, sir, I don't think you understood, I said it'll take two *years*.— Yes, that's right, but in two years' time, will it be the afternoon or, preferably, the morning?—This is ridiculous, sir, what can it possibly matter?—Well, you see, I've got the plumber coming in the afternoon.

This is a post-communist joke. I place it here anachronistically, around eighteen years ahead of its time, because it's a parable about people who, like Ormus Cama and Vina Apsara, are obliged by circumstances to take a long view. Whether these two, the loves of each other's lives, whose gift of loving is exceeded only by their talent for erecting mighty obstacles to that love, are the creators of their circumstances, or destiny's fools, I leave to others to decide.

Vina can't bear it. *Not this again, your fucking heroic oaths.* She rails, implores. He's throwing away what is wonderful between them in the name of an archaic convention. He must reconsider. He must come to bed at once.

You could have said ten days, he points out. You could have said ten minutes. The length of the engagement was your choice, its nature is mine.

Stopped in her tracks, almost panting in her desperation, Vina faces the crisis of her life. And, as always, when tenderness fails her, as she believes it always has failed her and always will, she has recourse to ferocity.

Fine, she says. Have it your way. Strictly business. Deal.

For ten years, he reminds her. Your word is your bond.

And you can live like a monk if you want?, she snaps her exit line, but don't expect this little lady to follow your lead.

When she's out of sight, Ormus Cama takes off his eye patch and the otherness streams in. He reels, then gathers himself. Little by little, he must learn to see double without growing dizzy and losing his balance. He will have, if not love, then whole sight. That, and music.

From the moment their pact is made, that devil's contract that will make neither of them happy, there's no stopping them. At the epicenter of the American earthquake that is VTO lies this very Oriental disorientation. Abstinence: it becomes their rocket fuel, and flies them to the stars.

13

ON PLEASURE ISLAND

A journey to the center of the earth. (Cab fare from Vina's place, $4 with tip.)

First stop, just around the corner from the center of the earth, is the artist Amos Voight's studio, alias Slaughterhouse-22. Amos was born Wojtyla, and years later, when the Polish Pope comes along, Amos in his great old age will seriously announce he's suing John Paul II for nomenclatural plagiarism.

At the Slaughterhouse, amid the printmaking and photography, small billionaires hang out in corners like gargoyles eager for rain, watching the curvy girls with the thick dicks go in and out of the movie studio. Amos never forgets a billionaire, never ignores them for longer than is enjoyable, so they're happy. At this moment Amos is holding forth to Vina about his dead friend Eric, who has been found naked in an empty bathtub in a seedy apartment on the Upper West Side. Like David's Marat, killed by tragic heroin, Voight says in that unsparing voice like a woman's sigh. It's too bad, he says. At least when the Lizard King went, his bath was full. Vina puts her arms round him, holds him. I took a ride up there, he says. It was horrible. $11 with tip.

To cheer him up, Vina takes Voight over to the center of the earth for champagne and orange juice and a steak sandwich ($36.93 including taxes). It's just a couple of blocks away. Its name is Sam's Pleasure Island, and there's no Sam, never was one, but if pleasure is your pleasure then you've come to the right place.

(Even those who never come to such places derive a form of perverse satisfaction, vicarious, perhaps malign, from knowing that they exist, that an essential part of America's contract with her citizens is being fulfilled. The pursuit of happiness; and of death.)

Oh, gee, says Amos, entering. I love New York. It's full of people still doing stuff they gave up years ago.

Lou's singing. *Wagon Wheel.* Boy, she's hot. Look, here are Rémy Auxerre and Marco Sangria, nobody knows more about music than Marco and Rémy. What do you say, boys, asks Amos, do you like what she's doing now.

Rémy answers, We must free our soul from the everyday and open it to *influxus mentium superiorum,* the influence of higher minds. To this end, our tools are vacantness and alienation. When influence finds our reason unoccupied, it shows it something of universal knowledge.

Oh, good, that means he likes it, Amos says to Vina.

How can you tell, she asks.

But it's so easy, because he's Martinican, you know, says Amos. It's that great French bullshit, he does it nearly as well as the French. People dance differently in different towns, most of us adapt, but not our Rémy. I love that, it's so great, so confident and empty, don't you think.

I want you to meet Ormus?, Vina says. We're now a band.

Just don't ask me to produce your album, Amos says. (He's really down tonight.) Just ask some other sucker, okay.

Nobody's asking you for anything. Vina smacks him playfully on the head, and his thatch of hair flies out like a soft explosion. Be nice now, Amos. You're on the Island.

Here's Ormus, wearing his eye patch, looking even gloomier than Voight.

I'll tell you what we've got in common, apart from almost having the same name, Amos confides, slipping an arm through his. We both came back from the dead. You had that crash, and somebody shot me, can you believe it, a woman, so butch. I wasn't supposed to make it but I just thought I would.

You old fraud, Vina scolds him. You know everything about everyone. You just pretend you're an ignorant blinking little mole just out of his hole.

Like a mole in the ground I will root this mountain down, says Ormus.

Oh, gee, a Negro spiritual, Voight snaps, deliberately invoking the archaic term in the age of Black is Beautiful. Suddenly direct, he peers at Ormus. Colored cels wash their faces in red and purple light. What color are you, anyway, it's so hard to tell these days, he demands, sharp as a rebuke. You know what they say about Vina. They say she's a brown girl trying to be black, which is just plain snippy and so unfair to a girl with naturally frizzy hair and a liking for trouble. Now I'm clear what color *she* is, but I am not fully briefed on the pigmentary orientation of Parsi males, so I guess I'll have to ask you straight out.

Do I have to be a color, Ormus mutters, coloring. Can't we get beyond, finally, I mean can't we get under our skins.

Aw, spoilsport, couldn't you even be lime green or something? green is nice. (Here Voight turns to the nearest femme of a group of sequinned gender illusionists.) And you, my dear, what color are you.

Oh, I guess velvet, honey, is that a color.

Sure, velvet, that counts; how about your pal.

Her? She's Gemini.

Voight turns back to Ormus. You see, here at Sam's they have every shade and variety of color in the book. Do you know Anatole Broyard, by the way? He's got the greatest trick. Every day when he enters the subway in Brooklyn he's black, but by the time he shows up for work at *The New Yorker* he's pure white. And did you ever hear of Jean Toomer? The most important writer of the Negro Renaissance. His book *Cane,* you know, way back in 1923, Waldo Frank called it a harbinger of the South's literary maturity, of its emergence from the obsession put upon its mind by the unending racial crisis. The dawn of direct and unafraid creation, that's what I believe he said. Seems to me you'd like that old book.

Ormus is tempted into unwariness. I've got an idea for a song, he offers. *At the frontier of the skin wild dogs patrol.*

You sure would've liked Toomer, Voight reiterates mildly. A light-skinned man like you. He disappeared, you know. The rumor was he'd crossed the color line. Arna Bontemps used to say that didn't mean he got away from the racial problem. The invisible cloak didn't get him out of the jam everyone else was in.

Excuse me, Ormus says, I don't want to spoil your evening but I'm tired, my head hurts, good night.

Ouch, Amos says, watching Ormus's back as it flounces off. Ooh, that hurt.

He's cheerful now. He squeezes Vina's arm. This was so good an idea, darling. This is so fun.

At the heart of Sam's Pleasure Island is the court of the Yul King. Sit, if you're so lucky, beside Yul Singh in his choice booth—blind Yul with his trademark Manhattan on the rocks and his thick Cohiba cigar—and sooner or later the whole world will pass by and pay homage. Nobody can out-dress, out-drink, out-smoke or out-cool the Yul. Vina slides in next to the man. Amos is on her left.

Everybody's in tonight, Yul grins. Which check it out check it out.

Here are the Vampire Lesbians of Sodom. Darlin', they say, we're all born naked; the rest is just a drag.

Here is a giant fat man, naked except for the zippered bondage hood on his head. Look, he's got his cock on backwards; it's poking out between the soft billow of his ass.

Here are Angel Dust and Nutcracker Sweet, two of Voight's own fabulous porno actresses, I call them all horses, he says, because every few weeks they get carried out to the glue factory, they end up on some brown envelope or ten-cent stamp or something. I guess at least they get to be licked again, one last time.

Here's Lou, she's finished her set. Isn't she gorgeous? There's her new squeeze, Laurie. What a hunk.

Here's the guy to see if you just got into town and you want to know where the party is and who to fuck later.

Here's the woman who was the last person on earth to see the guy who strangled himself with a noose, trying to get an erection for her, imagine how low her self-esteem must be, poor baby.

Here are the guys who set fire to money.

Here are penis-ironers, testicle-boilers, shit-eaters, penis-boilers, testicle-eaters. Over there is the world Spermathon Queen, who encountered one hundred and one men, four at a time, in a non-stop seven-and-a-half-hour megafuck. She's still in touch with all one hundred and one partners and refers to them as her Dalmatians. Naturally, her personal icon is the fur-loving Cruella de Vil.

Here's the earth mother who adopted nineteen babies from different international trouble spots. But when the trouble dies down she trades the babies in for needier kids from the new hot zones. (Every time I cover a war I wonder which orphaned tot will end up at her place, and who'll be out on the street.)

Here's Ifredis Wing. Her whole life is an act of worship, and she gives it all back to Jesus. Here's a brother with a crown of thorns on his head; he should get together with that poor girl. Otto's vamoosed already, he's now into Buddhism, he's flown to Dharmsala with a shaven-headed chick who's recognized as some sort of actual saint but she's also a martial arts maven so go carefully, Mr. Wing.

Here are more believers. They believe in the Divine Mother Goddess-Ma in her concrete high-rise in Düsseldorf. They believe in going for the burn. They believe in the name of God written in the seeds of a watermelon. They believe in the wise ones flying towards them in a comet's tail. They believe in rock 'n' roll. They believe reason and psychology are crutches you use until you find wisdom. Then, when you've found it, you throw away those crutches and dance. They believe they're the sane ones and it's everybody else that's crazy. They believe in Pleasure and its island. They do not believe the rumor about this island: that if you stay long enough, it'll make a donkey of you.

Hey, the space gods are in tonight. There's the guitar hero who was born on an asteroid in the general vicinity of Mars. There's Sun Ra, another alien. There's the thin Limey who used to work as a UFO spotter after he fell to earth.

And there's Neil. Neil from the Silver Spaceships. Neil, the living proof that there's rock 'n' roll on other planets.

Everybody. The whole Western world.

Voight is remorseless tonight. Isn't Ormus Cama the boy that sings about frontiers, he asks Yul, about going to the edge and crossing over? Well, dear, dear. He hardly got across the welcome mat tonight.

It can't be the edge as well as the center, says Vina, refusing to rise to the bait.

Sure it can, my pretty, says Yul Singh. Take a look around. Sure it can.

War-weary, divided, their belief in the mighty eagle's global ascendancy damaged by the humiliating withdrawal of U.S. personnel from Indochina, Americans find they want what Ormus Cama has to say. The helicopters circle over the Saigon embassy like angels of judgement; the living cling to them and beg for salvation. The dead have already been judged, and found guilty, by defeat. Limb-shorn veterans retreat psychotically into forests and mountain fastnesses, to dream of rice paddies and King Cong rising out of the water right in front of their screaming faces, here comes a chopper to chop off your head. You can get the boys out of the war but you can't get the war out of the boys. In this bereft moment, rudderless America is unusually open to the paradoxes of Ormus's songs; open, in fact, to paradox itself, and its non-identical twin ambiguity too. The U.S. Army (and its rock songs) went into one East and came out with a bloody nose. Now Ormus's music has arrived like an affirmation from another East to enter the musical heart of Americanness, to flow into the river of dreams; but it's driven by the democratic conviction, retained by Ormus from the days when Gayomart sang the future into his ears, that the music is his as well, born not just in the U.S.A. but in his own heart, long ago and far away. Just as England can no longer lay exclusive claim to the English language, so America is no longer the sole owner of rock 'n' roll: that is Ormus's unstated sub-text (Vina, always the loudmouth, the thrower-down of gauntlets, will come out with it soon enough, and put a few patriotic noses out of joint).

The story of the ten-year engagement and of Ormus's consequent oath of celibacy spreads quickly; and this, too, makes Ormus and Vina irresistible. The new band takes off almost at once, and the force of its ascending shakes the land. Starting as oddities, they grow quickly into giants. At once conqueror and celebrant, Ormus storms the citadels of rock, and Vina's voice, as Yul Singh foresaw, is his weapon. Her voice is the servant of his melodies; his singing the servant of her voice. And while Vina's is the exceptional instrument, capable of affecting the hairs on the back of your neck as it swoops and dives, Ormus's lower, gentler harmonies perfectly offset her pyrotechnics, and the two voices, when they blend, create a magical third, more Righteous than the Righteous Brothers, Everlier than the Everlys, Supremer than the Supremes. It's a perfect marriage. Ormus and Vina, put asunder by vows, are joined together in song. *V-T-Ohh!* America, disoriented, seeking a new voice, succumbs to theirs. Young Americans, in search of new frontiers, board VTO's Orient express.

That part of the American soul which is presently in retreat finds comfort in the new stars' restatements of the great American musical truths, the foot-tapper tempi that start out walking and then find the dance hidden in the walk; the placing of the beats that tug at our bodies; the speak-to-me rhythm and blues. And that America which by losing certitude has newly opened itself to the external world responds to the un-American sounds Ormus adds to his tracks: the sexiness of the Cuban horns, the mind-bending patterns of the Brazilian drums, the Chilean woodwinds moaning like the winds of oppression, the African male voice choruses like trees swaying in freedom's breeze, the grand old ladies of Algerian music with their yearning squawks and ululations, the holy passion of the Pakistani *qawwals*. Too much of the people's music settles for too little, Ormus says on the occasion of the issue of the self-titled first album (the one with the burgundy-colored velvet eye patch on the sleeve). It offers the people crumbs when they should have banquets.

He wants to work with what he calls the full orchestra, meaning not stiffs in tuxes but the full range of musical emotional intellectual yes and moral possibility, he wants this music to be capable of saying anything to anyone, but above all meaning something to someone. He's started to speak in this big new voice, and the someones out there are listening.

Angry America, too, is listening hard: the America of loss, the America that's taken a beating and doesn't fully understand how, or what it's done to deserve this pain (this America is looking not at the Indochinese dead but only at its own). This raging America responds to Ormus's wrath, because he's a very angry man, angry with Vina, himself and the cruel destiny thanks to which the decade of his high triumph has been rendered meaningless by the emptiness of his bed.

It responds in two ways. Only one of these is appreciative. Beneath the America that opens itself to VTO, there's another country that turns against him, that sets its jaw and closes its mind.

Ormus and Vina begin to acquire powerful enemies.

Someone should shut those uppity bigmouths once 'n' f'r all.

Melancholy and chastity make sublimation possible, according to the fifteenth-century Florentine Marsilio Ficino, and it's sublimation that sets free the *furor divinus*. First in the Peace Ballads of Ormus Cama, then in his legendary quake album, *Quakershaker,* fury is evident in every chord, every bar, every line, fury deep-drawn like black water from a poisoned well. Whether it be divine or earthly *furor* is a matter of some considerable dispute.

If Ficino believed that our music is composed by our lives, the contemporary Czech Milan Kundera thinks, contrariwise, that our lives are composed like music. "Without realizing it, the individual composes his life according to the laws of beauty, even in times of the greatest distress." To stand the old principle of good design on its elegant head: in our functioning we follow the dictates of our need for form.

Bravo, Ormus. I've got to hand it to the guy. Bearing a satchel full of hard-won images of the fall of Saigon I come trudging home with a lifetime supply of nightmares to the sweet-dream needlework merchants and powdered-happiness pashas clustered on the stoops of the brownstones of St. Mark's, and lo! there on the corner newsstand is our Ormie, already notoriously publicity shy, hitting a three-run homer, adorning the covers in the same week of *Rolling Stone* (with Vina), *Newsweek* (Vina's reduced to an inset) and *Time* (not a trace of Vina to be seen). Not only has he pushed the war news on to the inside pages but he's also marginalized one of the great beauties of the age, who is rapidly becoming one of the most famous women in the world. Some recluse! Some publicity! He must've really touched a nerve. Two quick albums, *VTO* and *Peace Ballads*—in those days before the omnipotence of videos and marketing, musicians put out records a whole lot more often—one, two!, and he's sitting on top of the world.

They made peace in the other world too. (Baby I've got one of my own.) Ain't no better than it is for you. (Good to know we're not alone.) Well the war is over and the battle's through. (But I can't reach you on the phone.)

I call your number but you ain't home. I call your number but you ain't home. Seems I made this long journey just to wait on my own. It's been a long journey home. A long journey home.

VTO's *Peace Ballads* defies the injunctions of the post-ironical cinéaste Otto Wing. "Picking up the Pieces," "(You Brought Me) Peace Without Love," "Long Journey Home," "Might As Well Live": it's easy enough to hear the bitter, disabused ironies in many of Ormus's songs. But the music he's come up with is jauntily, almost perversely up-tempo. The overall effect is oddly affirmative, even anthemic, and for many young people these jaundiced, dystopic tracks become unlikely, adult anthems of relief, a new beginning, release. On my own block I can hear the young dope peddlers—Nicely-Nicely Johnson, Harry the Horse, Sky Masterson, Big Julie, Nathan Detroit—whistling Ormus Cama's material. Peace without love: they are marketing this very product, the guaranteed top-grade genuine article, by the ounce. It's the only racket; always was. And when you run out of peace juice, bliss pills or sweet treats for your veins, you are always welcome to return to Happy Valley here and get yourself another tasty helping, as long as you are in possession of the requisite spondulicks. Which, the dealers at least would argue, is more than can be said for love.

Americans buy the *Ballads* by the wagonload, but the album's anti-war message causes a few subterranean rumbles. Agencies who see it as their rôle to protect the country from fifth columnists, from being *destabilized,* start taking a discreet interest. Yul Singh receives a polite phone call on his unlisted private line from a voice that calls itself Michael Baxter when it says hello and Baxter Michaels when it signs off. A warning shot across the bows. A word to the wise. We have some concern about certain lyrical content. There is naturally no question of infringing any individual's First Amendment rights, but the songwriter if we understand it correctly is not a U.S. citizen. A guest who wishes to remain welcome is not well advised to piss on his host's best rug.

Yul Singh summons Ormus and Vina to his suite of offices near Columbus Circle and then suggests a walk in the park. Ordinarily New Yorkers pride themselves on ignoring the fame of the famous but the exceptional success of *Peace Ballads* necessitates exceptional measures. For Ormus, an old hippie Afghan jacket, large round-lensed purple shades, a fright wig. Vina is harder to disguise. Her height, her Afro shock, her attitude, defy concealment. After much haggling she agrees to wear a floppy wide-brimmed felt hat in bright scarlet, because it matches her long Italian leather coat. Yul Singh refuses as usual to use a white stick, leans, instead, on Will Singh's iron forearm. Half a dozen more Singhs follow at a discreet distance, in case of crowd trouble. In the park, emboldened by foliage, Cool Yul passes on the content of the feds' phone call. Vina snorts her disdain, declines to take the threat seriously—*Everybody's got a fed on their tail right now, from Dr. Nina to Winston O'Boogie, it's like a fashion statement?*—and goes off at one of her zany tangents. What do they know, nobody ever gets rock lyrics right, anyway. For years I thought Hendrix was a faggot. You know, 'scuse me while I kiss this guy. And what *was* that about my feet begin to crumble. I used to admire the surrealism of rock lyrics?, the wild non sequiturs. Then I realized it was just my fucking ears.

Ormus, Yul Singh says quietly, these are what can I tell you sensitive times, people are touchy, skinless, you may be giving them too much truth. I'm just saying which it's a matter for you, okay, but you should keep under control your crazier sentiments and if I may say so also her many unscripted remarks.

That'll be the day, Vina snaps, flinging down her hat and shades and striding off fast through the dappled sunlight, a giantess at war. She turns heads, but the thunderclouds around her look too dangerous; people leave her alone.

There's no follow-up. Somebody's decided to let this one go. The attack on Ormus comes fifteen months later, after the earthquake songs.

The culture needs a vacuum to rush into, it is an amorphousness in search of shapes. Ormus and Vina's suspended love, that divine absence which we can fill with our fantasies, becomes the center of our lives. The city seems to organize itself around them, as if they are the principle, the pure Platonic essence, that makes sense of the rest.

I flatter myself that here I use the word "we" to describe a collectivity of which I am not a part.

They live separately. She's in a third-floor loft downtown, all the way west on Canal, a large space rescued from post-industrial decay in a building with brutalist common parts that satisfy some instinct of hers for roughness, though the loft itself is eminently creature-comfortable. She fills it with fish tanks for dumb company and whole walls of hi-fi equipment to shut out the noise of the West Side Highway and the no doubt even louder roar of Ormus's absence, which sounds constantly in her ear like the ocean in a shell. He's in a vast empty apartment uptown in the old Rhodopé Building, a classic-period Art Deco landmark; cocooned in space, looking east across the reservoir. Whole rooms contain nothing except a piano, a guitar, a few cushions. A fortune invested in soundproofing and air-purification systems. Ormus still wears his eye patch when he's out and about, and always when he's performing, as an aid to concentration, but here in this luxury padded cell he gives free rein to his craziness, his double vision: he rides it hard, busts it like a bronc. He shuts out the world and hears the music of the spheres. Though he is sworn to celibacy, he lets Maria come.

Their audiences, their arenas expand. The music gets louder. He goes on stage wearing earplugs but there's already damage to his hearing. Vina has her ocean-roar; in his case it's a ringing noise like a faraway alarm. This is the last sound he hears at night, the first that penetrates his consciousness each morning. Sometimes he mistakes it for air knocking in underfloor pipes or the wind whistling through a cracked pane of glass. *The ringing noise is my life,* he writes in his journal. *It's just another thing I can't escape.*

After a tense initial period during which they sometimes see each other in the evenings, with painfully awkward results, they agree to meet only to rehearse with the other band members, to discuss their finances and to perform. They are never alone together any more, they never eat a meal or take in a movie in each other's company, never phone each other, never go dancing, never feed animals in the zoo, never touch. Like divorced couples, they avoid each other's gaze. Yet mysteriously they continue to say they are both deeply, irreversibly, for-ever-and-a-day in love.

What can this mean?

It means that they are with each other constantly even while they are apart. When she stands in the shower she imagines him on the other side of the glass door, watching the water run down her body, pressing his lips to the steamy glass. She puts her own lips to the inside

384 • T H E   G R O U N D   B E N E A T H   H E R   F E E T

of the door, closes her eyes, imagines him waiting for her. The water becomes his hands, and her own hands run down her body, searching for and often becoming his touch. And when he lies in his bed he convinces himself there's a warm hollow in the mattress beside him, as if she has just left the room; he closes his eyes and she returns, she comes close. Their curled bodies are a pair of question marks at the end of the puzzling sentence of the day.

When he writes a line he always wonders what she'll think of it, he hears her goddess's voice take his music and hurl it into the sky, to hang there like a shining star. And when she eats, alone or with others, she never fails to think of his carnivorous habits, his high daily intake of red meat cooked medium rare, and a look of exasperated affection crosses her face, a look which (if she is not alone) she uncharacteristically declines to explain.

Her decision to live her private life in public embarrasses and even humiliates a man as private as Ormus has become; yet he wonders every day at the raw courage of her engagement with the world, of her willingness to walk naked in its streets in the service of what she thinks of as the truth. In response to her blabbering mouth, his own reserve grows around him like a wall. She beats her fists against it, as she does against his famous oath; but she also thinks of his choices, as she thinks of him, with a respect that she accords to no one else.

Entering the same room, they crackle with the electricity of their solitary loving. They quarrel, of course. What he thinks of as his commitment to monogamy, she calls his growing absolutism. She accuses him of tyranny, which he calls fidelity. It is her nature that separates them, he replies. Her determined infidelity, her refusal to value what is of value, namely the love of a good man, himself. What he calls infidelity, she calls freedom. What looks to him like promiscuity, she provocatively renames democracy. These arguments go nowhere; like, perhaps, all lovers' quarrels, though they cannot be ended, defused, as other lovers' quarrels are: by oblivion's kiss.

Everything is remembered.

And they can kiss only while they sleep; only in their dreams.

Vina continues to reveal everything to everyone all the time. The more intimate the detail the surer it is to see the light of day. When they go on stage Ormus stands with his back to the audience, facing his fellow musicians like a conductor, Karajan with a Stratocaster, while she yells out a number to the audience, which everyone knows by now is the number of days that have passed since she and Ormus last had sex. She announces the names of her latest stopgap lovers, her Reichian belief in the healing powers of orgone energy and multiple orgasms, and the precise nature of her sexual preferences.

(Domination, bondage, aggression alternating with submissiveness, punishment, surrender: long before her eighties imitators she was bringing out into the open the flimsy repetitive secrets of our forbidden hearts, flaunting beneath the intense weight of stage lighting what had previously skulked around in the dark; demolishing—by inhabiting—taboos. For this she was predictably called the pornographer of the phonograph, the stereotypist of the stereo, by those who did not care to notice what was staring everyone in the face, namely her colossal and growing need for him, that need which she shouted to the whole planet in order to belittle and thus survive it, which hit her with redoubled intensity every morning of her life—her heart's seismic scale, like the Richter, proceeded by doublings—and forced her into ever greater extremes of compensatory behavior, loudmouthings, promiscuity, drugs. Namely that there was only one person in all the world whom she was trying to offend: no matter how large the audience, how outrageously suggestive her performance, her true purpose was profoundly intimate, and her true audience numbered one.

Or perhaps, if I may be permitted a flash of vanity, two.

I say this because she, the queen of over-exposure, never exposed me.)

The arch-enemy of the hidden, she keeps me secret until the end. About our long afternoons on my outsize brass bed, Ormus will never learn as long as she lives. Why? Because I'm not nothing to her is why. We have *duration,* a present and a future, is why. Because a cat may look at a queen and maybe, just maybe, sometimes the queen looks right back at that hungry young tom.

Her casual amours, which she makes public, are rendered insignificant by being named. None of them lasts long, anyway: a few weeks, a couple of months at best. My love affair with her—or call it half a love affair, because half of the two of us was in love—will last for almost eighteen years.

Gayomart Cama skipped out of Ormus's head and disappeared. The great man lost a twin brother, but (without knowing it) gained me. I'm his true Other, his living shadow self. I have shared his girl. She doesn't tell him because this would matter to him. This would tear him apart. The people with whom you share a history: these are the people who can leave you shipwrecked and drowning.

This is how Vina will one day leave both of us.

If the Other cannot be named, the shadow self must also, by definition, be selfless. She gives me no rights over her, comes and goes as she pleases, summons and banishes me at her pharaonic whim. It's not for me to mind about her cavalcade of playmates; certainly not to be jealous of Ormus himself. Yet each new sexual revelation comes as what I'm learning to call a *zetz* in the *kishkes*. And the fact of Ormus, of the love that can neither be nor cease to be, is a knife slowly twisted in the heart. She makes public sport of his celibacy; I'm counting differently. Every day that passes is one day closer to his goal, the day when he'll ask her to keep her promise.

There's only one man for me, and I can't have him, she shouts to the crowds. Listen and I'll sing you his beautiful songs instead.

He keeps his back to the audience. He can't show them his pain.

The breakdown of boundaries, what Erwin Panofsky called decompartmentalization, gave rise during the Renaissance to the modern idea of the genius. The fifteenth-century manifestos and treatises of Alberti, Leonardo and Cennini leave us in no doubt that this decompartmentalization is intimately connected to the urbanization of artistic sensibility, or, rather, to the artist's conquest of the city. The Renaissance artist is no longer a worker bee, a mere craftsman dancing to a patron's tune, but polymathic, a master of anatomy, philosophy, mythography, the laws of seeing and perception; an adept of the arcana of deep sight, able to penetrate the very essences of things. The achievements of modern artists, Alberti proclaimed, prove that the modern world is not exhausted. By crossing boundaries, uniting many kinds of knowledge, technical and intellectual, high and low, the modern artist legitimizes the whole project of society.

Such is genius! Leonardo, Michelangelo: they claim kinship, even equality, with the gods. The opposed destinies of immortality and destruction are theirs.

As for Ormus, at first, upon his helicoptered arrival in Manhattan, he enters a condition of worship, marveling at this new Rome, open-mouthed and slack-jawed, as did Alberti in Florence in the 1430s. Every chord he plays will be a paean to the sky-high city, he promises himself. If it can conquer the heights, so too will he.

He should have been my mother's son. I should have been his dad's.

One might suggest simply that Ormus Cama's worship of the city has quickly been reciprocated; it has become the city's worship of him. And where this city leads, this Rome, all the world's cities quickly follow.

Alas, this is an over-simplification. If Ormus lands in Manhattan as a provincial with stars in his eyes, circumstances quickly sour his joy. The rusting decadence of the city at ground level, its shoulder-barging vulgarity, its third-world feel (the poverty, the traffic, the slo-mo dereliction of the winos and the cracked-glass dereliction of too many of the buildings, the unplanned vistas of urban blight, the ugly street furniture), and the bizarreries to which Vina initially insists on exposing him, at such boho meccas as Sam's Pleasure Island and the Slaughter-house, these things fuel his celebrated moral disgust. Groovy Manhattan is plainly no better than Swinging London. He retreats into high-rise heaven and watches the city float in space. This celestial Manhattan is what he loves. Against this backcloth of noble silence he will set his pet sounds.

He, too, is screaming inside. His agony will emerge as music.

Give me a copper and I'll tell you a golden story. Thus, according to Pliny, did the oral storytellers of old preface their fantastic tales of men transformed into beasts and back again, of visions and magic: tales told not in plain language but adorned with every kind of extravagant embellishment and curlicue, flamboyant, filled with the love of pyrotechnics and display. When writers adopted the mannerisms of these storytellers it was, says Robert Graves, because they "found that the popular tale gave them a wider field for their descriptions of contemporary morals and manners, punctuated by philosophical asides, than any more respectable literary form."

What hope can I, a mere journeyman shutterbug, a harvester of quotidian images from the abundance of what is, have of literary respectability? Like Lucius Apuleius of Madaura, a Moroccan colonial of Greek ancestry aspiring to the ranks of the Latin colossi of Rome, I should (belatedly) excuse my (post)colonial clumsinesses and hope that you are not put off by the oddness of my tale. Just as Apuleius did not fully "Romanize" his language and style, thinking it better to find an idiolect that permitted him to express himself in the fashion of his Greek ancestors, so also I . . . but look here, there is an important difference between myself and the author of *The Transformations of Lucius*, better known as *The Golden Ass*. Yes, you will say, there is the small matter of talent, and you'll hear no argument from me on that score; but I'm driving at something else: viz., that while Apuleius happily admits to the fictionality of his fiction, I continue to insist that what I tell you is true. In his work he makes an easy separation between the realms of fancy and of fact; in my own poor effort, I am trying to set down the true-life account of the life of a man who saw, long before the rest of us, the artificiality of such a separation; who witnessed the demolition of that iron curtain with his own eyes and courageously went forth to dance on its remains.

Thus:

When he is by himself in his gigantic empty apartment Ormus removes his eye patch and the double vision returns. He looks into the heart of the otherness, the streaming. The barriers between the world of dreams and the waking world, between the spheres of the actual and the imagined, are breaking down. There is a progression. Something is changing. Instead of the gashes through which he formerly saw these visions, the windows to the other quiddity now have blurry edges. Sometimes they grow very large; it's difficult to tell where this world ends and that begins. His apartment here looks exactly like his apartment there.

The frontiers are softening. The time may not be far off when they disappear entirely. This notion, which ought to excite him, instead fills him with terrible dread. If the forking paths are coming together, if a point of confluence is ahead, what does this mean for life on the earth he knows? If such a decompartmentalization were to occur, and all verities suddenly failed, could we survive the force of the event? Ought we to be building bunkers, arming ourselves, donning badges that identify us as fellow members of this reality and not the feared (perhaps soon the hated) other?

If each of us has alternative existences in the other continuum, which of our possibilities will live on, which will disappear?

If we are all twins, which twin must die?

Once she is convinced of the immutability of his self-denying oath, the wraithish Maria visits him less often. When she does come she's usually sulky, protesting Ormus's use of the eye patch to shut her out, to say nothing of the oath itself. She doesn't stay long, but never fails to remind him of what he's missing.

He notices that she often arrives out of breath, perspiring. She seems tired. Is it possible that as the two whatnesses join and meld it's getting harder for her to slide back and forth in her unsettlingly supernatural way? Could it be that when the blending is complete, the two worlds will obey the same natural laws, and Maria will have to enter and leave through the door just like anyone else?

If so, will there be an apartment—her apartment—awaiting him in Bombay? Will the Cosmic Dancer Hotel possess, in its ledgers, a record of the suite they booked for that supposed night of passion long ago?

How will he ever know fact from fiction again?

The headache begins. He replaces the eye patch and lies back on his bed.

That's enough for now.

It's not up to you no more, you can't choose if it's peace or war, just can't make choices any more, your nightmare has come true; and when the day becomes the night, and when you don't know wrong from right, or blind from sight or who to fight, don't tell me you feel blue.

For Jack and Jill will tumble down, the king will lose his hollow crown, the jesters all are leaving town, the queen has lost her shoe; the cat has lost his fiddling stick, so Jack be nimble, Jack be quick, as all the clocks refuse to tick, the end of history is in view.

The earth begins to rock and roll, its music dooms your mortal soul, and there's nothing baby nothing you can do. 'Cause it's not up to it's not up to it's not up to you.

The earthquake songs of Ormus Cama are rants in praise of the approach of chaos, paradoxically composed by an artist working at the highest levels of musical sophistication. The songs are about the collapse of all walls, boundaries, restraints. They describe worlds in collision, two universes tearing into each other, striving to become one, destroying each other in the effort. Dreams invade the day, while waking's humdrums beat in our dreams.

Some of the songs are intricate tapestries of driving, woven sound. In other pieces, however, Ormus with great deliberation abandons the juggling fantasies that come to him naturally and adopts a bare, discordant manner, demanding of Vina a raucous aggression to which she adds a terrifying intensity of her own. This is something entirely new in Ormus: this purposive disharmony. This is celibate misery speaking, the Miltonic pain of unconsummated love.

Untwisting all the chains that tie / the hidden soul of harmony.

Many of these raw songs are jeremiads addressed directly to Vina, so that when she sings them it's weirdly disorienting because he's putting into her mouth—that is, she's spitting out of her mouth—the words he needs to say to her. He isn't reclusive in his art. Music is his nakedness. This excites us. Watching them on stage, listening to them on our records and tapes, we can see and hear the tension in their strangely obstructed love. Their huge, rotten love, which they insist on denying themselves for so long, so long. It makes them the only lovers whose news we can't wait to hear.

Sung in Vina's swooping, belting voice, certain songs release something primal, even animal, in the listener. Though their message could be called nihilistic, their musical clothing is potent enough to captivate the world's disenfranchised, idolatrous young. Ormus, his own youthful excesses forgotten, a sensualist rendered simon-pure by a mighty promise of abstinence, a devotee of the flesh transformed into a preacher of the spirit by his horror at the profligacy with which the New World squanders its privileges, now berates his admirers for their wantonness, for the licentious debauchery of their ways; and though from the virtuous heights of his chastity he thunders about a generation mired in hedonism, lost in the archipelagoes of indulgence and desire, the objects of his fury love him for his wrath. Prophesying doom, he is the best beloved of the allegedly doomed. Vina in her magic voice sings Ormus's musical anathemas, and the anathematized young of the Western world are enchanted. They rush out to their rhythm centers and buy.

Whenever the *Quakershaker* songs are performed a wildness bursts out of the audience. There is a loud howling as of wolves. As floodlights rake the crowd, they reveal abandoned, Dionysiac scenes. The fans, possessed by the music, tear at their garments, at one another, at the air. Young women's arms snake upwards, entwined, their hands moving like wings. They sit astride their lovers' shoulders. The men's faces are turned inwards, towards their partners' splayed and naked groins, and there is much snuffling and slavering and many porcine grunts. When the crowd roars it is like a lion and beneath the roar there is sometimes heard a hissing, as of serpents.

There are disappearances. Young people fail to return home and are eventually marked down as runaways. There is loose talk of bestial metamorphoses: snakes in the urban gutters, wild pigs in city parks, strange birds with fabulous plumages perching on skyscrapers like gargoyles, or angels.

The laws of the universe may be changing. Such transformations may—incredibly, horrifyingly—become normal.

We may be losing our grip on our humanity. When we finally let go, what's to stop us from turning into dinosaurs, saber-toothed tigers, jackals, hyenas, wolves?

What's to stop us from sliding, as darkness falls and (as in the Orphic hymn to Night) *terrible necessity rules over all*?

There is much conservative condemnation of the new supergroup and its adherents, who are variously censured as neurotics, parasites, plunderers, libertines and cheats. At a concert in Toronto a thinly perspiring police chief with glasses like side-view mirrors warns Vina about certain explicit gestures she has been making during performances. *Keep it clean. No funny stuff. No grabbing yourself, okay?* Seeing that there's a tv camera present Vina gives the hapless police chief five minutes on the First Amendment and artistic freedom, and when she gets on stage she grabs herself so hard and so often there's a danger she might come off in her own hands. The police chief, faced with the likelihood of a riot, fails to intervene.

The cult of VTO—its adherents have started calling themselves New Quakers, a case of the wild stealing a name from the mild— grows larger every day, fueled by the rhapsodic exegeses of Ormus's lyrics and Vina's singing provided, in a series of landmark critiques, by the keepers of the flame of rock music, the Italian-American Marco Sangria and the Francophone Martinican Rémy Auxerre.

It is a characteristic of rock music that it drives otherwise reasonable men to rapture, to excess. Even by the gushing standards of music journalism, however, Marco and Rémy are extreme. They have access to levels of rhapsody that make them the envy of their peers.

Literally, Sangria screams, Vina Apsara's voice *is music;* music in its most profound essentials. The relationship of Vina and Ormus expresses the tension between wisdom and eloquence. And the intervals of the Ormic guitar may well be, *mathematically speaking,* the structural basis not only of the whole universe but of the human soul as well. When we explore our inner space, as both Buddhists and subatomic physicists agree, we find a microcosm there which is identical with the macrocosmos: Ormus's music reveals to our hearts the identity of the little and the large.

It spreads the music of the soul to our other limbs, and so, when we dance, we dance the dance not of the body but of the soul.

Rémy amplifies these claims in his own esoteric way.

This is the struggle of the great musician, Rémy writes: that he seeks not only to sing Apollo's pure, clean song but also to move to Dionysus's dirty rhythm. The reconciliation of the conflict between the Apollonian and the Dionysiac we may call *harmonia*. Where reason and light meet madness and darkness, where science meets art and peace meets battle; where the adult meets the child, where life faces death and scorns it, make your music there.

The singer uses the frenzy of the gods, Rémy says. The frontier between the empires of Apollo and Dionysus breaks down under the pressure of this divine fury. There are four levels of *furor divinus*. Poetic *furor* calms the soul, sacerdotal *furor* prepares the spirit for exaltation, prophetic *furor* lifts us to the level of the angels, erotic *furor* unites the soul with God. Ormus's music possesses them all in the highest degree.

There are two great spirits, Rémy writes: Spiritus Humanus, that links body and soul, and Spiritus Mundi, linking the sublunary and translunary worlds. These *lunatic* terms are Auxerre's version of Ormus's doctrine of the two realities, world and otherworld. *In VTO's music these two spirits are united.* This, Rémy concedes modestly, is perhaps a grand unified theory of the soul: at certain unimaginably high levels of heat and compression—that is to say, genius—we and the cosmos are one. Ormus Cama is the proof incarnate of this theory.

Starving for soul food, the stadium-filling legions swallow large gobbets of the above effusions. What really excites them, however, is catastrophe: Marco Sangria's line-by-line, image-by-image exposition of Ormus's eschatological world-view. *The Quake is coming, the Big One that will swallow us all. Dance to the music, for tomorrow, suckers, we die.*

Eschatology and gossip: the uranium and plutonium of the late twentieth century. Vina has made the story of her life, and Ormus's, into the world's soap opera. Such is the frisson engendered by the famous celibacy oath that half the world's women line up to offer Ormus what they hope will be irresistible temptation. These appled Eves are not unlike male bar-room boasters who back their improbable charms against the resistances of all forbidden women—movie stars, lesbians, their best friends' wives. Ormus, holding himself aloof from all blandishments, even engenders violence in some women who think it unreasonable of him to deny himself, who espy in his rejection of them an insult to red-blooded women everywhere. Threats are received, and the policing of VTO concerts, as well as security at the Rhodopé Building, is stepped up as a result. Such bacchic fury is one part of the temper of the times.

Vina has her own booth at Sam's these days. There, surrounded by lovers and disciples—Marco, Rémy, whoever's in town—she holds forth. She has wisdom of her own to impart, and wants the world to know her views on, for example, the latest quasi-sciences. Biofeedback and cognitive behavioral therapy, orthomolecularism and macrobiotics. She praises the beneficial effects of Jamaica dogwood, of cabbage rubbed against the skin, of the therapeutic use of sound waves. While her crusading vegetarianism prevents her from drinking the blood of lizards and bats, she graciously concedes that the beneficial effects of such beverages have been proven beyond much doubt.

Her diet book and her health and fitness régime will become world-wide best-sellers. Later, she will successfully pioneer the celebrity exercise video and license a range of organic vegetarian meals, which, under the name Vina's VegeTable®, will also succeed. (In the commercials, healthy young consumers make the tripartite gesture of her rock fans, the two-finger peace V, the time-out T with its connotations of sporty leisure, and the approbatory thumb-and-forefinger O. *VegeTable Organics* is what we are asked to believe the sign language recommends, but that's just standard adland doublespeak.)

She is the woman most cited by the world's young women as their rôle model.

She clenches her fist against racial injustice and sings from political platforms and amid charred buildings in the aftermath of racial troubles in the American South and West. Owing to her majestic bearing, her golden voice and, above all, her renown, nobody questions her right to sing out for American blacks. She, too, has crossed the color line: not away from, but towards.

She is a fiery, witty speaker on behalf of women's rights and against the sloppy *imperium* of men. This lays her open to attack by one segment of the women's movement. How is it, these sisters want to know, that this outsize, free-spirited female is so obsessed by the clearly obsolete male member, so anachronistically in need of penetration, that she actually boasts in public about her "conquests"? Is she not, as completely as the self-incriminating chauvinist Norman Mailer, a prisoner of sex?

Why does she sing only Ormus's songs?

Why doesn't she lend her voice to the artistic vision of today's women? Why doesn't she write her own material?

Can she be free if she's just the instrument of one man's art?

Such debate—passionate, informed, ideologue—is also a part of the turbulent spirit of the age. Vina ignores her critics and sails on, a great galleon in search of fabled treasure. She is the *Argo,* and Ormus sails in her. Music itself is the Golden Fleece they seek.

Breaking their own rule about not seeing each other outside work, simultaneously overcome by need, on a whim they drive to the Nevada desert and use the four-wheel drive to write their names in the sand, so big, Vina tells Ormus, that they'll be able to identify us from the moon, like the Wall of China. After that they start calling themselves the Chinese Wall. When Vina explains to a journalist back in New York what the joke means, it backfires, they are accused of arrogance, even of attacking religion, because being Vina she adds that they wrote their names over an area bigger than any church. *You can't see no churches from the moon.* That remark, added to the Black Power salutes she's been giving lately and the perceived anti-establishment contents of Ormus's lyrics, is enough. The long-delayed assault against them is launched. Vina's an American citizen, born in the U.S.A., so she gets unprovoked police visits in the middle of the night, when she is "invited" down to the precinct house to be grilled about her political associations with Yippies, Panthers, assorted unionists and leftists, and Amos Voight's crowd of weirdo undesirables. She gets drug raids (all unsuccessful; she's not that stupid), and the IRS turns her finances over as if they were rocks beneath which all sorts of poisonous snakes must lurk. Ormus, a foreigner, gets the Immigration and Naturalization Service. In March 1973 he is ordered by an immigration judge to leave the country within sixty days. The reason given is that he was once involved in a fatal car accident and though he was not the driver samples of his blood taken at the time revealed the presence in his veins of an illegal narcotic substance. When this is announced in court, Ormus understands he's up against power on a scale he's never encountered before, a power so great it can undo the good work of Mull Standish and Yul Singh and make public what has lain hidden for six long years.

(I say again: back then certain battles had not been won. It was still possible for the future to lose to the past, for pleasure and beauty to be defeated by piety and iron. One war ends, another begins. The human race is never really at peace.)

Nevertheless, discovering the tip of what will prove to be a broad stubborn streak, Ormus appeals. *America is a place to live in,* he tells the press in a rare news conference on the steps of the court. *I don't want to just scoot in and then duck out with the loot.*

There's not much chance of his scooting anywhere, to tell the truth. He's with three bulging, glitter-toothed lawyers, and Mull Standish, pushing sixty but still sleek, still looking like a contender, and Vina, who has chosen today to wear a molded golden breastplate over black T-shirt and leggings, putting Ormus, the classicist's son, in mind of Pallas

Athene girded for battle, a Pallas Athene with knuckle-duster rings and movie-star shades. They're surrounded by seven identically sunglassed Singhs, then by a second circle, of the NYPD's finest, who with linked arms and many menaces hold back not only the press corps but also the thrashing, ululating New Quakers, at whose extreme fringes lurk hairy charismatics with much the same psychiatric profiles as the self-impalers at the heart of Shiite Muharram processions: denizens of the psychotropics of Capricorn, the lands of the sacrificed goat.

Why don't you marry him, a reporter asks Vina, in her face, straight out. (This is New York.) If you marry him, it's over. He'll at once have the right to stay.

He should have that right, anyway, Vina answers, by reason of the gift he brings. He improved this town just by showing up.

Why don't *you* marry *her,* the same reporter then asks Ormus, as if Vina hasn't spoken. Hey, why take the long road when there's a short cut, right.

We have a bargain, Ormus answers, meaning the ten-year oath. There are disbelieving titters from the press corps when he spells it out for them. Ormus scowls, clams up. *I gave my word.*

Standish responds swiftly to the darkening mood; raps his cane on the step. (The British formality of his dress imposes itself on the crowd: against the three-piece Savile Row suit, the Jermyn Street shirt, the mother-of-pearl buttons, the tailored shoes, the Aquascutum loden coat, what chance do jeans and sneakers really have?) Okay, that's it, ladies and gents. Show's over for today. Thank you for your interest and attention. Officer, can we get some help here, let's move it to the limo right now.

Getting Standish back into full managerial harness was Vina's idea. Putting distance—the whole Atlantic Ocean—between him and the band had originally been her strategy too. Like many confident, talented people she saw no need to give a non-creative person a piece of the cake if she didn't have to; she could handle Colchis Records. Sure she could. She already had her solo deal, she'd held out for plenty (multi-record options, generous recording funds), she reckoned she knew her way around the insalubrious parts of Contract City as well as its glamorous, brightly lit boulevards—the mugger-shadowed back streets of small print as well as the shining royalty marquees—so now that Boss Yul was taking on VTO, she would negotiate that contract too.

After signing, she had begun to have her doubts. Record sales were huge, way up in the superstar bracket, multi-millions of units were being shifted, but the amounts paid into their bank balances were shockingly small. On her say-so Ormus had bought that white elephant of an apartment on the Upper West Side, and all his bank accounts were fiercely in the red. Ormus—always the more trusting one—left the business end to Vina and the lawyers and accountants she employed. At financial meetings he often actually fell asleep until Vina shook him and put a pen in his hand, whereupon he signed on whatever dotted line was indicated. Now she feared he might have done well to stay awake. She did not share her doubts with him but admitted that, if only to provide an objective second opinion, she wanted Mull Standish back on the team.

At first, to be honest, she confessed to Ormus, I was a little jealous?, because he's so in love with you?, pretty pathetic, huh. Of me, I mean. But we need somebody in between us and Mr. Yul Singh. We need cushioning, distance. It'll improve our bargaining power.

This was after the *Peace Ballads,* at around the time when YSL started to crack the whip about her political utterances et cetera. So when Vina went so far as to wonder whether they were being fleeced— golden fleeced, she called it—by Cool Yul, Ormus suspected a personal, non-business agenda. He wanted to protest, Yul has been pretty good to us so far, but he saw the look in Vina's eye and didn't argue. Besides, he'd been missing Mull Standish himself.

Standish had remained in England, unable to tear himself away from poor pickle-brained Waldo picking up leaves in Spenta Methwold's gardens. However, his continued presence was misinterpreted by Spenta as a sign of his long-term interest in her own forlorn offer of companionship, and there followed a slow, melancholy comedy of misunderstandings played out in a form of Noh theater, or as stylized dumb-show tableaux: neither did Spenta speak her own hopes nor could Mull Standish find the words to dash them; and Virus Cama watched everything but said nothing, while Waldo was now capable of only the simplest, most innocent insights about the birds and the bees and the flowers and the trees and the sky up above. Standish felt trapped between his gratitude to Spenta, for giving Waldo a semblance of a place in life, and his solicitude for her; things had been allowed to go too far, and the truth—that she had given her ageing heart to one who could never take it—would only humiliate her now. In this strangulated environment he felt energy flow out of him. He began to think the unthinkable: that life might after all be no more than a defeat.

Vina's telephone call came like a blood transfusion. At once he set in motion his long-prepared fast-track plan to divest himself of all his British enterprises, even his much-admired listings magazine, which had beaten off an upstart rival to maintain its grip on the market, with spin-offs successfully launched in Manchester, Liverpool, Birmingham and Glasgow. As for Spenta, he now had a face-saving way of leaving her. When he told her of his imminent departure her chin shook for just an instant. Then, reconciling herself in that moment to her fate, she said, Of course go. I will look after our two injured children. We are a sort of accidental family, after all, isn't it; a family of damage and loss.

Mull Standish bowed his head and withdrew.

In New York, facing the full horror of the Vina-negotiated contracts, he became once more his capacious, potent self. He insisted on absolute control, no arguments, and fired all the band's advisers five minutes after he finished reading himself in. Then he called Ormus and Vina to a crisis meeting in his reopened midtown office suite. Right now it was just a secretary and a Xerox machine, but expansion plans were at an advanced stage. It's a catastrophe, of course, he said, drumming his fingertips on the table. Only one more album under firm contract and eight more optioned. That means they can dump you whenever they like but you can't walk away from them or change the deal. Just eleven percent of suggested retail list price, for crying out loud, less three points for the producer, and will you look at these numbers on free goods and promo. Let me spell it out for you. One cassette of *Peace Ballads* has slapped on it an SRLP of, let's keep it in round numbers, seven dollars. Never mind what it's discounted at in the stores, this is what all the figures are based on. Then you take twenty percent off for packaging, that gives you a royalty base of five sixty. At eleven percent that's a royalty of sixty-two cents per cassette sold. But now you subtract twenty-one cents for Mr. Producer, which I take it is none other than our friend Mr. Singh, and then hello, we have this completely off-the-wall twenty percent for assorted freebies, so you can kiss goodbye to one fifth of what's left. That leaves just thirty-two point eight cents, out of which you've got to pay the other band members, LaBeef and the Baths, one percent each, generous to a fault, so that costs you another twenty-one cents. The pair of you are left with exactly eleven point eight cents per cassette, split two ways, but first you deduct the quarter of a million in recording costs and the full hundred and fifty thou for independent promotion—*one hundred percent of the total,* and you *signed?*—off the top of that, and what do you know, here's a thirty-five-percent reserve against returns. So what's it sold, six million units, call that one hundred thousand dollars each, maximum, and by the time you've paid your taxes you'll see maybe fifty-five percent of it, but that's only if you've got a good accountant, which is not the case. I'm guessing fifty thousand with taxes paid, bottom line, and that's on a mega-megahit. You *children.* And meanwhile you're spending money like it's going out of style, million-dollar apartments, fancy electronic toys, I bet your gigs lose money too, I haven't even started on Ormus's pathetic writing deal, and you're wondering why the numbers are red. Jesus Christ.

So what do we do now, Vina asked in an unfamiliar, deferential voice. I mean, are we permanently fucked? How do we play it?

Standish sat back in his chair and grinned. We start playing sneaky bridge, he said. We finesse.

Yul Singh's trans- and inter-continental movements make him a hard man to pin down. He owns a Napa Valley winery, a secret Arizona hideaway ranch, a Caribbean island and great stashes of classical-period sculptures in bank vaults in, allegedly, Toronto, Boston and Savannah. It is said he visits these vaults alone, at night, to fondle his winged marble Nikes and full-breasted Aphrodites in subterranean chambers with two-foot-thick walls of steel. He has mistresses and protégés, schemes and assignations, and always plays the cards close to his chest. He also owns cows. Sixty-six million dollars' worth of Holstein dairy cattle, a sizeable proportion of the entire Massachusetts herd. Cows are sacred, mystic, he tells people when they ask why. Also, business is doubleplus good.

For reasons nobody understands he has studied and now conforms to the arcana of maximum security, booking himself on several flights leaving at the same time for different destinations, using assumed names, avoiding predictability. You're just a high-rolling record-industry honcho, for goodness' sake, Standish scoffs to his face at their first meeting at Colchis, in a room full of circular platinum and gold. What, you're acting now like Carlos or Arafat?

To which Yul replies: Listen, Standish, no offense, I like you but you're behind the game, which the fact is it's signed sealed and delivered, your artists are bound and gagged on my personal sacrificial altar, am I making myself clear, I own them, the devil didn't own Faust the way I have these babies, they're mine.

Standish has good ears, close to the ground, contacts from his old days as one of the great builders of the city, and when Yul Singh unsurprisingly gives him the brush-off, he puts these eavesdroppers back on the active roster. I want him to know he is no longer playing patty-cake, he tells Ormus and Vina, he has to understand that the negotiation has entered the major leagues. For this I need inside material. He does not add that the first news he has received from his paid listeners is that he himself might be in need of security, his old jilted lover Sam Tropicana has heard he's back in town and certain explicit threats have been made, certain red-faced fulminations have been overheard both in the somber upscale setting of the exclusive Knickerbocker Club and also in the more unbuttoned environment of the sidewalk outside Catania's pizza place in Belmont in the Bronx, near D'Auria Brothers Pork Store and Our Lady of Mount Carmel on 187th Street. There is no getting round the fact that Sam Tropicana is now one large *fromage* but Standish declines to panic.

Forget about it, it's the past, he tells his ears. Time flows only one way and I don't believe in yesterday.

Finally the team comes up with the goods, and when Yul Singh holding Will's arm walks into the auction rooms in San Narciso, Calif.—the oldest building in town, actually pre-dating World War II—he is greeted in a cold lobby of gleaming redwood floorboards and the smell of wax and paper by Mull Standish tapping his cane. You what the fuck, inquires Yul inelegantly, genuinely discomfited. I guess your smoke screens weren't all they should be, YSL, grins Standish, I assume heads will have to roll.

So you're here for what, Yul demands, recovering fast.

First let me tell you why *you're* here, says Mull. Turns out you're interested in conspiracies, underground organizations, militias, the whole right-wing paranoid-America thing. Who knows why. You're here to bid for the memorabilia of some defunct immigrant cabal, used to go around writing DEATH on people's walls. Don't Ever Antagonize The Horn. They had a trumpet logo. Nice.

You're out of your depth, okay, Yul argues, his equilibrium restored. Lemme tell you the laws of the universe. The law according to Disney: Nobody fucks with the mouse. Which in my version, with the louse: that's me. The law according to Sir Isaac Newton: to every action an equal and opposite reaction. But that was way back, before television, and in Britain too. I say, no sir, that reaction's gonna be unequal if I got anything to do with it. You fuck with me, I fuck you two times and your kid sister too. Don't antagonize the horn, you got that right, did you know I played clarinet. So here's the deal. The law of laws. Heads Yul wins, tails you'll lose.

Nice talking to you, says Standish, and exits: slow, deliberate, like a matador turning his back on the bull. Contempt wins many bullfights. Sometimes, however, it gets you gored in the back.

The legal war between the two best-dressed men in the music universe, the legendary head of Colchis Records and the manager of the all-powerful VTO group, rocks the business. It is fought with weapons that cannot be described in English, on an esoteric legal battleground that might as well be made of moon cheese. Standish hires a team of Indian lawyers and launches against Colchis whole armadas of suits, entire arsenals of writs. The record company replies in kind. They are like battling spiders and VTO's music is the fly snared in their webs of sticky string.

Vina asks Standish, Couldn't we just somehow I don't know settle?

No, he answers.

Ormus says, This is never going to end, is it.

Yes, he replies.

Look, he says. What's happening here is we're trying to win a war we've already lost. He has your signatures, all we have is nuisance value. And if we're a big enough nuisance for long enough, if we tie up enough funds because they're under litigation, then in the end he'll come to our table and deal.

That's all? Vina asks, disappointed. That's all you've got?

That, and Indian lawyers, says Standish, deadpan. The maestros of the law's delays. *Jarndyce* v. *Jarndyce* is a stroll in the park for these guys. These are marathon runners, and Yul knows it. These are the gold medalists of stall.

But what if, Ormus begins, and Standish stops him.

This is the high road, the way in through the front door, he says. Maybe there's also a low road, a back-door entry. This, don't ask me. Maybe never, but anyway not now.

The *Quakershaker* album—self-produced in Muscle Shoals and Montserrat by Ormus; Yul Singh never enters the studio—sells over twenty million units and every penny of the money's tied up in court. Yul Singh invites Standish (who has been advancing living expenses to Vina and Ormus out of his own pocket) to come into the New York office when he's back from a trip to Europe, and *just talk*. The week before this meeting's due date, the authorities' attack against Ormus and Vina is launched.

Mull Standish is of the party that holds that there is no such thing as coincidence. He hires yet more lawyers, both Indian and non-, but behind the scenes he's the one orchestrating the defense. The greater the difficulties, the greater grows his energy, the more precise his focus. He arranges solidarity concerts at the Fillmores, East and West. Dylan, Lennon, Joplin, Joni, Country Joe and the Fish turn up to sing for Ormus. As character witnesses, Mayor Lindsay, Dick Cavett and Leonard Woodcock, president of the United Auto Workers union, speak to Ormus's integrity and value. A suit is filed demanding the government's case records and asking that the immigration service's ruling be overturned. There is also the appeal before the immigration board itself.

In July 1974 the appeal is lost. Once again Ormus is given sixty days to go, or be deported by force.

During those war years, there are no new VTO records. Ormus

retreats into the Rhodopé Building and if he's writing he's not telling anyone, not even Standish, not even Vina. Between Vina and Standish, both in love with Ormus Cama, a surprising intimacy forms, a friendship based in part on Ormus's denial of his body to them both, in part on their joint relish for the fray. She accompanies Standish to meetings of the gay businessmen's Greater Gotham Business League, joins in their lobbying of politicians on the subject of the recent increase in attacks on the gay community, and gains the League's support for Ormus's cause. Standish and Vina become a formidable pair of lobbyists. They brief Jack Anderson, whose Report then reveals both that the drug in Ormus's blood at the time of the Crossley accident had been administered in a spiked drink without his prior knowledge, and also that over one hundred aliens with worse drug records than Ormus's have been allowed to remain in the U.S.A. This in turn persuades a New York congressman called Koch to introduce a bill designed to allow the U.S. attorney general to grant residency to Ormus Cama. The tide, very slowly, turns.

In October 1975 the deportation order is overturned by the U.S. Court of Appeals, and a year later, Ormus receives permanent residence status. Once again, there is something like solid ground beneath his feet.

The celebrations are short-lived, however, like an opening-night party that dies when some killjoy comes in waving the *Times* critic's fatal panning of the show. Like the laughter dying on Macbeth's lips at the appearance of what Yul Singh once memorably called Banquet's Ghost. Now Singh himself is the specter at the feast. Openly dismayed by Ormus's victory, he hardens his own resolve. He meets with Standish and simply says, No deal. Then he digs in for a war of attrition, calculating that he can starve Vina and Ormus out. It's their money that's tied up, after all. He has plenty of access to funds elsewhere.

When it becomes plain that long litigious years stretch ahead, Standish begins to lobby Colchis's distributors, WEC, arguing that as the deadlock has taken the world's #1 band out of distribution, they, the distributors, are being hit in the pocket by Yul Singh's intransigence, his czarish refusal to come to the table like a reasonable man.

Ormus Cama is a tough cookie, he points out. He will sing for quarters on the sidewalk if he has to, but he will not be enslaved. Did they see the *Rolling Stone* cover, by the way, the one with Ormus and Vina naked and in chains? How worth it was that?

He gets a fair hearing, but Yul Singh is a big man, and can soak up a lot of pressure. It will be five more years before the battle ends. By 1980 Mull Standish has used up most of his personal fortune, and defeat has become a real possibility. By 1980 he has played all his cards.

Then the back door opens, and the low road to success is revealed.

At the nadir of the struggle against Colchis, Ormus has a bread oven installed in his apartment and spends his days baking his beloved loaves—crusty white, granary brown, flour-dusted buns—and discourages all callers. This is his way of going into retreat. On an impulse, Standish and Vina decide to head for a retreat of their own: Dharmsala in the Pir Panjal range, the place of exile of Tenzin Gyatso, the fourteenth Dalai Lama and, in Standish's opinion, the truest man in the world. Vina calls Ormus to tell him the news of their imminent departure. He speaks only of bread.

India is still there. India abides, and is the third thing that binds Vina and Standish together. Delhi is hot. It is blazing with discontents in the aftermath of the assault on the Sikh extremists who were cornered, and made their last stand, in Amritsar's Golden Temple. (This was the so-called Wagahwalé gang of terrorists, named after the egg-bald Man Singh Wagahwalé, a small bearded man deformed by the memory of the slaughter of his family during the Partition massacres and now fatally in love, like so many small, bald, bearded men around the world, with the fantasy of a micro-state to call his own, a little stockade in which to wall himself up and call it freedom.) The terrorists are dead now, but the sacrilege of the Indian Army's assault on Sikhism's holy of holies still reverberates. Reprisals are feared, and then counter-reprisals, and so on, the familiar sorry spiral. This is not the India Vina and Standish want. They make haste for the Himalayan foothills.

Indians—or let's say plains Indians—behave like children when they see snow, which seems like a substance from another world. The towering mountains, the lack of pretension of the wooden buildings, the people who seem free of all but the simplest worldly ambitions, the thin clear air as pure as a choirboy's soaring treble, the cold and, above all, the snow: these things render the most sophisticated urbanites open to what they would not normally value. The sound of small bells, the scent of saffron, slowness, contemplation, peace.

(In those days there was also Kashmir. The peace of Kashmir is shattered now, perhaps for ever—no, nothing is for ever—but Dharmsala remains.)

Vina once again finds herself playing second fiddle in the company of Mull Standish, and oddly doesn't mind. The origins of Tibetan Buddhism in the teachings of the Indian Mahayana masters, the formation of the different sects, the ascendancy of the Yellow Hats, the doctrine of the four noble truths: on these and other matters Standish is a fountainhead of information. Vina imbibes. Years ago, Standish met the Dalai Lama himself, and formed at that time a particular attachment to the deity Dorje Shugden, who, it is said, spoke to Gyatso through a monk in a trance state and told him the secret route by which he escaped from Tibet's Chinese conquerors and made his way to India.

Dorje Shugden has three red eyes and breathes out lightning. But he is one of the Protectors, wrathful as he looks.

On this trip there is unfortunately no question of an audience with the High Lama, who is abroad, but Standish plans to perform ritual devotions to Shugden. He, too, is a man looking for a way.

He asks Vina Apsara if she'd like to be a part of this.

Okay, Vina says. Why not. I came this far.

Then we'll be *vajra* brother and *vajra* sister, Standish tells her. *Vajra* is the unbreakable thing, a bolt of lightning, a diamond. It's the strongest bond, as strong as a tie of blood.

But at the doors of the down-at-heel Shugden temple Otto Wing is waiting for them with bad news. Shaven-headed and robed, every inch the true believer, the most faithful of the faithful, his heavy black-rimmed glasses the only remnant of the Otto who frolicked with Ifredis Wing in Tempe Harbor a lifetime ago, he informs Standish through pursed, disapproving lips that the Dalai Lama has broken with Dorje Shugden. These days he preaches against the deity, discourages his worship. He says that the Shugden cult detracts from the Buddha himself. To seek external help from such spirits is to turn away from the Buddha, which is disgraceful. You must not pray here, he instructs the shaken Standish. The road to the four noble truths no longer passes through this place.

Tense, embattled Shugden monks admit he's telling the truth. There is division in Paradise. Tibetan Buddhism has always been somewhat sectarian, and one of those divides has started to widen. Standish is so upset that he refuses to stay. Otto Wing flaps around, insisting that they all meditate together, but Standish brushes him off. *We're out of here.* Meaning: I no longer belong. Even in this haven I can find no peace.

No sooner have they slogged up into the mountains than they must take the slow buses and trains back down into the city heat. Vina goes along with this, because what she sees on Standish's face is an alienation that fills her with fear for him. This man has fought so hard and lost so much: children, illusions, money. She worries that he may not survive this latest blow.

They arrive in Delhi, to find the city in uproar. A quadruple assassination, by Sikh bodyguards, has resulted in the deaths of Indira Gandhi, both her sons, and the increasingly powerful political figure of Shri Piloo Doodhwala. Dreadful reprisals are being visited upon the city's Sikh population. The air is full of atrocity. Vina and Mull check in at the old Ashoka and sit together, stunned, not knowing what to do for the best. Then there is a knock on the door. A cockaded hotel employee hands Standish a thick, dog-eared file tied up in quantities of thin, hairy rope. The file was left at reception by a man who did not, however, leave his name. No description of the man is initially available. After much coaxing, the hotel front desk eventually concedes the slight possibility that the courier was wearing the saffron and burgundy robes of a Tibetan monk. Also seen briefly in the hotel lobby that day were members of the disbanded "magnificentourage" of Piloo Doodhwala, perhaps even—though this is unconfirmed—the great man's grieving wife, Golmatol Doodhwala herself.

In that overheated time it is easy for Vina, and even perhaps Standish, to believe in almost any rumor, any possibility; even that the package comes not from any mortal source but from a deity, which perhaps feels, in the hour of its own fall from grace, some kinship with the plight of VTO; that Shugden the Protector has in his wisdom sent them this priceless gift.

Inside the package is irrefutable documentary proof—in the form of facsimiles of signed documents, checks, etc., all duly notarized as true copies—that the celebrated Non-Resident Indian Mr. Yul Singh, the very same Yul Singh who has been taking such an interest in American underground cults and cells, Yul Singh the consummate rock 'n' roller, who has always presented himself to the whole world as the ultimate cosmopolitan, wholly secularized and Westernized, Boss Yul, Coolest of the Cool, YSL himself, has been for many years a secret zealot, a purchaser of guns and bombs, in short one of the financial mainstays of the terrorist fringe of the Sikh nationalist movement—of, in fact, the Wagahwalé cult, whose leaders were so recently murdered in Amritsar, and who have just exacted, for that assault, a terrible retribution, wrought from beyond the grave.

Is this new twist part of Piloo's posthumous revenge against *his* murderers?

Vina and Standish sit in air-conditioned coolness and contemplate this gift which India, greatest of all gods from the machine, has just dropped into their astonished laps. Outside, just a couple of miles down the road, the revenge slaughter of innocent Sikhs is being carried out by bloodthirsty mobs led by officials of the governing party.

Mull Standish, ordinarily the most fastidious, most thoughtful of men, is so carried away by what he has been given that he makes an observation which, in the circumstances, could be said to be in extremely poor taste.

The more I see of the West, he says, the more I realize that the best things in life come from the East.

When a great tree falls in the forest, there's money to be made from the sale of firewood. After Standish, back in New York, mails Yul Singh selected photocopies of the material in his possession—at his home address, for the sake of discretion—the record company boss invites him over to Park Avenue for a drink, and meets him at the elevator without a trace of rancor. You got me fair and square, he admits right off. I call that good work. I always told those kids they got a good one in you. A man wears many masks, few people strip him down to the bone. The criminal and the detective, the blackmailer and the mark, these are close connections which there's not many marriages more intimate. These are bonds of steel.

{}{}(){}

Vajra bonds, Standish thinks. Thunderbolts and rocks.

My wife reads the mail for me here at home, Yul Singh adds, which I don't have to tell you means I made a full breast of it all, so she's fully up to speed. He leads Standish into a vast room with much on the walls that is of interest to this India-loving man: an elephant's silver caparison, stretched and framed; small bronze Natarajas; Gandhara heads. Marie-Pierre d'Illiers is at the far end of the room, standing very still with a long flute of champagne in her hand. Her dark hair drawn tightly back, hanging in a chignon at the nape of her long and now slightly scrawny neck. She is tall, thin, utterly possessed, utterly unforgiving. She makes Standish feel like what he probably is: a blackmailer and, which is worse, the burglar of all her joy. I have for you just one question, Monsieur Standish, she says in faintly accented English. You and your charges will be owed now an immense sum of money, but truly immense; wealth beyond dreams. (*Question* and *immense* are spoken as French words.) So what I ask is this: If a good price can be made, will you buy my cows? I always detested that we were in the dairy trade, but in the end I grew fond of my Holsteins. I am sure you will be suited to the business ideally. The milking and so on.

There is a brief touch of hands between the blind husband and the all-seeing wife. At that moment, with her use of the past tense tolling in his ears as if it were a death knell, Standish understands what Yul Singh has told his wife about his future intentions, and what she has promised him in return.

Please, this way, Yul Singh shepherds him to a table covered in papers. The documents are retrospective, the terms are now at the outer edge of what is earned by any performer in the world, and there is favored-nation status. Please take your time and make any changes you care to make.

When the reading is done Standish takes out his pen and signs many times. Yul Singh's signature is already there.

He rises to go.

There is no possibility, Marie-Pierre d'Illiers murmurs, of an accommodation being arrived at regarding these documents?

The bull is on its knees waiting for the coup de grâce.

No, Mull Standish says. I am sorry. You must understand that I have simply been used in this matter, by a principal whose identity I don't know. If I do not move, the principal will surely bring these papers to light by another means. So, I can't help you. But as to the dairy herd, yes, if the price is right, we're interested.

He leaves them there, in long shot, at the far end of the great chamber of their lives, sipping Cristal champagne as if it were poison. Hemlock, Standish thinks, and then the elevator door closes and he's going down.

Their death (too many sleeping pills) is announced the next day. The obituaries are as large and as fulsome as any great star's. News of the end of VTO's dispute with the Colchis label is withheld for two weeks, as a mark of respect for the genius of the music man who has died.

The Sikh documents, interestingly, are not released into the public domain, even though Yul Singh, in a farewell message to the Colchis board, has sketched out their contents to explain his actions. The interests of the label are not served by making this final missive more widely known. Standish chooses not to say what he knows, and nobody comes forward in his place. Death has apparently satisfied the principal. Yul Singh is not pursued beyond the grave.

At Sam's Pleasure Island, Cool Yul's booth is left unoccupied for one full month, guarded against the incursion of the crass and ignorant by a formidable phalanx of Singhs. During this month, the Pleasure Island staff make sure that a Manhattan on the rocks and a thick Cohiba cigar are always waiting at Yul's absent elbow.

After that, however, the city's life moves on.

14

THE WHOLE
CATASTROPHE

More sadness, before joy. Mull Standish does not live to enjoy his great victory for long. The night before his 1981 disappearance he's working late at the office and makes midnight telephone calls to both Ormus and Vina to read them the riot act. Standish who never spoke up for himself hectors them both about their love, the pending, freeze-frame love which blots out his own. The ten years are almost up, he says, and it's time you both stopped acting like fools. To Ormus he says, that you were not able to return my feelings for you is of small concern to anyone but me, and I can handle it, thanks. (No, he couldn't, not really, but he carried his grief stoically, like the English gentleman he wasn't; he had acquired the stiff upper lip that went with the Savile Row tailoring he liked.) But that the two of you should squander what's left of the immense fortune of your love, he scolds, having already wasted so much time, that would be a thing I could not forgive. To Vina he adds, The suspense is killing me. Will you, won't you, will you, won't you. I say join the goddamn dance. And let me say that if you don't the disappointment might kill me too, and if it does and if there's light at the end of that famous tunnel maybe I'll come back and shine it in your eyes. If I have to haunt you into doing the right thing I'll find me a white sheet and howl.

The next day the richness of his life is reduced to the thin finality of a crime scene: a wrecked office, broken windows, an absence. Some, not much, blood on the carpet: a nosebleed, perhaps. A broken cane. Unexpectedly, there is what looks like a suicide note, in an open notebook on his desk. *Suicides are most frequent in the spring. When the world is falling in love, your own lovelessness hits you hardest.* Why would a man write such a note, then trash his office, punch himself in the nose, break his walking stick and vanish without trace? This isn't a suicide note, Vina tells the police, it's a diary entry. He was just talking to us about love on the phone and I guess it made him sad. But this was not a man to take his own life. This was a great fighter, a person who overcame.

This version is, after some initial hesitation, accepted as the most probable. The event is classified as abduction, and murder is suspected. Suspicion focuses on a certain jilted lover, but no hard evidence comes to light, nobody sends anyone a fish wrapped in the morning paper, no charges are ever laid. Nor is Standish's body found. Time must pass before he is legally declared dead and Waldo Crossley, Spenta's simpleton gardener, becomes a seriously wealthy man.

(When Spenta Methwold in a white mansion high above the rural Thames hears the news of Standish's disappearance she bundles Ardaviraf and Waldo into the back of her Mercedes and drives aimlessly for three hours through the surrounding country lanes. Spenta is an old woman these days, there are cataracts in both eyes, so it's like driving in blinkers, half blinded by a lifetime's accumulated tears, the stalactites of grief. In the local village of Fawcett, Bucks., she ignores a Give Way sign and is hit simultaneously from both sides by surprised farmers' wives in Mitsubishi 4WDs. It's a slow-motion accident, nobody is really hurt, but Spenta's car doors won't open. Without apology or complaint she drives to the nearest garage and the three of them wait patiently while mechanics cut them free. She goes home with Waldo and Virus in a mini-cab and when she reaches her front door she tells Virus and Waldo that this was her last journey, she is no longer interested in the world beyond her doors. *I will just sit on and think of the departed and you, our sons, will take care of me.* Then she calls her doctor and cancels the planned operation to remove the cataracts. Blinkered sight, tunnel vision, is all she now requires. The big picture is no longer a thing she wishes to see.)

Standish has gone all right. Ormus and Vina at a high window watch spring dance across the park. Here we are without family or tribe, having lost our greatest ally, he says. Now it's just you and me and the jungle. Can we stand together against whatever comes at us, the worst and the best of things? Will you? he asks her. Will you keep your word?

Yes, she says. I'll marry you, I'll spend the rest of my life with you, and you know I will love you. But don't ask me for high fidelity. I'm a lo-fi kind of girl.

There's a silence. Ormus Cama's shoulders drop in lovesick, dumb surrender. Just don't tell me, he says. I just don't want to know.

I like to remember Vina Apsara the way she was in those last years, the years of her marriage and greatest happiness, when she became the world's most dreamed about woman, not just America's Sweetheart like Mary Pickford long ago but the beloved of the whole aching planet. Vina in her thirtysomething prime striding down Second Avenue, wafting past the aromas of Thai, Indochinese and Indian food, the tie-dyed clothes, the African adornments and basketry. Her Afro had long departed, though her long hair would never escape frizziness, and her fist-clenching days were over. Her old fist-clenching buddies were Republicans now, successful community fat cats or gimcrack entrepreneurs whose designs for erotic bluejeans—with built-in penis pouches flapping absurdly beside the zipper—started to bomb the day they left the drawing board. What's gone is gone, Vina would say without regret of the old days, adding the half-complaining admission that, try as she might, and even taking into account her youthful troubles with Marion Egiptus, even allowing for her years of harassment by taxmen and policemen, she had never had to endure one hundredth of the racial abuse and hardship that came the way of her African-American friends. *Face it, Rai, we're just not the target here.* That's right, I confirmed, and didn't need to add that celebrity has a way of washing whiter too.

Nobody understood the workings of fame, upside and downside, better than Vina. Those were the days when the first crossover stars were making their way through the firmament: O.J., Magic, people whose talent made people color-blind, race-blind, history-blind. VTO was a high member of that élite, which Ormus always took in his stride, as if it were the most natural and proper thing in the world. He had taken to quoting biologists, geneticists. Human beings are just about identical, he'd say. The race difference, even the gender difference, in the eyes of science it's just the teeniest-tiniest fraction of what we are. Percentagewise, it really doesn't signify. But life at the frontier of the skin always made Vina uneasy. She still sometimes had nightmares about her mother and stepfather persuading a Virginia head teacher that her daughter wasn't no Negro, she was half Indian, not no redskin Pocahontas neither but Indian from faraway India itself, India of elephants and princes and the famous Taj Mahal, which pedigree naturally excused her from local bigotries and entitled her to ride on the yellow bus to the white kids' school. Vina also dreamed of lynch mobs, of burning crosses. If such horror was happening to anyone, anywhere, it might yet someday happen to her.

I remember Vina on fire with the dark flame of her adult beauty, flaunting on her ring finger another man's sparkler and platinum band, and, on her right hand, a cherished moonstone too. I truly believe she never knew how it tore me up when, using me as her confessor while lying in my arms, she told me about herself and Ormus, sparing nothing. Now that they were married she had somewhat reined in her public tongue and kept from the insatiable world a few at least of the privacies of her marriage bed, but she did need to talk to someone, and for all her liberation theology she was a woman without close women friends. I was her secret, to whom she told her secrets. I was what she had.

By the early 1980s I had moved a few blocks north, joining forces with three other photographers—Mack Schnabel, Aimé-Césaire Basquiat, Johnny Chow, all of them former Nebuchadnezzar hands who had quit, rebelling against the agency's worsening habit of treating its lensmen like dogs on a short leash—to buy an old whale of a building on a leafy stretch of East Fifth Street between Second Avenue and the Bowery, just across from the *Voice* offices on Cooper Square. This was an immense defunct dance and music space called the Orpheum, a name which, by conjuring up memories of my parents' cinema in Bombay, brought a lump to my throat and left me no option but to buy my share of what was then little more than a crumbling shell. Its purchase and renovation cost me more than I'd ever planned to spend on mere accommodation, but we'd got in on the ground floor of the property boom, so a big paper profit was quickly made, though by that time none of us would have thought of selling. We of the vagabond shoes, all four of us lifetime globe-trotters, had the strange, sure feeling that we had found our true home in the belly of our NoHo whale. I'd ended up with the vast top floor and a studio and terrace on the roof above. In addition, its ownership shared by the group, there was a cavernous double-volume former auditorium that could serve as giant studio, soundstage or exhibition gallery.

In the front lobby, carved into a stone wall, was a Latin motto. *Venus significat humanitatem.* It is love that is the sign of our humanity. This was a sentiment with which we were all prepared to live.

It was perfect. So this is what they feel like, I thought: roots. Not the ones we're born with, can't help having, but the ones we put down in our own chosen soil, the you could say radical selections we make for ourselves. Not bad. Not bad at all. I began to think about staying home more, but on the other hand I had a motive for travel which the three rebels didn't. I traveled, in part, to get away from Vina's absences. To get away from the brass bed she wasn't in, the empty bed which tormented me with memories of the times when she did turn up, usually unannounced, to remind me why I'd never married, and make our wretched liaison feel (almost) worth the pain.

Vina had moved uptown, into Ormus's Rhodopé Building super-apartment, now expanded with their limitless unblocked funds into a complex of four apartments, "to give ourselves space." Missing her old Canal Street haunts, she compensated by plunging into the property market. She started buying up historic houses all over the East Coast, sometimes sight unseen. I'd just look at the map and it would feel right? Also, she told me, I consulted numerologists sometimes. This is how she was right to the end, a strange mixture of high intelligence and the superstitious nonsense of her times. She loved the Orpheum, loved sunbathing naked beneath the winking spire of the Chrysler Building and, in the opposite direction, the giant gray henge of the

World Trade Center. Nearer to home, a dark water tower stood watch over her on Martian legs. Like a rocket, she'd fantasize. Look across town. A whole fleet of rockets standing on the rooftops. They're preparing to leave, to grab our water, blast the city to smithereens and take off, leaving us to die of thirst in our ruined urban desert. Vina was interested in Armageddon. Velikovsky's crank best-seller *Worlds in Collision* and its sequel *Ages in Chaos,* with their theory of "cosmic catastrophism," the new eschatological fiction by John Wilson, the ponderous old Cold War movie *Fail-Safe,* were all favorites. You could see why she liked *The Lord of the Rings.* This offered the end of a world too, but, unusually, it was a sort of happy ending.

Across the street from the Orpheum was a little coffee-and-vegetarianism store run by New York Buddhists. The coffee was good, the vegetarianism praiseworthy, but ever since her return from Dharmsala the omnipresent downtown tinkle of Buddhism had started to get Vina's goat. She was all in favor of noble truths but she was not comfortable with the way the Buddha, a wealthy and powerful prince who renounced power and wealth to gain enlightenment as a mendicant sage, now attracted followers among the wealthiest and most powerful class in the wealthiest and most powerful city in the wealthiest and most powerful nation on earth. The kids in the store were sweet and by no means were they zillionaires but they weren't carrying begging bowls or sleeping rough either, and their fellow Buddhists among the ranks of America's arts élite seemed to have an original definition of the simple life, of the Path. Vina was not sure how much renunciation was going on, but if the Dalai Lama wanted it, she said, and if the Constitution allowed?, with those backers he'd have a shot at President, or at least Mayor of New York. She had his campaign music all prepared. *Hello Dalai. Lama-Lama-Ding-Dong.* If you lost your sense of humor and pushed her into a corner she'd admit she was on the High Lama's side in his struggle against the Chinese, who wouldn't be, but she'd be annoyed at being forced into the admission. Most of the time she preferred to be sardonically out of line, out of step. To sound harsher than she was. Which fooled nobody, strangely enough. People saw through her tough-guy routine, even liked her for it, and the cruder her formulations, the harder she tried to be this radical alienated individual, the more profoundly she was loved.

India still called to her, and she couldn't understand my decision not to return. You and Ormus, she shook her head, just my luck to pick the two men in the world who turned their back on the old place. What?, I should go alone? Just me and a bunch of security guards?

Listen, I told her (her frankness lending added force to my own confessional promptings), the day doesn't pass when I don't think of India, when I don't remember childhood scenes: Dara Singh wrestling in an open-air stadium, Tony Brent singing, Sherpa Tenzing waving from the back of an open car outside Kamala Nehru Park. The movie *Mughal-e-Azam* bursting into color for the big dance number. The legendary dancer Anarkali strutting her stuff. The non-stop sensory assault of that country without a middle register, that continuum entirely composed of extremes. Sure I remember it. It's the past, my past.

But the tie is broken. There are conversations going on every day in India, conversations we'd be dragged into, that we no longer wish to have, that we can't stomach the thought of repeating even one more time, tired arguments about authenticity, religion, sensitivities, cultural purity and the corrupting effects of foreign travel.

We, she marveled. I suppose you think you're speaking for Ormus too.

Yes, I said. What do you think "Tongue Twistin'" was about, anyway?

("Tongue Twistin'" is, on the surface, one of Ormus's lighter efforts, cast as a simple song of teenage disappointment, a verse of yearning followed by a verse of disillusion. I like the way she walk and I even like the way she smell. Yeah and I like the way she talk and I really want to ring her bell. Now I know she's kinda crazy and a little too much, but I'm hopin' for the strokin' of her lovin' touch, and I'm really not insistin', but if we were tongue twistin', what a twistin' good time it'd be. The love story doesn't work out, alas: She don't like where I'm livin' so she don't care 'bout the way I feel. You know I had a lot of givin' but she told me that I was unreal. I tried to paint her picture but I had no luck, I tried to write her story but she said it sucked. Now I'm tired of her resistin', gonna go tongue twistin', with someone who wants to twist with me.)

In our weariness, Vina, I think we were always as one; as we are in our love for you, which is to say our love of the joy of life itself, which you embody. *Vina significat humanitatem.* That's the truth. It's you.

Well, that speech deserves a reward, she murmured, curling a hand around my head and drawing me down to where she lay, nude and splendid, beneath the blind skyscrapers and the all-seeing sky. Hug me, she ordered, and I did.

A kind of India happens everywhere, that's the truth too; everywhere is terrible and wonder-filled and overwhelming if you open your senses to the actual's pulsating beat. There are beggars now on London streets. If Bombay is full of amputees, then what, here in New York, of the many mutilations of the soul to be seen on every street corner, in the subway, in City Hall? There are war-wounded here too, but I speak now of the losers in the war of the city itself, the metropolis's casualties, with bomb craters in their eyes. So lead us not into exotica and deliver us from nostalgia. For Dara Singh read Hulk Hogan, say Tony Bennett instead of Tony Brent, and *The Wizard of Oz* makes a more powerful transition into color than anything in the Bollywood canon. Goodbye to India's hoofers, Vijayantimala, Madhuri Dickshit, so long. I'll take Kelly. I'll take Michael Jackson and Paula Abdul and Rogers and Astaire.

But if I'm honest I still smell, each night, the sweet jasmine-scented ozone of the Arabian Sea, I still recall my parents' love of their *art dekho* city and of each other. They held hands when they thought I wasn't looking. But of course I was always looking. I still am.

The party girl and the recluse, the loudmouth and the silent one, the promiscuous and the marrying kind: I never really believed they'd tie the knot, but they did, and right on schedule too. Vina's friend Amos Voight used to tell people that the celebrated ten-year engagement was just those kids' crazy game, a flirtation that acknowledged their mutual attraction but also resigned itself to the failure between them of trust, which left them no foundation on which to build any sort of marriage. Also, he'd say, it's just *so* good for business. The publicity, darlings, you couldn't buy it. Voight's philosophy of life was that you didn't read your clippings, you weighed them, and as long as your publicity was putting on weight, why then everything was just dandy. And it was true that as a publicity stunt the suspended love affair took some beating. Even during the band's long recording silence the unusual bond between Ormus and Vina kept them in or near the forefront of people's minds.

The contemporary public has had a long training in Voightian cynicism; it no longer believes what it's told. It's convinced there's a subtext beneath every text, a hidden agenda behind the overt one, an otherworld running parallel to the world. Because Vina shoved her promiscuity under people's noses, celebrated and satirized it, there were many who didn't believe it was "real." These citizens also openly queried Ormus's faithful restraint. The less scrupulous newspapers and magazines assigned their finest muckrakers to the case, and even put professional gumshoes on Ormus's tail to see who he was secretly sneaking around with, but they all came up empty. The desire to debunk the extraordinary, the urge to chop off its feet until it fits within the confines of the acceptable, is sired by envy on inadequacy. Most of us, on arriving at the notorious inn of Polypemon Procrustes in Corydallus, Attica, would find that the bed we were offered was far larger than ourselves. In the middle of the night he would seize us and stretch us screaming on the rack until we fit. Many of us who are racked by the knowledge of our smallness begrudge the few true heroes their great size.

Ormus, Vina and I: three of us came West and passed through the transforming membrane in the sky. Ormus, the youthful proselytizer of the here and now, the sensualist, the great lover, the material man, the poet of the actual, saw visions of the otherworld and was transformed into an oracle, a ten-year monk and an Art Deco–rated recluse. As for me, I must say at last that I passed through a membrane too. I became a foreigner. For all my advantages and privileges of birth, for all my professional aptitude, I was turned by the fact of leaving my place of origin into an honorary member of the ranks of the earth's dispossessed. Indochina helped, of course, unforgettable Indochina with its forgotten yellow dead, click, and the firestorm of bombing in neighboring Angkor that gave birth to a life-devouring beast, the Khmer, click, which walked like an evil phoenix out of the flames to declare war on spectacles, tooth fillings, words, numbers and time. (And on cameras too. That was my narrowest escape, needing much luck as well my old trick of invisibility. Khmer-sympathizing insects saw through my cloaking devices and assaulted me, and for weeks afterwards I was laid up with malaria as well as soul-sickness on Cheung Chau island in

Hong Kong harbor, but I was mightily relieved to settle for that, and for a slow convalescence eating waterfront fish and noodles.)

Over the years I saw the hand of Mighty America fall hard on the back yards of the world, click, not the helping hand-across-the-sea extended to America's friends but the fist which he-that-is-Mighty hammers on the green table of your country to tell you what he wants and when he wants it, i.e. right now, buster, assume the position, this means you. I came back from click the Angkoran slaughterhouse Tuol Sleng, after which I didn't find amusing any more the name of Amos Voight's studio; from click sickening Timor only to learn that officially, according to the word from Might Central at Foggy Bottom, there was no such place on the face of the earth; from Iran '79 where click the Puppet King forced his people into the arms of a revolution click that ate them alive; click from blasted Beirut; click from the revolution-speckled bananarama of Central America. I came home like Godard's soldiers bearing photographs of the dark wonders of the world, all my clicked body heaps and skull mountains and land-mined school buses and score-settling murderers and famines and full-blooded genocides, and when I opened my cheap suitcase to prove I'd kept my promise my sweetheart wasn't around, but there were photo editors who asked me, Mr. Merchant, do you love America? Ray—is that some kind of alias, Ray?—Ray, to what extent are you a communist stooge?

Our lives tear us in half. Ormus Cama the reluctant mystic, the surviving twin, lost the double in his head and discovered instead a doubling in the whole of existence. His two eyes, seeing different whatnesses, made his head and heart ache. Something of the same sort was my fate regarding this thing, America. Because the America in which I led my well-off, green-carded life, Orpheum-America in which love is the sign of our humanity, America below Fourteenth Street, loosey-goosey and free as air, gave me more of a sense of belonging than I'd ever felt back home. Also, with the dream America everyone carries round in his head, America the Beautiful, Langston Hughes's country that never existed but needed to exist—with that, like everyone else, I was thoroughly in love. But ask the rest of the world what America meant and with one voice the rest of the world answered back, Might, it means Might. A power so great that it shapes our daily lives even though it barely knows we exist, it couldn't point to us on a map. America is no finger-snapping bopster. It's a fist.

This, too, was like seeing double. This was where my heartaches began.

In combat zones there is no structure, the form of things changes all the time. Safety, danger, control, panic, these and other labels constantly attach and detach themselves from places and people. When you emerge from such a space it stays with you, its otherness randomly imposes itself on the apparent stability of your peaceful home-town streets. What-if becomes the truth, you imagine buildings exploding in Gramercy Park, you see craters appear in the middle of Washington Square, and women carrying shopping bags drop dead on Delancey Street, bee-stung by sniper fire. You take pictures of your small patch of Manhattan and ghost images begin to appear in them, negative phantoms of the distant dead. Double exposure: like Kirlian photography, it becomes a new kind of truth.

I'd started getting into quarrels, even into fights. Yes, in bars, with strangers, that too, fights about nothing. Me. I heard myself boring and bullying in a thick drunk's voice I barely recognized but I couldn't stop myself. As if the violence I'd seen had ignited some answering violence deep within me. The fires at my center ascending through faults in my personality to pour out through the volcanoes of my eyes, my lips. One evening not long after Standish's disappearance I escorted Vina to Xenon, then to 54. Ormus hated those places, so I could act as Vina's walker without arousing his suspicions. She on the other hand couldn't leave the clubs alone, it was an addiction, and anyway Vina never cared about what people might think. She wore black but it didn't look much like mourning dress; there wasn't quite enough of it for that. Well, anyhow, at 54 there was this slick-haired guy who made some wisecrack about it being too soon after Mull's last exit . . . oh, never mind. Vina pulled me away just in time. She said what I was experiencing was male anger, gender-based, *because you're losing control.* Meaning, men were. That felt like a shot so wide of the mark I didn't even know where to look to retrieve the arrow, so I started bitching about Ormus instead. These otherworld songs of his, I said, shouting over the music, what does he think he's doing, offering people a promised land or what. It makes me mad, I said, because even though if you listen to the small print he's just saying it's different, not better, that isn't what the kids are hearing. Who hears the lyrics properly anyway, you said it yourself. Those fucking New Quaker lunatics, you think they're hearing right? They're aching for doomsday, praying for the end, bring on the *dies irae,* the day of wrath, because then the fucking kingdom will come. I can't fucking stand it. Will you guys please stop.

That was when she told me. We're doing it, she shouted. We're getting married. I hope you'll cool down long enough to come.

The music had stopped, and she'd yelled into the sudden silence. It was quite an announcement. Everybody in the joint started applauding and Vina just grinned and took her bows. In the end, having no option, I clapped too.

Something unexpected was happening in the music world, the younger bands were failing, the glitter litter had lost its shine and the kids were looking to the older guys. As if the human race were to turn away from the present evolutionary moment and commence to reverence the dinosaurs who came before. It was disgraceful, in a way, but being older was getting to be an advantage. Ormus Cama was forty-four years old and this was working in his favor. The same age as the music, people kept repeating, the same age as the music, like a mantra, as if it meant anything, as if music didn't cross frontiers of time as well as space. To be the same age as the music was suddenly to know it all, like the ancient Delta blues brothers, like Old Adam himself. Wisdom was the hot commodity now, and Ormus had that, the wisdom of the recluse, of the Delphic oracle, of, oh, let's say Brian Wilson of the Beach Boys. And in addition, in the eyes of the record-buying public he possessed something which was not to be found in Delphi or the California surf: viz., the wisdom of the East.

VTO had a hit record again, and what a record it was, a jam-packed carnival of a double album, *Doctor Love and the Whole Catastrophe.* That was a phrase Ormus liked, he'd read or heard it someplace and it stuck. He used to say that music could be either about almost nothing, one tiny strand of sound plucked like a silver hair from the head of the Muse, or about everything there was, all of it, *tutti tutti,* life, marriage, otherworlds, earthquakes, uncertainties, warnings, rebukes, journeys, dreams, love, the whole ball of wax, the full nine yards, the whole catastrophe. The new album was a rich mosaic of all these: love songs and jeremiads, heart-stopping odes and visions of doom. It couldn't miss.

On the sleeve he and Vina posed in the fig-leafed nude, like classical statues wearing shades. Like mythical lovers, Cupid and Psyche, Orpheus and Eurydice, Venus and Adonis. Or a modern pair. He was Doctor Love and she, in this reading, was the Whole Catastrophe. This sleeve was afterwards called a prophecy of death by the same people who believed Paul McCartney was dead because he was the only one walking barefoot across the zebra crossing on *Abbey Road,* the people who insisted that if you put your stereo needle on the grooves in the reject-zone of *Sgt. Pepper* and then turned the platter anti-clockwise with your finger you'd hear John Lennon saying *I will fuck you like a superman.* The world of popular music—the fans as well as the artistes—sometimes seemed to be populated exclusively by people with troubled minds.

Vina and Ormus were finally allowing themselves just to be in love, and their flowering happiness was the damnedest thing. Soon after their marriage they paid for full pages of advertising space in the world's press to say how they felt: an idea that must have been Vina's. Much of the text sounded like her work too. This is what they told the world: that they had learned to love each other fully, trusting each other totally, through their dreams. They had discovered that each was dreaming of the other, every single night, *and they were the same dreams. We were actually, in reality, but without knowing it, leaving our bodies to enter the other's dream. Our spirits made love and taught our waking bodies to trust.*

So their wet dreams had got them through ten years, that was how I saw it. They, however, now had rather loftier ideas about the power of love, and of music, *which is the sound of love.*

Love is the relationship between levels of reality.

Love produces harmony and is the ruler of the arts. As artists we seek to achieve, in our art, a state of love.

Love is the attempt to impose order on chaos, meaning on absurdity.

It is inventive, double-natured, holding the keys to everything.

There is love in the cosmos.

Love was born before, and is more potent than, the laws of nature.

Love raises us above the limitations of our bodies and gives us free will.

We assert the love of man for his fellows.

We assert love as a cosmic force, bringing about creation.

We transform constantly and we remain constant. Music is the bridge between our worlds. Music liberates and unifies.

We are filled with the madness of love, which leads the mind beyond understanding towards a vision of beauty and joy.

Songs are love's enchantment. They are everyday magic. The Sirens' song drew men to their deaths. Calypso's song kept Odysseus enchanted by her side. No man can resist the song of Aphrodite, or of Persuasion, her singing witch.

Songs enchant away our pain.

May we, who are full of desire, always have song, sweet song, sweeter than any drug.

Love is harmony. Harmony is love.

(We dedicate this record to the memory of our friend and savior, Mullens Standish the loving pirate. May your skull and crossbones always fly high.)

The music was their real lovemaking. So much has been said and written about Vina's big-mouth attitude, but what I want to hear is more about the way she used that big mouth in song, along with those lungs, that brain. I want to hear about that voice-of-the-century voice. How she improved her phrasing by studying film of violinists—Heifetz, Menuhin, Grappelli—and, impressed by the bowing that created an apparently continuous sound (all teeth and no gaps was the way she put it), how she set out to sing the same way. To sing like a violin. To give herself that famous long-line fluidity she also studied the way horn players breathe, and spent hours improving her lungs by swimming underwater laps at her health club. Then she just stood up and let rip with (in the bad old days) a bottle of bourbon in her hand and it was as if she'd been born that way. The art that conceals art: the most flamboyant rock star in the world was a devotee of the philosophy of artistic discretion. Never let 'em see how you do it, that was her creed. She once said to me: What do they want to know, how? That's not for them to know. It's my job to do it and theirs to applaud.

The atom-splitter Oppenheimer, on beholding the power of his brainchild the Bomb, quoted the Bhagavad Gita. *I am become Death, the Destroyer of Worlds.* Death's magic mushroom, born of the marriage of fissile materials. In the eight years between Ormus and Vina's marriage and her untimely end, there were some harsh, carping voices, notably those of their erstwhile admirers Rémy Auxerre and Marco Sangria, who alleged that both leading members of VTO were highly unstable personalities, permanently on the verge of coming apart, and that if they weren't super-rich rock stars they'd be in the funny farm. I say only that if they were fissile, then at least the energy released by their union—love's own Manhattan Project—was a brightness rather than a darkness, a source of pleasure, not pain, an aspect of Life-the-Creator rather than the Destroyer, Death.

You must imagine me gritting my teeth as I write this.

Love made them irresistible, unforgettable. As performers, as people, deferral's end and the relief of consummation rendered them, if I may be permitted the pun, consummate. When they walked into rooms, hand in hand and glowing, people fell silent, in awe. They had been perfected by love. And there was plenty to spare. The long-dammed torrent of their joy poured over anyone within range, drowning strangers in unlooked-for happiness. Their stage act had been reinvented completely. Ormus turned round to face the audience. Legs planted wide apart, golden guitar sparkling in his hand, tall, thin, his face like a monument to his long wait and belated triumph, the golden eye patch adding to the power of the persona, lending it piratical overtones, he represented the danger and realism of the music as well as its underlying hope. Unfortunately, owing to his damaged, whistling eardrums, he needed protection against the decibels the band was pumping out, and so a soundproofed glass case had to be constructed for him, complete with air-conditioning and floor pedals which controlled and varied the sounds of his weeping guitar. At the focal point of the stage, brilliantly lit, was this object out of space opera or fairy tale, and Ormus Cama, who had once lain comatose in the glass coffin of a converted orangery, now sang and played, fully conscious, inside another glass box.

While he stood still, encased in glass, Vina ran and leapt, pranced and whirled, a super-fit, super-charged Vina, a Vina who was taking care of business and of herself. If he was Being, she was Becoming, and behind them the rhythm section laid down a succession of righteous laws; the drums beat their message to the skies.

And around and about them—perhaps to deflect attention from his own enforced static rôle—Ormus began to devise great spectacles, hyperbolic feats of showmanship that showed him to be a Bombay lad at heart, turning naturally to the mythic vulgarity of the Bollywood musical. Yes, showtime; science fiction dystopias, fabulated dragon-worlds, seraglio visions featuring platoons of harem-panted, rhine-stoned-naveled belly dancers, black-magic rings of fire o'ertowered by Baron Samedi inflatables, and the whole multiple-image videorama which is now the staple fare of stadium rock but in those days gave people the kind of shock Bob Dylan did when he went electric. (What could once be achieved by plugging a guitar into the wall now requires a military operation. We are not as easily shockable, not as innocent as we were.)

The addition of showmanship, of spectacle, gained VTO new legions of admirers. They entered that zone of celebrity in which everything except celebrity ceases to signify. Camamania, Vinamania were in full swooning, screaming swing, but some early exegetes jumped off the bus. Sangria and Auxerre attacked VTO for having betrayed their old fans, for selling out. Perspiration instead of inspiration, light shows instead of enlightenment, greed instead of need, wrote Marco Sangria, accusing the band of becoming little more than the biggest stick of bubble gum on earth. Ormus, that golden eye patch, that giant glass ear-muff, Sangria scoffed: why not just put your whole head in a fucking bag?

Later, when Vina and Ormus "went political," organizing the Rock the World charity concerts, meeting world leaders to demand action on global famine, protesting the cynicism of international oil companies in Africa, joining the campaign for third-world debt relief, demonstrating against health hazards at nuclear processing plants, documenting the growing invasion of personal privacy in America by the spreading tentacles of the secret state, highlighting the abuse of human rights in China, proselytizing the vegetarian message, the same commentators who had abused them for their superficiality now berated them for pomposity, for stepping out of their playpen to argue with the grown-ups.

Ormus Cama's second full-page press advertisement, *What Is the Whole Catastrophe?,* in which he publicly expressed his fear that some sort of apocalypse might be imminent, some sort of science fiction encounter between variant and incompatible versions of the world, was the last straw.

To be given the world as a toy must be pleasant, Rémy Auxerre wrote. But then one must have a certain aptitude for playing the world's big games. To be given the world as a stage is also a great privilege, he added. But on the world's stage there are only a few heroes and many babbling fools.

In a way they had ceased to be real. To Auxerre and Sangria, they had become little more than signs of the times, lacking true autonomy, to be decoded according to one's own inclination and need. Marco Sangria, whose most profound conviction was that the truth of the twentieth century is a secret truth, the century's history a secret history of antichrists and outcasts, announced that the VTO super-phenomenon was now too one-dimensionally *overt,* too vulgarly *apparent.* Their success was therefore a metaphor of the flatness, the one-dimensionality, of the culture. It was a rebuke to its own fans. The Martinican Auxerre, champion of racial and cultural admixture, of the *Creolization of the soul,* made it his task to expose Ormus and Vina—Vina, the honorary Panther!—as deracinated, even Tomist. After long researches he published a thousand-page hatchet job bringing all Ormus's family's skeletons out of their closets, the colonialist Anglophilia and examination fraud of Sir Darius Xerxes Cama, the braining of Ardaviraf, Cyrus the serial killer, Spenta playing the British milady by the Thames; and Vina's too, her murderer-suicide mother, her "willingness" to travel on school buses from which black kids were banned, and so on. From this work we learned that Marion Egiptus had "died in poverty" without so much as a phone call from the little girl she raised, but we did not learn of Vina's youthful miseries in Chickaboom, N.Y., or that she had paid all Marion's medical bills for years. We learned, too, that Vina's father, the disgraced Indian lawyer and ex-butcher Shetty, having filed for bankruptcy many years previously, was now a bum, a panhandler, living rough in an insalubrious quarter of Miami. *What sort of debased beings are these,* Auxerre demanded, *these great lovers who can love only themselves, but spurn their own family, their own people?*

One skeleton was not dragged out of the shadows to dance its hideous bone-clicking dance in the public eye.

One year and one day after their marriage, Vina had returned to my bed. Not often, not for long, but she came back. She came back to me.

I'll tell you why those poison-pen attacks flopped, Vina murmured in my arms. It's because everybody loves a lover. I'm a lover; everybody loves me.

Then what are you doing here, I asked.

It's that Amos dance pattern, she said. If you want to solve the riddle, you've got to step out of the frame.

But that was just a clever answer. There were others. One of these was that Vina wanted to save me. Look at your life, Rai, where you go, what you do. You dive with your camera into the cesspit of the human race, so obviously you think we're all made of shit. Then back home with the flat-chested knickerless clothes-ponies, that's hardly an improvement, is it. Those girls only open their mouths for one reason and it's not to fucking eat or speak. Look at your pathetic life. There was that girl who loved you, you left her behind, what was her name. (She knew the name. This scolding was a ritual. She wanted to make me say it.) Anita, I said. Anita Dharkar. She chose to stay home.

Did you ask her, Vina demanded. Even if you did, you didn't do it properly, your heart wasn't in it. Now I'm going to tell you a thing about your life. Your life is dirt. You're more like Ormus than you know only he's all cleanness and light and you're all mud and darkness. If you're the best on offer, we should all give up right now.

Thanks, Vina, I love you too, I murmured, more shaken than I cared to show.

Yet when I'm with you I feel you're part of something, some lifestream?, she went on. I think that's what each of us is, a part of some larger river, and no matter how muddy and poisoned any individual bit of the river might be, you can still pick up the sense of that larger flow, that great and generous water. This is the life and death business I'm talking about, Rai. You're a heathen, you pretend there's no life afterwards, but I'm telling you you're a part of something right here and now and what that is, whatever it is, it's good, it's better than just you on your own?, only you're just rolling along, you don't even know the name of the river of yourself.

Stop now, I said, it's Wednesday, on Wednesday I put out the garbage.

The way I saw it, my uninterest in her mystical side nagged at her, she needed to conquer that resistance, and that's one of the things that kept her coming back. But in the end the ordinary physical things, the man-woman things are primary. We were good together, end of story. Even though she was an old married lady now I allowed her to think she didn't have to be. I asked nothing, but gave what she needed. With me she was single again. She was free.

Oh, one more thing: Ormus, her one true love, was beginning to scare her.

About VTO's victory over the Sangria-Auxerre assault, however, she was spot on. In those days there were more women fronting bands and making solo careers. Some of them were angry because men and love had not been good to them, many of them had eating disorders, others were deranged on account of things that happened to them as children, *touch me daddy don't touch me, hug me mama don't hug me, love me daddy won't you leave me alone, love me mama wanna be on my own. You know that I remember too much. So I don't know what to do with your Tender Touch.* Still others were super-cool smooth operators with an empty thing in their eyes. Marco Sangria's angry sister Madonna, also now an influential critic, was already saying that gender, the body, was the only subject. Once upon a time the Crystals sang *he hit me and I'm glad.* Now it was *hit me and I'll break your fucking jaw.* (This was an improvement, evidently.)

In the middle of all this misery Vina, uniquely, looked like—she *was*—singing out of pure happiness. That single fact made our hearts soar, even when she was delivering Ormus's most jaundiced lyrics. The joy in her singing showed us there was nothing we could not overcome, no river too deep, no mountain too high. It made her the world's beloved.

(On this occasion, I use the words "we" and "our" to denote a collectivity of which I was certainly a part, as deliriously infatuated as any front-row fan.)

It began to be seen as her band. Ormus produced the records, dreamed up the shows with the design team, wrote the songs, and looked on stage like a small craggy god down from Rock Olympus, but he was encased in glass, which distanced him, made him abstract. He became more of a concept, an animatronic special effect, than an object for our dreams and desires. Also, we could tell he was a control freak. Those ten years of waiting, they hadn't been natural. This mythic monogamy of his, this excess of determination, there was something domineering about it, something obdurate that would not be denied. We could see how she might react against so possessive a love. How, even loving him, even adoring him, she might run to find room for herself.

So it was mainly Vina for us, Vina the Voice, Vina whose non-stop motion on stage was like a message saying Ormie, baby, Ormie, my only boy, I love you my darling but you can't tie me down. You can marry me but you can't catch me; if I'm the blithe spirit, you're the genie in the bottle. You can run the show but I can run. Yes, it was Vina we wanted, Vina of the horribly injured childhood who instead of whining on about it in a million interviews just shrugged her shoulders and made nothing of it at all, Vina who without ever asking for or expecting our sympathy told us about her abortions and barrenness and consequent grief, and thereby earned our love; Vina who took books by both Mary Daly and Enid Blyton with her when she went on tour, Vina of the thousand fads and cults who could look right into the future President's face and ask him how it felt to be named after a woman's pubic hair.

I will tell you now what I have not sufficiently expressed throughout this long saga: the thing with Vina, being her spare prick, coming off the bench for a few minutes per game, this was hard for me. There was too much time and room for my imagination to work. I imagined their lovemaking so often, and in such *Kama Sutra* variety, that I would break out in a rash. I actually would: whether of heat or fury I cannot say. Only a foreign war, a fresh batch of photographic models just off the plane from Texas, or a cold shower could bring my temperature down, restore to normalcy the beating of my heart.

I tried to make myself believe that the marriage with Ormus wouldn't last. When she told me that she had reached an understanding with him, that he would turn a blind or at least a patched eye to her *amours* as long as she didn't flaunt them in a crass and obvious way, at first I felt a spurt of hot joy because she had gone to such risky trouble to make room in her life for me. Later, in the shower, where sometimes when her absence became too painful I'd ask my soaped hands to play her part, just as her hands had understudied Ormus during his decade of non-performance, I felt my reactions becoming more complex. It was, I thought, as if I were a clause in their marriage. A sleeping partner in their merger. This doomed me to play second fiddle forever; it was in the contract. My rising anger informed me of a truth I had thoroughly suppressed: viz., that I still entertained hopes of having her all to myself.

Often I practiced feeling contempt for glass-boxed, reclusive Ormus. What sort of man would consent to become the *mari complaisant* of as major a beauty, a presence, as Vina Apsara? To which my mirror replied: And what sort would agree to take the droppings from another man's table, the leavings from his bed? There was a malicious and probably untrue story about the novelist Graham Greene according to which his mistress's husband would position himself on the sidewalk outside the apartment block in which the author of *The Quiet American* resided, and at the top of his voice shout abuse into the warm night air: *Salaud! Crapaud!* To which Greene, when asked about the story, allegedly replied merely that as his apartment was on an upper floor he would not have heard the cries, and so unfortunately he could not confirm or deny the tale.

Salaud! Crapaud! In my case, it was I, Vina's bit on the side, who felt the urge to hurl abuse. I, who with my photo-journalist's khaki hat on prided myself on my ability to blend into the background, to disappear, quickly came to loathe my invisibility in the story of Vina, the erasure from the public record of the great matter of my heart. But the more Vina and I were seen in public together, hiding in plain view, the less people were inclined to gossip. The blatantness of our association proved its innocence, yes, even to Ormus. Or so he always maintained.

One day in the Orwellian year of 1984—a time to dispense with doublespeak, to tear down the dreadful Ministries of Truth and Love— I could bear the situation no longer and rushed over to the Rhodopé Building, hot for certainty. In my hand was an envelope containing a set of photographs of Vina, nude photographs taken by me in the immediate aftermath of passion. She, who found it so hard to trust or to be trustworthy, had trusted me to make and keep private such explosive images as these; but it was the trustless marriage she preferred to her stolen hours with me. And as my behavior amply demonstrated, she would have done better not to trust me, either.

The point was that even Ormus Cama could not fail to understand what the pictures proclaimed: that for many years I had enjoyed the favors of his beloved wife. He must surely name his weapons. Prussian sabers, baseball bats, pistols at dawn by the Bethesda Fountain, I was ready for anything. For, as Vina would say, closure. I roared red-misted into the Rhodopé lobby, where I was restrained by a uniformed doorman.

It was Vina's father, the ex-lawyer, ex-butcher Shetty, now over seventy but looking ten years younger. His dreadful life had not marked him. Hearty, even jovial, he took what it dished out and stayed upright. Vina had hired a small army to find him after the newspaper article about his plight. When they unearthed him she'd flown to Florida for the big reconciliation scene and offered him whatever he wanted: retirement, a place of his own in the Keys, maybe, and of course a healthy allowance, but all that he had turned down flat. I'm the type that prefers to be in harness, he told her. Get me something where I can die with my boots on. Now he was installed in this new job, delighted with the uniform, beaming at the world. Cool in summer, warm in winter, a nodding acquaintance with the city's finest, he said. At my age and with my track record it's better than I could have hoped. India, forget about it. (His Indian linguistic education, which had stressed the importance of precise enunciation, made a strange match with his freewheeling U.S. idiom.) India, it's gone for all of us. I'll take Manhattan.

In my confrontational fury I hadn't remembered it might be Doorman Shetty's shift, but there he was, fit and ready and eager to please. Hey, Mr. Rai, sir, how is it hanging, what do you say, can I be of any assistance.

I just stood there holding my envelope, determination draining from me. Should I call upstairs, Mr. Rai? You want a ride in the elevator? Or just delivering a letter for Mr. Ormus or my daughter, can I get that for you, no problemo? Sure thing, leave it to me, it's my job.

Never mind, I said, exiting. Just a mistake.

He called after me, raising a cheery hand. Missing you already, Mr. Rai, you come back now, do you hear?

A terrible din was heard from the street outside; a junk band had showed up. Shetty's mood darkened. Charging past me, he confronted a group of youngsters playing a kitchen sink, a shopping cart, a dustbin, a wheelbarrow, buckets and, perhaps in VTO's honor, a strange chimeran fudge of a stringed noisemaker they called a guisitar, put together from the scraps of two wrecked instruments.

What do you call this, Shetty wanted to know. Where do you get off.

We're the Mall, said a red-eyed, goateed youth, asserting his leadership over his rag-haired, trembling tribe. (Not just a junk band but a band in search of junk, I noted silently.) We offer this serenade, he proclaimed, to the rock gods living in the sky. In the face of the radical uncertainty of the age we make odes to materialism, paradoxically utilizing items of no value to society. We celebrate donut culture, it's sweet and it tastes good but there's a void at the heart?

Get away from my canopy, Shetty commanded. Do it now.

There is no arguing with the authority of the New York doorman. The Mall obediently packed up and skulked away. Then, like an avatar of the Age of Greed, the leader turned back, shivering slightly, to glare at Mr. Shetty. When we're big, mister, I mean when we're monster big, I'm gonna come back here 'n' fucking buy this fucking building, and then it's your ass, baby, you have been warned.

My threat, the envelope I bore, was just as empty, I understood. Vina was right to trust me after all. I couldn't do it. I couldn't risk her withdrawal from my life. I too was an addict, hopelessly far gone, and she was my candy girl.

It occurred to me that in the field of love and desire Vina was just behaving like a man; showing herself capable, like most men, of loving wholeheartedly and simultaneously—halfheartedly—betraying that love without guilt, without any sense of contradiction. She was capable not so much of a division of attention as of multiplying herself, until there was enough Vina to go round. We, Ormus and I, we were her women: he, the loyal wife standing by her philandering husband, settling for him in spite of his roving eye, his wanderlust; and I, the simultaneously wanton and long-suffering mistress, taking what I could get. That way round, it made perfect sense.

I remember her hands, long-fingered, quick, chopping her beloved vegetables as if she were the high priestess of a pagan cult, matter-of-factly getting through the day's quota of sacrificial offerings to the gods. I remember her hunger for information, the way her bright, half-educated mind latched on to the many information-heavy intelligences her fame and beauty brought her in contact with (newspaper and tv bosses, Hollywood studio heads, rocket scientists, heavy hitters from Morgan Guaranty and D.C.) and how she pumped these sources for all she was worth, as if facts would save her life. I remember her fear of disease and early death.

Vina was a quick study, and by the time Mull Standish departed she was no longer the arrogant flake who had landed herself and Ormus in Contract Hell. Under his tutelage she had become a sharp businesswoman, as formidable as many of the big wheels for whose brains she showed an exaggerated respect they usually didn't deserve. She managed the stocks and bonds, the real estate, the growing art collection, the bakeries, the Santa Barbara winery, the cows. Ormus's fabled love of bread had led Standish naturally into this market; now Vina ensured that the high standards of the Camaloaf franchise were maintained from coast to coast. The bread was already an established brand; but few people thought of Vina Apsara and Ormus Cama as being amongst the finest viticulturists in California, to say nothing of the biggest dairy farmers in the northeastern United States, but that's what they had become. The winery thrived and the already huge herds of Holsteins acquired by Standish from the Singh estate had become even larger, their milk and cheese ubiquitously available. From goats to cows, Vina told me. Seems I can't help being on the udder side.

This in spite of the fact that during this period she had gone not only vegetarian but fully macrobiotic. No wine, definitely no dairy products. Occasionally, as a treat, she allowed herself a handful of those small Japanese dried fish. It was always interesting to me that she could make such a separation: that business, in spite of everything, was still business. Mull Standish had been an influential teacher.

Nowadays she was the worldly one, while Ormus's obsession with catastrophe had rendered him meditative, inward, strange. So, for example, it was Vina who decided for sound fiscal as well as strong sentimental reasons to buy Yul Singh's old Tempe Harbor place when it, like the cattle, was offered to the band cheaply by the estate lawyers, who informed her that it was the wish of the deceased that they be given first refusal at the most advantageous terms. (This was Yul's way of making a posthumous peace. He did not insult them by leaving them the property outright, as a gift. That would be to claim a friendship that had not existed for years. It was a finely judged decision. It showed respect.)

It was also Vina who decided to employ the Singhs. The new management at Colchis was dispensing with their services without explanation, and a deputation comprising Ormus and Vina's first chauffeur, Will, and Clea the châtelaine of Tempe Harbor, seamstress of Ormus's first eye patch, arrived at the VTO offices to plead the retinue's cause. Stripped of his black Valentino suit and sunglasses, no longer obliged to play the heavy, Will in jeans and white shirt turned out to be a hesitantly articulate young man. Clea was the same tiny, decent old lady she'd seemed at Tempe, only more worried. These were ordinary people sucked into the realm of the extraordinary and fighting back, playing their one and only card. Rumors had reached their ears of Yul's covert activities, they said, and they had, with some justice, concluded that they were being punished for their former boss's misdeeds. Just as innocent Sikhs in India were slaughtered after the Quadruple Assassination—the many suffering on account of the actions of the few—so the Colchis Singhs, too, had become the victims of American jitteriness. If Yul Singh had been a terrorist financier, then, in the view of the label, all his fellow Sikhs were tarred with the same brush. Yet we are not such people, madam, said Clea with simple dignity. We are persons of ability, willing and able to serve, and we ask you to grant our good wish.

Vina took on the whole entourage on the spot.

In 1987 Amos Voight died, Sam's Pleasure Island closed its doors for good, an era seemed to be ending, and Ormus Cama completed fifty years on earth. Turning fifty seemed to hit Ormus hard. His excursions from the Rhodopé complex had become few and far between, though once in a while Vina dragged him to a downtown music venue, accompanied by a clutch of Singhs, to hear a hot new act. These were disappointments more often than not, though just lately a young Irish quartet, Vox Pop, had impressed them as a possible start-up act. Mostly, however, their forays into Musicworld served only to confirm that the old order was, improbably enough, refusing to fade. The times were not a-changing. Lennon, Dylan, Phil Ramone, Richards, these old men were still the giants along with VTO themselves, while the likes of Trex, Sigue Spangell, Karmadogma and the Glam had been little more than blips.

Even Runt, the new rejectionism, all snarl and spittle, hadn't interested Ormus and, after a brief flare of scandal and attention, hadn't lasted. How could it, Ormus shrugged, you can't start a revolution in a clothes shop. Runt had been the brainchild of the resurfacing Antoinette Corinth, Tommy Gin and She, the Three Witches, Ormus Cama called them. Back in London, they had indeed dreamed up the angry new sci-fi look—rubber, slashed fabrics, bondage thongs, body piercing, the maquillage and attitude of android replicants on the run from exterminating blade runners—at their new Fulham Road store, and then invented a rock group to sell it. Inevitably they showed up in New York, acting as if they were the tastemakers supreme of London society, come to Manhattan to wreak a little British havoc. She, at Antoinette's bidding, did Daryl Hannah backflips in a distressed-leather miniskirt down the length of the bar at 44. No knickers, of course, darlings, Antoinette redundantly pointed out at the top of her voice. We call it Runt 'n' Cunt. New York gave them their fifteen minutes and forgot them. Their band, the Swindlers, the supposed shock troops of the new wave, fizzled in the face of American *pudeur* and ended up fatally shooting each other—and Corinth and Gin—in a suite at the Chelsea Hotel. She alone survived, having jumped ship five minutes before the fight that ended the revolution. She ran shrieking through the lobby wearing rubber and black lace, disappeared into the city night and never bothered to come back for her other clothes.

I remembered She's old loathing of Tommy Gin and wondered if this might have played a part in the shootings. But She had vanished for ever, and the question went unanswered. The Swindlers' violent stupidity was thought to be explanation enough.

Ormus barely responded to the news of Antoinette Corinth's death. This woman had in all probability tried to kill him once, had caused a car accident that deprived him of years of his life, but he seemed beyond resentment. He was thinking about the coming cataclysm.

They had been married in the Rhodopé Building looking out at the glory of the park. They honeymooned in that same private universe and needed nothing more, neither Venice nor the Hatshepsut Temple nor an island in the sun. And on the morning after his marriage Ormus Cama woke up and opened his pale eye and the otherworld was not there. The dark eye saw the world as it was, this joyous new world in which Vina lay beside him in his very own bed, and the other, accident-injured (accident-*opened*) eye saw nothing, or little more than a blur. The vision of doubleness had faded and he could not summon it back.

The years passed and the otherworld did not return, Maria no longer came to see him, and with the passage of time he began to have his doubts about its existence; it began to feel like a trick of the mind, a mistake. It was like waking from a dream; into happiness.

For a time he was tempted to let it go, to consign it to the realm of fantasy. To settle for joy, for the long-awaited arrival of completeness, of perfection: what a temptation! *I once was lost but now I'm found, was blind but now I see.* But the truth nagged at him, it wouldn't set him free. It's real, he told himself. It has turned away from me and hidden its face, but what is so, is so.

If the lost otherworld be likened to a Whale, then Ormus Cama had become its Ahab. He hunted it as a madman hunts his doom. On plane flights he stared out of the window searching for the slashes in the real. He went on wearing eye patches of various colors and fabrics because to admit that they weren't necessary was also to surrender to the fantasy that the otherworld didn't exist.

His music changed. In the eighties, as well as his VTO work he wrote long abstract pieces called *Sounds of the Otherworld,* which could not by any stretch be thought of as rock 'n' roll. He hired Carnegie Hall and a bunch of classically trained musicians and was greeted with derision for his pains, but he persisted, and a few people began to mention these new works with respect.

The longer the otherworld remained hidden, the more fearful he became.

Like Ahab, he knew that his whale had *sounded,* but he was determined to be near the great cetacean at its next rising. When sounding, a whale may plunge down through the waters, fathom after fathom, at bewilderingly high speed. There in the depths of the black water it may bide its time, then shoot upwards and smash through the surface of the sea, bursting upon the empire of the air as if it were the end of the world.

This was Ormus's greatest fear. In 1984 he published his thoughts in the international press and was immediately written off as another rock 'n' roll nut.

My greatest concern is that I feel the fragility of the fabric of our space and time, he wrote. *I feel its growing attenuation. Maybe it's running out of steam, coming to its predestined close. Perhaps it will fall away like a shell and the great granite truth of the otherworld will stand revealed in its place.*

Maybe the otherworld is the next world, not in a supernatural sense, not in the sense of an afterlife, but just the world that will succeed our own. (I am still convinced that when our scientific knowledge is greater, we will be able to explain such phenomena as these without recourse to superstition. It is simply a new aspect of the real.)

Maybe our own world is no more than a vision in some other accidental individual's damaged eye.

I don't know what I'm saying. I do know there is a danger of an ending, of a ceasing to be. I do know we can't trust our damaged earth. There is another cosmos hidden from us, sounding. When it bursts into our presence it may blow us away, as if we had never been.

We are aboard the whaleboats of the Pequod, *awaiting the final coming of the whale. As a man of peace, I am not shouting "Man the harpoons!" But I do say we must brace ourselves for the shock.*

As a matter of fact there was a Parsi aboard Melville's storied ship, and his rôle was that of the weird sisters in Macbeth: to prophesy Ahab's doom. *Neither hearse nor coffin can be thine,* he said. In the story I have to tell, the prophecy does not fit Ormus. But it fits Vina like a glove.

Call me Ishmael.

For all her fearsome competence, Vina didn't know how to deal with Ormus's deepening obsessions. I was her safety valve, her light relief. If you believe, she despaired, he wants me to get the mayor to agree to give us an acre of the park, a field for cows to graze in. That way, he says, when the earthquakes come, we'll get an early warning. He says everybody has to play music non-stop and there should be daily love festivals in major city centers everywhere because all we have to fall back on is harmony, all we have to protect us is the power of music and love.

That, and Ermintrude the cow, I observed.

I don't know what to do, she said. I don't know what to fucking think.

I remember her despair. I remember promising myself at that moment, I will break this crazy marriage if it's the last thing I do. If it's the last fucking thing, I will set this lovely woman free.

She still fought her daily bout against self-doubt and existential uncertainty, the universal bogeys of the age. Once when she was young, she told me, her mother took her to the state fair. There was a special kind of Ferris wheel with cages around the seats and a lever you could pull that would permit your little capsule to spin right over, turning you head over heels while the wheel took you up and around. Of course you could lock it off if you wanted and have the normal ride, but the bored little rat-toothed runt of an attendant didn't bother to tell them a damn thing about that, so when they started tumbling they both thought something had gone dreadfully wrong and they were about to die. Those five screaming minutes in the moving cage still returned to Vina in dreams. Now I know what it's like to be inside a laundromat appliance, she joked, but what she was talking about wasn't funny. She was talking about being out of control of your little bit of world, of being betrayed by what you counted on. She was talking about panic and the fragility of being and the skull beneath the skin. She was saying she was married to a lunatic and she loved him and couldn't handle it and didn't know what was going to happen, how it would end. She was afraid of death: his, her own. It's always there, death, in a Ferris wheel, in a loafing shed for goats. In a bedroom where something heavy swings from a slowly rotating ceiling fan. It's like a paparazzo waiting in the shadow. Smile, honey. Smile for the Reaper. Say *Die*.

In 1987, if you recall, Democratic presidential candidate Gary Stanton withdrew from the race for the nomination after the re-emergence of an old girlie scandal involving sex and death on Wasque Beach, Martha's Vineyard. Several of the smaller countries of Western Europe—Illyria, Arcadia, Midgard, Gramarye—voted against economic and political union, fearing it would result in a diminution of particularity, of idiosyncrasy, of national character. The Olympic 100-meter sprint was won by a Canadian man who was afterwards disgraced and erased from history. All official photographs of the event were retouched and videotapes were computer-doctored to show only the runners who finished second, third and fourth. There were bursts of unusually bad weather—blamed by the more meteorologically challenged Californians on a Hispanic handyman named Elvis Niño, who got beaten up in the street by irate Orange County residents—and there was also big trouble on the world's money markets, where the great fictionists behind the long-running *Currency* sitcom were having trouble with their creative processes.

But for millions of music-lovers 1987 would be remembered as the last great year of VTO. (Even the new leader of Angkor, the composer of over eighty songs, all of which dutifully topped the local charts, named Ormus and Vina as his "#1 Inspirational Lights" and invited them to play in Phnom Penh, an invitation which they were unable for pressure-of-work reasons to accept.) The year culminated in the huge free Concert in the Park at the end of the summer. After that they gave up performing in public—that is, Ormus retreated from view, he went home to bake bread, and the others had no choice but to accept his decision.

Goodbye, VTO, wrote Madonna Sangria. Once you made the city lights burn brighter, cars go faster, love taste sweeter. Once you lit the violence of our alleys like a Vermeer and turned the metropolis into our lyric dream. Then, guys, you turned into a pile of garbage I wouldn't throw at a f★cking cat.

Vina was upset about Ormus's unilateral *fiat*—at forty-three she was nowhere near ready to quit—but for external consumption she maintained full solidarity with her husband. In spite of all my urgings to run away with me, she stood by her man, declaring to anyone who would listen that their love was as strong as ever, that she looked forward to the exciting new phase of their careers which would shortly dawn.

The three other band members broke off all relations with the Camas and announced the formation of a breakaway shadow band called OTV, which failed to make any impression on the record-buying public, especially after Vina cruelly revealed that on *Doctor Love and the Whole Catastrophe* and other albums, including "live" albums, the entire rhythm guitar part played by the breakaway band's new frontperson, a stone-faced blonde named Simone Bath, had been replaced in the studio by jobbing axemen, because poor Simone's performance just hadn't been up to the mark.

Meanwhile, forty was proving as difficult a hurdle for me as fifty was for Ormus. Without success, I'd tried everything I could think of to prise Vina away from her increasingly cryptic partner. Don't start with me, Rai, she'd say. I don't come to you for a hard time. I can get plenty of that without leaving home. So much for the perfect love match, I thought, but I buttoned my lip and turned to lighter pleasures. Which failed these days to induce in me the old delirious joy. I had committed the back-door man's cardinal sin of hoping for more than was my right or due. I wanted the front-door key.

To console myself, and of course to provoke Vina, I turned to other women. I even got in touch with Anita Dharkar in Bombay, because I thought it might usefully provoke Vina if I took her tip and rekindled this old flame; but television had captured Anita as I never could. The Indian videocassette information and music services that were the forerunners of the imminent satellite invasion had made her a star. She had a weekly "Lite News" hour and a music show and, reborn as "Neata Darker," had become an icon of the Westernized—and the rapidly Westernizing—urban Indian young. She sent me promo shots of herself got up *à la* rock chick and I found myself mourning the serious, patriotic journalist I used to know.

There was no continuity in human lives any more, I thought. Nineteen eighty-seven was the year of *The Last Emperor,* the Bertolucci movie that proposed that a human being—Pu Yi, the eponymous

Emperor—could genuinely and sincerely change his nature so completely that, having been born the god-king of China, he could end up happily accepting his lot as a humble Chauncey of a gardener, and be a better person for it. A case of communist brainwashing, perhaps, dryly wondered Pauline Kael, but maybe it wasn't. Maybe we just jump tracks more easily than we think. And (I'm back on the subject of Anita now) maybe rock 'n' roll helps you do it better.

That year, to put distance between myself and Vina, I went back to Indochina to take the pictures which were afterwards published in my book *The Trojan Horse*. My idea was that the war in Indochina hadn't ended at the time of the ignominious U.S. withdrawal. They'd left a wooden horse standing at the gates, and when the Indochinese accepted the gift, the real warriors of America—the big corporations, the sports culture of basketball and baseball, and of course rock 'n' roll—came swarming out of its belly and overran the place. Now, in Ho Chi Minh City and Hanoi, too, America stood revealed as the real victor. Indochina became just another consumer-serf of (and supplier of cheap labor to) Americana International. Almost every young Indochinese person wanted to eat, dress, bop and profit in the good old American way. MTV, Nike, McWorld. Where soldiers had failed, U.S. values—that is, greenbacks, set to music—had triumphed. This, I photographed. I do not need to say that the pictures went down big. This (with the exception of the sweatshop material) was news that many Americans wanted to hear. Even the old-time anti-war demonstrators were pleased. To my eye, the pictures contained large dollops of ambiguity, of tension. They were, I suppose, ironic. The irony, however, was largely lost on many who praised them. What's irony when you can celebrate this new Cultural Revolution? Let the music play. Let freedom ring. Hail, hail, rock 'n' roll.

Timeo Danaos et dona ferentes. Discontinuity, the forgetting of the past: this is the wooden horse at the gates of Troy. Whose occupants burned, are burning, will surely burn the topless towers of Ilium. Yet I myself am a discontinuous being, not what I was meant to be, no longer what I was. So I must believe—and in this I have truly become an American, inventing myself anew to make a new world in the company of other altered lives—that there is thrilling gain in this metamorphic destiny, as well as aching loss.

On the subject of forgetting: after my return I briefly became involved with Ifredis Wing, who was now trying to be a photographer herself and arrived at the Orpheum as Johnny Chow's assistant. Chow lived on the first floor and Ifredis gradually worked her way up, via Schnabel and Basquiat, to the penthouse, and me. She still had the sexual appetite of a nympho rabbit—Vina, who else, had given me a detailed account of the shenanigans at Tempe Harbor—and her looks had, if anything, improved. Her blond hair now worn boyishly, spikily short, her body still womanly and long. But as a photographic assistant she was a total bust, on account of her terrible memory, which led to a number of film-processing disasters that none of us found funny. It's one thing to laugh about living in an amnesiac culture and quite another to have an amnesiac labeling your rolls of exposed film.

I'm sorry, I no remembrance have, she apologized when I screamed infra-red murder at her in the developing room. But this also means, she added, brightening, that I will not your discourteous words tomorrow morning remember, after I have slept on your arm.

Otto, by the way, had moved on from Buddhism to super-capitalism, had married a billionairess fifteen years his senior and was now a prominent figure both in Hollywood and on the Eurotrash party circuit. He no longer made art movies, having turned his attention to seventy-million-dollar action flicks instead. He had become the unquestioned master of what were known in the biz as *whammies:* the climactic set pieces, full of explosions and derring-do, on which such films thrived. (I once saw him on tv, being interviewed at the Cannes festival and shrugging off critical drubbings to explain his new cinematic philosophy: *First act, lots of whammies. Second act, better whammies. Third act, nothing—but—whammies!*)

For a time, I found myself strongly attracted to memoryless Ifredis Wing, who bore no mortal person any malice, reserving her wrath entirely for god. In the aftermath of her desertion by Otto she had entirely lost her faith. Once the god-squaddie supreme, she was now possessed of the zeal of the apostate and came on like an atheistic stormtrooper. Devotees of Indian mahagurus, Scientologist movie stars, Japanese cultists, British sports reporters repackaged as the Risen Christ, American gun-lobby crazies bunkered down in the desert with charismatic prophet-leaders telling them who to make babies with and how often: Ifredis spent a lot of her non-fucking time soliloquizing on the follies of such as these. The great world religions took a trouncing too, and I have to say I found all this pretty enjoyable. It wasn't often I met someone more thoroughly disenchanted with the world's credulity than myself. Plus, she really was wonderful in bed. Sometimes she lazily played at adolescent sex, all finger-fucks and blow-jobs; more often she just came at you like Octopussy, all arms and legs and whoops-a-daisy. Either way was fine with me.

It fizzled; she drifted away, as I knew she would. Nothing really went wrong between us, but then there really was nothing between us to go wrong. We were both filling in dead time, and one day she woke up and looked at me and had forgotten who I was. I went to take a shower and didn't hear her go.

After my return from Indochina, I began to rethink my work. Journalism and its sneering sidekick, cynicism, no longer seemed enough. In a way I envied Ormus Cama his madness. That vision of a literally disintegrating world held together, saved and redeemed by the twin powers of music and love, was perhaps not to be so easily derided. I envied its off-the-wall coherence, its controlling overview. Also, I confess, I was in the market for redemption myself. Something had to stop me dreaming about a dead man's shoe, about a heel that twisted sideways to reveal a roll of film that would change its finder's life. I had left so much behind, but that memory never seemed surplus to requirements. No matter how light I traveled, it was always there, in the pockets of my dreams.

These were days of guilty uncertainty. Ormus had found his way of dealing with the zeitgeist. Even that dreadful junk band, what did they call themselves, the Mall: they had a plan. My way seemed to have fizzled out in a dead end. With Vina, with myself, I was getting nowhere.

My fellow "Orphics" on East Fifth Street had all abandoned photojournalism for good, and the eagerness with which they were pursuing other interests aroused my envy, an emotion that's always reliable as a guide to the secret heart, *le secret-coeur*, as Hulot's Nebuchadnezzar partner Bobby Flow used to call it in his broad Yankee Franglais: that is to say, our deep neediness, the substitute in a climate of godlessness for the bleeding heart of Christ. Aimé-Césaire Basquiat, our beautiful young shaven-bodied Francophone, was using an old eight-by-ten plate camera, long exposures and gorgeous high-definition lighting to give a lapidary, Renaissance-classical look to a sequence of formal head-shot portraits and, more contentiously, to classically composed scenes of what were, to me, utterly stupefying sexual practices. The content of these out-there photographs made me feel like an innocent country boy who knew nothing of the world's true diversity, who in spite of staring into the maw of horror had never begun to guess what ancient impulses were really swimming in our lightless, hidden depths. It was Basquiat's simple idea to bring these things out of the dark into his sumptuous light and thus change our idea of what beauty is.

His third project was a sort of photographic reply to his namesake Césaire's celebrated poetic affirmation of *négritude,* the *Cahier d'un retour au pays natal.* Basquiat, who had left Martinique as a baby and defiantly stayed away ever since, was slowly creating a photo-essay—*Cahier d'un exit*—about exile, about rootless slip-sliders like himself, photographing them as if they were beautiful aliens floating an inch off the ground, as if they were blessed as well as cursed. Sometimes the three projects blended into one, and I was startled one day to see a powerful portrait of Basquiat's fellow Martinican Rémy Auxerre, haloed in light and ingesting, in extreme close-up, what was all too evidently Basquiat's own cock, an organ we all knew well because of its owner's penchant for nudity.

It's easy to say—and after his early death, all wasted body, wizened skin and frightened eyes, there were many who were quick to say it—that Basquiat was on a fast road to nowhere. But what I remember was the exaltation on his face each day. That was a room to which I also desperately wanted to find the key.

Johnny Chow and Mack Schnabel were involved in less edgy but equally rewarding careers: fashion and advertising work to support the high Manhattan society life they both adored, and more personal photo-essays for the good of the soul. Schnabel—a small man with a huge hawk's head and more than his share of nocturnal demons—would go to Italy twice a year for the Milan collections. Afterwards he headed off to Rome and took eye-popping pictures of the half-mummified, decayed, skeletal bodies in the catacombs. From that he progressed to taking pictures of civilian cadavers on a regular basis, fascinated by death's democracy. Violent death didn't interest him any more; just the fact itself, our shared inheritance, James's distinguished thing. The young and the old are the same age when they're dead, he'd say. They're *as old as it gets.* Other differences vanished also. Klansman and bluesman, Hamas fundamentalist and Jewish settler, Afrikaner and Sowetan, Indian and Pakistani, town mouse and country mouse, the farmer and the cowman, Mr. Tomayto and Ms. Tomahto, there they were, side by side on the slabs of his photographs, stripped of their frontiers, equalized for all time. To this continuing portfolio he gave the grandly Shakespearean title *Golden Lads and Girls,* who, you'll recall (*Cymbeline,* act IV, scene 2), all must, / As chimney sweepers, come to dust.

As for all-action Chow, that driven, gambling-crazy roadrunner who called himself the ideal New Yorker *because I'm like the city, man, I don't fucking sleep:* he was busy with his fifteen-year study *Queens,* a portrait of the polyglot borough. But he was at least as proud of the advertising photographs he took for Heinz. Multi-cultural street life, man, that's already rich, he told me. It's got texture, depth, does half your job for you. You got any idea what it takes to make interesting the surface of a cream of mushroom soup? Now that's a challenge.

One day Basquiat (fully dressed) came up to see me and wanted to hang out and play some music. Rummaging through my vinyl he came up with an oldie, *Exile on Main Street,* and put it on the deck. Rai, deed you evair see that tour movie, *Cocksuckair Blues,* they got Robair Fronk to make eet as well as thees covair, he wanted to know. Otherwise I can get eet, I know a man, we can run eet for ourselves some evening, que penses-tu.

Listening to "Sweet Virginia," the druggy music of another age, a strange, mouthy admixture of South London and the American South, I found myself staring at the album's collagist sleeve, its strips of film featuring a funeral (civilians and soldiers saluting a hearse), snapshots of faces both famous and not, a newspaper front page, a scrap of handwritten lyric, the repeated image of the road. The crudely handlettered credits. *Amyl Nitrate: marimbas. Clydie King, Vanetta, plus friend: background vocal. Bill Plummer: uprite bass.* The music inspired only nostalgia but the photographs still had plenty to say. Yes, Robert Frank, I thought. This was the sign I'd been waiting for.

Cocksucker Blues was okay, messy and of its unappetizing moment, but I was still primarily a stills man, and what really spoke to me was Mabou. In 1970, after separating from Mary Frank, Robert Frank bought a house in Mabou, Nova Scotia, with the artist June Leaf. The raw, strong work he made there was, is, a demonstration of how far a photograph can stretch, how much it can include, once it gives up the idea of including it all, once it accepts that it isn't going to break on through to some universal truth. A human eye, disembodied, floats against a high-contrast seascape. Words as well as images hang pegged and drying on a windblown clothesline. There are many photographs shot through glass on which words have been scrawled or else the words are written right across the image itself. *No Fear* over a type-writer with, once again, the ubiquitous sea. *Hold Still Keep Going.* Against that stark flat mournful landscape articulated by poles and frames the fading name of his dead daughter. *For Andrea who died. I think of Andrea every day. Look Out For Hope.* Pigs' carcasses. Hospitals. Cold. Ice. Packing cases. Nothing cropped, nothing aligned. Photographs like torn images in broken glass. A woman, I think it's June Leaf, lies on sand, full of joy. I had looked at these pictures before but never seen them. Now they led me to discard much of what I'd thought, they gave me what I wanted: a way of starting again.

Looking at the Mabou pictures, I remembered these lines of Virginia Woolf: A masterpiece is not the result of a sudden inspiration but the product of a lifetime of thought. Henri Hulot, my first master, had been a great believer in the sudden inspiration, the decisive moment that reveals an underlying harmony. Frank wasn't, and had probably put together his *Black White and Things* as an answer to Hulot's thesis, much as *Catch-18* is an answer to *The Naked and the Dead*. I realized I had been pursuing the unattainable, looking at atrocities in search of capital-A Atrocity, searching in so many deaths for Death. Now I decided to abandon universals and harmony to absolutists like Hulot and Ormus and concentrate on the inexhaustible happenstance of life.

I decided that nothing was forbidden. I was re-learning the imagination's alphabet and so it was okay to play with all the toys.

For some reason (I really don't think this needs to be spelled out) I became interested in double exposures. I constructed story sequences in which beautiful, often naked young men and women—Basquiat's perennial nudity had had its effect on me—were attended by see-through wraiths: a mother standing like the Christ of the Andes, arms spread wide, atop a skyscraper, a father hanging from a ceiling fan, a dream lover, a second self. As I opened myself to the language of dreams I was shown, and tried to re-create, images whose meaning was obscure, whose obscurity excited me. A man at a desk was visited by a phantom horse which put its hooves over his eyes. A naked man in an empty room talked to a white-masked version of himself. (This with sentences of text, scrawled by myself at the foot of each frame of the sequence: *Do you know who you are? Do you know what you want?*) To my surprise I found that much of the imagery that came to me had religious overtones: a double-exposure sequence describing a dying woman's out-of-the-body experience, another sequence in which a man suddenly explodes into pure light: first his head, then his body and clothes. I allowed myself the supernatural, the transcendent, because, I told myself, our love of metaphor is pre-religious, born of our need to express what is inexpressible, our dreams of otherness, of more. Religion came and imprisoned the angels in aspic, tied our winged beauty to a tree, nailed our freedom to the ground. In these sequences I tried to reclaim the sense of the miraculous without having to bend the knee before any god. The god of the imagination is the imagination. The law of the imagination is, whatever works. The law of the imagination is not universal truth, but the work's truth, fought for and won.

I invented an alter ego for myself, an enigmatic Mitteleuropean photographer, named Moosbrugger after the murderer in Musil, prowling the streets of New York looking for echoes in this New World of Vienna, of Budapest, of Prague. This pseudo-photographer photographed the love affairs of gargoyles, the Arthurian adventures of the great population of statuary living high above the city streets. The statues came to life, loved, fought, lived according to their personal codes. They were like the knights of Charlemagne, as well as the American pioneers. Moosbrugger's statue-work was some of my favorite stuff.

I worked with reflections, glass, shadows. Using mirrors, I became skilled at scale distortion. I learned how to hold the galaxy in the palm of a man's hand, and what happened if you placed mirror images inside other mirror images and photographs inside photographs, dizzying the eye, until the last image was crushed in a fist. First to create an illusion, then to show that it *is* an illusion, then finally to destroy the illusion: this, I began to see, was honesty.

One day I developed a roll of film and there was the ghost image of a woman I didn't know superimposed on several of the shots. I couldn't work it out. On this occasion I was certain I had not run the film through the camera twice, and anyway I didn't recognize the woman's silhouette. True, it was not unlike Vina's body, but it wasn't Vina's body. It was a stranger, moving through a space that was and was not mine.

As if I had penetrated a membrane and touched an otherworld.

That night while I slept the woman showed up in my dreams and told me her name. She said a little too contemptuously for my liking that she could read me as if I were a book. She said if she wanted to she could close me and put me back on her shelf and then my story would never finish, it would stop dead in the middle of a sentence. I was lying naked in bed and she leaned over me, murmuring threats. I tried to argue back. I told her the inside of a book is there whether you read it or not. Even if nobody ever reads it, it's there, doing its work. That's enough, I said. Being there is what counts.

She hissed, do you remember when we were lovers? Do you remember our wonderful first night of love? No, she said, you don't even remember me, do you, you bastard. Fuck you. I'm going. Maybe I'll never come back.

I woke up sweating and alone. Maria, I thought. I just met a girl called Maria.

I began to take pictures of infidelity: my apartment just before Vina entered the frame, or just after she left it. The rumpled bed of guilty passion. The water on the tiled floor by the shower. Used glasses. Half-eaten food. After a time Vina agreed to participate in the sequence. Her masked face. Her anonymous, naked body moving rapidly out of shot. Her extended arms, stretching towards the forbidden. These photographs brought us a new kind of closeness, and as she gave more and more of herself to the work, becoming more collaborator than subject, so I began superstitiously to fear the power of crazy Ormus's eye-patched, shamanic eye. Some days I could swear I could feel it roving the cosmos like a searchlight, like Robert Frank's eye at Mabou, like the cloud-razored moon in *Un Chien Andalou*. Like the eye of the Dark Lord Sauron searching for the Ring.

Thus I became an autobiographer, using whatever came to hand, drawings, stories, crayons, surrealism, Vina, texts. Realism isn't a set of rules, it's an intention, I pontificated at an amused, unusually tolerant Vina. The world isn't realistic any more, what are we going to do about that? Think of a photograph of people who never change, leading their grooved lives with if they're lucky a bit of bedroom psychodrama: *that's* the fantasy. A battlefield on which you don't see the undercurrents of history doesn't show enough of the truth. A battlefield on which you don't see so to speak angels and devils, the so to speak gods with their super-weapons, and the let's say ghosts. Somehow to show the metaphoric beneath the actual, driving what happens, making things so.

And how do you propose to photograph an undercurrent, she asked.

I don't know, I grinned. I guess start by looking in the right places.

You're changing, she told me. Don't stop?, I like it. I like it really a lot.

We were all changing. The change in Ormus, his sleep-masked retreat into locked and darkened rooms for days on end, his worsening migraines, his sobbing fits, his shrieks, these things gave rise to a great turbulence within Vina, tore her apart, made her feel helpless, alienated her, made her sit outside his locked door pleading to be let in. When she was let in she would attend at his darkened bedside for days on end, holding his hand, nursing him, while he thrashed like a great fish out of water and screamed about the imminent catastrophe. Doctors were brought to him, sedatives were prescribed. The condition of his mind was not good. Vina came to me more often now, fleeing the melodrama at the Rhodopé Building, leaving Ormus to be cared for by the infinitely patient Clea and the Singhs. She said, His breakdown leaves a hole where our relationship used to be. I still love him, you know, love's a mystery, right, but there's nothing between us any more. He's off in outer space or the fifth dimension, watching out for the end of the world. Sometimes I think he isn't coming back.

She knew she had to resume an independent life, to find her own new way. Gradually she became an enthusiastic participant in the alternative art scene, working with indie filmmakers, performance artists, dancers. Meanwhile she was writing her own songs for the first time, trying them out on me, jamming with her many A-list music-world friends. She made surprise appearances at small downtown music venues with a scratch band and was pleased by the reception she got. By the fall of 1988 she had an album, *Vina,* and was planning to go on the road. Not America or Europe to start with, she told me. I don't think I'm ready. Just a small tour of Latin America for a start?, the music is pretty much influenced by those guys anyway. Brazil, Mexico, just a toe in the water.

I want to remember her the way she was then, surging into her mid-forties full of beauty and courage, alone and scared but heading back out there, looking for her life. I want to remember that in those days before the tour she at last admitted what I'd waited my whole life to hear, namely that I had become a factor, a problem. I was no longer an occasional snack, a side dish. No longer containable. For too long it had been a case of Ormus and Vina sailing along with Rai clinging to the side of their racing yacht. It had been their story; now, at long last, it was mine too. Mine, at last.

She said she was disoriented, confused, she needed time to think, all of that. Yes, she was thinking of leaving him. She couldn't bear to be there any more. She couldn't bear to leave him. She couldn't stay.

She said, You don't know how alike you are, you two, except that he's going down for the third time and you're coming up for air.

She said, I have to get away. I'm going on this tour. I have to think.

I'll come with you, why don't I, I said. I could be your official tour photographer. All I'd ask is total access. You know? Total.

No, don't come.

I can't let you go. Vina, after all this. We're this close. I have to come.

Jesus, Jesus. I don't know. Okay, come. No, don't come. Come. Don't come. Come. Don't come. Don't come. Don't come. Come.

I'll come, then.

No. *Don't.*

We should have listened to Ormus. It wasn't just the great San Francisco earthquake of 1984: the 1980s had been a bad time for the whole faulty earth. In October 1980 twenty thousand people were killed by a 7.3-Richter event in El Asnam, Algeria, a quake so severe that it broke many local seismologists' measuring instruments. Three thousand people died in southern Italy a month later. In October 1983 a quake hit Hasankale village in eastern Turkey (two thousand dead); in September 1985 the Mexico City authorities were forced to use the baseball stadium as a morgue (over two thousand dead). A medium-size event wrecked San Salvador in August 1986, and then, two years later, a mysterious rash of quakes broke out along various international frontiers. A 6.7-Richter whopper rocked the India–Nepal border in August 1988 (over five hundred dead), and just three months later a thousand people died, this time on the China–Burma line. One month after that, a force of 6.9 on the Richter scale devastated the Armenian–Turkish border. The town of Spitak, with a population of fifty thousand, was totally destroyed; eighty percent of the buildings in Leninakan (a city with a population of three hundred thousand souls) tumbled down; one hundred thousand people died, and Gorbachev paid a visit to the scene. When, in January 1989, two villages in a border area of Tajikistan were buried by landslides and mudslides (one thousand people dead, also many thousand head of cattle), the so-called "borderline fault" phenomenon began to attract worldwide attention. *Is the world coming apart at the seams?* was the question asked by a cover story in *Time,* and even though the official, seismological answer was a resounding No, I began, for the first time, to wonder what Ormus Cama was seeing in his delirium. If dogs and pigs and cattle could feel quakes before our measuring instruments, was it possible that a human being could predict them months, years, in advance?

Yeah, but if we'd listened to Ormus, what then? Like all Cassandras, he was short on remedies. In the end such prophecy is useless. You just have to live your life, make your choices, move forward until you can't.

In February 1989 Vina Apsara and her new band flew to Mexico for a series of arena concerts. Without telling her, I caught a flight to Mexico City too. I had her itinerary, the list of her hotels and so on. This time I would not let her escape.

15

BENEATH HER FEET

When I show up at the Cattlemen's Club in downtown Mexico City she shocks me, trumps my ace, by beginning instantly, abundantly, to weep. She's slumped in a deep armchair and the liquid level in the bottle beside her confirms what I already know from the papers, i.e. that the first gig didn't go too well. Her band is still learning to play together, the papers say, and she looked oddly ill at ease on stage without Ormus there for reassurance, Ormus Cama in his glass box. They find things to praise, her beauty and so on, but she knows when she's being panned. She sniffs and snorts; the tears make it impossible for me to judge accurately the condition of her nose. How far do I have to run to get away from you, Rai, unfairly she sobs, fuck you, how deep a hole do I have to dig. Large men move menacingly in my direction but she waves them irritatedly away.

I call it the Cattlemen's Club because its fat-cat confidence is a Latin American echo of the establishment in *Dallas,* the soap not the city, where men in big hats clutched bourbon-and-branch and bitched about the price of oil. But this joint makes *Dallas* look like the boondocks, like any place where two roads cross and then make a low fast run for the horizon. It's a mighty stone-clad pyramid set on the upper floors of a shining high-rise near the Zócalo and it looks like all the extinguished peoples of the region have been exhumed to construct it: Olmecs, Zapotecs, Mayas, Toltecs, Mixtecs, Purépechas, Aztecs. It is a temple, in its monied way: a place of power with added settees and liveried waiters. You suspect the covert presence of altars, of knife-wielding priests. Vina, the sacrifice *du jour,* has been given a suite of rooms, where publicists and journalists and photographers and hangers-on and heavies come and go. To get past security I have to send in my card. She keeps me waiting just long enough for me to start worrying about a humiliating rejection. Then I am led into her presence to be greeted by her waterworks display, also the shocking red hair, and the strange thing is that my mouth is dry, my heart's pounding, I'm actually scared. I have come naked into this conference chamber, with, to paraphrase James Caan in *The Godfather,* nothing but my dick in my hand. I've got only my dumb love to offer, this love that is finally after all the second-fiddle decades insisting on taking over the orchestra. Take me or leave me, that's what I've come to say, knowing that if she doesn't want me I'm defenseless, a cap-in-hand schoolboy without even an apple for a bribe.

Meanwhile, this being one of the earth's buggier zones, I'm being bitten all over, scratching at my neck like Toshiro Mifune's scummy samurai (but without the sword skills). I'm in a nightmare. It's the beginning of the last act of the play and I've walked out on stage and there are no lines in my head, no prompter hissing from his box by the footlights. Vina, I say. She puts a finger across her lips, dries her eyes, waves me into a chair. Not that, she says. Let's talk about something else. In these last Mexican days it's a command she often gives.

She wants to tell me about the hot political scandal that's flaring up now, the President's brother who is on the run after embezzling the equivalent of eighty-four million U.S. dollars, there isn't a country prepared to give him asylum, not even Cuba, so he circles the globe like a ship carrying nuclear waste, unable to find a port. *And this is supposed to be the new, clean régime!* (The name of Piloo Doodhwala is on both our lips, so there is no need for it to be spoken.) She wants to talk also about the Argentinian footballer, Achilles Hector, who has been kidnapped by the revolutionists in the south. His amazing name, Greek

and Trojan?, winner and loser?, a double hero, she says. His captors gave
deadlines. They threatened to cut off his toes, one by one, if their
demands were not met. But the deadlines passed, and so far no toe in
the mail. The revolutionists are also football fanatics. It's a question of
which of their passions will prevail.

She wants to talk about the villa on the Pacific coast, the one she
stayed in for the first three days of her Mexican sojourn, to which she
will shortly return. The Villa Huracán outside Aparajitos, caught
between the jungle and the sea. From the jungle comes the singing of
the obscene bird of night, perhaps Lowry's *Trogon ambiguus ambiguus,*
his wonderful ambiguous bird. Deep in the ocean echoes the roar of
the *huracán,* the god of storms. The villa is actually not a villa at all but
a row of pink-washed edifices—"rooms"—topped with *palapas,* high
cones of thatch. It is jointly owned by the shockingly young new
Colchis boss, Mo Mallick, and a Hollywood heavy hitter named Kahn.
The death of Yul Singh and the retirement of VTO, his biggest act, has
holed Colchis badly, but Mallick has pushed his leaking boat out for
Vina on this tour, gambling that she can make it without Ormus.
Hence the offer of the Huracán. Hence, also, one reason for Vina's
present depression. She has been heavily backed to come through and
it looks as if she may not be able to deliver the required goods. Mallick,
at twenty-eight already a Vegas high roller, can take a hit if he has to,
like any player at the big tables he knows the money isn't the point, it's
just a way of keeping score. But he cares about the score. To win the
big ones gets to be a matter of pride. To lose? Let's talk about something else.

The other guests, she wants to tell me, were a famous Chilean novelist and his much younger, and strikingly attractive, Irish-American
wife. There was a breakfast terrace halfway down the cliffside, where
fruit and tortillas and champagne arrived in a picnic hamper that rattled through the air on ropes and pulleys. *El desayunismo magical,* the
novelist called it. The Irish-American wife spoke of her close involvement with the republican movement "back home," that is to say in
Ulster, whose bitter earth she had never trodden, telling of her fund-
raising efforts and the profound commitment with which the republican leadership was working for peace. Meanwhile the novelist ate and
drank heartily, refused to comment on the Irish question and pro-

nounced himself too frail to descend any further. *Sea level will have to do without me.* He sat on the terrace in an old polo shirt and khaki shorts. Vina kept him company while the entertainment executives gamboled at the ocean's edge below, competing for the attention of the young Boston-Irish aristocrat-revolutionary wife, splashing around her in the shallows like great lumbering hounds, all eagerness and dangling tongues. Speaking of dangling, Vina on the breakfast terrace observed that the writer's legs were wide apart and he wasn't wearing any underwear. His balls were big and smooth and pink, the same pink as the villa walls, and his cock was big and gray, the dull gray of the stone slab on which he sat with the ocean at his rear. I couldn't stop look-ing, Vina tells me, not bad for seventy-five, I thought. Afterwards I asked Mallick if the old gent had been trying to impress me, I mean, was this flirting?, or what?—but Mallick said no, he does it all the time, it's just innocent display. That's how I think of the Huracán now, she quips gaily. As a sacred place, the place where innocence is displayed.

She doesn't know how to make the choice I am obliging her to make.

She is brittle, over-bright, stretched.

She wants to talk about anything on earth except love.

Vina, I say again. She glares at me, furious now. This is one thirsty city, she says. The sub-soil water levels are falling alarmingly?, and any day now the place will just subside, just drop out of sight. Now that's what I call falling-down drunk. And then there's the Pope, I'm sup-posed to follow *his* act, how's that for lousy timing.

The Pope has just played Mexico City and he even talked about rock 'n' roll. *Yes, my children, the answer is indeed blowing in the wind, not in the wind of godless desolation but in the harmonious breeze that fills the sails of the ship of faith and blows its passengers all the way to heaven.* Vina, who couldn't match his audiences but knows that VTO could proba-bly have given him a run for his money, has to console herself by sneering at the over-extended metaphor and by retailing the latest papal gossip. His curt anger towards worker-priests, liberation theol-ogy, all that jazz. And there's this story doing the rounds about his driver, she says. No, not the chauffeur of the Popemobile. I mean his driver back in the old days when he was plain Cardinal Wojtyla? Apparently this driver had been with him for years, and when it was time to elect a new Pope the two of them drove down from Cracow in some little beat-up Polish pollution-wagon. What a road movie, right?, the future Pope and his workingman sidekick strikin' out for glory. Anyway, they get to the Vatican, the driver waits and waits, the smoke goes up, *habemus Papam,* and finally he hears the news, it's his good buddy, his road pal, his boss. Then a messenger comes to see him. Drive the car back to Cracow and then find yourself another job, says the messenger. Your ass is fired.

I've seen her in all kinds of moods before, but never so desperate. She's flying to Guadalajara in the morning—Guadalajara, where Pancho Villa shot the clock and stopped time, she says—and she knows the show isn't right, her life isn't right, and she doesn't know how to fix either one. She looks at my face and all she sees there is *leave him, Vina, come live with me and be my love,* and she can't handle that at present, *let's talk about something else,* she starts cracking Orpheus jokes. This is an old riff of hers, one she first laid down when she heard I was moving into an Orpheum; me, Rai, scion of the clan with the worst voices in Indian musical history. You should change the name, she said, out of respect you should name it after a different fucking god. Maybe Morpheus, the god of sleep. I played along: How about Metamorpheus, god of change. It went downhill from there. We came up with Endomorpheus and Ectomorpheus, the twinned gods of body type. Waldorpheus Astorpheus, god of hotels. Motorpheus, the biker god. Hans Castorpheus, the magic mountaineer. Shortpheus, god of anger. Conpheus, the head-scratching, puzzled god.

She wants to talk about gods because death-worshipping Mexico has startled her. Compared to the deities they've got here, she says, Apollo's just a theater, Poseidon's an adventure, Hermes is a fucking silk scarf.

She comes to a halt, looks at me. Vina doesn't often implore, but I see that right now she needs me to take up the chit-chat baton and run with it. She needs me not to force her to face what must be faced. Mutely, she pleads for compassion; even for mercy.

Incredible violence is the gods' stock-in-trade, I therefore commence obligingly to improvise. Rape, murder, terrible revenges. You go to them with open arms, but these are fatal embraces. The old gods, Hindu Norse Greek, laid down no moral laws, requiring nothing of us except worship. Reverence, the deified Herakles tells Philoctetes in Sophocles' play, is what Olympus digs above all else. On the surface this sounds preferable to the newer guys, no sermons on the mount, no Islamic how-to manuals, but watch out, there's an elephant trap. To revere the gods is to fear their wrath and therefore to seek constantly to propitiate them. Natural disasters are proofs of the gods' displeasure, because the world is our fault. Therefore incessant expiations. Therefore human sacrifice, et cetera.

That's what I love about you, Vina says, relief and gratitude concealed beneath her sardonic accents. Wind you up and you'll run off at the mouth for a good half hour; which allows a girl to tune out and get some rest.

It is at this point that I mention earthquakes.

Which isn't so surprising, given our location in notoriously quake-prone Mexico, not to mention the subject of VTO's biggest hit album and Ormus Cama's recent warnings about the coming apocalypse. I am not a superstitious man or, as I hope I have made plain, a religious one. I do not believe that by speaking of earthquakes I called down on our heads the anger of the gods. But for the record I note the fact that I so spoke.

Also, to be precise: not on my head. On Vina's.

Earthquakes, I point out, have always made men eager to placate the gods. After the great Lisbon earthquake of November 1, 1755—that catastrophe which Voltaire saw as an irrefutable argument for the tragic view of life and against Leibnizian optimism—the locals decided on a propitiatory auto-da-fé. The celebrated philosopher Pangloss was hanged (the more conventionally approved bonfire wouldn't light). His associate, Herr Candide of Thunder-ten-tronckh, a name like an occult incantation, likely to provoke earthquakes where none had previously occurred, was flogged rhythmically and for a long while upon his bloodied buttocks. Immediately after this auto-da-fé there was an even bigger earthquake, and that part of the city which remained standing instantly fell down. That's the trouble with human sacrifice, the heroin of the gods. It's highly addictive. And who will save us from deities with major habits to feed?

So god's a junkie now, Vina says.

The gods, I correct her. Monotheism sucks, like all despotisms. The species is naturally, democratically polytheistic, apart from that evolutionary élite which has dispensed with the divine requirement entirely. You instinctively want the gods to be many because you are One.

And the stories, she says, her mood improving. She's just kidding around now, shooting the breeze, getting her mind off her troubles. I've managed to put a faint smile back on her face. What about the stories, she repeats. Does a damned heathen such as you not even find pleasure there?

When we stop believing in the gods we can start believing in their stories, I retort. There are of course no such things as miracles, but if there were and so tomorrow we woke up to find no more believers on earth, no more devout Christians, Muslims, Hindus, Jews, why then, sure, the beauty of the stories would be a thing we could focus on because they wouldn't be dangerous any more, they would become capable of compelling the only belief that leads to truth, that is, the willing, disbelieving belief of the reader in the well-told tale.

The myths, you may have noticed, require their protagonists to be stupid. To walk blithely into mortal danger, blind to the most obvious traps.

(All this and probably more, I permit myself to say. I have not spoken like this, so exhaustively, so unrestrainedly, in a long time. And I repeat, I do not believe in hubris, the crime of thumbing your nose at the gods, and therefore I also do not believe in the coming of Nemesis. But I have sworn to tell everything and so I must also say that before what happened happened I made these, in the eyes of believers, no doubt injudicious remarks.)

Let's go to my hotel room and get fucked up, Vina briskly proposes. A snort of soma, a sip of ambrosia. Sure, I'm up for that. Lead on, my queen. It occurs to me, not for the first time, that I am in the position of a mortal man petitioning a so to speak goddess for love. Vina and Adonis: like that. I am aware that humans do not usually come well out of these encounters.

But the non-existent gods, too, can fall.

Her style, these days, is late-eighties ultraglamour; no more hippie (or radical) chic. Très movie star, with an extra shock 'n' roll twist of outrageousness. Tyler, Gaultier, Alaïa, Léger, Wang, but most often Santo

Medusa: his all-in-one technicolor-beaded catsuits, his shocking-pink *smokings* worn double-breasted over a shirtless torso, his chain-mail mini-dresses slit to the waist. Vina and Tina, people say, are slugging it out for the ageless-diva crown.

This is the hotel room. This is the woman I love. These are some of the last moments of her life on earth, her life above ground. Every stupid thing she says, every crack she makes, every heart she breaks, these are things I will forever hug to myself, to save them from the *barranco,* the abyss. This is the CD she plays: *Raindogs,* the honky-tonk blues as reinvented and growled out by Lee Baby Simms. She starts singing along with Simms, low and slow, and the hair rises on my neck. *Will I see you again / on a downtown train.* The walls seem to be swaying to the music. It's like Valéry, I remark. *Le roc marche, et trébuche; et chaque pierre fée / se sent un poids nouveau qui vers l'azur délire!* Valerie who, she shrugs, not caring, lost in music and smoke.

She's on her way to Guadalajara, the city where time stops. To Guadalajara and beyond.

This is us, making love. She always made love as if it were for the last time, that was how she did everything, how she led her life; but for us, though neither of us knows it, this in fact is the last time. The last time for these breasts. The breasts of Helen of Troy were so astonishing that when she bared them to her husband at the fall of Troy, Menelaus was unable to do her harm. The sword fell from his nerveless hand. This is the woman I love and these are her breasts. I run this tape over and over in my head. Did you show the earthquake your breasts, Vina, did you bare them to the god of storms, why didn't you, if you did you might, you surely would, have survived.

These are the breasts of the woman I love. I place my nose between them and inhale their pungency, their ripeness. I place my cock between them and feel their swollen caress.

This is Vina, talky as always after sex. She wants to beef about the problem of age for female singers: Diana, Joni, Tina, Nina, herself. Look at Sinatra, she says. He can hardly stand up, there are notes he can't even dream about any more, and somebody should kill that animal sitting on his head, but he's a guy, therefore these are not career problems. (Yes, she puts herself up there with the Voice. She's a Voice too. She has no false modesty. She knows her artistic worth. Tina and me, she says, we're re-writing the book. Not Fade Away, that's the new title, honey. We're telling you how it's gonna be.)

She's on to the younger generation, its inadequacies, its complaints. Here's Madonna Sangria again, still obsessing in *Rolling Stone* about the female body. Not its uses but its abuses. Not sex but gender. Will you listen to the low-grade grumpiness in this grouchy kid, Vina growls, talking mostly to herself. Man, we had high octane. We had *rage*. To whine about guys?, to complain about mom 'n' pop?, just wasn't in it. We had the generals and the universe to fight. *My boyfriend left me, men are assholes?* Give me a break. I'll take the good-time girls any day. Bop she bop. She bop shewaddywaddy. (She's singing now.) *She's so fine . . .*

Bullshit, she snarls abruptly. She's wasted and more than half asleep but she's arguing with herself. Always was a man pulling our strings. Ike Turner Berry Gordy Phil Spector Ormus Cama. Ike Spector Berry Turner. A man is for power and a woman is for pain. I'll say it again. Orpheus lives, Eurydice dies, right?

Yeah, but you're Orpheus too, I start to tell her. It's your voice that's making the enchanted stones of the city rise deliriously into the blue, that causes the city's banks of electrical images to dance. *Oraia phone,* the best voice, we all know to be yours, not his. And meanwhile he's the one sinking into his otherworld-underworld, and who's going to rescue him, I bite my tongue because this is the opposite of the line I have flown south to pursue: *Who if not you.* Instead I say, It's time men like him started rescuing themselves.

And I go on, Anyway, Orpheus dies too. And having said it, I want to rip out my tongue. Wrong, wrong! But what's said is said.

Vina's sitting up in bed now, stone sober and suddenly, illogically, mad as hell. You think you can walk in his shoes, she says. You think you can sleep in his hollow. In your dreams, Rai baby. Never in a million. You came all this way to tell me you want him dead?, maybe you'll want me dead too, if I don't bow down before your will, before your fucking *dick*. You came down here to murder love and call the murder love.

No, that's not it, I say uselessly. Dionysiac Vina has risen up in wrath, goddess of pleasure and destruction. Go, she orders, and miserably I obey.

The next day in Guadalajara—I've followed her there too, but I'm on my own, barred from backstage, unable to reach her by hook or crook or carrier pigeon—I wander wretchedly, with my thoughts *shooting out all over the place,* as Moses Herzog says. There's a woman bishop now in the U.S.A., maybe I could call her, she could probably get through to Vina and I don't know somehow on a sisterly basis intercede. Stroessner's out in Paraguay, a coup, but the day they announce a world shortage of dictators will be a cold day in Hell. I see where they executed the Sikhs who carried out the Quadruple Assassination. Say hi to Cool Yul for me, guys, maybe he's not so cool no more, not where he's at.

You're changing, she said to me. Don't stop.

Metamorphosis, this is what I need to explain to her, is what supplants our need for the divine. This is what we can perform, our human magic. I'm talking now not about the ordinary, quotidian changes that are the stuff of modern life (in which, as someone said, only the temporary is contemporary); nor even about the adaptive, chameleon natures which have become so common during our migrant century; but about a deeper, more shocking capacity, which kicks in only under extreme pressure. When we are faced with the Immense. At such a hinge moment we can occasionally mutate into another, final form, a *form beyond metamorphosis.* A new fixed thing.

Three of us passed through a membrane in the sky and were transformed by the experience. That's true. But what is also true is that those transformations were not at that time completed. It would perhaps be more accurate to say that we entered a transit zone: the condition of transformation. A transitional phase in which we might have been trapped for ever, which only the imperative force of the Immense can force towards completion.

The Immense has shown its face to Ormus Cama. He has become the agent of that revelation. For him, whatever the consequences, there can be no going back.

For Vina and myself—this is what I need her to understand—the Immense has taken the form of our lifelong, intermittent but inescapable love. Thus, if she will only leave Ormus for me, our lives will change entirely, we will both be altered in astonishing ways, but the new form which then emerges—she and I, together, in love—this will last for ever. For ever and a fucking day.

Putting the screws on her? You bet. I repeat: only under extreme pressure can we change into that which it is in our most profound nature to become. Lichas, hurled into the waters by Herakles, drained of life by fear, turned into a rock. Turned *for ever* into a rock, you can go and sit on it—on him—right now, in the Euboean Gulf, not far from Thermopylae.

This is what people get wrong about transformation. We're not all shallow proteans, forever shifting shape. We're not science fiction. It's like when coal becomes diamond. It doesn't afterwards retain the possibility of change. Squeeze it as hard as you like, it won't turn into a rubber ball, or a Quattro Stagione pizza, or a self-portrait by Rembrandt. It's *done*.

Scientists get angry when laymen misunderstand, for example, the uncertainty principle. In an age of great uncertainties it is easy to mistake science for banality, to believe that Heisenberg is merely saying, gee, guys, we just can't be sure of anything, it's all so darn *uncertain,* but isn't that, like, *beautiful*? Whereas actually he's telling us the exact opposite: that if you know what you're doing you can pin down the exact quantum of uncertainty in any experiment, any process. To knowledge and mystery we can now ascribe percentage points. A principle of uncertainty is also a measure of certainty. It's not a lament about shifting sands but a gauge of the solidity of the ground.

By the same token, as we say in Hug-me, I get annoyed when people misunderstand change. We're not talking about the goddamn *I Ching* here. We're talking about the deepest stirrings of our essential natures, of our secret hearts. Metamorphosis isn't whimsy. It's revelation.

In various bars around the Plaza de Armas, the Calzada Independencia Sur, the Calle de Mariachis, I'm learning to tell the difference between tequilas. Sauza, Ángel, Cuervo, the three big distilleries. For me it's between Sauza and Ángel, but then maybe I haven't tasted enough of the other guy's wares, hey, camarero, hit me again, hombre, muy pronto. The white tequila is the cheap hooch; then there's reposado, that's three months old; but for the good stuff you should stick with the tres generaciones, the name's an exaggeration but six to twelve years of ageing are well worth the wait. At some point I check out Orozco's *Man in Flames* mural. He's a national institution now, a major brand name, but back in the thirties he had to flee to America, where he made his reputation, the familiar story, you've got to leave home and get the gringos to love you before you get the time of day in your old neighborhood. Five minutes later, usually, you're called a sell-out, but Orozco is still in favor, lucky man.

She has made her choice and I'm not it. She has chosen not to change.

I wonder with the help of the three generations of the Ángel distillery how to make it through the rest of my life. I am only forty-two years old. Shit, she's older than I am, what is this, have all the under-forty women in the world written me off? I don't know. I guess if you drink down all these generations you get to be incredibly old. Three more generations, please, camarero. Here they come, begat begat begat. That's better. The women look younger all the time. The busboy's sprouting wings.

If I had a soul I would sell it now and gain my heart's desire. And another three generations, sir waiter, if you will.

Señor I think perhaps it is already sufficient. Where is your hotel. If you wish it, I will call for you a taxi.

On February 13, 1989, the last but one night of her life (we have been here before), the legendary popular singer Vina Apsara chooses the good-for-nothing greaseball playboy Raúl Páramo, a man given to the wearing of personal jewelry, to be the agent of my sexual humiliation. I'm waiting for her in the hotel lobby when she sweeps in, half naked, already oncefucked, in the arms of this pathetic nonentity who is grinning as dementedly as a village idiot who has won the lottery and whose doom, as things turn out, is even closer than her own. She pauses right in front of me, tongue-twistin', clutching at him not three feet from where I stand. She is making her point. *You're nothing in my life, Rai, you mean even less than this punk, so do me a favor, fuck off and die.*

I, however, have received from the lady a lifetime's instruction in the art of waiting for whatever scraps of herself she may care to throw in my direction. Surrendering the torn remnants of my pride, I bribe the floor security officer and am therefore allowed to spend the night in the corridor outside her suite, sitting on a small folding stool—every photographer has one, along with a nose for trouble and a light stepladder—and preparing to throw myself at her feet and beg to be allowed back into some dirty back room of her life.

As Vina once sat outside tormented Ormus's locked door, waiting to be let in, so that she could care for him, so I now wait for her. We are one another's echoes. We are the ringing in one another's ears.

Now it's noon on Valentine's Day. We have been here before. Here is Vina in the hotel corridor, panicky and uncertain, locked out of her suite, in flight from her dying lover; and here is doglike Rai, her faithful retainer, ready as ever to offer his abject, panting services.

We have been here before. It's two hours later and a helicopter is flying over blue agave. My brief exile is at an end; her feelings dictated by her needs, Vina again sees me as an essential ally, at present her onliest help and stay. I am a rock, like Lichas hurled into the sea. And a rock feels no pain.

We pass her retinue on the road below. *Of all you bastards he's the only one I can trust.* Vina, who thinks of trust as a prison, has declared her trust in me.

She's badly jolted by the Raúl Páramo business. In my headphones I hear the nostalgic sound of Hug-me, the argot of our youth. It's been a long time. Afterwards, remembering, I will be powerfully moved by the thought that Vina near her end circled back to our beginning. Of course the private language was useful, to shield our talk from the headphoned ears of the pilot and co-pilot, but for that purpose even English would probably have sufficed. She went further than she needed, resurrecting old Bombay in the hot dry Mexican air. Remembering, I can't help thinking of her decision as an earnest of our intimacy; as a promise of things to come.

We have been here before. We know that this promise won't, can't, be kept.

She is a worried woman: the police, Páramo, the drugs. She is even—astonishingly—concerned about me. Can I ever forgive her awful behavior et cetera, sometimes she just lashes out and hurts the people she cares for most, and how strong I was to still be there for her?, not to walk away?, to give her another chance. But can she please please take a rain check in the matter of love, because right now she can't think straight?, the tour, everything?, she owes it to me to wait until her head is clear. Rai, you've waited this long, honey, you can wait *do-teen* more days.

In the language of love's childhood I hear the words that thrill my still-besotted adult heart. Okay, I'll wait, I say. I'll hang on, Vina, but not for long.

Hug me honey honey hug me. Hang on Sloopy, come on come on.

The fierce heat of the day, the cheering crowd in the football field, the two silver Bentleys of Don Ángel Cruz, the frightened animals, the mariachis, and Vina singing: *Trionfi Amore,* the last song anyone ever heard her sing.

> . . . *il cor tormenta*
> *Al fin diventa*
> *Felicità.*

Then the earthquake. I take up my cameras and shoot, and for me there are no more sounds, only the silence of event, the silence of the photographic image.

Tequila! We have been here before.

In the time of Voltaire it was believed that underground seams of sulfur connected the sites of earthquakes. Sulfur, with its stench of Hell.

Faced with the blazing magnificence of the everyday, the artist is both humbled and provoked. There are photographs now of events on an unimaginable scale: the death of stars, the birth of galaxies, soup-stirrings near the dawn of Time. Bright crowds of suns gather in the wildernesses of the sky. Magellanic clouds of glory, heavenly Pisan towers set in a celestial Campo dei Miracoli, lean across the frame. When we look at these images, there is, yes, legitimate wonderment at our own lengthening reach and grasp. But it would be vain indeed to praise our puny handiwork—the mastery of the Hubble wielders, the computer enhancers, the colorizers, all the true-life-fantasist counterparts of Hollywood's techno-wizards and imagineers—when the universe is putting on so utterly unanswerable a show. Before the majesty of being, what is there to do but hang our heads?

This is irksome. This, naturally, pisses us off.

There is that within us which believes us worthy of the stars. Turn right on this forking path and you find god; turn left and there is art, its uncowed ambition, its glorious irreverent over-reach. In our hearts we believe—we *know*—that our images are capable of being the equals of their subjects. Our creations can go the distance with Creation; more than that, our imagining—our imagemaking—is an indispensable part of the great work of *making real*. Yes, I will even assert as much as that. (Usually I make such assertions when I'm alone in the sealed privacy of the bathroom, but today all bathroom truths must come out to play.)

For example: nobody has yet successfully photographed the gashes in the cosmos which, if Ormus Cama is to be believed, are responsible for the present rash of catastrophes. To get such a picture would be to effect a profound reality shift, a first-magnitude change in our understanding of what is.

However, there is a new picture of an earthquake on the sun. It made all the world's front pages in full, enhanced color. The earthquake looks like a heat bubble exploding through the surface of a hot thick golden porridge. But the seismic solar porridge ripples we see are apparently more than seven Everests high—over forty miles.

If we didn't have the photograph the news of the earthquake would lack felt reality. As it is, every newspaper reader on the planet is now asking the same tremulous question.

Is the sun in trouble too?

Thus, a photograph can create the meaning of an event.

Sometimes even when it's a fake.

In my last photograph of Vina the ground beneath her feet is cracked like crazy paving and there's liquid everywhere. She's standing on a slab of street that's tilting to the right; she's bending left to compensate. Her arms are spread wide, her hair's flying, the expression on her face is halfway between anger and fear. Behind her the world is out of focus. There is a sense of eruptions all around her lurching body: great releases of water, terror, fire, tequila, dust. This last Vina is calamity incarnate, a woman *in extremis,* who is also by chance one of the most famous women in the world.

After the disappearance of Vina Apsara at the Villa Huracán, my

earthquake picture will join that small stock of photographic images—
Monroe's flying skirt, the burning girl in Indochina, Earthrise—which
actually *become experiences,* part of the collective memory of the human
race. Like every photographer, I have hoped to end my days with my
name attached to a few powerful images, but the Vina picture will out-
strip even my most ambitious, self-glorifying aspirations. *The Lady Vanishes,* as it will come to be known, will surely be my bitter posterity. If
I am remembered at all, it can only be for this. So in one sense at least,
Vina and I will be joined together for ever, in spite of everything, a
consummation for which I've wished, all my life, even more devoutly
than I've wished for professional success. Yes, we're linked for all time,
beyond hope, beyond life: metamorphosed by the Immense into the
Eternal. But I was wrong about the nature of the metamorphic force
working its marvels upon us. In our case, it was not love but death.

Be careful what you wish for.

At the beginning of my life in photography I was guilty of an inglorious fraud: a dead man's pictures were passed off as my own. Ever
since then—as I have sometimes admitted to myself, though at other
points I have temporarily managed to suppress the memory of that
twisted boot heel, of the other hanged man in my life—I have needed
whatever is the godless equivalent of redemption; call it self-respect.
Here's an irony: when at last I do create one of the iconic images of
the age, I can only wish I hadn't, I at once and for ever concede that
she, the subject, was of a worth far greater than any photo I could take
of her; I cannot bear to be left with this single mute reflection of her
infinite variety.

You can have the fucking photo. I want her back.

Also, because the picture will first appear alongside news reports of
what I keep calling her disappearance because I'm finding it hard to
use the other word, it will be permanently associated in the public
mind with that final moment of terror. This is how people are. Even
though we all know there could not have been a photographer present
at Vina's end, we accept the authenticity of the image without much
trouble. My picture of Vina in a heaving Tequila street mutates under
the pressure of the world's need for last things, under the pressure of
this global manifestation of the Immense, into a portrait of the star at
the moment of her, say it, death.

So it's a sort of unintentional fake. Another fraud. And though I will try to set the record straight, telling the story of the photograph over and over again, nobody will really be listening. They will already know all they need to know. *The Lady Vanishes.* The world has made up its mind.

We have been here before.

This is a helicopter, hovering just above the broken ground. This is the woman I love, calling to me through the open door. *I'm going, then.* And I'm shouting back, I can't go. *What? Go. Fuck you. What? Good-bye, Hope.*

And this is what people are saying when they aren't saying what they mean.

I'm going, then. (Come with me, please, I need you, I can't believe you won't come with me.) I can't go. (My darling, I want never to let you out of my sight again, but goddamn it, you kick me around, you know that?, do you want to see the bruises?, and just this once I'm not putting you first. I'll be there soon enough, this time you can wait for me. If you want me, you'll wait. That's right, a test. Yeah. Maybe it really is.) *What? (You bastard?, you think you can hold out on me? Oh Jesus, Rai, don't play games, not now, not today.)* Go. (Okay, no games. I love you forever and beyond. But this is my work. I'll be there sooner than blinking. Go. I'm right behind you. I love you. Go.)

Fuck you. (I never wanted you to come to Mexico in the first place fuck you but you came anyway fuck you I guess that proves something yeah but I hurt you anyway I was mad I was wrong fuck you and then you helped me fuck you that really churned me up fuck you so I trusted you I really trusted you fuck you then the earth moved and you abandoned me fuck you you took your photographs I could have been dying I could have been broken and dying but you had your work to do fuck you and now you won't come with me fuck you now when I finally worked out that I need you fuck you I want you fuck you maybe I love you I do love you fuck you Rai I love you fuck you. I do.)

What? (What???)

Goodbye, Hope. (Goodbye for a moment, you bastard, but after this I'm never letting you out of my sight. The next time I see you will be the beginning of the rest of our lives.)

Every night for years, I replayed that shouted dialogue in my head, and now I think this may be what it means. Maybe *Goodbye* really was the never-to-be-completed beginning of *Hello*. I hope so, I hope so. Even though it's a meaning that makes the loss weigh more heavily and the pain harder to bear.

What the pilot says on Televisa: Señora, we took her over the mountains to the seacoast and everywhere below us was a destruction to break the heart. Our thoughts were urgent for our own families, it is true, but we discharged our duty to the end. Our calls ahead to the Villa Huracán were not fulfilled, the telephone was out of service, but the famous personage she insisted on going forward with the arrangement, always she was saying faster, can you not get there in a faster time. For her, to whom what man could say no, we have made our best effort, and when we come to El Huracán it appears she has been blessed with fortune, all is intact, in all our broken motherland this one corner has remained whole to receive herself. As was our pre-arranged plan we land on the sand at the foot of the cliff and she will climb up to Huracán. But on the beach is nobody to carry her baggages which you can easily imagine are plentiful for she is a fashionable one. Of course we can carry the bags, no problem, but understand sirs we are concerned for the machine and also, I confess it, there is a great desire to see once more my wife and sons in Acatlán. Also the personage she is insistent and is a personage of much force of expression, you comprehend, and so it is in compliance with her own desire that her baggages are reposed on the first step of the escalinata to the height and we say our farewells and that is the finish of it.—Excuse, please?—But naturally we were concerned for her safety. It is why we have made two circles over the establishment and have not departed until we have seen him, the other individual who was there.—No, regrettably, other than the distinguished lady personage on the sand we cannot identify any other person. However we have no way left her unattended. That is a scurrilous imputation. The situation at El Huracán at that point is still normal. By the time we leave no misadventure of any type is to be observed.

The Colchis boss Mo Mallick talks to Larry King on CNN. His shoulder-length blond hair, his earnest glasses, his fabulous profile. Excerpts: Sure, Larry, we were scared, I can admit that, who wouldn't be. . . . The house has, or I guess that should be had, that's still so hard to say, it *had* its own generator, so we had some quantity of power, but the phones, the water, that stuff was all down, for the whole coastline as it transpired, I'm telling you these were major heaves. . . . And I had guests, Larry, Chile's probably greatest living writer and his lovely American wife, these were responsibilities also, and what can I say, it simply never occurred to me that she'd make the trip, you know what I mean?, it wasn't the moment for a few super days by the old Pacific sea. Listen, the staff were out of there, I mean like bats out of, not meaning any disrespect, I understand how they felt, I'd probably have done the same myself, but they were *gone*. And I'm like, how quickly can I get myself and my guests to a place of safety, wherever that is, you know? Like, we've been lucky so far but don't push it. . . . It didn't cross my mind for a minute that she would just set herself down, with no plan for an exit, no direction home, you know?, on the *bleep*ing, excuse me, beach.—Excuse me?—Oh, the pilot said he saw . . . ?— No, Larry, I can't say who that would be. The staff are all accounted for, I believe, and my guests and myself, ditto. If there was somebody hanging around there, poor bastard, it's news to me. Maybe a looter, I don't want to be pejorative here, it would be the same way in California, no question, but uncertain times kind of bring forth thieves. I guess he paid a high price, huh.

The seismic moment of an earthquake is measured by multiplying its area (the length of the fault times the width), the amount of slip, and the stiffness of the local rock. The strength of an earthquake is usually characterized by using the logarithm of moment—known as the *magnitude*—rather than the moment itself. Thus all earthquakes, small to large, are ranked from one to nine, each unit of magnitude representing a tenfold increase in strength. A quake of the ninth magnitude is one billion times more powerful than a first-magnitude shock. This system of measurement is named after the American seismologist Charles Richter. Additionally, the intensity of an earthquake, defined as an index of its destructive effect, is classified from I to XII on the so-called Modified Mercalli scale. The monster quake that hits the Pacific coast of Mexico in the early evening of February 14, obliterating the Villa Huracán, the nearby hamlet of Aparajitos, the towns of Puerto Vallarta to the south and of Mazatlán to the north, and much else besides, measures a full nine on the Richter scale, which is to say: as bad as it gets. Also, XII on the Modified Mercalli, meaning complete destruction. Seismologists report the creation of a gigantic new fault, approximately one thousand kilometers long and one hundred kilometers wide, and running more or less exactly along the coastline. The worst earthquakes occur in subduction zones, where tectonic plates collide and one plate is pushed beneath the other. In 1960 a quake with an eight point five magnitude smashed up a big chunk of Chile. For the international seismological community, the 1989 Aparajitos quake signals the sudden, devastating extension to the north of that mighty subterranean war, the crunching encounter of the great plates. It is a major event in the geological history of the earth. A rift along the eternal frontier between the dry land and the sea.

Another possibility, of course, is that it is the first great calamity to be caused by the collision of worlds described by Ormus Cama in his much-derided worldwide bulletin; the beginning of an unimaginable end.

She is alone when it happens. Perhaps she stands on the breakfast terrace beneath a giant fresno ash, drinking a margarita made with tres generaciones tequila, thinking about an old novelist's exposed genitalia, or about Ormus Cama and his eye patch, his headaches, his prophecies. Or about the future; about me. Imagining her, I have again shrouded her in photographic silence. If the birds shriek, if the wind suddenly howls in the trees, if, as on Prospero's isle, the jungle behind El Huracán is filled with noises, I know nothing of these. A tempest is coming, but I am not interested in spells or usurpations.

Or, she is not alone. Some Caliban emerges from the jungle to reclaim his birthright. She is menaced. Or, she is not menaced. She struggles. No, there is no struggle. There is no Other. The pilot lied to seem more responsible than he was, to save face; that's all. The Other is a phantom, a figment. She is alone, with a margarita in her hand, there is a beautiful sunset. In her last minutes she is bathed in the beauty of the world. Perhaps she sings. I want to think of her singing, against the orange and purple sky.

Though I hear nothing else, yet can I hear her heroic voice raised in song.

Then the ground simply opens and eats her, like a mouth.

A great sweep of Pacific coastline is similarly, simultaneously, devoured. The slip of the earthquake is eleven meters: huge. The ocean boils in and fills the gash in the earth, the tear in reality. Water, earth, fire belch high into the sky. The deaths, the *disappearances,* are measured in the tens, the hundreds of thousands.

The earth closes over her body, bites, chews, swallows, and she's gone.

I cannot rightly organize my thoughts.—*I fear I am not in my perfect mind.*—O, she's rubble, and at the bottom of th'abyss!—Vina, the joy of life, the sign of our humanity—disappeared!, in this century of the disappeared, of disappearance—so many people missing from the record—the human race offers the earth god its greatest prize, Vina!!, and the deity, instead of being satisfied, feels its appetite whetted beyond all endurance and restraint, and gulps down a hundred thousand more—Ormus, she's lost to us both, crushed in that muddy embrace—you said it, Ormus, they're your words, the earth learns to rock 'n' roll—Madman, shall I blame you or embrace you?—by singing it, did you will it into being?—Then can you sing her back to life, for yourself, for me?

> *This was the woman for the love of whom*
> *more lamentation burst out from one lyre*
> *than from the throats of all lamenting women*
> *since the world began. Whose mourning*
> *made a world—brought all things back again,*
> *the forests, valleys, roads and villages;*
> *their cattle, fields and streams; a world like ours*
> *circled by sun and spanned by stars like ours—*
> *but set quite differently within*
> *those other heavens. So beloved was she.*

The scale of the emergency dwarfs individual tragedies. So many dead, so much damage both structural and infrastructural, such a hammer blow to the country's soul, and more: to the human race's sense of ease upon the earth. Roads, bridges, airstrips, whole mountains lie in ruins, or beneath the encroaching sea. A gargantuan relief operation is under way, and access to the devastated area, for all but military and relief-agency personnel, is denied. A few television news crews and stills photographers are given accreditation and taken in and around by army helicopters. International aid requires pictures. We can be of use. My Nebuchadnezzar Agency card—I never did get around to quitting formally—gets me a ride.

So I am deep in the heart of ruination when the Vina photograph goes boffo on the planet's front pages; when she becomes the face of the catastrophe. I am looking at scenes out of Bosch—the decapitated heads of children hanging from the branches of broken trees, women's naked legs sticking vertically upwards, like twin swords, out of "solid" rock—scenes that trouble even a war photographer's stomach. I have no awareness of having helped to create a myth. Even when the colonel in charge of press operations goes out of his way to arrange an over-flight of the site of the vanished Villa Huracán, I understand nothing. He is pandering to the Western world's cult of celebrity, I think. He's probably right: it's good for a few extra column inches, which, translated into dollars, makes this part of the itinerary a real money spinner. As pictures go, this one's no different from the others: the torn land, the intruding ocean, the uprooted trees. Standard disaster imagery, not a palapa or swimming pool or dead starlet to be seen. I am thinking these hard-bitten thoughts when unexpectedly I fall apart. I weep in my bucket seat until the thick marrow-snot comes down my nose. I weep like a howling dog on the grave of his fallen mistress. In the end one of the tv-crew sound engineers asks me to shut the fuck up, I'm louder than the rotor blades, my misery is wrecking the goddamn shot.

These fallen boulders are her tombstone, this brokenness her grave. I shout her name aloud. Vina, Vina.

When we land, back at the Guadalajara army strip, the colonel, a man my own age, comes up to me. You knew her, I think?—Yes, I say.—Then is it your picture? He takes out his wallet and there, folded up, is teetering Vina in the tequila-flooded street. I stare at the badly reproduced image on the worn and smudgy newsprint, while the wind tries to tear it from my hands. Señor, it is a sad time for you, the colonel says, and for sure I have much respect for your personal grief, but please, you can give me on this picture your amiable autograph?

Dazed, I sign my name.

Ormus Cama arrives in Guadalajara in a black linen suit and matching velvet eye patch, leaning on big Will Singh and tiny, antique Clea, with a phalanx of other Singhs to defend him from the world. He has taken two floors of the giant Hyatt on the Plaza del Sol in the modern, yanqui-style Zona Rosa: one entire floor for himself, the other for the Singhs. Clea comes looking for me in my humbler old-town abode. Please come, she says. In all the world it is you only he wishes to see.

Clea's grave, narrow face seems overly burdened by its cargo: a pair of outsize spectacles with clear plastic frames and lenses so thick that, without them, she must be all but blind. I can't guess at her age; she could be anywhere from sixty to a hundred. At her efficiency, her iron loyalty to Ormus, her indefatigability on his behalf, there is no need to guess.

It's been a long time, I say. (Meaning, what can I say to this bereaved and damaged heart? I, of all people. Should I tell him the truth? Where does honesty end and cruelty begin? What matters more: my need to be known as her lover, or his need not to know? Let him live in ignorance. He's got enough to worry about, what with the imminent end of the world and all.)

Clea is pursing her lips, smoothing her long, belted skirt, faintly shaking her head. My answer has not met with her approval.

Once you were friends, she says, as if that settles it. Meekly, I follow her down to the waiting limousine.

Ormus's floor of the Hyatt is like the *Marie Celeste:* uncannily still. A five-star ghost town at the top of the city. He has had it redecorated in accordance with his minimalist tastes. Almost all the furniture has been removed, all of the pictures and ornaments, and many of the doors. White sheets cover the walls, and the carpets too. There is a small sign by the elevator asking that shoes be removed. This is an unshod, segregated world.

I pad about the soft moonscape in my socks, looking for the great man. At length I hear the sound of an acoustic guitar emanating from a room which still boasts a door. It's an old song, but I know it at once, even though the words are new.

All my life, I worshipped her. Her golden voice, her beauty's beat. How she made us feel, how she made me real, and the ground beneath her feet.

And now I can't be sure of anything, black is white, and cold is heat; for what I worshipped stole my love away, it was the ground beneath her feet.

She was my ground, my favorite sound, my country road, my city street, my sky above, my only love, and the ground beneath my feet.

Go lightly down your darkened way, go lightly underground, I'll be down there in another day, I won't rest until you're found.

Let me love you true, let me rescue you, let me lead you to where two roads meet. O come back above, where there's only love, and the ground's beneath your feet.

Maybe in the otherworld she isn't dead, I'll have to look for her there, he says, seeing me standing flummoxed and trembling in the doorway. So this supposed alternative reality of his has become a version of Rilke's mourning-created world, a lamentation-cosmos *like ours, but set quite differently within those other heavens.* A world of grief made real by song, by art. Whatever. I shake myself out of the music's spell. She's dead, and these fancies are of no use to me.

She was right to trust in nothing, I say aloud. Even the ground betrayed her. Yet, trusting nothing, she was prepared to gamble on love, and that was heroic, nothing less. I stop there, not specifying: love of whom, or how many. Let it be.

He's sitting cross-legged on the floor of the empty room with a twelve-string country guitar across his knees. He looks terrible; his hair is almost white, and thinning. His skin is gray and ill. There was never any surplus weight on him, but he has lost a lot of pounds. He looks old. He is just fifty-two.

Was it you, he asks, without looking at me. At the villa, the other person, was that you. The photograph, et cetera. I need to know.

No, I say. The picture was before. I wasn't there till later, with the press corps.

A silence. He nods, slowly, twice. Okay. This, he accepts.

I always knew there were others, an other, he says, dull-voiced, still staring at the guitar strings. At my request she provided no details. All she said was, he was completely unlike me.

(I remember something else she said. *The two of you are more alike than you know. Only he's going down . . . and you're on the way up.*)

All she said, Ormus goes on, is it was a physical attraction, whereas what we had was the whole thing: love. (His mouth twists, bitterly. So, as it happens, does mine.) This was simultaneously hurtful, because obviously I was not fulfilling her needs, and comforting, because it told me she would stay. But now they're saying in the papers that the other person, whoever he was, looked exactly like me. In fact for a minute there they thought it was me, they called to ask if I'd been in Mexico. Clea and the office had to deal with that. It's pretty funny, right. I first heard about her death because people wanted to know if I was a corpse myself.

It's just speculation, I say. As far as I know there's no trace of any other person, let alone any description of him. Or her. It's just garbage in the papers.

When she was alive I managed not to care about him, he says. Now I need to know who he was. He's my gateway to her, you can understand that. To her underworld, her other reality. He, whoever he is, can help me find her. He can bring her back. Shall I tell you who I think it is?

My heart bangs. Who, I ask.

Gayo, he replies. Gayomart, my twin, who escaped from my head. It makes perfect sense, don't you see. She was fucking both of us, she needed to know both sides of that story. And maybe he died with her, but maybe he's still out there. I have to know which.

I see now that he really is not sane. His is a consciousness that surfaces intermittently, between long, damaging hibernations, and is no longer capable of seeing things as they are beyond his shrouded walls. You're wrong, I tell him. This is useless, stupid. Just sing your song, Ormus, sing it and say goodbye.

You don't get it, he says, looking me in the eye for the first time. The mystery of her life is now as horrible as the fact of her death. You were her friend, Rai. I know we drifted apart but she always liked you. Help me.

It's time to leave. I shrug and shake my head.

No.

He calls after me as I'm leaving. *The earthquake site,* he wants to know. *Was it flimsy?* That makes me stop and turn. It was a wreck, if that's what you mean, I tell him. As if you took a picture of beauty and then systematically broke everything in the picture. It was like that.

He's shaking his head. It's thinning out all over, he says. I don't think it can survive, it's not strong enough. So these places where it just gives out, where it rips, they must be almost translucent. You saw it, didn't you see it? The flimsiness. The weakness of it all.

I saw a catastrophe, I say. I saw the place she died.

Ormus will use all his considerable resources to pursue Vina's phantom lover. He will employ detective agencies, and rewards will be offered. When this becomes known in New York, that is to say, everywhere, people begin to laugh behind their hands. He is making himself ridiculous, and doesn't care.

On more than one occasion (as I afterwards learn from Clea Singh) the detectives he hires point their fingers in my direction. When this happens, Ormus just laughs, fires them and hires new investigators.

He believes he can see through the surface of things to another truth below, but remains incapable of seeing what's right under his nose.

Ormus and I have one thing in common. We're both trying to cling to the reality of the woman we loved, to preserve and deepen her memory. And yes, we both yearn for resurrection, for her impossible return from the dead: our Vina, just as she was. Our wishes, however, are ceasing to signify. Vina in death is assailed by a second seismic force, which swallows her up all over again. Which swallows her up and regurgitates her in a thousand thousand hideous pieces.

This force also goes by the name of love.

16

Vina Divina

*T*hat she was loved, of course I always knew. The facts about her public persona were not in doubt: that people in countries she had never visited cherished her for the beauty of her voice; that millions of males desired her body and dreamed of it at night; that women of all ages admired and were grateful for her outspokenness, her fearlessness, her musicianship; that when she campaigned against famine, or for the alleviation of the third world's burden of debt, or on behalf of various environmental and vegetarian agencies, the world's leaders, expecting to patronize her, to pat her on the backside and ignore her demands, were first impressed, then seduced and finally coerced into significant concessions by her quickness of intellect, her determination, her grasp; that she was intensely famous, fabulously photogenic, overwhelmingly sexy and great good fun; and that she was the first superstar of the age of confession, who, by her willingness to bare her scars, to live her private life in public, to talk about her wounds, her mistakes, her faults, found a direct line to the world's ashamed unconfident heart, so that, extraordinary and powerful and successful as she was, she came to be seen as an ordinary woman writ large, flawed yet worthy, strong and weak, self-reliant and needy. She was a rock goddess of the golden age, but she was, improbably, also one of us.

To know all this was nevertheless to be entirely unprepared for the scale of the worldwide response to her death. She was, after all, "only a singer," and not even a Callas or a Sutherland but merely a "low-culture" popular entertainer whose rock group, VTO, had been disbanded for almost two years. Her attempted comeback had hardly been a triumph, her solo record had sold acceptably but not well. These were the signs of a falling star. Given her fame, it was predictable that press, radio and television coverage of her demise would be heavy; that there would be small gatherings of grieving fans; that tears, many of them crocodile, would be freely or opportunistically shed; that there would be a number of determinedly jaundiced, professionally against-the-flow voices seeking to tarnish and diminish her memory; even that scandals hitherto concealed might come to light. But any more extreme reaction would be entirely without precedent. Retrospectives, tribute albums, charitable donations, a surge in back-catalog record sales, a memorial concert or two, and then on to the next business: these were the characteristic stages, the ordained rites of such a passage.

Dead Vina, however, had a surprise up her sleeve for us all.

This posthumous goddess, this underground post-Vina, queen of the Underworld, supplanting dread Persephone on her throne, grew into something simply overwhelming. Alive, and at her peak, she had been a beloved figure, even an icon, an electrifying performer and a charismatic loudmouth, but that was about the size of it, let's not get carried away. Dying when the world shook, by her death she shook the world, and was quickly raised, like a fallen Caesar, to the ranks of the divine.

After the great earthquake of '89, the footballer Achilles Hector is immediately released unharmed by his captors, thus becoming possibly the only person to benefit from the appalling tragedy. He tells a press conference that he feels as though he is beginning a new life, that having come so close to death it is as if this regained freedom were his afterlife, and our mortal earth Paradise itself. For these incautious words he is predictably condemned by Church leaders and ignominiously obliged to withdraw his happy, hyperbolic remarks.

Meanwhile, the astonishing afterlife of Vina Apsara is rapidly spiraling beyond the power of any authority, spiritual or temporal, to censure or control.

. . .

All over the world, when the news of her death breaks, people pour into the streets, whatever their local hour, pushed out of their homes by a force they can't yet name. It's not the news of the earthquake that galvanizes them, not the myriad Mexican dead they're mourning, it's just her. It's hard to mourn for strangers except conventionally, routinely; the true mourners of the hundred thousand casualties are themselves among the dead. But Vina is not a stranger. The crowds know her, and over and over again, in the streets of Yokohama, Darwin, Montevideo, Calcutta, Stockholm, Newcastle, Los Angeles, people are heard describing her death as a personal bereavement, a death in the family. By her dying she has momentarily re-invented their sense of a larger kinship, of their membership in the family of mankind.

On the front lines of the world's armed conflicts, amid the noxious fumes of ancient hatreds, men and women gather in cratered roads and sniper alleys, and embrace. It was always Ormus Cama's hope that it might be possible for human beings—for himself—to transcend the frontier of the skin, not to cross the color line but to rub it out; Vina had been skeptical, questioning his universalist premises, but in death she has indeed transcended all frontiers: of race, skin, religion, language, history, nation, class. In some countries there are generals and clerics who, alarmed by the Vina phenomenon, by its otherness and globality, seek to shut it down, issuing commands and threats. These prove useless. Inspissated women in sexually segregated societies cast off their veils, the soldiers of oppression lay down their guns, the members of racially disadvantaged peoples burst out from their ghettos, their townships, their slums, the rusty iron curtain is torn. Vina has blown down the walls, and this has made her dangerous. The love of her muddied radiance has spread deep into the territories of the repressed. Defying the authorities, dancing in front of their tanks, linking arms before the faltering rifles, the mourners move to her phantom beat, looking increasingly like celebrants, and even seem prepared to embrace martyrdom in her name. Dead Vina is changing the world. The crowds of love are on the move.

The standard model of the universe tells us that after the big bang, matter was not evenly distributed through the new cosmos. There was clumping, and from these aggregates of matter were born the galaxies and stars. Likewise, as the human race explodes out of doors, it clumps. The favored centers of congregation are not the high places of the world; not the palaces, parliaments, houses of worship or great squares. At first people seek out the low milieux of music, the dance halls, the record stores, the clubs. But these addresses prove unsuitable: not enough room. The crowds begin, instead, to gravitate to stadiums, arenas, parks, maidans—the major venues. Shea Stadium, Candlestick Park, Soldier's Field, San Siro, Bernabeu, Wembley, Munich's Olympic Stadium, Rio's fabulous Maracanà. Even the old Altamont speedway is thronged. In Bombay where she never performed professionally—there was just that one moment on stage with the Five Pennies more than a quarter of a century ago—the Wankhede is full. In Tokyo, Sydney, Johannesburg, Beijing, Teheran, they gather in great numbers and simply wait.

After a slow, even hostile start, the world's authorities are forced into grudging compliance. Days of public mourning are announced, services of remembrance are proposed. The gathered crowds have no interest in this belated reaction of the high and mighty. From their governments they demand only food, water and toilet facilities, and these begin to be provided.

In the packed stadiums, the sound systems offer her music to the crowds. This gift is accepted. Where possible, videotapes of her performances are played on stadium screens. In many countries, national sporting programs are suspended, cinemas and theaters are closed, restaurants stand empty. In all the world, or so it seems, there is only this single, uniting event: the miracle of the stadiums, the people gathered to share their loss. If her death was the death of all the world's joy, this life after death is like that joy reborn and multiplied.

In many stadiums the crowds call for stages to be constructed, and they duly are. Individual men and women walk up on to these stages and begin to declaim. They talk simply, personally but selflessly, about where they were when they first heard her music, and what it has meant in their lives, at their weddings, their children's births, the deaths of their lovers; in solitude and fellowship, on special days and everydays, in their dotage and their youth.

As if for the first time, the importance of this music—her music, and the music of which she has been part—is made manifest as people, motivated by her living-dead memory, find their voices and speak awkward or eloquent words of love. Music—Vina's voice, singing Ormus's melodies—surges round the world, crossing all frontiers, belonging everywhere and nowhere, and its rhythm is the rhythm of life. And Ormus singing his "Song for Vina" answers her. Disembodied, or rather embodied in song, their love hangs in the air, its story no longer limited by corporeal or temporal constraints. This love is music now.

Immortal, I think. Their immortal story, in which my own love's mortal tale is nowhere to be heard.

Here is a Gary Larson cartoon of Vina and Jesse Garon Parker, the grotesquely Vegas-rhinestoned Fat Jesse of his latter, pill-popping, burgerizing days. They're alone in a motel room, looking out at the world through the slats of a venetian blind. What's this supposed to be, the dressing room of the undead? A zombie transit zone on the Far Side? Ha ha ha.

The lords of information have been caught napping by the unexpected gigantism of the death and after-death of Vina Apsara, but within hours the greatest media operation of the century is well under way, dwarfing the Olympic games, the Cannes Film Festival, the Academy Awards, the Royal Wedding, the World Cup. Video packages are wrapped, sound is bitten. A global struggle begins, whose prize is something beyond even audience share or advertising revenue. Meaning itself is the prize. Overnight, the meaning of Vina's death has become the most important subject on earth.

Vina significat humanitatem.

Here is Madonna Sangria, speaking of women's pain as men's only access to an understanding of the transcendent—*she died that men might learn how to feel*—and expatiating, also, upon sublimation. *Now that she is safely dead they can say how much they lusted after her, without upsetting their wives.* (Madonna Sangria, who latterly reviled Vina and her music, is now, guiltily, reconstituting herself as the keeper of the flame.)

Here is a female music fan from Japan, a futuristically fashionable young beauty in a Planet of the Apes designer outfit, calling Vina

Apsara the great love of her life; no man or ape could ever come as close as this woman she never met.

Here is a fast-mouthed Italian woman admitting Vina to the pantheon of the century's female heroes, and as the true genius of VTO, whose voice could bring about miracles. Ormus Cama? Pah! A parasite. A leech.

Here is a fat Englishwoman, last of the Runts, stuck in her tongue-stud-and-leather time warp, boasting mendaciously of the time she told Vina she was too old to rock. Move over, grandma, and tell grandpa Cama the news.

Here is a great American intellectual's essay, "Death as Metaphor," in which she argues that Vina's life, not her death, was the liberating force; that death is merely death and should be seen as such: as the revenge of the inevitable upon the new.

Here is a recently ordained woman priest, deducing that the Vina phenomenon reveals the world's spiritual hunger, its need for soul food. She invites the stadium crowds to congregate each Sunday in their neighborhood church, *as Vina would very likely have wished.*

Here are Islamist women wearing birdcage shrouds. In their emphatic opinion this madness about a single immoral female reveals the moral bankruptcy and coming annihilation of the decadent and godless Western world.

Vina, who was driven from home to home, is claimed by the places that drove her out: rural Virginia, upstate New York. India claims her, because of her paternal bloodline; England, because it's where her singing career began; Manhattan, because all that is mythic on today's earth is a citizen of New York.

Here is a cultural-studies guru, Primo Uomo, repeating for the one millionth time the oft-iterated idea that Vina has become the patron divinity of the age of uncertainty, the goddess with the feet of clay.

Here are two British psychoanalysts. This one, the young lazy-eyed hunky one, author of *Winking, Nibbling and Licking* and *Sex: The Morning After,* speaks in awed tones of a mammoth spontaneous act of group therapy. That one, a grumpy codger of the old school, is haughtily contemptuous, criticizing the way in which the Vina event privileges raw sentimentality over reason, so that now we can no longer think, only feel. This one calls the phenomenon populist-democratic. That one fears it may be crypto-fascist, the origin of a new kind of intolerant mob.

Here are literary critics and drama critics. The literary critics are divided; the lisping old warhorse Alfred Fiedler Malcolm quotes Marlowe's Faustus—*Then will I headlong run into the earth: Earth, gape! O, no, it will not harbor me!*—and tries to build a complex theory about great celebrity being a Promethean theft of divine fire, whose price is this posthumous hell-on-earth in which the dead woman is actually rendered incapable of dying, and is constantly renewed, like the liver of Prometheus, to be devoured by insatiable vultures calling themselves devotees. This is eternal torment masquerading as eternal love, he says. Let the lady rest in peace. He is rudely ridiculed by the two young turks on the panel, Nick Carraway and Jay Gatsby, who mock his arrant élitism and offer a spirited defense of the place of rock music in society, though they are also fashionably scornful of the low quality of language used by the speakers in the stadiums, their repetitiveness, the use of doggerel rhyming and tabloid cliché, the worrying prevalence of received ideas about the afterlife (Vina living forever, in the stars, in our hearts, in every flower, in every new-born child). These ideas, Gatsby says sharply, are not very cutting-edge; not very rock 'n' roll.

The drama panel is divided too. There is praise for the spontaneous, improvisatory, street-theater rawness of the phenomenon, but the British participants bemoan the inordinate length of the global mourning, the French regret the absence of a firm directing hand, the Americans are concerned about its lack of leading players or a viable second act. All the theater people unite, however, to complain that their views are receiving insufficient attention, that they are as usual being treated as the poor relations, the beggars at the feast.

Here are tv biopic-film producers, advertising for look-alikes. Here are the open casting calls. Here are the lines of hopefuls, stretching round various blocks.

Here is Rémy Auxerre, calling the size of the phenomenon a product of the *feedback loop*. In the days before globalized mass communication, he argues, an event could occur, pass its peak and fade away before most people on earth were even aware of it. Now, however, the initial purity of what happens is almost instantly replaced by its televisualization. Once it's been on tv, people are no longer acting, but *per-*

forming. Not simply grieving, but *performing grief.* Not creating a phenomenon out of their raw unmediated desires, but rushing to be part of a phenomenon they have seen on tv. This loop is now so tight that it's almost impossible to separate the sound from the echo, the event from the media response to it. From what Rémy insists on calling the *immediatization of history.*

Here are two wild-haired New Quakers, a paranoiac and a mystic, probably both Gary Larson fans, denying her death.... Where's the body? Just show me the body, okay? She's not dead, somebody wanted her out of the way is all, we should be storming the Pentagon, the United Nations, you know? ... No, she's free, man, only we are not worthy of her, we have to purify ourselves, and at the hour of our cleanness she will cometh again, dig, maybe from a spaceship?, maybe from a chariot of the gods?, to liberate us. Like Buddha Jesus, man, she liveth.

Television.

Back at the Orpheum in the winter cold, alone and bereft, I hug myself and shiver while my white breath hangs in the air. I'm sitting out on the roof in my hat and coat with my hands over my cold-stung ears, trying to conjure up Vina sunbathing naked in the height of summer, Vina stretching her body and turning to me with a lazy faithless smile. But it's too cold, and anyway the racket is everywhere, there's no escape from the war of meanings, the white air is full of words. *Diachronically speaking, this is an event in history, to be understood within time, as a phenomenon with certain linear antecedents, social, cultural, political. Synchronically, however, all versions of it exist simultaneously, collectively forming a contemporary statement about art and life . . . its importance lies in the random meaninglessness of the death . . . her radical absence is a void or an abyss into which a tide of meanings can pour . . . she has become an empty receptacle, an arena of discourse, and we can invent her in our own image, as once we invented god . . . no possibility of the phenomenon fizzling any time soon because the phase of exploitation has now set in, the shirts bearing the last photograph, the commemorative coins, the mugs, the tackiness, her old schoolmates selling their stories, her army of casual lovers, her entourage, her friends . . . these are multiplier effects, she's caught in an echo chamber and the noise bounces round and round, getting boomier, fuzzier, less distinct . . . it's just noise now . . . and imagine, if she had lived, the dying of her flame, her slow descent towards non-fame, towards nothing . . . that really would have been an ending, a tumble into the Underworld, and the worst part is she would still have been alive. Maybe it's better this way. For ever young, right? Well, young-looking, anyway. Pretty fucking fantastic for a woman of her years.*

I find myself rising to my feet, bellowing formlessly, waving my arms at the blind sky, with cold tears freezing on my face. As if my rooftop's a Tower of Silence and Vina's living memory lies here, naked, beneath the circling vultures, helpless and unguarded except for me.

After forty days the crowds vacate the stadiums, in response to Ormus Cama's direct appeal, and slowly the surface regularity of the planet's daily life resumes. On Ormus's behalf, the Singhs are frequently in court, seeking to protect the "Vina property" from crass exploitation. The new Vina look-alike Quakette, a doll that sings a stupid song until its stand first begins to vibrate, then cracks open and gulps her down, is a particular target. It seems that all the cascading emotion of the Vina phenomenon will end in the slave market of capital. One minute she's a goddess, and the next she's *property*.

Once again, I'm underestimating her. It is true that commercial interests will do their damnedest to possess and use her, that her face will continue to appear on magazine covers, that there will be video games and CD-ROMs and instant biographies and bootleg tapes and cynical speculation about her possible survival and every kind of Internet chat-room baloney. It is also true that her own "side"—her record label and, in the rôle of her management and business team, Ormus and the Singhs—will capitalize on the Vina Effect too, putting her face on the milk, the bread, the wine, as well as the vegetarian meals and records.

(I once read a story about a woman who loathed her lazy slob of a husband. When he died she had him cremated and put his ashes in an hourglass, which she set on her mantelpiece with the words, *At last, you bastard, you're going to do some work.* Ormus's love for Vina is not in doubt, but he, too, is sending her ghost out to do business for the family firm.)

All this is true. But what will become evident during the course of the year is that something like an earthquake is building within people, that in countries all over the globe Vina's adoring constituency has acquired a taste for collective action and radical change. Instability, the modern condition, no longer frightens them; it now feels like possibility. This is Vina's true legacy, not the acres of mawkish commentary or the bad-taste dolls.

And the heaving earth, too, has more changes in store.

This is the way I remember it.

That whole first year after she died, I was badly off balance, not knowing what to do for the best, where to put my own distress, how to continue. I kept recalling a day on Juhu Beach, and a girl in a Stars-and-Stripes swimsuit bad-mouthing everything in sight. That was the day I drew my picture of the world as I wanted it to be, the picture I inhabited from that day on, until the day she died. Now it felt like somebody had snatched the picture out of my hands and ripped it to bits.

When you have no picture of the world, you don't know how to make choices—material, inconsequential or moral. You don't know which way is up, or if you're coming or going, or how many beans make five.

(Nineteen eighty-nine was also the year everybody else's picture broke, the year we were all plunged into an unframed limbo: the formless future. I'm aware of these facts. But that's politics and seismology, and I'll come to it later. I'm talking now about what happened to me.)

I'd wake up thinking she was in the room, and then lie in the dark, shaking. I'd see shadows move in the corners of my eyes and they were her too. Once I rang her private phone line at the Rhodopé and she answered after the first ring. *Hello. I can't come to the phone right now. Please leave a message and I'll get back to you as soon as I can.* I understood that Ormus had not been able to make himself erase her voice. After that I called the number a dozen or more times a day. Often, when I rang, the line was busy. I wondered how many other lost souls were pushing buttons on their phones, just to hear those two dozen words. Then I thought that perhaps there was just one other caller. Ormus Cama, like me, needed repeatedly to hear his dead wife's last recording.

I'll get back to you as soon as I can, a promise I needed her to keep. But what was the message I should leave? What was the communication that would bring her back from the dead?

Briefly, I felt my heart go out to Ormus Cama, my rival in love. Now my rival for nobody's hand. In the midst of that ocean of "love," here were these two shipwrecked lovers, Ormus and Rai, unable to open their hearts to each other, unable to help each other, making stupid telephone calls to the dead from their sinking rafts.

One year after her death, somebody erased the tape—I'm guessing it was Clea Singh, trying to haul Ormus out of his despondent slough—and that day I wept again, as if Vina had just that moment been gobbled up by the hungry earth.

Of all the things said and written about her, the comments that made most sense to me were the ones about death being just death, the arguments against interpretation. Don't make her a metaphor. Just let her rest in peace. I wanted to fight against the billowing firestorm of meanings, I wanted to put on my fireman's hat and turn a hose on the flames. Meanings beamed down from the satellite-crowded skies, meanings like amorphous aliens, putting out pseudopods like suction pads and sucking at her corpse. At one point I tried to construct a text of my own, some nonsense about the heroism of rejecting interpretation, the abrasive but desirable embrace of absurdity. But I got bogged down in ethics. How to live a moral life in an absurd universe, and so on. I didn't want to opt for quietism, to say it was better simply to cultivate one's garden. Something in me retained a desire for engagement with the world. I tore the piece up and spent my days leafing through my portfolio of Vina pix and, until the tape was wiped, calling her on the phone.

During that first year, noting that I had largely ceased to go out, that when I wanted to eat I would order in, that most of this food was liquid, and that my long-term cleaner had quit because the place was getting to be like a slum, my fellow Orpheum residents took it upon themselves to "save me." Johnny Chow came to advise, gravely, that I was paying too much attention to death. That was a laugh. Sugar Ray Robinson, Lucille Ball, the Ayatollah Khomeini, Laurence Olivier, R. D. Laing, Irving Berlin, Ferdinand Marcos, Bette Davis, Vladimir Horowitz, "La Pasionaria," Sakharov, Beckett *and* Vina, in one year, I pointed out thickly: it's Armageddon out there. Never a great debater, Chow withdrew, shaking his elegant head. Mack Schnabel suggested I make a selection of my Vina pictures and then hold a show in the building's gallery space. That was a tough one. Would such an exhibit look like a dignified personal tribute or just another case of an opportunist schmo jumping on the unstoppable Vina bandwagon? I couldn't make up my mind. Anyway, it was a while before I got round to finalizing the selection. Most days I suffered from blurred, or even double vision. Clarity was not my strongest point in those unhappy months.

Basquiat came up to talk to me about girls, which was sweetly conventional of him, considering his own astonishing preferences. Fantastique weemain are beursteeng out all ovair, he wanted me to know. Aftair so long, it ees no good to be alone 'ere weez your fantômes.

Fantômes is correct, I told him. There's a beautiful woman who keeps getting into my pictures, I don't know how. I photograph an empty room, my bathroom, maybe, I'm spending a lot of time in my bathroom, and when I develop the roll she's looking at me out of a mirror. No, it's not Vina, it's someone else completely. A haunting stranger. So you see that now there are two.

This dooble expozhair idée of yours, he said. Eet ees gone too far, I theenk.

Finally they approached me as a group to read me some loving version of the riot act. Say yes to life, clean up your act, take a minute to smell the roses, the usual formulae. I must admit they made quite an effort. They got the place into some sort of shape, cleaned out the drinks cupboard and the bathroom cabinet, dragged me down the street for a shave and a haircut, and threw a party in my apartment, featuring all the most desirable unattached women they knew (and this, given our profession, was a great many). I understood what was being done for me and why. Mostly friendship, yes, and for that I was and remain profoundly grateful. But there was also the other side of the coin. People don't like being around despair. Our tolerance for the truly hopeless, for those who are irremediably broken by life, is strictly limited. The sob stories we like are the ones that end before we're bored. I understood that I had good and true friends in these three men, that it was all for one and one for all and these were my musketeers. I also saw that I needed to behave better for their sakes. I had become their nagging toothache, their dose of gut-rot, their ulcer. I needed to get better before they decided to cure themselves of me.

If friendship is a fuel, the supply of it is not endless.

In the middle of my so-called coming-out party, I looked over at Aimé-Césaire and saw the mark of death on him, and the party began suddenly to seem like a wake for that beautiful man who, like Finnegan in the song, was sitting up gaily and enjoying his own farewell do. I knew about Schnabel also, that since his punishing divorce he continued to be at war with his ex-wife Molly, who had successfully obtained court orders preventing him from going within a mile of his two kids, and who visited Mack's father on his deathbed to tell him, falsely, that Mack was a heroin addict, guilty of both violence towards and sexual abuse of the boys. Johnny Chow had his own saga of catastrophes, mostly connected with gambling. Were these people from whom I was prepared to take advice?

Yes, I said to myself. Better a whore than a nun, better a wounded soldier than someone who never heard the crump of the guns.

At that moment I saw Johnny Chow forcing his way through the crowd of revellers, grinning demonically, with Vina Apsara on his arm.

I'd heard about the impersonation craze, the Vina supperclub/cabaret look-alikes, the underground, heavy-metal and reggae Vinas, the rap Vinas, the Vina drag queens, the Vina transsexuals, the Vina hookers on the Vegas Strip, the Vina strippers outnumbering the Marilyns and Long Tall Texans on amateur nights around these infinitely varied United States, the porno-Vinas on the adult cable channels and closed-circuit hotel tvs, the hardcore under-the-counter blue-video-Vinas, and the innocent biannual gatherings of dweeby karaoke Vinas whose numbers rivaled even the indefatigable *Star Trek* conventioneers. In point of fact Vina had once been a guest star on the *Next Generation* television series, conjured up on the holodeck to sing for an enamored Worf. He taught her Klingon and she taught him Hug-me, or another similar-sounding tongue. When the Trekkies remembered this they invited the Vina people to join forces with them, but Vina was bigger than the *Enterprise* now, she was in a continuum of her own, perhaps even the fabled Q.

There was a famous production of *Hamlet* in which Jonathan Pryce, the actor playing the Prince of Denmark, "produced" the Ghost from within himself, like a channeler or spirit medium, in an astonishing feat of body and voice control. The Vina impersonators did it the easy way, using costumes and recordings, but the idea was the same. In their own bodies they conjured up their fantasy beloved from the dead.

It's a few steps beyond Mizoguchi too, I thought. In *Ugetsu,* the poor yokel taken in by the mysterious aristocratic beauty was just in love with a ghost. But these people aren't merely under a dead woman's spell, they're actually trying to be her, wearing her kimonos, powdering their faces, walking the walk. This is a new form of auto-eroticism. Guised as Vina, these mimic women are making love to themselves.

There was some disagreement as to which Vina most merited commemoration, the firebrand Afro-Vina of her younger days, big-haired, big-voiced, big-mouthed and sexually rampant, or red-haired Mexi-Vina, older but still hot, her voice never better, her aura a little wiser, or Death-Vina, the sad-eyed lady of the broken lands. In the end, pragmatism ruled. The younger impersonators did the early Vina, the older men (yes, and women too) made the latter-day Vina their own.

This Vina, the one on Chow's arm, was unmistakably an older guy. Chinese too, which inevitably made the resemblance imperfect, but he'd put in some hard hours in front of his make-up mirror, darkening his skin, taking trouble with the shape of his eyes. He'd studied her swinging gait, the movement of her mouth, her attitude. And the red wig was very good. Tell me now if this is a bad idea, Johnny asked as they reached me, only we thought it might, oh shit, defuse something if she were in some sense here. Like Adult Children Of Alcoholics, you know that group, it can help to know you're not alone.

I so don't want to bum you out, this China-Vina said disarmingly in a fine baritone voice, and actually bowed. That's so not it. I much honored her, long time now, this is my way to give her respect.

It's fine, I told Johnny. Really. It's cool. Great job, I added to the gratified cross-dresser. Do you want to sing later, or what?

I mime, he said, breaking out in a big, proud smile. I brought my tape deck, if that's okay to do.

Go for it, I advised him, and forced myself to smile dazzlingly back. The look of relief on Chow's face told me I'd done the right thing. My friends would feel better about me now, and—with a sense of relief on all sides—they'd be more okay with leaving me alone.

. . .

For long periods, during year two after Vina, I lived alone by the sea in America. *What do you love?* I had asked her at Juhu, and she answered, *I love the sea.* That, at least, I regained, though she was gone: the ocean breezes on which I smelled her pungent, lost perfume; the beach. This long golden strand was a far cry from Cuffe Parade's urban gracious-ness, from Apollo Bunder's bustle, but it filled me with more than one kind of nostalgia. Cruising to the ocean past the potato fields, the corn-fields, the turning banks of sunflowers, the glistened polo horses, the sweet birds of youth and the tick-bearing deer; past the exotically casual American rich in their cut-offs, their halter necks, their chinos, their polo shirts, their classic convertibles, their Range Rovers, their monied old age, their gilded childhood and their potent prime; past the Shin-necock Indians trimming the hedges and cleaning the pools and main-taining the tennis courts and mowing the grass and in general tending to the high-priced, stolen land; past the honk of the railroad and the cry of the geese and the hissing of summer lawns, I was turned back, after a long age, towards thoughts of home. Home as another lost jewel, as something else swallowed up, by time, by choice. As something else now unavailable, glowing up through the water like sunken gold, breathing painfully under the plowed earth like a lover gone down to Hell.

I did pull myself together sufficiently to assemble that show of pho-tographs, *After Vina,* which was well and seriously received. I don't deny that this pleased me. The truth is that after all I was not immune to the disease of making Vina mean something, and what she meant to me was love, certainly, but also mystery, a woman ultimately unquan-tifiable and impossible to grasp, my window into the inexplicable.

The mystery at the heart of meaning. That was her.

I invited Ormus to the opening but he didn't show. I hadn't really expected it. There was one small fracas: at one point a group of New Quakers burst into the Orpheum gallery to denounce me noisily for implying that Vina was deceased, and these greasy, bikerish figures took some ejecting. When they had gone, I found myself standing next to a slender old Indian gentleman in a J. Crew check shirt and jeans, whom I did not at first recognize in this off-duty manifestation.

I want to thank you, he said in his curious, flat-accented way, for sharing my daughter with me. It surely is a positive and healing experience to be here. Yes, sirree, it surely is.

It was the Rhodopé doorman, Shetty. In the depths of my own grief I had callously forgotten that Vina's father was still alive.

My encounter with Doorman Shetty is like a whip of cold water across the face. It wakes me from my long unhealthy reverie, my heart-sick inwardness, and renews my awareness—which is the essence of the photographer's art—of the immediacy, the presentness, of things. At the end of his shift the next day I meet up with Shetty, who is back in uniform, and we go for coffee to the Buddhist-organic place across the street from the Orpheum, that Eastern-scented room with its oddly soothing combination of great dark coffee, stripped dark wood and pale barefoot waitresses in white dresses that drag on the floor and button all the way up to the throat. Shetty seems calm, though the joviality I recall is not in evidence. He is happy, he says, that Vina found him in his old age and that the distance between them was thereby at least a little reduced. This he tells me in the new vocabulary of self-regard. *We dealt with some issues. We confronted the anger that needed to be faced and we did some good healing work. We hugged. We became comfortable with each other. We had some quality time.*

They even went into therapy together, he reveals. The therapist, an Indochinese woman named Honey and married to a successful Wall Street arbitrageur of conservative Nicaraguan origins, one day hung a giant pink piñata in the shape of a rabbit from the ceiling fan in her office and handed Vina a wooden stick. As Vina slugged the piñata she was encouraged to say whom she was really hitting out at, and why. She went for it with a vengeance, and Shetty accordingly heard many painful complaints about himself, but the spectacle of his famous daughter beating the bejesus out of a giant salmon-colored papier-mâché bunny like a retard S&M queen was so absurd that he laughed. He laughed until he cried, especially when the piñata gave way under the force of Vina's assault and the usual children's sweets and fluffy toys tumbled out, all the gifts he had failed to give his daughter when she was a child.

How did that make you feel, Honey the therapist asked him. He wiped his eyes but the chortling wouldn't stop.

Let me tell you what I think, he began, and guffawed.

Never mind what you think, she interrupted. Let's stay with what you feel.

Shetty, unable to countenance the hilarious idiocy of this remark, got up and walked out, still laughing.

The trouble was, he tells me ruefully, Vina thought the piñata was a great idea, so she felt like I was laughing at her. After that we, ah, re-experienced our previous unresolved relational negativity. We remained on friendly terms but we didn't engage any more. This was classic avoidance behavior. We didn't confront. We sidestepped. We didn't heart-to-heart.

There is a great deal more he wants to confess: how his long decline from successful butcher to down-and-out hobo began the day after he took the young Vina to dinner at the Rainbow Room and then packed her off to live with the Doodhwalas in Bombay. He wishes to speak of fate, of a self-imposed curse, of having suffered the consequences of his failures as a parent deeply enough and for long enough. He is preparing to ask me for the expiation he never fully received from his dead daughter. Doorman Shetty is pursuing a dead Vina too, like all the rest of us he needs to raise her from the dead to give him peace.

Still too shaky myself to carry his additional weight, I cut him off in mid-flow. So as not to appear too rude, I inquire after his son-in-law, Ormus. How is the rock legend dealing with his loss? To my surprise, my pro-forma inquiry occasions a savage tirade.

Listen, this was all in the *National Enquirer*! This was in *People* magazine! What, you didn't hear, you were out of town?, I'm guessing on the moon?

Almost, I reply, thinking of the sea of forgetfulness, the sea of storms, the white white sand and the sea.

Shetty snorts, and dishes.

Ormus Cama, the notorious recluse, has added to his list of bizarre obsessions the growing imitation-Vina industry, making a full collection of the available pornographic film and video material, and showing up unannounced and surrounded by burly Sikh bodyguards at nightclubs and strip joints, to check out the quality of the impersonations. He is believed to be a patron of certain brothels and élite "home delivery" services specializing in celebrity look-alikes. On one occasion he was actually caught *in flagrante* with a counterfeit Vina in the back of a super-stretch, but when the sharp-eyed cop who saw the hooker responding to a signal and entering the limo understood what was going on, whose surrogate was doing what to whom, he didn't have the heart to take the matter further and let the participants go without further ado. (The whore in question, Celeste Blue, subsequently tried to parlay the incident into a financially beneficial little scandal but was foiled by the absence of any charges. Clea Singh, commenting on Blue's interview in the *Enquirer,* said only: It sounds like the lady has a big mouth.)

For many years the most private of men, Ormus—eye-patched and earmuffed—is now, says the Doorman, a regular attendee at the mushrooming Vina conventions, often agreeing to adjudicate at the lookalikes' beauty contest, stipulating only that he should be the sole judge. The winning Vina, if she is thought to be of a sufficiently high standard, is sent up to his suite after the contest, and afterwards escorted out by a firm-jawed Clea Singh and compensated so handsomely that, thus far, there have been no complaints.

Ormus has also—reversing the attitudes of a lifetime—been visiting a guru. Her name is Goddess-Ma, and as the upheavals of the age have become more numerous and dramatic her popularity among the élite of New York society, who are always easily alarmed by global instability and loud noises, has increased by leaps and bounds. Goddess-Ma is from India, allegedly illiterate, made her name in Düsseldorf and arrived in the United States "by a miracle." It is rumored that there is no record of her journey to New York in the files of any airline or shipping company. Yet her immigration status has never been investigated, which would indicate to the skeptical observer that the truth is more conventional than it is being made to seem, but is treated by the Goddess-Ma people as further proof of her existence within an impregnable aura of blessing and safety. Goddess-Ma is very small, but young and beautiful enough to be a movie star, and has powerful—and anonymous—backers who have installed her right in the Rhodopé Building, three floors down from Ormus. From this splendid residence she has issued a number of "Goddess Sayings" that have reverberated in the rarefied air of the city's better locales. India-blah, Bharat-burble, the so-called Wisdom of the East, is definitely back in fashion. In fact, India in general is hotter than ever: its food, its fabrics, its doe-eyed dames, its direct line to Spirit Central, its drums, its beaches, its saints. (When India explodes a nuclear device, the notion of Holy Mother India takes a few dents, but it is quickly agreed by *le tout* Manhattan that in this matter India's unwise political leaders have betrayed the land's true spirit. The valuable Oriental Wisdom concept suffers little lasting damage, unlike the much-shaken planet.)

Unsurprisingly, Goddess-Ma has been commenting on the Vina phenomenon. Beneath the unstable earth, she Says, there has always been a woman keeping things together, in all cultures. Our Indian earth mother parted her lips to receive pure Sita, falsely accused of having been defiled by Ravana, after Lord Ram rejected her on his spin doctors' advice. Our Greek mother Persephone sits beside Hades in his subterranean kingdom.

Now Vina, our beloved Vina, has joined these women, the greatest of women, who hold up the earth from below as mighty Atlas holds up the sky.

O dancing Earth, Says Goddess-Ma. In our Indian Puranas we learn that Lord Shiva danced You into being, He, the Lord of the Dance. Whereas the Greeks tell of Eurynome, the goddess of everything, who loved dancing and created the sea and the land so that she had some-place to groove. I Say that such also are We!, Men and Women!, danc-ing our world into being. I Say, Dance! And if the earth shakes, think that Vina dances, too, and see what new miracles She unveils.

As Goddess-Ma's popularity grows, as her beautiful face and her feel-good Sayings do their irresistible work on that city in which beauty and congratulation are the surest roads to success, there are dis-senting noises, from the followers of older spiritual Paths and from large segments of New York's Indian community. When asked about her critics, Goddess-Ma is sharp. Mine is the true Indian way, she Says with complete assurance. These converts and long-term expatriates are happier peddling and swallowing their glamorized exotica.

(Goddess-Ma has already learned the laws of spin. Take the worst thing that is said about you, accuse your accusers of the selfsame fault, be more beautiful and media-friendly than they, and you will carry all before you, like a storm.)

Writing this, I think of Darius Cama. I think of William Methwold. I remember their attempts to build bridges between the mythologies of East and West. I remember my own hours in Darius's library, my seduction by his storehouse of ancient tales. I wonder what the old gents with their love of scholarship and uninterest in hocus-pocus would have made of Goddess-Ma and her brass-bold bid for transcultural divinity, which includes a shameless attempt to co-opt dead Vina, to hijack her popular tragedy. New York, where you go to make it big, has no problem with Goddess-Ma's hard-sell tactics, which are, in fact, admired and increase her following. Also, the city's dance venues report a significant increase in numbers. The young of Manhattan are following the pint-size seer's terpsichorean advice.

Shetty is even-handedly contemptuous both of pretty, ambitious Goddess-Ma and of those who follow her. That Ormus Cama has been going down three floors to visit her a couple of times a week only proves that he's totally lost it, in the Doorman's forcefully expressed opinion.

And there's worse to come. Ormus is apparently chasing dead Vina down every rabbit hole he can find. It is Shetty's contention that the rock god is now a heavy user of major narcotics, pursuing his dead wife along trails of powder, reading her smoke signals, feeling her needle in his veins. The Singhs manage everything, the businesses, the royalties, the women, the drugs, they have enclosed him within their fierce loyalty, it's even harder to get anywhere near him than it used to be. It is probable that his devoted retinue—determined as its members are to fulfill his every whim, to slake his every thirst, to offer him whatever partial compensations might momentarily offset his irreducible loss— is in fact killing him with love.

It's the coward's way, Shetty tells me, and I'm surprised by the sudden brutality of his words. If he wants to be with my poor girl so much, then why not be a man and shoot himself in the mouth. Yeah. Why doesn't he just blow his head off and to hell with everything. Then they'll be together until the end of time.

I liked you better when you were cheerful, I tell him. When you were rolling with the punches, I liked you fine.

And the same to you, he says, leaving. Don't think you're the only SOB who can remember when.

Doorman Shetty doesn't know it, but he's echoing Plato. This is what the great philosopher has Phaedrus say in the Symposium's first speech about love: *The gods honor zeal and heroic excellence towards love. But Orpheus . . . they sent back unfulfilled from Hades, showing him a phantom of the woman . . . because he seemed to them a coward . . . [who] didn't venture to die for the sake of love, as did Alcestis, but rather devised a means of entering Hades while still alive.* Orpheus, the despised *citharode*—the singer with the lyre or, let's say, guitarist—the trickster who uses his music and wiles to cross boundaries, between Apollo and Dionysus, man and nature, truth and illusion, reality and the imagination, even between life and death, was evidently not to austere Plato's taste. Plato, who preferred martyrdom to mourning, Plato the ayatollah of love.

The pursuit of love beyond death is a harsh and joyless chase. I judge Ormus less harshly than would the Platonic Phaedrus, or that other, rather less eminent thinker, his personal gatekeeper and his dead wife's dad. I know what he's going through, because I've been down that tunnel too. I'm *there*.

Here he is, Ormus: unable to work, succumbing to Vina's weaknesses—the drink, the drugs—hoping to find her in her faults, by making them his own. And these are his chemically induced visions of her, of Vina in many guises. Here she is bearing the thousand faces of the women in whom he searched for her after she fled Bombay, also the thousand faces of all the women he gave up for her sake during the ten celibate years. They are all Vina now.

Here she is as herself. He looks on her and feels himself turn to stone.

As the Vina phenomenon swells and grows, he feels himself losing his grip on the truth of her; his Vina is slipping away for ever, dying a second time. The earthquake has already claimed her but after the earthquake comes the tidal wave, drowning Vina under the tsunami of her selves.

As she becomes all things to all people so she becomes nothing to him—nothing he knows or loves. And there is a worse thought: as she slides ever deeper into the abyss, buried beneath an avalanche of versions, as she enters the halls of the underworld to take her seat on her dark throne, is it possible that she is forgetting him?

Rilke's Eurydike, entering the nether realms, grows quickly forgetful of the light. The darkness stains her eyes, her heart. When Hermes speaks of Orpheus, this Eurydike terribly answers: *Who?*

The name Eurydice/Eurydike means "wide-ruler." The first recorded use of this name in tellings of the Orpheus story occurs in the first century B.C.E. It may therefore be a relatively recent addition to the tale. In the third century B.C.E. she was called Agriope, "savage watcher." This is also one of the names of the witch goddess Hecate; and of wide-ruling Queen Persephone herself.

Which precipitates an avalanche of questions: Did Eurydice—of whose origins we know little, although the official version is that she was a wood nymph, a dryad—actually bubble up from the Underworld to capture Orpheus's heart? Was she an avatar of the Queen of Darkness herself, hunting for love in the illuminated world above? And therefore, in being swallowed by the earth, was she merely going home?

Is the failure of Orpheus to rescue her a token of the inevitable fate of love (it dies); or of the weakness of art (it can't raise the dead); of Platonic cowardice (Orpheus won't die to be with her; no Romeo he); or of the obduracy of the so to speak gods (they harden their hearts against lovers)?

Or—most startlingly—is it a consequence of the reassertion by Eurydice of her true identity, her dark side, her citizenship of the night? And Gayomart, Ormus's dead twin, his own night self, his Other: is he her true husband, who sits beside her upon her obsidian chair?

Here's my answer. In the obsessive contemplation of death we may begin to hear, from the dead, whispers of how they lived. Hades, Persephone, all that belongs, for me, to the realm of the so-to-speak. But Vina's hidden self *during her lifetime* was no metaphor. The person she hid with was me, the self she concealed from her husband she revealed to me. Forget Gayomart; I was the flesh-and-blood Other beside her. I was her other love.

Maybe this is what Ormus can't admit to himself: that the Vina he doesn't know is not a construct of her death or afterlife. What he can't stand is the mystery of her earthly hours. Her nights above the ground.

This is a riddle I can solve but will not. *Yes, it was me,* I could say, *she was going to leave you, you crazy bastard, she was on the point of ditching you and your eye-patched visions and your whistling ears and your ten-year gestures and your famous grand passion, and making a beeline for my big brass bed.*

I am the King of her Underworld, I could tell him. *She belongs to me.*

I can't tell him this because I've lost her too, and now we're burning in the same fire. O Ormus, my brother, my self. When you scream the noise bursts from my throat. When I weep the tears seep from your eyes. I will not hurt you more.

And because I can't, I won't, he slides deeper into the bottomless pit: not Vina's abyss, but his own. He can't believe in her soiling, though she lie ever so deep in the soil. He sees her glowing up through the fog of earth and stone. He imagines her corpse as a blazing candle, phosphorescent, undimmed. His love illuminates her. He seeks her through the night.

He hopes each night to wake and see a familiar figure standing at his window, looking out at the shadowed park, the park before dawn. How often he pictures himself slipping out of bed to stand silently beside her sweet shade and watch the fingers of first light slip across the tall houses and the trees.

I know all his fears, all his hopes, all his dreams, because they are also mine.

Earthquakes, scientists say, are common phenomena. Globally speaking there are around fifteen thousand tremors a decade. Stability is what's rare. The abnormal, the extreme, the operatic, the unnatural: these rule. There is no such thing as normal life. Yet the everyday is what we need, it's the house we build to defend us against the big bad wolf of change. If, finally, the wolf is reality, the house is our best defense against the storm: call it civilization. We build our walls of straw or brick not only against the vulpine instability of the times but against our own predatory natures too; against the wolf within.

That's one view. A house can also be a jail. Big wolves (ask Mowgli, ask Romulus and Remus, ask Kevin Costner, we don't have to rely on the Three Little Pigs) are not necessarily bad. And anyhow, this new time of shocks and cracks is out of the ordinary, as even the seismologists agree. The number of tremors is up to over fifteen thousand a *year.*

Everybody reads the papers, right, so I don't have to spell out in too much detail how the world has changed in these last years, the sudden decrease in the height of the Himalayas, the crack across the Hong Kong–China frontier that turned the New Territories into an island, the sinking of Robben Island, the raising of Atlantis at Santorini-Thera in the southernmost Cyclades, the transformation of rock 'n' roll into a weapon that blasted Panama's dictator-on-the-run out of his hideout, and so forth. Everybody gets the new rolling-news stations, so we've all watched the earthquakes together, the old order falling, live, as it happens, we have seen the jails bursting open, the breaking of the so to speak seventh seal was a major breaking news story, and we're all wondering who those four horsemen are. Like Butch Cassidy and the Sundance Kid when the Pinkerton men just kept on coming after them, we turn to one another and ask, wonderingly, *Who are those guys?*

So to speak.

These frontier earthquakes are the wonder of the age, aren't they? Did you see that fault that just ripped out the whole iron curtain? "Unforgettable" doesn't even come close. And after the Chinese opened fire in Tiananmen, did you see the rift open up along *the entire length* of the Great Wall of China? So now there's nothing in China (but there's a big new airport in Japan) that can be seen from the surface of the moon, that'll teach 'em, right? Right.

Oh, man, the things these quakes are throwing up. Poets for presidents, the end of apartheid, the Nazi gold buried for fifty years deep in Swiss bank accounts, Arnold Schwarzenegger, the *Titanic,* and we guess communism just got buried in the rubble there somewhere. And those Ceauşescus? *So* not missed.

When the changes are this big, you can be sure there will be politicians lining up to take the credit. Seems that the iron curtain quakes were the result of years of covert Western activity underground. Seems we found where the pressure points were and used our best efforts to build that pressure until the whole house of cards came tumbling down. Seems that earthquakes, the ultimate weapons of mass destruction, are now at our disposal. Somebody gives us trouble, we literally pull the rug out from under his feet. This is what just happened to Saddam Hussein in what is quickly becoming known as the Shake of Araby. No, that's right, if you're being picky it hasn't been one hundred percent successful, he survived et cetera, but *did you see it?* You've gotta give our boys credit, they put on one hell of a show. Whoo-hoo! Whole lotta shakin' goin' on. And, as we hope you noted, no damage at all to the superstructures and infrastructure of that all-important Saudi oil. *Nada.* Zilcho. Zip.

What, now Mexico wants to know if United States or European Union agents were involved in their great quake? Was this some sort of dummy run, some Little Boy–Fat Man demonstration of extreme force? Jeez, there's always a killjoy. Read our lips. *Of course not.* Would we let Vina Apsara die in some sort of military-industrial megaconspiracy? That's just crazy. We loved that woman. What wouldn't we give to have her here, alive, and singing, right now. The Mexican earthquake was a natural phenomenon which we are doing our darnedest to understand. We have our best people on this. Mother Nature has her own bad moods, and we need to be in touch with those, to live well with the earth, our home. We need to build our knowledge so that we can work on setting in place systems and technologies that will minimize the risk of another such disaster. Our hearts go out to the Mexican people for their sad loss.

Okay? Are we okay on this? Okay, then. *Okay.*

The end of the Soviet Union was a good thing. The victory of the free world is a good thing. We are the good guys. The black hats lost. The new business of the world is business. Rejoice.

Peace.

Me? Don't ask me. As I've been telling you, my head's been in a spin ever since Vina died. If you ask me (don't ask me) the Vina phenomenon inspired people and they stood up and changed their lives. If you ask me, all you need is love. The quaking earth, don't ask. Maybe it's down to Mother Nature or NATO or the Pentagon. Me, I'm seeing ghosts. After a lifetime of refusing to accept the irrational it's here, in my work. The miracle of unreason: a woman's ghost-image in my photographs. Worlds in collision. I'm thinking wild thoughts; hypothesizing that—in spite of all the boasting and chest-beating, all the end-of-history rhetoric—the current cycle of catastrophes may have little to do with victory or defeat, the earthquakes may not be in our control, they may be little warning signs hinting at the proximity of the main event: which is, the end of the world. Or the end of one world. Ours, somebody else's, don't ask me which.

I repeat: Darius Cama's library of myths is as close as I have ever needed to get to fantasy. The old religions' legacy of living stories—the Ash Yggdrasil, the Cow Audumla, Ouranos-Varuna, Dionysus's Indian jaunt, the vain Olympians, the fabulous monsters, the legion of ruined, sacrificed women, the metamorphoses—continues to hold my attention; whereas Judaism, Christianity, Islam, Marxism, the Market, utterly fail to enthrall. These are faiths for the front pages, for CNN, not for me. Let them struggle over their old and new Jerusalems! It's Prometheus and the Nibelungs, Indra and Cadmus, who bring me my kind of news.

Additionally, ever since my youngest days, Ormus and Vina have added to my plate two goodly extra dollops of living myth. These have been more than enough for me.

Falling in love with Vina, I knew I was stepping out of my league. Nevertheless, I took the step and did not fall flat on my face. This is human heroism. Of this, as of little else, I am proud. Male love is a kind of self-assessment. We allow ourselves to love only those women to whom we feel we have a right to pay court, to whom we dare aspire. The young Ormus, a handsome devil, could legitimately dream of goddesses. He gave himself permission to imagine himself with them, to pursue, and (in his case) usually to attain his dreams. Then Vina, his true deity, came and went. The first time she left him he sought her in other women's bodies, her kiss on other lips. Now that won't do. It's Vina herself or no one.—But she's no longer of this world.—Then find her, wherever she is.

Which is, I confess, presently my attitude too. For, with less reason than Ormus Cama, I, too, dared to aspire to Vina; and she smiled on me also; and left me with an empty heart.

A word more about Ormus: his early gift of precognition, of hearing the future's music playing in his head, gave my anti-fantastic instincts their first severe test. In that instance I took refuge in the rea-

sonable man's partial-knowledge defense: to admit we do not understand a phenomenon is not to admit the presence of the miraculous
but merely, reasonably, to accept the limitations of human knowledge.
God was invented to explain what our ancestors couldn't comprehend:
the radiant mystery of being. The existence of the incomprehensible,
however, is not a proof of god. . . . Listen, if I'm reheating yesterday's
cold soup, it's because I'm about to set down matters strange to me;
strange because they belong to the realm of the "magical," the inexplicable. I have to speak of "Maria," and her "teacher," and in my adulthood concede what is hardest for full-grown men to grant, the same
truth which Hamlet, also upon seeing a ghost, obliges scholarly Hora-
tio to accept: that there may be more things in heaven and earth than
are dreamt of in his—in my—philosophy.

Returning to work after a long layoff—this is in the fall of 1991, some
time after the Vina show at the Orpheum—I decide to set up a
sequence of pictures about the remembered Vina, about memory and
the error-strewn, partial manner of its ownership of the past. I'm back
at the seaside, in Mack Schnabel's house near Montauk Point, a sprawling cliff-edge place to which the crashing ocean breakers give an air of
perpetual storm, even when the skies are clear. To design the sequence
I get hold of two hard, straight-backed chairs, two mirrors, a couple of
life-size dolls, a few other props. Here's how it's supposed to go. A
masked man—the mask is actually two eye patches, whose ties criss-
cross on his forehead, making an X—is to sit on one of the chairs,
against a wall on which hang oval frames containing indistinct images
of women from photography's early days: Niépces, Daguerres. On the
man's lap there's a circular mirror. In the first picture of the sequence,
a rectangular mirror containing the reflected image of a woman's
naked body will itself be seen reflected in the circular mirror, its outline proclaiming its femaleness, the body itself filled with light.

  In subsequent pictures in the sequence, the circular mirror containing the reflected rectangle takes up more of the frame, and the
woman's head gradually becomes distinct and takes up more of the
rectangular mirror. At one point it will clearly be Vina's head. Then it
will change and become the head of a woman very like Vina, but not
her. (I have to find this woman somehow.) As the sequence unfolds the

framing mirrors will be "lost," one at a time, and the not-Vina will be slowly pushed back into medium and then long shot. She will be seen to be sitting on a hard, straight-backed chair like the one used by the eye-patched man in the opening picture—it's similar, but it's not the same chair; she will be holding a rectangular mirror, and in it there will be the reflection of a circular mirror which in turn reflects the image of a man's naked body, its outline filled with light. The not-Vina will acquire eye patches. The man will be at first myself, then another person, less of a look-alike than the Vina double; just a not-me. Obviously the sequence is capable of infinite extension, but I plan to end it by bleaching the images into white. We change what we remember, then it changes us, and so on, until we both fade together, our memories and ourselves. Something like that.

To set up the shot, I prop a doll in a chair. Then I put together the zigzag of reflections, doll one into rectangular mirror, rectangular mirror into circular mirror held on the lap of the second seated doll, doll two into my own camera.

I'm alone at the house. When I've set up the shot I pour myself a glass of wine and sit looking at the set-up. I must be tired, because the wine sends me to sleep. Contentedly, I snooze.

I'm woken by the unmistakable noise of the camera's shutter clicking. Twice. I jerk upright, woozy with sleep and wine, and call out, but nobody replies. The set-up hasn't been touched. I check the Leica on its tripod. The first two frames of film have been exposed.

Vina, I whisper, all reason thrown to the wind. *Vina, is it you?*

But when I develop the film, Vina isn't on it. Somebody else is, though. It's the young woman who has appeared before, from time to time, as a ghost-image on various rolls of film. The photo-phantom. But this time she's sitting where the object doll should be—where, in the set-up, the object doll *still is*—and she's holding up a card with writing on it.

In the first frame this reads, *HELP*

In the second frame, the woman looks exhausted, beyond exhausted, as if the effort she has made has drained her completely. She has slumped back in the chair like a toy doll. The card dangles from her hand.

HELP OR

Who are you? I say to the photographs as they hang up to dry. What do you mean? Help how? Help or what?

But the photographs have said what they have to say.

It takes me a day to come up with the idea of the video camera, another day to drive back into the city, pick up the equipment I need and drive all the way back out to the house of perpetual storm. By the time I've got everything fixed up it's the middle of the night, and anyway, I have a notion that nothing will happen while I'm watching. I leave the camera running and go to bed.

In the morning I come into the room early, quivering with excitement, but the videotape counter reads 0000, it doesn't seem to have moved. Disappointment hits me hard. I sit down on the floor, and I'm being so sorry for myself that it's five minutes before it occurs to me that if the tape had been used until it ran out, the auto-rewind mechanism would have taken it all the way back to the beginning. I get up fast and come into a half crouch. This is what it feels like to be in one of those first-contact sci-fi movies. There are aliens on the video. Extraterrestrials who fell to earth. We come in peace, and so on. Surrender Earthlings your planet is surrounded. Don't panic. For some reason I begin to laugh.

The video camera has an internal-playback capability. I put my eye to the eyepiece and hit the Play button. The tape begins to run.

The woman sitting in the chair where the object doll should be is not the young phantom of the day before. This woman is older, in her mid-fifties, worried-looking, with a kind face and graying hair twisted into a bun. She looks and sounds Indian, but I'm sure I have never met her before in my life.

She coughs, an embarrassed little cough, and talks.

You see, one of our ancient philosophers says, consider the humble bat. You know what I'm saying, isn't it? That we should try to experience reality as a bat might. The purpose of the exercise being to explore the idea of otherness, of a radical alienness with which we can have no true contact, let alone rapport. You understand? Is it clear?

Bats live in the same space and time as we but their world is utterly unlike ours. So also: our world is as unlike yours as a bat's. And there are many such, believe me. All these bats, all of us, flapping around one another's heads. I'm not explaining this properly.

Well, we are one another's bats, that's it.

I'm sorry about Maria. The girl is brilliant but, as you see, not well. Also capricious by nature, vain, a meddler, a little bit nympho, okay?, the family has no control. I think perhaps she has been in your, what would it be, *dreams*? In your dreams, yes. Forgive her. She is, let me so express it, flimsy. I am afraid she will not survive what is to come. She does not have the strength of character. Perhaps even I do not. None of us knows how she will answer the question until it is asked. I'm talking about the great question, okay? Life or death.

You're not following me. Of course not. I'm so stupid.

(Pause.)

I don't know how to tell you so that you would get it. Suppose one day you turn a corner and there's a video store you never knew existed, and inside it there are whole walls of videos you never heard of before. Okay? Suppose a few of you find this store, quite a few, but not everybody, because many people when you send them to the street they come back saying it isn't there. The, store. The doorway to the store. It isn't really like this, but I'm doing my best.

You haven't noticed, how could you, but when we visit we don't age, okay? Like if you watch a video, a hundred years can pass in the story, but for you it's a hundred minutes, and you can skip about also. Fast-forward, freeze-frame, reverse, whatever you like. Your time is not like that of the people on the tape.

But this is wrong, because what we found, these few of us—or, not so few but not so many—is that if we, oh goodness, if we passed through the door we could be inside the video, do you see? Plainly my metaphor is not holding up, because I said the door was the door of the store, and the video was in the store, but really there is neither store nor video, just these doors, yes, these apertures, you are a photographer so you understand that word, the aperture opens and light flies in, light like a miracle, staining another reality, leaving its image behind.

I cannot explain it better. We are light from elsewhere.

I think some of the rest you have guessed. The accidentally entangled time lines, like the strings of kites. The worlds heading for collision, already it has begun, the earthquakes, you have perceived their meaning, I think. Your friend Ormus feared the worst long ago, it damaged him, I am sorry. He envisioned the end of your line. But the truth is, your line is stronger than we believed, and the damage to our line is terrible, completely terrible. Whole areas are simply devastated, torn and shredded, just no longer there. Where they were is now a non-being that drives people mad. Incomprehensible nothingness. Just think.

Can you conceive of such damage to the real? What was true yesterday—an anthrax attack by terrorists in the New York subway—is no longer true today: it seems there was no anthrax attack. Yesterday's *safe* is today's *dangerous*. There is nothing to hold on to. Nothing is any longer, with any certainty, *so*.

Do you understand? Your line is strong, like *kala manja* kite-gut. It seems you may cut us off and not we you. You will continue and we will come to an ending, to the edge, to grief. We will be your fading, what's the word, dream.

Already the damage is too great; we can't escape. The door, you see, the aperture, it is jammed. We can see through the glass, for a little while yet we can shout messages, like this, but we can no longer slip through and be there by your side. How mad we were to think that our time of free exploration, of blissful travel between universes, would not end! Perhaps we could have come to you as refugees, some of us say that now, but others say that when the line ends so do all the moments in it. All must be lost. We are lost.

This is all that will remain of us: our light in your eye. Our shadows in your images. Our floating forms, falling through nothingness, after the ground vanishes, the solid ground beneath our feet.

(The video-image begins to deteriorate. Sound and picture quality both become fuzzier. The image jumps and distorts, the audio crackles and beeps. The woman raises her voice.)

Long ago—on a plane—I spoke to your friend—I'm talking about Mr. Cama!—Ormus!—When she, Maria, approached him I at first thought maybe he was also one of us.—You can hear me? I thought he came from our side!—But he didn't—*he did not*—it was just her craziness—I'm saying she lives in a world of make-believe—fantasy! pretence!—poor girl.

Snap. Crackle. Pop.

Oh Lord!—Oh dear Lord!—It's tearing, it's shredding!—So thin, so flimsy!—It isn't strong enough.—Soon we will all be simply your make-believe world.

(It is becoming difficult to see the woman through the video "snow-storm," or to hear her through the mounting background noise. She is shouting; fading in and out and shouting as loud as she can. Her voice cuts out, returns, cuts out again, reminding me of poor cell-phone reception.)

Listen!—she fell for him!,—she truly did—she's not a bad girl, okay?—we are not bad people—our world is as beautiful as yours—but his love—Ormus's!—*for that woman, I'm saying!*—this was hard for Maria to handle.—Can you hear me?—This is what Maria wanted to say to you.—This is her last request.—My last also.—Care for him.—We are ending.—Can you hear me?—Do not let him die.

. . . HELP ORMUS . . .

Here the transmission cuts out for the last time. The snowstorm obliterates the image. I imagine that I am watching the end of a world. In the dancing video blobs I seem to see towers crash and oceans rise to swallow the alien land. In the hiss and roar of the white noise it is easy to hear the dying screams of an entire species, the death rattle of another Earth.

There is a change on the tape. The video snowstorm vanishes. In its place is the image of a doll in a chair, holding a circular mirror, in which is reflected a rectangular mirror, which in turn contains the reflection of another doll.

I stay there most of the day, alone with my dolls and their video images, thinking about Maria and her teacher and their story and everything that has melted into air. What comes to mind, absurdly, or not so absurdly, is a scene from a movie: Superman in his private polar ice palace, fitting crystals together and conjuring up his long-dead parents, a serene doomed couple offering wisdom from a vanished world beyond the arch of time. Flighty, deranged Maria with her scribbled messages, and my other lady visitor, nameless, composed, facing oblivion with high dignity: I barely knew them—they were aliens, after all, visitors from a familiar-sounding elsewhere, slipping into our awareness by an unimaginable route—and yet I'm profoundly stirred by their loss. I'm trying to work out why that is. In the end I decide it's because although I, we, didn't really know them, they knew us, and whenever someone who knows you disappears, you lose one version of yourself. Yourself as you were seen, as you were judged to be. Lover or enemy, mother or friend, those who know us construct us, and their several knowings slant the different facets of our characters like diamond-cutter's tools. Each such loss is a step leading to the grave, where all versions blend and end.

Which notion turns my thoughts back to Vina, to whom all my mental pathways still lead. Her knowledge of me was so deep, her version so compelling, that it held together my miscellany of identities. To be sane, we choose between the diverse warring descriptions of our selves; I chose hers. I took the name she gave me, and the criticism, and the love, and I called that discourse *me*.

Since Vina's death and the loss of her incisive vision, her Rai, I have at many points felt myself separating more and more into moments, disparate, contradictory: ceasing, as I now see, to cohere. The "miracle of the videotape" has shown me what I should long ago have spotted for myself: that there are two of us mourning the loss of her redeeming judgements; and that it's time we bridged the rift that has snaked between us over the years, widening by slow degrees. Now that she's gone, we perhaps hold each other's salvation in our hands.

Help Ormus. Yes. And maybe he'll help me.

I'm loading up the Jeep to head back to the city and thinking about the old Bombay days with Ormus, in his dressing room or up on the Apollo Bunder roof. As a matter of fact I'm cheerful enough, feeling the return of old affection, of happier childhood times. But here's Molly Schnabel in white shirt and khakis, Mack's embattled ex and world-class all-around poor mouth, strolling hands-in-pockets up the garden path, grinning her lippy, sidelong grin.

Well if it isn't the inconsolable Indian boyo, moping over the passing of another man's wife. You great girl, Rai, will you look at you. Like Niobe, all tears.

I keep things neutral. Hey, Molly, *quelle surprise.*

She switches accents from Irish lilt to Hug-me.

O, baba, what to tell? Wehicle broke down just close by. I am thinking, can I use the phone and give mechanic a tinkle? Sorry to inconwenience.

She has spent time in India—she's a multinational conglomerate babe, her father was big in Union Carbide until the airborne toxic event, the cloud of methyl isocyanate that ate the eyes and lungs of Bhopal; old man Molony was one of the executives who took the fall for that PR disaster—and she prides herself on her mimicry of Indian idiolect. Once at some Colchis bash she drove Yul Singh to distraction with this type of goodness-gracious, until finally he snapped, For God's sake, Molly, this is America. Talk American.

If she shows up don't let her in the house under any circumstances, Mack had warned. *I don't care if she's shot and bleeding. Barricade yourself in and hunker down for a siege if necessary. I mean it. One time when Chow was out there she showed up with a U-Haul panel van and tried to clear the place out.* Now here she comes with her head cocked on one side so that her golden Veronica Lake-y hair falls in waves over one enormous eye, with her trumped-up pretext and her ingratiating Hug-me dialogue. Listen, Molly, I say, you know I can't let you do that. If you want to make a call, sure, here's my mobile.

Mobile shobile, this instrument I also have, she says, instantly dropping the cover story with a shrug, her voice rising a couple of notches. You think so you can keep me out of my own residence? What, because it is the desire of that putter of his penis into the fist of his own son?

Stop it, I tell her. Molly, just stop right now.

What, because you have received instruction from that inserter of narcotic toxins into the noses of his own kiddiwinks? That indulger within and without the marital bed in sexual perwersions both bestial and coprophile? That whited sepulchre, in whom only I have seen the worms of corruption writhe?

As well as the version that holds you together, there's also one that tears you apart. This is it for my pal Mack, this thirty-three-year-old woman shrieking in counterfeit accents on the lawn of her own past, defaming what once she loved, making accusations which carry in many people's minds an automatic guilty verdict and using the authority of her beauty and of the words "wife" and "mother" to acquire for her falsehoods the support of the law itself. This brilliant adversary who has already stripped Schnabel of his good name but wants everything he's got. It doesn't matter what Mack does for the rest of his life.

This version has been branded on his forehead. It's a letter sewn on to his coat in scarlet thread.

I'll drive you to your car, I say. Or, if it really is bust, let's get the mechanic.

You'd make the perfect dogsbody courtier for some murderous third-world despot, Rai, she says, dropping the Indian voice. Or the Chairman's favorite lickspittle lackey and running dog. Or the little ratso soldier the big dons use to do their dirty work. There's a woman to abuse, to what's the argot injurize, to throw off her own land? Send for wiseguy Rai. Call him on his fucking mobile phone.

Get in, Molly, I tell her. And she does; and at once puts her hand in my lap. O, is that all, the old Adam is it, she says, feeling the movement I am unable to control. Is that where you're keepin' the keys now, why didn't you say so, poor darlin', just wait till I see you right, Molly's got the combination for your lock.

I move her hand away and start the engine.

Raincheck, okay?, I say too hotly, and drive.

When I reach the Orpheum, Clea Singh is waiting in the lobby, beneath the Latin tag about love, holding an envelope addressed to me in Ormus Cama's own—pretty unsteady—hand. Again he needs you, sir, Clea says. You must come.

The note inside the envelope is just five words long.

I've found her. She's alive.

17

MIRA ON THE WALL

Doorman Shetty isn't on lobby duty when we reach the Rhodopé Building. Tiny, purse-lipped Clea tells me he has finally been put out to pasture. Agelessly antique herself, she points out with some scorn and no irony that he, Shetty, was long past his superannuation date. *They only kept him on as a favor to Madam,* she says, *but now it is better he rests.* He's out in Mineola, N.Y., there's an excellent retirement home in that neighborhood, convenient for the crematorium, and he has what Clea describes as a *generous allowance, we were under no obligation but he was her Daddy after all.* There was never much love lost between Shetty and the Singhs, and once he lost Vina's protection his fate was sealed. After a suitable grace period had been allowed to elapse Clea made her endgame move. He had nothing to fight her with. Checkmate in one.

I offer up a silent valediction. Old man, you wanted to die with your boots on, but in old age our power to write our own scenarios wanes, and the shape of our last acts is decided by the rewrite merchants. Goodbye, Doorman. Enjoy the sunsets if you can.

In the matter of Doorman Shetty, Clea has acted with her habitual toughness and clarity, which makes it all the more remarkable that on our journey uptown in the limo this customarily unflappable lady has been profoundly agitated. I realize that few people outside the closed circle of the Singhs have been where I'm about to go: into the heart of the silence and shadow that now completely envelops Ormus Cama. Ormus has been invisible ever since I was last brought into his presence, in the Guadalajara Hyatt. I have Shetty's account of his activities—the visits to Goddess-Ma, etc.—but it's possible that no outsider has visited him in his heavily defended lair in all this time. Certainly Clea's acute concern is an indication of the exceptional nature of the event. No cameras, she insists before we leave. I hadn't planned on bringing any, but I am interested by the prohibition. How bad is Ormus looking these days? What is it that he, or his aides, don't want the world to see?

People in my line of work always think like this, I rebuke myself. There is no law which says that a man must agree to be photographed just because he wants to talk to a photographer. Give the guy a break.

Clea chatters without stopping all the way from the Orpheum to the Rhodopé. Mr. Rai, people have black tongues as you know, and maybe you have heard it said that we have not taken care of Sir. Probably you have read malicious comments on his physical and mental health, also cruel allegations regarding our husbandry of his assets. Mr. Rai, I beg you only to keep an open mind. If you desire I can open for you all the books, all the accounts, you will see that every cent is accounted for and all enterprises are in tip-top shape. If you require it I will present to you his personal physician who will confirm our absolute adherence to his orders. If it is your wish all things can be made plain.

He's dying, I suddenly realize. These are his last moments and Clea and her people are scared stiff.

I don't know why you're telling me all this, I say.

You see, Mr. Rai, Sir is such a lonely man. Twenty-four hours a day, seven days a week, he thinks only of dear Madam. To him, that you were Madam's good old friend makes you like his brother. It saddens him that you have been for so long absent from his side.

I decide not to challenge this remarkable statement. *Help Ormus.*

That is my new resolve, and there's no time for pettiness, old griev-
ances or ill will.

Clea in the limo has more to confess. Mr. Rai, Sir is in dire straits.
He is too much reliant on wrong things to help him bear his loss. I fear
for him, Mr. Rai.

Wrong things, I repeat. She looks harassed, and actually wrings her
hands. Then in a low voice she speaks the names of the illegal drugs.
The chauffeur today is Will Singh. He faces front and drives, stone-
faced, obscure.

How much stuff is he getting through, I demand, and when she
replies I know that disaster can't be far off. I ask, How did these substances come into his hands?

Clea looks defiant. I am able to acquire whatever Sir requires, she
says simply. It is my duty, as it was for Mr. Yul and Madame in the days
before.

I picture tiny Clea in her sari bargaining in the back rooms of
Dopeland with the likes of Harry the Horse and Candymaster C,
earning their respect by her calmness, her attention to detail, her insistence on the highest standards. You see, Clea, I say, keeping my voice
friendly, many people would not understand that when you fed
Ormus's habit and allowed it to grow so big, you were acting as a true
friend should. Many people would question your motives.

Clea Singh in the limo draws herself up proudly; straight-backed,
almost shocked. But Mr. Rai, I am not his friend, how can you think
it. I am his servant. Ever since Madam and Sir rescued us, we are all his
sworn subjects. I do not question or dispute his needs, Mr. Rai, I con-
cur. I accede.

And this physician, I say. Does he have qualms about what has been
going on?

He is familiar with the music business, Clea Singh replies, and the
old iron is back in her voice. Mr. Rai, you are a man of the world, I
am sure. Then what is the need for such innocent quizzery? The world
is what it is.

Even after these forewarnings, Ormus, waiting for me at the elevator
door, is a shock. He's upright, but only just. I have the feeling that even

this unconvincing display of well-being has been put on purely for my benefit. If I weren't here he'd be leaning on one of the Singhs. Strong young men dressed in white kung fu outfits wait anxiously in the corners of my eyes, looking concerned.

He was skinny in Guadalajara; now he's positively emaciated. I could probably hoist him shoulder-high with one hand. His hair has almost completely gone, and although what's left is shaved to the skull, the stubble I can see is all white. His nose looks dangerously narrow, and though he has a fine pashmina shawl pulled around his shoulders, he's shivering on a warm evening. He's walking with a stick, fifty-four going on ninety. It may be too late to help him.

There's no eye patch. I realize that he, too, knows about the end of the otherworld. About which he was both right—because there actually were two worlds on a collision course, I know that now—and wrong, because the otherworld was in no way intrinsically superior to our own. In the end, it was that version which failed. Ours succeeded—or let's just say survived.

This was the nature of Ormus's madness: that in his thinking he privileged another version of the world over his own. Maybe now, if he can only stay alive, he has a chance to regain his mental balance, to re-enter the actually existing world. Ours.

Thanks for coming, he whispers. There's just a thing you have to see: to, ah, confirm. At which he turns and totters away through his empty white universe.

The size of the apartment is astounding, dwarfing even his Mexican Hyatt billet: the endless albino spaces, the open doorways, the emptinesses, the *room*. In the distant corner of one enormous vacant zone I spy a white futon mattress and a white reading lamp on a low white table, in another gigantic area there's only a white concert grand piano and stool. Not a speck of dust or used glass or item of dirty laundry in sight. I can't imagine how many Singhs it takes to pick up after Ormus, to create this pristine unworldliness.

He's whispering as he walks. I have to stay close to hear what he has to say.

Curtis Mayfield's paralyzed, Rai. A lighting rig fell on him. And *then* his house burned down. Yeah. Steve Marriott burned to death, you hear that. Different fire. Right. And Doc Pomus died. David Ruffin

OD'd. I guess too much Temptation, huh. Will Sinott of the Shamen? Drowned. Leo Fender, Uncle Meat, Johnny Thunders, Professor Longhair, Stan Getz, RIP, baby. That little kid falling from the penthouse window too. Just terrible. And the word is Mercury doesn't have long, and Brian Jones was murdered, *Brian Jones,* they've got evidence. What's going on, Rai, I don't know what's going on. They're wiping us out.

This, I realize, is his strange, isolated, free-associative small talk. I do not judge him. I haven't forgotten my own list of the dead, which I'd reeled off at Johnny Chow not so very long ago. Different names, same obsession. These are Vina's new companions, the first social circle of her heaven or hell.

I follow Ormus through the white hectares until we turn a corner, a softly padded white door opens and shuts, and unexpectedly I'm in what looks like a minimalist version of Mission Control, Houston: floor-to-ceiling tv monitors on all four walls of a studio covering over a thousand square feet and, at the center, a space-odyssey command complex: computer banks, audio and video mixing-and-magic desks, Yamaha, Korg, Hammond, MIDI-B and Kurzweil keyboard equipment, and two white swivel chairs.

On every screen—there must be more than three hundred—a different phoney Vina pouts and twirls. The sound's muted; three hundred dumb not-Vinas dizzily mouth and prance. If I want a model to play the almost-Vina in my unfinished photo sequence—and I guess I do—I've come to the right place.

Even after all these years, the money generated by rock music still amazes me. The resources required to own all this space and to build, at its heart, this cutting-edge audio-video facility featuring beyond-beyond PixelPixie morphotech capability and massed floating-point musicomputers that could, if reprogrammed, efficiently run a medium-range-missile guidance system; then to hire a small army of video crews to track down and tape hundreds upon hundreds of Vina surrogates: unimaginable. Unimaginable, too, is the luxury of being able to ask for anything you want, and knowing people will make it so, and you won't even notice the cost.

To be given the world as a toy.

When my head stops spinning my heart starts to hurt, not only for myself but for Ormus too. Obsession is the enactment of hidden pain. I realize that I haven't taken his note seriously until now. I interpreted it, too glibly, as the cry for help of a drowning man; it never occurred to me to make a literal reading. Now, as my eyes swim with fake Vinas, I realize he actually believes that one of these pathetic counterfeits is the real thing, poor crushed Vina whom we loved risen from her abyss-grave and singing her old hits to cowboys, militiamen, possible Unabombers and drunks in Grand Island, Nebraska, or some such humming center of the musical world.

Then Ormus sits down at a control desk, says *Look at this,* throws a bunch of switches, and there she is, three hundred times over and more, blazing from all the monitor screens. He pushes a set of audio slide controls, and her wonderful—her inimitable—voice wells up and drowns me.

Vina. It's Vina, returned from the dead.

It's not up to you, she sings. And again and again, as the old song accelerates towards its conclusion, *no, it's not up to it's not up to it's not up to you.* Her voice is doing extraordinary things—new and familiar—with the song's melodic line, stretching and bending the sound, bringing a jazzy feel to it, the way Vina used to do when she felt in the Holiday mood. She even throws in a climaxing moment of Ella-ish scat.

> *Be-bop! Re-bop! Rreee!*
> *Skeedley-ooh!*
> *Oh, mam'! Rama-lam'!*
> *There's nothin' you can do . . .*
> *Wo, pop! De-dop!*
> *Mop! A-lop-a-doo!*
> *Oh it's not, no no not, whoo whoo*
> *Not up to you.*
> *. . . Oh, yeah . . .*

The invisible crowd goes crazy. She smiles: Vina's smile, that can light up the darkest room. Oh Vina, Vina, I think. Where did you spring from, this isn't possible, you're dead. Three hundred Vinas surround me, laugh and bow.

I don't recognize the performance, I stammer. What is it, an old bootleg, some gonzo recording from somewhere.

But I can see for myself that the tape carries a date ident. It was made less than a week ago. And I can see, too, that although this is Vina, it's her to the life, it's also an odd composite Vina, a Vina who never really was. She has the dyed red hair gathered above her head in that springy fountain I remember so well, that Woody Woodpecker crest, and she's wearing the sequin-glittered gold bustier and leather pants from Vina's last performance, but this is not a woman in her middle forties, this is not the mature solo artiste on the comeback trail. This Vina is no more than twenty years old. She is, however, wearing a moonstone ring.

When I turn to Ormus he has tears in his milky eyes.

I thought so, he whispers. I knew it wasn't just my imagination.

What's her name, I ask. I realize I'm whispering too.

He hands me a thin white file.

Mira, he says, coughing. That's what she goes by now.

Mira Celano, from right here in Manhattan, the file tells me. Born at Lenox Hill Hospital in January 1971, so I guessed right about her age. Nineteen seventy-one, the year of Ormus's celibacy oath, *that's* how young she is. She is an only child. Her father Tomaso was sixty-one when she was born. She remembers him (here I'm embellishing the detective agency's filed report with details gleaned from my later knowledge of her) as a short, chesty, thick-maned lion of a man, who became awkward in the presence of the adoring child of his old age, giving her quick rough embraces and handing her off, almost as quickly, to whatever female family member was closest. He was a man of honor, a high-flying corporation lawyer with an Upper East Side address, who nevertheless maintained close links with his community and prized his family roots in Assisi, Italy. He was also a decorated World War II hero with a distinguished service medal for his exploits as the oldest of the American dive-bombing aces who sank the Japanese aircraft carrier *Hiryu* at the Battle of Midway.

He is, additionally, recently deceased, at the age of eighty-one.

Mira's mother was not Italian. Surprisingly for such a conservative man, Celano, who remained single long enough to disappoint more than a generation of young Italian-American women, fell hard at the end of his sixth decade for an Indian woman doctor whom he "met cute," as they say in the movies, when her taxi's Ibo driver deliberately rammed his cab's Hausa wheel jockey on Central Park South. The two cab drivers, passionate supporters of the opposing sides in the bloody, escalating conflict over the attempted secession of Biafra from Nigeria, initially identified one another as enemies by their prominently displayed rear- and side-window flag decals and aggressive bumper stickers. They then wound down their windows and engaged in a stop-go exchange of insults—*Tree swinger! Oil slime! Gowon goon! Ojukwu oaf!*—as their cabs inched forward through the thick rush-hour traffic; until at length the young Ibo, hot for secession, or perhaps just plain overheated on that steamy summer afternoon, swung his wheels and smashed into the taunting Hausa's vehicle in a shower of breaking glass. The drivers were unhurt, but the passengers in the two rear seats were sent flying within their confined spaces, so they took some knocks.

Tomaso Celano, always the gallant gent, insisted on ensuring that the lady in the other cab had not been injured, but then confessed to having double vision himself and sat down on the parkside curb with a bad case, as he put it, of the tweet-tweet-tweets. Fortunately the lady was a qualified doctor. Mehra Umrigar Celano was born in Bombay (still no escaping these Bombay Parsis), came West to attend medical school, stayed on, married Tommy just nine weeks after the Biafran Taxi War, named their daughter Mira because it's a name in India as well as Italy, plus it's easy to say, and in spite of becoming a consultant oncologist at New York Hospital died of a perniciously aggressive breast cancer before her fortieth birthday, when her daughter was still only four years old. Old man Celano, declaring himself too antique to care for the infant, farmed Mira out to a series of relatives whom the little girl quickly discovered to be untypical Italians: that is, resentful of their extended-family obligations towards her, deficient in the provision of love, and unwilling to have her around for very long. In spite of this uncertain, peripatetic home environment, and the difficult discontinuities of an education spread across the high schools of three boroughs, Mira became a straight-A student, a model of diligence, who was accepted by Columbia University's School of Journalism and immediately ran wild, as if all her hard work and good behavior up to that moment had been a prisoner's ruse, a way of hastening the date of her release. She had hidden her wings all her life, and now she intended to fly.

In her freshman year she unfurled a singing voice that made her an instant campus star, ran with a fast crowd and got herself pregnant, all in a single semester. She decided to keep the baby, dropped out of college, and was instantly disowned by her father, after which he thoughtlessly dropped dead playing tennis in Cape Porpoise, Maine, thus making a reconciliation impossible. He'd been crouching to receive serve when he was murdered—aced—by a huge heart seizure, and fell face first on to the hard cement court, still holding his racquet, but unfortunately defaulting the game. He died before his arms had time to come up and defend his face, which consequently suffered a broken nose that sorely impaired his gravitas, making him seem, in death, far coarser than he'd ever looked in life. With that eminent nose squashed over to the right he wasn't a big shot any more but a plug-ugly boxer who'd lost the last in a series of losing battles. It was a quick end, but it didn't come fast enough to keep Mira in his will. *Not a red cent to my daughter Mira who has been the disappointment of my old age.*

The money was divided. Some went to charitable Italian community projects in Manhattan, Brooklyn and the Bronx, the rest to the same relatives who had blighted Mira's early life. The lucky heirs made no move to assist their disinherited relation and even snubbed her at her father's funeral, as if to say, forget about it, darling, don't call, don't write, you're out on your own. Mira accepted their challenge. After failing to break into journalism, even of the lowliest sort, she started singing for her supper in dingy piano bars, taking her baby daughter along in a carry cot and hiding her behind the stage-area drapes, or under the piano, or in the women's room, or anywhere, just praying she'd sleep through the set, bribing busboys and waitresses to take care of her if she woke up.

The girl is now a little over one year old. Her name is Tara, meaning—in Hug-me—*star.*

While I'm reading the file, Ormus hobbles off to the bathroom and takes his time there. I should be intervening but I don't know how to, not yet, anyway. Also, I'm reading. Also, I'm not too sure where the bathroom is.

Easy to see where this Mira Celano's interest in Vina comes from, I reflect. In spite of all the differences of community, opportunity and class, she has plenty in common with her idol: the mixed-race family, the early orphaning, the loveless childhood years, the outcast's deep-seated sense of rejection and exile. That thing about feeling out on the perimeter line and being pushed, by a powerful centripetal force, towards the heart of the game. And she's penniless now, just as Vina was when she started out.

And there's her voice, of course, the voice she kept under wraps for so long. Maybe, like Vina, she had secret places where she went to sing. Her own Jefferson Lick somewhere in the park.

I can readily imagine that when she started singing, during her solitary semester at Columbia, she was at once surrounded by admirers calling her the new Vina Apsara, or even better than that, and telling her to cut a demo, to forget journalism and reach for the stars. But then suddenly she was broke, the fair-weather college friends were gone and demos and producers and stardom seemed very far away. The repro-Vina business, however, was thriving. So, as she afterwards tells me: *If I couldn't be the new Vina, then I'd be the old one. That was the way I looked at it. I taped the picture you took—you know, Vina in the quake—on the wall of my room and decided, Okay, for now I'm her.*

Ormus is back from the john, looking both better and worse. I have other tapes, he says, and starts pushing buttons.

Here on three hundred screens is Mira Celano with her sleeping baby, watched by a spy camera high in a corner. She's in a tiny, unhappy dressing room, wearing a thin kimono-style dressing gown and preparing to take off her stage make-up. When she pulls off the red wig and the hairnet below it, I let out a small cry. Waist-length dark hair tumbles down her back. She shakes it loose, picks up a comb, bends forward so that the hair hangs over her face and all the way to the floor, and combs out her tangles. Then, at her mirror, she starts on her face. Once again, I'm amazed. Much of the dark skin color is coming off on the tissues. This girl has actually been blacking up to play dark Vina, crossing, in her own way, the heavily mined color line. Her own complexion—although the tape quality makes it hard to be certain—looks to be a light olive.

She's finished. Now in the mirror is a beautiful if kind of slutty young girl, more Latin- than Indian-looking, a young single mother fighting for survival in the badness of the city, and really pretty unlike her meal ticket, barren Vina, Mrs. Ormus Cama, my dead love. To realize this is like waking from a dream.

You shouldn't have done this, I tell Ormus, trying to work out the number of people downtown who have had to be paid off to allow us our uptown voyeurism. This is wrong, I say.

Look, he whispers, ignoring my qualms. On the monitors, Mira Celano is taking off her kimono. Underneath it is Vina's naked body. Vina with lighter skin, but Vina nevertheless, in every last detail, the weight and angle of the breasts, the jaunty sling of the hips, the full, the incomparable Vina ass, the thick unshaven bush. I am standing behind Ormus and push my fist into my mouth and bite down hard. If I were to gasp, it would reveal my secret, and now, more than ever, I want to keep that secret to myself.

Now that she's back, I hear myself madly thinking. Now that she has returned from the grave.

Ormus hits more buttons. Here is Mira Celano walking home alone with little Tara in a stroller. With another leap of the heart I recognize the Bowery, Cooper Union, St. Mark's. This girl is practically my neighbor. She waves at the mooching dope peddlers, works the stroller up half a dozen steps, unlocks a door. She's calling out something as she goes inside, but the sound quality is poor, I can't hear what she's saying.

Okay, wait a minute, Ormus murmurs, and I realize I've spoken aloud. In the next thirty seconds he performs a miracle of audio engineering, isolating her voice, cleaning out the background, compensating for the distorting effects of magnifying her faint words. Okay, here we go, he whispers. This is so good.

Yo, homes, I'm in the house! Yo yo yo homie-o!

If there's a man in there, I think, if she's calling out to a lover rather than a couple of girlfriends, it's possible I may have to kill him.

You understand what she's telling us, Ormus says, freezing the frame, trapping Mira Celano on her doorstep in mid-yo. She's saying she's come back. She's saying hi, honey, I'm home.

This is insane, I say, snapping out of it once more. Ormus, you have to stop this. It's like you're stalking her. You *are* stalking her.

Mary Virgin has a stalker who actually says that, he murmurs absently. Can you believe? The guy comes up to her house every night and calls into the entry system, making like he's her little hubby back from the old nine to five. *Hi, honey, I'm home.*

Yeah, I say, wiping cold sweat from my brow, I can believe it, and this time that nut is you.

More obstinate button pushing. Here on a long telephoto lens is Mira Celano in her room, it's a third-floor walk-up at the front, she has the lights on but is leaving the shade up. She's prowling around in a cream slip worn over a nursing brassière, making phone calls, putting things in her mouth that aren't chocolates or nachos, washing them down with gulps from a bottle that isn't Evian or Pellegrino, flopping down on her bed—she's got a brass bedstead!—zapping on the tv, watching basketball or maybe just stargazing, moondancing, planet-waving, while Tara, the little star in her arms, suckles contentedly. If Mira weren't still milk-heavy, I muse, her bosom would be less ample than Vina's. She'd have to pad out her bustier to get the right effect. On the other hand, Vina also liked to watch sports, especially hoop, so they have that in common. Vina knew her Magic from her Kareem and Bird and when the new kid arrived on the block she said to me, half seriously, Let's all move to Chicago so we can go watch Mike.

I think: There's no man in that room. This inordinately pleases me.

And I think: I'm thinking about this young woman as if she were my lover.

Abruptly, Ormus shuts the system down. Mira Celano vanishes and I miss her, so help me, I do. This total stranger into whose intimacy I have pried. This nobody with—if only temporarily—the only body that I truly loved. I'm pathetic, I tell myself, and Ormus is beyond that. Ormus Cama is a graybeard loon.

Ormus, you need help, I make myself say it. Now that you've asked me over here I have to tell you. If you don't get help you'll be dead inside a year, tops.

He's still staring at the darkened monitors. If it is her, he whispers, then anything's possible. If it's her then there's hope.

It's not her, I say. The likeness is incredible, but it's someone else. It's a Mira Celano, whoever that is. A person you don't know, whose privacy you have criminally invaded. A person less than half Vina's age, and able to have a child. And you saw the make-up tape. Come *on*.

He softly says, If she chose to come back this way, low key, sub rosa, incognito, step by step, I can understand that, tell her. Tell her, I'm waiting.

My own unexpected arousal makes me snappish. You require that I go into this woman's life and say what?, I demand. What, that a dying addict in rock-star heaven has been watching her every move, that he wants her to play his dead wife not only on stage for money but in his bed for the rest of her life?, or I should say *his* life?, it's sick, Ormus, don't look to me for this.

You have to go, he whispers, openly pleading now. It has to be you. I can't go. Look at me. I can't.

Skeedley-ooh, I'm remembering. *Mop! A-lop-a-doo!*

Even if I did go, I say, and we both know I'm surrendering, we both know that Mira Celano—that's *Selayno,* by the way, Americanized from the Italian *Chelahno*—is someone I too now need to meet, even just supposing I did go over there and take this crazy meeting, what the fuck is it for? Tell me why I'd be doing it, what you want me to offer her. Tell me the deal.

Just, come home, he whispers, so softly now that I have to lean right in to his cracked, dying-junkie lips. Just, Vina, my darling, come home.

The new places are Izvestia, a couple of blocks up from the Orpheum on the Bowery, which plays mostly trance music, ambient techno for the new acidheads (LSD is back), the grungy Soundgarten in the meat-packing district, and the post-CBGB's Voodoo Dollhouse at East Tenth Street and Avenue A, where bubbling-under indie bands play to an audience of sharp industry bloodhounds in search of the next big thing. None of these venues would ordinarily book a tribute act like Mira's Vina, but the spirals of postmodern irony twist tight and fast, and for five minutes that year they twist to Mira's advantage. Somebody at the Dolls decides that a "necro-themed" night—the crowd as well as the performers to arrive as their favorite dead icon—would be a fabulous one-off kitsch-camp event and perhaps even a celebration of the life of the music in what industry people are calling the year of death. So it's at the Voodoo Dollhouse, transformed for the occasion into a kind of neon graveyard, a necropolis with rhythm, and on the night of the biggest break of her musical life, that I first see Mira in person.

Waiting for her to come on, I sit through a series of—to me, at least—entirely forgettable acts, an electronica re-think of the Beach Boys doing the Monster Mash, a group of synchronized but soulless Temptations clones, a competent Mama Cass Elliot wearing a tent and drinking tea, even a no-holds-barred, utterly irony-deficient Liberace. Then Mira's up, and the moment she opens her mouth the mood of the night changes. This is no longer merely a fancy-dress ball. People are listening. She's *good*.

I haven't dressed up, but a word from Ormus's people—from Clea— has ensured my admission. I opt to listen from the bar, and as I drink my third margarita—the tequila is my own private tribute to Vina's memory—I wonder at the ease with which I've fallen back into an old routine. Once again, I'm Ormus's obedient "kid brother." Once again I'm playing Joe Cotten to his Citizen Welles, doing his dirty work. *Help Ormus.* I've come to plead his cause with this unknown woman, because I think it could save his life.

Up there on the Dollhouse stage, Mira Celano's Vina is sticking knives in my heart. I'm using the margaritas to ease the pain.

Success breeds excess. After the show it takes a while to get to Mira. There's a crowd of well-wishers and A&R men and would-be seducers in the way. I lean back in a narrow corridor outside the women's dressing-room door, waiting for the fan club and the other performers to leave: the Lady Day, the Bessie, the Judy, the Janis, the Patsy Cline, the Tammi Terrell, the Mamas Cass and Thornton, the upsettingly skinny Karen Carpenter, the pseudo-Icon whose "I'll be your mirror" was the only performance to come anywhere close to Mira's. By the time it's my turn Mira Celano is keen to leave. The wig and color are off, she's tired and wired—she seems fuzzy, fazed—and little Tara is beyond exhausted and cranky. So, what's your label, Abel, Mira drones, too wrecked to be polite. I'm not in the business, I answer, but you were wonderful, wonderful. (The margaritas have made me emotional.) Don't tell me, she shrugs, you were a huge Vina fan, she was the biggest thing in your life, left one hell of a heart-shaped hole, until I touched your soul. She turns her back on me and lights a cigarette with practiced, wasted cynicism, ignoring the squalling little girl, who has started throwing things on the floor, including a full glass ashtray. It smashes, there's glass and dead-cigarette detritus everywhere. Mira Celano doesn't jump. Feeling better now? Then relax, she says, and I'm interested to note that the little girl buys it, she slumps down on a cushion in a corner, sighs resignedly, calms down. Her mother rounds on me. What?, she demands, you have maybe an opinion? No opinion, I say. She nods, not really caring, then frowns. This is for an autograph, right? No, I say, it's not an autograph. It's important. I need you to come down off whatever you're on and pay attention.

I'm being intense, I've scared her a little. She puts herself between me and her daughter and says, Two minutes, then you're out. I point over her shoulder, to where Vina tottering in Tequila is taped to the wall. I'm Rai, I say, a photographer. She's a dropout journalist wannabe and a Vina student too, so she knows my name. Her eyes widen and suddenly the hardass crust cracks, she's a young girl again, just starting out and still able to be impressed.

You're *Rai*? *You're* Rai? My God, that's right. You really are Rai.

What you're acting out tonight, I tell her unnecessarily, it was my life, the love of, I loved her, I held her in my arms, she was going to, she would've, we would've, never mind, she got into a helicopter and I never, nobody ever. I just looked around and she was gone.

Gohohone. At this point, to my great discomfiture, I begin to cry. Again with the tears! What can she think of me, this man twice her age who took That Picture and who's now bawling like a baby in front of her with his hands over his face. I try to control myself. The girl and her mother are staring at me, genuinely astonished. I want to see you, I blurt out, I really need to see you again, and even I can hear how ridiculous I sound, how naked and premature. A few seconds later we're all laughing, the ice is broken, and the little girl is laughing loudest of all.

Okay, I was trying to work out if you're a serial killer or just a rapist, but I've decided you're cool, Mira Celano says, wiping her eyes. Now can we go, walk me home?, the kid needs to sleep.

An old guy followed me one day, she tells me as we walk (I'm pushing the sleeping Tara in her orange stroller), he said he was Ormus Cama, if you please. It's incredible that even someone like me gets followed around. What a town, right.

Right, I say. I'm thinking: wrong, wrong, this whole thing is off the rails, I'm supposed to be helping the big O, speaking for him. But I'm feeling the rebirth of urges which I thought had died with Vina: attraction, desire. The interesting thing is that it's not about the likeness, the impersonation, any more. It's Mira Celano herself, Mira *qua* Mira, that's responsible for these stirrings. Her long hair, as soft as Vina's was wiry, the spring in her step, the happiness bursting from her smile and giving the lie to the tough-cookie act. This is a girl permanently high on hope, with plenty of that rare commodity to spare.

I begin to feel my age, inhibiting me. If I say what I'm thinking she'll probably just laugh. Yeah right granddad in your dreams.

She's talking about herself, I haven't been paying attention, she talks fast and sometimes you get left behind, but when I do catch up with her I realize I'm being given an account of the false self she has chosen to inhabit since her disinheritance: That gig tonight, she's saying, half the performers were like upper-middle-class private-school types, you know?, slumming, I mean I don't understand those people, coming from the planet White Trash and all?, I've got tattoos, I'm subculture. Some kind of post-teen bag lady, that's me.

It's time to let her know I'm not fooled by this. Mira, I say, that's bullshit. I know where you're from. Then I tell her the short version of what I read in Ormus Cama's file. And all the time I'm thinking, under all that armor this is one very fragile person. Don't fuck around with her, Rai. Don't try for her heart unless you're serious. She has already been hurt too much.

We're turning in to her street. She stops in her tracks and snatches the handles of the stroller away from me and puts it behind her and starts screaming. What is this, what do you want from me, you fucking peeper, you fucking spy, she yells, reaching into her shoulder bag. Okay, okay, you should be aware that I am able to handle guns.

She shouts the warning with a harsh little hiss on the end: to handle *gunss.*

People are looking. I stand my ground.

Mira, I was sent to talk to you, I say. By Ormus Cama, the real one. He likes your act, had you checked out, what can I tell you, he wants to meet you, that's all of it, that's it.

She's calming down but she's still angry. I can understand that. It is an angering thing to be fingered as the self you're struggling to shuck off. To learn at twenty that the past goes on clinging to you, it bursts out of the grave when you least expect it and grabs your ankle in a stenchy decaying claw. She's still backed away from me, adopting a high-tension stance, legs apart, her right hand in her bag, bending slightly forward at the waist, the left arm stretched straight out at me, palm up, fingers splayed. *Keep away, fucking maniac,* says her body. And she's definitely trying to convince me she's got a pistol in there.

I put my arms up like a surrendering cowpoke. Don't shoot the messenger, I say unoriginally, with a grin.

Ormus Cama? she demands, still yelling. What's his problem? I mean is this what he's doing these days, he gets turned on by the impersonation industry? He sends out for look-alikes now? A pizza, some red Vina, maybe some jalapeños on the side, so what does that make you, mister, Domino's delivery? Or his pimp.

This is New York, late at night. Nobody makes a move towards us; Mira Celano's performance has emptied the street. There's just us now, and the sleeping infant, and the audience behind the darkened windows.

Close, but no cigar, I say quietly. Mira, calm down. This isn't a sex thing. It's more that he's dying, ever since Vina passed away he's been killing himself with junk, and it's my view that he urgently requires a reason to live.

So you're asking what? she says, quietening, her body relaxing, her mood swinging rapidly away from rage. I don't really get it. You want me to do what?

He thinks you're her, I say. He truly thinks she's come back. Or, you could say, untruly thinks it. It's like he half thinks it, wholly believes it while he's half thinking it, and at other times, not. The point is he needs to deceive himself and he needs the rest of us to go along with the deception, and if we do—if you do—that just may motivate him to clean himself up, to survive. Do this for him. Go see him, in costume. Give him hope.

Sounds like a sex thing to me, she says, back in charge of herself now, intrigued. This is a woman whose internal weather is unusually quick to change.

Right now he's too weak to even jerk off, I say. You know, we haven't really been close in a long time, Ormus and me. This is a mercy mission. A favor I promised to a late mutual acquaintance. To turn Ormus's face away from the gates of death.

She moves on, until we reach the steps to her front door.

So this must be some kind of incredible selflessness, she says in a new voice: playful, almost fond. You came to that terrible show, you waited in the corridor, and then you spent all this time with me just to speak up for another man.

No, I'm no saint, I say, that's not it. I mean, helping Ormus was part of it, but I would never have come if, if.

If what, she asks, beginning to smile, but it's not a laughing-at smile, it's too happy for that, it wants me to say what I'm almost too scared to articulate.

If I hadn't wanted to, I manage lamely.

And what's your desire, your wanted-to, she says, stepping in close. Does it also come necro-themed? You want Vina, but not that old lady of forty-five: you want Vina twenty years old all over again, isn't that it? You want her back from the grave, only younger?

Maybe in the beginning, I say, hanging my head. But now it's you, it's just you.

Do you read Longfellow? she asks suddenly, completely dropping the ignorant-white-trash pretense, staying very close, so that her breath fills my nostrils. No, I guess not. But there's a poem he has about this tongue-tied soldier, Miles Standish, who begs his pal John Alden to go on his behalf to ask for Miss Priscilla's hand, not knowing that John Alden loves her too. And good John Alden, for friendship's sake, does as he is bid, but Miss Priscilla won't go for it. You remember now?

. . . And here all of a sudden, conjured up by this miraculous young woman, is the ghost of John Mullens Standish XII at my elbow, urging me on. But I'm in uncharted territory, I don't know how to move forward, where to put my foot. The sidewalk has become unreliable, yielding. I can't move. . . .

Why don't you speak for yourself, John, Mira Celano softly quotes. That was what the lady said.

Yes, I remember, I say. (What I actually remember is Vina in my bed, Vina in the midst of one of her interminable soliloquies, her Ormusiads, telling me about Ormus's very first meeting with Mull Standish on the London plane.)

Then come again tomorrow, Rai, Mira Celano says, kissing me. Come not as a messenger, but to speak for yourself.

By the time I take her to meet Ormus I know some of her secrets and she knows all of mine. She lies in my arms, or I in hers, and I run off at the mouth for long periods (their actual length is determined by Tara's constantly changing sleep patterns). I find myself telling Mira all about Vina, just as Vina would once tell me about Ormus. So we repeat in ourselves the faults of the ones we have loved. I also photograph Mira in a hundred ways, learning her through the cyclops eye, and she gives herself to the camera with an openness and freedom that shocks. In conversation, however, she expresses herself with terseness and caution. It quickly becomes plain that I'm going to have to pay attention, because she says things once and refuses to repeat. If I forget a detail of her biography she hits me with a wide-eyed, betrayed look. *You didn't care enough to listen.*

At the very outset she tells me that she is interested only in that rarest of all emotional contracts between men and women: total engagement, total fidelity, instantly. All or nothing right away, the whole heart or else forget it. That's what she is prepared to offer and if I can't reciprocate, if I'm not in it for the long haul, then so long, it's been good to know you, no hard feelings, goodbye. Her daughter, she says, deserves a little continuity in her life, not a procession of inadequate men through her mother's bedroom; and so, she adds, does she.

In this she reveals herself to be Vina's polar opposite.

The more I learn about her the more I begin to think of her absolutism as heroic. The fearless courage of the innocent—the child who extends her trusting hand towards the fire, the student prankster who places a clown's hat on a tyrant's statue, the youth in his new uniform dreaming shiny dreams of derring-do, or the Beauty at the moment of her first plunge into the pit of love—this has never impressed me. Life's raw recruits go to the edge and over it because of the blinding immensity of what they do not know. But Mira's is the courage of experience, open-eyed, bruised and fearful. Rejected by her father and family, abandoned by the father of her child, bearing the unclosed wounds of her broken loves, she is nevertheless prepared to risk her heart once more. To try for the best in spite of being terrified of the worst. *This* is brave.

Mira has lost a lover too. She, too, has a ghost in her head, though she is trying hard not to act bereaved, pretending not to mourn. Tara's father Luis Heinrich killed himself, shot himself in the head and took three days to die, he even made a mess of that, Mira snarls, the tough-bitch accents back in evidence. Luis was a musician too, a troubled spirit, fronting an East Coast grunge outfit called Wallstreet. New York influenced by Seattle: how times change. The old idea of the periphery and the center, of music as a ticket from the sticks to the bright lights, seemingly no longer applies. Luis had been a Manhattan street-and-subway musician for years, he was a late starter, but it was the beginning of success that did him in, the acclaim at Soundgarten, the first record, all of that. The closer the album's release date came the more often he talked about killing himself. I told you we liked guns, she said, he had five or six, handguns, rifles, he took good care of them. When the death talk started I got somebody to take them all away but then one of his old street compadres brought him another, go figure, okay?, and a couple of days later he did it, plugged himself right in the record company lobby, so I guess he made his point, whatever it was.

Handgunss. Rifless. Compadress.

I half remember the incident. It made the papers in a small way at the time. Then she shows me his picture and I realize I've met him. The street band was the Mall in those days, I can see why they changed it, why they turned the M upside down. I remember Luis red-eyed and shabbily goateed, playing the hybrid guisitar and abusing Doorman Shetty as he was shooed away from the Rhodopé. *One day when we're big, I mean when we're monster big, I'm gonna come back here 'n' fucking buy this fucking building.* What, Mira is asking. No, nothing, I say, it's just that I heard about his death but I didn't know about you and him, that he was Tara's, so she's called Tara Heinrich, right.

No, she snaps, her lips thin and white with anger. Tara Celano, and don't you fucking forget it, I mean fuck that snake Luis, okay?, that coward and his fucking Latino-Teuton name. He's in the stupid club now along with Del Shannon and Gram Parsons and Johnny Ace and the Singing Nun. I'm the parent that stayed.

After he died she fell apart for a while, did every drug invented, had her stomach pumped once, so I know how your Ormus feels, she tells me, I've been there; almost stayed. In the ambulance two paramedics played hard man, soft man, one going *come on honey stay awake you can make it look at you you're a great big beautiful doll so stay awake baby you can make it baby baby we need you to live do it for me baby oh yeah yeah* like a fucking dirty phone call, she says, and the other guy was snarling *fuck you trash bitch cunt you want our fucking attention you fucking got it there's people in this city getting shot and sick for real but we gotta come here and take care of you fucking self-centered bitch slit we should put you out right here in the street and let you fucking die.* He was the one who saved me, the bad guy, she confesses. I kept thinking *man, I'm gonna live to slug that bastard right in the mouth if it's the last thing I do.*

After the stomach pump she discovered she was pregnant and then came the disinheritance et cetera, the triple whammy, but this time instead of cracking up she went to work. You never saw me when I was Pregnant Vina, she says, suddenly unleashing a wild cackle of laughter. Man, *that* was off the wall.

She won't say much about her family. I get the basic information and then the subject's permanently off-limits. I remember Vina's long silence about the bad childhood days in Chickaboom, and I want to tell Mira, honey, you don't know how like Vina you are, but I intuit that this would not go down well. Ever since we've started sleeping together it has become important for her to dissociate herself from her predecessor. She lists all the things Vina liked which she can't stand. *I hate Tolkien, you know?, and the fucking Faraway Tree, they should chop it down, and I* really *hate vegetarians, I'm a meat woman, give me meat.* As I listen to her I have to work to keep the smile off my face because she sounds exactly the way Vina did on the beach at Juhu, in the days when she was hating the hell out of India, before she discovered its good points, which included Ormus Cama and me.

One day Mira starts talking about sacred music. It seems that although her father's people were originally from Assisi they weren't all totally peace-loving St. Francis types. The original Tomaso di Celano (died *circa* 1255) was, Mira says, probably St. Francis's first biographer, but he also composed one of the great blood-and-thunder hymns of apocalypse, the *Dies Irae*. Not very love and peace and animals and birdies, is it, I reflect. Where there is discord may we bring harmony, that was the St. Francis angle, if I recall, but this Tomaso di Celano was apparently more interested in divine wrath than divine love.

She ignores my teasing. I can do the whole thing in Latin, she says proudly, and I actually let her. Such is new love.

> *Rex tremendae maiestatis,*
> *qui salvandos salvas gratis,*
> *salva me, fons pietatis.*

It ends, finally, with this remarkably financial burst of praise for the king of tremendous majesty, who saves those who are fit to be saved, free of charge. Mira's eyes are shining now. There's a new worldwide appetite for a spiritual approach, she preaches, I guess it's all the earthquakes and catastrophes, the sense of an ending, people are looking for meaning, you know what I mean?

Think about it, I say sardonically, there must be higher love. (I'm thinking, I hope she isn't about to rip off her mask and turn into the early Ifredis Wing.)

That's it, she says, missing my meaning entirely—irony is what people miss—and suddenly she's any bright, super-intense twenty-year-old, that's *so it,* she repeats, and have you *heard* this stuff? Sufi music, for example, it could be Azerbaijani or Uzbek or Moroccan, I mean I'm not au courant with the belief system, okay?, but there's this incredible drumming, and amazing layered syncopation, and trumpets, and dancing like you're possessed. But it's not just Sufi, there's so much of this music crossing frontiers now, music from all over, Yoruba drumming, the old songs of the expelled Jews of Spain, Persian-Iraqi maqam concerts using mystical poems, Shinto drumming, gospel, Buddhist chants, and do you know the work of Arvo Pärt, sort of minimalist meets New Age? Have you heard Fatty Ahmed, he's played with the Ruby Goo?

Yeah, him I've heard of, I say, laughing openly now. He just died weighing three hundred and eighty pounds, which is bad news for that finagling retinue of his, they were going for every dollar they could grab while the poor man, unworldly, unaware, sat singing his devotional songs at the Hollywood Bowl like a spider trapped in his own web. That's sacred music all right.

What's funny, she wants to know. People really want this, they want the magic and the security, the idea that there's something beyond, something greater, something more. Meditation, celebration, supplication, that's . . . fuck you, Rai, why is this making you laugh?

No, it's really okay, I say. I'm sorry, it's only nostalgia. I knew someone else who talked like this once.

Oh, shit, she says. My people were doing this stuff in the fucking thirteenth century but I should have guessed she'd still have gotten in first.

Here is seventeen-month-old Tara Celano on my roof terrace, wearing a furry pink bomber jacket and lime-green tights, serenading the watching Chrysler Building and World Trade Center towers with a lyric-free approximation of, I'm guessing, *Da Doo Ron Ron*. Mira, meanwhile, lounges on a rug, smoking, apparently ignoring her daughter completely. Left to her own devices, Tara is growing up as a strange mixture of precocious adult and lucky survivor. On the one hand, she can now wait in the wings during her mother's performances without complaining; she can do the twist, the stomp, the mashed potato too, and the wah-watusi and the hitchhiker and the locomotion, and if you don't know how to do it, she'll show you how to walk the dog; and she knows her way around the backstage areas and women's rooms of dozens of Manhattan clubs and bars, both salubrious and unhealthy. On the other, she picks pebbles off the tops of graveled cactus pots and tries to swallow them. My apartment's electric wall sockets exert upon her a potent magnetic attraction. I have the feeling I'm saving her life a dozen times a day, but she's come this far without me, so Mira must have been keeping an eye on her while pretending to turn her loose. That's what I choose to think, anyhow, while continuing to make sure Tara doesn't succeed in mounting the wall at the edge of the roof terrace and swallow-dive to an untimely death in East Fifth Street below.

The spiritual topic, interestingly, never recurs. Mira, always quick on the uptake, has understood two things about it: one, that I do not respond well to such remarks, and two, that it's a road leading back to Vina, with whose ghost she is beginning to feel, for the first time in her short life, a tad competitive. Thus it remains unclear whether she's genuinely religious or if this is some Catholic leftover mixed up with the remains of teenage mysticism. Or, to give her her due, maybe she sees sacred music simply as something to use, there's no need to become what did she say au courant, it's just a way of getting people to listen, a storehouse to ransack for her own purposes, as Picasso once ransacked Africa's visual motherlode, as the empires of the West once ransacked the world.

This is what a generation gap feels like, I realize. In some respects I simply do not understand the workings of so young and fresh a mind.

About the *gunss,* I have formulated a private theory. I think the weapons are linked to the *tattooss* (a butterfly on her ankle and a small dragon below her left shoulder blade), the whorey clothes, the exhibitionism (in spite of my repeated requests, she won't lower the window shades when she's walking around demi-nude at home)—in brief, to her whole trash act. It's all a class rebellion, a way of defining herself against those who rejected her. The guns are pantomime. When I check inside Mira's bag, I do find a little Giuliani & Koch .09 mm persuader, but it isn't loaded, nor is she carrying ammunition clips. The city is Mira's theater and the gun is just her prop.

On the morning of our appointment with Ormus she's as nervous as a teenager before her first date. Tara, on the other hand, is totally cool, except for a tendency to shout at anyone within range: *Go see old guy!* Johnny Chow has come up for breakfast and she yells the news at him. Big talker, huh, Chow grins, biting into a blueberry muffin. Careful, kid, nothing gets you in trouble like your mouth. Then Mira comes out of the bedroom in her Vina get-up and he chokes. I have to thump him on the back several times and when he recovers, wiping his eyes, he turns to Tara, gasping for air: See what I mean?

To Mira he wonderingly remarks, Rai told me you were good, but I never imagined, I never fucking dreamed. Damn! And you sing like her, too. Hot damn. I've got to tell you this totally weirds me out.

He leaves, shaking his head, still clearing his throat. Gee, you can't beat a good notice for building confidence, Mira exclaims, with an uncertain smile.

In the cab uptown—Ormus offered to send Will Singh with a car, but I thought it better to arrive independently—Mira goes through her Ormus checklist. Life story, discography, influences, touchy points, e.g. the tinnitus that doomed him to perform in a glass casket. That doesn't seem to bother him too much in ordinary life, I tell her. I'm remembering how he cleaned up the sound on his spy tape so that I could hear her voice. Even with his internal crackles and tweets he can still hear well enough to work a mixing desk. Oh, Jesus, I suddenly think, he's not crazy enough to play her the surveillance tapes, is he? If she sees herself on those three hundred screens she'll walk out of both our lives and never return and I can't say I'd blame her either.

So now I'm nervous too.

His heterotopian tendencies, his forays into alternative realities, both attract and alarm her. She has grown up with Ormus's songs and pro-nouncements about the otherworld, but she doesn't like the idea that it wasn't a better place, just a different one, no more than a variation that didn't quite work, and she doesn't at all like the idea that it's gone, that Ormus doesn't need the eye patch any more. I've also briefed her about Gayomart, who after all was Ormus's original heterotopic dis-covery. Gayomart and the songs of the future. Gayomart's escape from Ormus's head in a car smash long ago. Ormus's half-belief that it's Gayo with whom Vina spent her last moments, that maybe it's Gayo she's been with in her time below. It's still difficult for me to come out with this information neutrally, without making judgements, but Mira is fascinated. I love a good twin story, she says. It's all about the differ-ent sides of the brain, I mean we really have no idea of the untapped potential, of our own powers, okay? This guy has really penetrated his dark side. It's amazing. Rai?

I think the two of you will hit it off just fine, I say. (I'm starting to feel, and therefore sound, not only edgy but more than a little sour.)

Are you jealous? she asks, extremely pleased, I thought he was old and fucked up and had terrible buzzy ears. No contest, right? You are jealous, she says, punching me on the arm, grinning from ear to ear. *Now* she's relaxed.

Buzzy ear, says Tara from her corner of the cab. Buzzy ear fucked up.

Clea's waiting in the Rhodopé lobby wearing her thick-lensed glasses, looking more than ever like a tiny old sari-clad Mrs. Mole. When she sees Mira she gasps, Oh, Madam, thank god! Then she shivers slightly, as if making an enormous effort to rein in her feelings, and turns to Tara, greeting her like they're old buddies, low- and high-fiving her, instantly stealing her young-old heart. In the elevator Tara and Clea do the swim (VTO's on the sound system) while I look at myself in the mirror. I'm not in bad shape but next to Mira I look like the essence of square. I even use words like square. Ormus, in his current decrepitude, is, I suspect, still cool. I personally would call him more hip replacement than hip but then I'm not a twenty-year-old girl being granted admission to the inner sanctum of one of the sacred monsters of rock.

He's waiting at the elevator door, looking frail but expectant, dressed in Japanese martial arts whites and leaning on Will Singh. When he lays eyes on her his fingers tighten on Will's forearm, digging in painfully. Will remains impassive; impassivity is this big man's forte.

Yes, says Ormus Cama. Just that one word. He and Mira face each other for a silent eternity: fifteen seconds, ten years, something like that. I note with some satisfaction that the look on her face is one of disguised disbelief. She's acting as if she's seen a ghost, as if Ormus, this wasted entity that used to be Ormus Cama, is the revenant, the one who's come back from the dead. Which is of course supposed to be her rôle in today's little drama.

Please, says Ormus, and leads the way, still leaning on Will, towards the white Yamaha concert grand. After a few paces Mira touches Will Singh on the shoulder. Let me do that, she says, and offers her own young arm to Ormus. He nods, twice, his eyes filled with emotion, and they move forward again. Will hovers at the rear of the group. Tara has taken Clea Singh's hand. Everyone is silenced by the moment.

When we reach the piano, Ormus sits down and starts to play a slow, haunting gospelly tune. Mira stands by him, a little behind him. The rest of us wait awkwardly, feeling like intruders. For a few minutes she just lets him play, she lets the music take her body, closes her eyes, sways. One of her hands has alighted on Ormus's shoulder and she leaves it there, she even moves it across a couple of inches and rests her fingertips against the nape of his neck. I feel my face heating up but I do not intervene.

Then Mira sings, and the room fills with her ridiculously strong voice with its great river-deep-mountain-high range. Vina's voice. Ormus Cama hears it and is forced to stop playing because his fingers have begun to shake, but she keeps going by herself, like a ray of sunlight in a ruined church.

Lead me to your light, she sings, oh sweetheart lead me to your day, I'm down at the bottom in the endless night, won't you please show me the way. If you don't lead me baby then I guess I'm down here to stay.

The song is a VTO golden oldie, a lost soul's appeal to her lover, but Mira's the one leading Ormus out of the darkness now, the one saving him from the pit. He's down in that deep dungeon and it's her voice that's setting him free.

His hands go back to the piano, the tempo rises and her voice soars in answering joy. Clea and Tara are hand-clapping now. Even Will Singh, mister stoneface himself, is joining in. Me? I'm not clapping. I'm not the musical type.

Later, over dinner back at home, with Tara happily asleep in my bed, I look at Mira across the fettuccine and chianti I've set before her and I see a stranger: a tough, disenchanted young woman who is also sharp enough to seize her big opportunity, and under the eyes of her lover to flirt with another man. A woman who still isn't sure whether or not she has just had the most important encounter of her musical life. Maybe there's a future opening up for her, or maybe it's just a mad fantasy that will vanish with the dawn. I can see that she is imagining that future, she can't help picturing the rebirth of one of the legendary bands, with herself stepping into Vina's empty shoes.

Don't run away with it, I say, too roughly. You saw the shape he's in.

Maybe he'll break the habit, maybe he won't. The odds are not great, you know that, you know the addictive grip of what he's on, it could be stronger even than you. Anyway it's a long way from today to a stadium show.

Damn, listen to yourself, she says, setting her jaw. I thought this whole thing was your idea anyhow. It was even you who said we shouldn't tell him about us. *Help Ormus,* yeah, right, but let's not help Mira, let's not get carried away.

I can't think of a thing to say. I just sit and eat.

You don't trust me, is that it, she asks. You don't believe what I promised you. You think I'm a whore.

No, I say after much too long a pause, it's okay, I do trust you, I really do.

In fact I am sort of confident of her love, the unlooked-for surprise of it, I want to trust her blindly, but I'm also aware that I have badly miscalculated the power of what Ormus Cama still has to offer. His music, his legendary status and, yes, also his beauty. Mira is clear about that. You're so blind, she tells me, he's the most beautiful man. Those eyes, that soft, soft voice, he's fucking irresistible. Sure, he's taken a battering, but you can't be such a *man* that you actually think that makes him less attractive.

How about his age, I say, trying to sound light-hearted. This is a fellow with childhood memories of the 1940s, of World War II, "White Christmas," the Partition Riots, the New Look, *Oklahoma.* Is this what today's youth prefers?

That's just his shell, it's just the lantern protecting his flame, okay?, she waves me away. His spirit's still young, the flame's still strong, and that's what counts. Like your spirit, she adds consolingly, coming across to my side of the table, and p.s. I also like your shell.

At night when I've moved Tara into the room next door and she and Mira are both asleep, I stare at the ceiling and reflect on fate's little table-turning ways. With Vina I was always the secret lover, the backdoor man. This time it's Mira and I who are together, an item, in love, whatever, and it's my turn to fret about her secret life with Ormus. So we're rivals again, Ormus and I, and in this respect Mira has already filled Vina's boots. And even though the flow of this new triangle's energy has been reversed, some things remain the same: trust is the issue once more; and Ormus Cama still has no idea of my real importance in the story of his life.

The existence of the peekaboo videotapes is the secret Ormus and I are keeping from Mira, and must forever keep. That we have become lovers is the secret Mira and I have agreed to keep from Ormus. This is a secret I would now prefer to tell, but I am denied permission to do so by the woman I love, on pain of terrible retribution. As for Mira and Ormus, music is their secret language, in which they can commune in ways they don't trouble to explain to me.

Here is the last image in my photo-sequence about Vina. I'm sitting in a chair with a circular mirror on my lap. Reflected in the circular mirror is a rectangular mirror containing an image of Vina Apsara. No, not Vina, but the greatest of the not-Vinas. Mira Celano, my new torment, my love.

Mira, Mira, who is the fairest one of all?

On the fourth anniversary of Vina's death, Mo Mallick at Colchis summons the music press wearing a smile like the elated first chord of a surefire hit to announce the imminent emergence from retirement of Ormus Cama and the relaunch of the VTO supergroup in a phase-two lineup. The place of rhythm guitarist Simone Bath will be filled by the emerging gay icon lil dagover, who insists on lower-case initials, wears men's suits and a monocle and a Louise Brooks haircut, and plays like an expressionist dream. (Bath herself, embittered by Vina's old attack on her competence, is threatening to sue Ormus for the rights to the VTO name, a move that alarms nobody and comes to nothing.) The band will be fronted as before by Ormus Cama on vocals and lead guitar, Mallick concludes, and on lead vocals we'll be introducing the new singing sensation Mira Celano, the closest thing to our beloved Vina any of you will ever see.

It's like announcing a Beatles reunion, only bigger. The VTO back catalogue still outsells most functioning bands, and the classic *Quakershaker* CD, reissued with the revised version of "Beneath Her Feet" added as a bonus track, hasn't been out of the *Billboard* top three since the day of Vina's death. The hiring of dagover is widely applauded as a recognition of the need for the band to move with the times. diamond lil brings a formidable résumé with her. At the age of seventeen she was hanging out with the mystery men of Kraftwerk and devising music for the all-female Japanese-Western crossover Takarazuka dance company, in which half the women dress as men and are worshipped by legions of female fans, and she has never looked back. She is highly rated by production gurus as diverse as the Glimmer Twins, Mutt Lange and DJ Jellybean's sidekick, Whitney and Debbie H.'s producer, Toni C. A year or two with VTO should jet-propel dagover into the major leagues, so it's a smart move for her as well as the band.

Mira Celano, however, is being kept under wraps—no interviews, no photographs, no tapes—and this is not a popular strategy. It always used to be said that VTO was Ormus and Vina and anyone, but the circumstances of Ormus's decline are well known, his recovery is uncertain, and in the absence of hard evidence to the contrary Mira is considered unlikely to be worthy of standing in the great Vina Apsara's shoes. She is the subject of intense speculation and much skepticism, and when it's learned that she started out as a lowly impersonator the mood turns ugly. As ever, the Sangria siblings lead the attack, accusing Ormus of vandalizing his own legend and turning the VTO name into a joke, a theme park version of itself. (From Rémy Auxerre no more highfalutin Francophoneries will be heard. He is dead of the Illness, just a square in the quilt now. Rémy's gone, and his sometime lover, my friend Aimé-Césaire Basquiat, is Ill.)

As for the VTO operation, we're in rehearsal, locked away in a disused aircraft hangar in Nassau County and surrounded by an army-style security blanket. This, too, is an aspect of contemporary rock music: the move up to military scale and precision for no greater reason than to shake, rattle 'n' roll. Once upon a time Jerry Apple and his guitar could arrive at the stage door five minutes before showtime, collect his ten thousand bucks in cash from the manager and head out on to the stage, barely acknowledging the house band provided to back him. If anyone in the band dared to ask about the playlist he'd reply, *sonny, tonight we're gonna be playing some Jerry Apple songs.* It's different now. Those old-time duck-walkers were itinerant tinkers. These musicians are industrialists.

Here are the sequencers, the synthesizers, the sampling devices—Fairlights, Synclaviers. Here are the musicians, working out how to lay their own playing over the swirls and twirls, the technological sound-mattresses they'll be bouncing on throughout the show. Ormus and lil dagover, in particular, are currently in deep musical communion, swapping incomprehensibilities with the techno gandalf, Eno Barber. (Yes, Eno from Radio Freddie; these days he's the undisputed king of the loop, the czar of texture, King Ear. Our lives disconnect and reconnect, we move on, and later we may again touch one another, again bounce away. This is the felt shape of a human life, neither simply linear nor wholly disjunctive nor endlessly bifurcating, but rather this bouncey-castle sequence of bumpings-into and tumblings-apart.) Ormus has brought Eno in to work on the new show and its accompanying album, and there's a lot of this huddling at present. Mira hates it. As the singer, she's largely excluded from the instrumentalists' private club. This part of Ormus is not for her; when he's with dagover, she feels the way I feel when he's with her.

Today Mira is on edge, uncertain, she can't stop moving, a few steps this way, a few steps that, smacking the palms of her hands together, snapping her fingers, talking fast, her eyes concealed behind alarming night-black goggle-like curve-around shades. Tara is off somewhere in Mira's mobile-home private zone, being cared for by Clea Singh. She's a wise enough child to know that when Mommy's in this mood it's best to keep out of her way. I'm not yet prepared to be that wise. I'm there, trying to be a reassuring presence, mostly just flak-catching when she needs someone to yell at. I'm the wife.

She's soliloquizing, and when Mira is like this you just have to hang on for the ride. The negative speculation in the media has rattled her, the decision to seal her off from premature exposure has proved more stressful than she anticipated. It isn't easy to keep your head down when half the country's press corps is on your trail, to button your lip when what they're saying is cruel and you want to fight your corner. But Mallick had said, if we expose you now we're just showing them the target before we're ready to repel their fire. On stage you'll shut their fucking mouths so wait, just wait, please. And Ormus backed Mallick and they were the pros and so she agreed, but she's full of doubts, feels she shouldn't go out in front of audiences dressed up as Vina any more, feels caged in her impersonation and wants to be herself.

Come on, it wasn't Vina who awoke him from a coma this time, she growls, it was me, Mira, me hauling him back from the dead, me firing his crooked physician with the onion breath who came on to me while I was showing him the door, me getting him into rehab along with all the other guys with pointy teeth and spiralling eyeballs, and then me making sure he stayed with the program and graduated summa cum fucking laude. When he needed someone in the night he called out for me and baby, I got up and went to him every single time, well, okay, at least until one a.m. six nights a week, I mean not right in the middle of the night when we were, when, listen, you know what I'm saying here, I left my own child in your care, okay, yours and sometimes the babysitter's, okay and sometimes Clea Singh's too, when he sent her over, but goddammit nobody went to him more than me, I played all his crazy games, I let him hold on to Vina through me until he was strong enough to stand on his own feet, and look at him now, he's a man reborn, okay, bravo, kudos to him, what I'm saying here is he owes me, I'm holding his marker, it's time he set me free. I brought him back from Hell but that doesn't mean I've got to burn in the fire instead. This Vina crap, I know it's a mistake but I can't get myself heard and when we're out there in the bright lights it's me who's going to have to take the fall.

This is what I do not bring up at this juncture: that I'm sliding into Hell too. The deeper we get into rehearsals the further from me she moves, the more she resents lil dagover the more outrageously she comes on to Ormus. I continue to discover that there are few limits to Mira's pragmatism. Whatever works, is her motto. I keep wondering about Ormus's bedroom door. Is that an inviolable borderline? Or will she go beyond that, too, to find whatever works?

(Trust me. Don't you trust me?)

(Yes, darling, I trust you, baby, I truly do. But maybe I'm an idiot to do it, just one more fool for love. One more rock 'n' roll wife.)

Rumors reach the world outside the aircraft hangar of dissension within it. Mira suspects dagover of being the source of the leaks. The two women are increasingly at loggerheads; they're both opinionated, strong-mindedly pushing their ideas, competing for Ormus Cama's respect. Mira tells Ormus he's letting the technology turn his head, putting the cart before the horse, you're like the generals with their smart bombs, she says, boys and their fucking toys. I'm the one who knows the clubs, she adds, I've spent more time on the scene than the rest of you put together, you're just babbling science to sound cool but you don't know shit. In the clubs this stuff is already over, it wasn't enough. People are hungry, okay?, the machines aren't feeding them, I mean it's up to us to give them something to bite on, to give their spirits food.

Ormus is listening.

But lil dagover hits back with a well-developed theory that it's technology that has taken the music back to its roots, its origins in North African atonal call-and-response rhythms. When the slaves came across the sea and were forbidden to use their drums, their talking drums, they listened to the music of the Irish slave drivers, the three-chord Celtic folk songs, and turned it into the blues. And after the end of slavery they got their drums back and that was r&b, and white kids took that from them *and added amplification* and that was the birth of rock 'n' roll. Which went back across the ocean to England and Europe and got transformed by the Beatles, the first great rock group to use stereo technology, and that stereo mutation came back to America and became VTO et cetera. But the technology goes on changing, and with the invention of sampling you can graft the oldest music on to the newest sounds and then, shazam!, in hip-hop, in scratching, you're right back to call and response, back to the future. Technology's not the enemy, lil argues, it's the means.

What is this, Mira demands of Ormus, a history seminar or a rock 'n' roll band? If she's right then the music's a closed loop, it's dead, let's go home. To go forward, to break out of the loop, we've got to go on pushing what VTO started to do, what I always thought Vina stood for. Crossing frontiers. Bringing in the rest of the fucking world.

It's an impasse, and interestingly enough Ormus doesn't seem willing or able to offer leadership, to see a way forward. The solution comes from Eno Barber, who makes it look surprisingly easy. Eno still comes across as the brother from another planet, immaculately groomed at all hours of the day and night, never seen eating or drinking or taking a leak, unflappability incarnate. He calls Mira and lil to his mixing desk and says quietly, I was thinking, we could have it both ways. And as they listen to his loops, the tabla rhythms and sitar and yes vina riffs pushed through his sequencers along with pure synthesized sound, as he fades and balances and mixes his bubbling aural brew, something starts happening, lil picks up her guitar and starts playing along, finding the rhythms or letting them find her, riding the waves, and Mira's singing scat mixed up with Ormus's lyrics and Indian *bóls*, and Ormus Cama has actually begun to smile. All over the cavernous hangar electricians and grips and roadies and record-company stiffs stop doing whatever they're doing and listen. This is the sound of a baby being born. This is the rhythm of new life.

We've got a band.

There is hate mail. Well, there's always hate mail where there's attention, always the redneck *die commie perverts* messages, the religiomane *you may escape from me but you can't escape from god* fortune cookie menaces, the disappointed sexual fantasists, the fans of rival cults, the secret crazies who hold down mundane jobs and have back-yard cookouts on Sundays and fill their bedroom closets with magazine clippings over which they scrawl their epithets of existential loathing. And if the volume of the poison-pen material is greater than usual, it's partly because the band has been away so long, and the dirty water has been building up behind the dam. There's plenty of supportive fan mail too, of course, but it doesn't carry the same weight, doesn't become a part of what works on you as you go about your daily business. And this time the hostility is affecting the band more than usual, because, yes, theirs has been a long silence, and it's a new lineup, so there are uncertainties. Also, the hate mail is not just standard-issue nastiness. There's a new strain of virulence in much of it, an extra bitterness in the bile.

Vina wannabes write in to protest the choice of Mira rather than one of them, purists write to express disgust at the exhuming of the band, which should have been allowed to remain in the golden past where it belongs instead of being subjected to this zombified return, lesbian-haters send in their four-letter views of lil dagover and her Sapphic sisterhood, and that's just the polite stuff. Many correspondents send in near-illegible scrawls warning that VTO's quake songs may actually have been responsible for the current wave of seismic catastrophes and urging the band to keep away from that dangerous material. *Don't stir up yo uzual trouble again oar els, you've maid enouff money from uman mizry as it is.*

Another faction blames Ormus for the band's long silence, calling it a betrayal. Its members suggest that his envy of Vina's genius was the real reason for shutting down the band and that he must therefore be held responsible for what followed. If VTO hadn't ceased trading Vina wouldn't have needed to start building a solo career, and therefore in all probability she wouldn't have been in Mexico on that fateful Valentine's Day, so she'd still be alive, you fucking murderer, Ormus Cama, don't think we will ever forget or forgive.

Other correspondents, however, take a more positive line, praising the prophetic accuracy of Ormus's old songs, expressing the writer's belief that his music can literally change the world and begging Ormus to turn his magical powers towards the good. *Heal the breaking planet. Sing to us and soothe the aching earth.*

For everyone looking forward to Mira's début, there are five people hoping for various reasons to see her fail.

At one point during the months of gestation—this is before we get to the airplane hangar—I myself get a little carried away. Mira tells me that Ormus's plan is to make the new show an exploration of the ourworld/otherworld duality with which he's wrestled most of his life. He's interested in the theme of dissolving the frontiers between the worlds, so there's a narrative he's developing about an overworld/underworld love story, perhaps a rescue. . . . When I realize he doesn't know about the music that came before him—how much, subconsciously, he must still resent his scholarly father, how much he must be suppressing!—I get excessively hot and bothered and go out and buy a stack of early operas, Jacopo Peri's *Euridice* (1600) with the Ottavio Rinuccini libretto, Monteverdi's 1607 *Orfeo,* libretto by Alessandro Striggio, and of course the Gluck, from which Vina sang her last song at Tequila. I can't find Giulio Caccini's rival setting of the Rinuccini libretto, but I don't care because it really isn't very good.

When Mira next goes over to the Rhodopé I tag along and bring Ormus the CDs. He accepts my gift and puts on the Peri and even listens patiently to what I have to say, that not only does the whole history of opera begin with these works, but it's a myth that crosses all cultural frontiers, you hear echoes of it in the Odin story, in Celtic traditions, even, I believe, in certain Native American tales, and all those versions have their own songs too, you should really have someone hunt them down. I tell him about the birth of a new style of accompanied solo song—his own art form!—in sixteenth-century Florence, at the court of Count Giovanni Bardi in the late 1570s: a song aimed at expressing the meaning of the text. This radical departure from the madrigal principle of ornamentation by division of parts made possible opera, the aria, the whole modern tradition of song right down to the three-minute Tin Pan Alley hit single with a catchy hook. This, too, is a part of his history, I tell him, and he should know it.

I try to evoke for him the first performance of Peri's opera at the Pitti Palace, on the occasion of the wedding of Maria de' Medici to Henry IV of France, and the later première of the Monteverdi at the Accademia degli Invaghiti at carnival time in Mantua, whose Gonzaga duke was patron to both Monteverdi and Striggio. . . . But before I can start in on the technicalities, strophic variation, *stile concertato,* etc., he interrupts me, very gently. I get it, it's an old tale, it's been sung before, especially in Italian, he whispers, not unkindly. I guess that's always so with any story. But what I'm trying to make here is still mine, and I'll just keep going down this stumbling path I'm on, if it's okay with you.

Okay, excuse me, I mutter, embarrassed, I just wanted to mention that the problem everybody has is with the ending, because she isn't supposed to be saved, you know. Everyone gives it a happy ending one way or another, but that's wrong, I just wanted to mention that. After all, Vina wasn't, and here I stop and bite my tongue.

Good, says Ormus, giving no sign of having heard the last few words. Unhappy ending. Got it. Thanks for stopping by.

Vina knew all this stuff, I mumble foolishly, and perhaps just a tad mutinously, and go home.

(While we're on the classics, I should say that Ormus has set the *Dies Irae* to music. Mira must have recited it to him too, and clearly he didn't pat *her* on the head and shoo her away. *O Angry Day* may be the first-ever rock lyric to be translated from a Latin original written by a *duecento* Italian monk.)

• • •

To proceed: the idea is to do a first, short Anglo-American tour in smaller venues, Roseland, the United Center, the Cambridge Corn Exchange, the Labatt's Apollo, no more than half a dozen gigs in total, to let the band bed down before launching, six months later, into a full, eighteen-month-long, six-continent stadium program of performances. The famous stadium rock set designer Mark McWilliam is devising a grand fantasia of an environment for this grand tour. By contrast, these first evenings will have a stripped-down, raw, back-to-basics feel. Let's get the music right, Ormus murmurs, before we get into the show.

His own singing voice is in good working order once more, though it's smaller than it used to be, needs more amplification. However, his guitar playing, according to Eno, with whose ear I do not presume to argue, is perhaps even better, more emotional, than before. He's back all right, and the band's sound is fat and hot. On our last day in the aircraft hangar there's a full as-live concert before an invited audience, with nothing held back except that nobody's in stage clothes. Even in jeans and T-shirts, however, they sound right on the money. The applause is long and sincere. VTO lives.

We're at Roseland, September 1993, just one week after the concert in the hangar, and a couple of thousand fans are in a high state of excitement, stroked by roving spotlights into an ever greater frenzy of anticipation, and then the VTO engine room starts up.

One-two-three-four!

The drummer, Patti LaBeef, the original tall Texan and one of the first women drummers to make it into the big league, is in her own monosyllabic way as much a hall-of-famer as Ormus and Vina up front. In the early days young men in the audience would yell at her, *God, you're horny,* and she'd ignore them, spit, and get on with her job. The VTO bassman, Bobby Bath, comes from Montserrat, island of earthquakes and sound studios, and plays as if his life's ambition is stability, no more. *Plenty of players got more tricks,* he says, *but it was always the basics that I loved, to be rock solid, yeah?, to lay down that bass line and let them up at the front dance all over she.* Bobby Bath was briefly married to the outcast Simone, but he has no problem about being back in the lineup. *What she's against, I'm for, baby,* is his attitude. *That's a bad-tastin' drink of rum and I drunk me all I need.*

And here's dagover, there's a big cheer for diamond lil, her personal fan club's out in force tonight, and then the dry ice clears and Ormus Cama's in his bubble with his pedal steel guitar, plunging into the intro for the first song, a souped-up version of the hard-driving oldie "Ooh Tar Baby." He takes the first verse himself and it's just like old times, only better, because lil dagover is fitting in well and filling the band's old Bath-shaped hole, and then Mira runs out and things start going badly wrong.

I'm sitting with Mo Mallick and we both see the problem at once, we see that Mira was one hundred percent right and Ormus, blinded by his need to believe in Vina Apsara's return from the dead, was very, very wrong. The audience isn't pleased. *What, you're really sending out a girl in a Vina costume and we're supposed to swallow it?* The moment we see the reaction we know the evening's a bust, and VTO could die again tonight. Here in this old ballroom it's looking like Ormus Cama's last dance.

Or not-dance, because the kids in front aren't moving, they're just standing stony-faced and staring up at the stage, pouring out their dumb hostility at Mira. How long before they start to boo? How long before they walk out?

At this point Mira Celano does an astonishing thing. She holds up her hand and the band stops playing. Then she addresses the angry crowd.

Okay, fuck you too, she says. You don't like my look, and the truth is neither do I, but for now we're both stuck with it, so why not just let's see if the music's any good, okay?, I mean if the music's no good then shoot me, fine, you're entitled, but if it's music you came for we've got some to give, and if you don't like my outfit, take my tip?, open your ears and shut your fucking eyes.

Patti LaBeef comes in here: a thunder-roll on the drums, a cymbal smash. Patti's rooting for the girl, and Patti has a lot of money in the bank with the paying public, Patti's credible. The crowd settles, grumbling, half convinced. Then it's lil, it's dagover, who fought Mira most of the way to tonight, blasting out the famous "Tar Baby" riff. That does it. *Five-six-seven-eight.* Ooh Tar Baby won't you hold me tight. We can stick together all thru the nite.

Ormus and Mira have discussed stage-diving. He can't do it—he's fifty-six years old and trapped in a soundproof cubicle—but she thinks she should. If we're talking about blurring the frontiers, she argues, then we've got to erase the line between us and them.

I'm against it, but my being protective only drives Mira further into danger, and so it's settled, she's going to do it, about halfway through the gig in the middle of the sequence of *Quakershaker* songs. But now that the show has gotten off to such a rough start, and even though the band is playing brilliantly the crowd is only about eighty percent with them, surely she won't go through with it, I think, surely she'll be smart enough to hold back.

She dives.

For an instant I think *they aren't going to catch her,* I imagine her body broken and trampled beneath the crowd's surly lethal feet, I think of Tara. But the arms do go up, they're holding her, she's swimming over the sea of hands, she's safe.

That's what I think, but I can't see what she can—the anger in many of the faces below her helpless body—I can't feel the hands that are starting to claw at her body. Only when somebody rips off her red Vina wig does it become clear. I'm on my feet now, Mallick is yelling into his walkie-talkie, it's a riot, get her out of there, but before the security guards can wade in she has somehow managed to regain the stage, and when she stands up we can all see the cuts on her midriff, her back, even her face, her long dark hair is blowing wild and ragged at her back and the bustier has gone, but she won't stop singing, she doesn't miss a beat, she stands front and center in her ripped leather pants and sings bleeding and bare-breasted right into their goddamn murderous ungrateful faces and that's when I know, when every one of us at the Roseland concert hall knows for certain that Mira Celano is going to be a big, big star.

Afterwards, backstage, I want to hold her and comfort her and to hell with Ormus and his delusions. But she's on fire and needs encircling by no man's strength. She has come off stage to lay down the law. It's not much of a greenroom and we're all crowded in there and we all know what has to be said and that a woman with the guts to stage-dive into a crowd she can't trust also has the balls to face up to Ormus Cama and tear the scab off his deepest wound.

No more Vina, she says. She's standing toe-to-toe with him, she's the taller and stronger of the two and isn't planning on letting him get away. Okay, Ormus? We do it my way or let's forget the whole thing right now. Are you listening? Can you deal with this? Nobody comes back from underground. Nobody did return. Vina Apsara's gone.

But Ormus Cama is away in a Bombay record store, talking to a tall under-age beauty about the authorship of "Heartbreak Hotel."

Mira's shouting. Ormus? Did you hear what I said?

Yeah, Ormus whispers. He's actually humming the song.

Don't go crazy on me, Ormus. You're not so crazy now. I need to know your answer on this right away.

What's that? asks Ormus Cama, quietly. Vina Apsara? Oh, I'm sorry, she died.

18

DIES IRAE

O *angry day, O angry day, When Time, like ash, will blow away. That's what King David and the Sibyl say.*

In the West the earthquakes have stopped and the construction teams have moved in. Banks and insurance companies are building their new palaces over the faults, as if to assert the primacy of their authority, even over the misbehaving earth itself. The scars left by the quakes are being transformed into regeneration zones, gardens, office blocks, cineplexes, airports, malls. People have already started to forget and so, inevitably, resent those who remember. Ormus Cama and VTO, among others, are accused of negativity and scaremongering, because they continue to play the *Quakershaker* songs and their new gospel-influenced arrangement of Thomas of Celano's ancient minatory lines.

In the South, however, the devastation continues. It's as if the earth were discriminating against its most disadvantaged children. In India, where houses are built of mud and dreams, where the structures of life are fragile, their foundations weakened by corruption, poverty, fanaticism and neglect, the damage is immense. This is not pleasing to those who hold that India is not different from anywhere else, who deny that particularity of circumstance which makes a place itself. The fact is that the ground in America is not shaking, but some patch or other of Indian soil, one or another Indian city street, is hit by subterranean tremors almost every day.

To many third-world observers it seems self-evident that earth-quakes are the new hegemonic geopolitics, the tool by which the superpower quake-makers intend to shake and break the emergent economies of the South, the Southeast, the Rim. The boastful tri-umphalism of the West during the revolutionary upheavals of 1989–90 has come back to haunt it. Now all earth tremors are perceived as Euro-American weapons, what were once classified by insurance bro-kers as acts of god are now close to being treated by entire states as acts of war, and the altruism with which ordinary Western citizens con-tribute to disaster relief funds, and even the indefatigable efforts of the international aid agencies, look like post-facto attempts at salving the guilty consciences of the powerful after the damage has been done. India, Pakistan, Israel, Syria, Iran, Iraq and China all announce the allo-cation of gigantic "plate wars" budgets. A new kind of weapons scram-ble has begun.

Exhaustive efforts by skeptical Western journalists and politicians to investigate and challenge the claims of responsibility made by their own military-industrial complex for the 1989–90 transglobal quakeathon are treated as disinformation by the participants in the new quake race, and interventions by international peace movements are largely ignored. Appeals from world leaders to the quake-racers to freeze their dangerously destabilizing new "rift bomb" building pro-grams are branded arrogant and hypocritical. The U.N. Secretary-General's shuttle-diplomacy initiative to persuade all relevant parties to attend an urgently convened HARF (Hands Across the Rifts and Faults) symposium, where they might enter constructively into conflict-resolution talks, is ineffective. There are mass public demon-strations in support of the decisions taken by the leaders of all the Seis-mic Seven. Self-respect and national pride are invoked and people declare themselves ready to let their children starve in order to acquire the ability to shake the world, which they appear to equate with vic-tory in such other prestigious contests as the Miss World pageant and the soccer World Cup. The very walls of Delhi, Islamabad and the other seismohawk capitals shout pro-quake-technology slogans. *No HARF measures. When we can quake land will be time to shake hand.*

As the Indian earthquakes continue, local politicos continue to blame (as well as the West) the country's traditional enemies to the north and northwest, and this creates a fevered public climate in which war is a constant possibility. Golmatol Doodhwala, widow of the assassinated Piloo, is a particular political beneficiary of this fist-shaking. In a century marked by the frequent rise to power of the widows of murdered men, the spherical, illiterate Golmatol, with her unceasing demands for revenge, is the latest in the line—perhaps the last, if she gets her warmongering way, and the world ends. Not with a bang but a shudder.

Everyone's a New Quaker now.

Much that has lain hidden for years is thrown back into view by the unceasing tremors. When it is announced that the reborn VTO rock supergroup plans to add concert dates in Bombay and Delhi to its marathon tour schedule, and that at these dates *O Angry Day* and the *Quakershaker* songs will be played as part of the band's efforts to support Western peace initiatives, the opposition to Ormus Cama's return is orchestrated by an unexpected hand. From Tihar Jail, his elder brother Cyrus Cama issues a statement that wins wide public support.

Cyrus at sixty-one is still classified as dangerously insane and has never on any occasion requested parole. It is his firmly expressed view that he should remain in "my beloved Tihar" until the day of his death, for only in prison can he be safe from the fear that the Pillowman, who may yet sleep within him, might re-emerge to commit further hideous crimes. He is a multiple murderer, that is still true, of course; yet within the jail his gentle disposition continues to win him many friends. No matter how frequently his warders are changed they leave as his disciples, for Cyrus has become a wise man, having passed the years quietly, studiously, learning the ancient languages and mastering the old books, very much in the Darius Cama tradition. His *Meditations on Kalki*— Kalki, the last manifestation of Vishnu, who will come only to announce the end of the world—have been published in learned journals and reprinted as *feuilletons* and chapbooks by various small philosophical presses, and there are numerous university professors and excited students who consider him one of the deeper thinkers in the land, a voice for our troubled and conceivably terminal times. As a published writer of polish and note, and a man whose determinedly (if somewhat inevitably) simple life and principled self-denial are striking, Cyrus has become an emblem of what a man may do with his spell on earth once he accepts his given lot. His body is in prison but his spirit, as his fans admiringly put it, his spirit is a bird's joyous song, sounding in an open sky.

To Ormus Cama, Cyrus elects to write an open letter, more in sorrow than in wrath: *My brother, I regret so much to say, you have become a man who hates his own kind.* This opening sentence ensures the wide publication of Cyrus's ruefully polemical text in the Indian and then the global news media. Even Ormus's recent statement opposing the quake wars is turned against him. Ormus began wryly: *As for myself, I control no weapons of mass destruction, so I hope to be excused the charge of hypocrisy when I say* . . . ah, Cyrus offers mournful rebuttal, *but my brother is too modest; for who was it that penned the regrettable ditties that have become the totemic anthems of the new Quake Age? We must not take Ormus Cama at his own low estimate, as a mere troubadour or popster; for his self-hating, deracinated music has long been at the service, I would even say at very heart, of the arrogance of the West, where the world's tragedy is repackaged as youth entertainment and given an infectious, foot-tapping beat.*

What Cyrus initiates, others eagerly take up. The government's favorite godmen of the moment, Ulurishi and the Aurhum Baba, announce that the former Indian and lapsed Zoroastrian "seismopropagandist" Ormus Cama must indeed bear a heavy responsibility for the West's quake-inducing "doomsday scenario"; that his songs and performances are open attacks on intercultural as well as intracultural stability; and that accordingly he and his collaborators should under no circumstances be permitted to perform on Indian soil. Within days of the Rishi and Baba's unprecedented joint communiqué, Interior Minister Golmatol Doodhwala (whose Pilooist faction has just agreed to prop up the shaky governing coalition, the Interior Ministry being the price of Golmatol's support) confirms that all VTO tour personnel, including the band members, themselves have been refused entry visas in the public interest, and also in their own, because in the present heated climate their personal safety cannot be guaranteed.

So the past reaches up its claw for Ormus, grabs his ankle and seeks to drag him down. And after the Cyrus letter is published, the hate mail from India multiplies. Violence is threatened, but that's nothing new. For years a dozen Vina wannabes a week have been threatening to kill Ormus and/or themselves for his failure to love them, for restricting himself in what they consider an unhealthy way to the starvation diet of his dead wife's memory, thus denying himself the opportunity to partake of the banquets of love that are on offer all around. Ormus has never taken such menaces seriously, and in spite of Clea Singh's concerns, this new Ormus, Ormus in his cocoon, Ormus in the strangely absent mood he's been in ever since Mira made him face the Vina facts, this vague, wafting Ormus is also immune to his angry subcontinental correspondents' new darts. The Singhs, at Clea's insistence, are nevertheless on ready alert for trouble.

When news of the Indian ban reaches the Sangrias in New York, they decide that Cyrus Cama is the hot unwritten story of the VTO phenomenon, and make arrangements to travel to Delhi on the first available flight.

O angry days, O angry nights. This is how I think of the two long years of ending that followed the three deaths of Vina Apsara: as the nights and days of wrath. O final, departed times.

I think that Vina died the first time in the abyss at El Huracán, the second time very slowly, as the world turned her into its iconic Vina Divina and lost its grip on her quirky humanity until finally Clea Singh erased her voice from her own answering machine, and her third and final death occurred when my darling Mira Celano forced Ormus Cama who loved Vina best to speak the words that killed her for all time to come. After he spoke those words Ormus knew that he had severed the last tie that held him down to earth, and having lost all joy in life he began to look for death, to gaze into the faces of everyone he met as if he were asking, is it you? Please, friend, stranger, let it be you that brings me the gift I'm waiting for.

The *Into the Underworld* tour was conceived as a giant traveling memorial to Vina, whose Mira-simulacrum no longer appeared on stage but with whose silent, slo-mo image dancing across the giant Vidiwall behind the stage the show began and ended. This decision, too, was criticized in some quarters for over-commercializing the memory of a latter-day saint and was even described as a blatant attempt to cash in on a terminally rocky marriage, but Ormus continued to be impervious to criticism, to smile his quiet smile and go on down his chosen road. A man has to belong to something, even if it's just a golf club or a pet dog, and Ormus belonged to a memory now. Only the thing he had lost could hurt him; he belonged to her, and to music.

For most of 1994 and 1995 he lived exclusively in the world of the tour, an ersatz underworld environment tiered like the circles of Hell and enclosed in a giant arc by the largest Vidiwall ever built, from which the audience was nightly bombarded by incessant images of heaven and hell, both conceived of as places on earth, nuptial motels and flame-grilled-burger bars, video arcades and ballet schools, football crowds and war zones, ice deserts and political rallies, surf beaches and libraries, and it was up to each individual to decide which images were celestial, which infernal. This techno-inferno had been realized for him by the McWilliam design team but its essential concept was Ormus's own. Having created his fiction he plunged into it and did not come out for two years. The fictional universe of the show gave the impression of floating free of the real world, of being a separate reality that made contact with the earth every so often, for a night or two at a time, so that people could visit it and shake their pretty things. Voluntarily imprisoning himself within the private continuum of rock 'n' roll, Ormus Cama, too, became a floating entity, more otherworldly alien than human being, more show than O.

He moved from hotel floors stripped of superfluities, transformed into white spaces and supplied with white pianos, audiovideo editing suites and old Tuscan bread ovens, via limousines with blackened windows whose purpose was not so much to prevent people looking in as to make it impossible to see out, into that stadium environment which was always the same wherever in the world he might be, and in this illusion of continuity he found it possible for the moment to survive. When it was time to fly on the band's specially refitted 727 he took sleeping pills and did not wake up until it was time once again to enter the closed world of limousine and white hotel and underworld set which was now the only place on earth he needed to be or see.

It was as if the show were staying put while the world rushed past outside the stadium, as if the show were the permanence and human life the transient thing, as if the stadium was always the same stadium, and the limo was always the same car, always driven by Will Singh with . Clea Singh by Ormus's side, and the hotel floor where he spent all his off-stage time baking and eating bread was always the same hotel floor, but the cities outside its windows came and went like the lands at the top of the Faraway Tree.

Rio, Sydney, London, Hong Kong, Los Angeles, Beijing: these places weren't real. The Indian ban wasn't important, because India wasn't real, it was just another transit zone. The changing colors and races of the faces in the crowd, the parade of celebrities who came backstage to drink with him and eat the home-baked bread he insisted on offering them, the local heroes and tour sponsors and cover girl beauties who munched away politely on his loaves and told him lies about how well he looked, none of these mattered, because they were illusions too. Only the show was real. The show, the music, was home. Outside that fiction, the cosmos was a fake.

He stood on his imagination, on what he had conjured out of nowhere, what did not, could not, would not exist without him. Now that it had been made, he existed only within it. Having created this territory, he trusted no other ground.

During the show the weight of light hitting the stage was so burdensome that in truth he could barely see the crowd, just the first few rows and beyond it a great roaring beast he had to tame, to play as if it were an instrument, but this was something he knew, this was his real life. The lion tamer in the lion's cage, putting his head into the jaws of the beast, knows that this is his true reality and the cheering, brightly colored, balloons-and-popcorn world beyond the bars is trivial, a painted backdrop, a set. So also Ormus in the bubble of the show was perfectly comfortable, perfectly at home, and by general consent his performances were extraordinary, his guitar never more achingly clear, like a desert wanderer's dream of water in a cool clean well, his singing never so subtle or so strong. The weak voice of recent times had vanished and in its place was this mighty instrument, more powerful than it had ever been in the old days when Vina herself was pouring her coloratura music over the world.

At the end of each show the other band members would murmur to each other in wonderment, almost fearful of what was coming out of him. Even LaBeef and Bath had to admit they had never seen him be so unbelievable over so long a period. *It's like he's a jet on afterburners,* Patti LaBeef said one night, *he can burn double the fuel because he knows he don't have to save none for the journey home.* Once she had said that all the band members understood that he was dying, that the fuel he was using on stage was life itself. He was burning himself up in the fire of his art, each night's show was not only a gift to Vina but a step towards the oblivion, the not-being, where she lay with his joy in her keeping; he knew that when the show was over he would no longer need to sing or speak or move or breathe or be. After that the musicians began to think of him as a creature from another world, because they could see how hard he was trying to get there, maybe some world through a gash in the air, some variant dimension where Vina was still alive. But there were no longer such gashes for him, for anyone, to see. lil dagover said to Mira, Ever since I can remember I was a fan of theirs, this is so hard to watch, but listen, at least he isn't guttering and choking like some dime-store candle, this is a fucking flameout, a supernova, a real star's way to go.

(In reality the continuity of the show was maintained by doing everything in triplicate. Because the stage took a week to build, three different steel crews leapfrogged around the world, putting it up and tearing it down. There was always one stage being dismantled at the last venue, a second stage ready for action at the current stadium, and a third stage being built at the next stop down the road.

Then there was the energy requirement. Into the Underworld pumped out four million watts of power, produced by six-thousand-horsepower generators. The three hundred and fifty cabinets in the sound system accounted for one and a half million of these watts. There were also two thousand lights, which means you could have watched the show from the moon.

Six million people paid to watch the shows. Twenty million CDs and cassettes were sold. Hundreds of millions of dollars were made. If Ormus Cama

imagined he was standing still while the world revolved around him, maybe he
wasn't so very wrong. Such is the power of imagination.)

Out on the end of a long "finger" that ended in a great maw—
intended to suggest the Gate of Hell and guarded by a three-headed
animatronic Cerberus—was a small secondary stage on which Ormus
was initially discovered, alone, like Orpheus at Aornum in Thesprotis,
contemplating his terrible descent. On this stage Ormus played his
opening solo, an acoustic version of "Beneath Her Feet," while Vina's
image towered over the stadium on the Vidiwall. (As it was an acoustic
solo, he could perform it unenclosed, standing in the open air, without further damaging his ears.) At the end of the song the mechanical
dog lay down and slept and Ormus stepped into a clear bubble which
moved forward on a track and was "swallowed" by the Maw. Now,
under the catwalk linking the stages, he was transported to the main
stage at high speed by the fastest-moving walkway in production, and
burst into McWilliam's fantasy Hades where the other band members
awaited him, as well as a zoo of flame-belching iron demons, giant
inflatables and citizens of Pandemonium who were both costumed
mimes and machines. Inset into the stage floor was a complex system
of tracks and points, so Ormus was able to move around the great set
without leaving his bubble; at one point, in a tremendous coup de
théâtre, it was grasped by metal arms and became a glass elevator which
rocketed Ormus high into the sky above the shrieking crowd. Thus
bubbled Ormus no longer seemed separated from the action; the bubble became a metaphor of life, of his continued membership in the
world of the living during his adventure in the country of the dead.

And Mira was there, of course, she was the woman he had come to
rescue from the Prince of Darkness. Mira, dressed as herself now,
singing her heart out, growing day by day into the stardom that was
her destiny, stepping free of Vina's shadow and playing the part of Love
trapped in Hell and longing to be free.

Look, it doesn't matter any more, it's not important how they
behaved on stage, I understand that. I was jealous, all right?, let me
admit that right up front, I was half mad with jealousy, and I was
wrong. But boy, she turned out to be quite a performer, my Mira, you
could see it in the way she leaned against Ormus's curving bubble,

pressing her body against it, first her breasts and thighs, then her arched back and her ass, rolling across it as if she was making love to the damn thing, I couldn't watch. And at the end when she went inside it, when she was sealed in with Ormus and the bubble blazed with light and disappeared and then all of a sudden it was just Mira and Ormus back on the secondary stage, out of Hell, liberated from the bubble, and Ormus was playing his guitar as if it were sex itself and Mira was pouring herself over him like a free drink, well, hah!, I couldn't stand it!, I had to turn my back. I had to fucking leave.

I stopped going to the performances. I left the tour and went back to New York and got on with my work, I even went back to photo-journalism for the first time in years and ended up dodging bullets in places whose names I couldn't pronounce, Urgench-Turtkul on the Amu Darya, Târgul-Sačuesc in Transylvania, and the new post-Soviet hot spots of Altynaï-Asylmuratova and far-flung Nadezhda-Mandelstán; but still at night I dreamed pornographic dreams of Mira and Ormus. Sometimes my unconscious threw in lil dagover and a few Singhs to spice things up, and I'd wake up erect and sweating in some dirty murderous Cyrillic-scripted fleapit and understand that all human beings are capable of violence if they are sufficiently aroused, by the rape of their country, for example, or alternatively by the real or imagined seduction of their girl.

I know it's not the same thing, goddammit, I know the fucking difference between infidelity and genocide, but when you're out in woopwoopsky in a roachy sleeping bag in the back of a stranger's Jeep being bitten by Slavic and Asiatic insects, by Roman Catholic and Russian Orthodox and Zionist and Islamist bugs, while all around you is an exploding universe of disintegrating frontiers and crumbling realities, when you're in the midst of that kind of anarchy and mutability and you hope to make it back to East Fifth Street, New York, to read Page Six of the *Post,* just once more, while you're served a blueberry muffin and a cup of steaming organic coffee by a tall smiling barefoot Buddhist blonde, oh yes, just one more time, please, and you swear *you'll never make a single joke about designer Buddhism ever again, you want that peace-loving Buddha right now, give him to me, O Rinpoche Ginsberg, O Richard Lama, O Steven Seagal, take me, I'm yours,* and then you wake up with a head full of imaginary sex in which you were not personally involved, in which unspeakable acts are being performed on and by the body you recognize as pertaining to your beloved . . . let me assure you that at such a moment you don't think *così fan tutte,* whistle a happy tune, and turn over and go back to dreamland, you sit up ready to murder not just your little Fiordiligi, your beloved Dorabella, but whoever the rutting hog was who tempted them off the straight and narrow, just bring the bastard to me and I'll rip out his lecherous heart.

And I was wrong, all right? Wrong, wrong.

Once again I had misunderstood Ormus Cama. I'd allowed myself to forget that there was something so to speak superhuman about his love for Vina, something beyond the human capacity for loving. It was a love until the end of time, and after he failed to bring her back from the dead—after Mira made him see that Vina could not be restored to life—then women were finished for him for good. Now that Mira was just Mira he no longer wanted her to take Vina's place; even if she had come to him oiled and naked and steaming with desire, he would have simply patted her absentmindedly on the head and advised her to put some clothes on before she caught a chill.

So I admit also that Ormus's love for Vina Apsara was greater than mine, for while I had mourned Vina as I had never mourned any loss I had, after all, begun to love again. But his was a love which no other love could replace, and after Vina's three deaths he had finally entered his last celibacy, from which only the carnal embrace of death would set him free. Death was the only lover he would now accept, the only lover he would share with Vina, because that lover would reunite them forever, in the wormwood forest of the forever dead.

And lastly I admit—and I apologize to her now before the eyes of the world—that I should have trusted Mira. I was luckier than I knew: a new love had been born out of the ashes of the old. Mira wasn't interested in Ormus, or only professionally, and maybe a little bit as a way of keeping me honest. I was too stupid to believe it, but at the end of this long sad-luck saga, I was the jackpot boy.

Four hundred years ago, Francis Bacon believed that Orpheus had to fail in his Underworld quest, that Eurydice could not be saved and that Orpheus himself had to be torn to pieces, because, for him, the Orpheus myth was the story of the failure not only of art but of civi-

lization itself. Orpheus had to die, because culture must die. The barbarians are at the gates and cannot be resisted. Greece crumbles; Rome
burns; brightness falls from the air.

On their arrival in Delhi, India's odorous high-volume importunate
reality appalled Marco and Madonna Sangria, who had imagined it as
being perhaps one or two steps downscale from Queens. India can be
a tough country for Americans, who are seen as walking dollar signs
and, what's worse, as innocents abroad: legitimate targets, easy meat.
Within hours of checking in at their five-star South Delhi hotel, they
had been importuned, without leaving the grounds, by money chang-
ers offering them the best black rate in town for their greenbacks, vendors of semi-precious stones which could have been polished pebbles,
taxi drivers whose cousins ran a marble factory just close by, hotel-
lobby palmists, young men and women of quality offering serious
negotiable currency for their cameras and clothes, older men inquir-
ing of Marco whether Madonna was, in the first place, educated and,
in the second place, available, and if so, for what fee; and an elevator
pickpocket who was at once incompetent and unflappable, so that
when Marco pointed out that his hand was in the wrong pocket, the
fellow simply extracted the offending limb, smiled broadly and said
with a disarming shrug, It is an overcrowded country, what to do, we
are used to treating our neighbor's pocket as our own.

Tihar Jail was, unsurprisingly, much worse. The floor alone, never
mind the rooms or the prison staff and let's not even mention the
inmates, just the floor was a whole horror movie, *Scream Goes East,*
maybe, or *A Nightmare on Delhi Street,* the dirt, my dear, and when I
say bugs, I do not refer to a famous cartoon bunny. No place, anyhow,
for a high-maintenance dandy in Narciso pants to be wearing his
Jimmy shoes, or for a class filly of Madonna's pedigree to risk trailing
her Isaac cheesecloth skirt or her new Manolo slingbacks. And gosh,
Madonna noted, people seem to talk at the tops of their *voices* all the
time, and not always in English, what's *that* about?

But when Cyrus came into the interview room, shackled and man-
acled, Madonna suddenly started to have a very good time indeed. As
she afterwards told her circle, I just felt in the presence of *wisdom,* he
had this like *aura,* and I was, I don't know. Just blown *away.*

To him she said, Well, *you're* the sweetest jailbird I ever did see.

By the time they left Tihar Jail the Sangrias had sworn to launch an international campaign—celebrity fund-raisers, embassy pickets, Washington lobbyists, the works—to secure the early release of an exceptional human being. Marco returned immediately to America to set up the pressure group's HQ. Madonna remained in India, wore homespun and rope sandals, wiped the make-up off her face, pulled out her hair extensions, had henna patterns applied to the edges of her hands and the soles of her feet as if she were a bride, and visited Cyrus twice a week, which was the maximum allowable. She apologized to him for the way she looked at their first meeting—gee, I guess I looked like a *hooker, huh,* but it's my *culture,* but I so do not want to stay stuck in that like *error,* I'd like to learn your, what's the word, okay okay I remember, your *ways.*

We've been listening to the wrong Cama, she wrote to launch the Free Cyrus initiative in the first of her syndicated music columns to be filed after her arrival in India. Now let us turn from the ephemeral simplicities of Ormus's has-been rock 'n' roll to the profound contemplation of his elder brother's perennial philosophy. If we are not too old to learn, Cyrus Cama has much to teach. P.S. He's cute as a button, not that we love men for their steel buns, right? Yeah right.

During the long VTO world tour the Cyrus campaign gathered momentum. In New York, Goddess-Ma, always a trend spotter, moved out of the Rhodopé Building and denounced Ormus Cama in distinctly Cyrusian terms. *His suppression of race and skin modalities in the interests of the untenable Western dogma of universals is in reality a flight from self into the arms of the desired, admired Other.* Prominent lawyers in both New York and India took up the Cyrus case; the Indian authorities, embarrassed by the attention, indicated their willingness to be flexible; and at length Madonna Sangria proposed an attractive way forward. Hear me out, okay, she told Cyrus, all of an uncharacteristic fluster. I know this sounds like too *forward* and women in your culture just don't act this way but I guess I'm just, no, no, this is coming out all wrong, I'm saying that if I were to marry you, *okay, Cyrus?,* then you could get a *U.S. passport,* big thrill!, and we could put you on a plane and take care of you back home.

It was late in 1995, and the VTO tour was in South America, completing its last leg, when, after five months of thought, Cyrus Cama gave his reply.

Miss Madonna, when you and your brother first offered me help, I accepted, out of what I now see was weakness. You were so beautiful and persuasive and I thought, very well, if they believe in me then I am ready, I will place myself in their care and come out of my beloved Tihar. But I have also known all the time that if I came with you then soon I would feel obliged to kill you, yes, and your brother, too, and maybe also my mother who disowned me and my twin brother Ardaviraf and many other people along the way, and at the end of my journey, its only real destination and purpose, would lie the sweet murder of my younger brother Ormus, for hatred of whom I have ruined my life.

Now please see that this was most tempting. However, after due reflection, I have found it in myself to refuse. I thank you again for your interest, your declaration of love, your most generous offer of marriage, your gifts. Most particularly I thank you for providing as requested the video equipment and the tape of my brother's concert and for persuading the jail authorities to let me keep the same in my humble cell, contrary to regulations. On the video I watched my brother closely, and observed that he has already departed this life. Look in his eyes. He is dead and in Hell. So you see there is no longer any requirement for me to kill him, I am set free from the imperative of a lifetime. For me to commit other murders in this changed circumstance would be the height of bad taste, and so I will remain happily here in jail. Thanking you, Miss Madonna, and goodbye.

Now I am remembering the last things.

That winter after the end of the *Underworld* tour was the cruelest any of us could recall. Mira and I didn't see anything of Ormus, who was holed up in the Rhodopé as usual, but showed no inclination to get in touch. When I thought of him at all, I pictured him as an Indian chief who decides it's a good day to die, heads for the ground he has chosen and then just sits there waiting for the angel. But most of the time my attention was elsewhere. I had a relationship to repair. At the best of times it is hard for musicians to come home from tour. They get used to their own company, to killer schedules, nights without sleep and tearing up the floor at hot clubs around the world, to being the traveling center of the world's attention, to the coiling tension before the show, the rush of performance, the abandon and exhaustion of afterwards, the boredom with the music, the rediscovery of the music, the ups and downs with the other band members, the omnipresent sexual charge, the shipboard romances, the sense of playing hooky, of being outlaws on the run with raindrops falling on your head.

It is even harder for musicians who have taken their small children on tour. Tara Celano was old enough to go to school now, she had a place at Little Red, but while other little girls her age didn't even know the exact shape of Manhattan, Tara had circumnavigated the globe more than once and had seen more action than she was prepared to divulge, being afraid of offending her teachers' idealistic liberal sensibilities.

And the hardest return of all is the return to a steady relationship, because after the rootless years the very idea of steadiness seems like a fantasy, and in this particular case I had blotted my copybook and Mira knew it. I hadn't trusted her (hah!) with another man. In the midst of that maelstrom of infidelity I hadn't believed she could be true. There was trouble here, a problem we had to address.

I remember a Sunday in the park. It had begun to snow around Christmas and hadn't stopped. Tara loved the whiteness, space and still-ness after two years of garish environments, backstage trailers and con-stant movement. That Sunday making snowballs she was happy being home, happy with us, and her happiness helped draw us back together, we became conscious of our joint importance in her life, of her over-arching need. Such are the families of the modern epoch: elective alliances against terror or despair. This girl, this dead stranger's child, was the closest thing to a future I had found for myself anywhere in the world.

Mira took my mittened hand in hers and after that things were bet-ter between us. We went to a movie, some monsters or aliens were destroying New York as usual (this is L.A.'s way of telling Manhattan it cares), and when we got home there was a message from Clea on my voicemail.

Spenta was dead. It was cold in England too, and in a white house on a hill overlooking the Thames the octogenarian old lady had been huddling in her parlor with her "boys" around an antiquated gas fire. (Virus was sixty-three, Waldo in his mid-forties, and although they had both forgotten long ago that they weren't blood brothers, here, in truth, was another family relationship forged by circumstance rather than biology.) The heating system hadn't been serviced in years, and that night a slow leak developed under the exposed and gappy old floorboards, releasing a flow of gas which first put the three residents peacefully to sleep and then ignited, burning the great mansion to the ground and setting fire, also, to several beautiful oak trees which had stood in those grounds for over two hundred years. Ever since Spenta sequestered herself and left the details of daily life to Waldo and Virus to arrange, the house had gone into decline, and in the nearby villages after the fire people shook their heads and turned their mouths down disapprovingly. *It was an accident waiting to happen, that place,* was the general consensus. *Those sons of hers were never up to it. She should've had better sense.* The loss of the trees was, everybody agreed, a real country tragedy.

Clea's message said nothing about getting together to mourn the dead, nothing about a meeting of any kind. He just thought you'd want to know, she concluded, because of the old days. It was the last communication from Ormus I ever received.

Ormus didn't go to England for the funerals. He did send a couple of legal Singhs over for the reading of Spenta's will. When it was discovered that Spenta's only named heirs had perished with her, the assembled Methwold cousins girded themselves for battle. The house had gone, but the grounds and financial holdings were well worth a war. The Methwolds eyed the American Singh lawyers with open fear and distaste: more Indians! Will there be no end of them? Then the Singhs announced gravely that Ormus Cama wished to renounce all rights to the Methwold estate, rose to their feet, bowed courteously and left the other claimants open-mouthed, and free to fight their parochial, irrelevant, bloody, savage wars.

Although he maintained his distance from his mother's grave, her death had shaken Ormus. On the day after the reading of the will he told Clea that he was going out to walk in the frozen park alone. When she saw that it would be impossible to dissuade him she made him put on a pair of good snow boots, dressed him in his warmest coat, a navy-blue cashmere, wound his soft pashmina shawl around his neck, placed kid gloves upon his meekly extended old man's hands, and crowned him with his favorite cold-weather hat, a sixteen-dollar Chinese rabbit fur with ear flaps which Vina had bought for him in Canal Street long ago. Clea fastened the flaps with a bow knot under his chin, stood up on her tippytoes and kissed him on both cheeks. You're a good man, she told him. Your mother would be proud. Meaning that she thought of herself as his mother, had done so for years, but had never felt able to speak while Spenta lived. Meaning that she loved him and was as proud of him as any mother could ever be.

He smiled faintly and went down in the elevator and crossed the street and went into the park.

Of course she sent Will to follow him, but at a distance, she enjoined Will, don't you dare let him see. Which was not easy on that day of all days, the day when the snow and ice had forced all motor vehicles off the road and people were skiing down the city's empty avenues to work. New York was like the loveliest of ghost towns on that day and we were its shivering ghosts. It was a movie set and we were only actors. Reality seemed elsewhere, someplace that had not been blessed by this faery fall of snow.

He didn't walk for long. It was too cold, you could feel the air freezing the insides of your lungs. After perhaps twenty minutes he turned for home, walking briskly, and thirty-five minutes after he left he reached the high arched entrance of the Rhodopé Building. It was so cold that there was no doorman outside under the canopy. Everyone was sheltering within.

As Ormus reached the entrance, Will Singh, who was just arriving on the parkside sidewalk across from the Rhodopé, slipped and fell on the ice and sprained his right ankle. At the same moment a tall dark-skinned woman with red hair gathered above her head like a fountain stepped out of nowhere and approached Ormus. Astoundingly, given the weather conditions, she was dressed only in a sequin-glittered gold bustier, a pair of tight leather pants and stiletto heels. Her shoulders and midriff were bare.

Ormus Cama turned towards her and paused. I'm sure his eyes would have widened when he saw what she looked like, so he must have seen the small handgun that she aimed at him and emptied at point-blank range into his chest. After she had finished shooting she let go of the weapon, a .09 mm Giuliani & Koch automatic, she let it drop right there in the snow by his fallen body and walked quickly away, showing a surprising turn of speed in spite of the stilettos, turning right down a side street and vanishing from view. By the time Will Singh had hobbled slowly and painfully round the corner she was nowhere to be seen. There was a line of female footprints in the snow. Where the footprints stopped there was a red wig, a pair of leather pants, a sequinned bustier and a pair of stiletto shoes. Otherwise, nothing. No automobile tracks. Nothing, not even any witnesses, not at that time or any later date. It was as if a naked woman had flown through the air of Upper West Side Manhattan and disappeared and nobody saw a thing.

There were no prints found on the gun, either, although Will Singh remembered (but couldn't swear) that the assassin had worn no gloves.

It was the perfect crime.

Ormus died there in the snow a few minutes later with his head in Clea's lap. Clea had been pacing up and down in the lobby, worrying, and when she heard the shots she didn't need to be told who the target was. She ran out in time to see the woman's back disappearing round the corner, and screamed at Will to get after her, but she herself stayed with her Ormus, knowing that on so brutal a day the emergency vehicles would never reach him in time, even with their snow chains they'd skid and slide on the iced surfaces if they tried to hurry, and anyhow the holes in Ormus's beautiful coat told her what she needed to know. They were clustered so close together that it was obvious nothing could be done.

Ormus, she said, sobbing, and he opened his eyes and looked at her. Oh, my Ormie, she mourned, my little shrimpy boy, what to do for you? Do you know what you want? What you need?

He looked vague and didn't reply. Then in despair she asked, Ormus, do you know who you are? You still know that, don't you? Do you know who you are?

Yes, he said. Yes, mother, I know.

Because the murder weapon was the same make as the one known to be owned by Mira, she was briefly questioned by two embarrassed detectives. Because it was widely rumored that I had been dementedly jealous of Ormus's closeness to Mira during the *Into the Underworld* tour, I was questioned also, rather less shamefacedly. But we were each other's alibis, and Tara could vouch for both of us, and when they ran tests on Mira's gun they found it hadn't been fired in years. In the end the police decided the murderess must have been a random crazy, a loose cannon, maybe one of the many disgruntled Vina wannabes who had been sending in hate mail, in which case the use of the gun was either a coincidence or a deliberate attempt to send detectives down a false trail. When this theory was made public, several Vinas of both sexes immediately confessed to the crime, but their confessions didn't check out.

The investigators had no solution to the riddle of the killer's disappearance. Their best guess was that she had an accomplice in one of the apartment buildings along the street where she vanished, and somehow entered the premises without leaving footprints, put on a new set of clothes and later left. Maybe the accomplice had been waiting with a broom to wipe away the traces. It was all pretty speculative, even the detectives agreed. But hey, they wound up saying, many murders are committed to which no solution is ever found. This was one such crime.

If you ask me, I think it was Vina, the real Vina, Vina Apsara herself. My Vina. No: I have to accept this too, that she was still Ormus's Vina, always and forever his. I think she came and got him because she knew how much he wanted to die. Because he couldn't bring her back from the dead she took him down with her, to be with her, where he belonged.

That's my opinion. Oh, that's right, I almost forgot to add: so to speak.

So this was how it came about that on an icy day in January, Mira Celano, her daughter Tara, Clea Singh and I went up from the West Side Heliport in Mo Mallick's personal helicopter with Ormus Cama's ashes in an urn on Clea's lap, to perform the last rites of a life that began on the other side of the world, a life which was in reality lived not in one place or another, but in music.

(Clea and the Singhs got generously treated in the will, by the by; they'd never go hungry again. But apart from their lump-sum payments, all Ormus's money, plus the enormous future income from his back-catalogue royalties and sheet music rights, as well as the bakeries, the winery, the real estate, the cows, in short the whole multi-million-dollar Cama estate, went to set up an Ormus and Vina memorial foundation to assist underprivileged children around the world. This will was the only indication Ormus ever gave that he regretted not having had children of his own on account of Vina's barrenness. The enormous size of the bequest was a measure of the depth of his unspoken grief.)

Tara had brought a blaster. She turned it up to top volume, because of the noise of the rotor blades, and played the last VTO CD, the one featuring her mother's stellar performance, and I didn't like to tell her that I thought it was the wrong choice, because Vina should have been with us at such a time. Below us the city stood up iced and jagged and majestic as any Himalayas. The park was empty except for a couple of skiers and a few lone walkers wrapped up like bears. The fountains and reservoir were frozen, and as I looked down on Manhattan from the sky, it still seemed to be wrapped in winter, like a gift.

The pilot insisted on doing the ash-spilling. Clea gave up the urn reluctantly, and then Ormus was flying away from us, spreading out over the city he had loved, he was a small dark cloud dispersing over the great white metropolis, losing himself in all that whiteness; he merged with it, and was gone. Let his ashes fall upon the city like kisses, I thought. Let songs spring from the sidewalks and bushes where he lies. Let music be. From Tara's music machine came the voice of Mira singing the end of the *Dies Irae,* and Mira at my side sang along.

> *O King of tremendous majesty*
> *who saves the saveable for free*
> *O fount of piety, please save me.*

For no reason at all I suddenly thought of Persis Kalamanja, Persis the most beautiful girl in the world, who saved herself for Ormus and so lost herself altogether. I saw her again, still young and lovely, still standing on the roof of her long-demolished home, "Dil Kush" on Malabar Hill, Bombay, while above her the polychromatic kites of

India swooped and soared, simultaneously at play and at war. Stay where you are, Persis, I thought, don't move a muscle. Don't age, don't change. Let us all become ash and scatter on the wind, but stay on your old roof, Persis, stand forever silent in the evening breeze and watch the dancers in the sky. I want to think of you this way: eternal, unchanging, immortal. Do this for me, Persis. Watch those festive kites.

I see in the paper today that they shot another *rai* singer. There are more and more parts of the world now where they're trying to wipe out singing altogether, where you can be murdered for carrying a tune. This particular *rai* singer had even taken the precaution of going into exile, leaving his North African home for a lightless cell in Marseilles. The killers followed him there and shot him anyway. *Pan! Pan!* Now I'm reading his obit in the *Times* and I think to myself, what a wonderful world.

Rai is music. Rai is the ungodly forbidden sound of joy.

Not long ago there was a powerful earthquake in Italy and Assisi, the town of Mira's forebears, was badly damaged. When I heard the news I didn't think of quake wars and rift bombs. I thought of Maria from the otherworld, and her teacher talking calmly to my video camera while her world crumbled around her. Maybe it's starting again, I thought. Another variant version is on a collision course with our own, and we're starting to feel the first tremors, the pre-impact vibrations. Maybe this time it's the Big Crunch and we're the ones who won't make it, however tough we've proved ourselves to be, however long we've survived. Or maybe it's not necessary to hypothesize another reality smashing into our own. Suppose the earth just got sick of our greed and cruelty and vanity and bigotry and incompetence and hate, our murders of singers and other innocents. Suppose the earth itself grew uncertain about us, or rather made up her mind just to open her jaws and swallow us down, the whole sorry lot of us. As once Zeus destroyed the human race with a flood, and only Deucalion survived to repopulate the earth's surface with beings no worse or better than the dead.

I'm up early today, the coffee's on and I've squeezed the oranges and the muffins are warming nicely. It's the weekend. I can hear Mira and

Tara in the back, arguing, laughing, fooling with Tara's mongrel, Cerberus, a grateful old stray whom we seem to have adopted. They'll be out soon. We've moved in together at the Orpheum now—after Basquiat died Mira took over his floor, so there's plenty of room—and things are good, they're good. I'm not saying there aren't problems, because there are, mainly in the traditional new baby area, but with a twist. Here I'm the one who wants a child. Mira, she's got one, and she's got a career bursting out all over, her first solo album *After* went platinum in just weeks, she's just finished work on a new movie, the offers are flooding in. This is not a good time for her to be pregnant, or so she says. But we're talking about it. It's not out of court. It's on the agenda.

There's also my past. In Mira's opinion I haven't completely got Vina out of my system. She thinks I'm still silently making comparisons, physical, psychological, vocal. I tell her that if I am, I don't mean to, and I'm doing my damnedest to stop. She's a patient woman, and she's waiting for the day.

And Tara: Tara, I love. How it is that she's growing up with Vina's wiry, springy hair, with a complexion many shades darker than her mother's, I have no idea. Perhaps Luis Heinrich had a grandmother we don't know about. Anyway, Tara and I have one important trait in common: surrounded as we have been and will always be by singers, we can't hit a note. This makes us allies, musketeers to the death in a world of non-stop mockery by the self-satisfied croony-moony élite.

"After," the title song of the album, is Mira's elegy for Ormus. You were the stranger that I needed, she sings, the wanderer who came to call. You were the changer that I heeded. Now you're just a picture on my wall. And everything is stranger after you.

In all the old stories, in different ways, the point is always reached after which the gods no longer share their lives with mortal men and women, they die or wither away or retire. They vacate the stage and leave us alone upon it, stumbling over our lines. This, the myths hint, is what a mature civilization is: a place where the gods stop jostling and shoving us and seducing our womenfolk and using our armies to lave their poxy quarrels in our children's blood; a time when they move back, still leering, still priapic, still whimsical, from the realm of the actual to the land of so to speak—Olympus, Valhalla—leaving us free to do our best or worst without their autocratic meddling.

In my lifetime, the love of Ormus and Vina is as close as I've come to a knowledge of the mythic, the overweening, the divine. Now that they've gone, the high drama's over. What remains is ordinary human life.

I'm looking at Mira and Tara, my islands in the storm, and I feel like arguing with the angry earth's decision to wipe us out, if indeed such a decision has been made. Here's goodness, right? The mayhem continues, I don't deny it, but we're capable also of this. Goodness drinking o.j. and munching muffins. Here's ordinary human love beneath my feet. Fall away, if you must, contemptuous earth; melt, rocks, and shiver, stones. I'll stand my ground, right here. This I've discovered and worked for and earned. This is mine.

Tara's got hold of the zapper. I've never got used to having the tv on at breakfast, but this is an American kid, she's unstoppable. And today, by some fluke, wherever she travels in the cable multiverse she comes up with Ormus and Vina. Maybe it's some sort of VTO weekend and we didn't even know. I don't believe it, Tara says, zapping again and again. I don't *buh-leeve* it. Oh, *puh-leeze*. Is this what's going to happen now, for ever and *ever*? I thought they were supposed to be *dead,* but in real life they're just going to go on singing.